Chapter One

"CHLOE!" a voice bellowed down the hallway.

Chloe sighed to herself as she heard the dreaded voice calling for her yet again. She knew that he was calling her to complain about something, as always. It was impossible to do anything right for him lately. Reluctantly she placed one foot in front of the other and trudged down the hallway, wishing, not for the first time that day that she could escape the predicament that she found herself in on a near daily basis. As she walked into the dressing room and stood face to face with Lee, she remained silent, waiting for the slaughtering that she knew was coming.

"You can't honestly expect me to wear this." Lee said, gesturing to the hanger that Chloe had laid out for him. She bit her lip to keep herself from telling him how many hours she had spent searching for outfits for the band to wear for their photoshoot.

"Why don't you swap outfits with Nathan then, you are both the same size?" she suggested, knowing full well what the answer would be.

"Or you might fit into Steven or Adrian's outfits?" she added, beginning to panic a little.

"Because I don't like any of them." he snapped.

"Okay, well what do you want me to do then?" she sighed, trying to fight the tears that were filling her eyes.

"How about you get a sense of style..." Lee sneered as he slowly removed the outfit from the hanger, maintaining eye contact with her the entire time.

"And bring me something that I will actually look good in." he added. As soon as he removed the clothes from the hanger, he threw them at Chloe, smirking as they fell at her feet. Chloe could feel herself beginning to panic, the outfits all had the same theme, and there was less than an hour before the photo shoot, she wouldn't have time to find four similar outfits in such a short space of time.

She sat on the floor and silently picked up the clothes, folding them neatly as unlike Lee she knew how much they cost. Before she could stop herself, a warm tear flowed down her cheek. She angrily wiped it away, hoping that Lee hadn't noticed. She chanced a glance in his direction and breathed a sigh of relief when she saw that he was looking at something on his phone. Both Chloe and Lee's heads snapped up as Nathan walked into the room, frowning when he noticed Chloe sitting cross legged on the floor, folding clothes.

"What's going on in here?" he asked.

Chloe opened her mouth to answer, sighing deeply when Lee beat her to it.

"Our 'so called stylist' has messed up the outfits again." Lee sighed. Nathan glanced at Chloe as she shrugged and slowly stood up.

"The outfits look awesome, stop being a dick Lee and just wear it." he said firmly.

Lee rolled his eyes and fell silent, returning to his phone.

"It's okay, I'll try and find something else." Chloe said, turning to Nathan.

"Like another job." Chloe muttered sarcastically as she turned and left the room.

Chapter Two

Michelle and Kirstie were overcome with excitement as they walked towards the hall for the long-awaited university reunion. Ever since the annual tradition had started, they looked forward to it every year. As soon as they walked into the room, they could feel the party atmosphere. Kirstie peered around the room, searching for someone that she recognised. Her eyes lit up as she saw her best friend Matt waving at her from a corner table.

"I'm going to go and see Matt." she told Michelle.

"Okay, I'll grab us some drinks." Michelle replied as she headed off to the mini bar.

Kirstie beamed at Matt as she walked over to the table.

"Hey, my girl." he smiled at her, quickly wrapping his arm around her as soon as she sat beside him. Kirstie couldn't help but smile at how sweet Matt was. One of her biggest regrets in life was that things hadn't worked out with Matt. They dated all through school and university, until it suddenly dawned on them both that they weren't really in love and would be better off as friends. It meant a lot to the two of them to stay friends, since they knew each other better than anyone.

"How are you?" he asked, snapping her out of her thoughts.

"Good, you?" she replied.

"I'm always alright." he smiled. Matt laughed at her as she picked up his bottle of beer and took a long swig, playfully glaring at him as she did so.

"I see you're still an alcoholic." he bantered, bursting out laughing when Kirstie stuck her middle finger up at him. They both glanced up as Michelle returned to the table carrying a tray full of shots, wine bottles and a fishbowl.

"Holy crap Michelle!" Kirstie exclaimed when she saw the tray.

"Nah it's fine, it'll last us a while. Besides I'm planning to have a good night." Michelle smiled cheekily. Michelle giggled happily to herself as she handed Matt and Kirstie a straw for the fishbowl and quickly dug in herself.

"You really are a bad influence Michelle." Kirstie laughed, but her and Matt dug in anyway.

"Oh my god, Michelle!" a voice called from across the room. Their heads snapped up as they all looked towards the sound of the voice. Michelle quickly stood up and embraced Kathleen as she joined the group.

"Kathleen, it's been so long!" Michelle squealed when she eventually let go of her and allowed Matt and Kirstie to hug her.

"It has hasn't it." Kathleen agreed, quickly removing her jacket and sitting down.

"Are you still doing your column for the newspaper?" Kirstie asked her.

"Unfortunately, yes, I hate it though, my life is so boring, I never know what to write about." she sighed, slowly taking the glass of wine that Michelle poured and handed to her.

"Anyway, how about you guys, what's new?" she asked the group.

"I'm still working in the hospital, but that's pretty much it." Michelle said quietly.

"I'm still working as a Domestic Abuse Support Worker, I really love it, being able to help people." Kirstie stated proudly.

"And Matt over here is a talent agent." she added.

"Yeah, well that's what you do when you have no talent yourself you become an agent." Matt laughed, causing the others to burst out laughing too.

"Seriously though that sounds amazing!" Kathleen exclaimed when she finally stopped laughing.

"It's not as exciting as it sounds, I just look after some boy bands that's all." Matt shrugged, not particularly enjoying being the centre of attention.

"Oh wow, you have to tell us who!" Kathleen said excitedly, bouncing up and down in her seat slightly.

"I've been trying to get it out of him for months." Kirstie piped up.

"That's because I'm not allowed to say." Matt told them.

"Oh, c'mon Matt, don't be a spoil sport." Michelle tired.

"Seriously I'm not allowed, when you are associated with famous people you have to sign a gag order." Matt insisted.

"Famous people!" Kathleen spluttered, sending a small amount of wine shooting out of her mouth.

"I am so sorry, I got a bit carried away, I can't believe you know famous people." she said, slowly wiping up the drink with her napkin.

"We'll get him drunk, then he'll tell us." Michelle winked at Kathleen.

Matt shook his head slowly and mimed zipping his lips closed.

Michelle glanced at Kirstie as she felt her gently elbow her in the ribs. Kirstie nodded towards the hall door and Michelle turned to look and gasped as she saw Chloe walking in the door.

"Oh jeez, this could get awkward." Michelle muttered quietly.

"What are you talking about?" Matt asked, following her eye line.

"Have you and Chloe fallen out?" he asked, turning to Michelle and Kirstie when he realised what they were looking at.

"We're not really sure." Kirstie said, quickly filling the group in on the fact that despite Chloe and Kirstie being very close, neither Michelle nor Kirstie had been able to get Chloe to take any of their calls for a while.

"Don't take it personally you haven't fallen out." Matt said as soon as Kirstie had finished. Kirstie frowned at him, suddenly getting the feeling that he knew something that she didn't.

"How do you know that?" Michelle asked.

"She is going through a difficult time at the moment, I expect she got distracted." Matt told them.

"Too distracted to call back for the past few months." Michelle insisted, rolling her eyes.

"What do you mean, a tough time?" Kirstie asked worriedly.

"Just drop it guys." he said quickly as Chloe nervously walked over to the group.

"Hi everyone." she said quietly.

Even though Kirstie was still confused by what Matt had said and why he had suddenly gotten so defensive, she couldn't deny that she was happy to see her old best friend. Chloe hovered nervously on the edge of the group, appearing to be shyer than before. Kirstie couldn't help but look at her and frown to herself. Chloe had always seemed like one of those people that always had everything together, always a step ahead. Someone that people would look up to as Little Miss Perfect, but things had clearly changed. Her appearance was dishevelled and she had big dark circles under eyes, that she hadn't even bothered to hide with makeup.

"Maybe I should leave you guys to it." she whispered, after waiting a few moments and getting no response.

"Don't be silly Chloe, come and sit down." Matt piped up, patting the space on the bench between himself and Kirstie. She blushed as everyone watched her sit down and remained silent.

"So, how is everyone?" she piped up when she couldn't stand the tension any longer.

After a few moments of chatting, the group settled into having Chloe with them. Even Chloe herself seemed to relax when they told her about their lives and what had changed since she last saw them.

"So, what do you do Chloe?" Michelle asked.

"I am a personal assistant...kind of." she said quietly. Kirstie couldn't help but notice that Chloe was the only one not to have drunk anything since she'd been at the table. She clearly felt uncomfortable having everyone looking at her as she silently reached over to the table and poured herself a glass of water from the bottle provided for the table. Her hands shook as she quickly took a drink.

"To like a banker or something?" Kathleen asked.

"No not really, it's difficult to explain." Chloe replied.

Michelle and Kathleen glanced at each other and shrugged.

"You're very cagey about it." Michelle sighed.

"Ooooh!" Kathleen exclaimed, causing everyone at the table to look at her in shock.

"Matt was cagey too, maybe she is Matt's personal assistant!" she cried.

Chloe glanced at Matt who slowly shook his head at her, subtly giving her the cue to leave it alone.

"Oh well, we'll get you drunk too and then we'll find out." Michelle pouted, the alcohol clearly beginning to take an effect on her and Kathleen.

"More drinks?" Kathleen asked the group.

"I'll have another beer please." Matt said, handing her some money.

"A glass of red wine please." Kirstie asked, rummaging in her purse.

"Chloe?" Kathleen prompted.

"Nothing for me thank you, I'll stick with water." she smiled.

"Michelle?" Kathleen asked.

"I'll come with you Kathleen." she replied, following Kathleen to the bar.

Chloe sat silently watching Michelle and Kathleen queue at the bar.

"Oh great, I should have known he'd be here." Chloe said under her breath as her eyes wandered and she clocked her ex-boyfriend sitting at the bar talking to a beautiful young woman.

"Is that Andy?" Kirstie asked, following Chloe's eye line.

Chloe nodded silently.

"We're not together anymore." Chloe announced.

"Oh my god, since when?!" Kirstie exclaimed.

"Just over a year ago now." she said quietly.

"I can't believe it; you guys were together for like three years weren't you." Kirstie said.

Chloe shrugged and turned her attention away from the man that broke her heart, desperately trying to clear all thoughts of him from her mind. Despite her best efforts, her eyes kept wandering back to him. Memories swirled around her head as she remembered that fateful day when he'd told her that he had met someone else. The day that her life had been changed forever.

"In fact, I think it might be best if I call it a night, it was nice to see you guys again. It's been far too long." she smiled.

"Please keep in touch Chloe, I've missed you." Kirstie said.

"I'll try. See you later." she said before quickly walking away.

As soon as she left the hall, Kirstie rounded on Matt:

"What did you mean when you said that she's going through a tough time?"

"It's fine just leave it alone." he answered.

Kirstie stared at him; her eyebrow raised as she waited for him to tell her what was going on. She didn't like the fact that Matt seemed to be keeping something from her.

"You hardly know her though do you, apart from when we were at Uni together?" she tried again.

"I just meant that you should cut her some slack, she could do with a friend." Matt said, before standing up and walking away to use the restroom.

Chapter Three

Louise was rushing around backstage in a panic, desperately trying to find her hair curlers that she couldn't for the life of her remember where she had left them. This show was her debut and she only had a couple of hours to get her hair and makeup done, changed and complete sound check before she had to be on the stage. This was her big break; she had been trying to get here for the past ten years and now that it was finally happening, she was determined not to mess it up. She couldn't let all her hard work go to waste.

"Oh my god." she muttered, beginning to get flustered as she continued rummaging in drawers to no avail.

"Can I help with anything?" she heard a small voice from behind her.

She quickly turned around and smiled as she stood face to face with a young woman that she didn't recognize.

"I'm Chloe by the way, sorry I should have said." she smiled.

"I'm Louise." she smiled back at her.

"And I can't find my damn curlers, and I still need to do my makeup, I'm going to be so late!" she added, starting to panic again.

"Aren't these them up here?" Chloe asked pointing to the hook on the wall where the curlers were hanging.

"Oh god, I'm such an idiot." Louise chuckled, feeling slightly embarrassed that she had been looking for them for what felt like hours.

"I'm too stressed to think clearly." she told Chloe quietly as she picked up the curlers and slowly sat down. She sat staring at her own reflection, desperately telling herself over and over that she could do this, an opportunity like this was what she'd always wanted, and she wasn't going to mess this up now.

"I'm a stylist, I can help." Chloe smiled at her, the two of them locking eyes in the mirror.

"Thank you so much." Louise said as Chloe gently turned the chair around and rummaged in the makeup pouch that was always attached to her hip.

"The slight issue is, I don't normally do women, so I don't have much in here." she said thoughtfully.

"I have everything in here." Louise replied, handing Chloe her makeup bag.

"Perfect." Chloe smiled. Louise fell silent as she let Chloe get to work. Chloe couldn't help but smile to herself as she quickly applied the makeup. It felt so refreshing to be working with someone who didn't constantly belittle her.

"Thank you so much for doing this, I can't tell you how much I appreciate it." Louise said.

"It's okay, it gives me a break." she replied quietly.

"How long do we have?" Chloe checked as she applied the final touches of makeup.

"Half an hour or so." Louise replied, glancing at her watch.

"Okay, we need to get a move on." Chloe said, turning Louise's chair back to face the mirror so that she could work on Louise's hair.

"You've done an amazing job with my makeup, thank you so much." Louise stated as she looked at herself in the mirror.

"You are very welcome." Chloe smiled.

"Chloe, where are you?!" she heard Lee's voice calling from down the hall. Chloe jumped when she heard his voice, accidentally pressing the curler against her wrist.

"Damn it." she gasped in pain.

"Are you okay?" Louise asked when she heard the sizzle and smelt burning flesh.

"Yes, it's not too bad." Chloe insisted, trying to hide how much it hurt. She quickly placed her other hand over the burn, trying to hide it. She'd always hated fuss, but she couldn't stand to hear whatever sarcastic comment Lee was going to come out with. It was better to keep her head down and work.

"You need to put something cool on that." Louise said. Chloe opened her mouth to explain that she would be fine, but before she could say anything Louise stood up and left the room. As soon as Louise left the room Lee walked in.

"Where have you been?" he demanded as soon as he saw her.

"I was speaking to Matt about the logistics of the interview and then I stopped to help one of the singers with her makeup." she quickly explained.

"Right, well you do realise that you work for me and not 'one of the other singers'." he said, gesturing inverted commas as he did so.

"Technically I work for Matt." she sighed.

"Yeah, to look after us." he argued.

"Fine, what do you need?" she said sighing again as she gave up the fight. In all her life Chloe had never met someone who made her feel the way that Lee did, he was so condescending and patronising she literally felt like an ant under his shoe. Nothing that she ever tried to do for him was ever good enough, he still sneered at her from the high horse he seemed to think he was on. When she'd initially started working for the boys from Eclipse, she'd never been happier, but things had gradually got worse the past year; Lee's attitude had become more and more nasty. She knew that the fame was going to his head and that had to be the reason he treated her the way that he did.

"Well, aren't you forgetting something?" he said, smirking at her.

"Oh probably." she said, sounding defeated.

"I asked you for an Ice-Tea about twenty minutes ago." he said matter of factly.

"That's right you did, I forgot." she said quickly.

"Clearly." he snapped.

"I'll go and fetch it." she said quietly.

Chapter Four

As soon as Chloe left the room Lee sat on one of the makeup chairs and stared silently at his reflection. Ever since Nathan told him that he'd overheard Chloe say that she wanted another job, something had changed inside of him and he had no idea what it was. He'd always known that he continually pushed Chloe away, but he could never figure out why he treated her the way he did. He knew that it gave him a sense of satisfaction to make her hate him, but he didn't know why. When Nathan had told him a couple of weeks ago what he'd heard Chloe say, Lee felt his heart plummet. He didn't want her to go, even though she infuriated him, he didn't want her to leave his side. But he couldn't bring himself to say that to her or to even be kind to her. It was better that he pushed her away, better for everyone. He was snapped out of his thoughts by Chloe returning and silently placing the iced tea beside him. He glanced at her for a moment.

"Also, you might want to open a window, it smells in here." he said.

"Smells of what?" Chloe frowned.

"Burning." he said, not looking up from his phone. Chloe stared at him for a moment, her temper rising that he expected her to be his servant. She chanced a glance down at her wrist and saw that a blister was beginning to form over the burn.

"Window." he said matter of factly, clicking his fingers at her to get her attention. Chloe quickly walked over to the window and opened it, trying to calm herself down as she did so, she needed this job so she couldn't afford to answer him back.

Louise glanced questioningly at Lee as she walked back into the room.

"Here, it's all I could find." she said as she kindly handed Chloe a damp towel.

"Thank you so much." Chloe smiled, sighing in relief as she placed the towel on the burn and finally felt some relief from the pain.

"Hey, you made me look amazing, I owed you one." Louise smiled back.

They both turned to Lee who quickly stood up and walked over to Louise, taking her hand in his and gently placing a kiss on it, maintaining eye contact the whole time.

"Lee, nice to meet you." he said.

"Louise, I'm one of the support artists." she told him.

"You are also stunning." he breathed, unable to take his eyes off her.

She blushed and looked at the floor for a moment before her eyes turned back to his.

"I believe I have Chloe to thank for that." Louise said sweetly.

"Ah, so it was you who stole my stylist." he smiled.

"Yes, I believe it was, sorry about that." she giggled.

"That's okay, she's done everything we need her too anyway." Lee stated.

Chloe could feel her blood boiling as she listened to Lee talking to Louise. She hated the way that he was making out that he was a kind and considerate guy, when he was anything but with her.

"Do you want me to finish your hair Louise?" Chloe offered, trying to ignore the lump that was rising in her throat.

"No, it's okay, I'll finish it, your hand will be sore." she said.

Chloe couldn't deny that she was a little relieved, as Louise was right her hand was sore.

"What did you do to your hand?" Lee piped up.

"Burnt it on the curlers." she muttered.

"Show me." Lee told her.

"No, it's fine." Chloe argued.

Before Chloe could react, Lee reached out and took hold of her arm and pulled her towards him. He gently removed the towel and gazed at the wound for a few moments.

"It looks sore." he eventually said.

"Yeah well, I apologise for the smell." Chloe snapped as she quickly pulled her arm out of Lee's grasp. He opened his mouth to say something back but was interrupted by Matt entering the room, closely followed by Michelle, Kirstie and Kathleen.

"Right, I'll leave you in Chloe's capable hands." Matt announced before quickly leaving the room. As soon as she saw Chloe, Kirstie crossed the room and pulled her into a hug, Chloe stiffened at first but eventually she relaxed into it.

"Oh my god, I can't believe that we are backstage!" Michelle exclaimed, not quite able to believe what was happening.

"We now know why you couldn't tell us your job Chloe." Kathleen said. Chloe shrugged, her cheeks flushing.

"Louise you have ten minutes, Lee you have about forty-five before you have to be on stage." Chloe quickly told them. Lee nodded silently and returned to sitting on one of the makeup chairs, the conversation clearly boring him.

"I'm so excited about the interview!" Kathleen admitted.

"It's not until tomorrow, though right?" Chloe asked, starting to panic a little bit that she had got the date wrong.

"Yeah, I'm just getting over excited." Kathleen admitted. Chloe couldn't help but smile at how happy she was. Chloe took for granted the fact that she got to be around these celebrities daily, it was refreshing to realise how lucky she was.

"You two just want to meet some hot men." Kirstie said, rolling her eyes at them.

"So, do you Mrs." Michelle teased her.

"Chloe, close the window, it's cold in here." Lee demanded from the corner. She nodded silently and quickly did as she was told.

"OMG, Lee, I was so excited that I didn't really register that you were there." Kathleen said happily.

"Who are these people?" Lee asked Chloe, ignoring everyone else around him.

"Kathleen is doing the interview tomorrow and these are her friends." Chloe explained.

"Tomorrow?" Lee checked.

"Yes, I did tell you about it and your outfit is ready for the shoot afterwards." Chloe said defensively.

"Well get rid of them until tomorrow then." Lee snapped.

Chloe looked around the room awkwardly, not sure what to say or do.

"Actually, forget it, I'm out of here." he said. They watched as he walked over to Louise and handed her a piece of paper.

"Call me." he said quietly. He smirked at Chloe before walking out of the room and closing the door behind himself.

"He's a total tool." Kirstie announced, summing up what everyone was thinking.

"Tell me about it." Chloe agreed.

Chapter Five

"Hey, we just came to say goodbye and thanks again for allowing us to come along." Kirstie said, giving Matt a quick hug.

"Why are you saying goodbye?" Matt asked, a cheeky twinkle in his eye.

Kirstie frowned in confusion and waited for him to continue.

"I was just discussing with Chloe that we are having a little celebration tonight at a hotel, the record label has paid for a private function, free food, free drinks and a lot of fun. I could get the three of you in as my guests, if you're interested?" he smiled, turning to face Kathleen, Kirstie and Michelle.

"Are you serious?!" Kathleen exclaimed, unable to hide her excitement.

"So, we'll be rubbing shoulders with all the celebs?!" Michelle added.

Matt nodded, smiling at their reaction.

"I'd prefer it if there was no rubbing though." he chuckled.

"Are you going to be joining us Chloe?" Kirstie asked.

"Of course, she is, she's part of the company." Matt answered, before Chloe had a chance to respond.

"Yes, but like I explained, I don't have anything to wear. I can't exactly go dressed like this." she stated, gesturing down at her work clothes which consisted of leggings and a hoodie.

"Well, I already thought of that." Matt smiled, handing her a small key.

"Wait, is that what I think it is?" Chloe gasped.

"Yep, help yourself." Matt beamed. Everyone jumped as Matt's phone began to ring and he left the room to take the call.

Chloe's eyes lit up as she gazed down at the key in her hand.

"What is it?" Kirstie asked.

"The key to the storeroom where all the dancer's outfits are stored." Chloe explained as she walked over to the cupboard, quickly turning the lock.

"Wow." Kirstie breathed when she saw the large selection of stunning outfits.

Chloe nodded, slightly speechless that she was being given the opportunity to wear something that she could never hope to afford. As she scanned the rails, she finally found something suitable, rather than the other ridiculously short outfits.

Michelle and Kathleen sat down on the chairs and began to touch up their makeup. Kirstie joined them as Chloe left the room to go and get changed.

"She is so odd." Michelle announced as soon as Chloe left the room.

Kathleen nodded her agreement.

"I don't get why you are being so nice to her after she hasn't bothered with us for over a year and hasn't even bothered in the last two weeks since the reunion. She clearly isn't a good friend." Michelle pointed out.

"I'm just doing what Matt asked and cutting her a bit of slack, she doesn't seem herself." Kirstie told them.

"She's not your problem though. I'm just trying to be a good friend and protect you from being inevitably dropped again." Michelle stated.

"Also, that's another thing, do you think something is going on with her and Matt?" Kathleen added thoughtfully.

"No, I don't think so, but they work together so he probably knows more about whatever her situation is." Kirstie sighed, feeling a little bit disappointed that Michelle wasn't being more sympathetic towards Chloe.

They all instantly stopped talking as they heard Chloe's voice as she walked down the hall towards them.

"I don't know to be honest; I know Matt said something about staying in London for a while and doing a few shows here." she explained to someone.

They didn't hear the response as at that moment Chloe walked into the room closely followed by Ben from Saga.

"Well, I don't think it's a bad idea." Ben replied.

"It'll be easier than travelling all over the place anyway, I think I have the dates here somewhere." Chloe said, rummaging in her backpack for a few moments, before finally finding the piece of paper that she was looking for and handed it to Ben.

"Thank you." Ben smiled at her. Chloe smiled back at him and glanced at herself in the mirror. It had been so long since she'd worn something like this that she barely recognised herself. She'd chosen tight leather trousers with a white fitted corset style top that laced up at front and finished off the look with a leather jacket and black suede heels. She couldn't help but smile at how confident the clothes made her feel. Kathleen and Michelle glanced at her as she sat next to them and quickly began to apply her makeup, she decided on a subtle smoky eye look as that was her forte. She didn't have time to do anything with her hair, so she simply removed the hair band and brushed it through, feeling a sense of relief when her wavy hair sat just right.

"You look amazing Chloe." Kathleen smiled at her, feeling slightly envious of Chloe's amazing figure.

"I wish I had the confidence to pull off an outfit like that." Michelle admitted.

"We would have worn things like that a few years ago." Kathleen said.

"I am ten years younger than you guys remember." Chloe pointed out. They nodded at her thoughtfully. They quite often forgot that Chloe was so much younger than them. Kirstie, Kathleen and Michelle were older when they went to University and only met Chloe in their final year.

The three of them turned to face Kirstie when they suddenly realised that she hadn't said anything for a while. Michelle burst out laughing when she saw that Kirstie had turned in her chair and was watching Ben who was sitting at the table on the other side of the room, frowning at the paperwork Chloe had given to him. Kirstie's eyes were transfixed on Ben, like she was in some kind of trance. She opened her mouth to speak to him, but she was frozen. She'd adored this man since she was fifteen and here, he was sitting in front of her, it was like her teenage dream was finally coming true.

"Hey Ben, have you met my friend Kirstie?" Chloe called out to him, wanting to make sure that Kirstie got her moment with him.

"No, I don't believe I have." Ben smiled, as he stood up and walked towards the group.

Kirstie slowly stood up and shook his outstretched hand.

"Hey, aren't you the girl I threw the rose too?" he frowned.

"Yes, I still have it." Kirstie told him, finally finding her voice.

"I have been a fan for so long, I can't believe I'm finally meeting you." Kirstie admitted, suddenly feeling a little bit emotional. Ben smiled and quickly pulled her into a tight hug. Kirstie sighed and relaxed into him; she couldn't help but notice how amazing he smelt. Now that she was finally standing in front of him, she couldn't quite

believe how good looking he was, the posters didn't quite do him justice. She found herself a little disappointed when he finally let go of her.

"Are you going to the party?" Ben said quietly.

Kirstie nodded, not quite trusting her voice.

"Perfect, save me a dance then." he whispered in her ear, gently tucking her hair behind her ear as he said it.

He quickly stepped back as Matt walked back into the room, followed by Lee and Nathan. Lee froze as soon as he laid eyes on Chloe who was happily laughing about something with Kathleen.

"She looks stunning." Lee whispered under his breath to Nathan. Kirstie glanced at him and in that moment, he knew that she had heard him.

"Chloe!" Lee called out, quickly recovering himself and going on the defensive again. She turned to face him, the smile quickly fading from her face. Chloe quickly gathered up some items and walked over to Lee.

"Keys, phone, itinerary for tomorrow and the London show dates." she listed matter of factly as she handed him each item.

Lee stared at her, completely taken aback by how beautiful she looked as she innocently stood in front of him, gazing at the floor, as she always did when he was around. He opened his mouth to say something, but Matt quickly cut him off:

"Don't Lee, this is on her own time." he said firmly.

"Oh Chloe, I have some good news. The phone call earlier, was that company you applied too. They were calling me for a reference and don't worry I gave you a glowing one." Matt told her happily.

"Really, thank you so much Matt!" Chloe cried, throwing her arms around Matt. Matt glanced at Lee over the top of Chloe's head and raised his eyebrow at him. He knew from the pale expression on Lee's face that he'd heard the conversation, which is exactly what

Matt had intended. The last thing Matt wanted was to lose a talented stylist and assistant like Chloe. Maybe it would be the motivation Lee needed to start treating her better.

Chapter Six

Kirstie, Michelle and Kathleen gasped as they walked into the hotel and gazed around at the room. They had never seen so many celebrities in one room and couldn't help but feel a little out of place. As the three of them silently gazed around the room they saw the faces of so many famous people they recognised.

Chloe quickly led them over to a quiet table on the side of the dance floor. As soon as they sat down a waiter appeared and placed two bottles of wine and some glasses on the table.

"This is amazing." Kirstie breathed.

"It feels like we are famous." Kathleen agreed.

Chloe smiled at them as she poured them all a glass of wine.

"Do you ever get used to being around them all the time?" Kathleen asked curiously.

"Kind of most of them are pretty normal and some are a bit stuck up." she smiled, before quickly downing her glass of wine and pouring herself another.

"Cheers everyone." Kathleen said happily, raising her glass. A chorus of cheers echoed around the room as they clinked glasses.

"Hey Louise!" Chloe called as she spotted Louise walking past their table, looking a little bit out of her comfort zone. Chloe smiled at her and gestured for her to come and sit with them.

"Ladies, this is Louise, she is one of the singers. Louise this is Michelle, Kathleen and Kirstie." Chloe explained gesturing to each one in turn.

"Hello." Louise said shyly.

"We saw you on the stage, you were amazing!" Kirstie told her.

"Thank you, it was my first time singing in front of a crowd that big, I was terrified." Louise admitted.

"Well, you couldn't tell." Kathleen said kindly.

Louise smiled and fell silent again, her shyness taking over.

"How is your wrist?" Louise asked Chloe, relieved that she'd finally found something to say.

"It's not too bad now thanks." Chloe said.

"What happened?" Michelle piped up as she gazed down at Chloe's wrist.

"An accident with the curling tongs." Chloe told her.

"Ouch, you know Aloe Vera is really good for burns, it'll cool the skin and help to keep the wound from drying out too much." Michelle explained.

"Thank you, I'll see if I have any." Chloe smiled.

"If not, give me a shout, I'm pretty sure I have some at home." Michelle stated.

"I'm so excited about the interviews tomorrow." Kathleen randomly piped up.

"I bet you are, you're so lucky." Michelle said.

"If you wanted too, I'm sure the rest of you could come along and observe, I'm sure Matt won't mind." Chloe suggested.

"If you behave yourselves of course." she quickly added, giggling to herself.

Michelle glanced at Kirstie who nodded silently.

"We'd love to thanks Chloe." Kirstie smiled.

"I'm just so glad to have something positive after everything." Kathleen admitted.

"Huh?" Michelle frowned.

"Oh crap...I forgot to tell you guys.... David and I broke up." she said quietly.

"Wait, what?!" Michelle exclaimed.

"We drifted apart too far, neither of us was happy anyway." Kathleen explained.

"So now I'm single and ready to mingle." she added quickly.

"Wait are we all single?" Michelle asked, clearly sensing that Kathleen didn't want to talk about David anymore.

Kirstie and Kathleen nodded sadly. Michelle's gaze landed on Louise and she raised her eyebrow at her.

"Yes, I am very much single, but I don't want to meet anyone at the moment, I want to focus on my career. It's more important to me than a man." Louise answered.

"Preach to the choir sister." Chloe laughed, holding up her hand for a high five, which Louise quickly reciprocated.

"Aww Chloe, don't you want to find someone?" Kirstie asked.

"Nope." Chloe replied quickly.

"Why not?" Kathleen asked.

"I don't know, just things didn't end well with Andy and I guess it's kind of put me off the whole thing. Also, this is going to sound really silly..." Chloe started to stay but paused.

"What?" Kirstie frowned.

"I've only ever been with Andy, like he was my first and that meant a lot to me. I'd have to be in love to sleep with someone and I don't want to be in love." she laughed, surprising herself that she had said that aloud. Clearly, she'd had too much alcohol and it was affecting her judgement.

"Wait, so if one of these celebs wanted to spend a night with you, you would say no?!" Kathleen asked, not quite able to believe her ears. Chloe nodded.

"I certainly wouldn't." Michelle laughed.

"Me neither." Kathleen added, joining in with the laughter.

Chloe rolled her eyes to herself; she'd always been the one that was on the outside of the group, even at university. She knew that she was a lot younger than the others, but she felt like they just didn't understand her. Which is why she hadn't been able to tell them how much she was struggling at the moment. It was easier to pretend.

"What about Lee?" Michelle asked, wiggling her eyebrows at Chloe.

"What about him?" Chloe frowned.

"I hate that guy and can't wait to get away from him." she quickly added.

"If you say so." Michelle teased.

"Anyway, I'm going for a dance, anyone want to join me?" Michelle asked.

"I'll be your date." Kathleen giggled as she followed Michelle to the dance floor. Chloe poured herself another glass of wine.

"You might want to slow down a bit there Chloe." Kirstie laughed.

"I can't help it, I'm so nervous about tomorrow." Chloe said quietly.

"The interviews?" Kirstie frowned, not quite understanding why Chloe would be nervous about that.

"No not that, I have applied for a new job, I've had the interview and Matt gave them a reference and they are going to call tomorrow to let me know." Chloe explained.

"Oh no Chloe, you can't leave." Louise said sadly.

"I'm sorry, but I can't work with Lee anymore, it's dragging me down too much." Chloe told them.

"He seems quite nice." Louise frowned.

"That's because he was trying to charm you, he treats me like dirt, and I've had enough of it." Chloe said.

"It's true, he does, he's really not nice to her at all." Kirstie agreed.

"So, what's the new job?" Kirstie asked.

"It would be working with a new up and coming boyband, but not as a stylist. I would be their day-to-day manager, so it's a kind of promotion. And I would go back to travelling the UK, rather than just being in London." Chloe explained.

"Wow, that sounds amazing. I really hope you get it." Kirstie smiled.

"I hope you do to, it sounds great for you, but I don't want you to leave us." Louise said, quickly hugging Chloe.

"Thanks guys, right shall we dance?" Chloe suggested. Just as the three of them stood up, Ben walked over to their table and offered his outstretched hand to Kirstie.

"You promised me a dance remember." he smiled at her. She smiled back at him, butterflies swirling in her stomach as he led her to the dance floor.

Chapter Seven

Michelle laughed loudly as she took hold of Kathleen's hands and they began to spin each other around.

"This is not a good idea." Kathleen laughed.

Michelle laughed and continued. Kathleen gasped as Michelle accidentally let go of her hands and she fell against someone.

"I'm really very sorry." she said shyly, turning to face the person. She gasped as she stood face to face with Mark from Saga.

"That's quite alright." he said, aiming a perfect smile at her.

"My friend got a little bit carried away." she muttered, tucking a stray hair behind her ear.

"That's what you're meant to do at a party." he laughed.

"That's very true." she giggled.

"You have something on your face." he told her, before licking his thumb and gently brushing her face. Her skin tingled under his touch.

"I think it was a makeup smudge." he said, sounding slightly amused.

Kathleen could feel her cheeks colouring in embarrassment. She dreaded to think how long it had been there.

"My bandmates seem to have deserted me, so maybe you would like to join me for a drink?" he offered, gesturing to a table.

"Of course, I'd love too." she smiled.

Louise and Chloe had been dancing for what felt like hours. Hot and out of breath they both made their way to the bar and sat on the stools. Chloe removed her jacket and placed it on the stool.

"I think we might have got a bit carried away." Louise chuckled as she downed a glass of water.

"And we definitely shouldn't have worn heels." Chloe agreed, quickly removing her shoes and rubbing her sore feet.

Louise nodded in agreement and turned to gaze at the dance floor.

"I think your friends have found their guys." Louise grinned, gesturing to where Kirstie and Ben were dancing happily.

"Oh and there's Kathleen." Chloe pointed across the room to where Kathleen was sitting with Mark.

"Aww I'm pleased for them." Louise smiled.

"Me too, I wonder where Michelle got too." Chloe said thoughtfully.

"I can't see her." Louise replied.

Louise spun her stool back round to face Chloe, and impulsively pulled her into a hug.

"Thanks so much for making me feel so welcome." Louise whispered.

"Don't worry about it, we've been having fun." Chloe said.

Chloe jumped as she felt someone tap her on the shoulder. Louise let go of her and Chloe turned her stool to face the person.

"Oh, hi Shayne." she smiled when she saw Shayne standing in front of her.

"I'm sorry to interrupt, but I was wondering if you would like to dance?" he offered.

Chloe glanced at Louise who gave her a nod of encouragement.

"Sure." Chloe smiled, quickly pulling her heels back on and following Shayne onto the dance floor.

As soon as they reached the dancefloor Shayne pulled her into his arms. She glanced down at his hands that were in place on her hips. She wrapped her arms around his neck and gently swayed to the music.

"You look beautiful tonight." he whispered in her ear.

"Thank you." she smiled. Shayne slowly moved his hands and rested them in her trouser back pockets. They remained in place for a moment before they returned to her hips. Chloe frowned in confusion as he turned her so that her back was facing him. His hands slowly began to trail from her hips, up towards her waist, his hands roaming everywhere. She frowned as he gently placed a kiss on her neck, his hands reaching for the laces on her top. Before Chloe realised what was happening, he managed to get hold of them and slowly undid them. She quickly pulled away and turned to face him.

"What are you doing?" she demanded.

"Just having a bit of fun." he smiled.

"Not with me, you're not." she said sharply.

He smiled and placed his hands on her hips again, trying to gently pull her towards him.

"You're drunk." Chloe stated as she quickly stood back. Shayne shrugged and watched her closely. Chloe glanced down at her top, her hands shaking too much to tie the top back up, thankfully he'd only undone half of it, but that didn't stop the embarrassment that Chloe was feeling.

"I'm going to the restroom." Chloe muttered to herself. She quickly bent down to remove her heels and ran in the direction of the restroom.

"Are you sure you don't want me to come with you?!" he called after her. She remained silent and rushed into the bathroom.

Lee took another swig of beer as he tried to tune out what Nathan was saying to him. He was sat quietly at a table in the corner, unable to tear his eyes away from Chloe and Louise as he watched them dancing together.

"Lee snap out of it!" Nathan exclaimed clicking his fingers in front of Lee.

"What do you want?" he asked, finally turning his attention to Nathan.

"I was asking you about Adrian's surprise birthday party but never mind." Nathan sighed, frowning to himself when Lee's eyes flickered to look at something behind Nathan again.

"What are you looking at anyway?" Nathan asked, turning around to follow Lee's eyeline.

"Oh, I see." Nathan smirked.

"What?" Lee snapped.

"Nothing." Nathan said, smiling slightly to himself.

"I keep telling you that you should talk to her, before you push her away completely." Nathan added.

"She looks so beautiful." Lee breathed, completely ignoring what Nathan had said.

"Tell her then." Nathan insisted.

"I did tell her, and I gave her my number." Lee said, finally tearing his eyes away as Louise and Chloe went to sit at the bar.

"Wait...what?" Nathan frowned.

"I gave Louise my number earlier." Lee said quietly. Nathan stared at him in silence, his jaw set in frustration.

"Oh, I see, so you're going to pretend that you are staring at and talking about Louise. Nice try." Nathan said, the frustration finally starting to get to him.

"Stop being such a coward and admit how you feel!" he exclaimed.

"Fuck off Nathan, you don't know what you are talking about!" Lee hissed angrily.

Nathan raised his eyebrow sceptically but decided not to press the matter. He'd told Lee numerous times that if he didn't speak to Chloe, he was going to lose her forever, but if Lee wasn't going to listen to him then Nathan could do no more. He wasn't going to keep hitting his head against a brick wall.

Even though Lee knew he shouldn't keep staring at *her* he just couldn't help himself. He had no idea what was happening to him. His eyes wandered to Chloe again as she walked onto the dance floor with Shayne.

Lee took an angry swig of his beer as he watched them on the dance floor. He could feel his temper rising as Shayne turned Chloe around, his hands wandering all over her body. He grit his teeth and banged his beer bottle on the table, slightly harder than he meant too when he saw Shayne's hands making their way towards the laces. Even though Chloe and Shayne were a reasonable distance away from him, it was like he had tunnel vision and could see everything that was going on. Lee clenched and unclenched his fists as Shayne took hold of the laces and began to untie her top.

"What's going on?" Nathan asked, noticing the change in Lee's body language. Once again Nathan turned to follow Lee's line of vision. They both watched as Chloe turned and her and Shayne began to speak to each other. They couldn't hear what was being said, but it was obvious that it was heated. Chloe pulled off her heels and ran past them into the bathroom. In the very brief glance they got of her, it was clear that she was upset.

"Are you sure you don't want me to come with you?!" Shayne called after her. She didn't respond but that didn't stop Shayne from following her. Lee couldn't stand it any longer, he quickly stood up.

"Lee, leave it." Nathan appealed to him.

"I can't." Lee whispered to himself.

Chapter Eight

As Shayne made his way towards the bathroom, to follow Chloe, Lee quickly stepped forward into the doorway, to block him.

"Excuse me mate." Shayne said quietly.

"Not a chance." Lee said quietly, trying to control the deep pit of anger that he was feeling in his stomach.

"Also, I'm pretty sure that's the ladies." Lee added sarcastically.

"I'm aware. But I'm seeing a girl, she wants me to meet her in the bathroom." Shayne explained smugly.

Shayne made a move to walk past Lee, but before he could Lee placed a hand against Shayne's chest and pushed him away.

"What's your problem man?" Shayne asked, becoming angry.

"Maybe I'm just a bit old fashioned but I believe in consent." Lee said firmly, glaring at Shayne.

"And she definitely didn't consent to you following her. The fact that she ran away wasn't a clue." Lee added sarcastically.

"If she didn't want it, she shouldn't be dressed the way she is." Shayne pointed out. Once again, he stepped forward to squeeze past Lee.

"Back off." he warned, shoving him as hard as he could. The momentum caused Shayne to stagger backwards and fall over. Lee glared at Shayne as he slowly sat up, massaging his back.

"If you wanted her that bad you should have just said, I'm not going to fight you over her. I only went for her because she seemed easy." Shayne explained, sneering at Lee. As he said those words something inside of Lee finally snapped. Before he realised what he was doing he rushed forward

and straddled Shayne, grabbing him by his shirt and pulling him roughly towards himself. The other party guests began to scream as Lee hit Shayne across the face. As he raised his fist to hit him again, Nathan quickly pulled Lee off Shayne and positioned himself between them.

"Stop!" Nathan warned him.

"Don't start Nathan, he's a punk. He deserves it!" Lee shouted, still not in control of his temper. The room had fallen silent, not even the music was playing anymore. Everyone in the room was staring at Shayne bleeding on the floor and Lee standing quietly, taking deep breaths, trying to control his temper.

Michelle quickly rushed across the room and knelt beside Shayne, placing her hand under his elbow as she slowly helped him to sit up. He quickly tipped his head back, trying to stop the steady trickle of blood that was flowing out of his nose.

"Don't tip your head back, it has to go forward and pinch the bridge." Michelle told him. Shayne did as she told him, gasping in pain as he touched his nose.

"I think your nose is broken." Michelle stated, handing him a napkin.

"Yeah, no kidding, he's a psycho!" Shayne said angrily.

"At least I'm not a rapist." Lee retorted, loud enough for everyone to hear him.

"I didn't rape anyone. It's not my fault that you are possessive of her, even though you make her life a misery." Shayne said defensively. Lee made a move towards Shayne again, but stopped when Nathan placed a hand on his chest.

"You seriously need to cool off." Nathan told him.

"I'm fine, just keep him away from me." Lee warned quietly.

A few more moments of silence passed, before everyone became bored of staring and returned to the party.

"What's going on?" Lee heard a small voice from behind him. As soon as he heard her voice he instantly calmed down. Chloe glanced up at him as he slowly turned to face her. Lee couldn't help but notice that the upper section of her top was still undone. She held the two ends of fabric together to preserve her dignity. As Lee glanced down at her hands, he could see that they were shaking.

"Lee." she said shyly. He reluctantly tore his eyes away from the glimpse of her black lace bra and pale milky flesh and looked her in the eye.

"Do your shirt back up Chloe." he told her quickly.

"I can't, my hands are shaking too much." she whispered.

Lee shook his head silently.

"I know you hate me.... but please, I need you to do something for me." she whispered, her cheeks colouring. She hated having to ask the man that she couldn't stand for help, but she didn't feel like she had any other option. He raised his eyebrow at her and waited for her to continue.

"Can you get my jacket please?" she asked quietly. Lee sighed to himself and turned around to where Shayne was still sitting on the floor, just a few feet away from Chloe. He couldn't stand the idea of leaving Chloe with him. As soon as Lee saw that Nathan was still standing between Shayne and himself, he relaxed a little.

"Keep him away from her." Lee warned Nathan, pointing to Shayne, before quickly leaving to fetch Chloe's jacket. Nathan nodded and smiled at her reassuringly, feeling a little sorry for her.

"What happened?" Chloe asked, noticing for the first time that Shayne was bleeding on the floor.

"Long story." Nathan said quietly, not sure what he was supposed to say.

"I got attacked by your possessive psycho that's what happened!" Shayne exclaimed angrily from his place on the floor. Chloe frowned, not really understanding what he meant. She glanced across the room to where Lee was walking back through the crowd, carrying her jacket. As her eyes flickered back to Shayne, she saw him stiffen as he noticed Lee coming back towards them. Suddenly the dots joined in her head.

"Wait, did Lee attack him?!" Chloe asked Nathan. Nathan shrugged in response, clearly feeling uncomfortable.

"Why would he do that?" Chloe tried again.

"I think the two of you need to talk." Nathan pointed out. Everyone fell silent as Lee returned and gently held Chloe's jacket out to her. She nervously glanced at the jacket and then at her hands that were still clutching the material of her top. She couldn't face the idea of letting go of the material to take the jacket, the last thing she wanted was for everyone to see her bra. Lee glanced between her and the jacket, clearly realising the dilemma.

"Did you hit him?" Chloe randomly piped up, clearly trying to distract from her embarrassment. Lee remained silent and nodded slowly.

"Why would you do that?!" Chloe exclaimed.

Lee could slowly feel himself becoming angry again.

"Bathroom." he said quietly.

"What?" she frowned.

"Get in the bathroom." he insisted, pointing into the bathroom, waiting to take up the rear. He wanted to make sure that she was in front of him so that he could protect her. She sighed and did as he asked, feeling slightly nervous as he followed her closely.

"Don't judge me, you are the one who got yourself in that position Chloe, I just got you out of it." Lee said as soon as they were alone.

"Rubbish, I left the room, I got myself out of the situation." she insisted.

Lee scoffed and shook his head.

"What were you thinking wearing something like that?" Lee snapped.

"It was the only outfit I could find at the studio that wasn't ridiculously short." she said quietly, starting to feel six inches tall again. He seemed to have a way of making her feel stupid and worthless.

"Really and you couldn't have gone home and found something?!" Lee exclaimed.

"Not exactly no." Chloe whispered.

"You just don't get it." Lee muttered, shaking his head.

"Get what?" she asked.

"That outfit makes you look..." he started but she interrupted.

"I know, I look hideous and I have no sense of style, you've told me before." Chloe muttered.

"No Chloe...." Lee started but couldn't get the words out. He couldn't bring himself to tell her how beautiful she looked.

"You're just so naive sometimes." he said.

She nodded, his words once again cutting through her like glass. Warm tears began to slowly roll down Chloe's cheeks.

"Do you have any idea how close you were to getting raped?" Lee whispered, taking a step closer to her.

"He wouldn't do that." she sniffed.

"Ask Nathan then." Lee snapped, going on the defensive again.

"Even if he did, why would you care, you hate me remember." she sobbed, knowing in her heart that he was telling her the truth.

"Oh Chloe." he whispered, gently reaching out and brushing his hand against her cheek, wiping away her tears with his thumb as he did so.

Both of them jumped as the restroom door burst open and Kirstie and Ben walked in.

"Oh my god Chloe, are you okay?" Kirstie asked.

Kirstie pulled Chloe into a hug, as soon as she was in Kirstie's arms she began to sob.

"I'm such an idiot." she sobbed. Kirstie didn't say anything she just held her tightly and allowed her to let it out. Chloe eventually lifted her head slightly and locked eyes with Lee who was still standing, frozen in place, still holding her jacket.

"Right let's get you sorted." Kirstie said, taking charge when she eventually let go of Chloe. She took Chloe by her shoulders and gently spun her around so that Chloe's back was facing the boys. She stood in front of Chloe and held her hand out to Lee.

"Jacket." she said impatiently. Lee silently handed the jacket to her. Kirstie then took over holding the material so that Chloe could place her arms in the jacket. Chloe smiled at Kirstie as she quickly zipped up the jacket.

"You can go now." Kirstie snapped at Lee.

"What did I do?!" Lee exclaimed.

"You always make things worse, so just go and leave her alone." Kirstie told him. She couldn't stand this guy and didn't want him anywhere near her friend, particularly when she was upset. Lee glanced at Chloe, part of him hoping that she would stick up for him and ask him to stay with her. He wanted to stay beside her to make sure that she was safe.

"Go on Lee mate." Ben added when Lee still hadn't left.

"Chloe." Lee whispered, not entirely sure what he was going to say next.

"She doesn't want to hear whatever horrible thing you are going to say." Kirstie snapped.

"I'll see you tomorrow Lee." Chloe added quietly. Lee nodded, trying to ignore the lump that was rising in his throat. As he left the bathroom, he jumped as he almost walked headlong into Nathan.

"Is everything okay?" Nathan asked when he saw Lee's face. Lee remained silent for a second, taking a moment to compose himself.

"I need to get drunk." he eventually said.

"Well luckily there's a bar." Nathan chuckled.

"Not here, I want to go to a club or something where there's women." Lee said quickly, his jaw set in determination as he walked out of the hotel, allowing the door to slam behind himself.

Chapter Nine

Kathleen was so excited for the interviews that she could hardly contain herself. As she quickly walked towards the theatre where the bands were going to be performing later that evening, Mark following closely behind.

"Hey Kathleen, wait a second." he said quietly, taking her hand so that he could talk to her for a moment before she entered the venue. She turned around to face him and smiled as she looked into his eyes, trying not to become lost in them.

"Can we keep last night between us, I'm quite a private guy?" he asked her nervously.

"Yes of course." she smiled, still not quite able to believe that last night had happened.

"I won't even tell my friends." she added, trying to reassure him.

"Thank you." he smiled.

"I had a nice time though." she told him, her cheeks flushing.

"Me too." he said quietly. Kathleen smiled at him before leaning up and planting a soft kiss on his lips.

"We'd better go inside." he told her gently.

She nodded and they both walked inside together. Kathleen smiled happily as she gazed around the room and saw Eclipse lounging on the sofas in the corner of the room, waiting for their turns to be interviewed. Mark wandered over to the corner of the room and sat in silence, staring at his phone.

"Is she okay?" Ben asked Kirstie when they noticed Chloe hurrying into the room.

"I think so." Kirstie said instantly knowing who he was talking about.

"I took her back to mine last night to keep an eye on her and she seemed okay, thankfully nothing happened I think she just got a fright and is a little embarrassed about the whole situation." she explained.

"Right!" Kathleen called out as she stood and quickly took charge with her clipboard.

"I am going to start with Eclipse first." she stated happily, still not quite able to believe that she was in this moment.

"You might have to circle back to us, we are a man down." Nathan told her. It was only then that Kathleen noticed Lee wasn't with them.

"Is he in the bathroom or something, I can wait?" Kathleen asked, not wanting to deviate from her schedule.

"I don't know where he is, I haven't seen him since last night." Nathan said.

"Okay fine, we'll change the order a bit then, I'll do Saga first." Kathleen said, admitting defeat.

Nathan pulled out his phone and tried to call Lee, sighing in frustration as it rang out again. Nathan couldn't help but feel infuriated with Lee lately, it was bad enough that he treated Chloe badly when it was clear to Nathan that he secretly adored her, but now he was late for work. All because he'd been out partying most of the night. Mark stood up and quickly followed Kathleen into another room.

Chloe's eyes flickered up as Lee finally walked in the door, looking very dishevelled, Matt following closely behind.

"Where the hell have you been?!" Nathan exclaimed as soon as he saw Lee.

"Out remember." Lee replied shortly, sounding hoarse.

"All night?" Steven asked.

"Most of it." Lee admitted, throwing himself down in one of the chairs.

"I feel like shit." he added.

"You look like shit." Steven agreed. Lee raised his eyebrow and rubbed his eyes sleepily.

"Did you get any sleep last night?" Nathan asked.

"Nope, I was busy." Lee muttered.

"I took a couple of ladies home last night." he added.

"Sweet." Steven laughed, high fiving Lee.

"They were stunning." Lee said.

"Yeah alright, don't rub it in." Steven laughed.

"God, I'm so tired. I haven't even had a coffee. I literally only had time to shower and rushed here. Then Matt grabbed me, which made me even later." Lee explained, rolling his eyes.

"Oh shit, did you get a bollocking?" Steven asked.

Lee glanced at Chloe for the first time and shook his head.

"Okay everyone, I have an announcement to make!" Matt called out, waiting a moment for everyone to stop speaking and turn to face him.

"Shayne will no longer be a part of our label and will not be doing any shows with us, effective immediately." Matt told everyone.

"Good." Chloe heard Lee mutter under his breath.

"Chloe, I'll need you to put some makeup on Lee's cheek. He can't do the photoshoot like that." Matt sighed.

"That's fine." Chloe said quietly.

"Perfect, we'll get Saga to do their photos first and then they can be interviewed. Get a system going so that we are ready for the charity event tonight." Matt ordered. Chloe gathered up her makeup set and smiled at Kirstie as she watched her walk away with Saga, Matt following closely behind to supervise.

Chloe placed the makeup set on the counter in front of Lee, avoiding eye contact with him. She frowned to herself as she glanced at the cut and swelling on his left cheekbone. He winced slightly as she gently used a brush to try her best to conceal it.

"Please tell me you didn't go back and see Shayne again last night?" Chloe asked, feeling slightly concerned that all of this was her fault.

"No, I didn't. I think you are overestimating how much I am interested in your life. I didn't give you or him a second thought." Lee smirked. Nathan rolled his eyes from the corner, knowing full well that Lee had barely shut up about Chloe and Shayne when they left the hotel.

"Sorry." Chloe mumbled.

"For what, are you finally admitting that I'm right?" Lee grinned, looking up from his phone and locking eyes with her.

"Right about what?" Chloe paused, midway through what she was doing.

"That it was ridiculous of you to wear that outfit." Lee said bluntly. Chloe frowned to herself slightly confused as to what he meant. She'd worn trousers and a top, yes it was fitted but it wasn't like she'd gone out in a ridiculously short dress.

"I don't want to talk about it." Chloe mumbled. She took a step back from him and put down the makeup brush, relieved that she'd finally finished.

"Just remember if you dress like a tart, people will treat you like one." he said angrily before quickly standing up and joining the rest of the band on the couch.

Chapter Ten

Chloe glared at Lee's back as he sat on the sofa with his band members, giving them all the details on his 'adventurous' night in town. She was fuming with what he'd just said to her. How dare he judge her like that? It had nothing to do him what she chose to wear, and she refused to be made to feel guilty for it.

She smiled at Kirstie when she eventually walked back into the room, beaming from ear to ear.

"You had a good time then?" Chloe asked.

"It was amazing." Kirstie admitted, feeling a little bit lightheaded with excitement.

"He's so amazing." she whispered so that only Chloe could hear.

"Aww, I'm so happy for you." Chloe said as she quickly hugged Kirstie.

"Hey." Michelle said from behind them.

"Hey, where have you been?" Kirstie asked.

"Sleeping, I'm so hungover." Michelle sighed, running her hand through her hair.

"You did get a bit wild." Kirstie said.

"I always do." Michelle agreed, chuckling slightly.

"Right beautiful, are we going to lunch?" Ben appeared from behind them.

"Of course." Kirstie said excitedly, quickly picking up her jacket. Michelle and Chloe smiled warmly as they watched Ben and Kirstie take each other's hand. The two of them were so adorable together, Michelle and Chloe couldn't help but feel a little bit envious. They quickly averted their eyes as Ben seized the moment and gently placed a small peck on Kirstie's lips. Her skin tingled under his touch and she could feel her stomach swirling in excitement for their date.

"Have fun guys." Michelle called after them as they left the theatre.

"They are adorable." Chloe said, voicing what they were both thinking. Michelle watched Chloe as she took her phone out of her pocket and took it over to the sofa area, plugging it in to charge. Michelle smiled at Louise as she walked into the room a cup of tea in her hand.

"Chloe, have you heard about the job yet?" Louise asked as soon as she saw her. Dreading the fact that Chloe might get the job. Even though she wanted Chloe to be happy, she would miss her. Since they'd first met, Chloe had made her feel welcome and at ease.

"No not yet I'm hoping no news is good news." Chloe admitted, once again checking her phone just in case.

"Wait, are you leaving us?" Adrian piped up, overhearing their conversation.

"I don't know yet, but maybe." Chloe said politely, resisting the urge to say 'hopefully' as she didn't want to be rude to Adrian. Nathan smiled at her sympathetically, clearly sensing how she was feeling. Steven left the room, clearly bored by the conversation, and Lee stared at his phone pretending that he wasn't hanging on her every word.

"I'll be sad to see you go." Adrian told her.

"We'll just have to wait and see." Chloe smiled. She awkwardly perched on the end of the sofa, smiling at Nathan as he wrapped his arm around her and pulled her close.

"We don't want you to go Chlo Bo." Nathan said kindly.

"I'm pretty sure you'll be able to find someone else." Chloe pointed out. Nathan squeezed her tighter, causing her to giggle. Nathan smiled to himself, it had been so long since he'd seen Chloe laugh or even smile, that he'd forgotten how cute her laugh was.

He sighed slowly to himself, wishing that he could get Lee to stop treating her like a piece of dirt. In the past two years of working together Nathan had become very fond of her, she was like a little sister to him, he didn't want her to leave them. Chloe closed her eyes as she leant her head against Nathan's shoulder. She fell asleep almost instantly.

"Adrian, can you give us a minute please?" Nathan asked. Adrian nodded and quickly excused himself. Nathan glanced around the room, checking that everyone else was far enough away to not be able to hear them.

"What is going on with you?" he hissed at Lee as soon as they were alone. Lee glanced up at him, not entirely sure what Nathan was talking about.

"Last night you went all Rambo on us and now it's like you don't give a shit about her." Nathan tried again.

"Just because I don't condone rape doesn't mean that I care about her." Lee said matter of factly.

"I think you're forgetting who you are talking too." Nathan insisted. Nathan knew Lee almost as well as he knew himself. It was obvious to Nathan that Lee was head over in heels in love with Chloe, the only thing that puzzled Nathan was why Lee wouldn't admit it to himself, let alone Chloe. Or how he could be so cruel and heartless to someone that he loved. Chloe fidgeted a little in her sleep, causing Lee to glance in her direction. Even in a fleeting glance it was evident to Nathan how much Lee longed to hold her.

"I just don't want you to regret it when she is no longer with us, because that's what's going to happen if you keep on the way you are." Nathan said.

"If you feel that strongly about it, why don't you ask her to stay?" Lee said defensively.

"I have, and why would she stay when you treat her the way that you do." Nathan frowned.

"It's easier if she hates me." Lee muttered thoughtfully.

"What?" Nathan frowned, finally starting to feel like they were making progress and Lee's barriers were starting to lower ever so slightly.

"Nothing." Lee said quickly. As fast as the moment came, Nathan could tell that it was gone again.

"Just think about it." Nathan said.

"I can't believe we have had to wait until last, I literally feel like we've been here all day." Lee sighed impatiently, tossing his phone onto the sofa beside himself, the boredom finally setting in.

"Do you have somewhere else important to be?" Nathan said sarcastically.

"No, but I would quite like to get some sleep before the show tonight." Lee sighed, rubbing his dry eyes.

"Speaking of last night, what did Matt say to you about it?" Nathan asked, speaking in hushed tones, fearful that he might wake Chloe.

"Officially he told me off for the violence and embarrassing the label." Lee said.

"What do you mean 'officially'?" Nathan frowned.

"It was kind of funny actually." Lee chuckled, crossing his legs so that his left calf was resting on the thigh of his other leg and bounced his foot up and down. Nathan raised his eyebrow and waited for him to continue.

"Off the record, he thanked me for protecting her." Lee explained, his eyes wandering to Chloe again. He sighed as he watched her, he couldn't help but wish that she was asleep in his arms rather than Nathan's.

"That's nice of him, it's a shame that she doesn't realise how much everyone cares about her." Nathan said sadly, glancing down at her.

"Don't start this again." Lee warned. Both of them stopped talking and jumped as a phone began to ring.

"Whose phone is that?" Nathan asked, glancing behind Lee to the counter where the phone was ringing.

"Chloe's, I think." Lee said quietly, remembering that she'd placed it on charge there earlier. Lee turned and picked up the phone, his heart plummeting when it read unknown caller.

"It'll be the new job." Lee said quietly.

"Shit." Nathan muttered.

"Chloe wake up." he said, trying to gently rouse her. Her eyes suddenly snapped open.

"Is that my phone?" she asked, still not fully awake. She took a second for her eyes to adjust to the brightness of the room.

As soon as she realised that Lee was holding her phone in his hand, staring at the display as though he was in some kind of trance, she held her hand out to take it.

"Maybe I should answer it and ask why they are trying to poach our stylist." Lee said quietly.

"Is it the job?!" Chloe asked, beginning to feel nervous.

"Unknown caller." Nathan said quickly.

"Give me the phone." Chloe asked, still holding out her hand. Lee quickly stood up and walked over the other side of the room, still holding her phone tightly.

"Lee!" Chloe exclaimed. Chloe stood up to follow him but before she could get to him the phone rang out. Chloe's heart sunk; she wouldn't be able to call them back now as she didn't have their number.

"Why didn't you give me the bloody phone?!" Chloe cried.

"You won't have got the job anyway." Lee said quietly.

She remained silent, staring at him for what felt like an age for the both of them. No matter how long Chloe stood there, she couldn't quite process what had just happened or what possible reason he had for acting this way. Suddenly something inside of Chloe snapped and everything that she had been keeping in check for the past few months came bubbling to the surface and overwhelmed her.

"YOU REALLY ARE A MONSTER!" she screamed at him.

"I've done nothing but try and do my job, in fact I've gone above and beyond for you. What did I ever do to make you hate me so much?!" she exclaimed. Lee stared at her completely speechless by her outburst.

"Every day that I come in here you make me feel useless and worthless. You call me names you tear me down all the time and then when I can't take it any longer and look for a way out, you ruin that as well!" Chloe shouted.

"You must really hate me." Chloe said, standing frozen to the spot. Lee still didn't respond. Chloe put her head in her hands and began to sob uncontrollably. Lee and Nathan watched her sadly as she sobbed her heart out, neither of them entirely sure what to do or say to her. They were both completely powerless.

"Give her the phone Lee." Nathan whispered quietly so that only Lee heard him. Lee sighed and took a step towards the broken girl that was in front of him. In that moment he knew that she had reached her breaking point and he was the one who had done that to her.

"Stay away from me." Chloe warned as Lee stepped towards her.

"So, you don't want your phone back then?" Lee said sarcastically, once again going on the defensive. He slowly held the phone out to her, jumping slightly as she reached out and snatched it out of his hand.

"I will never forgive you for this." she whispered, before quickly walking out of the room.

"Not what I meant when I said you should ask her to stay." Nathan told Lee, before quickly going after Chloe, leaving Lee alone with his thoughts.

Chapter Eleven

Chloe rubbed her hands together as she blew on them, desperately trying to warm them up. She glanced around the dressing room, quickly placing her hands on the heater when she eventually found it. She sighed when she realised that it wasn't on.

"It's freezing." she said as she passed Adrian.

"I thought I could hear teeth chattering." Adrian chuckled. Chloe glanced over at Lee as she heard him sigh. He was sat at his usual place on the sofa, frantically writing something in a notebook. Chloe smiled at Nathan as he walked into the room and handed her a coffee.

"God your hands are cold." Nathan gasped as he accidentally brushed his hand against hers.

Chloe smiled at him as she wrapped her hands around the coffee, trying to warm them up.

"Did you forget to put your heating on?" Adrian chuckled.

"I don't have any heating at the moment." she admitted.

"You should get it fixed then; winter is on its way." Nathan pointed out.

"Is it, I hadn't noticed." Chloe snapped, instantly regretting her words as soon as they were out of her mouth.

"Sorry, I'm cold and tired and it's making me grumpy." she admitted. Nathan smiled at her and took the coffee out of her hands, placing it safely on the counter. She stiffened slightly as he pulled her into his arms, taking her cold hands in his.

"Jeez Chloe, you're freezing." Nathan whispered.

"Do you want me to have a word with your landlord about the heating?" Nathan offered, when a few moments had passed, and Chloe had finally stopped shivering.

"No, it's fine, I'll do it later." Chloe said, removing herself from his arms now that she felt warmer. Chloe suddenly remembered that Matt had asked her to figure out a set list for the band for their run of London shows that started tonight.

"Lee, are you working on the set list?" Chloe asked quietly. A couple of weeks had passed since the confrontation between Lee and herself and they had barely spoken since. Chloe couldn't help but feel relieved that she was finally getting less grief from him, which meant she could focus on figuring out everything else in her life.

"Nope." he replied shortly.

"What are you doing then?" she asked, not entirely sure if he was telling the truth or being petulant.

"If it's not to do with work, we aren't meant to be discussing it, that was one of your precious rules that you insisted on when you told us you'd got the job wasn't it." Lee said sarcastically.

"He is writing a song." Nathan quickly interjected, before things escalated between the two of them.
"Have you got a title for it yet?" he added.

"It's called Broken." Lee said quietly, before quickly turning back to the notebook to add some more.

"Well, we need to sort the set list, I only have an hour before I have to go and meet the band I'm going to be working with." Chloe sighed, feeling slightly frustrated that she was having to ask them again.

"Go now then." Lee said dismissively.

"We have to get this done first." Chloe insisted.

"What do you know about set lists, you're not even a singer?!" Lee scoffed.

"Lee." Nathan warned him.

"It's true though, all she knows how to do is make up and outfits and even then, she gets that wrong most of the time." Lee continued completely ignoring Nathan's warning.

"Just go." Nathan told Chloe. It was obvious that Lee was going to keep saying nasty things until he really upset Chloe and Nathan desperately wanted to prevent that. Every time that Chloe accidentally hurt Lee he always seemed to lash out, as if he was trying to prove that he was untouchable. Chloe sighed and left the room like Nathan suggested.

Chapter Twelve

As Chloe walked into the studio for her final day working with Eclipse, her heart felt heavy. Not every moment of the last two years had been a misery. Up until a few months ago the four of them had spent a lot of time together, regularly going out and doing things outside of work. They'd been like a small family, somewhere that Chloe had finally felt accepted and loved. She missed feeling like she was one of the lads. She'd have given anything to go back to those times, before Lee had suddenly turned on her, for no apparent reason. It was obvious that she'd done something to make him hate her like he did, but to this day, she still had no idea what it was. She hated the wedge that was now present between her and the boys. They were always with Lee and Chloe had started to avoid him for her protection, and as a result her relationship with the other boys had suffered.

She trudged one foot in front of the other, as she walked into the boy's dressing room. She jumped and frowned to herself as she opened the door and saw the four of them standing, staring at her.

"Um hi." she said nervously, not sure what was going on.

"We're not working today." Adrian said.

"You need to change out of your work clothes." Steven added. Lee remained silent and handed her a backpack.

"What's going on?" she frowned, looking between the four of them.

"We're taking you out for the day to say thank you for everything you've done." Nathan announced.

"Like we used too." Chloe said quietly, looking down at the backpack in her hand.

"Exactly, now go and get changed, we're on a schedule." Nathan told her. Chloe smiled happily and rushed out of the room.

"I still can't believe we're doing this." Lee muttered.

"Don't start." Adrian sighed.

"We meant what we said, if you ruin this day for her, we'll never forgive you." Nathan reminded him.

"Just rewind to a few months ago and be kind to her, you guys used to be close remember." Adrian added. Lee nodded slowly to himself, feeling slightly sad when he remembered those times. Back before things got complicated between them.

The four of them stopped talking as Chloe returned wearing the black skinny jeans and top, they'd given her.

"I'm tempted to say that you guys have no sense of style." Chloe said sarcastically, referring to the fact that Lee regularly said that to her. Adrian, Nathan and Steven burst out laughing, even Lee cracked a smile.

"Where are we going then?" Chloe asked when they eventually stopped laughing.

"It's a surprise." Steven grinned. Chloe silently followed them outside to the carpark. Chloe smiled as she listened to Lee and Nathan argue over car arrangements. Lee wanted to take his car but since it was a sports car, they couldn't all fit into it, so they finally reached an agreement. Eventually they agreed to take both Lee and Steven's car.

"Chloe, why don't you go with Lee?" Nathan suggested, hoping that if they had some time alone, they would finally talk. As much as Chloe would have loved to ride in a sports car, she couldn't bring herself to be alone with Lee. Once the car was moving, she would be trapped inside with him, unable to escape if he decided to be nasty to her. She glanced at Lee who was standing next to his car, waiting for her decision.

"No thank you, I'll go with Steven." she eventually said, feeling slightly embarrassed that everyone was staring at her.

The car journey passed quickly and before Chloe knew it, they pulled up at an amusement park.

"You guys do remember that I don't like heights, though right?" Chloe asked, feeling her stomach drop as they climbed out of the car.

"Don't worry, we won't drag you on the rides." Adrian laughed as he took her hand and walked with her towards the park, Steven following closely behind. Adrian led her into the park and over to the crazy golf. As they queued for their balls and clubs, Chloe glanced around, wondering where Lee and Nathan had got to.

"Knowing Lee, they probably stopped to speak to a hot girl." Steven laughed, when he noticed Chloe looking around.

"Yeah probably." Chloe agreed quietly.

Adrian handed her a club and ball and the three of them went to sit on the bench as they waited for the others. As Chloe sat on the bench with them it suddenly dawned on her that was this was probably the last time that she would spend time with any of them. Despite the hate and anger that she felt towards Lee she was determined to put that to the back of her mind and make sure that they all had a day to remember.

Eventually Lee and Nathan arrived, looking a little flustered.

"What took you so long?" Steven asked as soon as they walked over.

"We got lost, we couldn't find the bloody place." Nathan told them.

"It turns out that Nathan is the worst navigator ever." Lee agreed.

"Couldn't you have just followed the brown signs?" Chloe frowned.

"That probably would have been easier." Lee admitted glancing at Nathan who looked slightly uncomfortable. Chloe couldn't help but feel like they were hiding something, but she decided not to dwell on it.

"Right, who's ready to get beaten then?' Adrian said, quickly standing up.

"Clearly you haven't seen me play golf before." Lee said confidently, wiggling his eyebrows at him.

"Oh, it's on." Adrian countered, before quickly stepping up for his turn.

"Not bad but prepare to be amazed." Lee warned. Lee expertly hit the ball, smiling in satisfaction as he got a hole in one.

"What the hell!" Adrian cried.

"I warned you." Lee laughed.

"Indeed, you did." Steven chuckled.

As they continued playing their way around the course, they could see that Adrian was becoming more and more frustrated.

"What the hell dude, four out of six hole in ones?!" he exclaimed when Lee did it again.

"I told you, I'm good at Crazy Golf." Lee smiled.

"Either that or there is some foul play going on." Adrian muttered.

"Yeah, you're right, I put a giant arse magnet in the hole and one on the ball too." Lee bantered.

"I wouldn't recommend putting magnets on holes and balls Lee." Steven said with a deadpan face.

"He'll be even more drawn to the ladies when he gets dragged towards them by his balls." Nathan added. Everyone burst out laughing loudly.

"There's a lady present, we should probably behave." Lee smiled when they had stopped laughing.

"I know what you are like Lee, late night condom runs remember." Chloe said quietly.

"Wait, what?" Steven asked.

"You sent Chloe out to get condoms for you?!" Nathan exclaimed.

"Yep, more than once too." Chloe said, enjoying the fact that Lee was squirming.

"Lee for god sake." Adrian laughed.

"Why couldn't you get your own?" Nathan frowned.

"I was usually drunk and couldn't drive." he answered, beaming like a child when he got another hole in one.

"Definitely magnets." Adrian muttered.

"I just have an amazing technique." Lee winked, wrapping his arm around Adrian who quickly shrugged him off.

"We've heard." Steven laughed, starting up the innuendos again.

"Seriously though, how did you get so good at this?" Chloe asked.

"Do you want me to show you?" Lee offered.

"As long as it doesn't involve magnets in awkward places." Chloe answered. Lee smiled slightly at her.

"Right stand as though you are about to take your shot." Lee told her. She quickly did as he asked and waited for the next instruction.

"Now visualise where the ball needs to go and then you can estimate the speed required." he told her.

"How do I know?" she asked. Lee sighed and walked over to stand behind her.

"First of all, you are standing wrong." Lee said. He placed his hands on her hips and gently turned her to a different angle. Chloe was very aware of his hands still in place on her hips as she tried to ignore the tingling sensation that she felt all over her body.

"Turn your shoulders too." he said. She did as he asked, feeling the hairs on her arms stand on end as she felt his warm breath on the back of her neck. She could feel Lee hesitate for a moment before gently sliding his hands down her arms and taking her hands in his. Chloe stiffened for a moment feeling slightly uncomfortable, she felt Lee sigh slightly against her. Nathan smiled to himself as he watched the two of them.

"Right now, swing back." Lee said quietly, guiding her arms back.

"And through." he added.

"Oh my god, I did it!" Chloe said excitedly as the ball rolled straight into the hole.

"Although technically you did it." Chloe smiled over her shoulder at Lee who still hadn't let go of her. A moment later Lee reluctantly let go of her, smiling slightly at how happy she looked. The five of them frowned to themselves as they heard one of their songs start to play. The four boys glanced at each other for a moment as the song got close to the chorus. As soon as the chorus started playing the four of them executed the dance moves in perfect harmony. Chloe glanced around as she saw people start to stare at them and whisper amongst themselves.

"You guys can stop showing off now." Chloe laughed.

The group of people that were watching them began to take out their phones and film them. As soon as the song ended all four of the boys burst out laughing.

"I think you're going to have some fans to speak to now that you've drawn attention to yourselves." Chloe told them.

"But it's meant to be your day." Nathan said.

"It's fine, I'll go and grab a drink and you can come and find me when you are done." Chloe smiled.

Chapter Thirteen

Chloe smiled as the boys eventually came and found her at the table booth she'd selected. Steven and Adrian sat opposite her, whilst Lee and Nathan sat on either side of her.

"How were the fans?" Chloe asked, taking a sip of her drink.

"Intense and loud." Steven chuckled.

"Well, it was your own fault." Chloe smiled.

"True, we need some pizza!" Adrian exclaimed.

"Fancy helping me, Nath, Steven?" Adrian asked. Before he had finished asking the question the boys had already started to stand up. Chloe frowned at their backs as they walked away, leaving her and Lee alone again. From their body language she couldn't help but feel like this was a set up.

Chloe remained still and silent, almost hoping that Lee wouldn't notice her, a tactic she'd used quite a lot over the past few months. She glanced at Lee who was scrolling through his phone. The last thing she wanted to do was make conversation with him, but she also couldn't bear the uncomfortable silence. Lee's head quickly snapped up as he glanced over at Nathan who seemed to be mouthing something to him across the restaurant. Lee rummaged in his leather jacket pocket and threw his car keys at Nathan who swiftly caught them and gave Lee a thumbs up.

"He left his wallet in my car." Lee explained when Chloe looked at him questioningly. She smiled at him and returned to people watching around the restaurant. Her gaze wandered past where Lee was sitting, and she scanned the lower floor of the park. Her heart began to pound as she saw Shayne walking up the stairs towards the restaurant.

"Oh no" she muttered to herself, before quickly ducking under the table. As soon as she was safely under the table she crawled into the corner beside Lee's feet, hoping that she would be at a safe angle for Shayne to not notice her.

"What are you doing down there?" Lee asked, bending down to check on her.

"Nothing." Chloe said quickly.

"Well, you're doing something." Lee insisted.

"Please don't ask me." Chloe pleaded. She was afraid to tell Lee that she had spotted Shayne, she was afraid of what he might do. Lee nodded at her and grinned a cheeky smile. He hesitated a moment before climbing under the table beside her.

"What are you doing?" Chloe laughed.

"Seeing what it's like down here, it's surprisingly cosy." he teased her.

"It's quite hidden too." Chloe said, trying if possible, to move even further into the corner.
"It's a bit dirty though." he said, picking up an old chip and flicking it across the floor.

"Yuck." Chloe laughed.

"Are we going to sit down here the rest of the day, I'm not sure we will all fit." he said, smiling at how cute she looked.

"No, just a few more minutes." she told him, feeling slightly nervous about what she should do. If she came out from under the table too soon, she would be confronted by the man who had tried to take advantage of her.

"Seriously, we leave you two alone for a few minutes." Adrian's voice called out. Lee rolled his eyes at Chloe before quickly climbing out from under the table. Chloe slowly lifted her head out from under the table, peering around nervously.

"What were the two of you doing down there?" Steven asked, winking at Lee.

"I'm not really sure to be honest." Lee admitted, smiling slightly.

"Um hmm." Steven said, raising his eyebrow sceptically.

"Well, we weren't shagging if that's what you mean." Lee said quickly.

"He may not have many standards, but they are higher than me." Chloe said quietly as she finally stood up, her eyes scanning the restaurant. Lee frowned and turned to face her, not entirely sure what she meant by that. She seemed to be suggesting that she thought she was beneath him. Lee felt a pang of guilt as he realised it was his fault that she felt that way. He didn't see her as beneath him at all, if anything she was way out of his league. In that moment Lee knew that he would never forgive himself for making her feel the way she did. She'd always had insecurities and he had clearly added to them with his cruelty, even though he'd only been trying to protect her.

Lee could feel his legs going weak, so he quickly sat down. Nathan was right all along, he'd been cruel to this woman to keep her away from him. Someone like him wouldn't be good for her, so in order to protect her he'd made her hate him. Even though it was hard for her, to deal with the way he treated her, it was better than breaking her heart. As he sat silently, consumed by his thoughts, he made a vow to never hurt her again, he just had to get through today and then she would be taken from him, she would be happier that way. He could feel Chloe watching him closely as he slowly reached up and wiped away a stray tear that was rolling down his cheek.

"I have something in my eye." he said quickly, rubbing his eye to make the statement believable. Before he returned to staring into space, clearly deep in thought.

Steven and Adrian placed the pizza boxes on the table and went back to find Nathan who was sorting out the drinks. Chloe froze in her chair as she saw Shayne walking up to the bar, heading straight for Adrian and Steven. Nathan had noticed him too, because at that moment he looked across the room and locked eyes with Chloe. Nathan quickly walked over to the table.

"Get her out of here." Nathan hissed to Lee, quickly putting the car keys down on the table.

"What, why?" Lee frowned, finally snapping out of his thoughts.

"Because the creep is here." Nathan said, pointing to the bar where Shayne was talking to Adrian and Steven.

"Sneak her out whilst he is distracted." Nathan added.

"He wouldn't dare try anything with the four of us here anyway." Lee pointed out, glancing at Chloe who was sitting in place, looking like she wanted the ground to swallow her up. Lee could feel himself becoming angry.

"Maybe I should have a word with him." Lee said angrily, quickly standing up.

"No, you need to take her away from here, save her the humiliation." Nathan pointed out.

"He'll pay for that anyway." Lee muttered, starting to walk away.

"Lee please don't." Chloe pleaded from behind him. As soon as he heard her voice, he stopped, his feet frozen to the spot.

He desperately wanted to make Shayne pay for what he'd tried to do to Chloe, but he remembered his secret vow not to hurt her anymore. He nodded slowly. Lee quickly walked back to the table, grabbing his car keys with one hand and reaching out to take Chloe's hand with the other.

"We'll meet you at the beach." Nathan said quietly. Chloe quickly stood up and followed Lee, who was still holding onto her hand tightly.

"Excuse me." Lee called out to some passers-by as he ran down the escalator, gently pulling Chloe with him. They dodged through the crowd of people, a couple of them recognising Lee, and trying to get his attention, but he ignored them and continued walking. Eventually they reached Lee's car, he quickly unlocked it, waiting outside the car until he knew that Chloe was safely inside the passenger seat. Both of them remained silent as Lee quickly pulled away and began the long journey to the coast.

"Are you okay?" Lee eventually asked Chloe, sounding concerned.

"Yes." she said quietly.

"Chloe?" he tried again.

"I'm fine, nothing happened did it." she insisted.

"Yeah, it did, I kicked everyone's arse at golf." Lee smiled, trying to lighten the atmosphere. Chloe smiled slightly and remained silent. It was clear that she was upset, but didn't want to open up to him, and he couldn't really blame her.

"Why don't you call Nathan?" Lee suggested.

"What for?" she frowned.

"So that you can talk to someone you trust." he explained.

"This whole being kind and caring thing, is it real?" she piped up when she couldn't stand not knowing anymore. Lee glanced at her, not entirely sure what to say.

"The boys told me I had to behave." he eventually said. Chloe felt her heart sink.

"Well, you don't have to pretend to not hate me." she said sadly.

Lee sighed and gripped the steering wheel tightly, desperately trying to resist the urge to stop the car and pull her into his arms. Chloe sighed sadly and turned her back to him, gazing silently out of the window. She angrily wiped away the tears that were slowly rolling down her cheeks. She couldn't help but feel angry with herself for allowing herself to hope that her and Lee could be friends again. Despite how infuriating he was, she missed the way things used to be, when he was one of her best friends. She sniffed quietly, hoping that Lee wouldn't hear her.

"Are you crying?" Lee asked her, glancing to look at her, but quickly having to turn his attention back to the road.

"No." she lied, angrily wiping away the tears.

"Chlo." Lee whispered sympathetically. Chloe felt her heart flutter a little when he said that word. He hadn't called her 'Chlo' for months.

"I'm fine, can we just get there please." she said quickly. Lee nodded to himself and put his foot down. The rest of the journey passed in silence, as soon as they reached the beach Chloe quickly climbed out of the car, sighing in disappointment when she looked out over the quiet bay and saw that the others hadn't arrived yet.

"They probably got held up talking to the slime ball." Lee said from behind her. Chloe nodded and quickly removed her shoes, smiling happily as her feet made contact with the soft sand.

"I haven't been to the beach in so long." she admitted.

"Why, you clearly love it?" Lee frowned. As soon as they'd reached the beach, Lee had seen a surprising change in Chloe. She seemed happy and relaxed and the twinkle was back in her eye that Lee hadn't seen in a long time.

"It's a long way from the city and I don't have a car." she told him.

"See those rocks over there?" she asked, pointing out a cluster of large rocks at the edge of the coastline that started at the sand and headed into the sea.

"Yeah, what about them?" he answered.

"I used to come here with my parents and I used to climb them, I got quite good at rock hopping." she told him.

"It looks a bit dangerous." he said, looking at the jagged edges.

"Not if you do it properly." she said, turning to face him, a cheeky smile on her lips. Before Lee could say anything, she turned and ran towards the rocks.

"Chloe!" Lee called. She ignored him and continued towards the rocks.

"Damn it." he muttered under his breath. He stood for a moment, trying to decide if he should follow her or not. Lee's head snapped towards the carpark as he saw Steven's car pull in. Nathan quickly walked towards Lee, frowning when he saw that he was alone.

"Have you lost her already?" Nathan asked.

"No, she's over there." Lee said, pointing to the rocks in the distance.

"What is she doing?" Nathan frowned.

"Rock hopping apparently." Lee said.

"Trying to kill herself more like it." Steven said as he joined them.

"Did you get the presents out?" Adrian asked Lee.

"No, but I was panicking that she would look in the back of my car and see them." Lee chuckled. Adrian laughed and wandered over to Lee's car to get out Chloe's presents.

"I thought for sure she'd rumbled us when she said about following the brown signs to the park." Lee smiled.

"Me too, I nearly said the gift shop doesn't have signs, but I stopped myself." Nathan laughed. The four of them quickly got to work setting up the food, drink and presents on the sand, ready for when Chloe returned. Nathan laughed at Steven when Steven did a victory dance when he managed to light the makeshift fire that he'd made.

"So, what did Shayne have to say for himself?" Lee asked.

"Just speaking shit basically." Nathan said quietly.

"What does that mean?" Lee persisted.

"Well obviously he says that she led him on, and you overreacted, that he wasn't going to do anything to her." Nathan told him reluctantly, not quite sure how he was going to react.

"Bullshit." Lee said quickly.

"Yeah, like I said, just shit." Nathan agreed.

"How was she when you left?" he added.

"She didn't say much, but I think she was quite upset. She's been better since we got here though, I think the beach is her happy place." Lee told him, smiling to himself as he looked over to Chloe and saw that she was still expertly jumping between the rocks.

"Maybe you should talk to her." Lee added, turning his attention back to Nathan.

"What for?" Nathan frowned.

"She doesn't open up to me does she, maybe she would to you." Lee said quietly. The four of them stopped talking and turned their attention to the horizon as they heard Chloe let out a little squeal of excitement and jump into the ocean. They watched her closely as she swam back to the shore.

"Chloe, I didn't realise you were secretly bonkers." Nathan called out to her. She giggled and slowly walked towards them, wringing out her hair as she walked.

"You made a fire!" she called back to them.

"Yep, I'm quite proud of my fire." Steven admitted. As soon as she reached them, she gazed around at the pile of presents on the sand, looking slightly embarrassed that they'd gone to so much trouble for her. Lee glanced down at her as she stood in front of him, his eyes widening when he saw that her white shirt was now completely see through. He gazed at her flesh, feeling a deep sense of longing for her. The way that her blue lace bra gently cupped her breasts, the creamy white colour of her soft skin that he longed to touch.

His eyes wandered down to her perfectly flat stomach that had a small crystal piercing in her belly button. Eventually Lee was able to bring himself to stop looking at her. He closed his eyes for a moment, trying to focus on something else before he was unable to hide how attracted he was to her. Eventually Lee opened his eyes again and quickly removed his jacket.

"Put your arms in." he said hoarsely, holding the jacket out to Chloe.

"But I'm not cold." she said, frowning.

"No but you have wet T-shirt syndrome." Lee muttered, so that the other boys wouldn't notice. The last thing he wanted to do was to embarrass her. Chloe glanced down at her shirt and her cheeks quickly coloured.

"Oh my god." she said, sounding slightly mortified.

"It's fine, just put the jacket on." Lee said.

She did as he said and put her arms in his jacket. She glanced down at the zip, ready to do it up, but stopped herself when she saw that he was already doing it.

"Damn it." he muttered, getting angry with the zip when it wouldn't do up. It didn't help that his hands were shaking.

"Do you want me to try?" she offered, concerned that one of the boys might glance over and get the wrong idea.

"It always sticks, I need a new jacket really." Lee said, trying to keep himself talking so that he wouldn't think about how close his fingertips were to touching her. Lee smiled in satisfaction as the zip finally began to move. Chloe watched him closely as he slowly moved the zip upwards. Chloe shivered involuntarily as Lee accidentally brushed his fingers against the top of her sternum.

"Sorry." he whispered, mentally cursing himself.

"It's okay." she replied quietly.

"I thought you said that you aren't cold." he said.

"I'm not." she mumbled. They both hesitated for a moment, neither of them knowing what to say to the other.

"Thanks for the jacket." she eventually said. He nodded at her.

"C'mon let's open your presents." he said.

Chapter Fourteen

Chloe followed Lee towards the fire and sat down, the other three boys watching her closely.

"How was Shayne?" Chloe asked them.

"Fine, he was just waffling." Nathan smiled, hoping that she would drop the subject. He wanted her to enjoy the day, not to spend it being upset.

"Did he mention the video?" Chloe asked casually as she picked up a stick and stirred the sand with it.

"What video?" Adrian frowned.

"Never mind." she said quickly.

"Wait, did he film you Chloe?" Lee asked quickly.

"I'm not really sure, I haven't been able to bring myself to watch it." Chloe admitted quietly.

"Kirstie, just said that it's online." she added. Lee quickly pulled out his phone and did a quick search.

"Let's not focus on him, I don't want you to be upset today." Nathan said quickly when he saw what Lee was doing.

"Open some presents." Steven said, gesturing to the pile. Chloe smiled at them and did as they asked. She felt like the luckiest girl in the world as she opened all their thoughtful gifts. They'd kindly given her a blue faux fur blanket to keep her warm while she waited for her heating to be fixed, a year's membership to the zoo and a teddy that was wearing a t-shirt with a picture of her and the boys on it.

"He's so cute!" she exclaimed, placing the teddy on her lap.

"Thanks everyone." she said, hugging Adrian, Steven and Nathan. She glanced awkwardly at Lee who was still looking at his phone, deciding to herself that she felt too uncomfortable to hug him. Nathan opened the pizza boxes and placed them by the fire for everyone to help themselves too.

"I think I've found it." Lee piped up.

"Lee drop it." Nathan said quickly.

"Is it bad?" Chloe asked.

"I don't know, I haven't watched it yet." Lee said.

"Can I see it?" Chloe asked quietly.

Lee nodded and moved so that he was behind her, holding the phone in front of them. The two of them watched the video silently as Chloe finally got to see what had happened between Shayne and Lee when she was hiding in the bathroom. Whoever filmed the video must have been fairly close as Chloe could hear Lee warn Shayne several times before he finally lashed out at him. Chloe sighed quietly to herself as the video finally ended. Lee glanced down at her as he switched off the phone, frowning to himself as she relaxed against him, her back now gently resting against his chest. He put his hands down on the sand behind himself, making himself stable enough to take Chloe's weight and well as his own. Before he realised what, he was doing he gently placed his chin on her shoulder.

"You were right all along, I'm really sorry." Chloe said quietly, playing with the teddy that was still sitting on her lap.

"Right about what?" Lee asked her gently.

"He really was going to rape me wasn't he." she whispered, suddenly realising how close she had come to having her life changed forever. If it hadn't been for Lee, she didn't even want to think about what might have happened.

"I don't know for sure, all I know is that he was trying to follow you." Lee said quietly.

"And I wasn't going to let that happen." he quickly added. Chloe suddenly felt overwhelmed with emotion and gratitude towards Lee. She turned towards him and gently wrapped her arms around his neck. Lee hesitated for a moment before he wrapped his arms around her waist, gently pulling her onto his lap so that he could hold her tighter. He buried his head in her hair, inhaling her scent. He'd wanted to hold her like this for so long that he couldn't help but cherish the moment.

"Thank you for protecting me." she whispered, feeling slightly scared about what might have happened if Lee hadn't stopped Shayne from following her. Lee didn't answer but she knew in her heart that he'd heard her. Chloe couldn't help but frown to herself as she sat in Lee's arms, his grip on her firm and strong but gentle at the same time, as though he didn't want to let her go. She hadn't expected to feel like this, so calm and relaxed, like she was where she'd always wanted to be. Eventually the two of them reluctantly let go of each other. Nathan cleared his throat awkwardly.

"Right, we are going to play a game." Nathan announced.

"Uh oh." Chloe said quietly, suddenly feeling nervous.

"We've known you for the past two years, but we hardly know anything about you because you never talk about yourself." Nathan explained.

"That's because I'm boring." Chloe admitted.

"Nope, we're not having that, prepared to be grilled." Steven grinned.

"And there's a forfeit if you refuse to answer any question we ask." Adrian told her.

"Dare I ask." Chloe said.

"You have to drink a cup of seawater." Nathan chuckled. Chloe jumped slightly as Lee moved from behind her and walked over to the cool box, quickly picking out two beers, before sitting down next to the fire.

"You might need one of these." Lee said, smiling slightly as he handed her a beer.

"Yes, I think I will." Chloe smiled, taking a large swig.

"Fire away then, you can have one question each." she added, gazing around at the group.

"Okay, I'll start...why is no one allowed to know where you live?" Steven asked.

"Because I'm a very private person. Next." she said quickly.

"Why do you never talk about your family?" Lee asked.

"Because I don't have any, I am an only child, with no extended family that I'm in touch with." she answered.

"But you're only in your twenties though, what about your parents?" Lee frowned.

"Mum died about five years ago from cancer, Dad committed suicide a year later. He couldn't cope without Mum, but he waited until I was in a good place with Andy so that I had someone to take care of me." she told them sadly.

The four of them remained silent, not entirely sure what to say. They couldn't help but feel sorry for her, she'd been through so much, yet she never let on that anything was wrong.

"What happened with Andy?" Nathan asked, trying to fill the uncomfortable silence.

"He used to come to work with you every day, then all of a sudden we didn't see him anymore." he added.

"That's because he left." she said, quickly drinking more beer.

"So, he split up with you?" Nathan asked.

"Yes, he left me for someone else." she said quietly.

"I'd made dinner and when he got home, he told me that he'd been seeing someone else for the past few months and loved her more than me. So, he left." Chloe explained quietly.

"He sounds like a wanker." Lee said quietly.

"We could be your wing men and find you a nice guy to take care of you." Adrian suggested.

"No thanks, I've been rather put off the whole thing." she admitted.

"Don't say that." Steven said.

"It's true, and even if it wasn't, I'm not exactly a catch." she whispered.

"Says who?" Nathan frowned.

"If I was, Andy wouldn't have left would he. Besides I'm boring and plain." she said quietly, feeling her eyes start to fill with tears.

"Anyway, next question." she added quickly, just about managing to hold back the tears.

"How many people have you slept with?" Steven blurted, chuckling slightly to himself.

"Steven, you can't ask that?!" Adrian exclaimed.

"I'm trying to get her to drink the seawater." Steven laughed, winking at Chloe. Chloe could feel the boy's eyes burning into her as they waited to see what she was going to do. She didn't want to answer the question as not only was it her private information, but she knew that like most people they wouldn't understand, but at the same time she didn't want to give Steven the satisfaction of drinking the sea water. She smiled at them.

"Give me a cup then." she said. Steven smugly handed her a cup and the four of them watched as she walked down to the sea and filled the cup, quickly returning with it. She stood in front of them and raised the cup to her lips.

"Something else you should know about me, I'm quite stubborn." she smiled, raising her eyebrow at Steven as she poured the water on his 'precious' fire, causing it to sizzle.

"No, not my fire!" Steven cried.

"Serves you right." Nathan laughed.

"Right, you'll pay for that!" Steven grinned. Before he had a chance to stand up, Chloe had already sprinted down the beach. Steven laughed and quickly chased after her.

"I need to take a leak." Adrian said, before walking away. Nathan watched Lee closely who was sitting silently picking at the label on the beer bottle.

"You alright mate?" Nathan asked him.

He nodded silently.

"Lee come on man, tell me what's going on before the others come back." Nathan tried again.

"I think I need to go home." Lee said.

"Why?" Nathan frowned. Lee sighed and glanced over at Chloe when he heard her scream. Steven had picked her up and playfully slung her over his shoulder.

"I hope he doesn't dunk her in the sea, my car keys are in that jacket." Lee said quietly.

"Don't change the subject, what's wrong?" Nathan insisted.

"It's just really hard hearing everything she's been through. She's so amazing and she doesn't even know it." Lee said quietly.

Nathan opened his mouth to say something, but Lee cut him off:

"She just seems so sweet and vulnerable, but she's all alone. And I've probably made her life even worse." he said, angrily wiping away the tears that were rolling down his cheeks.

"You need to talk to her." Nathan said quietly, feeling a small sense of hope that Lee was finally, after all this time, starting to realise how he felt about Chloe.

"About what?" Lee frowned.

"How you feel." Nathan tried, rolling his eyes.

"I just feel sorry for her that's all, she's not had a good time of it." Lee said quietly.

"I've known you a long time Lee, I think it's more than that." Nathan insisted.

Lee raised his eyebrow at Nathan and waited for him to continue.

"Like the way you look at her, and how different you are when she's around. Even how you've been today..." Nathan started.

"That's because you all told me that I have to behave." Lee interrupted.

"Yeah, but the thing is you don't normally do what we ask you too. But on this occasion, you did, because you want her to have a nice day. And you know how much you are going to miss her, so you are cherishing this time." Nathan explained.

"What's your point?" Lee frowned, refusing to admit to Nathan that he was right.

"My point is...that you are in love with her." Nathan sighed, not quite able to believe that he was having to spell this out to Lee. Lee fell silent and started to pick at the beer label again, Nathan words swirling around his head. There was no way that Nathan was right in what he was saying, he couldn't be in love with her could he? His eyes wandered over to Chloe again, he watched longingly as she laughed and messed around with Steven, the smile on her face so wide that Lee found himself smiling slightly. He thought back to a few moments ago when Chloe had opened up about her family and how it felt like someone had punched him in the chest when she told them what Andy had done to her. How he'd faced down Shayne in order to protect her and wanted nothing more than to take care of her. How he wanted to constantly hold her in his arms so that he knew she was safe. Maybe Nathan was right after all...maybe he did secretly have strong feelings for her, that up until this point he hadn't even realised himself that they were there. Lee was snapped out of his thoughts when Nathan finally spoke:

"And you've never been in love before, so you don't know what it is or how to handle it." Nathan tried again, desperately trying to get Lee to open up.

"You're talking rubbish, I just feel bad for her." Lee snapped. Before Nathan could say anything else Lee quickly stood up and walked over to Steven and Chloe.

"Can I have my keys please?" he said sharply as soon as he reached them.

"Are you leaving?" Chloe asked as she rummaged in the jacket pocket and handed him his keys.

"Yeah, I have to be somewhere." Lee said.

"Booty call more like it." Steven chuckled.

"Good luck with your new job." Lee said, choosing to ignore Steven. Chloe nodded and tried to unzip the jacket, cursing under her breath when she couldn't get the zip to move.

"You can keep it if you want." Lee said, wanting to leave as quickly as possible before he changed his mind.

"I don't want it." Chloe snapped. She couldn't help but feel hurt that Lee was leaving early. Even though she knew better, she'd started to think that perhaps he didn't hate her after all, but clearly, he still did and the whole day had been an act. Eventually she managed to unzip his jacket and flung it at him roughly.

"Take care Chloe." Lee said sadly.

"See you." she said bluntly, quickly walking past him and back to the fire.

Chapter Fifteen

Kirstie awoke slowly, blinking as she adjusted to the bright light that was streaming in the window. She smiled to herself when she realised that she was curled up in Ben's arms, who was still fast asleep. She gently planted a kiss on his cheek and snuggled closer to him. Kirstie's eyes bolted open as she heard a knock at the front door, she frowned to herself wondering who it could be this early in the morning. Maybe Michelle had forgotten her keys again, she hardly seemed to be at the flat at the moment. Kirstie scrunched her eyes closed, hoping that whoever was at the door wouldn't knock again. She sighed as she heard another knock at the door. Kirstie sighed as she climbed out of bed, quickly pulled on Ben's shirt that was still laying on the floor and ran to answer the door. She frowned to herself as she answered the door and stood face to face with Nathan.

"Oh hi." Kirstie said.

"Hey, sorry it's early, but I need to talk to you about something." he said.

"Yeah, sure come in." she said, gesturing for him to come in. Kirstie hurried into the kitchen to make them both a cup of tea and quickly returned to the living room.

"Perfect thank you." Nathan smiled as she handed him a cup of tea.

"Hi Nath." Ben said as he walked into the room. Ben quickly sat beside Kirstie and wrapped his arm around her shoulder.

"So, what it is, I need your help to get Chloe to our show tonight." Nathan said.

"What, why?" Kirstie frowned, take a small sip of her tea.

"Lee wrote a song, and although he'd never admit it, it's about how he feels about Chloe. We are going to be performing it for the first time tonight, I think she should hear it." Nathan explained.

"He hates her, though doesn't he?" Ben frowned.

"No of course not." Kirstie said quietly.

"Wait, what, have I missed something?" Ben asked.

"It is kind of obvious." Kirstie smiled at Ben.

"Not to me it isn't." Ben chuckled.

"Anyway, she won't go if I invite her, maybe you could find a way of getting her there so that she doesn't suspect." Nathan suggested.

"I don't understand what you are hoping to achieve from it." Kirstie frowned.

"Maybe the two of them will finally realise how they feel about each other." Nathan said hopefully.

"But he's an idiot, he doesn't deserve her. She needs someone that will treat her right and take care of her." Kirstie pointed out.

"Trust me, he will. I think he pushes her away because he's afraid to hurt her, but he won't." Nathan sighed.

"Well obviously, but it's hurting her." Kirstie said.

"I know, I've tried to get through to him, but he's so closed off, that's why I'm hoping if she realises the song is about her that she will talk to him." Nathan said quietly.

"It'll have to be subtle though, we'll need to let her come to that conclusion on her own, otherwise it's forced." Ben piped up. Nathan nodded and glanced at Kirstie, hoping that she would agree to his plan.

"Don't tell anyone I told you this, but he is lost without her." Nathan tried, when Kirstie still hadn't agreed.

"What do you mean lost?" she asked.

"He's quiet, distracted, getting with even more women than before, which I'm sure is so that he can try and forget about *her.*" Nathan answered.

"Okay fine." Kirstie sighed.

"I still don't think he's good for her, but at the end of the day it has to be her decision." she quickly added.

"Awesome!" Nathan exclaimed excitedly, quickly standing up.

"Make sure she's listening to the song." he called back as he walked towards the front door.

"Which one?" Ben called.

"Broken." Nathan called back.

Chapter Sixteen

Kirstie smiled as she looked up from her magazine as she watched Chloe hand out outfits to the new band that she was now working with. Chloe had been working for them for a couple of weeks now and Kirstie had met them a few times, and all five of them seemed nice. She was pleased that Chloe was away from the toxic environment that she was working in before, but as she watched her best friend, she couldn't help but notice that something was different with her. Something that was so subtle that other people wouldn't notice but Kirstie could tell that something was missing with Chloe. She sighed to herself as she thought about what Nathan had asked her to do. Maybe he was right, maybe the two of them were secretly in love with each other and for some unknown reason they pretended to hate each other. Maybe Lee wasn't the only one that was struggling when they were apart. As much as Kirstie hated the thought of lying to her friend, she knew that she had to do this.

Kirstie silently put down the magazine.

Chloe, can I ask a big favour?" Kirstie said nervously.

"That depends what it is." Chloe smiled, as she continued applying makeup to Tom's face.

"I was meant to be going to a gig with Ben tonight, I've had the tickets for ages, and we had a huge row last night so now I don't have anyone to go with." Kirstie explained.

"And you want me to go with you?" Chloe asked.

"If you wouldn't mind, I don't have anyone else to go with." Kirstie said quietly, starting to feel more and more guilty.

"Is it that nineties gig you spoke about a while ago?" Chloe asked.

Kirstie nodded, feeling slightly nervous that Chloe was about to cotton on to the plan.

"Eclipse will be there, though won't they?" Chloe said quietly.

"Yeah, I guess so, but it'll be fine, you can put your hood up when they come on. It'll be busy, it's not like they will notice you in the crowd." Kirstie explained.

"Hmm...I'm still not keen." Chloe said quietly, feeling slightly awkward at the thought of being in a room with them again. She hadn't heard from any of the boys in the past two weeks and was still a little hurt by Lee's abrupt departure last time she saw him.

"Please Chloe, I really want to go." Kirstie pleaded.

"Michelle.....Louise.....Kathleen...anyone that's not me?" Chloe suggested desperately.

"All busy." Kirstie lied.

"Aww c'mon Kirstie." Chloe sighed.

"Please." Kirstie smiled, giving Chloe her puppy dog eyes. Chloe hesitated for a moment, wishing that she didn't have to be put in this position but knowing that she couldn't say no to her friend.

"Okay fine." Chloe sighed. Kirstie let out a little squeal of excitement and quickly rushed over to hug Chloe.

"It'll be amazing." Kirstie whispered in her ear.

Kirstie and Chloe laughed as they danced along to the music. The atmosphere in the stadium was so infectious, that even though Chloe didn't want to be there, she found herself having a good time. The music stopped for a moment as the announcer told the crowd that Eclipse were taking the stage next.

"I still can't believe you talked me into this." Chloe whispered in Kirstie's ear. Kirstie felt a pang of guilt once again that she was setting up her friend. She could only hope that everything would work out well. Chloe quickly pulled up her hood as Eclipse took to the stage. She could feel her eyes fill with tears as she laid eyes on them again. Chloe cringed slightly and moved to stand closer to Kirstie as Lee walked over to their side of the stage. She glanced up at him, even though he was a reasonable distance away, Chloe felt like she was close enough to touch him.

"This is an exclusive of our new song Broken!" Nathan announced.

Chloe's eyes were fixed on Lee as Adrian began to sing the opening of the song. Goosebumps rose on her arms as Lee held the microphone up to his mouth and began to sing:

My heart is yearning for you

I wonder if you feel it too

So many words I wanted to say

That never came out the right way

Now that I've lost you for good

I'd tell you I love you if only I could

I'm broken without you

As soon as the song finished the crowd erupted into enthusiastic applause. A few random girls screaming out the names of their favourite member. Kirstie gently wrapped her arm around Chloe's waist. Chloe watched Lee closely, it was difficult for her to see him closely under the lights, but she could have sworn that his eyes had filled with tears. He squatted down on the stage and pressed his microphone against his forehead, a look of pain etched on his face. It was only in that moment that Chloe became aware of the warm tears that were steadily rolling down her cheeks. She had no idea how long they had been falling or even why she was crying, all she knew was that she had to get out of this room. Kirstie watched in horror as Chloe rushed out of the room, quickly squeezing her way between the crowd and rushing into the bathroom.

As soon as she was safely in the bathroom, she leant her back against the wall and slowly slid down it, bringing her legs up to protect herself. She couldn't understand why she was so upset; something had stirred inside of her as soon as Lee had walked out onto the stage. As soon as Nathan had announced the song title, she'd recognised it as the one that Lee had been working on all those weeks ago when she still worked with him. Since the first moment that she'd heard the words, she hadn't been able to stop crying, but she didn't know why. How could someone so full of hate and anger write such a meaningful song? The way that he'd sung the song, he'd clearly meant every word.

Chloe jumped as the bathroom door burst open.

"Just wait a minute, we need to find a cubicle first." she heard a female voice giggling from the doorway. She couldn't see who the voice belonged to as it was around the corner from where she was sitting. Chloe quickly wiped her tears away, desperately hoping that whoever it was wouldn't notice. She gasped as a beautiful young woman walked around the corner, her hand holding on tightly to Lee. As soon as Lee locked eyes with Chloe he instantly let go of the woman's hand.

"Chloe!" Lee exclaimed.

Chloe remained silent, glancing between Lee and the beautiful woman standing beside him. She felt like someone was stabbing her in the heart repeatedly when she joined the dots in her head. As Chloe sat silently, she could feel herself becoming angry with herself, she shouldn't be feeling like this about him. This man hated her, he'd teased her, belittled her and tore her down repeatedly, so why was she getting butterflies in her stomach just looking at him and why now?

"Are you okay Chloe?" Lee asked gently when he noticed that she was crying. Chloe nodded silently, wishing that the ground would swallow her up.

"What happened?" he asked. Chloe remained silent, not really wanting to look at him or talk to him. The mystery woman smiled at Lee and took his hand.

"Laura, stop it." Lee snapped as he pulled his hand away from her, like he'd received an electric shock. Chloe glanced up as Lee crossed the room and squatted in front of her and placed his hands on her knees. Her skin tingled under his touch.

"Chlo, talk to me." Lee tried again, his tone almost pleading. Impulsively Chloe placed her hands-on top of his and gently played with his fingers. Lee glanced down at Chloe's hands and gently curled his fingers over hers, tracing small circles on them.

"Lee, don't we have something we should be doing." Laura said from behind them, sounding slightly frustrated.

"No, you can go." Lee said quickly, his eyes not leaving Chloe.

"But..." she started.

"Look, why don't you go and find someone else to get off with, try Steven." Lee sighed, finally turning to face Laura.

"It's fine, I have to go anyway, you get back to your beautiful guest." Chloe said quietly as she slowly stood up. Lee's heart felt heavy as he watched Chloe walk out of the bathroom. His heart was pounding seeing Chloe again, even though it had only been a couple of weeks, he felt like he was complete when he was with her. He knew that he missed her, but he hadn't realised how much until she was in front of him once again. His heart was pulling him to go after her, even though he'd vowed to stay away from her, he needed to see her. As Lee stood leaning his back against the sink, Laura walked over to him and slowly began to unzip her dress in front of him, smiling at him as she did so.

"Did you not hear what I said?" Lee sighed as he gently squeezed past her.

"I'll need my jacket back too.' he added, referring to the fact that she'd taken it off him on the way to the bathroom. She sighed and handed him the jacket.

"You're a dick!" she called after him as he left the bathroom.

"Yeah, I know." he muttered under his breath. He sighed and ran his hand through his hair in frustration, suddenly realising that he had no idea where Chloe had gone. He racked his brain for a moment, desperately trying to figure out where she might have gone. He suddenly remembered she said that she had to go. Before he could talk himself out of it, he ran out of the venue, quickly dodging between people, desperately hoping that he would catch up to her in time. As soon as Lee was outside the venue, he looked around, breathing a sigh of relief when he noticed her standing outside, the venue, her jacket collar turned up against the wind. He quickly walked over to her.

"What's going on Chloe?" he asked, slightly breathless from running.

"Nothing I'm fine." Chloe said quietly, trying to delete the thoughts of him with Laura that were swirling around her head.

"Well, what are you doing waiting out here?" Lee asked.

"Getting some fresh air." she said quietly.

"Why were you crying?" he asked, sounding concerned.

"I don't know really, just hearing that song made me feel really emotional." Chloe admitted.

"What song.....Broken?" Lee frowned, his heart pounding nervously. He couldn't help but feel concerned that Chloe might have realised that he'd written those words about her. She nodded slowly.

"Why?" Lee asked, his mouth suddenly feeling very dry.

"I just thought that...oh I don't know, I'm being stupid, same as usual." Chloe sighed. The more time that passed the more frustrated she was becoming with herself; she always knew her own mind, but right now she was so confused, she had no idea what she was feeling or why. Lee watched her closely, feeling slightly sorry for her. He hated it when she tore herself down.

"Anyway, you have a beautiful woman waiting in there for you, you shouldn't be out here talking to me. It's not like I am important, I'm a nobody." Chloe said quietly, her insecurities getting the better of her once again. Lee shook his head slowly, not quite able to believe that someone as naturally beautiful as her, constantly doubted herself. Lee made a snap decision.

Chloe glanced up at Lee as he began to stride purposefully towards her. She watched as he threw the jacket that was in his hand, over the venue railing on the way past. As Lee eventually reached her, Chloe impulsively stepped back, gasping as her back made contact with the venue wall. As soon as Lee reached her, he gently cupped her face before leaning down to kiss her. Chloe froze in shock for a moment but eventually relaxed into the tender kiss. After a few moments Lee broke the kiss, his face lingering against hers as he pulled away reluctantly. He gently planted a peck on her lips. Chloe slowly opened her eyes as she heard Lee sigh. She watched as he placed his head and hands on the wall behind her. Chloe sighed deeply, feeling comforted by Lee's warm body that was pressed against her.

"I shouldn't have done that I'm sorry." he whispered. Chloe gently placed her hand on his broad chest, frowning slightly when she noticed that his heart was pounding under her hand.

"Why did you then?" Chloe asked nervously.

"I don't know." Lee said quietly, as he slowly moved away from her, Chloe shivered as she felt his warm breath against her neck as he moved away.

"I like the ladies remember." Lee added quickly, starting to feel angry with himself for not being able to resist her.

"Yes, but beautiful ones normally." Chloe whispered. Lee silently walked over to the railing and picked up his jacket.

"But I was in the area, so I'll do right." Chloe said sadly.

"I didn't say that Chloe." Lee said quietly, before quickly walking away before he said or did something, he would later regret.

Chapter Seventeen

Chloe stood silently outside the venue; her head completely scrambled. She had never been this confused in her life, she felt powerless, as if she didn't know her mind.

"There you are!" Kirstie exclaimed, as she wandered over to her.

"Oh my god, are you okay?" she added when she saw Chloe's pained expression.

"Yes." Chloe said quietly.

"Come back inside, it's freezing." Kirstie said, rubbing her cold arms.

"I think I'd rather just go home." Chloe said quietly.

"No, come on, I'll buy you a drink." Kirstie insisted, taking hold of Chloe's hand and dragging her back into the venue.

Chloe sighed and allowed herself to be dragged into the bar. She frowned to herself as Kirstie led her over to a table where Ben sat smiling at them.

"I thought you guys had fallen out?" Chloe asked them as soon as she sat down. Kirstie and Ben glanced at each other, the two of them squirming slightly.

"Yeah...about that..." Ben said nervously.

"I'm really sorry, you seemed sad and I thought you might want to see Lee again." Kirstie explained.

"Why?" Chloe frowned.

"I don't know really, I was just trying to help you, I knew you were upset that you'd fallen out with him. I thought it might be good for the two of you to talk." Kirstie tried, if possible, feeling even more guilty than before.

"Well, you could have just said that you didn't have to lie to me to get me here." Chloe snapped.

"I'm sorry." Kirstie said again.

"Yes, so am I, I'm sorry that I trusted you and that I did something that I didn't want to do, to try and be a good friend for you!" Chloe exclaimed angrily.

"C'mon now ladies, let's not fall out over it. Technically it was Nathan's idea anyway." Ben said quickly.

"Wait, what?" Chloe frowned.

"Nathan asked us to get you here, we were just helping." Kirstie said.

"Yes, but I don't understand why." Chloe said quietly.

"You need to speak to him about that, we're not getting involved." Ben said quickly.

"But you are involved Ben, the moment the two of you got me here, you became involved." Chloe muttered angrily.

"It's not worth falling out over, I said I'm sorry." Kirstie said quietly.

"I'll get some drinks in and we can just forget about the whole thing." Ben said, before quickly standing up and walking over to the bar.

"I really am very sorry Chloe; I really was just trying to help you feel better. You haven't seemed yourself and I thought seeing him might cheer you up." Kirstie said as soon as Ben walked away.

"I know, I just wish you hadn't lied to me." Chloe said quietly.

Kirstie fell silent for a moment, feeling slightly awkward as she sat opposite her friend. Chloe had barely looked at them, she sat watching herself twirling the beer mat.

"Maybe you should speak to Lee before you go, he's probably still here somewhere." Kirstie suggested when she couldn't stand the silence any longer.

"I already spoke to him briefly." Chloe muttered. She sighed to herself before quickly bringing Kirstie up to speed on what had happened between Lee and herself. Even though she was still a little angry with Kirstie, she needed to open up to someone, to try and figure out what was going on in her head.

"And how was the kiss?" Kirstie asked, wiggling her eyebrows. Ben glanced between the two of them as he returned to the table and handed out the drinks.

"Bacardi and Coke, I made it a double." Ben grinned as he handed Chloe her drink. Chloe smiled her thanks at him. Kirstie raised her eyebrow at Chloe, still waiting for an answer to her question.

"It was actually really good." Chloe admitted, her cheeks colouring. Ben and Kirstie watched as Chloe quickly downed her whole drink and placed her head in her hands.

"This is such a mess." Chloe said quietly.

"No, it's not." Kirstie said, reaching over to take one of Chloe's hands and squeezing it reassuringly.

"Yes, it is, I can't believe I'm this stupid. I think I'm falling for someone that hates me." Chloe muttered.

"He doesn't hate you Chloe." Kirstie said gently.

"I'm so confused, when I heard that song. I felt like it was trying to tell me something." Chloe said thoughtfully.

"Like what?" Kirstie prompted, trying to get Chloe to reach the correct conclusion herself.

"I don't know like it was telling me that I have feelings for him but have never realised." Chloe said.

"Not exactly." Ben frowned, not quite able to believe how low Chloe's confidence was that it didn't even enter her head that someone could care about her or maybe even love her. Kirstie gently elbowed him in the ribs, giving Ben the silent signal to him not to say anything, Chloe needed to figure things out for herself.

"And the way that he kissed me." Chloe sighed.

"You need to talk to him, tell him how you feel, who knows he might feel the same way." Kirstie suggested.

"I doubt it." Chloe replied.

"You'll never know unless you talk to him, what's the worst that can happen." Ben said.

"That he'll be nasty, and I'll be humiliated again." Chloe muttered.

"Chloe, you have to speak to him. You'll regret it if you don't." Kirstie insisted.

"Maybe." Chloe said thoughtfully.

She sat silently with her thoughts. As nervous as she was about talking to Lee, she knew that Kirstie and Ben were right. She would regret it if she didn't, and the way that he'd kissed her, surely, he did feel the same. Chloe knew it was a chance that she had to take, before it was too late.

Chapter Eighteen

The following day dawned bright and clear, Chloe slowly rubbed the sleep out of her eyes as she sat up, waiting a moment for her eyes to adjust to the bright sunlight. She sighed to herself as she gently rubbed her sore back muscles, gazing around the park as she did so. She quickly stood up and brushed the dirt off her trousers. Chloe jumped slightly as she saw a young couple walking towards her, they whispered something to each other and smiled at her sympathetically on the way past. Chloe sighed to herself, this was the part of her life that she found the hardest, the constant judgement and pity. She didn't want anyone to feel sorry for her, she didn't want pity. Danny waved at her from the other side of the park, she waved back and quickly hitched her backpack on her back. As soon as she reached Danny, he quickly hugged her tightly.

"It's going to be a nice day." Danny said, as soon as he let go of her.

"It's a shame it's so cold." Chloe replied, pulling down the sleeves of her jacket so that they covered her hands. Danny nodded at her. Chloe sighed to herself when she saw the look of sadness etched on Danny's face. He was reasonably new to living rough and she knew that there were still moments that he missed his home comforts. Even though she knew that it was selfish of her she couldn't help but feel slightly pleased that Danny had come into her life. Despite the fact that she'd only knew him for a couple of weeks, the two of them had a strong bond. They understood each other in a way that nobody else did and they knew the hardships that they both faced on a daily basis.

"I'm going to go busking later if you want to come?" he said, snapping her out of her thoughts.

"I can't, I need to be somewhere." she said quietly, suddenly remembering her conversation with Ben and Kirstie last night.

She'd had plenty of time to think last night and she knew in her heart that they were right, she had fallen for Lee and she needed to tell him.

"Are you working today?" he asked her.

"No, there's just something I have to do." she said quietly, trying to control the butterflies that were swirling in her stomach.

"Speaking of which, would you look after my bag please?" Chloe asked him. Danny nodded and smiled as Chloe removed her backpack and handed it to him. She felt slightly sad as she handed it to him, the small bag which contained the only items she owned.

"I'll keep it safe." he told her, clearly sensing how she was feeling.

"Thank you, I'll see you later." she said, quickly walking away before she talked herself out of what she was about to do.

About an hour later Chloe finally reached Lee's house. She gasped as she saw just how big it was. Despite the fact that she'd been to his house before, it never failed to take her breath away. Since she'd reached Chelsea, the people that she'd passed had sneered at her, all of them clearly thinking that she was beneath them. Like she was a piece of mould that needed to be eradicated from the neighbourhood. Chloe quickly walked up the driveway, stopping when she reached the front door. She took a deep breath to steady her nerves and knocked.

Chloe heard movement in the house and a few moments later the front door opened. Her heart fluttered a little as Lee stood in front of her, his shirt unbuttoned and fluttering in the slight breeze. She couldn't help but notice how attractive he looked with his hair messed up.

"Sorry, did I wake you?" she asked suddenly realising how early it was for a weekend.

"Nope." he gestured for her to come in, quickly closing the door behind them.

"Laura just left and I haven't showered yet." he added, slowly doing up the buttons on his shirt.

"You went back to her then." she said, her heart breaking a little.

"Of course, I did." he said matter of factly.

She nodded slowly, trying to ignore the lump that was rising in her throat.

"So, I'm guessing you've come to apologise then?" he prompted her after a few moments of silence.

"Apologise for what, you kissed me?" she frowned.

"Not that, the article." he said. Chloe frowned in confusion, having no idea what he was talking about. Lee rolled his eyes and picked up the newspaper, quickly handing it to her.

"Turn to page nine." he told her sternly. Chloe quickly did as he asked, feeling slightly afraid of what she was going to discover.

"Oh my god." Chloe whispered, her heart sinking as she saw a photo of her and Lee kissing outside the venue last night. The headline read: *Notorious Ladies Man Lee Knight's New Mystery Woman?*

"Yeah, my thoughts exactly." Lee snapped.

"I know you are struggling with money, but I didn't think that you'd stoop that low." he said angrily.

"Wait, you think I sold them the story?" she asked.

"And what, got you to follow me outside because I knew that you would kiss me!" she exclaimed, starting to lose her temper.

"Well, it wasn't a chance encounter because they know your name." he argued.

"Yes, but only my first name and they've got my age wrong. I think I know how old I am." she pointed out.

"Well, you're obviously not going to admit it or apologise so I don't understand why you came over." he said dismissively.

"Nor do I." she muttered to herself.

"I didn't do this, but you can believe what you like." she added, folding up the newspaper and throwing it down on the counter.

"You're just annoyed that you got caught kissing someone that wasn't one of your hot models." she added angrily. Lee shook his head angrily.

"Why are you even here?" he sighed. Chloe smiled sarcastically to herself, her blood boiling that he thought she was capable of doing something like that to him. She wasn't calculating and manipulative and even if she was, she wouldn't do anything to hurt him. Least of all something that hurt her too, the last thing she wanted was to see her photo in a newspaper. Chloe swallowed the lump that was in her throat as she suddenly realised that he really didn't know her at all. In just over two years he knew nothing about her.

"I don't know anymore." she said quietly. The realisation dawning on her that he didn't feel the same. If he did, he wouldn't be accusing her of something like this. Before Lee could say anything, else Chloe walked out of his house slamming the door behind herself.

Chapter Nineteen

Ben glanced up from his book as he watched Kirstie rushing around her flat, frantically setting out plates of food.

"Exactly how many people are you expecting?" Ben frowned as he noticed a large selection of nibbles.

"Quite a few, it's better to have more food than not enough." she told him, slowly removing the cling film from the plates.

"You're meant to be helping." she added.

"What do you want me to do?" he sighed.

"Set out the drinks and some glasses and stuff." she told him.

Ben nodded and quickly set to work.

"Also, you can be doorman." she quickly added when the doorbell rang. Ben sighed and did as Kirstie asked.

Ben felt like he'd been opening and closing the door for hours when he finally closed it behind what he hoped was the final guest. He gazed around the crowded room checking that everyone had arrived. Ben mentally checked them off in his head: Michelle, Kathleen, Louise, Matt, Mark and Nathan. He cursed under his breath when he noticed for the first time that Nathan had brought Lee with him. Ben scanned the room, searching for Kirstie smiling to himself when he saw Kirstie beaming with happiness.

"Right, I think that's everyone, so help yourself to food and drink, don't get too drunk as we will be playing Truth or Dare later." Kirstie announced to the room. Some of the group glanced at each other nervously, whilst others groaned loudly.

"Oh, lighten up, it'll be fun." Kirstie said shortly.

As the group turned their attention away from Kirstie and began to mingle with each other, Ben quickly made his way through the crowd. Kirstie frowned at him as he gently placed his hand on her back and guided her away from the group.

"What's wrong?" she asked him.

"Nathan has brought Lee." he hissed under his breath.

"What, but he wasn't invited?!" Kirstie exclaimed. "I can't believe he'd come here after how he treated Chloe." she added, her blood boiling as she remembered her devastated friend showing up on her doorstep in floods of tears, only two days ago. Kirstie knew that Lee would be lucky to have someone as special as Chloe, but when she'd visited him to reveal her feelings, he'd hurt her yet again.

"Maybe I should have a word with him." she said angrily.

"No, just leave it." Ben said quickly.

"I don't want him near her." she said quickly.

"Chloe isn't here anyway." he pointed out.

"What?" she frowned, craning her head to gaze around the room, frowning when she realised that Ben was right. She couldn't help but feel a little worried. When Kirstie saw Chloe a couple of days ago, she had been excited to come along to the party, and Kirstie had promised her that out of the Eclipse boys she would only invite Nathan.

"It's probably a good thing if *he* is here." she said quietly. As if Lee knew that they were talking about him, he glanced across the room at them, locking eyes with Kirstie almost instantly. Kirstie's heart sunk as she saw Lee making a beeline for her, Matt quickly noticed what was happening and followed him.

"Oh god, he's coming this way." Kirstie muttered.

"Be nice." Ben said quickly.

"I'm not the one who's a dick." she said firmly, instantly stopping speaking when Lee stood in front of her.

"Where is Chloe?" he demanded instantly.

"How should I know?!" Kirstie said defensively.

"Nathan said she'd be here." Lee said thoughtfully, almost as if he was talking to himself.

"She was invited, I don't know why she isn't here." Kirstie said.

"Maybe she'll be here later." Lee said quietly.

"Why, what's the big deal?" Ben asked.

"I need to apologise." Lee said quietly.

"You mean for accusing her of selling a story." Kirstie said sarcastically.

"Yeah that, it wasn't her, Laura admitted that it was her." Lee said.

Kirstie frowned, she had no idea who Laura was, and she didn't really care, all she cared about was keeping this cruel man away from her friend.

"Call her or text her then." Ben piped up.

"I tried calling, there's no answer." Lee said quietly.

"That usually means that someone doesn't want to talk to you." Kirstie snapped.

"It's not that, her phone broke, and she can't afford a new one." Matt interjected.

"I bumped into her yesterday when I was in town. I took her for a coffee, and she told me that her phone is broken." Matt explained.

"Who can't afford a new phone?" Lee frowned.

"Quite a lot of people actually, just because you don't have to worry about money, normal people do." Kirstie snapped quickly, her tone cutting.

"Okay, why don't you go and see to your guests?" Ben suggested, quickly trying to diffuse the situation. Kirstie nodded and quickly walked away before she said something that she would later regret.

"She's okay, though right?" Lee asked, softening slightly as soon as Kirstie walked away. "Yeah, I think so, she seems to be enjoying her new job." Matt said.

"It's a shame it came to that though, all the boys miss her.... even you." Matt prompted. Lee nodded slowly. Matt sighed to himself, knowing that he was going to regret it, but he could see on Lee's face how desperately he wanted to speak to Chloe and Matt was still hopeful that one day that her and Lee would reconcile so that Chloe would come back.

"You could always call Danny and ask to speak to her." Matt said.

"Who the hell is Danny?" Lee asked sharply.

"I don't know, I just know that she said she's not living on her own anymore, she has Danny and that if we need her to call him." Matt said.

"Yeah, but who is he?" Lee asked again.

"I honestly don't know." Matt said quickly, holding his hands up in defence. Lee thought for a moment, trying to swallow the lump that was rising in his throat, but his mouth was too dry.

"I've lost her haven't I." Lee whispered to himself.

"What?" Matt asked.

"Nothing." Lee said quickly. Before Matt could say anything Lee quickly walked away. Matt's gaze followed him, slightly nervous that he was going to do something stupid, like the loose cannon that he was. He couldn't help but breathe a sigh of relief when he saw Lee leave the house. Matt glanced at Kirstie, smiling slightly when he saw her visibly relax.

"Right truth or dare everyone!" Kirstie called excitedly. As soon as everyone settled on the floor, Kirstie happily piped up:

"Michelle your turn." Kirstie announced.

"I'll go with truth." Michelle said.

"Who was the last person you kissed?" Michelle glanced at Mark for a moment.

"Actually, I want to do a dare instead let's have some fun." she added. Everyone frowned at her wondering why she wouldn't just answer the simple question but then Nathan quickly piped up:

"Okay lick either an armpit or foot of every person in this room." he laughed as everyone groaned.

"That's gross" Michelle sulked.

"Should have just answered the question then shouldn't you." Nathan laughed as Michelle got up and started licking body parts.

"I'll have truth as well please." Kathleen said.

"So, Kathleen, your question is why are you not joining us in the shots and cocktails?" Louise laughed.

Kathleen gazed around at everyone waiting for her answer, feeling very uncomfortable wondering if she should really tell them the truth or if she could pass.

"If you pass on the truth you have to do a forfeit and that is to run around the block in just your underwear." Louise added sensing the hesitation.

"Erm well, this isn't really how I planned on announcing this, but I guess it's as good a time as any, I... well, I'm pregnant." Kathleen said staring at the floor and playing nervously with a loose strand of her hair.

The group let out a chorus of "Wows" and "Congratulations" that echoed around the room except one murmur of "You're what?" Kirstie looked around in the direction of that voice, she's was almost certain it was Mark who was stood back from all the others hugging Kathleen and looking a little bit confused. As soon as he noticed Kirstie staring at him, he quickly hugged Kathleen awkwardly.

"I'm going for truth." Matt said.

"Tell us about when you lost your virginity." Nathan asked. Matt shifted a little and looked around at the others, he glanced at Kirstie who was giggling with Ben and not looking his way, he felt so uncomfortable sharing when it wasn't just about him.

"We were at college and had been dating for a few months and we had gone away for a weekend to see a show, we had a really nice meal followed by a walk along the beach in the moonlight." Matt started describing how nice and romantic the night was.

"Okay enough of the boring stuff get to the good bit." Nathan laughed.

"Well after we went back to the hotel, I told her for the first time that I loved her and thankfully she said it back." Matt laughed.

"Well things just happened" he said looking slightly awkward.

"Ahh you're a soppy one aren't you, how cute." Louise laughed.

There was a moment of silence before Michelle suddenly realised something:

"Wait a minute, weren't you dating Kirstie back in college?" she said.

The group glanced at Kirstie who looked slightly mortified, her cheeks slowly colouring.

"Okay who's next, Mark?" Ben said, quickly taking charge of the situation before anyone could say anything else to embarrass Kirstie further. He was shocked by the latest revelation but could feel how tense Kirstie was beside him and that she didn't want to discuss it front of everybody.

"Well after that shocker I think I'll stick to dares." Mark laughed.

"Switch clothes with one of the girls for the next 30 mins." Nathan said with a cheeky grin.

"Okay, come on then, do you mind switching with me?" he said to Kathleen motioning for her to join him in the next room so they could swap clothes. He was secretly hoping he would be able to ask her about the baby when they were alone.

"Aww that sounds fun I could have switched with you." Michelle said looking a little disappointed he hadn't picked her.

"Too late." Kathleen grinned, before following Mark into the spare room.

Chapter Twenty

"Do we have to keep going over the same section over and over again?!" Lee snapped at Matt as he asked the band to run the song for what felt to Lee like the hundredth time.

"When everyone gets it right, we can stop." Matt insisted, starting to get frustrated with Lee, who'd been in a foul mood the whole day.

"I don't see the point; we know the words and we know the bloody dance routine." Lee argued.

"Well, you obviously don't otherwise we wouldn't have to keep redoing it." Matt sighed.

"I bloody did it right the first time!" Lee snapped, angrily putting his microphone back on the stand.

"You guys want to do the reunion tour, I'm just making sure that it's perfect, so that the four of you don't go out on stage unprepared." Matt argued back.

"Well, I'm not running it again." Lee smirked.

"Oh, c'mon Lee, just do as you're told." Steven sighed.

"Sometimes you are more hormonal than a pre-menstrual woman." Adrian said, rolling his eyes.

"Well, I'm done." Lee stated before quickly walking off stage and into the dressing room.

"I'll go after him." Nathan said sighing slightly. Nathan quickly walked into the dressing room, sighing when he saw Lee sitting on one of the sofas, watching the television.

"What's with you today?" Nathan asked impatiently.

"Not a lot." Lee replied dismissively. Nathan shook his head and rolled his eyes.

"Is this all because Chloe wasn't at the party last night?" Nathan asked.

"Nope." he said quickly.

"So, it has absolutely nothing to do with the fact that she's living with a guy then?" Nathan tried. Lee sighed and picked up the television remote and turned to face Nathan.

"You keep saying that I'm into Chloe, but maybe it's you. You're the one that keeps going on about her." Lee said defensively.

"You're such a child sometimes." Nathan sighed.

Lee shrugged and glanced back at the television frowning as he listened to the news announcer:

Police are appealing for witnesses after a young woman was stabbed in the Park late last night. The victim is said to be in her early twenties and of slim build. She is said to be in critical condition.

Lee gasped, the television remote falling out of his hand as a picture of the victim was displayed on the screen. He would recognise those deep blue eyes anywhere.
"It's Chloe." Lee whispered to Nathan.

"Huh?" Nathan frowned, glancing up from his phone screen to look at the television.

"Oh my god!" Nathan exclaimed.

"I have to go and see her." Lee said, quickly standing up, his legs feeling weak. He quickly steadied himself against the wall and took deep breaths, trying to calm down the intense fear that he was feeling. It felt like someone had stuck a screwdriver in his heart and was slowly twisting it. Nathan remained silent, not quite able to process what was going on.

Lee quickly walked through the corridors, hurrying out to the carpark.

"Where are you going, you can't just leave?!" Adrian called after him.

"Matt will go mental!" Adrian tried, not aware of the severity of the situation.
"You can cover my parts." Lee told him, as he carried on walking.

"Yeah right." Adrian laughed.

As soon as Lee reached the carpark he quickly climbed into his car, pulling away so fast that the tyres screamed against the tarmac. He made it to the hospital at record speed, desperately hoping that he'd chosen the correct hospital. All he could do was to pick the hospital closest to where Chloe had been stabbed and hope that he was correct. He ran into the A and E department, quickly resting his hands against the reception desk, trying to get his breath back.

"Is there a Chloe Evans here?" he asked the receptionist. She glanced up at him and typed on her computer.

"She's not long out of theatre, Room B." she said, sounding slightly disinterested. Lee nodded and quickly walked down the hallway, searching for her room.

He quickly stopped as he walked past the window to Room B and saw Chloe lying motionless on the bed. Her eyes were closed tightly, her chest rising and falling very slowly. Lee leant against the window frame, suddenly feeling an overwhelming wave of relief to know that she was still alive. He couldn't bring himself to tear his eyes away from her, she looked so frail and vulnerable that he found himself longing to protect her.

"Are you one of her friends?" Lee heard a male voice from behind him. He quickly turned around and frowned as he stared at a young man. Lee quickly glanced down at the man's white shirt that was stained with blood.

"Yeah, I'm one of her friends." Lee eventually said.

"Danny." the man said, holding his hand out for Lee to shake.

"Lee." he said quietly, shaking Danny's hand.

"Did you see her picture on the news?" Danny asked. Lee nodded slowly.

"Yeah, that was me, she doesn't have any next of kin and her phone is broken so I was kind of hoping that someone would recognise her and do something to help her." Danny explained.

"Help her?" Lee frowned; not entirely sure what Danny was trying to say.

"Yeah, she's too proud to ask." Danny sighed, glancing in the window at his friend. He knew that Chloe couldn't go back to the park, at least not until she was fully recovered. She needed to be somewhere warm and safe with adequate meals for a change. As much as he would miss her company, Danny couldn't help but feel pleased that Lee was here, maybe he would be able to help her.

Lee frowned to himself again, he really couldn't figure this Danny guy out. It almost seemed like he was trying to ask something but wasn't making it clear what he wanted. Danny was living with Chloe; it was his responsibility to keep her safe and he'd failed.

"Speaking of helping her, how come you didn't manage to protect her, you walked away injury free?" Lee asked accusingly.

"I'd have taken the knife for her if I'd have been there." Lee continued quietly.

"Well, I wasn't there. I just found her afterwards." Danny said quickly.

"What?" Lee whispered. Danny opened his mouth to respond but Lee cut him off.

"You let her go to the Park on her own, that place is dodgy it's full of hookers and smack heads!" Lee exclaimed.

"Go there?" Danny frowned.

"Someone got raped there last week." Lee continued, his temper growing.

"Yeah Megan, we know her." Danny said sadly.

"She's one of the 'smack heads' you so politely described." Danny quickly added, gesturing inverted commas.

"You know her?" Lee frowned.

Danny gasped as he suddenly realised that whoever this Lee was, he clearly had no idea about Chloe's situation and the fact that she lived on a bench in the park.

"Yeah." Danny said quietly, his mouth suddenly very dry. He couldn't help but feel slightly uncomfortable, he'd just assumed that Chloe's friends knew her situation, but clearly, he was wrong.

"You do realise this is all your fault, if you hadn't let her go to the park on her own, she wouldn't be laying in that bed right now." Lee said angrily. The anger was slowly building in the pit of Lee's stomach, this man who was supposed to care about Chloe had let her down and now she was paying the price. He felt sick to his stomach as a thought suddenly popped into his head.

"And if she has been sexually assaulted then you'll have me to deal with." Lee warned him, his tone slightly aggressive.

Danny rolled his eyes and shook his head slowly, not in the mood for an argument. He had no idea who this Lee guy was or why he was suddenly acting like Chloe's protector, when he clearly didn't know her that well, otherwise he would know that she was homeless.

"I need to go and get cleaned up." Danny said quietly, glancing down at his shirt that was still covered in Chloe's blood. He closed his eyes for a moment, desperately trying to get the images out of his head. For as long as he lived, he would never forget the sight of her laying helplessly on the ground, in a pool of her own blood. Danny sighed to himself and quickly walked away.

Lee rolled his eyes as Danny walked away. He couldn't help but feel frustrated with him, if Chloe was his he would never leave her side at a time like this. Lee took a moment to compose his thoughts before he quickly walked into the room, his breath catching in his throat as he gazed at Chloe fondly. He crossed the room and perched beside her on the bed, taking her hand in his and gently stroking the back of her hand with his thumb. He slowly brought her hand up and gently rested it against his face, sighing deeply to himself.

"Oh Chloe." he whispered, slowly planting a soft kiss on her hand. Lee sat in silence, gazing at her, desperately wishing that he could do something to help her. She was the kindest person Lee had ever met; she didn't deserve the life she'd been given. He couldn't understand why anyone would want to do anything to hurt her.

I'm broken without you. he sang softly.

"Aww you have such a good voice." a voice said from behind him. Lee jumped and quickly let go of Chloe's hand. He turned behind him and smiled as he laid eyes on a nurse.

"You should audition for a show or something." she smiled at him, trying to fill the uncomfortable silence as she quickly picked up Chloe's clipboard from the end of her bed. Lee smiled at her, not entirely sure what to say. He watched intently as she checked Chloe's vitals.

"She will be okay, won't she?" he asked nervously, slightly afraid of her answer.

"She should be the surgery went well. And she's young which is good. But it's a long road to recovery. We'll keep her in overnight because she's quite anaemic, we need to keep giving her blood." she explained.

"I can give her some if she needs it." he said quickly.

"We already have a supply honey." she told him gently, smiling warmly at him.

Lee nodded slowly, unable to tear his eyes away from Chloe.

"The biggest thing is the psychological aspect." she said, smiling sympathetically at him.

"What?" Lee asked, finally turning to face her.

"She's been through a huge ordeal; it's going to take its toll. She'll need someone to look after her for a while." she explained.

"But luckily she has you and that will help, having someone that loves you makes all the difference." she added, when Lee didn't respond. Lee frowned at her as she quickly walked away, he couldn't understand what she was talking about.

"Wait...I'm not her boyfriend!" he called after her, suddenly joining the dots in his head. Lee sighed to himself and turned back to face Chloe, watching her closely.

"Not that your boyfriend deserves you anyway." Lee said quietly, sighing deeply to himself. As he sat gazing at her fondly, he couldn't resist reaching out and gently running the back of his fingers down her cheek.

"If only you were mine, I would have protected you." he whispered softly. Lee breathed a sigh of relief as Chloe's eyes slowly fluttered open. She glanced at him nervously for a moment, before a look of realisation crossed her face.

"What are you doing here?" Chloe said quietly.

"I saw that you'd been hurt on the news." Lee mumbled.

"I was on the news?" she frowned.

"Yeah, Danny wanted to track down your friends, I'm not really sure why though." he told her.

"He was probably just trying to help." she said thoughtfully. Chloe could feel Lee's eyes burning into her as she sat staring at her hands that were in place on her lap. She tried to focus on stopping them from trembling but no matter how hard she tried, she couldn't get control of it. Lee noticed her staring intensely at her hands, his stomach churning when he noticed they were trembling. The nurse's words were still ringing in his ears, he couldn't help but worry about the psychological impact that this would have on her. He couldn't stand the idea that she would be changed by this, he loved her the way she was and didn't want her to change. Lee hesitated for a moment before gently placing his hand on top of her hands. Chloe glanced up at him, trying to figure out why he was here. She could still hear his words, like they were on reply in her mind:

"If only you were mine, I would have protected you."

Her thoughts were swirling, she hadn't meant to pretend to be sleeping but she'd wanted to avoid speaking to him. The last time she saw Lee he was accusing her of betraying him by selling a story to the press and yet here he was, making sure that she was safe in her time of need.

"Do you want to talk about what happened?" Lee asked her gently, snapping her out of her thoughts.

"Didn't they say on the news?" she asked.

"No, just that you'd been stabbed." he told her.

"Well, that's what happened then." she said quickly.

"Chloe." Lee tried.

"I don't want to talk about it." she whispered. Lee nodded slowly. He desperately wanted to know what had happened to her, but he resisted the urge to keep asking questions.

"You can go if you want too." she added after a few moments of silence.

"I'm not leaving you." he told her quietly.

"I'll be fine, Danny will be back soon." she told him.

Lee scoffed sceptically.

"Besides you shouldn't be seen with me, I might sell another story." she said.

"I am sorry for accusing you of that. I know that it wasn't you." he said quietly.

"Finally." she muttered under her breath.

"I'm sorry." he told her again. She hesitated a moment before nodding slowly. Lee glanced down at her hands as she moved them out from under his and slowly lifted the corner of her hospital gown, gazing sadly at the large dressing in the middle of the left side of her abdomen. She brushed her fingers against the dressing, sighing sadly to herself. Lee gasped in horror as something in her suddenly changed and she angrily pressed hard against the dressing, crying out in pain as she did so.

"Chloe, what are you doing?!" he asked her.

"I shouldn't have fought back; it was so stupid." she said angrily.

"Chloe stop it." Lee said sternly, quickly taking both of her hands and holding them tightly to prevent her from hurting herself any further.

"Let go of me." she said sternly. Lee shook his head slowly and tightened his grip on her hands as Chloe tried to free them.

"Lee." she pleaded. His heart broke a little at the sadness in her voice, but he couldn't bring himself to let go of her, in case she hurt herself again. After a few moments, Chloe eventually stopped struggling, sighing as she admitted defeat. Chloe sat quietly, the flashbacks from last night suddenly swirling around her head. She glanced down at her bare neck, remembering the moment when *he'd* roughly ripped the chain off. Her eyes filled with tears as she thought about her parent's wedding rings that had always sat on the chain, close to her heart and now she would never see them again.

Lee seemed to sense that she had finally calmed down as he slowly let go of her hands, watching her closely in case she started to hurt herself again. He watched as the tears that she was trying to hold back slowly spilled down her cheeks. She placed her hands on either side of her and slowly sat forward, wincing slightly as she did so. She took a few deep breaths, trying to control the intense pain that was shooting in her abdomen. Chloe didn't even wipe her tears away, she just let them fall, too focused on the pain to care.

"It's maybe not a good idea to sit up." Lee said quickly, unable to stand seeing the pain on her face. She nodded and slowly sat back, gritting her teeth to stop herself from crying out. She carefully turned on her side, pulling the blankets up under her neck, trying to feel safe.

"Are you cold?" Lee asked her gently.

She shook her head slowly, finally wiping away her tears.

"Is there anything I can do to make you feel better?" he asked sadly. Lee glanced down at his hand as Chloe reached out to take it gently in hers. She quickly moved his hand towards her and hugged it tightly.

"You could stay with me until Danny comes back." she said quietly.

Chapter Twenty-One

Lee stirred in the chair and slowly opened his eyes, frowning slightly when he realised that he wasn't in his bedroom. As he laid eyes on Chloe, his stomach plummeted as the events from yesterday suddenly came flooding back. She smiled at him as they locked eyes.

"You alright?" he asked her worriedly.

"Yes, did you get much sleep?" she asked.

"I got some." he told her, stretching in the chair.

"Thank you for staying, I feel bad." she said.

"It's fine, I don't mind." he reassured her. Lee fell silent for a moment, his brain spinning. He'd spent most of the night watching her as she slept, feeling comforted by watching her breathe. It had suddenly hit him last night, just how much she meant to him. He needed to be by her side always, making sure that she was safe. It was only when he thought that he was going to lose her that he realised how much he needed her.

He sighed quietly to himself as he realised that Nathan had been right all along, he was madly in love with her and had no idea how to handle what he was feeling.

Images kept swirling around his head, his imagination running overtime about what Chloe may or may not have been through.

Lee knew that she didn't want to talk about what had happened to her, but he couldn't stand not knowing any more.

"Chloe, I need to know what happened." he said quietly.

"Why?" she asked.

"Because I keep imagining things, and I need to know." he said firmly.

"I was on my way to Kirstie's party and I got ambushed by someone. He tried to rob me, and I stupidly fought back so he stabbed me." she said quickly, trying to get the words out quickly before she got upset.

"So, it was a burglary then." Lee said thoughtfully.

"Yes, why?" Chloe frowned.

"No reason." he mumbled.

"No, what?" she insisted.

"Someone got raped there last week, I remember hearing about it on the news." he said, rambling slightly as he was too terrified to ask her the question that he was dying to know the answer to.

"Danny shouldn't let you go there on your own, that park isn't safe, especially at night." he continued.

"Please don't blame Danny, none of this is his fault." she said quickly.

"It kind of is though, it's his job to protect you." he said quietly.

"No, it's not, I can take care of myself." she countered.

"Yeah clearly." he muttered, feeling slightly frustrated that she didn't seem to grasp the severity of the situation. How easily her injuries could have been so much worse. Chloe rolled her eyes at him but decided not to argue. She knew that he was upset about what had happened, not that she understood why he would care.

"Chloe, promise me that nothing else happened." Lee said nervously.

"I promise." she said quietly.

"Thank god, I was so afraid that you'd been raped or something." he whispered.

"No, just stabbed." she sighed. Lee watched as she slowly shuffled over to the side of the bed and sat for a moment, slowly swinging her legs nervously. The two of them turned to the doorway as Chloe's nurse Paula walked in.

"How are you feeling this morning sweetheart?" Paula asked Chloe.

"A little better, I'm not so tired." Chloe told her.

"Well, your vitals look good." Paula said after she'd checked Chloe over.

"But we'll need to check your PCV again." she added. Chloe nodded and remained silent as Paula collected a small amount of blood from Chloe's arm.

"I'll go and run this, hopefully we should be able to get you home today." Paula smiled.

"Thank you." Chloe said softly.

"You can change into your clothes if you want too, it'll be more comfortable than the gown." Paula told her. Chloe glanced at Lee who smiled at her reassuringly, clearly sensing that Chloe suddenly felt tense.

"I don't have any clothes." Chloe admitted, her cheeks colouring.

"Yes of course the paramedics cut them off you didn't they. " Paula said, before quickly leaving the room to run the tests.

"I can go to your place and get you some?" Lee offered.

"No!" Chloe said sharply. She gazed at the ground, suddenly realising that whoever had robbed her and ran away with her bag was now in possession of everything that she owned, even her clothes. She literally had nothing, not even the photos of her family and the letter that her father had written for her. Things had been bad for her before, but now they were even worse. She didn't even have her blankets to keep her warm on the cold winter nights in the park.

"Oh, here comes boyfriend of the year." Lee muttered under his breath as Danny finally walked into the room.

"You look better." he smiled at Chloe as soon as he saw her.

"I'll be fine." she said smiling falsely.

"I couldn't find your stuff, by the time I finished the audition it was dark and there's not a hope in hell of finding anything in the dark." Danny quickly told her when she raised her eyebrow at him hopefully.

"That's okay, we can go and look once I'm discharged, hopefully it'll be soon." she replied.

"You do realise it's unlikely that we'll find anything." Danny told her gently.

"I know, but I have to try." she said quietly.

"Wait, hold up!" Lee said sharply. Both Chloe and Danny turned to face him.

"You're not taking her back there." Lee said sternly. Danny glanced between the two of them, not entirely sure what to say. Chloe clearly still hadn't told Lee that she lived there.

"It's not up to you." Chloe told him.

"Are you mad, you almost died there and now you want to go back?!" Lee exclaimed.

"It's not happening." Lee added when they didn't respond.

"I want to see if I can find any of my things, and besides I can't avoid the park forever."
Chloe argued, glancing at Danny awkwardly.

Lee shook his head angrily as she glared at him defiantly. In that moment he realised that
it didn't matter what he said, she was determined to go anyway, and there was nothing he
could do to stop her. The only thing that he could do was to go with her, so that at least
he could protect her.

"Fine, but I'm coming with you." he sighed.

"I'll be fine, Danny will be with me." she said.

"I'm coming too." Lee said quickly. He didn't trust Danny to protect her, not after in Lee's
mind, he'd failed her last time.

"I got you some clothes by the way." Danny said, trying to fill the silence. Chloe watched
as he rummaged in his backpack and pulled out a carrier bag, gently handing it to her.

"I thought you said you couldn't find any of my stuff?" Chloe frowned.

"No, I didn't, I went to a shop." Danny told her. Chloe frowned to herself, she knew that
Danny only just made enough from his busking to cover his food, so she couldn't
understand how he had been able to afford to buy clothes. She quickly pulled out the
clothes, frowning as she saw a pair of leggings, a jumper and some trainers. As soon as
she saw them, she knew they wouldn't have been cheap.

"I tried to pick something warm." Danny told her.

Chloe nodded slowly and sighed when she saw that the price tags were still on them. A
thought suddenly popped into her head:

"Did you steal these?" she asked nervously.

"No, they fell into my backpack." he said quietly.

"Danny, I don't want you getting into trouble for me." Chloe said sadly.

"It was the only option." Danny told her.

"This just gets better and better." Lee said angrily. Lee could feel himself becoming angry, first this man had failed to protect Chloe, then he'd abandoned her during her time of need and now he was a thief. Chloe deserved so much better.

"Lee stop it." Chloe warned, before he could say anymore. Danny was trying his best in what was an incredibly difficult situation for them both and the last thing Chloe wanted was for Lee to be nasty to him in the same way that he used to her.

The three of them fell silent as Paula walked back into the room.

"Your PCV is a lot better so the doctor is happy to discharge you." she told Chloe happily. Chloe nodded to show that she understood.

"You'll have a lot of meds to take and you'll need to change your dressings every day, so I'll go through all that with you now. I'll help you get dressed too, as it'll be sore." she explained. Lee and Danny silently left the room, to give Chloe some privacy. Lee turned his back on Chloe's room and leant against the window frame, his eyes burning into Danny who was perched on a chair across the other side of the corridor.

"You don't like me very much do you?" Danny asked when he couldn't stand the silence any longer.

"Nope." Lee said quickly.

"You shouldn't be so quick to judge, the situation is more complex than you think." Danny told him.

"I don't want you near her." Lee warned.

"What?" Danny frowned.

"I'm serious. She's innocent, kind and pure and I won't allow you to tarnish her." Lee said his tone soft but with an edge of aggression to it.

"I don't know who you think you are, you don't *own* her." Danny pointed out.

"She can make her own decisions." he quickly added.

"I know, but she's naive." Lee said quickly.

Danny nodded.

"I mean it though; you stay away from her. You don't want me as your enemy." Lee warned him. Danny opened his mouth to reply but quickly closed it when Paula came out of the room and walked over to them.

"I'll show you guys how the dressings work and her medication in case she forgets." she told them.

Chloe sighed to herself as she perched on the end of the bed, gazing down at herself wearing stolen clothes. She couldn't believe that she had fallen this far, her parents would be turning in their graves if they could see her now. Her eyes flickered up as Lee walked back into the room.

"Are you ready to go?" he asked her gently.

Chloe nodded and placed her hands on the bed, using it for support as she slowly stood up. Her legs shook as she stood motionless, trying to get used to supporting her own weight. Whenever she moved her hands from the bed, she wobbled and had to quickly grab it again. Lee could see that she was struggling so he moved to her side and gently wrapped his arm around her waist, holding her body against his to support her weight.

"Are you sure you can walk?" he asked her, as she took a few careful steps.

"Um hum." she squeaked, clearly in a lot of pain.

"Do you want me to carry you?" Lee offered.

"No, it's okay, I can do this." she said stubbornly.

"Just don't let me fall." she quickly added when she wobbled again.

"I won't, we'll just take it slowly." he told her.

Chloe sighed in relief when after what felt like an age, they finally reached the car park. Lee quickly took his keys out of his pocket and unlocked his car, his arm still wrapped around Chloe.

"Is that your car?!" Danny exclaimed from behind them when he noticed Lee's car.

"Yep." Lee said sharply.

"Wow." Danny breathed.

"There's only two seats though so you'll have to walk." Lee told him shortly.

"I'll see you at the park then." Danny said to Chloe before quickly walking away, clearly keen to escape the tense atmosphere. Before Chloe could protest Lee picked her up and gently placed her in the passenger seat. Chloe quickly put on her seatbelt as Lee walked around the other side of the car and climbed in.

The two of them remained silent as Lee pulled away, Chloe took deep breaths, still trying to recover from the exertion of walking through the hospital. She placed her elbow against the car door and rested her head against her fist, struggling to keep her eyes open.

"I really don't know what you see in that Danny guy." Lee said.

"You should cut him some slack; you hardly know him." Chloe sighed.

"I know enough." he said quickly.

"No, you don't, you have no idea." she argued.

"You're right, I have no idea why you don't seem to matter to him." he snapped.

"What are you talking about?" she frowned.

"Firstly, he let you go to the Park alone, at night and then he disappeared all night, if I hadn't been there, you would have been alone in the hospital." he pointed out.

"Well, I'm sorry for being such an inconvenience." she snapped.

"That's not what I meant; the point is he didn't care enough to be by your side." he said quickly.

"He had an audition, I spoke to him about it before you got to the hospital, I didn't want him to miss it." she explained.

"It means a lot to him; he really needs to get work." she added.

"He doesn't have a job?" he frowned.

"No, he goes busking, the audition was for a part in a theatre show." she told him.

"So that's why he has to steal, because he doesn't even have a bloody job!" Lee exclaimed incredulously.

"Well yeah." Chloe said, sighing sadly as she glanced down at her clothes and felt another wave of guilt.

"You need to get away far away from him Chlo." he told her.

"I can't." she mumbled.

"Why not?" he frowned.

"Chloe?" he asked again when she didn't respond.

Chloe remained silent, unsure what to say to him. She couldn't bring herself to tell him her living situation, she was too ashamed.

"Please tell me it's not because you're in love with him?" he tried again.

"No of course not." she said quickly.

"Because you deserve so much better." he added thoughtfully.

"I don't deserve anything; I'm sitting here in stolen clothes." she whispered.

"Yeah, well that's your boyfriend's fault." he said quickly.

"He's not my boyfriend." she told him.

"What?" he frowned.

"We're just friends." she said.

"But you live together." he frowned.

"Yes, but we are still just friends." she insisted.

"Good." Lee whispered, suddenly feeling a huge wave of relief.

"Good?" Chloe asked.

"It'll be easier to keep him away from you if you are just friends." he told her.

"Who said anything about keeping him away from me?" she frowned.

"I've already warned him to stay away from you." he told her.

"It bothers me, you being around someone like him." he said quietly when Chloe fell silent, staring at him in disbelief.

"It has nothing to do with you." she snapped.

"I'm just trying to look out for you." he said.

"Well don't, I need Danny, he's the only person who understands me, so stay out of it." she said sternly. Lee frowned at her words, not sure what she meant by that, but he decided not to push her as at that moment they pulled up at the park. Chloe sighed as she gazed out of the car window at the park, the memories from that fateful night swirling around her head. She closed her eyes and took deep breaths, desperately trying to steady her nerves.

"Are you sure you're ready to do this?" Lee asked worriedly, watching her closely.

"I don't have a choice." she whispered.

Chapter Twenty-Two

Chloe glanced up at Lee and smiled at him as he helped her to the bench. She sighed to herself as she sat on *her* bench, gazing around at the familiar surroundings. As much as she disliked being in the hospital, it was better than being here, at least the hospital was warm and comfortable. Lee perched on the bench beside her, watching her closely, still concerned about her. Chloe began to shiver so she pulled down the sleeves on her jumper, trying to keep her hands warm.

"It's going to be cold tonight." she said quietly, her heart plummeting at the thought of spending a night outside in the middle of winter without so much as a blanket. Lee nodded in agreement and glanced around, looking for Danny. He wanted Danny to get here so that the three of them could search for Chloe's possessions and get out of this park as soon as possible. Chloe glanced up as Megan quickly walked over to her.

"Oh my god Chloe, I heard what happened are you okay?!" she exclaimed as soon as she reached Chloe.

"I'm fine." Chloe said quietly. Megan smiled and quickly hugged Chloe.

"Be gentle with me." she winced as Megan squeezed her tightly.

"Sorry." Megan said, quickly letting go of Chloe.

"Everyone has been really worried about you. The police were all over the park yesterday, looking for evidence." Megan told her. Chloe smiled at Megan, not quite believing her that everyone was worried about her but appreciating that she was trying to be kind. Megan kept glancing at Lee and then raising her eyebrow at Chloe questioningly. Chloe shook her head slowly at Megan, subtly giving her the cue to leave it alone. Chloe chanced a glance at Lee and frowned to herself when she saw that he hadn't moved. He was still sitting, with his arms resting on his thighs, his eyes scanning the park, almost like he was checking for danger. Lee jumped slightly when Chloe slowly linked her arm through his and snuggled against him, trying to get warm when she couldn't stand being cold any longer. He glanced at her for a moment, before quickly returning to gazing around the park.

"Chloe, you look like you're freezing." Megan said quietly when she noticed Chloe shivering. Chloe nodded slowly.

"I'll check if I have a spare blanket." Megan told her, before quickly walking away.

"Are you okay, you haven't said a word since we got here?" Chloe asked Lee as soon as Megan walked away.

"I'm just on high alert, I really don't like you being back here." he said quickly.

"No one will try anything in the daylight." she told him. Lee sighed and eventually turned to face her, frowning to himself when he noticed for the first time that Chloe was shivering. He unlinked their arms and gently took her hands between his, blowing warm air onto them to try and warm them up. Chloe eventually locked eyes with him and smiled slightly under his gaze. She liked this softer side to him that he liked to keep hidden.

"What?" he frowned.

"Nothing." she said quickly. She was saved from any further questioning by Danny quickly walking over to them.

"Shall we go and look for your things?" Danny said as soon as he reached them. Chloe frowned at him, not entirely sure why he was in such a rush.

She suddenly remembered what Lee had told her in the car about him warning Danny to stay away from her, clearly Danny was keen to rush in the hope that Lee would leave once they'd found Chloe's belongings.

"Do you remember where you got stabbed?" Danny prompted when Chloe didn't answer.

"I got changed here." Chloe said thoughtfully, trying to mentally retrace her steps during that fateful night.

"You got changed on a bench?" Lee frowned.

"Yes, it was dark, nobody saw anything." she said quickly, suddenly realising that in her weakened state she'd let something slip. Chloe reluctantly removed her hands from Lee's warm grasp and pointed north.

"Kirstie's house is that way, so I would have headed that direction." she told them.

"Surely you remember where you found her?" Lee blurted at Danny; his eyes fixed on Chloe as he watched her slowly stand up.

"Not really, it's a bit of a blur." Danny said quietly. Lee watched Chloe shuffle along for a moment before he quickly walked over to her and picked her up.

"Put me down!" Chloe protested as he carried her in the direction that she'd pointed out. Danny quickly bringing up the rear.

"I can walk!" she added when he didn't respond.

"I know, but it takes ages, and I don't want to linger." he told her. Chloe sighed to herself, deciding not to argue with him. Even though she liked her independence, she couldn't help but enjoy the feeling of being in his strong arms. Even though she was still in the park, she suddenly felt safe and protected, like nothing could touch her.

"I'm guessing it was here." Lee mumbled, his stomach churning when he noticed a pool of blood on the grass. Chloe looked around and nodded slowly.

"How did you know?" she asked Lee as he carefully set her down.

"There's blood on the ground." Lee told her, his mouth suddenly feeling very dry. Chloe followed his eyeline and gasped as she saw a pool of her own blood on the ground. The realisation suddenly dawning on her of exactly what she had been through.

"If any of your things have been dumped, I think it'll be over there." Danny said quickly, pointing to a wooded area across the park.

"Yeah probably, I don't care about my clothes and things, just the sentimental items." she sighed, leaning her back against a tree.

"We might find the photo album and your Dad's letter, but whoever robbed you will have kept your parents wedding rings, since they are the only thing of value you own." Danny told her gently.

"I know." Chloe whispered, gently stroking her bare neck. Danny nodded slowly before walking away, towards the wooded area.

"I feel so weird not having them round my neck anymore." Chloe admitted thoughtfully. Lee stared at her, wishing there was something that he could do to help but knowing there was nothing he could say or do to make her feel better.

"That's when I fought back when he ripped them off my neck." she continued, gazing at the pool of blood on the ground, almost as if she was talking to herself.

"Well, they meant a lot to you didn't they." he sighed sadly as he watched her heart slowly breaking. Chloe nodded slowly before quickly pushing herself up off the tree. She kept her eyes fixed on the wooded area as she slowly walked towards it, determined to reach it on her own. Lee followed closely, making sure he was beside her in case she fell again. He couldn't help but feel a surge of pride at the determined expression on her pretty features. She'd been through so much in her twenty-four years, but she was mentally stronger than a lot of people that he knew. No matter how much she got knocked down she refused to be beaten. Eventually they caught up to Danny who was still rummaging through the bushes. Chloe glanced at Lee as he stood glaring at passers-by that were watching Chloe struggling to hold herself up. He heard them whispering to each other, suggesting that Chloe was one of the park junkies.

"This really isn't good; you should be at home resting." Lee sighed when Chloe wobbled again, and he quickly reached out to steady her.

"I'm fine." she whispered, shivering against him.

"No, you're not, I'm taking you home." Lee insisted.

"You can't take me home." she said quietly. Her heart pounded against her chest as she suddenly realised that Lee wasn't going to stop pressuring her until she caved in and told him the truth. She'd never wanted to tell anyone about her living situation, to see the pity on their faces as they realised just how pathetic she really was. Chloe glanced up as Danny pulled her backpack out of a bush and walked over to her, quickly placing it on the floor and rummaging through it.

"I think most of your clothes are still in here." Danny told her.

"I don't care about my clothes." she sighed.

"Why don't you look through the bag and I'll check the surrounding area?" Danny suggested.

Chloe nodded and slowly placed her bag on a tree stump, before carefully leaning over and rummaging through it. Lee watched her closely as she frantically pulled out her belongings, desperately searching for something. He glanced at the bag as she suddenly stopped rummaging and slowly pulled out a photo album, her hands trembling slightly. She opened the album, sighing in relief when she saw the letter from her father still safely tucked inside the front cover. Before Lee could react, she dropped to her knees, clutching the photo album tightly against her heart, her fingernails digging into it. His heart broke as she began to cry, her breath coming out in loud sobs that she couldn't control. The relief of finding the only connection that she now had to her parents, overwhelming her and bringing everything to the surface that she had been keeping in check for some time. Lee stared at her, not entirely sure what to do as he watched her emotionally breaking down in front of him, her sobs filled with such anguish that he could feel himself becoming emotional.

Danny glared at Lee accusingly as he walked back over to join them, clearly thinking that Lee had said something to upset her.

"Why couldn't *he* have just killed me?!" she sobbed sadly.

"I have nothing left to live for anyway." she continued.

"Don't say that." Lee sniffed, trying to keep his emotions in check, even though he was struggling with seeing the woman he loved in so much pain and anguish. Chloe ignored him and continued to sob, unable to control her emotions anymore. Every time that she let out a sob, she felt a searing pain tear through her abdomen, but she didn't care. She'd been holding back on how she was feeling for so many months that she just couldn't pretend any longer. She had nothing, not even a home to call her own and nobody that cared about her. Her existence seeming small and insignificant.

"I want my family back; I'd give anything to feel loved again." she whispered sadly. Lee opened his mouth to say something but quickly closed it again, not entirely sure what he was going to say anyway. He watched her as she sat silently, not even moving, too exhausted to even cry anymore. Lee couldn't stand seeing her like that anymore, when he knew that there was nothing, he could do to take her pain away.

"I need a minute." Lee muttered, before walking away from her. He knew that he had to get away from her before he could no longer control his emotions. Chloe glanced up at him as he walked away, slightly confused as to why he was leaving her side when up until now he'd refused too. She decided not to dwell on it and opened the photo album, slowly leafing through the pages, smiling as she stared at the happy memories of her and her family, before everything was torn apart.

"I'll go and see if I can find any more of your things." Danny said awkwardly, feeling slightly uncomfortable that he had no idea what to say to her. Chloe nodded, sighing quietly to herself as she sat alone with her thoughts.

Chapter Twenty-Three

Chloe glanced up as Danny walked back towards her a few moments later. As soon as he reached her, he quickly held out his hands to her and gently helped her to stand. Danny took the photo album from under her arm and placed it safely in her backpack.

"I found your teddy." Danny smiled, pulling it out of his pocket and showing it to her. She smiled slightly as she gazed at her only remaining present from the 'Eclipse' boys.

"I didn't realise Lee was in that band that you used to work for." he added, gazing at the photo of the five of them on the teddy's shirt. Chloe nodded slowly as Danny put the teddy in the backpack.

"I think I need to sleep." she told him quietly.

"You need to ask Lee if you can stay with him." he told her.

"No!" she said sharply.

"You can't sleep in the cold, you're not well." he argued.

"I'll be fine." she insisted.

"But you don't even have your blankets." he pointed out.

"Megan thinks that she might have a spare." she told him. Before he could say anything else, she slowly began the long walk back to her bench. Danny picked up her backpack and fell into step beside her. Chloe linked her arm through his, leaning on him for support as she walked.

"Isn't Lee going to be annoyed when he realises you've disappeared?" Danny asked.

"Yes probably, but tough. He's not in charge of me." she said quickly.

"If we don't lose him, he's not going to leave me alone in the park." she added.

"Good, you should go and stay somewhere warm." he sighed.

"I can't tell him that I'm sleeping rough." she said quietly.

"Why not?" he frowned.

"Why do you think, it's humiliating." she said.

"Surely if he's your friend, he won't judge you." he frowned.

"I don't know if he would or not." she said quietly, gritting her teeth at the pain in her abdomen as she walked. After what felt like an age, Chloe sighed in relief when she eventually sat on *her* bench. She closed her eyes taking slow, deep breaths, trying to control the intense pain that she was in. She felt Danny sit beside her, trying to provide some warmth as she began to shiver.

"Well, that was obvious." Danny muttered under his breath.

"What?" Chloe asked, slowly opening her eyes. Danny glanced at her and looked back across the park to where Lee was walking towards them.

"You do realise you're going to have to tell him." he told her.

"I can't." she muttered.

"Why did you wander off?" Lee asked as soon as he reached them.

"You don't have to follow me, Danny is back now, you can go back to your life." Chloe said quietly.

"I need to make sure that you get home safely." he told her, frowning in confusion as to why she was being so dismissive with him all of a sudden.

"It's fine, Danny will take me home." she snapped.

"Chloe...." Danny whispered, trailing off when she glared at him.

"Please just go Lee." Chloe whispered, her eyes filling with tears.

"I can't leave you here." Lee said quietly. Chloe blinked slowly, sighing quietly as she felt warm tears slowly roll down her cheeks.

"Chloe, I know you don't want to, but you need to tell him." Danny prompted, glancing up at Lee as Chloe remained silent. Lee's eyes wandered across the park as he saw Megan walking towards them, carrying a blanket under her arm. Suddenly everything finally made sense in his head, the fact that Danny had 'allowed' her to be alone in the park late at night, the two of them knowing Megan, the fact that Danny had needed to steal clothes for Chloe to wear and finally the realisation that Chloe had been carrying around her belongings and clothes in her backpack.... clearly because they were all she had, and she had nowhere else to store them.

"Have you been sleeping rough Chloe?" Lee blurted before he could stop himself. Chloe hesitated for a moment before nodding slowly. She kept her eyes fixed on the ground, wishing that it would swallow her up. She hadn't told anyone about her living situation because she was so embarrassed. Lee was the last person that she ever wanted to feel vulnerable in front of.

"How long for?" Lee asked quietly.

"Almost a year." she muttered, quickly wiping away the steady stream of tears that were flowing down her cheeks. Lee watched her sadly, his heart sinking as he thought of her sleeping on a park bench. She'd always seemed so small and vulnerable to him, like she needed someone to protect and take care of her, yet here she was struggling to get by on a daily basis. He could feel his stomach churning as he thought about the woman that he loved curled up on a bench, shivering every night, as she lay alone in the cold.

"Why didn't you tell me, I could have helped?" Lee whispered sadly, his voice breaking slightly.

"Like you would have cared." Chloe said quietly. She rested her head against Danny's shoulder, suddenly feeling very weak. Lee felt a pang of guilt at her words. He wished that he could find a way to tell her the real reason for him pushing her away and it had nothing to do with him hating her.

"You could help now, she needs somewhere to stay, she can't sleep outside in the cold." Danny quickly piped up.

"Of course, she can stay with me." Lee said quietly, feeling slightly pleased that he was able to do something to help, but wishing that he could do more.

"I don't need to stay with anyone, I'm fine here." Chloe argued.

"There is no way in hell, that you are spending another night in this god forsaken park." Lee said quickly.

"But I don't want to stay with you." she said quietly. Even though Lee had been good to her since she'd been in the hospital, she couldn't help but feel apprehensive about living with him. She knew from experience that he could turn on a dime with no warning and she didn't have the strength to deal with his nasty comments and taunts.

"Maybe you should stay here then!" Lee snapped, before he could stop himself. As soon as the words were out of his mouth, he instantly regretted them. Even though he'd made a promise to himself to treat Chloe better, he couldn't seem to stop himself from becoming defensive whenever she said or did something that hurt him. He'd only been trying to help her, to be there for her in her time of need, but she refused his help. Lee wanted nothing more than to be able to take her home and take care of her, to be able to know that she was safe.

"That's what I've been saying." Chloe whispered, snapping him out of his thoughts. Lee watched her sadly as she slowly closed her eyes, unable to fight to stay awake anymore. Danny glanced at her nervously as he felt her body relax against him.

"Is she okay?" Danny asked quickly. Lee frowned for a moment, before quickly placing his fingers on her neck, a wave of relief washing over him when he felt her pulse.

"I think she's just sleeping." Lee said quietly.

Danny nodded slowly, hesitating for a moment as he glanced at Lee nervously.

"I'm sorry I judged you, I totally misread the situation." Lee said.

"It's fine, it happens a lot." Danny replied.

"She can't stay here though, she's not well enough." Danny added, trying to change the subject.

"I know...I'm not going to leave her here." Lee told him. Danny nodded slowly, watching as Lee leant down and carefully picked Chloe up. Lee gazed down at her as she moved slightly.

"Make sure you take care of her." Danny said quietly, feeling slightly sad that he was now going to be alone in the park. Lee nodded slowly; his eyes still fixed on Chloe as he held her in his arms.

"She's going to be so angry when she wakes up at your house." Danny said, smiling slightly.

"I'll take her to Kirstie's." Lee said thoughtfully, sighing quietly to himself as he once again found himself wishing that he could take her home with him. As tempted as he was to go against her wishes, the last thing he wanted to do was upset her any further. Lee quickly walked to his car, gently placing her into the passenger seat, taking care not to wake her. He couldn't help himself from intermittently glancing at Chloe as he drove, to make sure that she was still okay.

Chloe's eyes fluttered open, she frowned to herself as she gazed around, her eyes landing on Lee as she suddenly realised that she was in his car.

"What's going on?" she asked weakly.

"You can't sleep outside in your condition, so I'm taking you to Kirstie's." he said quickly. Chloe nodded slowly, not really having the energy to argue anymore. She fell silent, taking slow breaths, to try and control the constant pain she was in. She frowned as Lee changed gear and she noticed that he had split his knuckles.

"What did you do to your hand?" she asked quietly, trying to rack her brain to figure out when she last looked at his hand. Lee remained silent as he slowly pulled into Kirstie's driveway and switched off the engine.

"Lee?" Chloe tried again, when she heard him sigh quietly.

"It's nothing." he said quietly, not quite able to bring himself to tell her what had happened. He couldn't find the words to tell her how it had felt when he stood watching her breaking down in front of him. The deep anguish and frustration that he'd felt and had to find a way of releasing it. As soon as his fist had made contact with the tree, Lee had felt at least some of the anger dissipate.

Lee glanced at Chloe as she picked up his hand and gently pulled it towards herself. Lee winced slightly as her thumb gently grazed over his knuckles.

"It looks sore." she said quietly.

"I think you win on the wound front." he said quietly. Chloe smiled slightly, fighting to keep her eyes open.

"You can sleep if you need too, I won't let anything happen to you." he told her gently, when he noticed that she was struggling to stay awake. Chloe sighed quietly, her vision blurring slightly. As she sat in Lee's car beside him, she suddenly felt lightheaded, almost like she was having an out of body experience.

"I just don't have the energy to fight anymore." she admitted quietly.

"You have to fight Chloe, there are people that care about you." Lee said quickly, his heart breaking slightly at the thought of losing her.

"I meant, that I can't fight how I feel anymore." she whispered. Lee watched as Chloe slowly moved towards him, glancing down at his lips as she did so. At the last second, she moved her head sideways and collapsed against his chest, her eyes finally closing.

"I'm so tired." she admitted, not able to fight how weak she felt anymore. Lee sighed to himself as she instantly fell asleep against him. He gently stroked her hair, trying to provide at least a small amount of comfort to her. His brain swirled with a mist of thoughts as he sat silently, desperately wishing that she'd been able to finish her sentence. He had no idea what she was going to say or whether she even realised what she was saying or who she was speaking too. All he knew was that it felt like she was going to say something important, but the moment had gone.

Chapter Twenty-Four

Kirstie opened the door, gasping to herself as Lee stood in front of her, gently cradling Chloe. Chloe lifted her head slightly, but she quickly slumped back into Lee's arms, feeling too weak to even raise her head. As Kirstie gazed at her pale features and dishevelled appearance, she could feel herself growing angry.

"What have you done to her?!" she rounded on Lee.

"I haven't done anything to her." he snapped defensively.

"She was stabbed in the Park a couple of nights ago." he added.

"Oh my god.' Kirstie whispered, gesturing for him to come in.

"Don't you watch the news?" Lee said shortly as he carefully carried Chloe inside. Kirstie remained silent, rolling her eyes to herself at his words. She'd been arguing with Ben almost constantly for the past couple of days, the last thing she wanted was to argue with Lee as well.

"So, you just happened to find her?" she asked suspiciously.

"No, her friend Danny found her, I heard about it on the news and went to make sure that she was okay." Lee explained.

"She looks awful." Ben piped up as him and Kirstie watched Lee gently place Chloe on the sofa. As soon as Lee set her down, her eyes bolted open and she attempted to sit up, crying out in pain as she did so.

"You need to keep still." Lee told her, gently placing his hand on her shoulder. Kirstie frowned to herself as she saw Chloe visibly relax.

"You're not leaving, are you?" Chloe asked softly.

"No, I'll stay for a bit." he reassured her. Chloe nodded slowly and closed her eyes, bringing her arms up in front of her chest as she began to shiver.

"I'll fetch some blankets." Ben said quickly.

"Can she stay with you for a few days?" Lee asked Kirstie.

"Yeah of course she can." Kirstie said quietly, still a little confused as to why Lee suddenly seemed to care about her so much.

"I have everything from the hospital." he told her, quickly removing Chloe's backpack from his shoulder and pulling out a carrier bag.

"Okay, so she has pain relief and strong antibiotics to take. She's also on high dose iron tablets because she's anaemic. These are some sleeping tablets in case she can't settle, but hopefully she won't need them." Lee explained as he slowly pulled out the different items and placed them in front of Kirstie.

"These are spare dressings for the wound, we need to change it once a day. They said that we should clean it very carefully with hibiscrub but very dilute and just kind of wipe it gently." Lee continued. Kirstie nodded slowly, trying to take in all the information that he was telling her, but not quite able to process what was happening. Ben returned a few moments later and carefully placed a blanket over Chloe.

"Thank you." Chloe said quietly, smiling up at him as she took hold of the blanket and held it tightly.

"Other than that, she's not allowed to shower for a while, and she needs to eat little and often because if she bloats then it could compromise the stitches in the muscle layer." Lee told them quietly, his eyes fixed on Chloe. As he stood watching her shiver, he couldn't help but wish that he could curl up beside her and hold her in his arms, in a desperate attempt to provide her with some warmth.

"So, she had surgery then?" Ben asked, snapping Lee out of his thoughts. Lee nodded slowly.

"Why would anyone attack her?" Kirstie whispered sadly.

"It was a robbery." Lee said quietly. Ben sighed quietly and perched on the sofa beside her. Chloe quickly reached out to take his hand, desperately trying to find a way to feel safe.

"Chloe, you're freezing." Ben gasped when she took his hand.

"I'll make her a hot water bottle." Kirstie said, quickly walking into the kitchen. As soon as Kirstie walked away Lee quickly followed her.

"I need to speak to you about something." he said as soon as they were alone.

"What?" Kirstie said dismissively.

"She's going to hate me...but I think you need to know..." Lee started.

"She already hates you." Kirstie interrupted. Lee nodded slowly and sighed to himself.

"You can't let her leave here, she's been sleeping rough and we can't let her go back to the park, even when she's recovered." Lee explained, choosing not to rise to the bait.

"Oh my god." she whispered, suddenly feeling guilty that her friend had been struggling and she had no idea. Ben watched Chloe closely as she tentatively sat up, biting her lip hard to keep herself from crying out in pain.

"Where's Lee?!" Chloe said quickly, sounding slightly panicked as she looked around and realised that he wasn't in the room.

"He's in the kitchen." Ben told her gently.

"Okay good." she whispered, resting her head against the back of the sofa.

"You look awful Chloe." he sighed, feeling really sorry for her. Even though he'd never been close to Chloe, he was still fond of her and didn't like seeing the grimace of pain that was constantly etched on her face.

"I'll be okay." she said quietly. Chloe reached down to her neck, feeling the need to hold her parents wedding rings, like she always did when she was upset or afraid. A lump rose in her throat when she suddenly remembered that she no longer had them anymore. She quickly wiped away the tears that were slowly rolling down her cheeks, hoping that Ben wouldn't notice.

Chloe glanced up as Lee and Kirstie walked back into the room. Kirstie silently bent down and gently placed the hot water bottle on Chloe's lap. Chloe smiled her thanks and placed her hands-on top of it, trying to warm them up.

"I should probably head home." Ben said, quickly standing up.

"I thought you were staying over." Kirstie frowned.

"There's not much point is there." Ben said dismissively.

"Do you have to be such a child." Kirstie said, rolling her eyes. Ben shook his head and quickly left the room, slamming the front door behind himself.

"Are you guys fighting?" Chloe asked, quickly wiping away the last of her tears.

"Yep, I'll tell you later." Kirstie said quickly, glancing awkwardly at Lee.

"I should probably go too; you need to get some rest." Lee said reluctantly. Chloe nodded slowly, her stomach sinking at the thought of him leaving her.

"Are you coming back?" she asked tentatively.

"I'll come back in the morning, I can change your dressing then, since I've been shown what to do?" Lee suggested, glancing at Kirstie for permission. Kirstie sighed quietly when she saw Chloe's face light up at the thought of Lee coming back tomorrow. Even though she didn't want Lee around, she couldn't deny her friend of the small shred of comfort that she needed. Kirstie nodded reluctantly.

Lee sighed sadly to himself as he watched Chloe curl her arms on the back of the sofa and gently rest her head against them, softly closing her eyes. She looked so innocent and vulnerable that he found himself longing to hold her in his arms. He couldn't help but notice that even in her injured state, she was still strikingly beautiful. He found himself wishing, not for the first time that he hadn't treated her so cruelly. Before he could stop himself, he slowly reached towards Chloe and gently tucked her hair behind her ear, making sure that it wasn't in her face.

"I'll come back first thing tomorrow." Lee said quietly, quickly walking away.

Chapter Twenty-Five

Kirstie sighed in frustration as she looked at her phone for about the tenth time that morning. She still hadn't heard from Ben since he left in a huff the night before.

"I'm sure you guys are okay." Chloe said sympathetically when she instantly realised what was bothering Kirstie.

"He can sulk all he wants; I haven't done anything wrong." Kirstie stated.

"He clearly cares about you a lot though, it's kind of cute." Chloe said.

"Not enough to call though." Kirstie sighed.

"Maybe you just need to give him some time to think about it, I'm sure he'll realise that there's nothing going on with you and Matt." Chloe said. Kirstie nodded slowly, watching Chloe closely as she picked up one of the sofa cushions and hugged it tightly.

"Did you manage to get some sleep last night?" Kirstie asked her worriedly.

"I got some, it's difficult to get comfortable though." Chloe admitted.

"I felt so guilty, sleeping in a comfy bed while you were stuck on the sofa." Kirstie sighed.

"I like being on the sofa, I meant because I'm sore." Chloe smiled.

"If I'd known that Michelle wasn't going to be home, you could have slept in her bed." Kirstie continued.

"It's fine honestly." Chloe told her.

"She's hardly ever here these days anyway." Kirstie said thoughtfully.

"How come?" Chloe frowned.

"I think she said she's seeing someone." Kirstie shrugged. The two of them stopped talking as the doorbell rang.

"That might be Ben." Chloe smiled.

"It's probably more likely to be Lee." Kirstie said as she slowly stood up to answer the door. Chloe glanced up as Kirstie returned a few moments later, closely followed by Lee and Nathan.

"Hey, my little Chlo Bo." Nathan said, quickly sitting next to her on the sofa and carefully pulling her into his arms. Chloe sighed and relaxed into his arms.

"You doing okay?" he asked her, placing a soft kiss on top of her head. Chloe nodded slowly.

"Lee and I have been talking and we were thinking that once you are recovered you can move in with me." Nathan announced quietly, glancing at Lee as he perched on the end of the sofa.

"Then you won't have to go back to the park." Nathan added when Chloe didn't respond. Chloe sat up quickly, wincing slightly. Her eyes wandered to Lee as she could feel herself becoming angry, first he'd told Kirstie her secret and now he'd been discussing it with Nathan. Lee was the first person that she'd told about her living situation. Even though she'd been working at the studio with Matt for the past two years, she hadn't even been able to bring herself to tell him, even though he often asked her why she would shower at work and bring her backpack with her.

"I really wish people would stop trying to interfere in my life, I'm not a child!" Chloe snapped.

"We're not interfering, we just don't want to see you back on the streets." Nathan said quickly.

"I'm not your responsibility or yours." she argued, glaring at both of them in turn.

"I can take care of myself." she added, quickly standing up, forgetting in her anger that she was wounded. As soon as she stood up, she yelped in pain and fell to her knees.

"Chloe, calm down. We just want to help." Nathan said gently.

"I'm not a charity case that everyone needs to feel sorry for." she muttered sadly, her eyes brimming with tears.

"We don't think that Chloe, we just care about you." Lee said quietly.

"It's okay to accept help when you need it." Nathan told her.

"I don't like being a burden." she said quietly, fighting to hold back her tears.

"You're not a burden Chlo." Lee said softly. Chloe sat silently, not believing their words.

"I just really want my Mum." Chloe whispered to herself. Nathan sighed quietly to himself and quickly knelt down beside her. As soon as he sat next to her, she quickly snuggled into his arms, holding onto him tightly.

"You will miss your family at a time like this." Nathan whispered in her ear.

"I just want to be with my parents again." she admitted sadly. Nathan sighed sadly as she sat in silence, tears flowing steadily down her cheeks.

"I'm sorry, I've made your shirt wet." Chloe said quietly.

"You don't need to apologise, it'll dry." Nathan said, smiling at her as she sat back and glanced up at him.

Lee watched Chloe as she sat in silence on the floor, occasionally glancing up at Nathan and smiling warmly at him. As he sat watching her, he sighed quietly to himself, wishing that he had the courage to tell her how he felt. Then he would be able to hold her in his arms and never let go.

"I got you a present." Lee blurted when he couldn't stand the silence anymore. Chloe watched closely as the pulled a small box out of his pocket and handed it to her. She gasped as she stared at the box and saw that it was a new mobile phone.

"You need to have something to use if there's another emergency." Lee explained.

"I can't accept this.... it's too expensive." Chloe whispered, feeling slightly guilty.

"It's the least I can do." Lee said. Chloe fell silent, not entirely sure what he meant.

"Call it an apology." he added. Chloe nodded slowly.

"Thank you." she said quietly. She stared down at the new phone thoughtfully.

"Do you think I'd be able to get my videos and pictures back?" she asked.

"That depends, did you have them backed up?" Lee asked her.

"I think so." she said tentatively, not entirely sure what he was talking about.

"I'm not very good with technology." she admitted.

"I could probably sort it; I could access it on my laptop and then put them on your phone." Lee said thoughtfully.

"I hope you don't have any embarrassing photos that he's going to be looking through." Nathan laughed, smiling at Chloe when he saw her cheeks colouring. Chloe glanced at Lee nervously, quickly racking her brain to try and remember exactly what had been on her old phone. Lee couldn't help but smile slightly as he noticed her squirming.

"As long as you haven't got any nudes on there, I'm sure it will be fine." Nathan teased her, gently wrapping his arm around her playfully.

"I've never done that." Chloe said quickly.

"What, never?!" Nathan said incredulously. Chloe shook her head slowly.

"I'm pretty sure nobody would want to see that." she muttered sadly. She could feel Lee's eyes burning into her as she sat silently, picking her fingernails.

Lee couldn't help but stare at her as he tried to process her words. Even though she often hid her body under baggy clothes, he couldn't help but remember the night of the record label party, on the night that he'd attacked Shayne. The way that the fitted clothes had clung to her body perfectly. Her figure was breath-taking, but she didn't realise it, she was completely oblivious to the eyes that always followed her when she entered a room, and the people that were unable to stop themselves from staring at her. Everyone knew how naturally beautiful she was.... except her.

"Do you want me to go and get your laptop then?" Nathan offered, snapping Lee out of the thoughts.

"Yeah, you could do actually." Lee said, quickly throwing Nathan his car keys.

"I actually get to drive the precious sports car." Nathan grinned.

"If you damage it, I'll be fuming." Lee warned him. Nathan nodded slowly before quickly leaving the room, closing the front door behind himself. Chloe glanced up at Lee as she saw him stand up and rummage in her backpack, quickly pulling out the bag from the hospital.

"I need to change your dressing." he told her as he turned to face her.
"I can do it." she said quietly.

"It's fine, I don't mind." he said.

"I'm quite capable of doing it, if you give me the stuff." she argued, holding out her hand for the bag.

"I said I'll do it." he said shortly. Chloe sighed to herself as she scowled up at him. She knew how stubborn he was and that he wasn't going to allow her to change it by herself. She couldn't help but feel slightly uncomfortable at the thought of having to pull her shirt up in front of him. Even though she knew how difficult it would be for her to change it herself, due to the angle of the wound, she couldn't help but feel apprehensive about him touching her.

"It'll be easier if you lay down on the sofa." he told her firmly. Chloe nodded and stood up tentatively, carefully making her way over to the sofa. Lee perched on the end of the sofa, watching her closely as she slowly laid down.

"You'll need to move your shirt up." he said quietly, resisting the urge to do it himself. Chloe's hands shook slightly as she slowly lifted her shirt up. Lee quickly shook the spray bottle that they'd given him at the hospital and sprayed some on the dressing. Chloe gasped as the cold liquid made contact with her skin. Lee couldn't help but stare at her as he waited for the spray to soften the glue on the dressing. His eyes were drawn to her bare stomach, he couldn't tear his eyes away from her pale, silky skin that he longed to stroke. Chloe flinched slightly as she felt Lee's fingers gently pick at the corner of the dressing. She squirmed as she felt the dressing slowly being removed.

"Just relax, I'm not going to hurt you Chlo." Lee said quietly. Chloe nodded silently.

"It's quite bruised." he said thoughtfully.

"That's probably normal." she said quietly.

"Okay done." Lee announced a few moments later when he'd applied the fresh dressing.

"Is that it?!" Chloe exclaimed. Lee nodded slowly.

"I told you, I wouldn't hurt you." he said quietly, watching her closely as she quickly pulled her shirt down and slowly sat up. She rested her elbow against the back of the sofa, placing her chin on her hand. Lee couldn't help but smile at her as she gazed at him.

"What?" she frowned.

"Nothing." he said quickly, not quite able to bring himself to tell her how beautiful she looked. The two of them jumped slightly as the front door opened and Nathan walked in, quickly handing Lee his laptop.

"Jeez, you must have floored it!" Lee exclaimed.

"Kind of." Nathan smiled. Lee rolled his eyes and shook his head, suddenly feeling slightly apprehensive about his car. Lee opened up his laptop, glancing at Chloe as she watched him closely.

"Do you remember your password for the backup?" Lee asked her.

"I think so." she replied thoughtfully. Lee's skin tingled as she reached across him and typed in her password, her bare arm brushing against his as she did so. Chloe sat back, her eyes scanning the laptop as her pictures slowly began to appear.

"You're not in very many of these pictures." Lee stated, frowning slightly as he scrolled through the pictures.

"I don't like having my picture taken." she admitted. Lee smiled to himself as he suddenly noticed a selection of pictures from a few months ago, when the two of them were still close.

"Oh my god, I can't believe you kept these." Lee said quietly, smiling as he remembered the happy times they'd spent together.

"We used to have fun didn't we." Chloe said. Lee nodded, bursting out laughing when he saw the picture of Nathan and himself sitting on horses.

"I remember that day.... when you convinced us to go horse-riding on the beach." Lee laughed.

"Oh god!" Nathan groaned, smiling slightly.

"It was so much fun." she smiled.

"For you it was, remember when you galloped off and our horses bolted after you!" Lee laughed.

"And you ended up falling off." she giggled, turning to face Nathan.

"At least I had a soft landing." Nathan smiled. Chloe fell silent, her heart sinking slightly as she thought back on those times and how much she missed them.

"The two of you used to be so close." Nathan stated quietly, trying to prompt them. Lee nodded sadly, wishing that he could turn the clock back and go back to the way things were.

"That was before everything that I did annoyed you." Chloe said quietly, glancing at Lee sadly.

"You didn't annoy me." Lee muttered.

"I clearly did." Chloe argued.

"Either that or you realised that you hate me." she added, sighing quietly. Lee glanced at Nathan who was watching him closely, raising his eyebrow at him, almost like he was giving him a silent cue to tell Chloe the truth about his feelings for her. Lee swallowed the lump that had risen in his throat and frowned as he noticed a folder containing videos.

"What are these?" he asked Chloe, quickly changing the subject.

"Oh, those are Dad's." she told them. She watched as Lee opened the folder, his eyes widening when he saw the large number of videos that were in the folder.

"He was a professional photographer, so he liked to record everything. Memories were a big deal to him." she explained, smiling fondly as Lee clicked on one of the videos and her father's face appeared on the screen.

"You have your Dad's eyes." Lee smiled as the two of them sat silently, listening to her Dad speak.

"I know, everyone used to tell me that." Chloe sighed.

"What was his name?" Lee asked.
"Paul." she answered.

"Dad!" Chloe's voice called out in the video.

"Oh no, I've just remembered which video this is." Chloe said, her cheeks flushing.

Paul instantly stopped talking and turned to face the doorway.

"What is it munchkin?" Paul asked.

"I need boy advice." Chloe said, appearing in the doorway, looking slightly flustered.

"I think I just got asked out." she added.

"You're not allowed to date; nobody is ever going to be good enough for you." Paul said, smiling at her as he teased her.

"Oh, c'mon Dad, I'm being serious." Chloe giggled as she quickly crossed the room and sat on his lap.

"I don't know what to reply." she said quietly, handing him her phone so that he could read the message.

"That you can't possibly go out with someone until your father has interviewed him." he told her, pretending to be stern. Chloe groaned and hid her head in her hands.

"You're only sixteen, maybe you should hold off on dating until you are a bit older?" he suggested.

"I don't want you to get taken advantage of." he lectured.

"I won't be." she replied, rolling her eyes.

"You'll be a prime target because you are so kind and you have your Mother's looks." he told her firmly.

"I give up, I'll go and ask Mum." she sighed, quickly standing up and walking away.

"Chloe, I love you!" he called after her.

"I love you too Dad." Chloe whispered to herself, sighing quietly as the video ended.

"Aww, that was really cute." Lee smiled, watching her closely to make sure that she wasn't upset.

"He always used to lecture me about boys." she said quietly, smiling to herself.

"Good, he was being a good Dad." Nathan piped up.

"He liked to tell me I look like Mum too, but I think I'm more like my Dad." she said thoughtfully, her head suddenly full of the happy memories of her family, before everything had been ripped away from them. Chloe could feel her eyes filling with tears as she thought about her parents and how much she loved them and missed them every day. Chloe shuffled closer to Lee, sighing sadly as she placed her head on his shoulder. Lee watched her closely as she carefully wrapped her arms around his waist.

Nathan couldn't help but smile to himself as he watched the two of them together. Lee didn't even tear his eyes away from Chloe when Nathan stood up and left the room, clearly realising that they needed some time alone.

Chloe sat silently for a few moments, enjoying the fact that she was curled up against Lee. Despite the fact that she hadn't felt safe since she was attacked, she suddenly felt relaxed and secure, almost as if she was where she was meant to be. She slowly lifted her head, her cheeks colouring as he watched her closely. Her eyes flickered to his lips for a moment before she quickly realised what she was doing and sat back, tentatively moving away from him.

"Sorry, I shouldn't have done that." she whispered, staring down at her lap.

"It's okay, you were keeping me warm." he said softly, longing to pull her back into his arms. He hesitated for a moment before finally giving into his feelings. He quickly reached over and wrapped his arm around her waist, carefully pulling her towards him. Chloe sighed in contentment as she wrapped her arms around his waist. The hairs on the back of her neck stood up as he carefully wrapped his arm around her shoulder, his fingers gently stroking her bare arm. She watched for a moment as he continued working his way through her pictures, carefully uploading them to his laptop. Chloe rested her head on his chest as she felt her eyelids becoming heavy. Lee glanced at her, his fingers still softly stroking her arm. He smiled to himself as he felt Chloe relax against him, her breathing becoming steady as she slept. As he watched her, he found himself unable to tear his eyes away from her, a warm feeling of contentment spread through him as he watched her sleeping peacefully in his arms.

"I love you." he whispered, softly placing a kiss on her forehead. Lee closed his eyes and gently rested his cheek against her forehead, cherishing every moment that he held her in his arms.

Chapter Twenty-Six

Michelle sighed to herself as she walked into the flat, flinging her bag onto the floor, frowning to herself as she saw Chloe curled up on the sofa. She slowly peered over her, feeling slightly confused when she saw that she was asleep.

"Why is Chloe asleep on our sofa?" Michelle asked Kirstie as soon as she walked into the kitchen.

"Nice to see you too." Kirstie said quickly, rolling her eyes.

"I do live here." Michelle stated.

"I know, but I haven't seen you for ages." Kirstie pointed out, feeling slightly frustrated that Michelle seemed to come and go as she pleased, without even keeping in contact with Kirstie.

"I told you I was seeing someone." Michelle snapped, getting slightly defensive.

"You've been seeing him a little while now, when do I get to meet him?" Kirstie asked.

"I don't know." Michelle sighed. Her heart sinking as she thought about her and Mark. She knew that she had strong feelings for him but couldn't help but feel like they weren't reciprocated. Even though she'd been trying to get Mark to commit to her for weeks, he still seemed as distant with her as he was at the beginning. She couldn't help but be plagued by insecurities that maybe she wasn't enough for him.

"Anyway, why is Chloe here?" Michelle asked, changing the subject.

"She was stabbed, so she's been staying here the past few days." Kirstie said quickly.

"Why?" Michelle frowned.

"I don't know why anyone would want to hurt her, but apparently it was a robbery. Kirstie explained.

"No not why was she stabbed, why is she staying here?" Michelle sighed.

"So that we can take care of her." Kirstie said quietly, frowning in confusion at Michelle's attitude.

"Surely she can take care of herself." Michelle pointed out.

"That's a bit heartless Michelle, I thought you are a nurse." Ben stated as he walked into the room. Michelle opened her mouth to respond but quickly closed it, her cheeks colouring.

"Where's Lee?" Ben frowned when he suddenly realised that Lee wasn't in the room.

"He's gone for a shower." Kirstie told him.

"What?" Ben gulped.

"Not like that, he's been at the studio all morning, he came straight here to check on Chloe." Kirstie said quickly, slightly nervous that Ben was going to kick off again.

"Lee is here?!" Michelle asked quickly.

"Yeah, he's been taking care of Chloe." Kirstie told her.

"He's been amazing actually; he hardly leaves her side." she added. Kirstie rolled her eyes at Ben as she heard him snort sarcastically. Michelle glanced at the doorway, smiling widely at Lee as he walked into the room. She couldn't help but notice how handsome he looked with his messy hair and casual sweatpants and shirt look.

"Thank you for letting me use your shower." Lee said quietly, picking up on the awkward atmosphere but not entirely sure what was causing it.

"You did kind of smell." Kirstie smiled at him.

"We have a new choreographer and he's kind of a tool." Lee smiled.

"Is he overworking you?" Michelle said, smiling sweetly.

"A little, his routines are very fast paced and he likes to make us do them over and over." Lee explained, his eyes wandering into the living room as he saw Chloe fidgeting in her sleep.

"How's she been today?" Lee asked, turning his attention back to Kirstie.

"She's alright, very emotional. She's not getting much sleep either, because the nightmares are getting worse." Kirstie told him. Lee sighed sadly, his gaze wandering to Chloe again.

"Maybe she should take the sleeping tablets." Lee said quietly.

"They are quite addictive though." Michelle piped up. Lee nodded slowly.

"I'll speak to her when she wakes up, to see what she wants to do." Kirstie said, sighing sadly.

"Did you say yesterday that you and Ben are going shopping today?" Lee asked.

"Yeah, why?" Kirstie frowned. Lee rummaged in his pocket and quickly handed Kirstie his credit card.

"Can you get Chloe some new clothes, then we can get rid of her old tatty ones?" Lee asked.

"I'll text you the pin number, just get her whatever she needs." he quickly added.

"Are you sure?" Kirstie asked. Lee nodded slowly.

"Have I missed something, I thought you hate her?" Michelle piped up, frowning in confusion.

"I don't hate her." Lee said quietly, glancing at Kirstie who smiled at him warmly. She had seen a completely different side to Lee over the past few days, a secret soft side to him that he liked to hide. Kirstie sighed as she glanced into the living room and saw Chloe fidgeting frantically on the sofa.

"She's doing it again." Kirstie announced quietly. Lee followed her eyeline, his heart sinking as he saw Chloe, still asleep but clearly in distress.

"Maybe we should wake her." Lee whispered, struggling to watch the fear on her pretty features.

"You might make things worse if you do that." Michelle told him. The four of them jumped as Chloe let out a small scream and bolted awake, clutching her abdomen in pain as she did so. Without hesitating Lee quickly left kitchen and walked into the living room.

"Aren't you going to check on her?" Ben asked Kirstie, frowning in confusion when Kirstie remained in the kitchen.

"I'm not the one she needs." Kirstie said.

"If you say so." Ben replied shortly.

"She needs Lee, not me!" Kirstie snapped, rolling her eyes at him. She couldn't understand what had gotten into Ben the last few days, but he was beginning to frustrate her.

Chloe jumped slightly as Lee sat beside her on the sofa. He watched her closely as she sat silently, taking deep breaths, trying to calm down. Her whole-body trembling in fear.

"He's going to find me." Chloe whispered to herself.

"Who's going to find you?" Lee asked her gently.

"The man who stabbed me, he wants to come back and finish the job." she rambled, still not completely awake. Lee watched her closely as she curled into a ball, resting her head on his lap. She quickly took hold of his trouser material and curled it into a fist in her hand. Lee could feel her whole-body trembling against him.

"Please don't let him hurt me." she whispered. Lee sighed sadly and gently stroked her hair, trying his best to provide at least a small amount of comfort.

"I won't let anyone hurt you.... ever." he told her softly. As Lee sat in silence, stroking her hair, he could feel her slowly starting to relax.

"You need to rest." he told her as she slowly sat up.

"I can't." she whispered, afraid to go back to sleep and return to her nightmares.

"I need to use the bathroom." she added, carefully standing up. Lee watched her as she slowly stood up, her eyes filling with tears. He knew that she was still upset by her nightmare but was trying to hide her feelings. Lee quickly stood up and followed Chloe as she slowly walked away. She stopped walking when she felt him reach out and take hold of her wrist.

"Chloe." he said quietly, trying to get her to face him. He heard her sniff quietly to herself. Lee gently pulled her towards himself and wrapped his arms around her tightly, trying to help her feel safe. Chloe placed her arms across her chest, finally allowing the tears that she'd been holding back to flow down her cheeks.

"You'll always be safe when you are with me." he whispered in her ear.

"I know." she muttered, her skin tingling as Lee softly stroked her hair. She sighed to herself as she finally felt herself calm down.

"I really need to use the bathroom though." she said smiling up at him. Lee nodded, reluctantly letting go of her.

He watched her as she slowly walked away. Lee's eyes snapped up as he saw Kirstie gesturing to him through the glass panel between the kitchen and living room. Lee quickly walked into the room.

"Did you want me for something?" he asked.

"Is she okay?" Kirstie asked quickly.

"I think so." he replied quietly.

"I was wondering if you could maybe stay over for a few days, she's so much more relaxed when you are here?" Kirstie asked. Lee thought for a moment, he didn't want to leave Chloe's side, particularly now when she needed him. He nodded quickly.

"I think she needs you; it took me ages to calm her from her nightmare last night." Kirstie said thoughtfully.

"Yeah, I know she needs me." he said quietly. He couldn't help but feel slightly sad that in a few days' time when she was feeling better, Chloe wouldn't need him anymore. He'd been by her side almost constantly for the past few days, and he couldn't quite bring himself to be torn from her side again.

"There's space in my bed." Michelle offered, snapping Lee out of his thoughts. Michelle wiggled her eyebrows at Lee as he glanced at her.

"There's no need for that, the sofa is a big corner one, so you can have one side each." Kirstie said quickly. Lee's eyes flickered to the living room as Chloe returned. He quickly left the room, making sure that he was there for her.

"I'll go and find some blankets." Michelle said, quickly walking away. Kirstie glanced at Ben nervously, picking up on the tension in his body language.

"What's wrong?" Kirstie asked, when she couldn't stand the silence any longer.

"I just don't understand why you are inviting other men to stay over." he said quietly.

"I'm trying to do right by my friend, she needs him right now." she told him.

"I mean look at her." she added, gesturing to the living room where Chloe was curled up on the sofa, her head gently resting on Lee's lap.

"I know, but I can't help but wonder if you have a thing for Lee?" he asked.

"Well, I don't. I can't understand why you are so insecure, you're the one who has all the girls throwing themselves at you, and I haven't given you any reason to doubt me." she explained.

"I guess I know that I do trust you, I just don't trust Lee, I know what he's like with women." he sighed.

"Well, you're the one I love, you big idiot." she smiled. Ben smiled slightly before quickly placing a soft kiss on Kirstie's lips.

"You could stay over too, if it would make you feel better?" she offered, smiling slightly. Ben nodded and kissed her again.

"We need to go and get these clothes." Kirstie reminded him. Ben nodded as he followed her out of the back door.

Chloe glanced up from Lee's lap as Michelle walked into the room and perched on the coffee table opposite her.

"I found you some spare blankets." Michelle told Lee, smiling at him.

"Thanks." he replied.

"Are you staying over?" Chloe asked, lifting her head to look at him.

"If you want me too?" he asked nervously. Chloe nodded quickly, placing her head back on his lap and snuggling against him. He glanced down at her and smiled.

"I had an idea Chloe." Michelle piped up.

"Okay." Chloe said sleepily.

"Since you're staying here, you could always do our makeup for the masquerade ball?" Michelle asked.

"She's not up to doing that." Lee said quickly, before Chloe could respond.

"It's not for a few days yet anyway." Michelle said quickly, rolling her eyes at him.

"You could earn your keep." Michelle prompted when Chloe didn't respond.

"I'm happy to do it, who is going?" Chloe said quietly, her mouth suddenly feeling very dry, when she heard Michelle's words.

"Great!" Michelle exclaimed happily.

"Me, Kathleen, Kirstie and Louise." she added.

"It's a shame you won't be able to go." Michelle said, smiling slightly to herself when she realised that Chloe wouldn't be able to join them. Chloe nodded slowly. Michelle couldn't help but feel pleased that Chloe wouldn't be coming along, even though she didn't have anything against Chloe, she didn't want to be upstaged by her beauty. Whenever they went out as a group, Chloe was always the one that got most of the male attention.

"I can't afford a dress anyway." Chloe said sadly.

"Because you're homeless?" Michelle asked.

"What, how do you know about that?" Chloe said quickly, her head snapping up as she looked at Lee.

"Don't look at me, I didn't say anything." he said quickly.

"It's in the local paper that a homeless person was stabbed in the park." Michelle told her.

"Great." Chloe muttered, her cheeks colouring as she felt a wave of shame wash over her.

"What's it like, sleeping rough?" Michelle asked.

"Hard going." Chloe muttered. Lee placed his arm around her waist, taking her hand in his and squeezing it reassuringly.

"I just don't understand how you have a well-paid job but yet you can't afford accommodation." Michelle frowned.

"I don't want to talk about it." Chloe said quickly.

"I'm just curious, it doesn't add up." Michelle continued.

"She said she doesn't want to talk about it, so back off." Lee told her sternly.

"Alright, I was just asking!" Michelle snapped.

"Well don't, you're upsetting her!" Lee snapped back.

"I'm pretty sure that's your area of expertise." Michelle muttered under her breath as she walked away.

Chapter Twenty-Seven

Chloe jumped as she awoke, frowning to herself as she gazed around the room and saw that it was still dark. She glanced over to the other end of the sofa, smiling slightly as she saw Lee. She stretched slowly, slightly confused as to what had woken her, it was the first time in a while that she'd managed to sleep without having a nightmare. She couldn't ignore the feeling in her gut that something was going on. Chloe gasped as she heard a crash from along the hall. She quickly reached over and switched on the lamp, gazing around nervously, not entirely sure what to do.

"Lee?" she whispered.

"What?" he said quickly, sounding slightly sleepy.

"Did you hear that noise?" she asked. Chloe gasped as she heard Kirstie squeal from down the hallway. Chloe could feel herself beginning to panic, she couldn't get the thought out of her head that Kirstie was in danger.

"Where are you going?" Lee asked her as she quickly stood up. Chloe's feet froze to the spot, her cheeks colouring as she heard a headboard repeatedly banging against the wall.

"I think they are fine." Lee laughed when he saw the realisation finally dawn on Chloe's face. Chloe quickly climbed back onto the sofa and pulled the blanket over her face, desperately trying to hide her embarrassment. She reached out and quickly switched off the lamp, trying to ignore the sounds that she could hear.

"This is so embarrassing." she muttered a few moments later.

"At least someone is getting laid." he replied, sounding slightly frustrated.

Lee sighed angrily to himself and quickly put the pillow over his face, trying to tune out the sounds that were travelling up the hallway.

He hadn't slept with anyone for the past few days, ever since Chloe had been stabbed and he realised how he felt about her, he didn't want anyone else other than her. Being able to hear Kirstie and Ben sleeping together was causing Lee's thoughts to wander to Chloe and what sleeping with her would be like. He desperately wanted her, to be able to feel her perfect body against his. Having Chloe under his nose was making it difficult for him to resist her. Lee slowly removed the pillow from his face and glanced over at Chloe, smiling slightly as he saw her silhouette illuminated by the moonlight beaming in the window.

"Oh, thank god." Chloe whispered when the house fell silent. Lee ran his hand through his hair in frustration and slowly sat up. Chloe sat up and switched on the lamp, frowning when she noticed Lee sitting up, a look of frustration on his face.

"Are you okay?" she asked him. He nodded slowly, not looking at her. The two of them glanced at the doorway as Ben walked into the room.

"Oops sorry guys, I didn't mean to wake you." Ben said, when he saw them staring at him.

"Did you have to make so much noise?" Lee rounded on Ben as soon as he entered the room.

"Sorry, I didn't realise it was an issue." Ben said shortly.

"It's not." Chloe said smiling at him as she walked past him on her way to the bathroom.

"Are you jealous or something?" Ben asked, clearly picking up on Lee's frustration.

"Yeah." Lee said quickly.

"Well, you need to get over it, she's with me and we are happy." Ben said sternly. Lee frowned in confusion for a moment, before he finally realised what Ben was suggesting.

"I'm not into Kirstie, it's just really difficult hearing that when you're sleeping next to a beautiful woman." Lee said quietly.

"Plus, it's been a while." he quickly added. Lee sighed as he slowly stood up and stretched, his back feeling slightly stiff from sleeping on the sofa.

"Whoa, sit back down and cover up before Chloe comes back!" Ben said quickly, glancing nervously at the doorway. Lee glanced down at himself, before sitting back down and pulling a blanket onto his lap.

"She has that effect on me." Lee muttered.

"I want her so bad." he added.

"I noticed." Ben chuckled.

"I've never wanted someone this much before." Lee admitted thoughtfully.

"That's probably because you can't have her, whereas normally you get the women you want." Ben pointed out.

"I don't think it's that, I can control it when I'm with her normally, but hearing you guys and having her just a few feet away, it's a bad combination." Lee sighed.

"I have got to stop fantasizing about her." Lee added, shaking his head quickly, to try and clear the thoughts that were swirling around his head.

"You seriously need to get laid." Ben laughed. The two of them stopped talking as Chloe walked back into the room. She'd felt her heart sink as she walked around the corner and heard Ben tell Lee that he needed to get laid. She hated the thought of him sleeping with someone, but she knew that she had no right to feel that way. Lee glanced at her awkwardly as she sat cross legged on the sofa, hoping that she hadn't overheard the conversation between him and Ben.

"Maybe you should go out to a club or something, it's still early ish?" Chloe suggested quietly.

"What for?" Lee frowned.

"To meet a girl." she told him.

"I don't want to go out and meet a random girl." he said quietly.

"You do it normally, and it'll stop you from being frustrated won't it." she tried.

"And you don't have to stay in all the time because you feel sorry for me." she added quietly.

"I'm not here because I feel sorry for you." he told her.

"You don't need to be with me twenty-four seven though, I'll be alright. You shouldn't put your life on hold because of me." she told him quietly, feeling slightly guilty that she was keeping him from living his life. Lee opened his mouth to respond, but quickly closed it when Michelle walked into the room. Lee and Ben frowned at each other as she walked past them, wearing a sexy underwear set. The material was almost see through and clung to her tightly, most of her flesh on show. She smiled sweetly at them as she walked into the kitchen.

"What on earth is she wearing?" Ben hissed, glancing at Michelle as she stood in the kitchen, making a cup of tea.

"I know, I was just thinking that." Lee laughed.

"There's no way she sleeps in an outfit like that." Ben muttered. Lee shook his head slowly. Chloe glanced up as Michelle walked back into the room, carrying a cup of tea.

"You look amazing Michelle." Chloe told her kindly, trying to make the effort with her after things had been awkward earlier in the day.

"Thanks honey." Michelle smiled.

"Whoops." Michelle said as she conveniently dropped her biscuit, slowly bending down to pick it up. Lee flinched as Michelle bent down in front of him, her rear perfectly positioned right in front of his face. He locked eyes with Ben, who was biting his lip, to prevent himself from bursting out laughing.

"Night everyone." she said sweetly, smiling over her shoulder at them as she slowly walked away. As soon as she left the room Ben and Lee burst out laughing, neither of them entirely sure what had just happened.

"I wish I could pull off an outfit like that." Chloe said thoughtfully, sighing to herself.

"The only thing stopping you is your confidence." Ben told her kindly, when he'd finally managed to stop laughing.

"You'd also look a hell of a lot better." Lee said quietly. She glanced at him for a moment, assuming that he was being sarcastic, frowning to herself when she saw that he was smiling warmly at her.

"Anyway, I need to get Kirstie a glass of water, she'll wonder where I've got too." Ben laughed as he walked into the kitchen. Chloe shuffled over to her part of the sofa and curled up, quickly pulling her blanket over herself. Lee couldn't help but smile to himself at how cute she looked as she snuggled under the covers. As soon as Ben walked back along the hallway, Chloe quickly switched off the light.

"Night Chlo." Lee said softly.

"Night." she replied quietly.

Chloe awoke with a start for the second time that night, glancing at the clock on her phone and sighing when she saw that it was only six am. She frowned to herself when she noticed that Lee's section of the sofa was empty. She sighed to herself, she knew how frustrated he was last night, and she couldn't help but feel concerned that he'd finally succumbed to Michelle's charms and joined her in her bed. Chloe could feel the bile rise in her throat as she thought about the two of them together. The thought of Lee being with someone else was painful enough for her, but the thought of him being with one of her friends made her feel like she wanted to vomit. She angrily wiped away the stray tear that was rolling down her cheek, feeling slightly frustrated with herself. It shouldn't matter to her what Lee did, but somehow it mattered. Her eyes snapped up as Lee walked into the room, her heart fluttered when she saw that he was only wearing his boxers. She watched as he rummaged in his suitcase, quickly pulling on his jeans and a shirt. Lee turned to face her as he felt her watching him closely.

"You alright Chlo?" he asked her worriedly, slightly concerned that maybe she'd had another nightmare.

"Yes, I was just wondering where you were." she said quietly.

"In the bathroom." he told her.

"I thought maybe you were with Michelle." she whispered to herself.

"Nope." he said quickly. Chloe's cheeks coloured when she realised that he'd heard her.

"I have to go; we have some early interviews to do." he told her as he pulled on his jacket. Chloe jumped slightly as he quickly crossed the room and squatted in front of her.

"You'll be okay, if you need me you can call me." he said gently.

"I know, I'll be fine, you don't have to worry about me." she said quietly.

"I'll be back later." he told her, softly touching her cheek with his thumb for a brief moment.

Chloe's skin tingled under his touch as she nodded slowly. She sighed in disappointment as he moved away from her and quickly left the house. Chloe sighed and slowly sat up, afraid to go back to sleep now that Lee wasn't there.

A few moments later Kirstie walked into the room, still dressed in her pyjamas. She smiled at Chloe as she sat beside her on the sofa.

"Did you get some sleep?" Kirstie asked quickly.

"Yes, I got the most sleep I've had in a while." Chloe said.

"It makes you feel better when Lee is here doesn't it." Kirstie smiled. Chloe nodded slowly.

"I don't really understand why, he was horrible to me when I worked with the boys." Chloe said thoughtfully.

"He's been good with you recently though, he barely leaves your side, even when you are asleep." Kirstie pointed out.

"I think he feels guilty and sorry for me too probably." Chloe said quietly.

"Or maybe...." Chloe started but trailed off.

"No, there's no chance of that." she added quickly.

"What were you going to say?" Kirstie asked.

"I was going to say that maybe he has feelings for me, but I don't see why he would." Chloe sighed sadly. Kirstie remained silent, smiling to herself as she listened to Chloe finally joining the dots in her head.

"What?" Chloe asked, when she noticed Kirstie smiling at her.

"Of course, he has feelings for you, anyone with eyes can see it." Kirstie told her. Chloe fell silent, trying to process Kirstie's words and figure out how she felt about the revelation that Lee reciprocated her feelings for him.

"This is such a mess." Chloe whispered thoughtfully.

"Why, isn't it a good thing?" Kirstie frowned.

"How could I ever trust him?" Chloe asked quietly.

"You give him a chance to earn your trust." Kirstie told her.

"You'll never know unless you talk to him, you don't want to live to regret not telling him how you feel, and I can guarantee you he feels the same." Kirstie added. The two of them stopped talking as Michelle walked into the room, dressed in the underwear from last night. Kirstie rolled her eyes as she saw that her dressing gown was undone, perfectly displaying her underwear.

"Is it really appropriate for you to be walking around wearing that when the boys are here?" Kirstie snapped.

"Oh, don't worry, Ben is still in your bed isn't he." Michelle said sarcastically.

"And Lee is single anyway so who cares." she added.

"That's not the point, I know Ben felt uncomfortable about you walking around in your underwear last night and I expect Lee felt the same." Kirstie told her sternly.

"Well, I didn't hear them complaining last night." Michelle said smugly.

"Just do your dressing gown up!" Kirstie snapped. Michelle sighed and quickly did as Kirstie asked, pouting slightly.

"Where is Lee anyway?" Michelle asked sweetly.

"He left early; he has work stuff to do." Chloe told her.

"He looked so handsome last night with his bed head." Michelle said, giggling slightly.

"He was always my favourite one in Eclipse." she added.

"I always liked Nathan." Kirstie said, trying to get Michelle to stop talking about Lee.

"Lee seemed a little wound up last night." Michelle said, turning to Chloe.

"Yes, he was a bit frustrated with certain things. " Chloe agreed.

"Yeah, Ben told me." Kirstie said quickly.

"Oooh spill, what was wrong with him?" Michelle asked quickly.

"I think he was just tired and ratty." Chloe lied quickly. She couldn't help but feel guilty about lying, but she couldn't bring herself to tell Michelle the truth, as she knew that it would encourage her to flirt with Lee even more than she already did. Chloe glanced at Kirstie nervously, feeling slightly concerned that Kirstie might let on to Michelle that Chloe was lying. Kirstie smiled at her reassuringly, before quickly standing up.

"Let's get breakfast sorted." Kirstie announced, before walking into the kitchen.

Chapter Twenty-Eight

Kirstie smiled at Lee as she walked into the kitchen and saw him cooking dinner.

"Wow, something smells amazing!" she exclaimed, sniffing the air.

"Yeah well, I'm not a bad cook." he smiled at her.

"I'm making my famous stir-fry for everyone." he added, quickly chopping the vegetables.

"You don't have to make us all dinner." Kirstie told him.

"I know, but I want too. You've been good enough to let me stay here and you won't accept any money, so I thought I'd make dinner." he explained.

"You're secretly quite sweet aren't you Mr Knight." Kirstie said, bursting out laughing when his cheeks coloured.

"You hide it well though." Kirstie added.

"I personally love a man who can cook." Michelle piped up from where she was sitting at the dining room table.

"I think all women do." Lee said, smiling slightly.

"What are you doing up?" Lee said quickly as Chloe slowly walked into the room.

"It doesn't hurt as much now." she told him.

"That's not the point, you're meant to be resting." he said, smiling slightly as she stared at him defiantly.

"I can't sit around all the time; I could help you chop the vegetables or something." Chloe argued.

"Chloe Olivia Evans, you had major abdominal surgery a week ago, so get your arse back on that sofa, before I throw you over my shoulder and carry you there." he told her sternly.

"Alright fine." she sighed, glaring at him. Lee glared back at her, pretending to be angry with her, a small smile playing on the corner of his lips. Chloe burst out laughing, no longer able to keep up her poker face.

"Ow." she muttered, clutching her side. Lee raised his eyebrow at her, nodding his head towards the living room. Chloe rolled her eyes at him and reluctantly left the room.

"Remind me I need to change her dressing in a bit." Lee said to Kirstie.

"I don't think you'll forget." she replied, smiling slightly at how cute Chloe and Lee were together.

"I could do it?" Michelle offered.

"No, it's okay thanks. I was shown how to do it at the hospital." Lee said quickly.

"I am a nurse, I'm pretty sure I know how to change a dressing!" Michelle snapped.

"Even so, it's fine." Lee told her firmly. Michelle shook her head slowly, feeling slightly frustrated with how overprotective Lee was over Chloe. She couldn't help but feel even more envious of Chloe than before. Not only did she have her beauty and figure that caused all the men to swarm around her, but now she had one of the men that Michelle had always fancied at her beck and call. Even though Chloe and Lee weren't together, it was clear that he would do anything for her, she would only have to say the word. Michelle quickly left the room and walked into the living room, smiling at Chloe as Chloe glanced up from her magazine.

"You okay?" Chloe asked Michelle when she perched on the sofa beside her, watching her strangely. Michelle nodded slowly.

"I was going to speak to you about our makeup for the ball." Michelle said.

"Okay." Chloe said, placing the magazine on the coffee table.

"I can change your dressing at the same time if you want?" Michelle offered. Chloe nodded, quickly rummaging in her backpack and handing Michelle the hospital bag. Chloe slowly laid down and lifted her shirt.

"What did you want to ask me?" Chloe asked.

"I just wondered what kind of makeup choices we have?" Michelle asked.

"I can do pretty much whatever you would like, the only slight issue is that I don't have any makeup, so I'll need to use your products." Chloe explained, as Michelle carefully removed her dressing.

"My dress is black, so I was thinking of a dark eye look." Michelle stated.

"I can easily do that for you." Chloe smiled.

"Has Lee been cleaning the wound?" Michelle asked as she inspected the wound.

"Occasionally, just when it needs it though." Chloe replied. Michelle nodded slowly, quickly picking up the cotton wool and soaking it with the hibiscrub solution.

"Anyway, I want gossip, what's going on with you and Lee?" Michelle asked, winking at Chloe.

"I don't know really, I need to speak to him, Kirstie thinks he might have feelings for me." Chloe told her thoughtfully.

"It's difficult though isn't it, I'm really not very brave with things like that." she added. Chloe whimpered quietly as Michelle scrubbed the wound, being slightly rough.

"It needs a good clean." Michelle said quickly. Chloe nodded slowly, biting her lip to try and control the pain.

"Are you sure it's a good idea to speak to him, you know he'll just upset you like he always does?" Michelle asked. Chloe remained silent, unable to focus on anything other than the pain she was in. Michelle eventually stopped scrubbing the wound and discarded the cotton wool onto the coffee table.

"He must feel something for me though, the way he's been over the past week." Chloe insisted, finally able to concentrate now that Michelle had stopped scrubbing her wound.

"I highly doubt it." Michelle said shortly. She picked up a bottle, frowning as she realised that it contained surgical spirit. She glanced at Chloe and then back at the wound.

"Lee said that's for sterilising your hands before touching the wound." Chloe told her.

"Well, it's not, it's for the wound, to kill any potential microbes." Michelle replied. Chloe nodded and watched as Michelle hesitated for a moment before slowly pouring a small amount of liquid onto the wound. Chloe gasped as the cold liquid made contact with her bare skin. She cried out in pain as it slowly soaked into the wound, causing an intense burning feeling. Chloe quickly curled into a ball, clutching her abdomen as she cried out in pain again, warm tears flowing down her cheeks.

Lee's head snapped towards the doorway as he heard Chloe crying out. His initial thought was that Chloe had another nightmare, but as he quickly assessed the situation, he soon realised that wasn't the case. He saw Chloe curl herself into a ball, clutching her abdomen tightly as she cried out in pain once again.

"What the hell is she doing to her?!" Lee exclaimed angrily, when he noticed Michelle sitting beside Chloe, looking slightly smug. Lee quickly threw the wooden spoon onto the kitchen counter and strode into the living room.

"What have you done?!" he said angrily, his heart breaking as he watched Chloe writhing in pain.

"Lee, make it stop!" Chloe cried.

"I put surgical spirit on to disinfect the wound." Michelle quickly explained.

"Well, that was fucking stupid, even I know that surgical spirit hurts like hell!" Lee shouted. Lee turned on his heel and rushed into the kitchen, quickly returning a few moments later with a damp cloth. Chloe glanced up at him as he quickly knelt in front of her.

"Move your hands." he told her. She quickly did as he asked, breathing a sigh of relief as he gently applied the cool cloth to the wound. Chloe scrunched her eyes closed.

"You're such an idiot, you're meant to be a nurse." Lee said angrily.

"I didn't mean to hurt her." Michelle said, suddenly feeling slightly afraid of Lee and his temper.

"You shouldn't have been doing it anyway, I told you I would do it!" he shouted.

"Lee, it's fine." Chloe said quietly, slowly opening her eyes, breathing deeply to get her breath back. Chloe frowned to herself as she gazed into his eyes, in all the years that she'd known Lee, she'd never seen him so angry.

"It's not fine!" Lee snapped.

"She really hurt you." he added, his tone softening slightly as he gazed at her.

"I'm alright." she told him quickly. Lee sighed and gently wiped the wound with the cloth, trying to cool the wound down as much as possible. Chloe sighed in relief as the pain finally stopped.

"Is there anything I can do?" Michelle asked quietly leaning over to peer at the wound. Lee moved quickly, blocking her from getting near Chloe. Michelle jumped slightly as

Lee moved towards her quickly, not entirely sure if he was angry enough to want to hurt her or not.

"You can back the hell off!" Lee exclaimed angrily.

"Lee stop, it was an accident." Chloe said quietly, gently placing her hand on top of his, in a desperate attempt to try and calm him down. She knew from experience how nasty Lee could be when he was angry and the last thing, she wanted was for Michelle to be exposed to his temper.

"I highly doubt it was an accident, she knew exactly what she was doing." Lee argued.

"I'm really sorry Chloe." Michelle said quietly suddenly feeling guilty at what she'd done.

"It's fine, accidents happen." Chloe said quietly, glancing at Lee nervously as she slowly sat up.

"Accident my arse." Lee muttered angrily.

"You really think I would do that on purpose?" Michelle asked quietly.

"Yeah, I do, I know how jealous of her you are, and I wouldn't put it past you." Lee said quickly.

"The truth is you have a lot to be jealous of don't you." Lee added, smirking slightly.

"Lee." Chloe said quietly.

"It's true though." he insisted. Chloe watched in horror as Michelle's eyes slowly filled with tears. Michelle blinked slowly, causing the tears that she'd been holding back to slowly fall down her cheeks. Lee rolled his eyes and quickly looked away from Michelle, turning his attention back to Chloe who was watching Michelle sympathetically. Chloe winced as Michelle placed her head in her hands and began to sob. Lee raised his eyebrow at Chloe as she glanced at him, shaking her head slowly.

"How did I suddenly become the bad guy." Lee muttered under his breath. Chloe raised her eyebrow at him, causing Lee to feel slightly guilty under her intense gaze.

"I'm so sorry." Michelle sobbed. Lee sighed angrily, not entirely sure if he believed that Michelle's tears were genuine. Before he could talk himself out of it, he turned to face her and gently hugged her. Michelle clung to him tightly, instantly stopping crying as soon as she was in his strong arms.

"Dinner is done!" Kirstie called from the kitchen.

"Thank god." Lee muttered, relieved that he could finally let go of Michelle. Chloe started to stand up, pausing when Lee gently placed a hand on her knee.

"You stay there, I'll bring a plate through to you." he told her. Michelle rolled her eyes as she walked into the kitchen.

"But shouldn't we eat with the others?" Chloe asked, feeling slightly guilty that they were being antisocial.

"No, I need to keep away from *her* for a bit." he said quickly. Chloe sighed, realising instantly who he was talking about. Chloe watched Lee as he quickly pulled a fresh dressing out of the bag and carefully applied it to her wound.

"Don't let anyone else do it next time." he told her firmly, before quickly standing up and leaving the room.

Chapter Twenty Nine

Lee slowly put down his book and glanced at Chloe, who was sitting on the sofa beside him, her earphones in, watching a video on her phone. He'd been dying to give her the clothes he'd brought for her for the past few days but had been waiting for an opportunity when they were alone in the house. The last thing he wanted was for Chloe to feel self-conscious in front of everyone. Chloe glanced up at him as he quickly stood up and walked to his car, returning a few moments later with a large box.

"What have you got in there?!" Chloe exclaimed, switching off the video and quickly removing her earphones.

"A present for you." he smiled, carefully placing the box on the ground and returning to the sofa.

"You need to stop buying me things just because you feel guilty." she said quietly, feeling slightly guilty.

"I didn't get it for you because I felt guilty, I got it because I want to help you get your life back on track." he sighed. He smiled at her as she slowly climbed onto the floor, sitting cross legged beside the box. Chloe slowly opened the box, her eyes filling with tears as she saw the collection of new clothes. It had been so long since she'd owned something that wasn't tatty, she couldn't help but feel slightly emotional.

"I don't deserve all of this." she said sadly, a stray tear rolling down her face as she saw a selection of shoes at the bottom of the box. She knew that all of the items wouldn't have been cheap.

"You deserve the world." he told her sadly, his heart sinking slightly when he noticed the stray tear that was slowly rolling down her cheek.

"You can throw out all of your old clothes now, it's a new start." he quickly added when she glanced up at him. Chloe shuffled across the floor so that she was sitting in front of him, glancing up at him nervously for a moment before she quickly hugged him.

"Thank you." she sniffed. Lee stiffened for a moment, before he eventually relaxed, smiling slightly to himself as she hugged him tightly.

"It's fine." he told her.

"And don't feel bad, they weren't that expensive." he added when she sat back. Lee watched as she rummaged in her backpack, quickly pulling out her belongings. She smiled slightly to herself as she placed her photo album on her lap, carefully stroking it with her fingers.

"That's a big photo album." Lee said laughing slightly.

"Dad liked taking pictures." she smiled.

"Show me then." he said, quickly sitting on the floor beside her.

"Why?" she frowned.

"Because I want to know everything about you, you never talk about yourself." he said quietly.

"Only because I don't want to bore people." she told him.

"Well, I want to know." he said softly. Her skin tingled as he gently placed his hand over hers and opened the photo album.

"Oh no, not the baby photos!" Chloe groaned, quickly hiding her head in her hand. Lee couldn't help but laugh at her as she squirmed slightly.

"They look besotted with you." he smiled as she turned the page.

"They went through a lot to get me." she said quietly.

"Tell me." he prompted.

"They had problems and had a few years of IVF before I happened. That's why I don't have any siblings, because they didn't want to go through all of that again." she explained.

"So technically I'm a test tube baby." she added, smiling slightly.

"I bet they were so happy when you came along." he smiled. Chloe nodded.

"They definitely cherished me, I was so lucky, the three of us were so close. It was us against the world." she explained, a lump rising in her throat when she was reminded yet again just how much she missed them.

"Wow, is that your Mum?!" Lee exclaimed when Chloe turned the page and he saw a professional picture of a beautiful woman.

"She's stunning." he added.

"Yes, she was a model." Chloe told him.

"That figures." he said quietly, glancing at Chloe as he suddenly realised where she got her stunning good looks from.

"That's how she met my Dad, he was her photographer." she continued.

"And she taught me how to do her makeup, because she wanted me to feel involved." she said.

"Is that why you went into makeup?" he asked.

"Not exactly." she said quietly.

"What?" he frowned, turning to face her as he sensed a change in her body language.

"I've never told anyone this before." she muttered.

"I won't tell anyone." he reassured her. She glanced up at him and sighed quietly when she remembered what Kirstie had said about giving him a chance to earn her trust.

"I wanted to study Zoology which I applied for and I applied to do makeup as a backup in case I didn't get in. I got accepted onto both, but I lied and told my parents that I got rejected from Zoology." she said hesitantly.

"Why?" he frowned.

"Because Mum always wanted me to do makeup because I was good at it, and she'd just been told that she had cancer, so I wanted to try and do something to make her happy." she explained.

"Aww Chloe." he said sadly.

"And plus, the course was a lot cheaper, and Mum and Dad wouldn't let me take out a student loan and I knew how tight money was." she added.

"So, you sacrificed your happiness for your family?" he whispered.

"Yes of course." she muttered.

"You can't tell anyone though." she said quickly.

"I won't. You don't realise what a good person you are do you?" he said softly. Chloe shrugged and continued leafing from the pages.

"Oh no." she burst out laughing when she saw a picture of herself in a formal dress with a young man.

"What is it?" Lee asked. He couldn't help but join in with her laughter as she erupted into a fit of giggles, her cheeks colouring.

"That's Darius." Chloe said, trying to stifle her laughter.

"He's the one that I was talking to Dad about in the video we watched the other day." she explained.

"The first person I dated." she giggled.

"Why are you laughing?" Lee laughed.

"Oh, it was just awful." she laughed.

"So basically, he invited me to prom and I'd never been on a date before, so I was really nervous and he was my first kiss and it was so bad." she said quickly, starting to laugh again.

"And because I was so embarrassed, I avoided him for the rest of the night and got so drunk that I ended up dancing on a table." she added.

"Did you actually?!" he exclaimed in disbelief.

"Yes, I did. I'm pretty sure I did a kind of strip tease at one point too." she giggled.

"You stripped?" he laughed.

"Only a little, but Dad was furious." she said, smiling to herself.

"I didn't realise you had a secret wild side." he smiled.

"Only when I'm drunk." she said.

"And to be honest I had more confidence back then, even though I've always been self-conscious." she added.

"That's probably because you had your parents." he told her quietly, feeling slightly sad that her confidence was almost non-existent.

"I don't think being homeless helps, you feel so worthless and insignificant. Like nobody cares." she sighed.

"Society doesn't care in general do they." he sighed. Chloe shook her head sadly.

"When Megan got attacked nobody cared, not even the police." she told him.

"Yeah, I heard about that." he said quietly.

"It's always the same, society just labels her as some drug addict that got what she deserved." she said quietly.

"No one deserves that though." he said quietly.

"I know. I wouldn't wish it on anyone." Chloe agreed.

"Did you get a lot of hassle living rough?" he asked her, feeling slightly nervous about the answer.

"Only a little." she said quietly.

"What does that mean?" he asked quickly.

"You get a lot of drink and drugs going on in the park, but I just kept my head down." she told him.

"Although there was one time that some random guy thought that I was one of the prostitutes." she added.

"He didn't touch you, did he?" he asked.

"He just got a bit grabby." she said quietly.

"Worse than Shayne?" he replied, his mouth suddenly feeling really dry.

"I guess so." she muttered.

"Chlo, don't make me keep asking questions, just tell me." he whispered, his tone almost pleading.

"He was really drunk and didn't believe me that I wasn't a prostitute, so he kept grabbing me and stuff....and then he tried to put his hand in my underwear..." she started but trailed off for a moment, her cheeks colouring in embarrassment.

"I don't know if I want to hear the next part." Lee whispered.

"I did something really bad." she admitted.

"Wait, you didn't let him have you, did you?!" he exclaimed. Chloe screwed up her face in disgust and shook her head. Lee's heart was pounding against his chest as he waited for her to answer. He felt sick to his stomach at the thought of anyone touching her, particularly if it was against her will.

"No, I kind of panicked, it was only a few days after Megan was attacked and I kept thinking about what almost happened with Shayne....so I kind of kicked him in his sensitive place." she told him.
"You kicked him in the nuts?" he checked.

"It was more of a knee to be fair." she said quietly.

"Good." he said quickly, suddenly feeling a wave of relief wash over him.

"I still feel guilty about that." she added thoughtfully.

"You're so cute." Lee laughed, quickly wrapping his arms around her shoulders and rocking her playfully.

"Someone tries to sexually assault you and you're the one that feels guilty for hurting them." he said, smiling at how adorable she was. He'd never met anyone as selfless as Chloe, her kind heart was so big that she always thought of everyone else before herself.

"I did knee him quite hard, hopefully I didn't make him sterile." she said giggling slightly.

"Well, that's one thing settled.... you're never going back there." he told her sternly. Chloe slowly removed herself from his grasp and sighed quietly, suddenly remembering that she still had nowhere to live.

"I keep wondering if he was the one that stabbed me." she said thoughtfully.

"Wait, I thought you said it was a robbery?" he frowned.

"It was, but maybe he wanted revenge or something. I didn't see the face of the man that stabbed me so it could have been." she pointed out.

"Don't think about it too much, that's the police's job." he told her quickly, trying to make sure that she didn't drive herself crazy by over analysing what had happened to her.

"They won't catch him, or care, I'm a homeless person remember." she reminded him. Lee fell silent, watching her sadly, his heart breaking a little for her. She had such a kind and pure soul that she didn't deserve all the terrible things that had happened to her. Chloe silently turned over the page of the photo album, sighing quietly as she saw pictures of Andy with her family.

"I still can't believe he left you for someone else." Lee said quietly.

"Nor could I at the time, but looking back, neither of us were happy." she sighed.

"I was so broken from losing both of my parents in the same year and I think he stayed with me because he felt guilty." she explained.

"Don't say that." he muttered. It always broke his heart a little when she put herself down.

"It's true though, when Dad left me a letter, he left one for Andy too asking him to take care of his little munchkin, so I think he didn't feel like he could split up with me." she said quietly.

"You loved him, though didn't you?" he asked.

"I did, but I think I fell in love with him because I needed him after everything that happened and partly because I was afraid to be alone. When I look back on it, he never once told me that he loved me." she sighed.

"He started to resent me in the end and that's when the gambling started. I only found out when he left that he had taken out four different credit cards in my name and left me with twenty thousand pounds of debt." she admitted.

"He did what?!" Lee asked, sounding slightly angry.

"That's why I live on the streets, most of my wages go on interest, I don't even have enough money left over to pay off any of the loans." she sighed.

"I can't believe he did that to you." he whispered, shaking his head in disbelief.

"Plus, I didn't get any money from my parents because Dad remortgaged the house to pay for Mum to get private health care, because he was so desperate to save her." Chloe told him, her eyes filling with tears.

"And because he committed suicide the life insurance was void so the house went to the mortgage company." she continued.

"Oh my god." he whispered, not entirely sure how to respond to what she'd just told him.

"He loved her so much that he wanted to be with her." she whispered thoughtfully.

"He literally tried everything to save her, that's why we moved from Nottingham to London, because he wanted her to have access to the best private health care in the country." she added.

"That explains why you talk so much nicer than I do." he said, trying to lighten the mood as he could sense that Chloe was getting upset.

"And yet it was all in vain anyway." she whispered, appearing to not hear him. Lee glanced at her sadly as she began to cry silently. He sighed to himself, wishing not for the first time that he could take her pain away. Chloe jumped slightly as Lee gently placed his head on her shoulder. She turned her head to face him, smiling slightly when she saw that he was gazing up at her. She couldn't help but notice how handsome he looked, peering up at her with his deep blue eyes. She sighed quietly and turned her attention back to the photo album, carefully resting her head against his.

Chapter Thirty

"Please don't tell anyone about any of the things I told you." Chloe said nervously, as she wiped away the last of her tears.

"I won't, I promise." he told her, slowly lifting his head off her shoulder.

"If anyone asks you why I'm homeless, just tell them I'm in debt or something." she said quietly.

"I don't think anyone is going to ask me." he said.

"No probably not, I just really don't like people feeling sorry for me. I'm not some pathetic person that needs pity." she explained.

"No one thinks that, you're one of the strongest people I've met, to have gone through everything that you have and come out the other side of it. I think you are stronger than you realise." he told her gently.

"That's what Danny says." she smiled.

"It's true though." he smiled at her. Chloe glanced at him, quickly looking away when she blushed under his intense gaze. She smiled to herself as she turned the page of the album and stared at the pictures of her and her Mum at the zoo, feeding a range of animals.

"You look so happy in those pictures." Lee said smiling to himself. As he gazed at the pictures, he couldn't help but notice how Chloe was even more beautiful when she was happy. She had a twinkle in her eyes that he'd never seen before.

"Mum and Dad paid for me to be Keeper for a Day for my eighteenth birthday." she told him.

"I bet you loved that." he said. Chloe nodded quickly.

"I was definitely in my element." she smiled.

"Have you used your London Zoo membership that we got you yet?" he asked.

"No, and I don't have it anymore." she said sadly.

"It was one of the things that *he* kept." she added.

"Along with the wedding rings." he sighed.

"Yes, I gave the police a picture of them, but I doubt I'll ever get them back, they've probably been pawned somewhere by now." she said quietly. Chloe fell silent for a moment, desperately wishing that she still had her parent's wedding rings in place around her neck.

"That's the last of the pictures." she said, trying to distract herself.

"What about the other pages?" Lee frowned, pointing at the album, where he could see some pages that were left.

"I never look at those ones." she said quietly.

"Are they embarrassing ones?" he chuckled.

"No, they are from when I was nineteen, which is the year Mum got sick. I don't like to look at them because you can see her gradually getting more and more frail." she explained. Lee sighed, the smile slowly fading from his face.

"I'm really sorry." he said quietly.

"It's okay, I just kind of blocked that year out of my mind." she told him sadly. Lee watched her closely as she carefully closed the album and reached up to place it on the coffee table. She gasped as an envelope fell out and slowly fluttered to the floor. Lee carefully picked it up and handed it to her.

"Is that the letter from your Dad?" he asked. Chloe nodded slowly.

"I remember being in a lecture at university when the police came and pulled me out of class to tell me what he'd done." she said quietly.

"It was horrible." she whispered.

"Yeah, I bet." he said.

Chloe sighed quietly as she stared silently at the letter in her hands. Despite the fact that she hadn't read the letter since the day the police gave it to her all those years ago, the words were ingrained in her memory. Her thoughts wandered to Lee as he sat beside her watching her closely, if her father was here, he would tell her to seize the day and tell Lee how she felt. He always told her to never live with regrets. Chloe carefully placed the letter safely inside the photo album, her heart pounding against her chest as she sat wracking her brain, trying to find the words and the courage to tell him how she felt. She took a deep breath, trying to calm her nerves. She quickly brushed her hair out of her face, suddenly noticing that her hands were shaking.

"Are you okay, you look a bit stressed?" Lee asked worriedly.

"I need to tell you something, but I don't know how too." she admitted.

"Just tell me." he said, feeling slightly nervous. Chloe nodded slowly, taking a deep breath.

"Do you remember that day, after the gig that I came to your house?" she started.

"Yeah, and I was a dick to you." he replied quietly, suddenly feeling very guilty. Chloe nodded, smiling slightly.

"I came over to tell you that I think I have feelings for you." she blurted before she could stop herself. Lee's eyes widened as he stared at her silently. The silence seemed to stretch for an eternity as he stared at her, not able to process what she'd just said.

"And I was wondering if you maybe felt the same?" she prompted nervously. Lee remained silent, not even looking at her, his head a mist of swirling thoughts that made it difficult to even think, let alone speak. Chloe sighed to herself as he remained silent.

"Clearly I misread the situation, I'm really sorry." she said, slowly standing up and pulling the sleeves of her hoodie down over her hands, wishing that she could hide her flushed cheeks.

"I shouldn't have said anything, I know that you are way out of my league." she rambled, starting to panic slightly.

"Can we just pretend I didn't say anything and go back to being friends please?" she asked quietly, finally glancing at him and frowning as she saw him staring at his hands.

"I don't think we can Chlo." he muttered, finally managing to speak. Chloe's heart sunk as she heard his words, it felt like someone had stabbed her in her chest as he rejected her. She nodded slowly, finally realising how ridiculous the thought of him being with someone like her really was. He was handsome, rich and successful, the last thing he would want is to be saddled with a pathetic homeless person. Before Chloe could stop them, warm tears began to roll down her cheeks.

Lee couldn't process anything; he didn't know what to say to her. Ever since she'd been attacked and he thought that he was going to lose her, he knew that he was in love with her. But never for a moment did he dare to hope that she felt the same. Given the way he'd treated her over the past few months, he knew that he didn't deserve her but here she was telling him that she had feelings for him. He suddenly realised that if he didn't tell her how he felt now, there would be no going back....and he would regret it for the rest of his life.

"Maybe you should go then." Chloe said, a small sob escaping her lips. Lee sighed quietly and eventually looked at her.

"Come here a minute." he said quietly. Chloe shook her head slowly.

"Please." he muttered, holding out his hand to her. Chloe sighed and slowly walked over, sitting awkwardly beside him on the floor. She placed her hands on her lap and stared at them, too embarrassed to look at him.

"I meant we can't go back to being friends because of the way we feel about each other." he said quietly.

"You think you feel something too?" she asked tentatively, still staring at her hands.

"No, I know how I feel..." he started, but trailed off when he suddenly felt nervous to tell her. Chloe shivered as he leant towards her and she felt his warm breath on her neck.

"I'm in love with you Chloe." he whispered in her ear.

"What?" she whispered, flinching slightly when she turned to face him and realised that his face was virtually touching hers.

"You heard me." he told her softly. Chloe glanced down at her hands as she felt him take them gently in his.

"Why would you love me, I'm a nobody." she muttered sadly.

"Don't say that." he sighed, gently resting his forehead against hers.

"But...." she started. Before Chloe could finish her sentence, Lee placed a soft lingering kiss on her lips.

"I've wanted to do that for so long." he whispered, gently resting his forehead on her shoulder, breathing in her familiar scent. Chloe remained silent for a moment, not quite able to process what he'd said to her. She watched Lee closely as he slowly raised his head from her shoulder and gazed at her longingly. She couldn't quite comprehend why someone would fall in love with her, least of all someone like Lee, who could have anyone he wanted. Before Chloe could say anything else, he kissed her deeply. A shiver travelled down her spine as he gently rested his hands on her hips.

"Why are you crying?" he asked her gently, when he eventually broke the kiss. Chloe thought for a moment, not entirely sure why she was crying, she hadn't realised that she was until he asked her.

"I don't know, it's just a lot to process." she admitted.

"And...." she started but trailed off, sighing to herself.

"What is it?" he asked nervously, slightly afraid that she didn't reciprocate his feelings for her.

"I'm afraid that you are going to hurt me." she admitted quietly. He closed his eyes for a moment, sighing deeply. Chloe slowly took his hands and removed them from her hips. He watched her closely as she placed them on her lap and squeezed them reassuringly.

"I'm sorry." she whispered, feeling slightly guilty that she might have hurt his feelings with her comment.

"You have nothing to be sorry for, I'm the one to blame." he said quietly.

"I am so sorry for the way I treated you." he added. Chloe nodded slowly.

"I didn't understand what I was feeling, so I pushed you away." he explained.

"To protect yourself?" she asked.

"No, I knew you wouldn't hurt me, I was just so confused and angry at myself for not understanding what I was feeling, and I guess in the back of my mind I knew that I'm not a good person to be in a relationship with." he told her.

"You've never tried though have you." she pointed out. Lee shook his head slowly.

"I will never treat you like that again." he said quickly.

"And I don't deserve you right now, but I will earn you." he added. Chloe smiled at his words, butterflies swarming in her stomach at the thought of being in a relationship with him.

"If we're going to do this, can we take it slowly?" she asked nervously.

"Oh wait... you're a really sexual person, that's not going to work." she added quickly, suddenly remembering the conversation between him and Ben that she'd overheard a few nights ago.

"It's fine, I want to cherish this." he said quietly.

"Sex has always been a big deal to me." she explained.

"Honestly, it's fine. I think it's a good idea to take things slow, it'll give me time to earn your trust, and you can get some of your confidence back." he told her.
"Which I helped destroy." he added sadly.

"It's fine, you don't need to feel guilty about it." she said.

"Yeah, I do, I was vile to you." he insisted.

"You've made up for it since I was attacked though, you've been taking care of me." she pointed out. Lee nodded slowly.

"I'll always take care of you." he said, smiling warmly at her.

"You don't need to take care of me, just don't hurt me." she muttered. Lee sighed to himself as Chloe wrapped her arms around his neck and hugged him tightly. The two of them quickly sprung apart as the front door opened. Lee glanced at Chloe as her cheeks coloured. Chloe's eyes snapped up as Michelle walked into the room, smiling sweetly at the two of them.

"Hey guys." she said, glancing between the two of them. Lee glanced at Chloe as she subtly moved away from him, hoping that Michelle wouldn't notice how close they had been sitting to each other.

"I got my dress for the ball." she smiled proudly, holding up the shopping bag in her hand.

"Good, I bet you're excited." Chloe smiled, trying to make the effort to get on with Michelle.

"Are either of you going?" Michelle asked innocently. Chloe shook her head slowly.

"Lee?" Michelle asked.

"Not that I know of." Lee replied, glancing at Chloe, suddenly realising that Chloe might want him to go with her.

"I was actually wondering.... if maybe you would like to escort me to the ball?" Michelle asked him.

"No thank you." Lee said quickly.

"Are you sure?" she tried again.

"I can't anyway, I have a girlfriend." he told her, smiling slightly to himself as he thought about the fact that he could now officially call Chloe his girlfriend.

Chloe smiled to herself and quickly looked at the floor, her heart fluttering as he called her his girlfriend.

"Really, since when?!" Michelle exclaimed in shock. Lee shrugged.

"So, you'll have to find someone else to take you." Lee told her.

"Alright no problem." she shrugged, quickly walking into the kitchen. As soon as Michelle walked away, Chloe turned to face Lee, smiling slightly.

"I'm glad you didn't tell her about me." she said quickly.

"Why, what difference does it make?" he asked.

"I just feel a bit awkward, because she likes you." Chloe admitted.

"So, she'll need to get over it." he shrugged.

"Although we haven't discussed whether you want to be public or not have, we." he added.

"Maybe we keep it quiet just for now, so that there's no pressure." she suggested.
"If you're happy with that?" she added quickly.

"If you're happy, then so am I." he said.

"Did you particularly want to go to the masquerade ball, because if you do, I could escort you?" he offered, wiggling his eyebrows playfully.

"As a friend of course." he winked.

"No, it's okay, I'm really not that bothered." she said quickly.

"We can go if you want too?" he tried again, not entirely convinced that she didn't want to go. Chloe shook her head. Lee watched her closely as she pulled her clothes out of her backpack and began to rummage through them, separating them into piles of what she wanted to keep and what she didn't. Lee couldn't help but notice how different she was now that Michelle was home, when it had been just the two of them, she was relaxed and showed her vulnerable side, but now she seemed uncomfortable and tense. He glanced into the kitchen as he felt Michelle watching him. As soon as he locked eyes with her, she quickly looked away, pretending to be preoccupied with something. Lee quickly turned his attention back to Chloe, smiling at her as they locked eyes.

"You need to promise me something." he said quietly. She raised her eyebrow and waited for him to continue.

"That you won't keep living your life for other people, you don't want anyone to know about us because Michelle likes me, and you don't want to go to the ball because you think she doesn't want you there." he explained.

"I didn't say it was about Michelle." she muttered.

"But now that you mention it, I don't want to rock the boat with her, especially since I'm staying here at the moment." she admitted. Lee stared at her for a moment before quickly standing up.

"I need to make a phone call." he told her as he left the room.

Chapter Thirty-One

"Oh my god, I look amazing!" Kathleen squealed excitedly, as she gazed at her reflection in the mirror. Chloe smiled at her, carefully putting down the makeup brush.

"You've done such a good job, thank you." Kathleen said, hugging Chloe gently.

"You're welcome, I'm surprised I remembered how to do it, since I always do men these days." Chloe said, smiling slightly.

"Well, you've done a great job of mine too." Kirstie piped up.

"Okay my turn." Michelle said, sitting next to Chloe as soon as Kathleen left the room to change into her dress.

"Do you still want a smoky eye look?" Chloe checked. Michelle nodded quickly. Chloe jumped slightly and glanced into the kitchen as she heard Ben and David laughing about something.

"I have been meaning to ask if you are coping okay with finding out that Lee has a girlfriend?" Michelle asked gently. Chloe nodded slowly, feeling slightly awkward.

"I told you not to tell him how you feel, I bet you're glad you didn't now." Michelle said smugly. Chloe's cheeks coloured further as Michelle and Kirstie stared at her.

"Oh no, you didn't tell him did you...you poor thing." Michelle said, her tone slightly patronising.

"Can we talk about something else please?" Chloe said quickly, feeling slightly uncomfortable at not being able to tell them the truth.

"You shouldn't let it get to you Chloe, there will be other guys in your life." Michelle said, completely disregarding what Chloe had just said.

"Speaking of guys, who is taking you to the ball Michelle?" Kirstie said quickly, trying to change the subject when she noticed Chloe squirming.

"Nobody, I am going to get my hands on a man while I'm there." she said, smiling falsely.

"What about that guy you are seeing?" Kirstie asked, trying to keep her talking so that she wouldn't start pestering Chloe again.

"He can't manage." she said shortly. Kirstie couldn't help but roll her eyes. She couldn't understand why it seemed to be okay for Michelle to grill Chloe about her love life but when the shoe was on the other foot, she wasn't so keen.

"Okay you're done." Chloe announced a few moments later. Michelle quickly stood up and left the room to change.

"You're welcome." Chloe muttered sarcastically under her breath.

"I'm beginning to think that she doesn't like me." Chloe added sadly.

"But I don't understand why, I've never done anything to her, at least not that I know of." she added thoughtfully.

"I think she's just jealous." Kirstie said quickly, her heart breaking a little at Chloe's sad expression.

"That's what Lee says." Chloe sighed, completely unable to understand why anyone in their right mind would possibly be jealous of her.

"Speaking of Lee, I need to tell you something, it's a secret for now, but I feel bad lying to you. We're kind of dating." Chloe said in hushed tones, glancing around nervously, in case she was overheard.

"Ooh, see I told you to tell him how you feel." Kirstie said happily, quickly pulling Chloe into a hug.

"I'm so happy for you." Kirstie whispered in her ear. Chloe smiled slightly when Kirstie eventually let go of her. The two of them instantly stopped talking as Kathleen and Louise walked back into the room, both of then twirling excitedly in their dresses.

"Wow, you guys look amazing." Chloe said, smiling at their happy expressions.

"I need to put my dress on." Kirstie said, before excitedly running along the hallway. Chloe sat silently, applying some makeup to her face.

"Have you decided to come along Chloe?" Louise asked hopefully.

"No, I just fancied putting some makeup on." Chloe said quietly.

"I don't have anything to wear anyway." she quickly added.

"I can't believe that David is taking you, that's so exciting!" Chloe said turning to Kathleen, quickly changing the subject.

"Are you guys back on track now?" Louise asked.

"We are seeing how things go, but hopefully." Kathleen said, smiled slightly, sighing as her thoughts wandered to the baby. She still had no idea who the father of her child was, but even though she'd been honest with both Mark and David she couldn't help but hope that the baby was David's. Mark had shown no interest at all in his potential child, he was more interested in going out in search of women. Kathleen couldn't help but feel disappointed that her idol had turned out to not be as nice as he appeared.

"Is he excited about becoming a father?" Chloe asked. Kathleen swallowed the lump that was rising in her throat. David and Mark were the only people that knew about her doubts as to who the father of her baby was, she'd been honest with both of them from the start. Kathleen nodded slowly, not entirely sure what to say.

"You're so lucky, I would love to have a baby." Louise said, a dreamy expression on her face.

"What happened to focusing on your career?" Kathleen laughed.

"I know...I just get a bit broody sometimes." Louise giggled, quickly putting on her masquerade mask. Chloe smiled at Kirstie as she walked back into the room, closely followed by Michelle.

"I bet I'm the only one who doesn't get asked to dance tonight." Louise sighed.

"Aww don't say that honey." Kathleen said gently.

"I think Steven is going, he'll dance with you, he's always had a little soft spot for you." Chloe told her.

"Has he?!" Louise exclaimed. Chloe nodded, smiling slightly at Louise's shocked expression. The three of them glanced up as the front door opened and Matt walked in.

"Hello everyone!" he called, smiling to himself as he received a chorus of replies.

"Looking good ladies." he smiled at them as he gazed around the room.

"Are you going too Matt?" Michelle asked when she noticed that he was wearing a suit.

"Yep, but I have some business to attend to first." he told her. Chloe glanced up at him shyly as she felt him watching her closely.

"What have I done?" Chloe said quickly, her cheeks colouring as everyone stared at her.

"You haven't done anything." Matt laughed.

"I want you to come back to work for me." he told her. Chloe stared at him, not entirely sure what to say.

"The Eclipse boys have decided to do their own tour with a new album, so we're looking for a kind of manager for them." he said.

"So, you'll be styling them, helping me sort out their schedules and just generally keeping things running." he explained.

"Isn't that your job though?" Chloe frowned.

"I have loads of bands to do, you'll be allocated to them. You'll be perfect for it, you're organised, you know the industry and the boys know you, so they respond well to you." Matt said.

"Plus, it's a promotion, so there'll be a nice pay rise." Matt added. Chloe sighed to herself as she thought carefully. She'd always enjoyed working with the Eclipse boys, before things had turned sour with Lee. Even though she had a small nagging doubt in the back of her mind that Lee might return to his old ways, she knew in her heart that if their relationship was going to work, she had to give him a chance. She also knew that if the boys were going on tour for a few weeks or months, then she would be parted from Lee, which would have a negative impact on their relationship.

"Lee's not going to bully her, again is he?" Louise piped up, an edge of concern present in her voice.

"No, he won't." Matt said quickly.

"He's been a really good friend to her lately." Kirstie piped up.

"Has he?" Kathleen frowned.

"Yeah, he was the one that heard about her being stabbed, so he's been helping out." Kirstie agreed.

"The boys and I have barely seen him the past couple of weeks." Matt told them.

"I'll take the job." Chloe said quickly, before she could talk herself out of it.

"That didn't take much, I thought it would take ages to convince you." Matt chuckled. Chloe smiled awkwardly.

"Are you not enjoying your job?" Kirstie asked her, sounding slightly surprised. The last time she'd been to visit Chloe at work to invite her to the gig, she seemed to be enjoying working with the new band.

"They are really nice, but it was starting to get a bit awkward." Chloe admitted.

"Ooh what happened?" Kathleen piped up.

"I ended up going on a date with one of them, and I wasn't feeling it." Chloe told them.

"What, but they are so good looking?!" Louise exclaimed.

"Which one was it?!" Kathleen asked excitedly.

"Max." Chloe said quietly.

"He's hot." Kathleen said, smiling proudly at Chloe.

"How come *she* gets all the famous people after her?" Michelle muttered under her breath.

"Only Max." Louise snapped, quickly leaping to Chloe's defence. Michelle rolled her eyes at Louise's back as she leapt to Chloe's defence. She couldn't understand why Chloe didn't seem to get under everyone else's skin in the same way. She was so sickeningly sweet that Michelle couldn't stand it. For some unknown reason, she seemed to get a lot of attractive, famous people attracted to her, first Shayne and now Max.....even Lee, who even though he had a girlfriend, he clearly still fancied Chloe. Yet she couldn't even get Mark to commit to her!

Is everyone ready to go?" Ben asked as he walked into the room, closely followed by David.

"Oh Ben, there you are, could you do me up please?" Michelle asked sweetly, turning her back to face him.

"Err....sure." Ben said hesitantly, glancing at Kirstie who shrugged in response. Ben zipped up Michelle's dress as quickly as he could before walking over to stand behind Kirstie. She smiled as he gently wrapped his arms around her waist and rested his chin on her shoulder.

"You look beautiful babe." he whispered in her ear. Kirstie giggled as he took her hand and carefully twirled her around.

"Oh, I almost forgot." Matt said, winking at Chloe as she finished her makeup and carefully put the brush down on the coffee table. The group watched him as he rummaged in a bag and slowly pulled out a white lace masquerade mask, quickly holding it out to Chloe.

"You shall go to the ball." Matt beamed at her, slowly pushing a gift bag along the floor towards her. Chloe silently took the mask from him and stared at it.

"It was a bit last minute to get you a dress, so I borrowed one from the costume department." Matt told her.

"Wow." Chloe breathed as she pulled out a beautiful purple dress with a white lace bodice.

"It looks really expensive." Chloe whispered. Matt nodded slowly.

"We didn't want you to not be able to go because you couldn't afford a dress." Matt told her.

"Who's we?" Chloe asked quickly.

"I mentioned it to Matt the other day." Kirstie piped up.

"I can't wear this, it's too expensive." Chloe muttered.

"You can't make a silk purse out of a sow's ear." she added quietly. Chloe glanced up at Michelle as she burst out laughing.

"Just go and try it on." Matt said firmly. Chloe sighed quietly and reluctantly stood up, carefully carrying the dress.

"I'll help you get ready." Kirstie stated, quickly following her. Chloe nodded and walked into Kirstie's room, standing awkwardly as Kirstie stood, watching her closely.

"Can you turn your back while I change?" Chloe asked nervously.

"Aww, it's no different than seeing you in a bikini." Kirstie said, smiling slightly at Chloe's flushed cheeks.

"I don't do that though." Chloe said, quickly pulling off her clothes as soon as Kirstie turned her back.

"Oh no, it's really fitted." Chloe whispered a few moments later when she had finally pulled on the dress. Kirstie slowly turned back around and walked over to carefully zip up the dress.

"It really suits you Chloe." Kirstie told her, gazing in wonder at her figure. Chloe remained silent, staring sadly at her reflection in the mirror. Kirstie quickly picked up the curling irons and began to curl Chloe's hair.

"We need to tie your mask on so we can hide the tie under your hair." Kirstie suddenly realised. Chloe silently handed Kirstie the mask and watched as she tied the mask in place, quickly returning to curling her hair.

"Can you just make my hair wavy please, I don't suit curly hair." Chloe asked her. Kirstie nodded slowly.

"I don't know if I want to go." Chloe whispered to herself.

"Why not?" Kirstie frowned.

"There's going to be a lot of people there and I'm just not feeling it." Chloe admitted.

"If it's because of the dress, you look stunning." Kirstie told her as she gently set down the hair curlers and admired her handy work.

"Plus, it'll be a fun night and you haven't been out since the attack." Kirstie pointed out.

"Yes exactly." Chloe said quietly, suddenly feeling afraid at the thought of leaving the house. Chloe jumped as she heard Ben's voice calling down the hallway:

"Hurry up, we have to go!"

Kirstie quickly took Chloe's hand and gently led her down the hallway. Chloe felt herself squirming as she walked into the living room and everyone turned to stare at her.

"Matt, you could have picked something that actually suits her!" Michelle exclaimed, her stomach churning when she saw how mesmerising Chloe looked.

"It does suit her." Matt argued.

"I really don't want to go." Chloe whispered, slowly stepping backwards as she felt herself beginning to panic.

"Well, nobody is forcing you." Michelle said, rolling her eyes. Michelle quickly linked arms with Kathleen and Louise and walked out of the house, the three of them slowly making their way up the driveway towards the cars. Michelle smiled sweetly as she noticed Lee climbing out of his sports car.

"What are you doing here?" Michelle asked sweetly.

"I brought my suit, in case Chloe wants to go to the ball. I did tell her that I could take her." he told them.

"I don't think she does." Louise said, sighing sadly as she thought about how self-conscious Chloe was.

"Besides you have a girlfriend remember." Michelle pointed out.

"I know, I meant I would take her as a friend." Lee said quickly, suddenly realising that he'd almost put his foot in it.

"How come I didn't get that option?" Michelle pouted.

"Probably because we're not friends." Lee said shortly, as he walked past her.

"Do you think something is going on with him and Chloe?" Kathleen said thoughtfully.

"Nah he has a girlfriend, some beautiful model probably." Michelle muttered bitterly.

"She certainly is." Lee called back when he heard Michelle's comment, smiling to himself when he turned back and saw Michelle squirming.

Lee jumped as he opened the door and stood to one side as David, Matt and Ben walked out.

"Where's Chloe?" Lee asked Ben.

"She's still inside, Kirstie is trying to convince her to come along." Ben answered.

"I'll speak to her." Lee said quietly.

"You're going to struggle to keep your hands to yourself tonight, wait until you see her." Ben chuckled. Lee quickly walked past Ben and into the living room. His eyes widened as he gazed in wonder at Chloe. Her figure perfectly highlighted by the fitted dress. Her dark hair perfectly curled around her face, the white lace of her mask that matched the lace on the tight bodice. He locked eyes with her, smiling slightly at her kind blue eyes that were gazing up at him.

"Holy shit." Lee breathed when he realised how breath-taking she looked.

"Maybe you can convince her to come with us." Kirstie said, turning to Lee. Lee remained silent, unable to tear his eyes away from the beautiful woman that was standing in front of him.

"Lee?" Kirstie tried again, smiling to herself when she noticed Lee gazing longingly at Chloe.

"Hmm?" he asked, finally tearing his eyes away from Chloe.

"Chloe needs to come with us." Kirstie insisted.

"Why don't you want to go Chlo?" Lee asked her softly.

"I just don't feel comfortable, Michelle clearly doesn't want me there and keeps making comments." Chloe said quietly.

"Who gives a shit what she thinks!" Lee snapped quickly.

"And there's going to be so many people there, and I don't want to be stared at when I don't feel comfortable wearing this." Chloe explained. Lee smiled gently at Chloe; he could sense that she was getting upset.

"You guys go, I'll stay with her." Lee said, quickly turning to Kirstie. Kirstie nodded slowly, feeling her heart sink a little in disappointment that Chloe wouldn't be joining them.

"I feel like I'm being so ungrateful." Chloe whispered as soon as Kirstie left, and she was alone with Lee.

"Why?" Lee frowned.

"Because Matt has gone to a lot of effort to find me a dress and Kirstie really wants me to go." she said quietly.

"I just really don't want to be surrounded by a lot of people. I feel safer here." she added.

"It's not about other people though, it's about what you feel comfortable with. You have to stop putting other people first." he told her. Chloe nodded slowly, placing her arms across her chest, in an attempt to protect herself. Lee sighed quietly as he walked over to her and carefully held her tightly in his arms.

"Why are you trembling?" he whispered in her ear.

"I don't know, I think it's the thought of going out." she mumbled against his chest.

"I won't let anyone hurt you." he sighed, his heart breaking a little at her words.

"I know, the only time I feel safe is when I'm with you." she admitted.

"I'd have gone with you if you wanted." he reminded her.

"I'm happy here." she smiled, sighing to herself and closing her eyes.

Chapter Thirty-Two

Lee glanced down at Chloe when she eventually removed herself from his arms, sighing quietly to herself as she stared at the floor.

"You look stunning in that dress." he told her.

"Did you see the girls on your way in?" she asked, not acknowledging what he'd said to her.

"Yeah, Michelle was whining about the fact that I wasn't going with her." he told her.

"She was being a bit flirty with Ben earlier too, I don't know what's gotten into her." she frowned. Lee raised his eyebrow, deciding not to comment.

"The girls looked amazing though, their dresses were so pretty." she said.

"Speaking of dresses, I really need to take it off." she added, glancing at herself.

"Why, you look amazing...I kind of want to take you out and show you off." he admitted, smiling slightly. Chloe glanced down at her hand as she felt Lee take it and twirl her, gently pulling her close. She smiled at him and wrapped her arms around his neck, her fingers gently stroking his hair. Lee slowly ran his fingers down the length of her arm, smiling slightly when she shivered. He still couldn't believe how breath-taking she looked, standing quietly in the dress. Chloe glanced down at her hips as Lee placed his hands on them and pulled her towards him, no longer able to fight the deep longing he was feeling for her. Before Chloe could react, he leaned towards her and kissed her gently, his hands slowly tracing their way up her torso. As Lee deepened the kiss, Chloe quickly pulled away, turning her head away from him.

"Sorry, I shouldn't have done that, I know you want to take things slowly." he said quickly.

"It's okay." she said quietly, feeling slightly guilty that she'd pulled away from him.

"You just look so good, I couldn't resist." he said, smiling slightly. Chloe unwrapped her arms from around his neck and quickly stood back from him.

"I'm going to get changed." she told him, before quickly walking away. Lee nodded slowly, running his hand through his hair in frustration as he threw himself onto the sofa. He couldn't help but feel like he'd pushed things too far with her, it hadn't been his intention to lose control for a moment, she was just so stunning that he struggled to resist her. He knew how delicate she was and the last thing he wanted to do was push her too fast, when he knew that she wanted to take things slowly. His eyes flickered to the hallway as he saw Chloe hovering nervously, still wearing the dress.

"I have a problem." she said quietly, glancing at him shyly.

"Me too." Lee muttered under his breath, so quietly that she didn't hear him.

"I can't reach the zip." she admitted, her cheeks colouring. Chloe quickly reached behind her head and untied the mask, carefully placing it safely back in the bag. Lee hesitated for a moment before slowly crossing the room and standing in front of her.

"Turn around then." he mumbled, staring down at her. Chloe glanced up at him briefly, before slowly turning her back on him. She carefully reached behind herself and gathered her hair, pulling it to one side. Lee carefully took hold of the dress material, his hands shaking as he slowly unzipped it. He gasped quietly as he laid eyes on the back of her white lace bra. His hands lingered at the base of her spine, when he finally reached the end of the zip. Lee couldn't resist placing his hands on her hips, enjoying the feel of her soft, warm skin under his hands. His eyes wandered to her bra, as he found himself longing to unfasten it.

"You're so beautiful." he breathed, gently placing his chin on her shoulder and planting a soft kiss on her neck. Chloe sighed quietly, feeling content that her back was resting against his chest, her skin tingling under his touch. She frowned to herself as he quickly moved her away from him, towards the doorway.

"Go and get changed then." he said quietly, quickly turning away from her. She turned to face him, frowning in confusion when she realised, he had his back to her.

"Is everything okay?" she asked.

"Yeah fine, you get changed, I'll order a takeaway." he said quickly, still not turning to face her. Lee glanced behind himself as he heard her walking away from him. He quickly sat on the sofa, pulling a cushion on his lap and resting his phone on it, as he ordered the food. As soon as he'd ordered the food, he put down his phone and closed his eyes, trying to think about something else other than how stunning Chloe looked. His eyes snapped open as he felt her sit down on the sofa beside him, carefully wrapping her legs under her. Chloe smiled at Lee as he glanced at her. She felt much more comfortable now that she was wearing her leggings and a jumper.

"I've ordered the food." he told her.

"How did you know what to order?" she asked.

"Because I remember what you like and don't like." he told her, smiling slightly. She smiled, raising her eyebrow sceptically.

"I ordered pizza, and I remembered that the vegetable one is your favourite." he stated.

"Did you order garlic mushrooms?" she asked, a smile playing at the corner of her lips.

"Nice try, I know that you hate mushrooms." he smiled.

"Damn it." she giggled.

"See, I'm good." he chuckled.

"I'm surprised you remembered to be honest." she admitted, smiling slightly at how sweet he was.

"The five of us used to hang out a lot didn't we." he reminded her.

"Yes, but that was a while ago." she pointed out.

"I remember loads of random facts about you." he said smugly.

"Really?" she asked.

"Yep, I know that you hate having flowers inside the house because it reminds you of funerals. You're allergic to peanuts."

"Your favourite food is pasta, Winter is your favourite season because you think it's beautiful and you've always wanted to go to Svalbard to see the Polar Bears." he continued, smiling slightly at her shocked expression.

"Wow, that's a lot." she breathed, slightly impressed that he'd remembered so much about her.

"Oh, and your favourite boyband is Eclipse." he chuckled.

"I wouldn't go that far." she said, smiling slightly.

"And I'm your favourite member obviously." he grinned.

"Oh, I don't know though.... what about Nathan?" she giggled, playing along with his banter. Lee smiled at her before kissing her lips tenderly.

"Still Nathan?" he winked.

"No, I think I'll give you that one." she laughed.

"Speaking of the boys, I'm coming back to work with you." she told him.

"Awesome." he smiled.

"Why aren't you surprised?" she frowned. Lee sighed nervously, not entirely sure how she was going to take what he was about to tell her.

"I knew that we needed a tour manager to work with Matt to organise our schedules, so I suggested to Matt that he offered it to you." he explained.

"Why?" she asked.

"The boys and I miss you, and the tour won't be the same if you aren't there with us." he said quietly. Chloe nodded slowly.

"Matt gave me a bit of a talking too." he chuckled. Chloe raised her eyebrow and waited for him to continue.

"He wanted to make sure that I treated you better than last time." he said quietly. Lee quickly stood up as the doorbell rang, returning a few moments later with the food.

"I feel bad that you keep buying me things." she said quietly when Lee handed her a pizza box.

"It's not a big deal." he told her gently.

"You can have half of it anyway, I won't be able to eat the whole thing." she told him.

"I don't need yours; I have my own." he said.

"Why don't you eat much?" he asked.

"I've never really eaten much." she admitted.

"What did you do about food when you were living in the park?" he asked nervously, slightly afraid that he was going to upset her.

"We scavenged food that people brought for the ducks." she said quickly. Lee paused mid mouthful and turned to look at her, bursting out laughing when he noticed her smiling at him cheekily.

"I always had a small amount of money left for food, but I kind of lived off sandwiches. It's been so nice having hot food since I've been staying here." she told him.

"Danny earned money from busking for his food." she said. Lee nodded slowly. Lee glanced at Chloe as she quickly placed her slice of pizza back in the box.

"Oh no....Danny." she whispered.

"What?" he frowned.

"I've been living here in the warm, with three meals per day, while he's still in the park. I haven't even given him a second thought the past couple of weeks." she explained. "You've been recovering that's why." he told her quickly.

"That's no excuse, I'm such a bad friend. We were supposed to look out for each other." she sighed.

"Well why don't we go for a walk tomorrow; we can go and see him when he's in town busking?" Lee suggested, not comfortable with taking her back to the park to see her friend.

"We can take him some food." she said. Lee nodded, feeling pleased that she had agreed to leave the house. He couldn't help but hope that if she was able to leave the house for a short time in a quiet location that she would eventually start to feel more comfortable in larger gatherings.

"You forgot the garlic bread." she teased him, trying to lighten the mood.

"Are you trying to put me off doing this?" Lee smiled, slowly leaning over and kissing her tenderly. As soon as his lips left hers, he gently rested his forehead against hers, watching her closely.

"Why would I want to put you off kissing me?" she smiled, before kissing him softly. Chloe rested her head on his shoulder and closed her eyes, suddenly feeling very sleepy.

"I think you need to go to bed." he told her. Chloe nodded slowly, watching Lee as he gathered up the food and quickly put it safely in the kitchen. She curled up on her section of the sofa and pulled her blanket over herself.

Lee smiled at her as he watched her, he couldn't help but notice how adorable she looked curled up on the sofa. He lay down on his section of the sofa, glancing over at her as he saw her face illuminated by her phone as she looked at something on it. She smiled to herself and placed one of her earphones in her ear, safely putting her phone under her pillow and closing her eyes. Lee sighed as he thought about Chloe, laying just a few feet away from him, he didn't want to be apart from her.

"Sod this." Lee muttered under his breath. Chloe opened her eyes slowly as she heard Lee muttering, she watched him in the faint light as he shuffled along the sofa. She turned her head around, smiling slightly as he laid down behind her, gently wrapping his arms around her waist and pulling her close.

"Are you alright there?" she teased him.

"Yep, you're my girlfriend now, so I can do this." he whispered, planting a soft kiss behind her ear.

"What are you listening too?" he asked her, snuggling his face against hers.

"You'll laugh." she said quietly.

"No, I won't." he told her. Before Chloe could react, he gently picked up the spare earphone and placed it in his ear.

"Wait, is that your Dad's voice?" he asked.

"Yes, he liked to write books and he recorded them as audiobooks too for me and Mum, I like to listen to them at night sometimes." she explained.

"That's really cute." he said, closing his eyes, feeling comforted by holding her tightly. Chloe closed her eyes and placed her arms over Lee's, quickly linking her fingers with his.

Chloe bolted awake as she heard the front door close and the sound of voices from the hallway. She quickly turned over, noticing that she was still asleep in Lee's arms.

"Lee?" she whispered, trying to wake him so that she could remove herself from his tight embrace before the others noticed.

"Lee?" she hissed again, when he continued sleeping.

"Damn it." she muttered when she tried to squirm out of his arms sighing when she realised that his grip was too strong for her.

"Where are you going?" Lee asked groggily as he slowly woke up, instinctively pulling her closer.

"The others are back." she said quickly.

"Let go of me...quickly." she told him, as she heard footsteps approaching.

Chloe glanced up at Kirstie and Louise starting to panic slightly. She sighed in relief as she finally managed to loosen his grip slightly and squirm out of his arms. She avoided eye contact with Kirstie and Louise as she quickly shuffled over to the other side of the sofa, rolling her eyes at Lee as he fidgeted slightly and fell back asleep. Kirstie switched on the lamp and raised her eyebrow at Chloe as she sat cross legged on Lee's side of the sofa, gazing at her lap, her cheeks a deep shade of red. Kirstie bit her lip to stop herself from bursting out laughing, glancing behind herself as Ben and Matt walked into the room, the four of them staring at Chloe, who was squirming slightly.

"She must have had another nightmare, the only way to calm her down is to hold her." Kirstie said, thinking quickly.

"Oh, really, is that the excuse we are going with." Louise giggled.

"Nothing happened." Chloe said quickly.

"You shouldn't have worn that dress in front of him." Ben teased her, laughing when her cheeks coloured even further.

"Well, nothing happened, they are both still dressed." Kirstie said sternly, glaring at Ben to subtly tell him to drop the subject. Ben shrugged and walked out of the room.

"Right, where is everyone sleeping?" Kirstie said, quickly changing the subject when Michelle walked into the room.

"Louise can have the other half of my bed." Michelle stated.

"Okay cool, Matt, will you be okay on the air bed?" Kirstie asked him.

"Yeah, that's fine." Matt slurred, quickly leaning against the wall as he staggered slightly.

"If it's a pain we can get a taxi?" Louise offered.

"No, it's fine, the more the merrier, Ben can cook his famous fry up for everyone that he keeps bragging about." Kirstie said, smiling slightly.

"Also, you can all tell me about the ball in the morning." Chloe smiled, relieved that the subject had been changed, especially since Michelle was now in the room, her eyes fixed on Lee who was sleeping peacefully. Louise quickly linked her arm through Michelle's and walked down the hallway, trying to get her away from Lee before he woke up. Ben quickly walked into the room, placing the air bed onto the living room floor and handing Matt a blanket, before disappearing back down the hall.

"I get to be in the room with the lovebirds." Matt sighed, half falling onto the mattress as he tried to climb on it.

"Nothing happened!" Chloe insisted.

"At least now I know why he wants you to come back and work with us." Matt chuckled, completely ignoring her. Chloe sighed and glanced at Kirstie who shook her head slowly, subtly giving her the signal to not worry about it.

"See you in the morning." Kirstie said quietly.

Chapter Thirty-Three

Lee squinted in the daylight as he slowly opened his eyes, frowning when he realised that Chloe was no longer in his arms. He sat up slowly, frowning further when he saw that she was asleep on his section of the sofa. He quickly stood up and walked into the kitchen, racking his brain to try and figure out what had happened last night. He remembered spending a magical evening with her, just the two of them and he remembered holding her close as he fell asleep.... but after that nothing...he also had no recollection of Matt coming home and why he was asleep on an air bed on the floor.

As soon as Lee made himself a coffee, he quickly returned to the living room, sitting beside Chloe carefully so as not to wake her. She glanced up at him, gently placing her head on his lap and snuggling against him.

"Did something happen last night?" he asked her, taking a sip of his coffee. He frowned to himself when she ignored him, smiling slightly when he realised that she'd fallen asleep again.

Lee smiled at Louise and Kirstie as they walked into the room, still dressed in their pyjamas.

"Ugh, I'm so hungover." Louise sighed as she sat on the sofa. Kirstie smiled at her as she sat beside her.

"Yeah well, you did get a bit carried away didn't you." Kirstie smiled.

"I know, it was awful." Louise agreed.

"That guy you were dancing with seemed nice though and he seemed really into you." Kirstie pointed out.

"What was his name again?" she added.

"Peter." Louise said, her cheeks colouring slightly.

"He gave me his number too." she added, smiling slightly as she felt her heart flutter.

"Awesome, that's really exciting!" Kirstie said, clapping her hands happily.

"And I woke up to a text from him this morning, so now I don't know what to do." Louise told them. Before Kirstie could stop herself, she let out a squeal of excitement, causing Chloe to jump and open her eyes. She blinked slowly for a moment, rubbing the sleep out of her eyes.

"Sorry Chloe." Kirstie said quickly as Chloe slowly sat up.

"It's fine." she mumbled, still not fully awake.

"Are you tired?" Lee asked her, gently brushing her hair out of her face. Chloe nodded slowly, smiling at him as he handed her his coffee.

"You look like you need it more than I do." he told her.

"That's because you slept like a baby." Chloe sighed, quickly taking a sip of his coffee.

"Yeah, you were out for the count." Kirstie laughed.

"Didn't you hear us come back at all?" Louise asked. Lee shook his head, glancing at Chloe for a moment as he finally made the connection in his head. The reason she wasn't in his arms when he woke up must have been because she was trying not to let the others know about them. Chloe quickly rummaged in the bag at her feet and pulled out her hairbrush, quickly running it through her hair as she suddenly felt self-conscious.

"Anyway, tell me about last night, what did I miss?" Chloe asked when she sat back against the sofa beside Lee.

"Well Louise was just telling us that her mystery man from last night has sent her a text this morning." Kirstie said, wiggling her eyebrows at Louise.

"Ooh, what are you going to do?" Chloe asked her, taking another sip of coffee.

"I don't know." Louise admitted.

"I think I need to meet this guy first, to check out his intentions." Lee piped up. Louise rolled her eyes as both Chloe and Kirstie turned to face Lee, frowning in confusion at him.

"I didn't realise the two of you were close." Kirstie frowned, looking between the two of them.

"We just see each other at work a lot." Louise said.

"I think we kind of bonded over missing you." Lee said thoughtfully, gently stroking Chloe's hair.

"And I felt really guilty that you left because of me and Louise was missing you. I wanted to try and make up for it." Lee explained.

Chloe smiled at him, her heart swelling with pride that he cared about her friend enough to want to protect her from being hurt. She glanced down at his lips, desperately wishing that she could kiss him, quickly turning away from him before she was unable to resist any longer.

Chloe felt her heart plummet as Michelle walked into the room and sat on the sofa beside Kirstie. Kirstie frowned at her when she realised that she had a bottle of vodka in her hand.

"Speaking of men, where did you disappear to for like an hour last night?" Kirstie rounded on Michelle as soon as she sat down.

"I don't know what you are talking about." Michelle said quickly.

"You definitely disappeared, and you were grinning like a Cheshire cat when you came back, so spill." Louise laughed.

"And you disappeared more than once too." Kirstie insisted. Michelle rolled her eyes and remained silent, not really in the mood for being teased. Ben smiled at them as he walked into the living room.

"Fry up for everyone?" he offered, smiling when everyone nodded. He winked at Kirstie and quickly walked into the kitchen.

"It sounds like you all had a really nice time." Chloe smiled at them.

"It would have been better if you were there though." Louise smiled at her.

"It's probably a good job you didn't go though." Kirstie said quickly.

"Why?" Chloe frowned, glancing at Matt as he let out a loud snore.

"Shayne was there." Kirstie announced, screwing up her face in disgust.

"The slime ball himself." Louise agreed. As soon as he'd heard Shayne's name, Lee impulsively wrapped his arm around Chloe's shoulders, to make sure that she was protected and felt safe.

"It's okay." Lee whispered in Chloe's ear, when he felt her becoming tense as she thought about Shayne.

"He wouldn't dare touch her anyway, because I'd kill him." Lee said quickly, his tone slightly fierce.

"He didn't give any of you any trouble, did he?" Lee quickly added, glancing at Chloe as she reached up towards his arm that was still around her shoulder and carefully took his hand.

"No, we didn't speak to him." Kirstie said quietly.

"He was probably busy spending the whole evening trying to take advantage of drunk women." Lee muttered bitterly.

"He didn't actually, he spent most of the evening with me." Michelle piped up. The four of them turned to face her, staring at her in shock as they tried to process her words.

"Are you serious?!" Kirstie exclaimed.

Michelle nodded slowly.

"Even when you know what he's like?" Kirstie asked.

"I'm not entirely sure I believe that to be honest." Michelle said.

"He told me that it all got exaggerated and twisted to make it look like he was the one in the wrong." she added.

"Well, he's not going to say anything else is he." Louise said, rolling her eyes.

"I believe him, it's not like there are any witnesses, and it's very much an accusation of he might have tried to rape me, rather than he actually did." Michelle pointed out.

"So, you don't think that trying to undress someone on a dancefloor is wrong then?" Lee asked, trying to keep his tone level.

"No, not really, it's not exactly rape is it." Michelle said, rolling her eyes.

"And when Chloe ran away from him into the bathroom and he tried to follow her?" Lee asked, demanding her to try and justify Shayne's behaviour.

"Was she running away, or did she want him to chase after her?" Michelle pointed out.

"That's what he told me." she added taking a swig of vodka.

"Why would I make something like that up?" Chloe frowned, feeling slightly hurt that her so called friend thought she was capable of something like that.

"Because you like pretending to everyone that you are Little Miss Perfect and it's exhausting!" Michelle exclaimed.

"You need to shut your mouth." Lee warned her angrily.

"I don't know why everyone else seems to fall for it, when the truth is, you're an attention whore who likes to have everyone fawning over you." Michelle continued.

"You're one to use the word whore, given that you'd spread your legs for anyone." Lee said quickly, glancing down at Chloe when he heard her sniff.

"Oh look, here come the tears, just because you don't have any parents, doesn't mean you need to try and get attention from other people all the time." Michelle sighed, rolling her eyes. Lee quickly stood up, angrily walking towards Michelle.

"Lee don't!" Chloe said quickly.

"BEN!" Kirstie yelled, desperately hoping that Ben would hear them from the kitchen. Lee stood in front of Michelle, slowly clenching and unclenching his fists, trying to get control of his temper as she sat smirking up at him.

"Lee, stop, you'll never forgive yourself." Chloe called out to him, slightly afraid of what he was going to do. Ben rushed through from the kitchen, quickly assessing the situation. He quickly pushed his way between Michelle and Lee, placing his hand on Lee's chest and moving him backwards.

"Oh Ben, thank god." Michelle squeaked from behind him.

Lee scoffed, shaking his head angrily as he heard Michelle pretending to be the victim.

"Michelle stop, you're the cause of this!" Kirstie told her sharply.

"You need to go and cool off." Ben told Lee quickly, when he could see him steadily becoming angrier by the minute.

"Come on, we'll go and see Danny." Chloe suggested, taking hold of Lee's hand, in a desperate attempt to calm him down.

"Louise, could you grab the leftover pizza from the kitchen please?" Chloe asked, afraid to leave Lee's side in case he lost control and lashed out.

"Lee please, she's not worth it." Chloe said quietly, when Lee still hadn't torn his eyes away from Michelle. After a few moments of silence, Lee took a deep breath and nodded slowly, eventually turning to face Chloe. Louise smiled as she handed Chloe a sandwich bag with the leftover pizza inside.

"Thank you." Chloe said quietly. Chloe rummaged in Lee's suitcase and handed him his jacket, before quickly pulling on her own and placing the pizza safely in her pocket. She quickly picked up their phones and put them in her pocket.

"Lee, let's go." she said quietly when he hesitated for a moment. Lee sighed for a moment before walking out of the front door, slamming it behind himself. Kirstie smiled at Chloe as she mouthed *sorry* at her on the way past.

"Thank you so much Ben." Michelle whispered as soon as Lee and Chloe had left.
"Cut it out, you caused the problem, so don't play the bloody victim!" Kirstie said angrily.

"Are you guys talking about Shayne?" Matt piped up. They turned to face him, not realising that he was awake. Kirstie nodded slowly, still not quite able to believe that Michelle had been so cruel to Chloe.

"The guy has form, after I fired him from the label, a couple of other staff members came to me and told me that he'd behaved inappropriately with them too." Matt told them.

"Oh whatever, you're all under Little Miss Perfect's spell anyway, I don't know why I bother." Michelle snapped, before standing up and quickly leaving the room. Louise, Kirstie, Ben and Matt fell silent, the four of them still confused as to what had caused Michelle's outburst and why she hated Chloe so much. They jumped as they heard the smoke alarm ringing loudly.

"Oh shit, the food!" Ben exclaimed, before quickly running into the kitchen.

Chapter Thirty-Four

Chloe quickly walked down Kirstie's driveway, hurrying to catch up with Lee. She jumped as she rounded the corner and saw him perched on the wall, a look of anger etched on his handsome features.

"Are we going then?" she asked quickly, trying to get him moving in case he decided to go back inside the house.

"In a minute." he said quietly, quickly reaching out to take her wrist and gently pulling her towards him. Chloe wrapped her arms around his neck, sighing in contentment as she stood between his legs.

"Are you alright, you look a bit upset?" he asked her gently.

"I'm fine." she said quickly, trying not to let him see how upset and hurt she was by Michelle's words.

She knew that he was already struggling to control his temper and the last thing she wanted to do was make him angrier than he already was. He gazed at her for a moment, not entirely sure if he believed her or not. Before Chloe could say anything else, he wrapped his arms around her waist and pulled her close. As Chloe rested her head on his shoulder, she felt the tears fall that she'd been fighting to hold back.

"Oh Chloe." Lee whispered, holding her tighter when he heard her sniff quietly.

"I'm alright, I know that I shouldn't care what she thinks, I just can't help it." she mumbled.

"No, you shouldn't. She's really not a very nice person." he said quickly. Chloe quickly wiped the tears from her face and sighed quietly.

"You're right, it doesn't matter what she thinks, what's important is what you think." she said quietly.

"Because I love you." she added, before Lee had a chance to respond. Lee placed his hands on her hips and gently removed her from his arms, staring at her closely.

"You don't have to say that just because you know that I'm pissed off." he said quickly.

"And you don't have to hide the fact that you are upset, it's not okay that she said those things." he added, gently wiping away the last of her tears with his thumb.

"That's not why I said it, I really do love you." she insisted.

"And I appreciate how you much you've been there for me lately." she added. Lee took a deep breath, smiling down at the amazing woman standing in front of him. He couldn't quite comprehend how someone as special as her would love someone like him. She was so precious to him that he knew he would cherish her forever.

"I really do love you." she tried again, smiling up at him. Chloe's skin tingled under his touch as he gently placed his hand on her cheek and stroked it with his thumb.

"I love you too." he whispered, kissing her lips softly. Chloe jumped as her phone buzzed loudly in her pocket.

"Oh, I forgot, I still have your phone." she said, taking it out of her pocket and quickly handing it too him, before gazing down at her own.

"Danny says he'll meet us at the cafe." she told him.

"Let's go then. And try and forget about that vile woman." Lee said shortly as he quickly stood up and took Chloe's hand.

"I've missed you so much Chloe." Danny told her, quickly pulling her into a hug as soon as he saw her.

"Be careful with her, she still hasn't healed fully yet." Lee told him quickly. Danny nodded slowly, before quickly sitting opposite Lee at the table.

"How have you been?" Chloe asked Danny as she sat beside Lee.

"Fine, just the usual, you know how it is." Danny told her. Chloe nodded slowly.

"I didn't get that job I auditioned for." Danny said sadly.

"Oh no, you really wanted that part didn't you." Chloe said, slowly reaching over and squeezing his hand gently.

"Yeah, but it's okay, there'll be other auditions. I have an interview for a supermarket next week so hopefully I get that, at least then I can start saving to rent a place." Danny told them.

"Chloe mentioned that you go busking quite a lot?" Lee asked him.

"Yeah, to pay the bills, I've always had a passion for song writing." Danny said.

"I could come with you at some point if you want, we could put out a post online or something." Lee offered.

"You'll make a lot of money if Lee goes with you, there'll be fans turning up probably." Chloe said, smiling at Lee and how big his heart was, despite the fact that he tried to hide it.

"Okay that sounds good, thanks." Danny smiled.

"Maybe you should show him some of your songs too, Lee writes a lot of songs for the band?" Chloe suggested.

"Really?" Danny said.

"Yeah, I wrote some of them." Lee said quietly.

"The last one you wrote was amazing, it made me cry." Chloe said, turning to face Lee.

"The one that was about you?" Lee asked.

"No." Chloe said, frowning in confusion.

"Yeah, it's about you." Lee told her, smiling slightly.

"Is it?!" Chloe exclaimed.

Lee nodded slowly, laughing slightly as he finally saw the look of realisation on her face.

"Oh." she said quietly, her heart fluttering.

"Hi there, what would you like to order?" a waitress interrupted them.

"Nothing, I'm good." Danny said quietly.

"We'll have three coffees and he'll take a full English." Lee said quickly. The waitress smiled at them before walking away.

"My treat." Lee said quickly. Chloe glanced at Lee for a moment, before quickly looking at Danny, slightly concerned that he was going to feel like a charity case.

"You don't need to do that." Danny said awkwardly.

"I need to do something to thank you for looking out for my girl." Lee pointed out, gently wrapping his arm around Chloe's shoulders.

"Is there no way you could reconcile with your parents and maybe they would let you move back in?" Chloe suggested, feeling slightly sorry for Danny.

"They don't want anything to do with me, they won't even take my calls." Danny told her sadly.

"That's ridiculous." Chloe muttered angrily.

"Did they kick you out?" Lee asked. Danny nodded slowly, falling silent.

"Why would they do that?" Lee frowned in confusion. Danny glanced at Chloe nervously, not entirely sure what to say.

"He's alright, he won't judge you." Chloe quickly reassured him.

"My parents are devoted Christians and they didn't take very well to having a gay son." Danny said quickly.

"They kicked you out for being gay?!" Lee exclaimed in disbelief.

"Yep." Danny said sadly.

"That's a bit messed up." Lee stated.

"Just don't judge me please." Danny said, suddenly feeling slightly embarrassed.

"I won't, my best friend is gay, I don't see it as an issue." Lee told him. The three of them instantly stopped talking as the waitress returned and carefully handed out their order.

"I need to use the loo." Lee announced, before quickly standing up and walking away.

"Is there something going on with the two of you?" Danny asked, as soon as Lee was out of ear shot.

"We're dating." Chloe nodded.

"Good, I'm glad you've found someone, and he seems much nicer this time." he said, smiling slightly.

"You seem a bit sad though, what's going on?" he asked. Chloe sighed to herself and quickly told him about the altercation with Michelle.

"She clearly hates me and doesn't even bother to try and hide it." she sighed.

"She sounds like a nightmare." he agreed.

"I just really don't want to be there anymore; the atmosphere is just awful. I need to get away from it." Chloe sighed.

"Yeah, I was going to speak to you about that, you are definitely not staying anywhere near her." Lee said when he returned to the table and quickly sat back down.

"I was actually thinking that you might want to move in with me?" Lee offered.

"There's no pressure or anything, because I know that you want to take things slow, but I have plenty of space and you could have one of the spare rooms if you want?" he continued, rambling slightly. Chloe thought for a moment, suddenly feeling slightly nervous about the thought of living with him.

"Or if you prefer, Nathan offered for you to live with him." Lee added when Chloe still hadn't responded. Even though Chloe knew that moving in with him was a big step and she was nervous, she couldn't help but feel excited about the idea of spending more time with him. Her heart plummeted at the idea of sleeping in the spare room, she'd become so used to sleeping beside him, feeling comforted by his presence that she couldn't help but feel afraid that her nightmares might return if she was alone.

"I'd like to move in with you, but only if you're sure?" she checked.

"Of course, I'm sure." he smiled at her, his heart pounding against his chest happily.

"But....maybe...." Chloe started but trailed off when she became too embarrassed to finish the sentence.

"What were you going to say?" Lee asked her.

"Maybe I could sleep in your bed with you.... but just sleep for now?" she asked nervously. Lee smiled at how adorable she was.

"I think I can allow that." he teased her, quickly wrapping his arms around her waist and pulling her onto his lap.

"She's so cute isn't she." Lee said, locking eyes with Danny as he rested his chin on her shoulder.

"Yep, you'd better not hurt her." Danny told him quickly.

"Never again." Lee said quietly.

"Besides I'd have so many people to answer too." he added, chuckling slightly.

Chloe sat cross legged on the floor beside Lee, quickly gathering her clothes and carefully placing them into her backpack as Lee did the same with his belongings. Chloe glanced up and smiled as Louise walked into the room and sat beside her, gently pulling Chloe into a hug.

"Are you alright babe?" Louise whispered in her ear.

"I'm fine." Chloe replied quietly, glancing at Lee, who was smiling at her reassuringly.

"That was just awful earlier, I can't believe she said those things to you." Louise said thoughtfully, sitting back and watching Chloe and Lee pack.

"She's wrapped up in a lot of jealousy that's why." Lee said bitterly. Louise nodded in agreement.

"That's what everyone keeps saying, but I don't get it, I'm nothing special." Chloe sighed sadly.

"It's because she's insecure and she desperately wants attention. Ironically the things she said about you, apply more to herself." Lee pointed out.

"And you're an easy person to be jealous of." Louise told Chloe.
"What?!" Chloe squeaked.

"You are though, you don't realise the effect you have on people, especially men, you are able to mesmerise them without even trying." Louise explained.

"That's not true, I just go about my business, hiding under jumpers and I don't even wear makeup most of the time." Chloe argued.

"Yeah, but having worked with you, so many of the guys want you Chloe, you'd only have to say the word." Louise insisted.

"It's because she's so beautiful, without even trying." Lee pointed out.

"And her demeanour too, she comes across as sweet and kind." Louise agreed. Lee smiled at Chloe as her cheeks coloured in embarrassment.

"I'd kill for your looks Chloe." Louise said kindly.

"She is stunning enough to be a model, like her Mum." Lee said, smiling at Louise. Louise nodded in agreement.

"Changing the subject slightly, but I need guy advice." Louise piped up, looking at Chloe.

"I think you are asking the wrong person." Chloe said quietly, still not quite able to process what Louise had just told her.

"Advice about what, whether to message him back or not?" Lee asked. Louise nodded slowly.

"Well, if you like him, then why wouldn't you message him back?" Chloe frowned.

"I just have so much going on at the moment and I need to focus on my career." Louise reminded them.

"It is possible to have both though, it just takes a bit of effort on both sides." Chloe told her.

"If you decide to meet him, I think we should come with you, so that you're not meeting a mysterious stranger on your own." Lee told her firmly.

"Alright Dad." Louise said, rolling her eyes at him.

"He might turn out to be like Shayne." Lee pointed out, glancing at Chloe for a moment.

"Yeah, I guess so." Louise said quietly.

"Why don't you send him a reply and see what happens?" Chloe suggested. Louise nodded.

"And make sure you keep me in the loop." Lee told her.

"You do realise I'm not your sister." Louise laughed.

"You kind of are." Lee smiled at her.

"How come you guys are packing?" Kirstie asked as she walked into the room and perched on the sofa.

"I am moving in with Lee." Chloe announced, glancing up as she saw a movement in the doorway, her heart plummeting as she locked eyes with Michelle.

"Really, since when?" Michelle asked.

"Since now." Chloe said shortly, not even able to bring herself to look at Michelle.

"Surely your girlfriend won't be very happy about that?" Michelle asked, turning to face Lee.

"Just ignore her, she just wants a reaction." Louise whispered.

"And don't you feel guilty for taking his time away from his girlfriend all the time?" Michelle tried, rolling her eyes at Lee as she turned to face Chloe.

"I would never do that." Chloe said quietly, glancing at Lee.

"And she would never steal someone that was taken either, because she's a good person." Lee said through gritted teeth as he felt his blood starting to boil.

"Really?" Michelle said, smirking slightly as she glanced at Chloe.

"Even though she has feelings for you?" she said smugly. Chloe felt like she had been kicked in the stomach as Michelle said those words. Even though she'd already told Lee how she felt, Michelle wasn't aware of that. She was prepared to stab her in the back and reveal what she thought was her biggest secret to the man she loved, just to prove a point.

"I'll never forgive you for that." Chloe whispered, her eyes filling with tears. Michelle shrugged slowly, unable to remove the smug smile from her face. Lee shook his head at her as he finally realised just how heartless she could be.

"I already know how Chloe feels and she knows how much I love her." Lee announced, suddenly realising in that moment that he couldn't keep it a secret any longer. Chloe glanced at him as he leaned towards her and placed a soft, lingering kiss on her lips. Chloe smiled slightly at the smug expression on his face. Lee quickly turned to face Michelle, smiling in satisfaction when he realised that he'd finally managed to wipe the smirk off her face.

"Right, on that note we are going." Lee said quickly, standing up and picking up his suitcase, trying to leave the house before Michelle could hurt Chloe any further. Chloe stood up and carefully put on her backpack.

"Give me that." Lee said quickly, gently taking it off her back.

"I can manage." Chloe argued.

"You haven't healed fully yet; you need to be careful." Lee insisted. Chloe sighed and handed him the backpack.

"Thank you so much for letting me stay." Chloe said quietly, quickly hugging Kirstie.

"It's okay, anytime." Kirstie said awkwardly, feeling very guilty that Chloe felt forced into leaving because of Michelle's behaviour.

"The two of you are welcome to come over anytime." Lee said, smiling at Kirstie and Louise.

"C'mon then beautiful, let's go." Lee smiled at Chloe, waiting for her to walk in front of him so that he could make sure that she was safe.

Chapter Thirty-Five

Chloe sighed to herself as she perched on the bed and began to trawl through the mountain of paperwork that she had to do. Her eyes flickered upwards as she heard the front door open and close and Lee walked into the bedroom.

"Hey." she smiled. She couldn't help but notice how attractive he looked in his casual dance wear.

"Hey beautiful." he smiled, bending down to peck her on the lips.

"How was rehearsal?" she asked.

"Good, we've figured out all the routines now I think." he told her, before throwing himself down on the bed behind her. Chloe nodded slowly and returned to her paperwork, very much aware that she had to have it completed before the end of the day. Lee slowly sat up on the bed and crossed his legs, before wrapping his arms around Chloe's waist and gently pulling her onto his lap.

"I've been waiting all day to be back here though." he admitted, placing his chin on her shoulder, his fingers slowly tracing small circles on her stomach.

"You've only been gone for a couple of hours." Chloe giggled.

"I know, but it feels like all day." he said.

"Smooth." she smiled, turning her head to face him and gently kissing his lips. Eventually she broke the kiss and turned back to her paperwork, desperately trying to focus and not become distracted by the feeling of being in his arms. Whenever he touched her, it was like something inside her ignited, her skin constantly tingled like an electric current was flowing through it. The hairs on the back of her neck stood up as Lee slowly began to plant soft kisses on her neck.

"I have to get this done, stop distracting me." Chloe said quietly.

"What are you doing anyway?" he asked. Chloe found herself feeling slightly disappointed when he stopped kissing her.

"It's a contract for the band, I'm checking it, before I speak to the four of you about it." she told him, turning over to another page.

"That sounds boring." he smiled. Chloe jumped slightly as he returned to kissing her neck. Lee smiled to himself as Chloe continued trying to resist him, determined to pretend that she was engrossed in the contract.

"Chloe." he whispered hoarsely in her ear.

"I think this contract looks amazing." she said quietly, completely ignoring him. Lee smirked to himself and gently stroked her hair, smiling in satisfaction as she shivered.

"They want to use a song as a soundtrack for a film." she told him, a slight catch in her throat. Lee ignored her. Chloe glanced down at his hands as he gently lifted the material of her shirt and placed his warm hands against her bare stomach. He could feel Chloe trembling nervously as his hands took hold of her shirt and gradually made their way upwards.

"Lee stop." Chloe squeaked as he was about to remove her shirt. Lee instantly stopped what he was doing and watched her closely as she slowly climbed off his lap and stood up.

"What's wrong?" he asked as he watched her rummage in a drawer and pull out her sportswear.

"I need to get changed, I'm going for a run." she told him, standing in front of him, holding onto her change of clothes. Lee raised his eyebrow and waited for her to get changed.

"Don't look." she told him.

"Why not?" Lee challenged her, refusing to look away.

"I'll get changed in the bathroom." she said quietly, quickly walking away. Lee sat silently for a few moments, waiting for her to return.

"Did I do something wrong?" he asked as soon as Chloe returned. He couldn't stop himself from gazing in wonder at her beautiful hourglass figure.

"Of course not, why would you say that?" Chloe frowned as she put her foot up on the bed and began to tie the shoelaces.

"Because we've been dating a few weeks now and I feel like you're not really into me. If that's the case, I'd rather you just said." Lee said nervously, feeling slightly sick at the thought of losing her.

"Of course, I'm into you, I love you." Chloe frowned. Lee smiled at her, suddenly feeling relieved.

"Why don't you let me see your body, you always move away from me?" Lee asked. Chloe sighed silently to herself, not sure how to answer his question.

"You won't even get changed in front of me.' Lee prompted her.

"I know." Chloe sighed.

"You've seen me naked loads of times." Lee said.

"Yes, but that's because you have a lot of body confidence, you walk around the house naked." Chloe said, smiling slightly.

"And then forget that I'm naked and answer the door to the post woman." Lee laughed.

"Well, I think she enjoyed it." Chloe giggled.

"You're so cute when you laugh." Lee told her. Chloe blushed and looked at the floor, like she always did when she received a compliment.

"I'm sorry if you feel rejected, I can't help it." Chloe said quietly.

"I know, I get that you have confidence problems." Lee said reassuringly.

"That's putting it mildly, I literally hate the way I look, my body most of all." she admitted, surprising herself at how easy it was to admit.

"Oh Chloe....I wish you could see how beautiful you are." Lee said sadly. He always found it upsetting listening to Chloe tear herself down all the time.

"You're so naturally beautiful, people stare at you all the time when you are out, you just don't notice it." he tried when she remained silent.

"I think they are staring at you." she argued.

"Some of them recognise me, but Chloe everyone says how beautiful you are." Lee insisted, desperately trying to make her see how amazing she is. Chloe couldn't help but smile at how sweet he was being, even though she didn't believe him, she appreciated that he was trying to make her feel better.

"Also, you look really hot in your lycra." Lee smiled.

"This is easier than getting undressed in front of someone, when you are naked you are completely vulnerable." she told him. Lee sighed sadly as he stood up and walked over to Chloe. She smiled as he pulled her into a tight hug.

"You know how much I love you and I wouldn't judge you." he whispered in her ear.

"I'm really sorry." she whispered.

"Sorry for what?" he asked gently.

"I've made you wait too long, you are a highly sexed person, it's not fair of me." she said quietly, feeling slightly guilty.

"It's not just about me, I admit I really want you, but I can wait until you want me too." he said, finally letting go of her and looking her in the eye.

"I do want you, I'm just nervous and embarrassed." she told him.

"I know, I remember you saying sex is a big deal to you. Did you feel like this when you were with Andy?" he asked gently.

"Not exactly." she said quickly.

"So, if you can undress in front of him, then why not me?" he frowned, feeling slightly hurt that maybe Chloe didn't trust him.

"You don't think that I'm going to cheat on you like he did do you?" he asked, his hand gently stroking her cheek.

"You know I'd never do that." he added.

Chloe remained silent, quickly wiping away stray tear that had escaped her eye. She knew that the moment she'd been dreading would come eventually, but that didn't make it any easier to tell him.

"Chloe, I feel like there's something you're not telling me." Lee said nervously.

"I didn't undress in front of Andy; we didn't do anything." she sighed.

"But you were together for years." Lee frowned.

"He said that he was religious and didn't believe in sex until after marriage, so we had to wait, but then I obviously found out that he'd been sleeping with other people behind my back. So, he clearly didn't want me." she explained.

"That'll destroy your body confidence." Lee muttered, sounding slightly angry.

"I wasn't very confident before then to be honest, but it's worse now." she said quietly.

Lee nodded slowly, feeling slightly emotional at what she'd just told him. Andy had always seemed like such a nice person, but he'd ripped out Chloe's heart and stomped on it. Not only had he left her to pay off his debts, but he'd left her with scars too. All of her insecurities that were following her around and hindering her life were a direct result of his actions. Lee really wished that he could make him pay for hurting the person that he loved.

"So, I've never actually undressed in front of anyone." Chloe admitted nervously, not entirely sure how he would take it. Lee stared at her and slowly stepped back.

"Wait, are you saying you're a virgin?" Lee asked quickly.

Chloe nodded slowly.

"Shit." he muttered under his breath, his complexion suddenly turning pale.
"Why didn't you tell me?" he asked quietly.

"Because it's embarrassing." she said. Chloe watched Lee closely as he began to pace, his facial expression looking slightly flustered.

"Are you angry?" she asked.

"No, I just don't know what to do." he muttered, still pacing.

"What to do about what?" Chloe frowned.

"Why did you have to be a virgin?" he said quietly, running his hand through his hair.

"I didn't realise that it would be such a big problem." she said, her heart plummeting when she realised that he was disappointed in her. Even though she was nervous to tell him, part of her had hoped that he would respect her for it and feel honoured that she wanted to give her virginity to him. Never in a million years would she have guessed that he would hate the idea. Clearly, he didn't want to be with someone who didn't know what they were doing.

"I'm sorry." she said, fighting back the tears that were threatening to spill.
"What are we going to do?" he muttered, almost to himself.

"I don't know what you mean." she said quietly.

Eventually Lee stopped pacing and turned to face her, a sad expression etched on his handsome features.

"I'm not taking your virginity Chlo." he told her firmly.

"You wouldn't be taking it; I would be giving it to you." she whispered. Chloe slowly walked over to him, placing her hands against his chest to stop him pacing. She wrapped her arms around his waist and held him tightly, craving some comfort as she tried to fight back her tears. She frowned as Lee took hold of her arms and quickly removed them from his waist, pushing her away slightly.

"I need to think." he said quietly, almost like he was talking to himself.

"Think about what?" she asked nervously. Lee remained silent and stared at the ground. Chloe felt like she had been punched in the chest. It felt like history was repeating itself, first Andy didn't want her and now Lee didn't either. She could feel her legs becoming weak, so she subtly leaned against the wall, determined not to let him see how upset she was. She couldn't even bring herself to ask why he didn't want her; she knew the answer anyway. She'd always known that he was way out of her league. He was used to beautiful young models; she was kidding herself that he would be happy with her.

"I'm not good enough for this, I can't be your first." he said thoughtfully.

Chloe stared at him in numb shock, not entirely sure what he was thinking or why they were having this conversation. He remained silent and started to pace again.

"I'm done with this conversation." Chloe snapped as she turned and walked out of the room.

Chapter Thirty-Six

As soon as Chloe returned from her run, she quickly rushed upstairs and climbed into the shower. She was still furious with Lee for how he'd made her feel. She'd thought the days were long gone, when he'd been able to make her feel stupid and insignificant, but apparently not. She'd shared her biggest secret with him, one that she'd never told anyone before and he'd managed to make her feel like being a virgin was something to be ashamed of, like she was a disappointment to him.

The time had come to put a stop to it, she wasn't going to tolerate it anymore. She needed to prove a point to him. Once she had finished in the shower she quickly pulled on a tight dress and heels, her heart sinking slightly as she heard footsteps climbing the stairs. She quickly sat at her dressing table and carefully began to apply her makeup.

"What are you doing?" Lee asked, locking eyes with her in the mirror as he hovered awkwardly in the doorway.

"I'm going out." she snapped.

"What, now?" he asked quickly, his heart sinking in his chest.

"Yes now. " she replied.

"But we need to talk, I made dinner." he said quietly.

"Invite someone over to eat with you then, you could always invite one of your booty calls over." she said sarcastically, cursing herself as she smudged her eyeliner. Lee sighed quietly, not wanting to rise to the bait.

"We need to talk though." he tried again.

"I think you've said enough, I know how you feel." she said.

"No, you don't, you've just assumed." he told her quietly.

"Well don't worry, I won't be a problem for you to fix anymore." she snapped, too angry to listen to him.

"Please just stay. We can talk about it." he pleaded with her.

"I can't, I'm ready to go." she said sharply. He watched as she stood up and squeezed past him in the doorway. As he watched her walk down the stairs and out of the front door, he found himself wishing, not for the first time, that he hadn't reacted the way he did. He was shocked.... he'd never imagined that Chloe wouldn't have had sex before, especially given how beautiful she is. He knew that she was hurt by his reaction but if only she would stop and listen to him, he would be able to explain. He hesitated for a moment, not entirely sure what he should do, he knew that she would be angry if he followed her but at the same time, he couldn't leave her alone and defenceless late at night. He ran down the stairs, desperately hoping that he could catch her up.

Chloe sighed quietly and massaged her sore temples as she sat at the bar of the pub, trying to drown out the loud music. The last place she wanted to be was in a pub, but she knew that she had to prove a point to Lee. If she was going to make sure that he treated her better, she had to make him realise she wasn't wrapped around his finger. She knew as she sat there that she had no intention of spending time with any guys, she wouldn't do that to him. She loved him so much that she would never hurt him. Chloe quickly downed the rest of her drink as her mind raced as to why he didn't want to sleep with her. She couldn't help being a virgin, in some ways she wished that she wasn't, but she couldn't understand why he was so put off by the idea. She jumped as she felt someone place a hand on back. She turned slightly and sighed to herself as she saw Lee standing beside her.

"Have you come to supervise?" she asked him sarcastically.

"No, I've come to take you home, it's not safe for you to be on your own in a pub in the middle of the city." he explained.

"What are you doing here anyway, you hate pubs?" he frowned.

"Well, I figured if I came out and pulled a random guy then the problem would be solved...after all, it's what you were saying wasn't it." she snapped sarcastically.

"There's so many guys in here with no standards, I doubt many of them would say no to me." Chloe added, quite enjoying the fact that she was making him squirm.

"No probably not." Lee said quietly, his mouth suddenly feeling very dry.

"Chloe, please come home." he begged her, unable to stand the thought of her being with anyone else. Chloe looked up at him, sensing a change in his body language. She nodded and climbed off the stool. He gestured for her to walk in front of him, wanting to have her in front of him so that he could make sure she was safe. They walked home in silence, neither one of them wanting to talk about their situation until they were safely home.

As soon as they got home, Chloe pulled off her heels and wandered to the back of the house, smiling to herself as she pushed open the large wooden door and gazed in wonder at Lee's indoor swimming pool. She hadn't been in this room for so long that she forgot how stunning it was, both of the front walls lined with glass, overlooking the large garden. She slowly sat at the side of the pool and placed her legs into the water. She sighed to herself as the coolness of the water helped to calm down some of the anger that she was feeling.

Her eyes wandered over the other side of the room, towards the hot tub area, in a few short weeks Chloe felt like she was living a completely different life. It felt a world away from living on a park bench. She glanced at Lee as he sat beside her.

"I'm really sorry." he said nervously. Chloe nodded slowly, not sure what to say or where they went from here. Lee sighed sadly as he watched Chloe sitting beside him, gently swinging her feet in the water. He hated that he'd managed to upset her.

"It was just a shock." he told her.

"I know, I was shocked too, I didn't think you'd react like that." she said.

"I didn't mean too, I was panicking." Lee admitted.

"Panicking about what?" she frowned.

"Sex has never been a big deal to me, it's always just been about doing what's fun, no feelings involved. But for you, it's different, it's about a connection." he said quietly.

"But if you love me like you say then we would've had a connection anyway, so I don't see what difference it makes." she said.

"I know, and I was nervous about that side of it anyway, but when you said you are a virgin that's a completely different situation." he replied.

"I don't understand, surely it's a privilege for you to be my first?" she asked.

"Yeah, but I don't deserve it." he said quietly.

"What?" she frowned, turning to face him.

"I've been with so many people Chloe, I've lost count, you need to give your first time to someone better than me." he muttered.

"It's up to me to decide who I want to give myself too and I want it to be you." she whispered, feeling slightly embarrassed.

"But I don't want to hurt you Chlo." he told her gently, his heart breaking slightly at her sad tone. Lee hated being in this situation, he could finally see how much this meant to her but at the same time, the thought of her being in pain because of him made him feel sick. Chloe felt her heart flutter as he said those words. She'd been convinced that he didn't want her, but the truth was that he did, but he was afraid to hurt the person he loved.

"But you won't." she said gently, desperately trying to convince him to agree.

"It will hurt Chloe, you know it will." he said, gently planting a soft kiss on her cheek.

"I know, but it'll hurt less with you because you'll be careful, some random guy won't be." she told him.

"I don't want anyone else touching you anyway." he said, his tone slightly fierce. Chloe felt her heart flutter as he said those words.

"Nobody else is allowed?" she smiled, raising her eyebrow.

"No, that's never an option. " he said quickly.

Chloe sighed in pleasure as Lee placed a series of soft kisses on her neck, gently sucking on the sweet part of her neck, just above her collarbone.

"Are you marking your territory?" she asked hoarsely. Lee ignored her and continued his determination to leave a mark.

"I really want to give myself to you." she whispered, gently resting her head on his shoulder. Lee instantly stopped kissing her and sighed to himself.

Chloe lifted her head and sighed quietly, sensing that Lee needed some time with his thoughts, to figure out what he wanted to do. She slowly slipped into the pool, smiling to herself at the feeling of the cold water. Lee smiled at her, before quickly removing his shoes and socks and climbing into the pool beside her. Chloe quickly swam over to him and wrapped her arms around his neck.

"I have a condition." he said quietly, placing his hands on her hips. Chloe raised her eyebrow and waited for him to continue.

"We wait until tomorrow, so that I have time to make it special for you." he whispered in her ear.

"Really?!" Chloe exclaimed, not quite able to believe that he had finally agreed. Lee nodded, smiling slightly at her happy expression.

"I don't want lots of fuss though, I hate fuss." she told him happily. He smiled at her as she gently stroked his hair, a cheeky glint in his eye.

"Lee?" Chloe asked nervously.

"Just trust me." he smiled, pulling her closer and resting his head on her shoulder.

Chapter Thirty-Seven

Chloe rushed around Lee's house, frantically checking that she had got everything that she needed. She quickly picked up the contracts and stuffed them into the bag.

"I feel like I'm forgetting something." she said, turning to face Lee as he walked into the kitchen.

"Your breakfast probably." Lee smiled as he handed her a bowl of porridge that he'd made.

"I'm running so late, I won't have time for a run, I'll have to go after work." she sighed in between mouthfuls.

"Good, that'll give me a chance to make some preparations." he smiled, wiggling his eyebrows at her. Chloe smiled slightly, afraid to ask.

"Right, let's go." Chloe said, quickly placing her bowl in the sink.

"Hey, the future Mr and Mrs Knight are here!" Steven exclaimed as soon as Lee and Chloe walked into the gymnasium they were currently using as a rehearsal space.

"You're so funny." Chloe said sarcastically, rolling her eyes at them.

"Keep your voices down, the rest of the team will be here in a minute." Lee warned them sharply. Chloe smiled at the boys reassuringly when they sighed at Lee's waspish tone. Shortly after Chloe and Lee had finally started dating, they'd told the Eclipse boys who had been thrilled, but Lee had sworn them to secrecy. The last thing he wanted was for Chloe to be exposed to the press and the fans.

"Chloe, are you dancing with us?" Nathan asked.

"No, why?" Chloe frowned.

"You're dressed for exercise." Nathan pointed out.

"It's comfortable and I'm going for a run after work." she told him.

"Also, it means I can do this." Chloe said, laughing at their faces as she performed the splits.

"Woah Chloe, who knew you were so flexible." Adrian laughed.

"I wanted to be a dancer when I was growing up, until I got older and hated people looking at me." she told them. Nathan gasped as she quickly performed a side aerial.

"You guys must have really good sex, with his experience and her flexibility." Steven teased them, pointing at Chloe and Lee in turn. Chloe glanced at Lee awkwardly who remained silent. The five of them stopped talking as the door opened and the other dancers came in, followed by someone that Chloe didn't recognise.

"Hi, I'm Jonny, I'm the choreographer." he said to Chloe when he reached her, holding his hand out to shake her hand.

"Chloe, I'm the day manager." she told him, shaking his hand.

"Can I run through the routines with the boys or do you need them for something?" he asked her.

"No, you're fine." Chloe smiled warmly. She wandered over to the bench area in the corner, gently spreading out her paperwork on the bench beside her. She couldn't help glancing up occasionally, smiling to herself as she subtly watched Lee dance. He was even more attractive to her when he was dancing. After they had rehearsed a few songs Jonny finally called to them to take a break. Steven, Adrian, Nathan and Lee sat on the floor in a circle, the four of them out of breath. Lee glanced over at Chloe, winking at her. She smiled at him and quickly walked over to join them.

"I need the four of you to read through these contracts please." she told them, handing each of them a copy.

"The only slight issue I could find is that they want you to film the video in Germany so that some of the cast can be there. It might be difficult with your schedules so it might be worth saying to them that it needs to be filmed here. I think they'll go for it." Chloe explained. The four of them remained silent as they read through the contracts.

"Chloe, I need to speak to you about the set!" Bobby the set designer called her from the hallway.

"I'll be right back." she said.

Lee glanced up as Chloe walked out of the room to speak to Bobby. He couldn't help but roll his eyes to himself as he noticed Jonny watching her walking away. Chloe had no idea how many people around her admired her looks, if only she could see it. Almost every man that was in the room, hadn't been able to stop themselves from checking her out, her flawless body perfectly highlighted by her gym wear. He found himself wishing, not for the first time that she had more confidence in herself.

"That Chloe girl is stunning; I'm surprised the four of you have managed to keep your hands off her." Jonny said, trying to banter with the lads.

"She is a pretty girl." Nathan agreed as everyone else remained silent.

"Is she single?" Jonny asked them. Nathan glanced at Lee not entirely sure what he wanted them to say. Lee hesitated for a moment, part of him wanting to tell Jonny that she was seeing someone so that he would back off, but another part of him wanted Jonny to ask Chloe out, in the hope that it would boost her confidence.

"You'll need to speak to her about that." Lee eventually decided. Nathan quickly stood up and followed Chloe.

"Hey, can I speak to you?" Nathan asked when he reached her.

"Yeah sure, let's go in here." Chloe said, leading him into an empty room and closing the door.

"So, what's wrong?" she asked, perching on the windowsill.

"I'm just checking in, are you feeling okay about tonight?" he asked gently.

"What?" Chloe whispered, feeling a lump rise in her throat.

"He told you." she quickly added.

"Only because he's worried about you." he told her. Chloe nodded slowly, suddenly feeling very humiliated. The thought of Lee and Nathan discussing her virginity was making her feel unwell.

"I think I'm going to be sick." Chloe admitted, feeling the colour drain from her face.

"Chloe, it's not like that, he wasn't gossiping. He was asking what he should do and how to make it easier for you." Nathan said quickly.

"Doesn't make it any less humiliating." she whispered.

"I won't tell anyone, I promise." he reassured her. Chloe nodded silently, feeling very troubled that someone else now knew her biggest secret.

"I want to help, both of you can speak to me if you want." he tried.

"I'm not talking about my sex life or lack of it." Chloe snapped defensively.

"Sorry, I'm tired, I didn't get much sleep last night." she quickly added, feeling guilty for snapping at him.

"Why, because you are nervous?" he asked.

"Partly and I kept having bad dreams." she told him.

Nathan smiled slightly.

"It's not funny." she said quickly.

"No, it's not that, the two of you are so cute together. Lee had bad dreams too." he explained.

"He did?" she frowned. Nathan nodded.

"About me?" she asked.

"I think you should ask him that." he said quickly.

"You make him better you know." Nathan told her. Chloe scoffed sceptically.

"I'm serious, he's much calmer. We don't have to walk on eggshells anymore." Nathan chuckled.

"He's still an idiot though." she sighed, not quite able to bring herself to look Nathan in the eye anymore.

"I know but one problem at a time." he smiled. Chloe quickly stood up and walked back into the gymnasium, Nathan following closely behind.

"Chloe, help settle something for me!" Jonny called as soon as she walked back into the room.

"What?" Chloe sighed when she reached them.

"I think we should have girls dancing with the boys during Broken, but the boys aren't keen." Jonny told her.

"We didn't say that we just said that the song means a lot to Chloe so she should decide." Adrian said awkwardly, clearly not wanting to tell Jonny that Lee had written the song for Chloe and it would cheapen it if girls were added in.

"You could come on and do your tricks Chloe." Steven laughed, trying to lighten the atmosphere.

"I'd rather watch from backstage." she smiled.

"You can do tricks?" Jonny asked.

"Just a few, it's been a while though so I'm rusty." Chloe smiled.

"Show me then." he asked her.

Lee watched as Chloe quickly performed a selection of tricks, including a cartwheel, side aerial and a back handspring. He couldn't help but smile at how seamlessly she performed them.

"Did you know she could do all of that?" Nathan whispered to him. Lee shook his head slowly.

"I might still be able to do a turn sequence, but it's been a few years." Chloe said, slowly taking her shoes off. They all watched mesmerized as she completed a flawless turn sequence.

"Wow." Jonny said.

"Have you done partner work before, we could get you dancing with the boys?" he added.

"No, I haven't. Besides you are not getting me on stage." Chloe told him sternly. Lee watched her proudly as she stood up for herself, there was a time when she would have gone along with whatever anyone told her, but now she had the confidence to stand up for herself. He couldn't help but feel a little bit of hope that her confidence was finally starting to grow.

"Okay that's fine, you could help me teach the boys a trick for when the girls get here tomorrow though." Jonny said. Chloe nodded slowly and watched as Jonny knelt on one knee in front of her.

"So, use my legs to climb up and sit on my right shoulder." he told her. Chloe did as she was asked. Jonny placed his hands on her hips to steady her as he slowly stood up.

"Jeez, you're really light." he smiled up at her. Chloe held her arms out at either side of her, trying to engage her core and find her balance.

"You guys won't have this problem as the girls will be on a higher stage than you, so you'll just have to stand still, and the girls will get on your shoulder." Jonny told them. He slowly let go of Chloe's hips when he realised that she had herself balanced.

"Now Chloe you need to get some forward momentum like you are going to do a cartwheel, but you want your hands to land halfway down my thighs. Stop halfway over, hold yourself with your core and then arch your back towards me, lift your head up and do something pretty with your legs." Jonny explained.

"I'm not sure my core is strong enough for that." Chloe told him.

"I'll hold your stomach to start with." he said. Chloe locked eyes with Lee who slowly shook his head, subtly telling her that she shouldn't attempt it. Chloe hesitated for a moment before she did as he asked. As she arched her back and pointed her legs, she could feel her momentum going too far forward. Jonny quickly placed his arms around her stomach to stabilise her.

"There's no way in hell we're going to be able to do that, we'll end up dropping someone." Adrian said, summing up what the others were thinking.
"They will hold themselves; this is just because Chloe hasn't done it before." Jonny said.

"You should be higher up though, it'll be easier to balance." he told Chloe, gently moving her so that she was further up. Chloe's arms began to shake as he moved her, as he continued to move her, his hand slipped. Lee watched in horror as the effort of pulling Chloe's weight higher up his legs caused one of his hands to slip. Before Lee could react, Chloe lost her balance and fell to the floor with a loud thud that echoed around the gymnasium. Chloe lay in a heap on the ground for a moment, slightly winded from her fall. She glanced up as Lee knelt beside her.

"You okay?" he asked her quietly.

"Yes, I'm fine." she said slowly sitting up.

"You'll be fine Chloe." Jonny said from behind them.

"She would be if you weren't such a fucking idiot." Lee said angrily.

"Chill out man, there's no need to be a dick about it." Jonny said, rolling his eyes.

"It wasn't a bad fall and dancers fall all the time anyway." Jonny added.

"She's not a dancer, she's our manager, you shouldn't have put her in that position." Lee snapped.

"No that's true, if she was a dancer, she'd have been able to hold herself in that position." Jonny pointed out.

"Are you seriously blaming her, from where I was standing it looked like your hand slipped." Lee said angrily, quickly standing up.

"Whatever." Jonny shrugged.

"You don't put her in that position again do you understand." Lee warned.

"I didn't hear her complaining about it." Jonny said, wiggling his eyebrows. Everyone's eyes turned to Chloe as she slowly stood up, wincing slightly.

"The two of you can stop talking about me like I'm not here." she told them.

"You could have been seriously hurt." Lee said.

"I know, I chose to go along with it and I don't need you to fight my battles for me, I can take care of myself." she told Lee.

"As for you...it was your hand slipping that caused me to fall and you know it. And as for me wanting to be in your arms or whatever you were insinuating you can dream on. I have a boyfriend and even if I didn't, I wouldn't be interested in you anyway." she said, turning to Jonny.

"Oh, and as for Broken, I'm the manager and it stays the way it is, just the four boys on stage." she added. Lee stared at Chloe in shock, a warm feeling inside his chest. He couldn't help but smile proudly at his girlfriend who was slowly turning into a little firecracker.

"I need to go and walk it off." Chloe told them before quickly leaving the room.

Chapter Thirty-Eight

Chloe slowly closed the front door behind herself when she got back to Lee's. She took a moment to steady her nerves about the evening before she walked into the living room, smiling as she saw the open fire burning. Lee glanced up from his laptop as she walked into the room.

"Something smells good." she said, suddenly noticing the smell wafting through from the kitchen.

"It's probably me." he teased her.

"Well, it's definitely not me, I need to shower." she smiled.

"Don't be too long, dinner is almost done." he told her, watching as she quickly left the room. As soon as she left the room, he folded down the laptop and sighed quietly to himself. Despite the fact that he wanted to make this night as special for Chloe as possible, he still wasn't entirely comfortable with the situation. But he knew in his heart that it meant a lot to her, to give her virginity to him and so he had to do it for her. He wandered into the kitchen to serve the food, Chloe reappeared a few moments later.

"Where do you want to eat?" he asked Chloe as he handed her a plate of steaming risotto.

"We could eat in the living room in front of the fire?" Chloe suggested.

"Sounds good." Lee said, picking up his own plate in one hand, a bottle of wine and two glasses in the other. He frowned at Chloe as she rummaged in the medicine drawer, quickly taking out a tablet and swallowing it, before walking back into the living room.

"You alright Chlo?" he asked as he followed her.

"Yep, just making sure I don't bloat, I'm pretty sure you don't want to see that." she smiled, sitting cross legged on the sofa.

"I keep telling you that you are beautiful, when are you going to believe it?" he sighed, sitting beside her.

"Probably never." she admitted.

"It was so hot when you stood up to Jonny earlier." he told her, deciding that it wasn't the right time to keep talking to her about her looks.

"He's horrible." she said matter of factly.

"Yeah, I know." he chuckled.

"Speaking of which, are you hurt?" he added.

"Nope not really, it wasn't a bad fall." she told him.

"He totally fancies you though." he said. Chloe nodded and remained silent.

"So does Bobby." Lee told her.

"What, no he doesn't." Chloe frowned.

"He definitely does, he's like a lost puppy when you are there." Lee insisted.

"Chloe can you help me with this, Chloe I need to ask you something." he laughed, imitating Bobby.

Chloe burst out laughing. "Not a bad impression." she laughed.

"I keep telling you that everyone wants you." Lee grinned smugly at her. Chloe remained silent and stared into the fire.

"I have something I need to get off my chest." she eventually said quietly.

"Uh oh." Lee said nervously.

"I'm really unhappy that you spoke to Nathan about us." she told him.

"Yeah, I get that I regret doing it. I was just really worried about everything and I needed to ask someone who knew more about it than me." he explained. She frowned.

"I've never been with a virgin before, but Nathan has so I was able to ask him about it." he added.

"Like what?" she frowned.

"Mostly he just gave me reassurance and a few tips." he said, being slightly vague. Chloe sighed and put her plate of unfinished food on the coffee table.

"It leaves a bad taste in my mouth, the thought of you and your best friend gossiping about something which is my personal business. You are the only person that I've told, I lied to my friends, they all think that I lost it to Andy." she said quietly.

"Oh my god Chloe, I didn't know that." he said quietly, suddenly feeling really guilty.

"We weren't gossiping or anything though I swear, I just needed someone to speak to about it. Nathan actually thought it's really cute, so he doesn't think less of you." he added.

"I don't care if he does, that's not the point." she sighed.

"No, I know, I'm really sorry." he told her. She nodded slowly.

"I'll have a word with him about not speaking to you about it anymore." Lee said.

"He shouldn't be speaking to either of us about it, it's none of his business." she said.

"I know, he means well though." he pointed out.

"Yes, but it doesn't help. I felt so exposed earlier." she told him.

"What?" Lee frowned.

"When I went out to speak to Bobby, Nathan pulled me aside to ask me how I was feeling about tonight. I get that he wants to help, and if it wasn't for him, we probably wouldn't be together now, but I felt really uncomfortable." she explained.

"I'll have a word with him." Lee said sternly. Lee quickly poured them both a glass of wine and handed one to Chloe who smiled her thanks.

"Just one glass though, I'm not going to take advantage of a drunk girl." he winked at her. She smiled slightly.

"He did mention that you had bad dreams last night, it wasn't about me was it?" Chloe asked.

"Oh, for fuck sake." Lee muttered under his breath.

"I told him that in confidence." he quickly added.

"Great so he's a blabber mouth, that bodes well." Chloe said, shaking her head.

"He won't tell anyone your secret Chloe." he said, trying to reassure her.

"He'd better not. To be fair, he only told me about the dreams because I said that I had them." she told him. Lee stopped chewing mid mouthful and stared at her.

"You had them too?" he checked.

"Yes, I think we are both getting too stressed about it." Chloe said quietly, quickly finishing her glass of wine.

"Yeah probably." Lee agreed quietly.

"Just promise me something." Chloe whispered, her cheeks colouring as she thought about her dream. Lee nodded and waited for her to continue.

"If it gets too much and I ask you stop you will." she said nervously. Lee stared at her quietly, his heart breaking a little at her sad expression.

"Chloe you know I would." he told her gently.

"I know, the dream just freaked me out a bit." she admitted. Lee winced at her words, not quite able to bear the thought that he had done something to her, even though it was just a dream. She watched him closely as he placed his empty plate beside hers on the table and laid down on the sofa.

"Come here." he said, lifting his head to look at her and holding his arms open. Chloe quickly shuffled over to him and gently laid sideways on top him bending her legs into the foetal position. He wrapped his left arm around her waist and placed his right hand on her legs. Lee smiled at her as she sighed and snuggled her face into his collarbone.
"You need to make me a promise in return." Lee told her.

"Okay." Chloe said quietly.

"If it gets too much or you change your mind you tell me." he said.

"I won't change my mind." she muttered.

"You might." he told her.

"I won't but I promise anyway." she said.

"Just don't break my heart okay." she whispered, her eyes filling with tears. He sighed and planted a soft kiss on her forehead.

"Once we do this, there's no going back, so don't cheat on me." she continued.

"I would never cheat on you; I have everything that I want right here." he reassured her.

"Don't get your hopes up, you haven't seen me naked yet." Chloe laughed.

"Please don't start putting yourself down again." he said quickly. Chloe sighed happily as she closed her eyes.

"This is my new happy place." she said.

"Me too." he said.

"Although I've just realised, I'm probably crushing you." she laughed when she suddenly realised that he was taking all of her weight. Lee glanced down at her. Despite the fact that she was on top of him, Lee still felt as though his large broad frame dwarfed her petite one.

"You're really light Chloe, it's fine." he said quietly. His mouth suddenly felt dry as he thought about their plans for later tonight. She seemed so small and fragile in comparison to him, he felt like he was going to break her. Chloe had fallen silent and he knew by her steady breathing that she had fallen asleep. Lee took deep breaths, trying to steady his nerves. He couldn't understand what this woman had done to him, he'd never been vulnerable before, but she'd managed to get under his skin, so much so that he would do anything for her. She'd managed to bring out a caring and protective side in Lee that he didn't even realise that he had. He wanted to hold her and touch her all the time, to feel the fire that felt like it was flowing through his veins every time they touched. Despite the fact that he'd never been in love before and didn't really know what it felt like, he knew that what he and Chloe had is something special and he would do anything to protect that. Chloe stirred slightly in her sleep as he gently rested his head against hers and closed his eyes, feeling comforted by the sound of her steady breathing.

Chapter Thirty Nine

Lee glanced down as Chloe slowly stirred in his arms. He watched her as she slowly sat up.

"Sorry I didn't mean to fall asleep on you." she yawned.

"It's fine, mind your bum a minute though." he smiled as he gently pushed her onto the sofa.

"Ow, I've got cramp." he hobbled as he stood up.

"Sorry, that was my fault." she said quietly. He turned to face her, a cheeky glint in his eye.

"I was just teasing you." he laughed. Before Chloe could say anything he quickly leant down and planted a soft kiss on her lips. Chloe smiled as he picked up the plates and took them into the kitchen.

"I'll wash up, you cooked." she called after him.

"It's fine, I'll put yours in the fridge for tomorrow and the other things can go in the dishwasher." he called back.

"Are you remembering that we are meant to be going to Mum's tomorrow?" he reminded her.

Chloe groaned quietly, glancing into the kitchen slightly nervous that he might have heard her.

"No, I forgot about that." she admitted.

"She's been nagging me to meet you for weeks." he told her.

"Why?" she frowned.

"Because this is the first serious relationship I've had, she's a bit over excited about it." he smiled as he walked back into the room, carrying some kebab sticks and a bag of marshmallows. Lee quickly skewered a marshmallow on a stick and handed it to Chloe. Chloe smiled at him and sat beside him at the fire.

"Try not to set it on fire." he chuckled as the two of them held their marshmallows over the fire.

"I'm more worried about it dripping on your carpet." Chloe giggled.

"Everything in this house is so expensive, it's stressful." she added.

"It's fine, everything in this house can be replaced." he told her.

"Only one thing is priceless." he grinned at her. Chloe smiled at him, realising instantly what he was suggesting.

"You mean worthless." Chloe muttered to herself. She slowly removed her marshmallow from the stick, gasping slightly as the gooey mixture burnt her finger.

"Why do you say things like that about yourself?" Lee sighed sadly.

"Because they are true, I'm homeless remember, a stray." she said quietly.

"You're not feral enough to be a stray." Lee smiled.

"I hate it when you say negative things about yourself." he told her gently.

"I only say it because it's true." she said.

Chloe glanced at Lee as he reached out and took hold of her wrist, gently pulling her hand towards himself. He maintained eye contact as he guided her finger towards his mouth and gently sucked off the marshmallow residue. Chloe smiled at the mischievous grin on his face.

"It's not true, and you are not homeless, this is your home." he told her in between seductively licking the marshmallow from her fingers. Chloe sighed quietly to herself, she didn't want to argue with him, but she knew that this house was Lee's home. Technically her home was still a park bench. She suddenly realised that if the worst was to happen and Lee and herself split up, she would have nowhere to go but back to the park.

"What are you thinking about?" Lee asked her, clearly sensing that she was deep in thought.

"That I really need to sort my life out." she said.

"If anything happens with us, I'll be homeless again." she added thoughtfully.

"No, you won't, I wouldn't kick you out." he told her. The two of them glanced at the fire as it eventually went out. Lee took hold of Chloe's hand and stood up, gently helping her to stand up too.

"Is it that time already?" she asked nervously, her voice trembling slightly as Lee led her upstairs.

"Not quite yet I'm going to run you a bath first." he told her.

"Why, I had a shower earlier?" she frowned.

"It's part of my plan, you'll see." he smiled.

"Okay you wait here, you can open your present while you wait." he told her when they reached the bedroom. Lee quickly let go of her hand and walked into the bathroom.

"Oh, I forgot this is for you." Lee said, peering his head around the bathroom door and handing her a tablet.

"Are you trying to drug me now?" she smiled as she took the tablet in her hand. He smiled slightly.

"It's a paracetamol." he told her. Chloe sighed and stared at the tablet in her hand, her heart pounding nervously as she was reminded of their plans.

"It probably won't make much difference." she muttered.

"I know but it makes me feel better." he told her quietly. Chloe nodded and quickly swallowed the tablet.

"Open your present." Lee told her, pointing towards the bed before disappearing back into the bathroom. Chloe slowly walked over to the bed and picked up the small gift box. She gasped as she opened it and saw a silver necklace with a heart shaped pendant on the end. In the centre was a blue sapphire.

"Wow." she whispered, feeling slightly guilty at how expensive the gift looked. She hated that she was in so much debt that she couldn't afford to buy him anything at all, let alone something as expensive as this. She gently stroked the pendant with her finger, turning it over and frowning when she noticed an engraving on the back. As she peered closer, she noticed that her name was engraved on one side of the heart and Lee's name was on the other. Tears pricked Chloe's eyes as she stared, transfixed by her beautiful gift. Lee really was the most thoughtful person that she'd ever met.

"Do you like it?" she heard Lee's voice from behind her.

"I love it, thank you so much." she whispered, not turning around to face him so that he wouldn't notice her tears. She heard him cross the room and felt him stand behind her. He reached around her and took the necklace out of the box. Chloe remained silent as he gently placed it around her neck and fastened it, his fingers brushing against her neck as he did so. He hesitated for a moment before gently wrapping his arms around her shoulders and holding her tightly.

"I love you so much Chloe." he whispered in her ear.

"I love you too." she smiled, her legs feeling weak as she felt him sigh in contentment.

"Does being in love normally feel like this?" he whispered in her ear.

"No, I think this is unusual." Chloe replied, planting a soft kiss on his hand and resting her head against his arm.

"It's a good job we eventually stopped pretending to hate each other." he smiled. Chloe nodded silently, smiling to herself.

"You'd better get in the bath, before it gets cold." Lee told her, reluctantly letting go of her. She nodded slowly and walked towards the bathroom, briefly glancing behind herself when she realised that Lee was following her. As soon as she walked into the bathroom, she gasped as she saw the mound of bubbles on the bathtub, the room in darkness except for a few candles that were dotted around the room.

"Did you get carried away with the bubble bath?" Chloe giggled.

"Nope." Lee smiled, at her before miming zipping his lips closed.

"Get in then." he prompted her, laughing at her confused expression.

"Don't worry, there's not someone hiding in the bath." he quickly added. Chloe burst out laughing, before taking a deep breath and slowly removing her hoodie. She placed her hands on the material of her shirt and hesitated, suddenly feeling very nervous again. Lee smiled at how cute she looked before quickly turning his back. He heard her undress and climb into the bath. He waited a few moments just in case and slowly turned back to face her.

"I feel like I'm suffocating in bubbles." Chloe giggled. Lee smiled in satisfaction when he saw that only her head was visible in the bathtub.

"That was the plan." he smiled at her.

"To suffocate me?" she laughed.

"No, you don't like being naked in front of me because you are embarrassed so this way, I'm in the room when you are naked, but I can't see anything. Baby steps." he explained.

"Oh my god." Chloe mumbled, her voice breaking slightly.

"Too much?" he asked her, as he quickly picked up the hair clip from the bathroom counter and twirled it around in his hands. Chloe crossed her arms and leant them against the side of the bathtub.

"I just...." Chloe tried, but she couldn't hold it back anymore she buried her head in her arms and began to cry.

"I knew it was too much, I'll leave the room." Lee quickly said, his heart breaking a little for her.

"No, wait!" she called. Lee stopped in the doorway and turned to face her.

"Come over here." she said quietly, holding out her hand to him. He quickly walked back towards her and took her hand. As soon as he sat on the floor Chloe quickly leaned towards him and kissed him deeply, the tears still flowing freely down her cheeks.

"Please tell me these are happy tears." Lee said wiping them away with his thumb when Chloe eventually let go of him.

"Of course, they are, you are so amazing. You're everything I ever wanted." she sobbed. He smiled at her, his hands quickly gathering up her hair and placing the grip in. Chloe smiled slightly as Lee scooped up some of the bubbles and gently placed them on her nose. She laughed and scooped some up in her hand, gently blowing them at him, bursting out laughing when they stuck to his face.

"That's better." he said when he heard her laugh.

"My Dad would've loved you. I've finally found someone to take care of me." Chloe smiled at him.

"And I'm never going anywhere." he told her.

"Unless you ask me too of course." he quickly added, grinning mischievously. Chloe rolled her eyes at him and kissed him again.

"The necklace really suits you." Lee smiled, slowly running his finger down the chain and onto the pendant.

"It's so beautiful." Chloe agreed.

"Like it's owner." he smiled at her.

"I did notice that the stone is blue." she giggled, completely ignoring the compliment that Lee had just given her.

"It's a sapphire." he told her, noticing that she had completely disregarded the compliment but deciding that it wasn't the right time to push it. Chloe smiled and rested her head against his shoulder.

"I'm so nervous." she whispered.

"I know, me too." he said.

"At least you actually know what you're doing, you're like a pro." Chloe giggled, trying to diffuse her tension.

"I'm just afraid that I'm going to hurt you." he whispered, gently planting a kiss on her forehead.

"Even if you do, it won't be on purpose." she told him gently, removing her head from his shoulder and looking him in the eye.

"I trust you." she whispered. Lee smiled at her. His heart pounded against his chest as he processed her words. He couldn't believe how lucky he was to have her. This young, naturally beautiful woman who was so pure and innocent, like all of her hardships hadn't tainted her. Her sweet, kind nature still shone through and he knew that she would do anything for him. And here she was, ready to place her trust in him of all people.

"And you think it's you that doesn't deserve me." he whispered so quietly; he wasn't entirely sure if she heard. Chloe smiled at Lee as he placed a soft kiss on the corner of her lips before slowly trailing kisses along her jawline, finally stopping when he reached her neck.

"Seriously though, how do I know what to do?" Chloe asked him nervously. Lee instantly stopped kissing her neck.

"You don't have to do anything." he told her.

"You're supposed to teach me though so that I know how to keep you happy and stuff." she squeaked, her cheeks colouring as she gazed at the ground, too embarrassed to look him in the eye.

"Not tonight though, tonight is about making you as comfortable as possible." he told her. Chloe nodded slowly, still gazing at the floor. Lee cupped her chin and gently tipped it upwards so that she was finally looking him in the eye.

"So, you let me take the lead okay." he told her.

"Okay." she replied quietly.

"Are you on the pill?" he asked her.

"I started taking it after I recovered from the stabbing, just in case." she told him.

"Good." he said.

"I think I'm ready to get out now." she said quietly.

"Okay, I'll wait in the bedroom." he told her, quickly standing up.

"You have your clothes there, so you have the choice to come out wearing as much or as little as you are comfortable with." he said, standing in the doorway.

"Okay." she smiled at him.

"There's no rush, take as long as you need." he smiled at her before quickly closing the bathroom door behind himself.

As soon as Lee left the room, Chloe climbed out of the bath and wrapped a warm towel around her slender frame. She reached up to unclip her hair and quickly brushed it through. She sighed sadly as she caught a glimpse of her reflection in the bathroom mirror. If only she was beautiful, she'd have given anything to be able to walk out of the bathroom with her head held high, but she knew that was never going to happen. She slowly unwrapped the towel and pulled on her underwear. Her eyes wandered to the very visible scar on her abdomen. She traced it with her finger, desperately wishing that it wasn't there, just another thing to make her feel unattractive. Chloe reached out to the doorknob; her hand frozen in place on it. She closed her eyes and took a few deep breaths, trying to calm her nerves. *You can do this.* she told herself over and over again. She quickly opened the door and walked into the bedroom before she could talk herself out of it. As soon as she walked into the room, she saw Lee was perched on the end of the bed, his leg bouncing up and down nervously.

She stood for a moment, hovering nervously, not sure what to do with herself. Lee eventually glanced up at her, his eyes widening as he gazed at her flawless figure.

"Wow Chloe." Lee breathed, his heart pounding against his chest.

"Please don't tell me things that aren't true just to make me feel better." she said quickly, before he could say anything else.

"I wouldn't, I honestly think you are stunning." he told her. She watched him closely as he slowly unfastened his shirt, struggling slightly because his hands were shaking. When he eventually removed it, he quickly stood up in front of Chloe. He gazed down at her, the two of them not touching but so close they could feel the heat radiating from each other's body. Lee gently placed his hands on her ribs, gently stroking the material of her bra with his thumb. He could feel her trembling nervously under his touch.

"Are you ready to do this?" he whispered in her ear. She hesitated a moment before nodding. Lee took her hand and slowly led her over to the bed. He waited until she laid down and climbed onto the bed, laying on his side beside her. Chloe turned on her side to face him and smiled nervously, her cheeks colouring. Lee wrapped his left arm around her head and began to slowly stroke her hair. His other hand gently traced circles on her bare stomach. Chloe leaned forward to kiss him tenderly. After a few moments they broke the kiss, the two of them slightly breathless. Chloe glanced down at Lee's hand that was still gently stroking her stomach and winced slightly.

"What's wrong?" he asked worriedly, noticing her change in expression.

"I really hate that scar." she said quietly.

"I don't." he told her, tracing his thumb along it.

"It's part of you." he added, leaning down to plant a kiss on it. Chloe sighed in pleasure and gently stroked Lee's hair as he continued to plant kisses on her abdomen, slowly trailing his way upwards, along her sternum and collarbone. As soon as he reached her, he slowly made his way back down the way he came, teasing her. When he reached her abdomen, Chloe arched her back towards him. He smiled to himself when he heard Chloe sigh disappointingly when he stopped kissing her. As soon as Lee's face came back to hers, she quickly wrapped her arms around his neck.

"You doing okay?" he asked her.

"Um hum." she mumbled, not really trusting her voice. Lee kissed her lips gently for a moment before quickly deepening the kiss. He could feel the goosebumps on Chloe's slender legs as he gently ran his hand up them. Chloe gasped against his mouth as she felt Lee gently place his hand inside her underwear.

"It's okay." he told her gently.

"I know, I'm fine." she whispered. As Lee continued what he was doing, Chloe snuggled closer to him, her whole body now pressed against him, her forehead pressed against his collarbone. Her whole body trembled against Lee as an occasional whimper escaped her lips.

"I actually can't cope with how hot you look right now." he admitted hoarsely. She lifted her head slightly and placed a soft kiss on his lips, gently resting her forehead against his, enjoying the feel of his warm breath on her face. Chloe could feel her legs becoming weak as Lee continued with his hand in her underwear.

"Lee....I..." she said in a small voice.

"I know, just relax and go with it." he reassured her. As soon as Lee said those words Chloe closed her eyes and felt herself release. Shockwaves rippled through her body as she collapsed against him. Lee placed his hands on her hips and sat up, gently pulling her with him so that she was on his lap.

"You really are a pro." she whispered, still slightly breathless.

"You've no idea how hard it is for me to not just take you right now." he breathed, glancing down at Chloe when she began to plant a series of gentle kisses on his bare chest. Chloe quickly looked up at him and smiled slightly.

"Do it then." she said quietly. Before Lee could say anything, Chloe reached down and began to undo his belt, her hands fumbling slightly. Lee slowly reached around her and unclasped her bra. As soon as it fell onto the bed, Chloe instinctively wrapped her arms across her chest, covering her breasts.

"Sorry." she whispered when she realised what she'd done.

"You don't have to apologise." he told her gently.

"Just take a minute." he added, slowly climbing off the bed and removing his trousers and boxers, before climbing back on the bed beside her.

"I really wish I had your body confidence." she admitted.

"You will one day." he reassured her. He held his hands out in front of her and raised his eyebrow, waiting for her to place her hands in his. After a few moments she reluctantly lowered her arms and placed her hands in his. Lee's eyes were drawn to her perfectly formed breasts, but he didn't allow himself to stare, the last thing he wanted to do was to make her even more self-conscious than she already was. Chloe stared at her hands as Lee placed them on her lap and let go of them. His hands trailed up to her knickers and he expertly removed them.

"Lay back then." he told her gently. She remained silent and quickly did as he asked, feeling slightly embarrassed as she lay in front of him, completely naked. Chloe gazed into Lee's eyes as he gently climbed on top of her.

"Ready?" he asked her. She nodded slowly and closed her eyes, bracing herself for the pain. Chloe gasped and bit her lip as Lee slowly pushed part of the way into her.

"Don't bite your lip, you'll make it bleed." he said gently, before brushing his finger along her lips and carefully pulling her lip out from between her teeth.

"It's not actually too bad." she said quietly.

"That's only part of it." Lee told her sadly. He propped himself up on his elbows and quickly took Chloe's hands, gently guiding them to the bed post.

"Here, grip this." he told her, curling her hands around the rails.

"It might help." he added quietly. Before Lee could talk himself out of it, he gently pushed the rest of the way into her. Chloe cried out in pain and gripped the rails tightly. She screwed her eyes shut, trying to ignore the searing pain between her legs. Lee's stomach turned with guilt as he watched the woman that he loved in pain because of him.

"I knew this was a bad idea." he muttered under his breath. Chloe's eyes snapped open. "I'm fine." she said, trying to reassure him.

"No, you're not." Lee whispered, gently kissing away the tears that were rolling down Chloe's cheeks.

"Please Lee, I want this." she told him. He sighed to himself, afraid to move in case he hurt her more. In the turmoil of his thoughts an idea suddenly popped into his head.

"Alexa, play Broken by Lee Knight." he said loudly. Chloe smiled slightly as she heard their song start to play. She frowned to herself as she heard Lee's powerful voice sing the opening.

"Did you record a new version?" she asked.

"Yeah, I recorded a version where I sing the whole song. I was saving it for your birthday, but it seems more appropriate now." he explained. Chloe smiled at him, her heart fluttering in her chest. Whenever she listened to Lee sing it made her feel light and fluffy, even more so when he sang *their* song.

"Just focus on the song." he whispered in her ear.

Chapter Forty

Chloe sighed quietly and slowly sat up in bed, glancing over at Lee who was still laying on his back, staring silently at the bedroom ceiling. She watched him closely, feeling slightly concerned as to why he was so quiet. Chloe reached down to the end of the bed and picked up Lee's shirt, quickly pulling it over her naked frame, feeling comforted when she realised that it smelt of him. Chloe jumped as Lee suddenly sat up and climbed off the bed.

"Is something wrong?" she asked him, when he still hadn't looked at her.

"I need to shower." he said quietly, quickly walking into the bathroom and closing the door. Chloe sighed, her shoulders sagging in disappointment. She hadn't really known what to expect, nor did she know how she felt. All she knew was that she wanted Lee to hold her in his arms and tell her that everything was okay.

She gazed down at her hands that were in her lap and silently picked her fingernails, like she always did when she was uncomfortable. She couldn't help but feel like Lee was disappointed in her. Chloe gasped as she suddenly noticed spots of fresh blood on Lee's sheets. Even though she was alone in the room, she could still feel her cheeks flush in embarrassment. She quickly climbed off the bed and frantically pulled off the sheet, before screwing into a ball and angrily throwing it on the floor. Chloe suddenly felt overcome with emotion, she dropped to the floor, tears steadily rolling down her cheeks. She couldn't understand why she was feeling this way, she'd wanted this. It was her that had talked Lee into it, she knew in her heart that she didn't regret it, but at the same time she felt strangely emotional. Her eyes flickered upwards as Lee walked out of the bathroom, a towel wrapped around his waist.

"Are you okay?" he asked quickly as soon as he noticed her sitting on the floor, beside the crumpled bed sheet.

Lee's heart ached for her a little when he saw that she was crying quietly.

"Yes, I just need to get this washed." she said. She quickly gathered the sheet into her arms and slowly stood up, wincing slightly as she did so. Lee remained silent, watching her closely, not sure what to say to her. He glanced down as something caught his eye, his breath catching in his throat as he saw a trickle of blood slowly running down the inside of her leg.

"Chloe, you're bleeding." he told her gently. Chloe quickly glanced down at herself and gasped when she saw that he was right.

"I'll take that, you go and clean yourself up." he told her, holding out his hand to take the sheet from her. She nodded slowly, before handing him the sheet and quickly disappearing into the bathroom.

Lee sighed deeply as he quickly walked downstairs and angrily stuffed the sheet into the washing machine. He closed his eyes for a moment and rested his head against the machine. He couldn't get the image of Chloe being in pain out of his head. Even though she'd wanted this, he still couldn't help but feel guilty that he was the cause of the pain that she was feeling. As soon as he realised that he'd made her bleed he'd been even more racked with guilt than before. She was so precious to him, the likes of which he'd never felt before and even though he'd been as careful as possible, he'd still managed to injure her.

Lee slowly stood up and made his way back upstairs, glancing at the bathroom door on the way past when he heard Chloe switch off the shower. He quickly found a fresh sheet in the cupboard and began to make the bed. His head snapped up as Chloe finally walked out of the bathroom. She glanced at him for a moment before leaving the room. He frowned to himself as he heard her walking downstairs.

Chloe breathed a sigh of relief as she sat down on the sofa, her legs curled up beside her. She quickly placed a hot water bottle on her groin and took a sip of her tea. As she sat alone with her thoughts, she found herself longing once again to be curled up with Lee. Even though she felt strange and vulnerable, she knew in her heart that he wasn't to blame. It was her own insecurities playing on her mind again. Her eyes wandered across the room as Lee walked into the room, looking slightly nervous.

"Aren't you coming to bed?" he asked her quietly.

"Yes, in a minute." she said quietly. Lee nodded slowly and crossed the room, awkwardly perching on the sofa beside her. She glanced down at his hand as he gently placed it on her knee.

"I'm so sorry Chlo." he whispered.

"Sorry for what?" she frowned.

"The last thing I wanted to do was hurt you." he sighed. Chloe sighed quietly, feeling slightly sorry for him. She quickly shuffled forward and wrapped her arms around his neck. Lee remained still and didn't even react when she placed a soft kiss on his cheek.

"You're overthinking things, it only hurt at the beginning." she reassured him. Eventually he turned to face her and raised his eyebrow sceptically.

"And I wanted this." she added.

"Are you sure you're okay?" he asked gently.

"Yes, I'm fine, honestly." she whispered. Lee glanced down at Chloe as she gently shuffled onto his lap, her arms still wrapped tightly around his neck.

"I love you so much." she whispered, gently resting her forehead against his cheek.

"I love you too." he whispered back. The two of them sighed quietly, finally feeling content now that they were where they both needed to be.

"Thank you for being so gentle with me." Chloe mumbled sleepily.

"You don't have to thank me." he said quietly. Lee turned his head slightly and placed a tender kiss on her lips.

"We should probably go to bed, before you fall asleep." he smiled when he noticed that Chloe was slowly getting sleepier by the minute. Chloe nodded slowly. She winced as she started to move off Lee's lap.

"Wait a minute." he said, quickly wrapping his arms around her hips to hold her in place on his lap.

"Does it hurt more when you walk?" he asked. Chloe nodded, her cheeks colouring slightly. Lee smiled at her reassuringly as he quickly placed one arm around her back and used the other arm to scoop up her legs. She smiled happily at him as he gently stood up, carrying her carefully in his arms. Lee glanced down at her as she gently wrapped her arms around his neck and placed her head on his shoulder. He couldn't help but smile at how adorable she looked. He opened his mouth to tell her but stopped himself when he noticed that her body had relaxed, and her breathing was steady. For the second time that evening she had fallen asleep in his arms.

Chapter Forty-One

"Chloe, wake up." Lee whispered gently in her ear. Chloe sighed quietly and slowly opened her eyes, jumping slightly when she saw that Lee was standing at the side of the bed, leaning over to whisper in her ear. She frowned to herself when she realised that he was dressed.

"What time is it?" she asked sleepily.

"Almost lunchtime." he told her, smiling slightly.

"Oh god." Chloe whispered, slowly rubbing her eyes.

"I have to go to Mum's." he told her, smiling at how adorable she looked.

"Wasn't I meant to be coming with you?" she asked.

"It's fine Chloe, I'll just go." he said quietly, placing a quick peck on her lips before he stood up.

"Are you sure?" she asked, feeling slightly guilty.

"Yeah, it's fine, just have a quiet day. You look tired." he said quietly, suddenly feeling a little bit worried about her. He gently placed his hand on her forehead to check that she wasn't running warm.

"You feel okay." he told her, an edge of concern present in his voice.

"I'm fine, I'm just tired." she reassured him.

"Just make sure you get plenty of rest." he said. Chloe nodded and watched Lee sadly as he walked away, stopping for a moment in the doorway.

"Oh, I forgot to say, the Eclipse boys are coming over for dinner this evening...." Lee started.

"Why?" Chloe interrupted, sighing slightly. She'd been looking forward to having a quiet weekend.

"Because we have a surprise for you." he smiled.

"Anyway, depending on what time they come over they might get here before I'm back." he quickly added.

"Oh great....so Nathan is going to grill me about last night." she said quietly.

"Just tell him to mind his own business." he said.

"Yeah, I'm sure that'll work." she said sarcastically.

"I have to go. I'll see you later." Lee said, before quickly walking away.

Chloe smiled to herself as she carefully set out the cardboard boxes on the kitchen counter and began to share out the tins of food between them. She jumped as she heard the front door open and close, glancing up as Steven, Adrian and Nathan walked into the kitchen.

"Hey Chlo Bo." Nathan smiled when he saw her.

"Hey." she smiled. She frowned to herself as when she suddenly noticed that they were carrying suitcases.

"Are you guys going away somewhere?" she frowned.

"We are flying to Germany in the morning remember, that's why we are staying over here and heading off first thing." Nathan told her.

"To Germany, is this to film the soundtrack video?" she asked.

"Yeah, we decided to go along with it and film it in Germany." Adrian piped up.

"Didn't Lee tell you?" Steven frowned.

Chloe shook her head slowly, feeling slightly confused as to why Lee wouldn't have told her.

"To be fair, we only got told this morning." Nathan said quickly.

"It's a bit last minute, I'll need to pack some things." she sighed.

"Erm..." Adrian said awkwardly but trailed off.

"What?" she said quickly.

"Matt is standing in for you." Nathan told her gently, not entirely sure how she was going to react.

"Why?" she frowned.

The three of them shrugged awkwardly and quickly looked away from her, clearly not sure what they were supposed to say. Nathan sighed quietly to himself, wishing not for the first time that Lee wasn't such an idiot. He should have already had this conversation with Chloe, before the three of them arrived to save her the embarrassment and them the awkwardness that they were feeling.

"Does Lee not want me there?" she asked in a small voice.

"I'm going to go and get settled in my room." Adrian said quickly, clearly trying to avoid the uncomfortable atmosphere. Steven nodded and quickly followed him.

"Nathan?" Chloe asked again.

"He just said that Matt should go." he told her quietly.

"So, he doesn't want me there then.... great." she whispered. As she stood angrily packing the tins into the boxes, she couldn't help but feel disappointed in herself. She'd given her virginity to the man that she loved last night and now he didn't even want her around. She gasped as a thought suddenly entered her head, maybe this was his plan all along, and in her naivety, she'd fallen for someone who just wanted to take advantage of her. Or worse.... maybe he wanted to go to Germany without her so that he could go out clubbing with the beautiful models just like he used too. She had been such a disappointment to him last night, because she didn't know what she was doing that he needed to get some decent sex.

"You alright?" Nathan asked her, when she accidentally banged a tin into the box, much harder than she meant too.

"Yep." she replied shortly.

"There's quite a lot of media attention around this video, I think he just wants to protect you from it." he told her.

"Or he's embarrassed to be seen with me." she said quietly.

"No, he's not, there's been a rumour going around that he has a girlfriend, so I think he wants to make sure they don't find out it's you." he tried again.

"How long are you going for?" she asked.

"Four days I think." he told her.

"Great." she muttered. Chloe bit her lip to try and control the tears that were slowly filling up her eyes.

She didn't want to live in Lee's pocket, and she knew that she couldn't follow him everywhere, but four days seemed like a lifetime to be apart from him. Four days that he would be away from her, with beautiful models and fans throwing themselves at him, just like they always did. He's such a highly sexed person that she knew he wouldn't be able to resist.

"He's going to cheat on me isn't he." Chloe whispered sadly, folding her arms across her chest that was suddenly feeling very tight.

"No Chloe, I don't think he would do that to you." he said quietly.

"Like hell he wouldn't." she muttered.

"I made him wait weeks and last night wasn't fun for him." she added thoughtfully.

Nathan opened his mouth to reply but Chloe interrupted him:

"Oh my god, he's going to cheat on me, I'm such an idiot." she said, beginning to panic.

"He won't Chloe and even if he tries to, I won't let him." he reassured her. She sighed quietly, trying to calm herself down from the panic she was feeling. Nathan gently pulled her into a hug, squeezing her gently to try and provide some comfort. He couldn't help but feel sad for her, that her insecurities were so bad that she couldn't imagine anyone ever loving her enough to not want to hurt her.

"I can't lose him, he's all I have." she whispered against Nathan's chest. Chloe closed her eyes, feeling the tears that she'd been holding back, finally flow down her cheeks. Nathan frowned as he heard the front door open and close and what sounded like a female voice coming from the hallway. He glanced down at Chloe, who didn't seem to have noticed, she still had her eyes closed.

"What's going on?" Lee asked as soon as he walked into the kitchen and saw Nathan holding an upset Chloe. Chloe slowly removed herself from Nathan's arms and quickly wiped away her tears.

"Nothing, I'm just being stupid as usual." she said quietly.

"You'd better not have been grilling her about last night." Lee rounded on Nathan, assuming that was the reason for Chloe being upset.

"I didn't even mention it." Nathan said.

"Good, because that subject is off the table." Lee said sharply. Nathan nodded and glanced between the two of them awkwardly, not quite sure what to say or do. Chloe glanced at Lee, quickly looking away when she saw that he was watching her closely. Even though she was hurting at the thought of him not wanting her to come to Germany with him, she knew that she couldn't allow herself to pull back from him. If she did that, Chloe knew that he would be even more likely to cheat on her, and then she would lose him forever. Before she could talk herself out of it, she crossed the room and quickly placed herself in his arms. He stiffened for a moment in shock, then quickly relaxed and wrapped his arms around her small frame, holding her tightly. Her skin tingled as he rested his head on her shoulder and gently stroked her hair.

"What's wrong Chlo?" he asked gently.

"I just love you so much." she whispered, her voice breaking slightly.

"Who's that?" Nathan asked as the heard a woman's laugh coming from the living room.

"Mum insisted on coming back with me to meet Chloe." Lee said, rolling his eyes.

"What?" Chloe whispered, letting go of Lee and gazing up at him. Lee nodded slowly.

"Oh god, what if she hates me?" she said nervously.

"She won't." Lee said quickly.

"Oh, and I need to talk to you about tomorrow." he added when he suddenly remembered.

"You mean Germany, I already know." she said quietly.

"Yeah, sorry that was our fault, we thought you'd already told her." Nathan quickly piped up.

"I was going to, but you were still sleepy when I left." Lee told Chloe. She nodded slowly.

"I messaged Kirstie and asked her to get the girls together, they can come and stay here with you while I'm away." he added when she didn't say anything.

"Fine." she said shortly, not sure why he'd done that. She couldn't help but wonder if he didn't trust her.

"What's with all these boxes anyway?" Nathan asked, trying to break the tension.

"Food parcels, I take them to the park every week." Chloe said.

"That reminds me, I have the rest of the food in the car." Lee said quickly.

"And who funds all of this?" Lee's Mum Sheila asked as she walked into the room. Chloe jumped and dropped a tin onto the floor.

"So presumably it's you?" Sheila asked, staring at Lee.

"Nope." Lee said quickly, glancing at Chloe who looked like she wanted the ground to swallow her up.

"Well, I highly doubt a homeless person can afford to buy all this." Sheila pointed out.

"Chuck me the keys, I'll get the stuff out of the car." Nathan said quickly. Lee nodded and threw Nathan the car keys, which he swiftly caught.

"I got a promotion, so the little bit of extra money that I have, I use it to make food parcels for the people that really need it. I have a deal with the local shop that I buy the short-dated food because it's a bit cheaper." Chloe explained quietly.

"Instead of paying for your keep?" Sheila asked raising her eyebrow.

Chloe opened her mouth to respond but Lee beat her to it:

"She gives me food money Mum." he sighed. Sheila rolled her eyes at Lee and fell silent. Lee couldn't help but feel disappointed in how his Mum was behaving. He knew that if she would just give Chloe a chance, she would see how special she is. But as she'd spent the past few hours telling Lee, she couldn't help but feel that Chloe was just another beautiful girl trying to take advantage of her son.It didn't help that she knew about her living situation, so as far as Sheila was concerned, Chloe was with Lee for purely financial reasons.

"I think I'll go and help Nathan." Chloe said sadly, before quickly leaving the room. Lee smiled at her reassuringly as she walked past.

"You need to cut her some slack Mum." Lee said sternly as soon as Chloe was out of earshot.

"I'm just worried that she's with you because she wants your money." she replied.

"She's not like that Mum, she has a heart of gold. She's in so much debt that she goes to work and hardly has any money left over. The small amount that she does have left she spends on the food parcels and she gives me some for her keep." Lee explained.

"Well, she shouldn't have got into debt in the first place." she said quietly.

"It's not her debt, it's her exes." he said shortly, becoming more and more frustrated that his Mum didn't see Chloe the way he did.

"So, she's with you so that you can pay for her to go out and do fun things." she said, rolling her eyes.

"She doesn't really like going out, she prefers nights in." he said quietly.

"She's not like you think Mum, it's not her that doesn't deserve me, it's the other way around." he added.

Lee glanced around as he heard Chloe and Nathan coming back.

"Just give her a chance, please." he whispered. Sheila sighed and nodded reluctantly. Chloe slowly placed the bag of food on the counter and glanced around awkwardly. Lee stared at Sheila and cleared his throat, giving her a subtle signal to talk to Chloe.

"I'm sorry about before, I went all overprotective Mum on you." Sheila said reluctantly.

"That's okay, I understand." Chloe replied shyly.

"I'm Chloe by the way." she added.

"Sheila." she replied awkwardly.

Lee crossed the room and silently helped Chloe to share the food out between the boxes.

"Would you like a cup of tea?" Chloe offered Sheila as she sat at the breakfast bar.

"Yes please, black with one sugar." Sheila smiled. Chloe nodded and began to make the tea. Lee stopped packing the food as a thought suddenly entered his head.

"Make sure you don't take the food to the park until I'm home." he said.
"I won't." she said quietly.

"I don't want you going there on your own." he told her sternly.

"No, I know, I won't. We could take them over on Wednesday when we go and see Danny." she pointed out.

"Sounds like a plan." he agreed.

"Who's Danny?" Sheila asked, smiling her thanks at Chloe as she placed her cup of tea in front of her.

"One of my good friends, I used to live with him at the park. We always had each other's backs so I try and help him out as much as I can." Chloe explained.

"He's a good singer, he goes busking to earn money and I've started going with him." Lee told her.

"You, going busking?!" Sheila frowned.

"Yeah, it's actually quite good fun and I put it out on social media the last time we did it and he made a lot more money. A lot of Eclipse fans came to see him because I was singing with him, it was nice to do something to give back." Lee said. Chloe smiled at him proudly and gently wrapped her arms around his waist. He smiled at her and placed his arm protectively around her shoulders.

"He's written a song too and it's really good, we're trying to convince Matt to let us release it as our next single." Lee added.

"Hopefully he should make enough from the royalties to get himself off the street." Chloe agreed. Sheila shook her head slowly in disbelief.

"What?" Lee frowned.

"You're turning soft." she said proudly.

"That's this one's fault." Lee said smiling down at Chloe, gently planting a kiss on top of her head. Sheila couldn't help but smile to herself as she watched the two of them together. She'd never seen Lee look at someone the way that he looked at Chloe. With such love and admiration, it was clear that he adored her. She couldn't help but notice that Chloe seemed to melt every time that Lee looked at her.

Despite her initial reservations Sheila could clearly see how in love the two of them were. Lee needed someone good like Chloe in his life, she just hoped that he would do the right thing by her. That he would end his womanising ways and hold onto this chance he had for a deep and meaningful relationship. Chloe came across as so kind and innocent that she couldn't help but feel concerned that Lee might break her heart.

"I should probably go and pack. We're leaving early in the morning." Lee said quietly. Chloe sighed and reluctantly letting go of him.

"I'll leave the two of you to bond." he winked as he left the room.

Chapter Forty-Two

"I think my Mum is officially in love with you." Lee told Chloe as he climbed into bed beside her.

"Why?" she laughed.

"I've just spent the past hour being lectured about how I must make sure that I take care of you and that if I break your heart I'll be in trouble." he chuckled.

"Aww that's sweet, I thought she didn't like me." she admitted.

"Well, she loves you now, I'm pretty sure she would adopt you if she could." he laughed. Chloe smiled slightly and continued reading her book. She glanced at Lee as he rolled over on his side to face her and gently began to stroke her arm.

"Did Nathan say something that upset you earlier?" he asked.

"No, I was just being silly. It wasn't his fault." she sighed, slowly placing her book on the nightstand.

"Tell me." he insisted. Chloe glanced down at his hand, that was still gently stroking her arm and sighed.

"I was just a bit upset about you going away." she told him.
"Aww Chloe." he whispered.

"And that you don't want me there." she added.

"I do want you there, but I want to protect you more." he told her.

"The media storm is going to be quite big, and they are letting some fans on set to watch the filming, I don't want you exposed to it. You're an easy target for trolls and stuff." he explained.

"What's that supposed to mean?" she frowned.

"The media are good at finding out everything about people, they'll find out all about you and you'll get trolled for being after my money and fame and stuff. I don't want that for you." he told her gently. Chloe nodded slowly, still feeling slightly uneasy about the potential of him cheating on her, but she decided not to mention it. She wasn't going to believe him anyway when he undoubtedly told her that he wouldn't. Part of her felt a little bit sorry for him, that she'd made him wait so long and he wasn't able to be sexually satisfied by her anyway.

"What are you thinking about, you've gone red?" Lee chuckled, snapping her out of her thoughts. Chloe turned on her side to face him and gently placed her hands on his bare chest. She glanced up at him nervously as she leaned forward and kissed him softly. She wrapped her arms around his neck and gently stroked the back of his neck. Lee watched Chloe as she gently trailed her hands down his chest. He shivered under her touch and closed his eyes, desperately trying to resist her. Before she could do anything else, he took hold of her hands and held them gently.

"Not tonight Chlo." he whispered, gently pushing her body away from him, as he was unable to concentrate with her perfect body pressed against him.

"You don't want me." Chloe sighed sadly.

"I have to get up early." he said matter of factly. Chloe nodded slowly and turned her back to him. She closed her eyes tightly, trying to ignore the fear that she was feeling about him going away. Chloe rushed to answer the door as she heard the doorbell ring. She smiled as she saw Kirstie, Kathleen and Louise standing in the doorway. Her heart sunk as she suddenly noticed Michelle standing behind them. Even though Michelle had finally called Chloe and apologised for her behaviour, that didn't mean that Chloe wanted to spend time with her. Chloe knew that the group had decided to forget about what had happened for the sake of their friendships, but Chloe knew in her heart that she would never forgive her for what she'd done.

"Hi guys, come in." she smiled. Kirstie couldn't resist pulling Chloe into a tight hug as soon as she saw her.

"I didn't invite her, it was Kathleen." Kirstie whispered in Chloe's ear.

"Hi Louise, it's been so long." Chloe said quickly composing herself and hugging her.

"Aww Kathleen, look at you." Chloe smiled at her.

"I'm due in three months." Kathleen replied quietly.

"Oh wow, that's so exciting!" Chloe exclaimed.

"I'm going to be godmother." Michelle stated smugly.

"I haven't decided that yet." Kathleen said quickly.

"Do you guys want to come through to the kitchen, we can get teas and coffees?" Chloe offered as she led them through to the kitchen. Michelle smiled to herself as she placed a carrier bag of alcohol on the kitchen counter.

"Help yourselves to food and drink whilst you are here." Chloe told them.

"I came prepared." Michelle told the group.

"Oh yay!" Louise exclaimed.

"You do realise I can't drink." Kathleen piped up.

"The rest of us can though." Michelle said dismissively.

"I'll stay sober with you Kathleen." Chloe told her, feeling slightly guilty that Kathleen was being left out.

"Why, are you pregnant too?!" Michelle snapped.

"No of course not." Chloe said quietly, frowning at Michelle's harsh tone.

"Well stop being such a prude then." Michelle said firmly.

"You can drink all you like, but I don't want any drunken antics, this isn't my house, and I don't want things getting broken." Chloe warned her.

"How do you work this damn coffee machine?" Kirstie said, running her hands through her hair in frustration.

"It's a bit technical, like everything in this house. Everything is automated and confusing." Chloe laughed and quickly helped Kirstie work the machine.

"This house is stunning though, it's like something out of the movies." Louise breathed.

"You could probably get lost in it." Kathleen agreed.

"Do we get a tour later?" Louise said excitedly.

"If you really want one, it's just a house though." Chloe smiled.

"A luxury house, you're so lucky." Louise said smiling at Chloe. She couldn't help but feel pleased that after everything she'd been through things had finally worked out well for Chloe.

"Yes, but remember ladies, it's not actually Chloe's house." Michelle reminded them. Everyone fell silent and looked at Michelle, not entirely sure what had gotten into her today.

"Are you ladies staying the whole four days?" Chloe eventually asked, trying to break the uncomfortable silence. Kathleen, Kirstie and Louise nodded.

"I shall personally be making the most of living in luxury for a few days." Michelle beamed, as she rummaged in a cupboard and pulled out a wine glass, before quickly pouring herself one.

"It's a bit early in the morning for wine isn't it?" Kirstie chuckled.

"Nope." Michelle replied shortly. The five of them stopped talking as Lee and Nathan walked into the room.

"Right, we are leaving Chlo Bo." Nathan said, quickly pulling Chloe into a hug.

"I'll keep an eye on him." he whispered in her ear so that the others couldn't hear him. Chloe nodded slowly and let go of Nathan.

"Oh shit, we forgot to give her the surprise!" Nathan suddenly exclaimed.

"We'll do it when we get back." Lee said quietly.

"Do you want a glass of wine?" Michelle offered, looking at Lee.

"No thank you." Lee said shortly. Even though Chloe had decided to try and make the effort with Michelle for the sake of the group, he couldn't bring himself to be nice to the person who'd hurt the woman he loved.

"I hadn't realised that you were still going to be here, otherwise I would have worn makeup." Michelle said, smiling flirtily at Lee.

"I hadn't realised that you would be here either." he frowned an edge of anger in his voice. He quickly turned his back on her, giving her the silent signal that he didn't have time for her.

"You know how to work the security system don't you?" Lee asked Chloe.

"Yes, I think so." Chloe said quietly.

"Don't forget Emma will be coming in at some point over the weekend." Lee reminded her.

"Who's Emma?" Kirstie frowned.

"He has a housekeeper." Chloe said, rolling her eyes. Lee smiled slightly.

"Come here then." Lee grinned at Chloe. Chloe shook her head slowly, dreading having to say goodbye to him. Lee chuckled and reached out to take her hand, gently pulling her towards him. As soon as Chloe was in his arms, she wrapped her arms around his waist and held him tightly. Kirstie couldn't help but smile at them as they both held each other tightly, as if neither of them ever wanted to let go.

"I'm going to miss you Chlo." he whispered in her ear.

"I'll miss you too." she whispered sadly.

Eventually Lee reluctantly let go of Chloe and placed his hand on her cheek. Chloe's cheeks coloured as he gently planted a tender kiss on her lips.

"I love you." she whispered.

"I love you too." he smiled, gently kissing her again.

"Right c'mon, we really have to get going, otherwise we are going to miss our flight." Nathan called out, chuckling slightly at the fact that they didn't want to let go of each other. Lee placed his hand on Chloe's neck and gently stroked along her jawline with his thumb.

"Look after her for me." Lee said quietly, turning to Kirstie. Kirstie smiled and nodded. Chloe felt her heart sink as he moved away from her and followed Nathan, glancing back for a moment when he reached the doorway. She couldn't help but feel like he was taking her heart with him. Four days was going to feel like a lifetime to be away from him.

"You alright Chloe?" Kirstie asked, gently wrapping her arm around Chloe's shoulders.

"Yes, I'm fine." she replied quietly.

"You guys are too cute." Louise said smiling warmly at Chloe. Chloe smiled her thanks, suddenly feeling very quiet.

"Do you want the tour then?" Chloe offered, trying to keep busy and distract herself from how she was feeling. Chloe couldn't help but sigh to herself as she led the girls around the house, everywhere that she walked she was reminded of Lee and how much she missed him already.

"Oh my god!" Kathleen exclaimed as Chloe led them into the pool room.

"Yes, I know." Chloe said quietly.

"It's like a leisure centre." Louise breathed.

"What's through that door?" Kirstie asked, pointing down the end of the room, behind the hot tub.

"It's just an empty room at the moment, I think Lee wants to turn it into a gym." Chloe told them.

"You're so lucky to live here." Louise smiled.

"It's not my cup of tea to be honest, it's too grand for my taste. I'm more of a cottage in the countryside kind of person." Chloe admitted.

"Oh, boo hoo, life must be so difficult for you." Michelle snapped.

"What's gotten into you today?" Kirstie frowned.

"Nothing I'm fine." Michelle said shortly.

"Can we go for a swim?" Louise asked hopefully.

"If you want too." Chloe smiled at her. Louise giggled happily and quickly pulled off her clothes, before jumping in the pool in her underwear.

"Come on then." she said excitedly, looking around at the others. Kirstie and Michelle quickly followed suit.

"I can't do that either." Kathleen said quietly. Kathleen removed her shoes and socks and placed her legs in the pool.

"I thought you could go swimming when you're pregnant?" Kirstie frowned.

"Can you?" Kathleen asked.

"I think you can." Louise said.

"It's okay, I'm actually alright here." Kathleen said quietly. Chloe perched awkwardly on one of the sun loungers and watched the girls messing around in the pool, smiling slightly at their laughter.

"Chloe stop pining and come and join in!" Kirstie called.

"I'm not pining." Chloe said quickly.

"Well come and join us then." Kirstie insisted.

"No thank you." Chloe said.

"What's the problem, it's no different than being in a bikini?" Michelle said rolling her eyes.

"Well then it's a good job I've never worn a bikini isn't it!" Chloe snapped, finally reaching the end of her tether with Michelle's constant point scoring. Michelle laughed loudly.

"I thought you were meant to be the young, beautiful one with the banging body." Michelle said smugly.

"I don't know where you got that from, I've never said that or even thought it." Chloe said quietly. She couldn't help but feel confused and hurt by how Michelle was treating her. She had no idea what she had done wrong or why Michelle seemed to be on the warpath against her. Chloe jumped as she heard the doorbell ring. She glanced down at her phone to check the security camera to see who was at the door.

"I need to go and let Emma in." Chloe said quietly, feeling slightly relieved that she had an excuse to leave the room for a few moments.

Chapter Forty-Three

Chloe sighed in frustration as she rummaged through the kitchen drawers, searching for the takeaway menus. She glanced up as Kirstie walked into the room.

"What are you up to?" Kirstie asked her.

"It's getting late, so I'm trying to organise dinner, but I can't find the menus." Chloe sighed.

"Isn't this them here?" Kirstie frowned as she noticed them behind the rolling pin. Chloe nodded and closed the drawer silently.

"Are you alright Chloe?" Kirstie asked worriedly.

"Yes, why?" Chloe frowned.

"Lee messaged me, he's worried about you." Kirstie said.

"He said you didn't answer his calls last night and you are just messaging back short answers to let him know you are okay but not really wanting to talk." Kirstie prompted when Chloe didn't respond.

"It's just easier to put my head in the sand and pretend that it's not happening." Chloe said quietly.

"He's only away for a few days Chloe." Kirstie frowned; not entirely sure what Chloe was talking about.

"I know, it's not that, I'm paranoid he's going to cheat on me." Chloe admitted.

"Don't tell anyone though, I don't want to be an annoying insecure girlfriend." she quickly added.

"I won't tell anyone." Kirstie smiled.

"I don't think it will work long term, someone who is insecure, dating a lady's man." Chloe said thoughtfully.

"That was before the two of you started dating though, everyone has a past, and people can change." Kirstie told her.

"Hmm." Chloe replied sceptically.

"He clearly adores you; he won't want to hurt you or risk what the two of you have." Kirstie reassured her.

"We'll see." Chloe said quietly, still not believing her. She couldn't ignore the bad feeling in her gut that Lee wouldn't be able to resist the temptation.

"You can't keep avoiding him though." Kirstie said.

"It's just easier though, he'll know that something is wrong, he'll keep asking and I'll either have to lie or tell him. He doesn't like hearing about my insecurities." Chloe explained.

"So just tell him that I'm fine, I'm busy playing hostess." Chloe added. The two of them stopped talking as Kathleen, Michelle and Louise walked into the room.

"What are we doing for dinner then?" Kathleen asked.

"I was thinking a takeaway." Chloe said quietly.

"Sounds good." Louise smiled as she began to leaf through the menus.

"How do I switch the tap on?" Michelle frowned as she stood in front of the kitchen sink.

"Hold your hands under it, I told you everything is automated." Chloe told her shortly.

"When you've decided what you want, you can order it on the laptop" Chloe added, placing it in front of them.

"Ooh, is it going on Lee's tab?" Michelle said excitedly.

"No, we'll change the payment method at the end." Chloe snapped, over the past couple of days Michelle was slowly starting to make her blood boil. Chloe glanced at her phone on the counter as it began to ring.

"Who's Sheila?" Kathleen asked as she handed Chloe her phone.

"I need to get that." Chloe said, quickly excusing herself.

"Did you see how defensive she got about spending Lee's money?" Michelle said as soon as Chloe left the room.

"Probably because she thought you were suggesting that he should pay for our food." Kirstie said.

"More likely, she's defensive because she knows that's why she's with him." Michelle pointed out.

"I mean, why else would someone date a guy like him." Michelle tried again when she got no response from the group.

"I don't think that's true Michelle, she clearly loves him." Louise piped up.

"Loves the lifestyle more like it, I mean look at this place, it's easy to pretend to be in love when you get all of this out of it." Michelle said, gesturing around the house.

"If that's the case, do you think that about me and Ben?" Kirstie frowned.

"No, I don't, because you're not homeless and then you conveniently move into his luxury house. It just seems to have all fallen into place for her, almost like it was planned." Michelle explained.

"Well, it sounds to me like you are jealous." Louise said.

"I'm not actually, I'm seeing a celebrity of my own." Michelle said smugly.

"Really, who?!" Kathleen exclaimed excitedly.

"I'm not allowed to say." Michelle said quickly. Kirstie scoffed sceptically, not entirely sure if she believed Michelle or not.

"What was the point in telling us then, if you're only going to tell us half of the story." Louise said, rolling her eyes.

"Because you accused me of being jealous, and I'm not." Michelle insisted.

The four of them stopped talking as Chloe walked back into the room, frowning as everyone stared at her silently.

"What's going on?" Chloe asked nervously.

"We're just figuring out the food." Kathleen said quickly.

"I fancy pizza." Louise piped up, feeling slightly sorry for Chloe that one of her so-called friends seemed to have it in for her.

"I'll only eat half of one if someone wants to share?" Chloe asked.

"Sounds good." Kirstie smiled.

"Maybe we should sort it out in the living room, then I can light a fire while we are getting organised." Chloe suggested. The group nodded and quickly followed Chloe into the lounge. Kirstie and Louise sat on the floor, the laptop between them on the coffee table as they figured out the orders. Chloe glanced at Michelle as she threw herself roughly onto the sofa and poured herself yet another glass of wine.

"Kathleen, why don't you have a look on the TV and pick something for us to watch." Chloe said, handing Kathleen the tv remote. Chloe tuned the girls out as they sat, debating what pizzas they wanted to order. She snapped a piece of kindling in half and placed it in the fireplace.

"Ooh what this one?" Kathleen piped up.

"The guy looks hot." Michelle giggled.

"Oh shit, what have I done?!" Kathleen exclaimed as the television screen changed and the sound of a phone ringing echoed around the living room. Chloe frowned and glanced at the television screen, her heart sinking a little as she saw the display.

"Lee is trying to video call." Chloe said quietly.

"I didn't realise you could do that on a tv." Kirstie said. Kathleen smiled at Chloe and reached out to hand Chloe the remote so that she could take the call. Chloe shook her head.

"Just ignore it." Chloe said shortly. Chloe's cheeks coloured as everyone turned to stare at her, clearly confused by her words.

"Do I sense trouble in paradise?" Michelle said, a slight smile present on her face.

"No, we're fine." Chloe said quietly, glancing at the screen as the call rang out.

"So, you don't have to worry." she added sarcastically, looking Michelle in the eye, almost as if she was daring her to show her true colours. Michelle nodded and quickly looked away, squirming slightly under Chloe's intense gaze.

"Right, I think that's the order done." Kirstie piped up, trying to break the uncomfortable silence.

"I hope they deliver it soon, I'm so hungry." Kathleen sighed.

"That's because you're eating for two." Louise smiled at her.

"I think that's just an excuse for pregnant women to binge, but I'm sticking with it so oh well." Kathleen giggled.

"Put the movie on now then, while we wait for the food." Louise smiled. Chloe moved away from the fire and lay down on the sofa. She slowly picked up a cushion and hugged it against her chest. She couldn't help but remember the last time she'd laid on this part of the sofa. It was the night that she'd curled up with Lee and fell asleep on him, on the night that she'd given her virginity to him. She hugged the cushion tighter, wishing that she could hug Lee. She hated how much her insecurities affected her life, as much as she tried to fight them, they were always there, in the back of her mind, almost like they were whispering to her.

Part of her knew that Lee didn't want to do anything to hurt her, but she couldn't stop the nagging doubt. Chloe jumped as the movie stopped as Lee tried to call her on Skype again.

"I need a drink." Chloe said, before quickly standing up and leaving the room. Even though she was trying to protect herself she couldn't help but feel guilty for avoiding him. Kirstie stood up and quickly followed Chloe.

"Hand me the remote." Michelle hissed as soon as Chloe left the room, leaning across to swipe the remote out of Kathleen's hand. Kathleen and Louise watched in horror as Michelle answered the call. Lee looked relieved for a moment, his eyes quickly scanning the room, his face falling when he realised that Chloe wasn't there.

"Hi everyone." he said quietly.

"Hello." Louise said awkwardly, feeling slightly uncomfortable that Michelle had deliberately gone against Chloe's wishes. Kathleen waved silently.

"You look very handsome this evening Lee." Michelle said smiling sweetly.

"Erm...okay." he said awkwardly.

"Germany clearly suits you." Michelle said.

"Not really, my girl isn't here." Lee said shortly.

"Where is she anyway?" he quickly added.

"She's around somewhere." Michelle shrugged.

Louise watched Michelle in a state of numb shock as she watched her flirting with Chloe's boyfriend. Even though Lee was handsome, Louise would never dream of flirting with someone who was taken, especially when that someone meant the world to one of their friends. She couldn't understand why Michelle would want to do anything to hurt Chloe, no matter how jealous she was of her.

"How is the filming for the video going?" Louise asked, trying to stop Michelle from being able to speak to Lee.

"It's going really well; we've pretty much done all of it. It's been fun having the cast on set too." Lee smiled at her.

"Wow, that's amazing, so will you be coming home earlier than planned?" Louise asked, desperately trying to keep him talking.

"No unfortunately not. We have some promo stuff to do for the new album while we are here." he replied.

"Are you ladies enjoying your girls' weekend?" Lee asked. Louise opened her mouth to answer, but before she could say anything Michelle piped up:

"Your house is amazing." Michelle said. Lee smiled slightly.

"If ever you need any company when Chloe isn't around, I'd happily spend some more time here." she quickly added, flashing him a big smile. Lee stared at her in shock, not entirely sure what to say in response to her comment.

"Michelle!" Louise warned sternly.

"I was only joking, lighten up." Michelle said quickly.

"Speaking of Chloe, can you put her on please?" Lee asked firmly when he'd eventually recovered himself.

"I'll go and get her." Louise smiled.

"Thank you." Lee smiled at her.

Louise quickly walked into the kitchen, smiling at Kirstie and Chloe as she saw them attempting to mix cocktails.

"Lee wants to speak to you." Louise said quietly.

"But I ignored him." Chloe frowned.

"Yeah, well.... Michelle answered it." Louise said nervously.

"What, why would she do that?!" Chloe exclaimed.

"I don't know, but I think you should come and talk to him." Louise said.

"I don't want too." Chloe said sadly.

"Do you want me to go and say that you are busy?" Kirstie offered. Chloe nodded slowly.

Kirstie walked into the living room, frowning at the uncomfortable silence. She couldn't help but wonder what had happened to cause such a tense atmosphere. Lee felt his heart drop when he saw Kirstie walking into the room. He couldn't understand why Chloe had been avoiding him for the past two days. He knew she was upset about him going away, but he was becoming more and more worried that something had happened or that he'd somehow done something to upset her.

"Where is she Kirstie?" Lee sighed sadly.

"She's busy." Kirstie said quickly, suddenly realising she hadn't thought through an excuse before she came into the room.

"She's not really, she's just saying that." Michelle piped up.

"Doing what?" Lee asked, completely ignoring Michelle.

"In the bathroom." Kirstie said.

"Yeah, well she's been busy for the past two days, even though you are all having a quiet weekend." Lee sighed in frustration.

"You can just speak to me instead." Michelle giggled.

"What for?" Lee snapped.

"Well, you didn't mind speaking to me that night in the club did you." Michelle grinned.

Lee sighed and rolled his eyes.

"Wait, she didn't go to the park, to drop off those bloody food parcels, did she?!" Lee exclaimed suddenly, sounding slightly panicked.

"No, she didn't, she's in the house. She's safe." Kirstie reassured him. She couldn't help but smile at him as she saw him visibly relax.

"Chloe, I think you should go in and speak to him." Louise suggested as she watched Chloe lean against the counter, silently biting her fingernails. She shook her head slowly.

"But Michelle is flirting with him, quite a lot. I think you need to put a stop to it." Louise told her.

"People flirt with Lee all the time, it's just what happens." Chloe sighed.

"Yeah, but she's doing it when she knows he's your boyfriend, in his living room, on his tv, just to get to you. Don't let her get away with it." Louise insisted. Chloe glanced at Louise and nodded slowly, knowing that she was right. Lee and Chloe had tried to make the effort with her, even after everything that she'd done, and she was continuing to bitch and point score. And now she was trying to take the thing that was most precious to Chloe, just to prove a point. Chloe quickly walked into the living room before she could talk herself out of it.

"There's my girl." Lee said happily as soon as he saw her. Chloe smiled at him and rested her arms on the back of the sofa, leaning over slightly.

"You alright, you're not still sore, are you?" he asked worriedly. Chloe shook her head slowly, wincing at his words.

"Sore, what happened?" Kathleen frowned. Lee glanced at Chloe nervously for a moment, suddenly remembering that the others were still in the room. As soon as he'd seen Chloe, he was so focused on her, he'd forgotten they were there.

"Our idiot of a choreographer tried to perform a trick with her and ended up dropping her." Lee said, thinking quickly.

"It was a few days ago, I'm not sore anymore." Chloe said quietly, locking eyes with Lee, the two of them almost speaking in code.

"How is Germany?" Chloe asked awkwardly.

"It's alright, we've been very busy so it's tiring." he answered. Chloe nodded slowly, the two of them falling silent once again.

"I spoke to Matt about Danny's song." Lee told her.

"What did he say?" she asked.

"He thought it was a really nice idea, and we are going to release it as our next single off the album." he said.

"That's great, Danny will be so happy." Chloe smiled. Lee nodded slowly.

"The other thing I need to talk to you about is that Matt wants to have your song on the album and for it to be the third single. But I want to check that you are happy with the idea?" he asked her.

"I don't mind either way. It's your song anyway, you wrote it." Chloe pointed out.

"Yeah, about my feelings for you." he said quietly.

"It should be fine, just don't tell anyone that it's about me." Chloe sighed.

"No, I wouldn't, the media would definitely latch onto that." he agreed. Lee glanced up as the door to his hotel room opened.

"What are you doing?" Chloe heard Nathan's voice say.

"Speaking to Chloe." Lee told him. Nathan smiled and quickly peered around the laptop screen, beaming at Chloe cheekily. Chloe couldn't help but smile at the cheeky glint in his eye.

"Have you shown her the picture yet?" Nathan asked, grinning mischievously.

"No, I haven't, stop it." Lee said quickly.

"What picture?" Chloe frowned.

"He took a nude photo of himself, just for you." Nathan laughed, winking at Chloe.

Chloe's cheeks coloured as everyone burst out laughing.

"I think you'll like it." Nathan added, teasing her. Chloe hid her face in her arms as everyone stared at her.

"Stop it, you're embarrassing her." Lee said quickly.

"Let's see the photo then." Michelle said, sounding slightly excited.

"Yeah Lee, let's see it." Nathan bantered.

"Chloe." Lee said softly, trying to get her to take her head out of her arms and look at him.

"What?" she asked nervously, wincing slightly as she raised her head, slightly nervous about what she was going to see.

"I didn't take a nude photo." Lee said, smiling slightly at how adorable Chloe looked when she was embarrassed.

"He did Chloe." Nathan insisted.

"I didn't, he's just being a shit." Lee laughed, elbowing Nathan firmly in the ribs. Nathan fell out of shot, a loud thud echoing around the room as he landed roughly on the floor.

"Ow, you dick!" Nathan exclaimed.

"It's your own bloody fault." Lee chuckled.

"So, there isn't a picture then?" Chloe frowned in confusion.

"No there is, it's just not a nude." Lee said, glaring over at Nathan.

"Aww that's a shame." Michelle said.

"Is it?" Lee snapped.

"Oh definitely." Michelle giggled.

"Michelle, back off." Kirstie hissed under her breath.

"Okay don't be mad, but you know how you hate having your picture taken?" Lee said nervously. Chloe nodded and waited for him to continue.

"Well, I wanted a photo of us together, so I took this the other day." he told her, quickly picking up his phone and entering the pin. He smiled slightly as he glanced at the photo, before slowly turning the phone around to face the computer screen. Chloe gasped as she looked at the picture. It was a black and white photo of Chloe sleeping peacefully in Lee's arms. Lee had closed his eyes and turned his face so that he was snuggling against her.

Chloe could feel herself melting a little as she stared, transfixed at the photo of the two of them.

"Aww, that's adorable." Kirstie said, smiling happily. It was so evident, even just from a photo, how much they loved each other.

"Is that from the night I fell asleep on you?" Chloe asked, her voice catching slightly.

"Yeah, I couldn't resist, you looked so beautiful." Lee said quietly. Chloe's cheeks coloured again, and she quickly looked at the floor.

"Also, I need a picture of my girlfriend on my phone, so I caught you unawares." he chuckled. Chloe felt her heart flutter a little, like it always did when he called her his girlfriend.

"Isn't love beautiful." Nathan laughed, poking his head around to the screen again.

"Seriously, will you go away." Lee laughed.

"Fine, I'll leave you to it." Nathan said, holding his hands up in defeat and finally leaving the room.

"So, do you like the picture then?" Lee smiled at Chloe.

"I guess." she replied quietly.

"I'll send it to you later." he told her.

"Once I crop myself out of it, I'll like it a lot more." she sighed. Lee sighed sadly to himself. He couldn't help but wish that he was beside her, so that he could kiss her and hold her tightly, like he always did when she spoke negatively about herself.

"I really hate it when people say stuff like that to fish for a compliment." Michelle said angrily, before quickly downing her glass of wine.

"Chloe hates compliments so you clearly don't know her very well." Lee snapped quickly, before anyone else could say anything.

"Sure, she does." Michelle laughed.

"You know what, either you wind your neck in or you can leave my house!" Lee told her angrily.

"Lee, it's fine, just leave it." Chloe said quietly.

"Can you go and get the spare laptop please Chlo?" he asked her, trying to distract himself from the anger that was slowly building inside him.

"What for?" Chloe asked.

"So that I can transfer the call over, I need to talk to you about something." he said quietly.

"But I..." Chloe started.

"Chloe, please just do it." he said firmly.

"Okay fine." she sighed.

Chapter Forty-Four

Lee remained silent as he waited for Chloe to return with the laptop. He kept his eyes fixed on Michelle, an intense gaze that was silently warning her not to say anything. Chloe returned a few moments later, hurrying to get back before Michelle could flirt with Lee again.

"How do I do it then?" Chloe asked Lee as she switched on the laptop.

"Turn it to face me." he told her. Lee pressed a button on his laptop and suddenly he disappeared from the television screen and reappeared on the spare laptop.

"Wow, that's awesome." Kirstie laughed.

"I like my technology." Lee smiled. Chloe quickly picked up the laptop and left the room. Lee watched her closely as she sat on their bed and placed the laptop on her lap.

"So, what do you want to talk about?" she said quickly.

"Is the door shut?" he asked.

Chloe nodded slowly.

"I need to know why you are avoiding me, I'm terrified that I have done something to upset you." he said nervously.

"I'm not avoiding you." she said quietly.

"You are though." he insisted. Chloe sighed quietly and silently picked her nails, avoiding Lee's gaze. Lee sighed as he watched her closely, he couldn't stand seeing her looking sad.

"Please tell me it's not something that I've done?" he said quietly. Chloe shook her head silently. She couldn't bring herself to look him in the eye, she felt too embarrassed by her behaviour.

"Is it something to do with the fact that you think I'm going to cheat on you?" he asked. Chloe's head snapped up.

"What?" she whispered.

"Nathan told you?" she asked quietly. Lee nodded slowly.

"For god sake, I'm never speaking to him about anything important again!" she said angrily.

"I'm not going to cheat on you Chloe." he said quietly.

"I don't really want to have this conversation." she said quickly.

"Why not?" he frowned.

"Because what's the point, my insecurities are never going to go away and I'm never going to think that I'm enough for you." she admitted.

"That's not true Chloe." he sighed.

"You know what I was like before I fell in love with you, I was selfish, all I cared about was my own ego. You make me better, even my Mum said it the other day.

You've taught me to open up, to care about people that are less fortunate than me." he told her gently.

"I even went busking, which I would never have done before." he added, chuckling slightly.

"I'm not taking credit for you being a good person." she said quickly.

"I didn't mean that I meant that we make each other better, your confidence is growing every day. You stood up to Jonny, which you wouldn't have done before." he explained. Chloe sighed sadly.

"I know, I'm just so afraid that you are going to cheat on me." she whispered.

"I don't want anyone else, just you." he told her. Chloe remained silent. She couldn't help but feel confused that his words didn't match his actions. He'd barely been near her since she'd given him her virginity.

Even on the night before he left when she tried to make a move on him, he had rejected her. She knew in her heart that he didn't want her anymore, part of her wouldn't blame him if he did cheat on her, he's a lady's man and she knew that someone like her wouldn't be enough for him.

"Chloe, I promise I won't do anything to hurt you." he said quietly, when she didn't respond. She nodded slowly.

"Can we talk about something else please?" she said quickly. Lee sighed to himself, he couldn't help but feel slightly frustrated that she didn't seem to believe him. Her self-confidence was so low that she constantly doubted that the people around her actually cared about her. Even though he knew it was a result of her past, he found himself wishing that he could do something to stop her from feeling the way she did.

"Are you doing much tomorrow?" he asked her, changing the subject like she'd asked.

"I think the girls want to go shopping." she told him. She quickly moved the laptop off her lap and turned onto her front.

"Do you need me to get you anything while I'm out?" she added. Lee shook his head slowly.

"Are you sure?" she asked, frowning at the fact that he'd suddenly fallen silent.

"Lee?" she prompted, when he still didn't respond. He blinked quickly, suddenly snapping out of his trance.

"Can you move the laptop forward a bit." he muttered.

"Why?" she frowned.

"I can see down your top and I can't concentrate on what you are saying." he said, smiling slightly. Chloe glanced down at the corner of the screen, gasping when she realised that he was right.

"Whoops, sorry." she said, quickly changing the angle of the laptop.

"I wasn't complaining." he smiled.

"I can't believe I just did that." she said, suddenly erupting into a fit of the giggles. She placed her head on her arms, unable to stop laughing.

"You're killing me right now Chloe." he laughed.

"Why?" she giggled, finally looking up at him.

"Because I wish I was there, I could show you what you do to me." he whispered hoarsely. Chloe smiled slightly, her cheeks colouring.

"In fact, I'll show you now, fair is fair." he grinned cheekily.

"You wouldn't." she laughed. Lee beamed at her, before gently pushing the laptop off his lap.

"Try me." he grinned, maintaining eye contact with her as he slowly unfastened his belt.

"Is one glimpse of my bra all it takes?" she smiled as she glanced at his crotch. He instantly removed his hand from his belt and glanced up as his hotel room door suddenly opened. He sighed as Adrian and Steven entered the room.

"Shit that was close." he whispered to Chloe.

"Lee, we've been waiting for you for ages, we need to go." Adrian said.

"Someone has got a party in their pants; have you been looking at porn again?" Steven chuckled.

"Of course not. I don't need porn; I've got a beautiful girlfriend." Lee said, grinning at them smugly. Lee glanced at the screen as he saw Chloe quickly pull up the zip on her fleece, just in case Adrian and Steven looked at the screen.

"Well hurry up, the bar will be closing soon, and I want to hit the clubs afterwards." Steven sighed. Chloe sighed to herself as she felt her insecurities swirling around her head once again. She couldn't help but feel nervous about him going clubbing and being surrounded by beautiful girls.

"I'll be down in a minute." Lee told Adrian and Steven, trying to get them to leave the room. They rolled their eyes at him and left the room.

"I'm not going clubbing; I'm just going to have a drink with the boys." Lee told Chloe.

"It's okay if you want too." she said quietly.

"I don't." he said quickly.

"I should probably go though, otherwise they'll just keep coming back." he added. Chloe nodded slowly.

"Yes probably." she agreed, smiling slightly.

"We can continue this when I'm home." he said, winking at her.

"Two more days to go." she sighed.

"I'll be back before you know it." he smiled.

"I know, you know how much I love you right." she said sadly. Lee nodded.

"Not as much as I love you." he said quietly.

Chloe sighed and reluctantly closed the laptop as Lee ended the call. She quickly left the bedroom and walked back towards the lounge, freezing in place as she heard Michelle's voice coming from the living room:

"You guys are having a go at me, but shouldn't you be having a go at Lee. It's quite clear that he wants me." Michelle said.

"I don't think so, he was pretty snappy with you." Louise answered, her tone sounding slightly angry.

"He was like that with Chloe to start with, he's like a shark, that's how he hunts." Michelle argued.

"I don't believe that for a second, him and Chloe are so happy together." Kirstie piped up. Michelle scoffed sceptically.

"What?" Kirstie asked.

"Someone like him is never going to be satisfied by Little Miss Innocent, the novelty will soon wear off." Michelle said smugly. Chloe gasped as she heard Michelle's words, feeling like she'd been punched in the stomach. This person was supposed to be her friend, yet here she was slating her and Lee to the group. Even though she knew Michelle's words were true, Chloe had been feeling that way for days, it didn't stop the hurt she felt at hearing someone else say it.

"You hardly know him; I don't understand why you think you have all the answers." Louise sighed.

"I know him better than you think." Michelle stated. She paused for dramatic effect and then continued:

"The night that he got into a fight with Shayne, we ended up in a club together. So, put it this way.... I know him *very* well." she told them. Chloe couldn't take it anymore, she took a deep breath and quickly walked into the room. The group fell silent and turned to look at her as she hovered in the doorway awkwardly.

"You and Lee have slept together?" Chloe whispered, her stomach churning at the thought of the two of them together. Chloe knew that unlike her, he had a past, but she couldn't stomach the idea that he had been with one of her so-called friends.

"He's slept with a lot of people Chloe; I don't understand why you are so shocked." Michelle frowned.

"I don't believe you; he would have told me." Chloe said quietly, her chest suddenly feeling tight.

"Would he?" Michelle asked. Chloe opened her mouth to respond, but her mouth was too dry. It suddenly made sense to her, why Michelle had been flirting with Lee, clearly there was something between them.

"When was it?" Chloe eventually asked.

"We were together the night after he attacked Shayne." Michelle said.

"Just that night?" Chloe checked. Michelle nodded. Chloe thought for a moment, her head a swirling mist of thoughts. She had no idea if Michelle was telling the truth or not, all she knew was she had to know for certain.

"I don't know if I believe you or not." Chloe said quietly.

"Well, I can't exactly prove it can I." Michelle said, rolling her eyes.

"Although actually.... he has a small birth mark on his left hip." Michelle added.

"Yes, I know." Chloe mumbled.

"And he does this thing where he puts his hand on the neck and strokes along the jaw with his thumb." Michelle tried.

"Oh my god." Chloe whispered, her eyes filling with tears. She stood, racking her brain to try and think of how Michelle could possibly know that. The only possible conclusion Chloe could come too, was that Michelle was telling the truth.

"I have to say though, he is really good isn't he." Michelle smiled.

"Michelle!" Kathleen exclaimed, clearly noticing that Chloe was becoming more and more upset.

"It's okay, we weren't together then anyway." Chloe said quietly, trying to convince herself that she was okay as much as them. She stood silently, desperately trying to fight the tears that were filling her eyes.

"I'm sorry Chloe, I just think you need to know the kind of man he is." Michelle said.

"I know that he likes the ladies." Chloe said quietly.

"That's putting it mildly, you're being played, he makes out he loves you, but people like him always look for sweet, innocent women." Michelle explained.

"Michelle that's enough!" Kirstie snapped loudly. Chloe closed her eyes, feeling the tears that she'd been fighting finally flow down her face, but she didn't care. It felt like someone was sticking a screwdriver in her heart and slowly twisting it.

"I'm just trying to protect her." Michelle argued.

"I said that's enough!" Kirstie exclaimed, quickly crossing the room and pulling Chloe into her arms.

"Don't listen to her Chloe." Kirstie whispered in her ear.

"I'm okay, I think I'm going to get an early night." Chloe said quietly, quickly removing herself from Kirstie's arms and running upstairs. As soon as she left the room, Kirstie rounded on Michelle, her stomach churning when she saw that Michelle had a smile playing on the corner of her lips.

"How could you do that to her?" Kirstie said quietly.

"It's not my fault that the truth hurts." Michelle said quickly.

"Jealousy is such a vile trait." Kirstie said angrily. Michelle shrugged and glared at Kirstie. Kirstie shook her head angrily and left the room to check on her friend.

Chapter Forty-Five

As soon as Chloe reached the bedroom, she quickly pulled on her pyjamas and climbed into bed. She sighed sadly as she pulled the covers under her chin. She couldn't help but feel sick to her stomach at the thought of Lee being with someone else, and it felt even worse that it was someone she knew. Michelle's words kept replaying on a loop in her head. Chloe had known all along, even before her and Lee got together that he was a lady's man and that she probably wouldn't be enough for him, but she'd always known in her heart that he loved her. But maybe Michelle was right...maybe he was pretending in order to take advantage of her. Was she secretly tangled in a web of lies with the man that she loved? Chloe glanced up at Kirstie as she climbed into bed beside her.

"You alright?" Kirstie asked.

"Yes." Chloe said quietly.

"Don't let her get into your head, you know Lee better than anyone." Kirstie said.

"Do I though, maybe I don't. Maybe she is right." Chloe sighed.

"He can't help that he has been with Michelle before the two of you got together." Kirstie pointed out. Chloe sniffed and slowly wiped away her tears.

"I know, but he could have told me though." she said quietly.

"He makes me so insecure because of the way he is with women and all the ladies want him because he's good looking, rich and famous. I can't compete with that." Chloe explained.

"And now one of my so-called friends is after him." she quickly added.

"He won't hurt you Chloe, he loves you." Kirstie said gently.

"Or he's just playing me." Chloe sighed.

"He's not, he adores you. Remember when you were injured and he was by your side day and night, to make sure that you were safe." Kirstie reminded her.

"Michelle is just saying that because she's jealous." she added.

"Why would she be jealous of me?" Chloe frowned.

"Because you have everything that she wants." Kirstie said.

"And she may not want to admit it, but she knows how much he loves you, it's obvious from the way he looks at you. You're so lucky." Kirstie added.

"It's no different than Ben is with you." Chloe said quietly.

"It is different, Ben and I love each other, but you and Lee are different. He would literally take a bullet for you." Kirstie explained.

"I guess I know that." Chloe whispered.

"So, you don't have to worry." Kirstie smiled at her. Chloe nodded slowly, still not quite able to ignore the doubts that she was having.

"It's just difficult to think about." Chloe admitted.

"I know hun." Kirstie said quietly. Chloe sighed and closed her eyes, wishing that she could fall asleep, to escape her thoughts.

"I'll stay with you if you want?" Kirstie offered. Chloe smiled at her and nodded slowly.

"Thank you." Chloe smiled, feeling lucky that she had such a good friend.

Chloe awoke with a start and slowly opened her eyes, frowning to herself when she realised that she was still in bed. As she glanced at the clock on the bedside table and saw that it was only eleven pm, she couldn't help but wonder what had woken her. She pulled the duvet under her chin and snuggled against it, closing her eyes once again. Chloe jumped as she heard movement from the hallway. She slowly opened her eyes, freezing in place, afraid to turn over in case someone was there. As her eyes slowly adjusted, she squinted in the darkness, silently cursing Lee's blackout blinds that meant she couldn't see a thing. She quickly felt under her pillow, breathing a small sigh of relief as she finally located the torch. Chloe jumped as the bedroom door slowly opened. She quickly climbed out of bed as she saw the slight outline of a silhouette in the doorway. The hallway was in darkness, only a few small beads of light coming from around the curtains. All Chloe could see was a small phone torch light and what appeared to be a figure walking into the room. Her heart began to pound against her chest as she stood, frozen to the spot, not entirely sure what to do. She jumped as the figure dropped the phone, suddenly plunging the room into complete darkness. Chloe seized her moment and ran, quickly heading for where she knew the doorway was, desperately heading towards the specks of light that she could see coming from the hallway. She gasped as she ran into someone. Chloe hesitated for a moment. Before she could bolt again, the figure quickly took hold of her arms and held her in place. Chloe screamed as she squirmed away, trying to break free.

"Chloe, it's just me." Lee said quickly.

"Lee?" Chloe checked.

"Yeah, it's me." Lee told her. He bent down to retrieve his phone, quickly using the torch on it to locate the light switch. As soon as Lee switched on the light, Chloe fell to her knees in relief.

"You really scared me." she whispered.

"I'm sorry, I didn't mean too." he said quietly.

"I thought I was going to be attacked again." she said, breathing deeply to calm herself down.

"Oh shit, I was trying not to wake you." he told her.

"I'm really sorry Chlo." he added worriedly, slowly squatting down beside her. She nodded, still trying to calm herself down.

"What are you doing home?" she asked.

"I missed you too much, so I decided to come home early." he told her.

"You look terrified." he added, quickly sitting down beside her.

"I was a bit, but I'm alright now." she admitted. The two of them glanced up as Kirstie rushed into the room, quickly stopping when she saw Lee sitting beside Chloe.

"Oh, thank god, it's you!" Kirstie sighed in relief.

"I heard you scream and panicked." Kirstie said, laughing slightly.

"I believe I owe you an apology too then." Lee said.

"No of course not, it's fine." Kirstie smiled.

"I think maybe we all need a cup of tea." Lee suggested.

"Yes, or some Valium." Kirstie laughed. Lee glanced at Chloe again as she shuffled towards him and gently placed herself in his arms. He wrapped his arms around her and held her tightly, feeling slightly guilty when he realised that she was trembling.

"C'mon let's go downstairs." he whispered in her ear, after holding her for a few moments. Lee took her hand and slowly helped her to stand.

As soon as they reached the kitchen, Kirstie quickly put on the kettle and began to set out the mugs. Lee sat on one of the chairs at the breakfast bar, his eyes fixed on Chloe as she hovered awkwardly. Chloe glanced at Lee and smiled slightly as he gestured for her to come and sit with him. As soon as she perched on his lap, Lee quickly wrapped his arms around her waist and pulled her against him. He placed a soft kiss on her neck, before gently resting his chin on her shoulder.

"I really missed you." he whispered.

"I'm glad you're home." Chloe said quietly, turning to face him and softly kissing his lips.

"So, why are you home?" Kirstie asked when they eventually stopped kissing each other.

"I assume it wasn't just to scare everyone." Kirstie giggled as she handed out the cups of tea. Lee smiled slightly.

"There's just the promo stuff to do, technically I should have been there, but I wanted to get back to my girl." Lee explained.

"I bet Matt wasn't happy." Kirstie smiled.

"No not really, I told him if he's not happy then he can fire me." Lee said quickly.

"The boys are on television tomorrow, a livestream from Germany, to show everyone around the set." Lee told them.

"Cool, we'll need to get up and watch it." Kirstie said. She couldn't help glancing at Chloe, wondering why she was so quiet. Clearly Michelle's comments were still playing on her mind. Lee could sense that Chloe was upset about something, as soon as he'd got home, he knew that something was going on with her.

"Are you alright Chlo?" Lee asked her quietly.

"Yes, I'm fine." she said quickly.

"You're very quiet." Lee tried again.

"I'm just tired." she told him. Lee gazed down at her as she placed her hands on his and gently moved them so that she could extract herself from his arms. Kirstie and Lee watched her as she stood up.

"I need to use the bathroom." she told them as she left the room.

"Is she alright?" Lee asked Kirstie as soon as Chloe had left the room.

"I think so, she's had a rough weekend." she replied.

"Because I wasn't here?" he frowned, slightly confused.

"Partly, but Michelle has been stirring up a lot." she told him.

"Stirring up about what?" he asked.

"You mostly." she said.

"Me?!" Lee spluttered, coughing on his tea. Kirstie nodded slowly.

"Has anything ever happened between you and Michelle?" she asked him. Lee thought for a moment, quickly racking his brain.

"I think there was a drunken kiss one night, but that was ages ago. I think it was actually the night I stopped Shayne from taking advantage of Chloe." he said thoughtfully.

"Just a kiss?" she checked.

"Yeah, why?" he frowned.

"Wait, has she been saying that it was more?" he added quickly, before Kirstie had a chance to respond. Kirstie nodded slowly, slightly nervous about how he was going to take it.

"That's bullshit." he snapped.

"I know, but I think she got under Chloe's skin, she had details of things and was saying that you are playing Chloe because she's innocent." she explained. Lee smirked and shook his head angrily.

"How dare she come into my house and start talking shit about me!" he exclaimed.

"I did speak to her about it earlier." she told him. Lee raised his eyebrow and waited for her to continue.

"She just said that she's looking out for Chloe." she said.

"More fucking bullshit." he said angrily.

"She was flirting with me like crazy on the video chat, that's not someone who cares about their friend. She's always been jealous of Chloe and she wants to stir up between us." he added.

"Plus, she likes to get her claws into famous people and not let go." he added.

"What do you mean by that?" she frowned.

"Nothing just forget it." he said quickly.

Lee fell silent, his brain swirling in anger as he thought about this person and what she was trying to do. Lee had never done anything to her and yet she seemed hell bent on taking the person that was most precious away from him. Chloe was already plagued by insecurities, the last thing she needed was someone whispering in her ear, making them worse, like an annoying parrot.

"I'll be having a word with Michelle in the morning." he muttered under his breath.

"I also feel like I owe you an apology." she said tentatively.

"Why, did you say that I slept with you too?" he snapped.

"Sorry, I'm really angry." he quickly added.
"It's okay, I understand." she said gently.

"I'm sorry that I prejudged you. I really didn't like you to start with." she said.

"I'm aware of that." he said, smiling slightly as he remembered how difficult his relationship was with Kirstie at the beginning.

"And I thought you'd be bad for Chloe, but I was wrong. It's so obvious how much you love her." she smiled.

"She's my world, she just doesn't realise it." he said, sighing quietly.

"I think she does, she knows that you take care of her and would do anything to protect her. She just struggles with her confidence." she told him. Lee's eyes flickered to the doorway as Chloe walked back into the room. As soon as he saw her, he quickly stood up and crossed the room. Chloe glanced down at her hand as Lee gently took it in his.

"I think we need to talk." Lee said quietly.

Chapter Forty-Six

Lee sat opposite Chloe as she sat cross-legged on their bed. Chloe placed her hands on her lap and silently picked her fingernails.

"What do you want to talk about?" Chloe asked, when she couldn't stand the silence any longer.

"I heard that Michelle has been shit stirring again." Lee said angrily.

"Yes, a bit." she said quietly.

"You could have told me that you slept with her." she added.

"I've never slept with her." he said quickly. Chloe sighed and shook her head, not believing him.

"I haven't I swear, it was just a kiss." he insisted.

"But she knew details about you." she argued.

"Like what?" he sighed, his temper starting to grow with Michelle again.

"About your birthmark.... about that thing you do with stroking the jawline." Chloe told him, tears filling her eyes.

"She probably saw me do it to you." he said, sighing quietly. Chloe sighed and nodded slowly, wishing that she could believe him, but she wasn't quite able to ignore the doubt that was niggling in her gut.

"You believe me, don't you?" he asked her quietly. Chloe thought for a moment, not entirely sure what to say. She still didn't believe him, she knew that he wouldn't have been able to resist any advances that a woman made on him and judging by the fact that Michelle had been flirting with him, she clearly had feelings for him. If Michelle and Lee were together in the club that night, it seemed a logical conclusion to assume that something more than a kiss would have happened between them. Chloe didn't want to speak or even think about the idea of them being together anymore, but she knew that he wasn't going to drop the subject until he thought that she believed him.

"Yes, I do." she lied, feeling slightly guilty about lying to him, but knowing that it was the only way for them to drop the subject. Lee frowned at her words, not entirely sure if he believed her, but he decided not to push the subject.

"Is something else going on Chlo?" he asked her as she sat silently once again.

"Not really, I'm just being stupid again." she said quietly.

"Tell me." he said gently.

"There's no point, you don't like it when I speak about my insecurities." she muttered.

"I didn't cheat on you I swear, I wouldn't do that to you." he said quickly.

"I'm just never going to think I'm enough for you." she told him sadly.

"You're more than enough Chloe, you always have been. And you are more than I deserve." he told her. Lee's heart sunk as he watched a stray tear slowly roll down Chloe's cheek. He sighed and gently brushed it away with his thumb.

"If that's true, then why don't you want me?" she whispered.

"What are you talking about?" he frowned.

"You clearly don't, you haven't been near me since that night." she muttered. Lee stared at her in numb shock, not entirely sure what to say. He couldn't quite fathom why someone as beautiful as her, didn't realise how difficult it was for someone like him to resist her all the time.

"I know that I don't really know what I'm doing yet, and I'm not very good at it, but it's not my fault." she added, her cheeks colouring.

"Are you serious?" Lee checked. Chloe nodded slowly.

"I can learn." she whispered, wiping away the tears that were rolling down her cheeks. She couldn't stand the idea that the man she loved and adored didn't want her.

"It's not like that, I do want you." he told her.

"I've wanted you for years, since the moment I first laid eyes on you. We've been living together for the past few weeks and it's been killing me not grabbing you every chance I get." he explained, smiling slightly at her.

"Well, why didn't you then?" she asked, finally looking him in the eye.

"I didn't want to put too much pressure on you, because I love you." he said quietly.
"You wouldn't have been putting pressure on me." she sighed.

"You know what you do to me Chloe." he whispered, reaching over and gently placing his hand on her bare leg.

"Why did you reject me the night before you went to Germany then?" she asked.

"I was worried that you might still be sore." he admitted. Chloe sighed and rolled her eyes.

"Remember the video chat....all it took was a glimpse of your bra and hearing you laugh." he said, flashing her a cheeky smile. She nodded slowly, a small smile playing on the corner of her lips.

"I just feel like you will be comparing me to all the other women you've been with." she sighed quietly.

"There's no comparison Chloe." he said quickly.

"You're just saying that to make me feel better." she whispered.

"No, I'm not. This is all new to me too, I've never been in love with anyone before and my feelings for you are so strong. We make love, it's not sex and it's more powerful. You are my whole world, and I think deep down you know that." he explained gently.

"Don't for a second think that I don't want you because I do." he told her firmly.

"I could happily stay up and make love to you all night." he added. Chloe glanced down at his hand that was still resting on her leg. Goosebumps rose on her leg as he gently traced small circles with his fingers.

"I wouldn't have a problem with that." she said nervously, swallowing the lump that was rising in her throat. Lee smiled slightly before quickly leaning towards her and kissing her gently, suddenly realising just how much he'd missed being this close to her. The kiss deepened as Lee placed his hands on her hips and slowly lifted the material of Chloe's night dress, the tips of his fingers running up her side as he did so. Chloe reluctantly pulled away from the kiss and watched his hands closely as they slowly made their upwards, the material of her night dress still firmly in his grasp. Just before he uncovered her breasts, Chloe reached up and took his hands between hers, placing them on her lap. Lee frowned at her, slightly confused as to what he'd done wrong.

"Do you think that maybe we could turn the light off?" she asked nervously.

"Why?" he frowned. Chloe's cheeks coloured as she gazed down at Lee's hands, gently playing with his fingers.

"Don't you want me to see you?" he tried when she didn't respond. Chloe shook her head slowly.

"I've seen you before though." he reminded her.

"I know, I just thought it might help to make me feel more confident." she admitted. Lee sighed sadly and wrapped his arms around Chloe's waist, quickly pulling her onto his lap and holding her tightly against himself.

"When are you going to see yourself the way that I see you." he whispered in her ear sadly. It broke his heart a little to think of the woman that he loved constantly doubting herself and living with no confidence in herself or her looks. Chloe felt herself relax into Lee as he held her tightly.

"I don't think I'll ever like my body." she admitted quietly.

"Your body is literally flawless." he told her.

"The problem is, you've never been told how special you are and how beautiful you look." he added thoughtfully. Chloe opened her mouth to say something, but he interrupted her.

"Andy has so much to answer for." he said, sounding slightly angry.

"It's a combination of a lot of things, not just him." she said quickly. Lee watched Chloe closely as she slowly removed herself from his arms and rested her forehead against his, sighing in contentment.

"Yeah, I know, I just hate that you feel like that." he admitted sadly.

"I've just thought, if we switch the light off, it'll be pitch black won't it." Chloe said quickly, trying to change the subject.

"We can use the lamp." he said, quickly reaching over and switching on the bedside lamp.

Chloe stood up and switched off the bedroom light, sighing to herself as she gazed around the bedroom and saw how much light was still in the room. Lee sensed Chloe's trepidation, so he quickly removed his shirt and placed it over the lamp, smiling in satisfaction as the room was plunged into almost darkness, the only light being a faint amber glow.

"It's not going to catch fire is it?" Chloe asked as she lay down on the bed.

"No, it should be fine." he told her. Before Chloe could say anything else, Lee quickly laid down beside her and kissed her passionately. After a few moments he planted a trail of kisses along her jaw, slowly making his way down to her neck. Chloe closed her eyes, sighing in pleasure, her hands gently stroking Lee's hair.

Chloe jumped and bolted up as she heard a bedroom door closing down the hallway.

"It's okay, it'll just be Kirstie going to bed." Lee said from behind her. Chloe nodded and turned to face Lee, who was still laying on his side on the bed.
"Speaking of the girls, we'll need to be quiet." she told him.

"I'm sure they won't care." he chuckled.

"I'm serious." she insisted. Lee fell silent as he suddenly remembered that Michelle was still in the house. Even though he wasn't proud of it, he couldn't resist the temptation. If he could get Chloe to call out his name, it would prove a point to Michelle.

"Is that a challenge?" he grinned at Chloe, wiggling his eyebrows mischievously.

"No, just a request." she giggled.

"Well, I'm not making any promises." he smiled.

"Damn it." Lee muttered under his breath as he dropped an egg on the floor. Chloe quickly picked up some tissue paper and bent down to wipe it up.

"When you said you were going to make eggs, I thought you meant in the pan and not on the floor." she teased him, smiling as she placed the tissue paper in the bin.

"I'm going to blame tiredness." he laughed, rubbing his eyes.

"Tell me about it, when you said that we could stay up all night, I didn't realise you meant it literally." she yawned.

"It was worth it though wasn't it." he grinned at her. Chloe nodded happily, before walking over and standing beside him, watching as he stood at the cooker, keeping a close eye on the eggs. She sighed happily as she wrapped her arms around his waist, squeezing him tightly. Lee glanced down at her, before gently placing his arm around her shoulders and kissing her forehead. The two of them glanced at the doorway as Kirstie walked in, smiling when she saw them.

"Morning guys." she smiled.

"Hey, would you like some breakfast?" Lee offered.

"That would be great actually." Kirstie replied.

"He's making Eggs Benedict, it's his speciality." Chloe told her.

"Oooh yum, I can make the coffee if you want?" Kirstie suggested. Lee nodded, smiling at Chloe as she yawned again.

"I think I need a double shot one." Chloe said sleepily.

"Well, you didn't get much sleep last night did you." Kirstie grinned. Chloe shook her head slowly, quickly looking at the floor. Kirstie couldn't help bursting out laughing as Lee beamed at her, raising his eyebrow, almost like he was proud of himself.

"We were literally up all night." Lee told her.

"That must have been a long 'talk'." Kirstie laughed, gesturing inverted commas.

"We had a lot to *talk* about." Lee smiled.

"So, I heard." Kirstie laughed.

"Oh god, you didn't did you?" Chloe asked shyly.

"Kind of." Kirstie smiled.

"That's your fault, I told you we had to be quiet." Chloe rounded on Lee.

"Technically you were the one making most of the noise." Lee smiled, feigning ignorance.

"Yes, well you made me." Chloe giggled, her cheeks colouring even more.

"You shouldn't have challenged me then." Lee grinned.

"I wanted to make sure that a certain someone heard." he added under his breath.

"Were you trying to rub Michelle's nose in it?" Kirstie laughed.

"Maybe a little." Lee said, smiling slightly.

"Yet you managed to rub my nose in it instead." Kirstie laughed, her smile fading slightly when she suddenly realised how much she had missed Ben over the past couple of days.

"Not intentionally." Lee told Kirstie.

"I am so embarrassed." Chloe said quietly, burying her face into Lee's shoulder.

"You slept with your boyfriend, it's not something to be embarrassed about." Lee told her, smiling slightly at how adorable she looked. Chloe giggled quietly as Lee squeezed her tightly against himself playfully.

"You clearly had a good time." Kirstie giggled.

"That's because I'm a professional." Lee laughed.

"Sssh." Chloe whispered as Kathleen and Louise walked into the room. The three of them instantly stopped talking. Louise and Kathleen glanced around awkwardly, both of them looking shocked to see Lee home and feeling slightly self-conscious when they realised, they'd clearly interrupted something.

"What are you guys talking about?" Kathleen asked, when she couldn't stand the silence any longer.

"We're talking about sex." Lee blurted.

"Oh, for god sake." Chloe whispered, burying her head in Lee's shoulder once again.

"Is that why you are back early?" Kathleen laughed. Lee grinned cheekily.

"Partly." Lee smiled. He quickly handed Kirstie her plate and smiled down at Chloe as she reluctantly removed herself from his arms.

"Thank you." Chloe said quietly as Lee handed the plate of food to her.

"I need to shower." Lee announced. Chloe nodded and smiled slightly as he quickly leant down and gently placed a kiss on her lips.

"The boys will be on the tv soon." he reminded the group

Chapter Forty-Seven

"I can't believe he came back early; Matt is going to be fuming." Chloe said quietly as she sat on the sofa beside Kirstie. She took out the remote and switched on the television, quickly putting it on mute until the Eclipse boys were on.

"It shows how much he cares about you though, he obviously really missed you." Kirstie pointed out.

"Oh my god, this food is amazing." Kirstie said as soon as she put the first mouthful into her mouth.

"Yeah, how come we didn't get any?" Louise chuckled as her and Kathleen walked into the room and sat on the sofa beside them.

"Lee didn't know you guys were awake." Chloe said.

"It's fine, I was just teasing you." Louise smiled, glancing up at the tv and frowning in confusion.
"What are we watching?" Louise asked.

"Apparently the Eclipse boys are doing a livestream from Germany to show the set of the video." Chloe explained.

"Oooh, that sounds interesting." Michelle said as she walked into the room, trying to make the effort with the group to fix the tense atmosphere. Kathleen wrapped her arm around Michelle and snuggled into her as soon as Michelle sat beside her.

"They're on!" Louise exclaimed a few moments later. Chloe carefully put down her plate of food and switched on the sound.

"And now we can cross live to Eclipse in Germany, can you guys hear us?" the presenter asked.

"Hello, we can hear you." Nathan answered as he stood in the shot with Adrian and Steven.

"We're missing someone aren't we, where is Lee?" the presenter asked.
"He had a previous engagement." Adrian said quickly.

"Where is Lee?" Michelle frowned.

"He's upstairs." Chloe said shortly.

"He came home early because he missed her." Louise piped up.

"Hence why Chloe's so tired." Kirstie smiled when Chloe yawned for about the hundredth time.

"I thought I heard something going on in the early hours." Louise said thoughtfully.

"Yeah probably, they pulled an all nighter." Kirstie laughed, smiling at Chloe when her cheeks coloured. Kirstie couldn't resist glancing over at Michelle, smiling slightly to herself when she noticed her squirming.

"You're as bad as Lee." Chloe whispered to her.

"Sometimes you need to prove a point to people." Kirstie whispered back.

"Chlo, have you seen my shirt?" Lee called as he walked into the living room.

"What this one?" Chloe asked, glancing down at herself and smiling when she remembered she was wearing Lee's shirt over the top of her leggings.

"I forgot you were wearing it, I'm so bloody tired." Lee said, smiling slightly.

"Do you want it back?" Chloe offered.

"No, it looks better on you anyway." he said, smiling slightly at how hot she looked wearing his shirt. Even though it was large on her, she still looked stunning. Lee pulled on his fleece and quickly zipped it up when he noticed Michelle staring at his bare chest.

"Oh, I have a bone to pick with you Lou." Lee said, pretending to be stern with her.

"Wait, what have I done?!" Louise exclaimed, turning to face him as he stood behind her.

"A little birdie told me that you've been on two dates with this Peter guy." he said, raising his eyebrow at her.

"Yeah, so." Louise smiled.

"So, I thought we were going to double date so that we could check him out." Lee said, smiling slightly. Louise burst out laughing at his stern expression, the hint of a smile playing on the corner of his lips. Before Louise could say anything, Lee threw his wet towel over her.

"Ew, is that the one you just used?!" Louise cried, quickly trying to get the towel off herself.

"Yep." Lee grinned.

"That's gross, your bits have been on it." Louise said, screwing her face up in disgust as she quickly flung the towel across the room.

"You deserved it." Lee laughed.

"You're such an arse." Louise laughed with him. Lee nodded proudly.

Kirstie moved along the sofa slightly, to give Lee space to sit beside Chloe. As soon as he sat beside her, he wrapped his arm around her shoulder and gently placed his head on her shoulder, closing his eyes. Chloe carefully rested her head against his, sighing in contentment.

"I think the two of you need an early night." Kirstie said, smiling at them. Lee's eyes snapped open as he beamed at Chloe.

"Sounds like a plan." Lee winked.

"I think we need sleep first." Chloe said, smiling slightly.

"The two of you are gagging for it." Kirstie laughed.

"He is, I just go along with it." Chloe said quietly, feigning innocence.

"Erm excuse me, that's not how I remember it." Lee laughed. Chloe squealed as Lee quickly grabbed her playfully and pulled her onto his lap, squeezing her tightly.

"I also don't remember hearing you complaining." Lee teased her, gently brushing her hair to one side and placing a soft kiss on her neck. Chloe giggled, her cheeks colouring when she glanced up and saw everyone staring at them.

"They are so cute aren't they." Louise smiled, summing up what everyone else was thinking.

"How did you guys first meet?" Kathleen asked.

"It'll be when Chloe went to work for them won't it." Michelle said quickly, rolling her eyes.

"I'll always remember that I was so nervous." Chloe said, smiling slightly.

"Why?" Lee chuckled.

"I don't know really, I knew I had the job by that point, but I wasn't sure if you guys would be nice or not. Some celebrities are full of themselves aren't they." Chloe explained.

"Or slime balls." Louise said.

"Technically that wasn't the first time we met though." Lee reminded her.

"Yes, it was." Chloe said. Lee frowned at her, slightly confused as to whether she was joking or not.

"We met a few years before that." he tried.

"Did we?" Chloe frowned.

"At the pub gig we did in two thousand and eight." Lee told her.

"Wait, that was five years ago, I didn't know you then!" Chloe argued.

"No but we met and spoke for a bit." he told her.

"I remember being on the little stage and you walked in wearing that white lace dress and you looked so beautiful that I couldn't tear my eyes off you. I ended up missing my cue to start singing." he explained, smiling slightly.

"And I knew then that I wanted you." he added.

"That's quite normal for you though to want someone as soon as you see them." Chloe pointed out.

"Not like that, it felt different." he told her.

"Wait a second." she said, quickly climbing off his lap and running upstairs. Lee watched her as she returned a few moments later, carrying her photo album under her arm. She sat beside Lee, resting her back against his chest. He quickly wrapped his arm around her shoulders, gently stroking her arm. He watched her closely as she carefully opened the photo album, hesitating for a moment when she reached the section from when she was nineteen.

"Are you sure you want to do that?" Lee asked her quietly. She nodded slowly. Even though she didn't want to look at the images, she needed to know if Lee was correct and they did meet all those years ago and she had blocked it from her memory, along with most of the other things that happened that year. Chloe's hands shook as she turned the page, trying not to look too closely at the pictures as she searched for what she was looking for. She gasped and let go of the page, almost like she'd received an electric shock, as she noticed a picture of her standing with Lee, smiling for the camera, wearing the white dress he'd described.

"Oh my god." Chloe sobbed when she noticed a picture of him standing with her Mum.

"See, I told you." Lee smiled at her.

"You met my Mum." Chloe whispered, burying her head in her hands as she began to cry. Lee held her tightly against himself, feeling slightly guilty that he'd managed to upset her. She couldn't help but feel emotional at the thought of Lee meeting her Mum. It meant the world to her that the man she loved had met her family. Chloe eventually lifted her head, staring silently at the photographs, the memories of that day suddenly coming flooding back.

"You spoke to us at the bar, didn't you?" Chloe said quietly.

"Yeah, you were there with your Mum, we only spoke briefly but I remember you telling me that you'd got a place at Uni to study makeup and were due to start that September." he told her.

"I also remember thinking you seemed really confident, when you walked into the pub you lit up the room." he added.

"I was a lot more confident back then." she told him.

"But I thought you had a sadness behind the eyes." he said quietly.

"Mum had not long been diagnosed, I took her out to try and cheer her up." she explained.

"I actually do remember that when Mum and I went back to our table, she kept pestering me to go and speak to you." Chloe said, smiling slightly.

"She kept saying that you seem nice and clearly like me so I should go and speak to you." she added.

"I got her approval then." Lee smiled.

"Yes, I guess you did." Chloe said quietly, gently stroking the picture of her Mum.

"I can't believe you remembered all of that, if the two of you barely spoke." Kirstie piped up, smiling at the two of them.

"I couldn't stop thinking about her for ages, and when Eclipse became a big thing again about three years later when we reunited officially, I asked Matt to head hunt her for us, because I knew she'd have finished at Uni by then." Lee explained.

"Why would you do that?" Chloe frowned, turning to face him.

"I just felt something that I'd never felt before and I knew that I had to get to know you." Lee said.

"That explains why Matt just randomly offered me a job one day, I always wondered why it was a job working with a boyband when most of my course was doing makeup for women." Chloe said thoughtfully.

"I was so gutted when you came to work with us, and I found out that you were dating Andy." Lee said quietly.

"You must have been happy when we broke up then?" Chloe said, smiling slightly at him.

"A little, but I didn't like seeing you upset." he admitted.

"If you knew you had feelings for her, then why did you bully her for so long." Michelle said, rolling her eyes.

"He didn't to start with, just towards the end." Chloe said, quickly jumping to Lee's defence.

"And Chloe knows why." Lee said quietly, feeling slightly guilty again for the way he'd treated her back then.

"And you've more than made up for it since." Chloe told him, smiling warmly when she noticed a change in his body language.

"I still can't believe we met all those years ago." Chloe said thoughtfully, her heart filled with pride.

"I can't believe you didn't remember me." Lee chuckled.

"You know why though." Chloe told him quietly. Lee nodded, gently placing a soft kiss on her cheek as he continued to stroke her arm. Chloe couldn't tear her eyes away from the photograph of Lee with her Mum. It meant so much to her that the two of them had met and that her Mum had encouraged Chloe to speak to Lee, almost as if in a small way he had gained her approval.

"I love you." she whispered impulsively, finally turning to face him. He smiled at her, gently caressing her cheek with his hand. Chloe kissed him softly, forgetting for a moment that the others were in the room. The two of them jumped as Lee's phone began to ring.

"It's Mum." he said, as he quickly pulled the phone out of his pocket and looked at the screen.

"She's probably phoning me to check that I'm still taking care of you." he smiled, rolling his eyes.

"More likely she watched the livestream and wants to know why you weren't on it." Chloe laughed. Lee nodded as he stood up and left the room to take the call.

"I'm so in love with you two." Kirstie smiled at Chloe as soon as Lee left the room.

"Me too, where do I find myself a Lee." Louise agreed. Chloe remained silent, not entirely sure what to say.

"Speaking of Lee, has he admitted it yet?" Michelle piped up when she couldn't stand listening to them fawning over Lee and Chloe any longer.

"Admitted what?" Chloe frowned.

"That me and him spent a night together." Michelle said impatiently.

"Because presumably you spoke to him about it, given how upset you were?" Michelle tried again when Chloe remained silent.

"He says that it didn't happen and the two of you just kissed." Chloe sighed, her brain swirling again as she was reminded of the possibility that Lee might have slept with Michelle. Michelle raised her eyebrow and smiled sarcastically.

"Maybe he's not as open with you as you think." Michelle pointed out.

"And has he told about his little kink that he likes?" Michelle asked.

"I don't know what you're talking about." Chloe said quietly, her heart pounding against her chest.

"I guess that's a no then." Michelle chuckled.

Chloe sat silently, her thoughts a tangled web of information. She had no idea what to do or who to believe. She felt sick to her stomach at the thought of Lee sleeping with Michelle and a deep sense of hurt that he'd been able to open up to Michelle about his desires and not her.... the woman that he claimed to love. Before she could stop herself, Chloe stood up and walked into the kitchen, heading towards the sound of Lee's voice. As soon as he saw her walk in, he smiled at her.

"You alright Chlo?" he asked when he saw her hurt expression. Chloe shrugged in response, not entirely sure what to say.

"I'll speak to you later Mum." Lee said, quickly hanging up.

"What's going on?" Lee asked her quickly.

"Michelle just told me you have a sexual kink that you haven't told me about?" Chloe blurted before she could stop herself.

"How does she know about that?" Lee said quietly, instantly regretting the words as soon as they were out of his mouth.

"So, you do?!" Chloe exclaimed in disbelief. It felt like someone had punched her in the chest, the thought that he was able to open up to Michelle and not her.

"Well.... no....I..." Lee started but trailed off.

"You totally slept with her didn't you?!" Chloe snapped angrily.

"I didn't sleep with her." Lee sighed, slowly starting to get angry that Michelle was stirring up yet again.

"Stop lying to me." she whispered, her eyes filling with tears.

"I swear to you, I've never slept with that woman!" he exclaimed.

"I've never lied to you Chloe." he added quietly. Chloe sniffed quietly and angrily wiped her away her tears, her head snapping up as Michelle walked into the room.

"I feel really bad that I've caused this, I never wanted to come between the two of you." Michelle said quietly.

"Like hell you didn't!" Lee snapped angrily, his temper rising as soon as he saw her. Lee glanced at Chloe as she rummaged in the tumble dryer and pulled out her tank top.

"I can't do this anymore!" Chloe said angrily, her temper finally snapping.

"What are you doing?!" Lee asked Chloe as she quickly unbuttoned Lee's shirt that she was still wearing. His eyes widened in shock as she removed the shirt, so blinded by anger that she didn't seem to care that she was stood in front of Lee and Michelle wearing only her bra and leggings. She quickly pulled on her tank top and roughly flung Lee's shirt along the counter towards Michelle.

"Maybe you want to wear that, since you clearly know him better than I do!" Chloe said angrily. Michelle stared at Chloe silently, slightly shocked at her outburst. In all the years they'd known each other Michelle had never seen Chloe so angry.

"Where are you going?" Lee asked as Chloe turned and walked away.

"Out, I need some air." she snapped.

"Chloe!" he called after her as he watched her walk away, slamming the front door behind herself.

Chapter Forty- Eight

"I'm really sorry." Michelle said quietly, gently placing her hand on Lee's arm.

"Don't fucking touch me!" Lee said, angrily slamming his hands onto the kitchen counter, hanging his head in frustration.

"When are you going to sort out your own insecurities, rather than keep tearing Chloe down all the time?" he said through gritted teeth.

"Who said anything about me being insecure?" she frowned.

"It's glaringly obvious, and it's clear that you are so wrapped up in jealousy of her." he muttered angrily.

"What's going on, we saw Chloe leaving the house?" Kirstie asked as she walked into the room, closely followed by Louise and Kathleen.

"I think I accidentally upset her." Michelle said quietly.

"It wasn't an accident!" Lee exclaimed, struggling to get control of his temper.

"We spent ages listening to you apologise after you hurt her last time, and the first opportunity you get, you do it again!" Lee added angrily.

"Just because you don't want to admit it." Michelle muttered under her breath, suddenly feeling slightly nervous about Lee and his temper.

"There's nothing to admit, I haven't bloody slept with you!" Lee shouted.

"It was a drunken kiss in a nightclub and that's it!" he added angrily. Michelle raised her eyebrow at him sceptically.

"And as for this secret kink thing or whatever you called it that apparently, I told you about, we never discussed that!" Lee continued.

"So, you're saying you don't have one then?" Michelle said smugly.

"Most people do." he argued. Lee's eyes snapped up as he heard the front door open and close, he breathed a sigh of relief as Chloe walked into the kitchen. She quickly crossed the room and stood in front of Michelle; her jaw set in anger.

"Promise me that what you said is true." Chloe said, carefully scanning Michelle's face to try and figure out if she was lying or not.

"Which part?" Michelle asked, trying to give herself time to think.

"Both parts." Chloe said sternly. Lee couldn't help but smile slightly at how confident she was being in her angry state.

"The kink part was a lucky guess...I know he's a very sexual person, so it wasn't a big leap to make...." Michelle started but trailed off. She couldn't help but feel a pang of guilt as she looked between Chloe and Lee and finally realised what she was doing to them. She'd never set out to hurt anyone, but she'd become so consumed by jealousy, as Chloe being so perfect highlighted her own intense insecurities.

"Come on Michelle, you need to tell the truth, we all know you haven't slept with him." Kirstie prompted. Michelle shrugged, not entirely sure what to say, not quite able to bring herself to admit to everyone that she'd lied, in a desperate attempt to tear Chloe down from the pedestal that she seemed to occupy.

"Clearly you've been confusing me with one of the hundreds of other people you've chased that did actually sleep with you." Lee muttered smugly. Chloe sighed and stepped away from Michelle, leaning her back against the counter.

"Are you calling me a tart?!" Michelle exclaimed, suddenly turning angry again at his words.

"Yeah, because it's true." Lee smirked, enjoying the fact that he was clearly getting under her skin.

"That's your type though isn't it, that's why you're shacked up with one!" Michelle snapped.

"Come again?" Lee muttered, a note of warning present in his tone.

"You've basically found someone who gives you sex on tap in return for somewhere fancy to live. I doubt it's the first time she's done it either!" Michelle shouted, so angry by Lee's comment that she was seeing red.

"You have no idea what you are talking about." Lee laughed sarcastically, glancing at Chloe for a moment, wishing that he could tell everyone the truth that she'd only ever been with him.

"It's not my fault that comment hit home, because you know how much you chase men and would basically sleep with anyone that smiles at you." Lee added firmly.

"You have no right to judge me, you're the biggest man slut around and *she's* some dirty hooker that you picked up from the park!" Michelle shouted. Before anyone else could react, Chloe stood in front of Michelle and quickly slapped her across the cheek. Everyone fell silent, staring at Chloe in shock, as Michelle carefully placed her hand on her burning cheek.

"Don't you *ever* judge me, I can count on one hand the amount of people I've slept with, I doubt you can say the same." Chloe muttered angrily, taking deep breaths to try and calm down.

"Sometimes the truth hurts, but it'll all come out eventually." Michelle said quickly, smirking at Chloe. Chloe quickly stepped backwards and perched on a stool, Michelle's words still swirling around her mind.

"If you like the truth so much, how come you haven't told everyone about your secret relationship with Mark?!" Lee piped up. Michelle's cheeks coloured as everyone turned to look at her.

"Mark?!" Kathleen exclaimed.

"Oh my god, is he the guy you've been seeing?!" Kirstie piped up. Michelle gazed around the room in embarrassment. Lee smiled slightly as he watched Michelle squirming uncomfortably.

"Who's making up lies now." Michelle snapped defensively.

"Nathan and I saw you in a club with him a few days after the record label event, and I've seen you backstage with him a lot recently." Lee pointed out.

"The little secret rendezvous in the bathroom at the studio, the fact that you follow him around like a lost puppy because you are so desperate to get him to commit to you, even though he never will because he's a player." Lee continued, not quite able to wipe the smirk off his face, that the tables had finally turned on her. He glanced at Chloe for a moment, his temper growing again when he noticed that she was biting her lip, trying to keep herself from crying now that her anger was slowly fading.

"You don't know what you are talking about." Michelle muttered. Lee raised his eyebrow sceptically.

"How long have you been seeing him for?" Kathleen piped up.

"I haven't been seeing him, he's just trying to deflect from his own problems." Michelle said quickly.

"It would be just after you interviewed all of the groups." Lee said, turning to Kathleen.

"Oh my god." Kathleen whispered, leaning on the kitchen counter for support as she suddenly felt very weak. She had secretly been seeing Mark herself at that point, before she'd realised that he wasn't going to commit. Shortly after she'd started seeing Mark, she'd quickly realised how much of a player he was, but she couldn't help but feel upset at the thought that he'd been secretly seeing her best friend behind her back, even though he'd repeatedly called Kathleen paranoid about her concerns that he was seeing other people. Everyone turned to stare at Kathleen as they heard her sniff quietly and saw warm tears slowly rolling down her cheeks.

"Oh no, Kathleen, what's wrong?" Kirstie asked.

"I was seeing Mark back then too." Kathleen admitted, letting out a small sob.

"Shit." Lee muttered under his breath, suddenly feeling very guilty that he'd outed Michelle. Even though he'd wanted to hurt her and humiliate her, in the same way that she had done Chloe, the last thing he wanted to do was upset Kathleen, particularly when she was heavily pregnant.

"What....no you weren't." Michelle muttered, her stomach churning at the thought of it.

"I was, we started seeing each other the night of the record label event.... I went home with him on the night Lee and Shayne had their altercation." Kathleen explained, quickly wiping away her tears.

"I didn't know you were seeing him too Kathleen, if I did, I would never have done that to you!" Michelle cried, starting to panic that she was going to lose the only person in the group of friends that didn't hate her. Lee rolled his eyes, biting his tongue to prevent himself from smugly pointing out that she'd finally admitted it. Even though he wanted to hurt Michelle, he knew that he would upset Kathleen further.

"He sounds like a total dickhead; he's basically played you both at the same time." Louise said thoughtfully, summing up what everyone else was thinking. Kathleen took a deep breath, trying to control her tears.

"Are you still seeing him now?" she asked Michelle nervously. Michelle hesitated for a moment, before nodding slowly.

"That explains why he doesn't give a damn about the baby then." Kathleen muttered bitterly.

"Wait, what?!" Kirstie exclaimed.

"Are you having *his* baby?" Michelle asked, sounding slightly shocked.

"Maybe, I don't know." Kathleen sobbed, unable to control her emotions any longer. Louise quickly pulled her into a hug and held her tightly as she sobbed quietly, suddenly feeling betrayed by both Mark and Michelle.

"I had no idea Kathleen I swear." Michelle whispered, a wave of guilt washing over her as she watched her friend.

"I think maybe I should go home." Kathleen muttered, quickly removing herself from Louise's arms.

"I'm sorry Kathleen, I didn't know." Michelle tried. Kathleen nodded slowly, before quickly leaving the house. Louise sighed sadly before quickly following her to check on her.

"Maybe I should go too." Michelle stated.

"Feel free. Don't let the door hit you on the way out." Lee said shortly. Michelle nodded slowly and quickly left the house.

Kirstie watched Chloe as she sat silently on the stool, her eyes fixed on the floor.

"Are you alright Chloe?" Kirstie asked worriedly. Chloe nodded slowly; her gaze still fixed on the floor. Lee sighed sadly as he walked over to stand behind her and gently wrapped his arms around her shoulders, squeezing her tightly. He frowned to himself as she quickly removed herself from his arms and stood up.

"I'm used to it by now, first I'm an attention whore and now I'm a dirty hooker." Chloe said sadly, Michelle's words finally hitting home.

"I need to get some sleep." she announced as she quickly walked away. Lee sighed and ran his hand through his hair in frustration.

"That woman has managed to come between us yet again!" Lee said angrily.

"I think she knows you didn't sleep with Michelle; she's just upset about everything." Kirstie said.

"I'm sorry for how the weekend ended." Lee said, suddenly feeling guilty that he'd invited them into his home and most of them had left upset.

"It's fine, it's not your fault is it." Kirstie sighed in disappointment that Michelle had managed to cause problems in the group yet again.

"You need to go and check on Chloe." she added. Lee nodded slowly, glancing up the stairs as she said those words.

"Can you apologise to the others for me?" Lee asked her. Kirstie nodded slowly, smiling slightly as Lee gently hugged her.

Chapter Fifty-One

Chloe sighed to herself as she curled up in bed and quickly pulled the covers under her chin, holding them tightly to try and provide some comfort. Michelle's comments had cut her to the quik, she'd always been proud of her virtue and the fact that unlike a lot of her peers at school and university, she hadn't slept with a lot of people. It made her blood boil that people judged her to be something that she wasn't just because, due to a set of unfortunate circumstances, she'd ended up sleeping rough. Just because she'd ended up on the streets, didn't mean she was a hooker and she certainly wasn't dirty. She quickly wiped away the tears that were slowly rolling down her cheeks as Michelle's words swirled around her head. When she'd said those words, Chloe had felt a deep surge of anger, the likes of which she'd never felt before. It was bad enough that Michelle was continually trying to take the man that she loved from her but to question her virtue was another matter entirely. Chloe had always prided herself on her high moral standing that her parents had instilled in her from an early age. Her moral code was the only thing about herself that she liked. The events of what had happened kept playing over and over in Chloe's mind, she couldn't help but feel a pang of guilt that she had lashed out and slapped Michelle. She hadn't meant to lose control and hurt someone.

Chloe glanced up as Lee walked into the bedroom, pulled off his fleece and climbed into bed beside her. Chloe jumped slightly as he laid down behind her, wrapped his arms around her waist and pulled her close.

"Are you okay?" he whispered in her ear.

"I'm fine." she said shortly.

"Are you annoyed with me?" he asked her.

"No." she replied quickly. She didn't mean to be short with him, she was so angry with Michelle and with herself for lashing out that she wasn't in the mood to speak to anyone.

Lee sighed against her and rested his face against hers, gently planting a soft kiss on her shoulder. He knew that she was upset about Michelle's comments and was trying to hide it.

"You do believe me that I haven't slept with her, don't you?" Lee asked nervously.

"Yes." she replied quietly. As soon as she'd stood in front of Michelle and looked her in the eye, Chloe knew that she was lying. The only thing she couldn't understand is why she seemed to be so desperate to take Lee away from her, particularly when as it turned out she was seeing Mark anyway. Lee breathed a sigh of relief and snuggled against her, sensing that she needed some time to calm down before speaking to him about what had happened. He closed his eyes, feeling comforted by holding her in his arms.

"I think I need to phone Michelle and apologise." Chloe said thoughtfully a few moments later.

"No, I really don't think you do." he said quickly.

"I shouldn't have slapped her; it was uncalled for." she muttered sadly.

"It really wasn't, she called you a dirty hooker!" Lee exclaimed.

"Besides it was a good job you slapped her, otherwise I would probably have done it." he quickly added. Chloe remained silent and nodded slowly, her stomach still swirling with guilt. Lee sighed quietly and held Chloe tighter, trying to provide her with at least a small amount of comfort.

"Don't feel guilty, she got what she deserved." he told her firmly.

"I still can't actually believe she said that about you." he added thoughtfully. Chloe nodded and quickly wiped away her tears.

"We know it's not true though." she said quietly, trying to put on a brave face.

"I so badly wanted to tell her the truth about you." he admitted. Chloe smiled slightly to herself. She knew how much it meant to Lee that he was the only person she had given herself too. He knew that he was the only person that she'd trusted enough to make the commitment to him, and to allow him to be her first.

"I'm glad you didn't." she said, turning her head slightly to place a soft kiss on his lips.

"I need to ask you about that comment she made about you." she added quietly.

"The fetish thing?" he asked. Chloe nodded slowly.

"She admitted that was a lucky guess, I hadn't told her anything about it." he said quickly.

"I know, but why didn't you tell *me* about it?" she asked quietly, feeling slightly hurt that he wasn't able to open up to her.

"Because it's not a thing anymore." he said quietly. Chloe frowned to herself, quickly turning to face him.

"What does that mean?" she asked.

"I liked to try and pick up two women because I was into having threesomes, but I'm not anymore." he said quickly.

"Why, because you think I'll say no?" Chloe asked, her stomach churning slightly.

"No, because I don't want to do it anymore." he told her.

"You're more than enough for me." he added, before kissing her lips tenderly.

"But...I don't understand." Chloe said when they eventually broke apart.

"If that's your thing, then why would you suddenly not want to do it anymore?" she added.

"It was my thing, but that was before, when I was just having sex. With you it's different. Making love with you is the best sex I've ever had." he told her. Chloe smiled slightly, her cheeks colouring.

"There's another reason too..." he said, smiling slightly. Chloe raised her eyebrow and waited for him to continue.

"I couldn't bring myself to have a threesome with you, because I don't want to share you." he smiled. Chloe felt her heart flutter as he said those words.

"Nobody else is allowed to touch you....ever." he whispered in her ear, smiling slightly to himself when he realised the effect his words were having on Chloe. She was laying silently on the bed, gazing up at him through her long eyelashes, a look of longing etched on her pretty features.

"Well thankfully I don't want anyone else anyway." she said softly. Lee smiled at her words as he placed his hand on her neck and softly stroked her cheek with his thumb.

"I can't believe how lucky I am to have you." he whispered. Chloe smiled slightly, as she wrapped her arms around his neck and kissed him deeply.

"I just wish people would stop trying to take you from me." she said thoughtfully, when they eventually broke apart.

"Nobody is going to take me from you, I love you and I know how special you are." he told her reassuringly. "I love you so much." she whispered as she lovingly stared into his eyes. As Chloe stared into his eyes, she could feel herself becoming lost in them. She'd never felt this way about anyone before, she would literally do anything for him.

"I still can't believe we met all those years ago." she whispered as Lee gently placed a series of soft kisses on her neck.

"I always wondered how different things might have been if I'd been brave enough to ask you out that day." Lee said thoughtfully when he eventually stopped kissing her. Chloe's skin tingled as she longed for him to kiss her again.

"I would probably have said no." she admitted.

"Nice." Lee said quietly, smiling slightly.

"I was so focused on Mum at that time, there wasn't time for anything else." she explained.

"I know." he said sympathetically. He smiled at Chloe as she softly stroked the hair on the back of his neck, her eyes twinkling happily as she stared at him. Lee kissed her lips tenderly, quickly deepening the kiss. Chloe slowly pulled away, hesitating for a moment before unwrapping her arms from his neck and slowly removing her top, her cheeks colouring slightly as Lee stared at her longingly.

"You're so beautiful Chlo." he whispered hoarsely, unable to tear his eyes from her. Chloe's hands shook slightly as she slowly reached behind herself and unclasped her bra. Lee's eyes widened in shock at this new level of confidence that she was showing, that if possible, made him long for her even more than normal.

"Please don't stare at me." she said quietly, her cheeks colouring further as he watched her intently.

"I can't help it, you're breath-taking." he whispered in her ear, reluctantly tearing his eyes away from her perfect body. Lee placed his hands on her waist and pulled her close.

"Are you sure you're not too tired?" he asked her when he noticed her yawning.

"No, I'm fine." she said quietly, trying to hide how desperately she wanted him.

"Besides since I'm your dirty hooker I don't really have a choice do I." she said sarcastically, an edge of bitterness present in her voice as some of the anger she'd felt at Michelle's words suddenly came flooding back.

"Please don't ever say that about yourself again." Lee said quickly, sounding slightly angry as he was reminded of what Michelle said to her.

"I was just being sarcastic." she said quickly.

"I know, but I don't want to even think about that piece of work. And I don't want her near you anymore, she just hurts you every time you see her." he said quietly.

"I don't want to see her anymore anyway; she crossed the line." she agreed.

Lee nodded trying to focus on Chloe rather than the anger that was slowly building inside of him. Chloe shivered as he placed a soft kiss on her collarbone methodically making a trail along it and down her sternum, maintaining eye contact with her the entire time. His eyes twinkled cheekily as she shivered under his touch. Chloe squirmed nervously as he quickly removed her underwear.

"How come I'm naked and you're still dressed?" she frowned, feeling very self-conscious.

"Because I like looking at your perfect body." he smiled, sitting back and gazing at her. Chloe could feel her cheeks colouring as he continued to stare at her, unable to tear his eyes away. She could feel herself becoming more and more self-conscious, so she quickly took hold of the bed sheet and pulled it over her naked frame.

"That's coming off." he chuckled, smiling at her cheekily.

"Is it?" she said, smiling mischievously at him.

"Most definitely." he laughed. Chloe stared at him, raising her eyebrow, a small smile playing on the corner of her lips. Chloe giggled and curled her hands into fists around the sheet, clinging onto it tightly as she glared at him defiantly. Chloe laughed as the two of them playfully fought over the sheet, both trying to pull it towards themselves. She couldn't help but glare at him playfully, her stubborn streak kicking in. Chloe suddenly jerked the sheet towards herself, the sudden motion causing Lee to lose his balance. Chloe gasped as his full weight landed on top of her small frame.

"Shit, I'm really sorry." he said, quickly moving to lay beside her. Chloe laid still for a moment, trying to get her breath back as she was slightly winded.

"Are you alright Chlo?" Lee asked worriedly, starting to panic slightly that he'd hurt her. She nodded slowly and turned to face him, frowning slightly when she saw him staring at her, a look of concern on his handsome features.

"Don't look so worried, I'm okay." she quickly reassured him.

"It was an accident." he said quietly, clearly not listening to her.

"You didn't hurt me, I'm not made of glass you know." she said softly, shuffling over to him and resting her head against his collarbone.

"You just always seem so fragile, you're so small compared to me." he whispered in her ear, still feeling slightly guilty.

"I'm not that small, I come up to your shoulder." she said quickly.

"Only just." he argued, gently stroking her hair. Chloe sighed to herself, quickly realising that whatever she said, he was determined to feel guilty for what was a complete accident.

"Are you sure you're okay?" he asked.

"Yes, I'm fine." she said, closing her eyes as the lack of sleep from the night before finally overwhelmed her.

Chapter Fifty

Chloe couldn't help but smile to herself as she sat at the breakfast bar, watching Lee rush around the kitchen, looking slightly stressed as he prepared what he'd described as the best meal ever. He'd been so racked with guilt for the way the weekend had ended that the first opportunity he'd got, he'd invited Kathleen, Kirstie and Louise over for dinner, in an attempt to make it up to them.

"Do you not think it would have been easier to get a takeaway?" Nathan chuckled, glancing at Chloe for a moment as they both sat watching Lee.

"Probably, but that lacks the personal touch." Lee pointed out. Nathan burst out laughing, quickly stopping himself when he realised that Lee was being serious.

"Will you at least let me help?" Chloe offered.

"It's fine, everything is under control." Lee said, quickly pecking her on the lips as he walked past.

"Are all three of them coming?" Chloe asked him.

"No, Kathleen said she can't manage." Lee said quietly, feeling slightly guilty that he'd managed to upset Kathleen. When he'd exposed Michelle's behaviour the last thing, he expected was that Kathleen would be involved with Mark too.

"She's probably just embarrassed to be with the girls at the moment, she might need some time to get her head around things." Chloe said, trying to reassure him.

"They'll be here, soon won't they?" Nathan piped up, glancing at his watch. Lee quickly glanced up at the clock on the kitchen wall and nodded slowly.

"I'd better head off then." Nathan said, quickly standing up.

"Make sure he behaves himself." Nathan added, smiling at Chloe.

"Excuse me, I'm six years older than her." Lee pointed out, smiling slightly.

"Yeah, but she's more mature than you." Nathan laughed. Chloe quickly stood up and pulled Nathan into a hug.

"Thank you so much for my present." she whispered in his ear. She couldn't help but smile to herself as she thought about what the Eclipse boys had done for her. To thank her for all of her hard work over the years the four of them had decided to split her debts between them and pay them off as a surprise. So, for the first time in years Chloe was now free of the debts Andy had left her with. Even though she felt guilty that they'd done that for her, she'd felt a huge weight lift from her chest, like she was finally free of the chains that were holding her down.

"You're welcome Chlo Bo, we just wanted to do something to help." Nathan said quietly, squeezing her tightly for a moment before letting go of her.

"I'll never be able to express how grateful I am." Chloe said quietly.

"It's fine honestly." he said quickly, before walking away.

"I still can't believe the four of you did that for me." Chloe muttered as soon as Nathan had left.

"We wanted too. I told Nathan that I was thinking about paying off your debts for you and he suggested that I approach the boys and we split it four ways as a surprise present." Lee explained.

"Your face was so cute when I gave you the letters from the credit card companies." he smiled at her.

"I just couldn't believe it." she muttered, smiling slightly when she remembered how shocked she'd been to read the letters that told her all her debts had been settled.

"So how does it feel to be a free woman?" he added, smiling warmly at her, trying to lighten the mood as he could sense that she was feeling guilty.

"Pretty good actually, I never have to go back to that bench again." she said quietly.

"You wouldn't have needed to go back to it anyway, I've told you this house is yours as much as it is mine." he smiled at her. The two of them fell silent and turned to face the door as the doorbell rang. Chloe quickly climbed off the stool and hurried along the hallway to answer the door.

"Hey ladies." she smiled as she quickly beckoned for Kirstie and Louise to come in.

"Ooh, something smells amazing." Louise said, as she removed her jacket and hung it on a hook.

"Lee's making carbonara." Chloe told them.

"Wow, he's quite the chef, isn't he?" Kirstie laughed.

"He tries." Chloe giggled.

"I think he feels really guilty that he might have upset everyone." she added.

"He didn't upset me, I thought it was adorable that he was sticking up for you." Louise smiled as the four of them walked into the kitchen.

"Lou Bear!" Lee exclaimed as soon as he saw her.

"No, you stay away from me, I swear to god if there's another contaminated towel coming my way then I'm going to kill you!" Louise laughed as Lee moved towards her and quickly pulled her into a hug.

"There's no more towels....at least not today anyway." Lee laughed. Chloe smiled as she watched the two of them, she couldn't help but feel happy that the two of them were such good friends.

"Are you making apology food?" Kirstie teased Lee.

"Yeah, kind of." he smiled.

"It's Michelle that was the one in the wrong, not you two." Kirstie told them.

"The things she said about you were disgusting." Louise said, sounding slightly angry.

"And the biggest load of bullshit I've ever heard, if you're a hooker then what does that make her?!" Lee exclaimed, suddenly feeling very angry.

"She's never liked that you don't sleep around though has she, don't you remember at Uni, before you and Andy got together, she kept trying to set you up with people." Kirstie reminded her.

"That's right she did, I'd forgotten about that." Chloe said thoughtfully.

"Maybe she was so jealous of you that she wanted to steal your virtue, so that you didn't seem so perfect." Louise said, rolling her eyes. Chloe glanced at Lee, smiling slightly as he raised his eyebrow at her.

"This is what I don't understand, she called me Little Miss Perfect the time before, but my life isn't perfect, I don't have any family and I was homeless for a year." Chloe said quietly.

"I wouldn't worry about it Chlo." Lee said quickly, trying to diffuse the situation before Chloe got upset.

"Your story last night about when the two of you met was so cute." Kirstie said, changing the subject.

"I spoke to the boys about it this morning and they don't remember me from back then." Chloe told them.

"Nathan said he remembers me keep going on about you though." Lee laughed.

"I'm pretty sure he was joking." Chloe smiled.

"He wasn't, I did keep going on about you." Lee smiled.

"Aww, could you not stop thinking about her?" Louise piped up, a slightly dreamy expression on her face.

"Nope, and there were a lot of random bathroom visits too, so that I could 'think' about her some more." Lee laughed, gesturing inverted commas. Louise and Kirstie burst out laughing, glancing at Chloe who was sitting silently, her cheeks slowly colouring.

"He's joking." Chloe said quickly, squirming in embarrassment.

"I'm really not." Lee winked at her. Chloe sighed quietly to herself, even though she knew that Lee didn't mean any harm with his comments it was just the way he was, she couldn't help but feel embarrassed. She was a very private person that didn't like to broadcast things, especially in front of her friends.

"You're so cute." Lee laughed when he noticed her coloured cheeks. Lee quickly served the food and handed each of them a plate. They smiled their thanks and followed him through to the Dining Room.

"It's a shame Kathleen couldn't manage to come over." Louise said thoughtfully.

"We were speaking about that earlier, she's probably a bit embarrassed." Chloe told them.

"Yeah probably, it's a shame really. She seemed quite upset." Kirstie sighed.

"Mark's a dick though." Lee stated.

"I mean fair enough, I used to get with a lot of women, but I was always upfront with them, Mark is sly with it." he quickly added.

"Michelle is literally going to have no friends left, the way she is going." Louise said thoughtfully.

"Speaking of which, I asked her to find her own place." Kirstie announced.

"What?!" Chloe spluttered, coughing slightly on the spaghetti that was in her mouth. Lee watched her closely, slightly concerned that she was going to choke.

"Please tell me it wasn't because of me?" Chloe asked when she recovered herself.

"It's a combination of everything.... I basically said to her that she's obviously got things going on right now, but I don't want to be dragged into it, so for the sake of our friendship she needs to find her own place." Kirstie explained.

"But where is she going to go?" Chloe said quietly, feeling slightly sorry for Michelle, despite everything that she had done. Chloe knew better than anyone what it was like to be homeless.

"She's gone to stay with a friend I think." Kirstie said, smiling at Chloe when she realised once again how big her heart was. Even though Michelle had caused Chloe and Lee nothing but problems, Chloe still couldn't bear the thought that Michelle might be suffering.

"I don't want everyone to fall out with her on my behalf though." Chloe said quietly,

"It's not really, she's the one who has been out of line, you haven't done anything." Kirstie quickly reassured her.

"I guess I know that." Chloe said quietly. The group fell silent, each of them deep in thought about what could have possibly prompted Michelle to suddenly turn so nasty.

"You know what we need!" Louise randomly piped up, pausing for a moment for dramatic effect.

"We need to plan a weekend away." she added.

"Ooh that would be amazing!" Kirstie exclaimed.

"In our couples, just the six of us." Louise continued excitedly.

"So, we'll finally get to meet Peter?" Lee asked, wiggling his eyebrows at her.

"Only if you promise not to do your overprotective brother mode." Louise laughed. Lee raised his eyebrow at her, smiling slightly.

"Maybe we could do like a resort type thing, they have nice lodges and cool activities on site, don't they?" Kirstie suggested.

"Oh yeah they do, that could be fun." Louise agreed.

"Could we maybe go to the Woburn Forest one, I've always wanted to go to the zoo there?" Chloe asked.

"It's the biggest zoo in the UK." she added.

"Sounds like a plan, where is it?" Louise asked.

"Bedford, I think." Chloe told them.

"I need to go home and get my laptop, so that we can book it now!" Kirstie said excitedly, quickly standing up.

"Why don't you just use mine?" Lee laughed.

"Oh yeah, that would be easier." Kirstie laughed.

"Where is it then?" she quickly added.

"Upstairs probably." Lee said, bursting out laughing when Kirstie left the room and dashed upstairs before he'd even finished speaking.

Chapter Fifty-One

Chloe couldn't help but smile as she sat in rehearsals and watched Lee, Nathan, Adrian and Steven practicing the lyrics for the songs on their new album. Goosebumps rose on her arms every time that Lee sung his parts, his powerful voice causing butterflies to swarm in her stomach. Matt smiled at her as he walked over and sat on the bench beside her, his eyes fixed on the band.

"I think they are almost ready for the tour." Matt said.

"Have you figured out dates for when it starts yet?" Chloe asked.

"Nothing for definite yet, but probably within the next few months." he told her.

"We need to get the album out first though don't we." she said.

"Yes indeed. We're getting the album promo shots done today, so that's one less thing to do." he said.

"If they ever bloody turn up." he added, glancing at his watch.

"Lee mentioned that the photo shoot was today, do you want me to do the boy's makeup now?" Chloe asked.

"I think they are okay at the moment." Matt sighed, starting to get slightly stressed that they were already behind schedule with the organisation for the tour and now the photo shoot was running behind.

"You might need to do the girls when they get here too, I'm not sure if they are doing their own or not." he quickly added. Chloe couldn't help but glance at Lee and sigh quietly when she realised that once again, he was going to spend the day surrounded by beautiful women. Matt glanced at Chloe and followed her eyeline as her gaze remained fixed on Lee.

"Is he taking good care of you?" he asked quietly, nervous that they might be overheard.

"Yes, he's been amazing." Chloe smiled. Lee glanced over at her, as he felt her watching him from across the room. As soon as their eyes locked, Chloe quickly looked away, fearful that it would be obvious that something was going on between them.

"Maybe I should go and sort out the boy's outfits?" Chloe asked.

"Yeah, you could do." Matt said, smiling at her.

Lee couldn't help but watch Chloe as she stood up and walked out of the room. As usual he found himself wanting to follow her, like an invisible bungee rope that was constantly trying to pull him after her. Matt quickly stood up and walked over to the band. The door to the room opened and Jonny walked in, followed by three young female models.

"We have a bit of a problem." Jonny told the group as soon as he reached them.

"What now?" Matt sighed.

"One of the models has gone down with a stomach bug, so we are short." Jonny said quickly, slightly nervous about how Matt was going to take it.

"Great." Matt said shortly.

"I don't know if you want to reschedule?" Jonny suggested.

"We can't, we only have the photographer for today and plus there is no room in the schedule, we still have so much other stuff to do." Matt said, running his hand through his hair in frustration.

"It's going to look stupid with just three models, I thought you wanted them to have one each." Jonny pointed out.

"I did, does the agency not have a stand in or anything?" Matt asked.

"Not at such short notice." Jonny replied.

"For god sake." Matt muttered under his breath.

The two of them instantly stopped talking as the door opened and Chloe walked in, carrying four bags of clothes. They watched her as she walked towards the group, struggling slightly under the load she was carrying.

"I have your outfits." she told Adrian, Nathan, Steven and Lee as soon as she reached them.

"Although I'm not sure they are right, they seem a bit basic." Chloe added, turning to Matt after she handed each of the boys a bag.

"What's in them?" Matt frowned, starting to feel like this day couldn't possibly get any worse.

"Black skinny jeans and a simple white suit shirt." Chloe told him.

"Yeah, that's right, we're going for a simple look, the shirts need to be left unbuttoned." Matt explained.

"There's no shoes either, are they going barefoot?" Chloe asked. Matt nodded. Chloe turned her back to allow them to get changed. As she stood with her back to them, she rummaged in her makeup pouch, quickly pulling out the powder and a brush. Chloe frowned as she saw Matt and Jonny watching her closely. After a few moments had passed Chloe slowly turned back to face them, smiling cheekily at them, knowing how much they hated having makeup put on.

"Don't give me that look, it's not my fault you have spots." Chloe giggled, quickly applying makeup to Nathan's face.

"I have *a spot.*" Nathan corrected, smiling slightly at her. As soon as Chloe had finished Nathan's makeup, she quickly moved onto Lee, desperately trying not to stare at his chest as she stood in front of him.

Lee stared down at Chloe as she stood in front of him. Even though they'd been dating for a few months, he could still feel his heart pounding against his chest whenever she was close to him. He longed to reach out and touch her, to be able to stroke her cheek or to hold her perfect body against his. Lee reluctantly tore his eyes away from Chloe and glanced up. He frowned to himself as he noticed Matt and Jonny watching Chloe, the two of them glancing at each other and raising their eyebrow.

"Are you thinking what I'm thinking?" Jonny eventually asked.

"It did enter my head, but it's probably not the best idea." Matt said, glancing at Lee.

"Of course, it is, she'll be perfect." Jonny insisted.

"I know." Matt said nervously, slightly nervous about how Lee was going to react. Lee glanced at Chloe again and sighed quietly, he knew what they were suggesting, and found himself wishing that he could give her a heads up in some way. The last thing he wanted was for her to be put on the spot, when he knew how self-conscious she was.

"Hey Chloe." Jonny called out to her. Chloe quickly stopped what she was doing and turned to face him.

"Would you be able to do us a big favour?" Jonny asked.

"I am not performing tricks with you again." Chloe said quickly.

"No something else. You need to go and do your hair and makeup, make yourself look beautiful." Jonny told her. Chloe frowned in confusion, not entirely sure what he was talking about.

"What Jonny is attempting to communicate is that we are a model down for the shoot and need you to stand in." Matt explained.

"No way." Chloe said quickly.

"I'm not a model, I wouldn't have any idea what to do." she quickly added.

"You'll be fine, the photographer will keep you right." Matt told her.

"Besides I'm not beautiful like them, I'll stick out like a sore thumb." Chloe said quietly, gesturing to where the models were sitting in the corner, applying their makeup.

"You can hold your own with all of them." Jonny told her. Chloe stared at the floor, her cheeks colouring. She could feel her palms getting sweaty at the thought of standing in front of a camera, everyone staring at her and silently judging her. These were the situations she spent most of her life trying to avoid. Chloe shook her head, slowly stepping back from them as she began to panic slightly. She gasped when her back made contact with Lee, as she suddenly remembered that he was still standing behind her. As she stood in place, her back gently resting against Lee's chest, his warmth radiating against her, she could feel herself slowly calming down.

"You might actually enjoy it, and we'll be there with you." Nathan piped up.

"I don't feel comfortable." Chloe said in a small voice, feeling slightly guilty.

"If you don't feel comfortable then don't do it, we can always reschedule." Lee said quietly.

"We don't have any space in the schedule to reschedule it!" Matt exclaimed.

"We'll make do with three then." Lee argued.

"The dynamic won't look right with the four of you if we do that." Jonny said shortly. Chloe sighed quietly, glancing at Nathan who was watching her hopefully. Even though she didn't feel entirely comfortable with the situation she knew how important it was that they didn't fall even further behind schedule. The Eclipse boys had been good to her over the years and they'd never asked her for anything, until now. She knew in her heart that she couldn't let them down. Chloe sighed deeply.

"Fine, I'll do it." she told them nervously.

"Brilliant, go and do your hair and makeup, I'll bring you the outfit!" Jonny said happily. Chloe nodded, glancing briefly at Lee, who gave her a small reassuring smile.

Chloe gasped as she stood in the bathroom at the studio and stared in horror at her reflection. When she'd agreed to step in and help, she'd had no idea that the outfit would be so revealing. She'd been expecting to wear clothes, not a white lace corset with matching panties. Her stomach sunk as she realised how ridiculous she looked, there was no way she could pull off an outfit like this, she wasn't a model. As soon as one of the wardrobe team had finished lacing up the corset, Chloe had grabbed her makeup bag and run into the bathroom, desperately trying to hide before anyone caught sight of her. Chloe racked her brain, desperately trying to think of what to do, all she knew was that she felt too naked and exposed to leave the bathroom. She rummaged in her makeup bag and pulled out her phone, quickly sending Lee a text. While she waited for him she quickly applied the finishing touches to her makeup, trying to do whatever she could to give herself a small shred of confidence.

Chloe jumped and dropped the makeup brush as she heard footsteps approaching the bathroom. She ran into one of the cubicles, quickly locking the door behind herself. She listened carefully as she heard the door to the bathroom open and squeak closed again.

"Chloe?" Lee called as he looked around the bathroom and realised that Chloe wasn't there.

"I'm in here." she called back.

"I got your text, what's wrong?" he asked quickly.

"I can't wear this outfit; I don't know what to do." she told him sadly.

"Why not?" he frowned.

"Haven't you seen the other models' outfits?" she asked him.

"No, I think they are still faffing about with makeup." he told her, rolling his eyes. Chloe fell silent and sighed quietly to herself. She slowly opened the cubicle door and peered around it, smiling nervously when she saw Lee, standing quietly, waiting for her.

"Are you going to show me then?" he chuckled. Chloe took a deep breath, desperately trying to steady her nerves. Even though she felt self-conscious about showing him, she knew that she had to show someone and that he was the best person.

Before she could talk herself out of it, she slowly stepped out from behind the door, her eyes fixed on the floor as she walked out of the cubicle and stood awkwardly in the bathroom.

"Holy shit." Lee breathed when he laid eyes on her. He couldn't tear his eyes away from her. His eyes roamed her body as she stood in front of him in a white lace corset, which perfectly held her breasts, pushing them upwards slightly, the tightness of the fabric highlighting her tiny waist. His eyes widened as he noticed the small white lace, matching panties, just visible under the lace trim that ran around the base of the corset.

"I know, I look ridiculous." she said sadly, sounding slightly tearful.

"That's not the word I would use." he replied hoarsely.

"Stunning maybe or perfect." he added quietly. Chloe's eyes flickered upwards as she finally locked eyes with Lee. He took a deep breath and maintained eye contact with her, desperately trying to resist the urge to stare at her body.

"I wouldn't have agreed to step in, if I knew the outfits were so revealing." she admitted.

"It suits you though." he told her, clearing his throat.

"I'll stick out like a sore thumb, standing half naked with a bunch of models." she said sadly.

"Only because you'll be the most beautiful one there." he told her quietly. Chloe raised her eyebrow sceptically.

"It's true, they are fake pretty, but you're naturally beautiful." he mumbled.

"I guarantee you that every man that sees you out there will want to sleep with you." he said, when she still hadn't responded.

"I'm pretty sure Nathan won't." she giggled.

"Sometimes I hate that we are a secret." he sighed.

"Why?" she asked.

"Because sometimes it would be nice for people to know that you are with me and to keep their hands off." he said thoughtfully.

"Wait, are you getting insecure?" she frowned.

"Maybe a little." he admitted.

"I just know how difficult it is to resist you right now and I won't be the only one struggling." he told her.

"I would never look at anyone else." she told him.

"I know, I trust you. I just don't trust guys." he said smiling slightly. Chloe smiled slightly and walked towards him, stopping when she was stood in front of him. Lee quickly turned away from her, knowing that he needed to resist her. He closed his eyes for a moment, trying to focus his mind on anything except the beautiful woman standing silently beside him.

"Is something wrong?" Chloe asked, placing her hand on his shoulder, clearly having no idea the effect she was having on him. Lee slowly opened his eyes, he sighed to himself as he caught sight of Chloe in the bathroom mirror.

"I can't do this anymore." he whispered.

Before Chloe could respond, he placed his hands on her hips and gently picked her up, placing her on the bathroom counter.

She giggled and wrapped her arms around his neck as he gazed down at her, breathing deeply. Chloe watched Lee's hands as they quickly trailed all over her body, eventually coming to a stop on her thighs. He gently spread her legs and stood between them, pulling her closer so that her body was pressed against him. He smiled slightly as Chloe giggled and wrapped her legs around him. Lee kissed her passionately, finally able to give into some of the deep desire that he was feeling for her.

"How am I going to concentrate on posing for photos, with you in that outfit." Lee said quietly when he eventually stopped kissing her lips. Chloe gasped as Lee began to kiss her neck.

"Be careful you don't leave a mark." Chloe said quickly when she suddenly remembered that they still had the photo shoot to do. Lee sighed and quickly stopped kissing her, gently resting his forehead against her collarbone. Chloe shivered as she felt his warm breath against her bare skin. After a few moments, he eventually lifted his head to look at her.

"I've kind of ruined your makeup." he smiled at her as she carefully climbed off the counter.

"That's because most of it is on your face." she laughed. Chloe quickly picked up a makeup wipe off the counter and gently wiped away the traces of her lipstick from his face.

"I think I have a bigger problem than my face." he said quietly, glancing down at his crotch. Chloe followed his eyeline.

"I thought I could feel it before." she smiled.

"It's your fault you know." he grinned.

"Technically you kissed me." she smiled.

"It was there before that, as soon as I saw you in that damn outfit." he muttered. Chloe giggled, her cheeks colouring slightly.

"You'd better go, we can't be seen leaving together." she reminded him as she started to quickly reapply her makeup. Lee nodded and quickly left the bathroom, before he was unable to fight the urge to kiss her again.

Chapter Fifty-Two

As Chloe eventually emerged from the bathroom and began the short walk back into the studio, she could slowly feel her nerves starting to settle slightly. Even though she still didn't feel entirely comfortable in the outfit, Lee's reaction had given her a small amount of confidence that maybe she could pull this off after all.

"Wow Chloe!" Adrian exclaimed as she walked into the studio and quickly made a beeline to stand with Steven, Adrian, Nathan and Lee.

"You look gorgeous Chlo Bo." Nathan told her, quickly giving her a reassuring hug when he noticed how nervous she looked.

"You are a lucky guy." Steven told Lee. Lee nodded slowly, feeling slightly uncomfortable watching his bandmates check out his girlfriend. Even though he could understand why they couldn't help themselves, it still didn't sit well with him.

"Chloe, can you come over here for a second!" Matt called from across the room. Chloe glanced at Lee who smiled at her reassuringly, wishing not for the first time that he could pull her into his arms and tell her how much he loved her.

"You need to stop looking at her like that." Steven said as soon as Chloe walked away.

"Like what?" Lee frowned.

"A mixture of loved up and that you want to take her right now." Steven chuckled.

"Maybe I do." Lee muttered.

"People are going to notice, and you want your relationship to be a secret." Adrian reminded him.

"I'm sick of it being a secret." Lee muttered bitterly as he glanced across the room and saw Jonny staring at Chloe. Lee sighed as Jonny wrapped his arm around Chloe's waist and led her over to the other models.

"You could always tell everyone, if that's what you want?" Steven suggested.

"I can't, I have to keep her protected for as long as possible." Lee sighed sadly.

"I want her paired up with me though." he quickly told them. The four of them instantly stopped talking as Jonny walked over to them.

"The four of you are very welcome." he said as soon as he reached them.

"For what?" Nathan asked, frowning in confusion.

"Getting Chloe to wear that outfit, I mean what a show." Jonny said smugly, his eyes wandering to Chloe again.

"We were just saying that she scrubs up well." Steven agreed.

"She's so beautiful, the best part is the innocence though, she won't have been with many men." Jonny said thoughtfully.

"It's better to have someone with experience though I think." Nathan said quickly, trying to put Jonny off. Nathan could sense that Lee was growing angrier by the minute and he couldn't help but feel concerned that if Jonny kept speaking about Chloe that Lee was going to lash out and say or do something that he would regret.

"Yeah, most of the time, but I reckon she'll be nice and tight." Jonny smirked.

"I'll let you boys know tomorrow." he quickly added, laughing slightly.

"Tomorrow?" Nathan asked.

"Yep. All women succumb to me eventually." Jonny said smugly wiggling his eyebrows. Nathan, Steven and Adrian fell silent, the three of them feeling slightly awkward.

Lee could feel his blood slowly simmering as he listened to this vulgar man speak about the woman, he loved like she was a piece of meat. He bit the inside of his lip to stop himself from giving Jonny a few home truths.

"How long have you four been working with her?" Jonny asked, almost like he was desperate to get the four of them to join in with his 'banter'.

"Just over two years." Adrian said, shuffling his feet awkwardly.

"Christ, I'm surprised none of you have had a go on her.... especially you." Jonny said, looking at Lee. Lee remained silent, glaring at him, desperately wishing that he didn't have to keep their secret, so that he could defend Chloe's honour.

"She's like a little sister to us." Nathan said quickly, before Lee could respond.

"Oh well, less competition for me then." Jonny grinned before finally walking away.

"I really want to deck him." Lee said angrily as soon as Jonny was out of earshot.

"Yeah, me too and she's not even my girlfriend." Nathan admitted.

"How dare he speak about her like that." Lee hissed.

"Just forget about it, who cares what he thinks." Steven said quickly.

"That's easy for you to say." Lee snapped.

"Please don't start anything, we need to get this shoot done." Adrian sighed, afraid that their resident loose cannon was going to kick off again. Lee rolled his eyes and quickly walked over to where Matt was gesturing for them to join.

"Do you want Chloe with you?" Matt said quietly to Lee. Lee nodded slowly and walked over to stand beside Chloe. Matt quickly took charge of the situation and assigned each of the other boys to a model.

"Chloe, you need to take off your necklace." Jonny told her as he stood behind the camera.

"Why?" Chloe asked.

"No one else is wearing jewellery, we are going for a simple look." he explained. Chloe glanced down at the necklace Lee had given her on the night she'd made, what was to her, a big commitment to the man she loved. She couldn't help but feel slightly tearful at the thought of removing it.

"It means a lot to me; I haven't taken it off since I got it." she said quietly.

"But..." Jonny started.

"I've agreed to help out, so my necklace stays on." Chloe interrupted firmly.

"It's fine, it can stay on." Matt told Jonny.

"Right, everyone, this is Sam, he's the photographer. I have some paperwork to do so I'm going to leave him in charge." Matt announced.

"Okay guys, we are going to start off with some shots of the individual couples." Sam explained.

"We'll go first." Lee said quickly, keen to get their photographs out of the way so that Chloe could cover herself up. Sam nodded and watched as Lee took Chloe's hand and gently helped her to step over the wires and take her position in front of the backdrop. Chloe giggled as Lee twirled her slowly, gently placing his hands on her waist as her back rested against his chest.

"Chloe, slowly bring your left arm up towards Lee's neck and look back at him. The two of you need to pretend that you fancy each other." Jonny instructed. Chloe frowned slightly at his words, but she decided not to dwell on it and quickly did as he asked. As she gazed into Lee's eyes, she could feel her legs getting weak, she'd never loved anyone as much as she loved him. He was her whole world, the one who made her feel complete.

"Now turn to face each other." Sam instructed. Chloe turned to face Lee, quickly wrapping her arms around his neck. Lee sighed quietly, desperately trying to focus his mind as he gazed down at Chloe, gently placing his hands on her waist.

"Maybe we could incorporate some of her tricks somehow?" Jonny suggested. Chloe turned to look at them, frowning in confusion.

"Tricks?" Sam frowned, seemingly equally confused.

"Yeah, like she can do the splits and stuff, so maybe she could do that against Lee or something?" Jonny asked, smiling slightly.

"Don't do it Chlo." Lee quickly whispered in her ear, realising instantly that Jonny had ulterior motives. Since Chloe was wearing a revealing outfit, Lee knew that she would unknowingly reveal more than she meant too. Lee couldn't help but feel slightly angry that Jonny clearly wanted to put her in a compromising position, but he wasn't going to let that happen.

"I think I'm okay like this." Chloe said quietly.

"We should be fine with what we have, we'll do the group shots and then move on to the other individual couples." Sam stated. Chloe remained close to Lee as she watched the other Eclipse boys and their models join them. Lee went into autopilot as he followed the photographer's instructions, the more time that he spent in Chloe's presence the more difficult he was finding it to hide how he felt about her.

"Maybe we should switch up the couples?" Steven suggested, snapping Lee out of his thoughts.

"Actually, that's not a bad idea, I'm not really feeling these couples." Sam agreed. Lee glanced at Chloe as he noticed her peering around nervously.

"I'm happy with mine." Lee said quickly.

"No, I think we need to switch." Sam said.

"I could take Chloe?" Steven suggested.

"Yes, let's do that, we'll swap Kate and Chloe." Sam said firmly. Lee felt his heart sink a little as Chloe reluctantly walked away from him and stood in front of Steven. She stood in front of Steven awkwardly, feeling slightly uncomfortable at the thought of having to pretend to be flirting with him and potentially drape her half naked body over him.

"Okay if everyone can press your foreheads against your partner, pretend that you are about to kiss." Sam told them. Chloe sighed and did as the photographer asked. She couldn't decide what was making her feel worse, the fact that she was being asked to flirt with someone who wasn't her boyfriend or that the same thing was happening to Lee.

"Chloe, you need to try and sell it." Steven told her quietly.

"Right now, pick up the girls, and they will wrap their legs around your waists." Sam instructed. Steven quickly picked Chloe up, she blushed as she reluctantly wrapped her legs around his waist. Chloe grimaced as she felt Steven place his hands on her hips to support her weight.

"Trust me, you have to pretend." Steven told her. Chloe sighed and tried to relax against him. She closed her eyes for a moment, desperately trying to convince herself that she was in Lee's arms.

"Okay, that's great everyone, let's take a break." Sam announced. As soon as Sam said those words, Chloe jumped down from her position and walked over to her clothes, quickly pulling her leggings on over her bare legs. She sighed in relief and perched on the windowsill.

Lee quickly chanced a glance over at Chloe, watching her closely as she sat quietly, gazing down at her phone. Even sitting silently in leggings and the corset, he was struck by how beautiful she looked. He'd seen a lot of beautiful women in his time, but never one like her. She seemed to light up a room without even trying.

"Lee, did you hear me?" Adrian asked, snapping Lee out of his thoughts.

"What?" Lee frowned.

"I said that I think Matt wants a word with us about the album." Adrian said, smiling slightly when he followed Lee's eyeline and noticed what he was staring at. Lee nodded slowly, eventually tearing his eyes away from Chloe and reluctantly following the boys to Matt's office.

Chloe glanced up from her phone as she saw Nathan, Steven, Adrian and Lee walk past her. She frowned to herself as she saw Lee deliberately avert his eyes away from her as he walked past. She sighed quietly, suddenly feeling slightly concerned that maybe he was unhappy that she had been posing with Steven. As soon as the boys left the room, Jonny quickly walked over to Chloe and sat next to her on the windowsill. Chloe's heart sunk as he sat beside her, watching her closely. As he sat, staring at her in silence Chloe nervously glanced at him, raising her eyebrow questioningly.

"Has anyone told you how breath-taking you look in that outfit?" he muttered. Chloe shook her head slowly, feeling slightly uncomfortable as he gazed at her longingly.

"Well, you do." he told her. Chloe remained silent, not entirely sure how to handle the situation.

"You could come over to mine for dinner tonight?" he suggested hopefully.

"I have a boyfriend remember." she reminded him quickly. Jonny scoffed, smiling slightly to himself.

"I can be very discreet." he smiled, gently stroking down her arm with his fingers.

"Good for you." she snapped quickly standing up and slowly backing away from him.

"I know you don't want to make it awkward with everyone at work, but it could be our little secret." he said.

"I'm not interested in you; I have a boyfriend." Chloe stated, gasping slightly as her back made contact with the wall.

"And I would never cheat on him, especially not with someone like you." she added, glancing behind her as Lee, Nathan, Steven and Adrian walked back into the room. Lee locked eyes with Chloe, his eyes darkening as he quickly assessed the situation.

"You don't need to keep pretending, it's obvious that you want me." Jonny smiled, resting his hand against the wall behind her.

Chloe watched as he slowly moved closer to her, his face gradually getting closer to hers.

"I could make you feel things that your boyfriend couldn't. You'll always remember a night with me." he whispered softly in her ear. Chloe flinched slightly as Jonny planted a soft kiss on her cheek. She squirmed to get away from him, unable to get away as she was trapped against the wall. She quickly glanced down at his lips as he gradually edged closer to her....

Chapter Fifty-Three

Lee couldn't tear his eyes away from the corner where Jonny was talking to Chloe. He had always known that men fancied Chloe wherever she went, and he couldn't blame them, but that didn't make it any easier for him to stomach. He desperately wanted to get Chloe away from Jonny, but he knew that he had to be careful. If anyone had any inclination that something was going on between him and Chloe, they could potentially expose them to the media and Lee knew that Chloe would struggle to handle it. Lee could feel anger rising in his stomach as Jonny leaned towards Chloe and whispered something in her ear, before placing a kiss on her cheek. Before he could stop himself, Lee quickly stood up and walked over to them.

"Chloe, we need to speak to you about one of the songs on the album." Chloe heard Lee say from behind Jonny.

"We're busy." Jonny quickly told him, not even turning around to face him.

"No, we're not." Chloe snapped, suddenly feeling more confident now that Lee was close by. Jonny sighed and reluctantly turned to face Lee.

"Does it have to be right now?" Jonny asked.

"Well, you were the one who said we are on a tight schedule." Lee said, smiling smugly. Jonny rolled his eyes, glancing back at Chloe who was staring at the floor silently. Jonny smiled slightly as he turned back to Lee.

"I get it now; you've been thinking about what I said earlier haven't you." Jonny smirked.

"Which part?" Lee asked, feigning ignorance.

"You know which part." Jonny snapped.

"So now you are cock blocking me because you've realised that I am right, and you want to get there first." Jonny added, sounding slightly angry.

"No one is cock blocking you, I've told you three times now that I have a boyfriend." Chloe sighed indignantly.

"Yeah, and I've told you that it doesn't bother me." Jonny said.

"Well, it bothers me, so accept it and move on." Chloe said angrily, her temper slowly starting to rise.

"Speaking of your precious boyfriend, does he know that you are prancing around in sexy underwear in front of all of us?" Jonny asked smugly.

"He won't mind." Chloe said quietly.

"Why, because he doesn't exist?" Jonny laughed.

"No, because he knows that he's the only one who gets to see what's underneath." Chloe replied shortly. Lee smiled slightly at her words, quickly looking away from her. Lee glanced behind him as he saw Nathan walk over to join them.

"It's lunch time isn't it?" Nathan asked, quickly trying to take charge of the situation. He knew that he needed to get Chloe away from Jonny before Lee lost his cool with him.

"You guys go, I'm fine here." Jonny told them, quickly turning back to face Chloe. Before Jonny could react, Nathan moved to the other side of him and took Chloe's hand, quickly pulling her under Jonny's arm.

"Hey!" Jonny protested, as Nathan led Chloe away. As soon as Nathan noticed Jonny starting to follow them, he quickly turned to face him.

"When I told you earlier that she was like our little sister, I meant it." Nathan snapped.

"Why is everyone cock blocking me today, you don't even like women!" Jonny said angrily.

"Back off." Nathan warned him.

"Unless you want to have the four of us to deal with." Nathan quickly added, glancing over at Adrian and Steven who were hovering nearby, watching closely. Before Chloe could protest Nathan picked Chloe up and draped her over his shoulder in a fireman lift. Lee followed closely behind as Nathan quickly walked away, carrying Chloe.

"You do realise I can walk?" Chloe giggled.

"Yeah, but this way, he can't get to you." Nathan grinned.

As soon as they reached the next room, Nathan gently placed Chloe down, smiling slightly at her embarrassed expression. Nathan laughed as Chloe playfully glared at Nathan, pretending to be angry with him.

"You're welcome." Nathan chuckled. Chloe smiled slightly, her facade finally dropping. As soon as the door was safely closed behind them, Lee walked up behind Chloe and wrapped his arms around her waist, gently resting his chin on her shoulder. Chloe placed her hands-on top of Lee's and sighed in contentment.

"Why do I always seem to attract the slime balls." Chloe said thoughtfully to herself.

"I think you attract most people, but the slime balls can't hide it as well." Lee whispered in her ear. Lee slowly brushed her hair to one side and gently placed a series of soft kisses on her neck.

"What did Jonny mean when he said you'd been thinking about what he said earlier?" Chloe asked, trying to distract herself from the desire that she was feeling for him. Chloe glanced across the room, locking eyes with Nathan who quickly looked away from her.

"Nothing, he's just vile." Lee said quickly.

"I want to know what he said." Chloe insisted, removing herself from his arms and turning to face him. Lee remained silent, not quite able to bring himself to tell her. Chloe could feel the tension as she glanced around the room, looking at each of the boys in turn.

"Is someone going to tell me then?" Chloe asked, sounding slightly impatient.

"Steven?" Chloe tried, when there was still no response from anyone.

"Basically, he said that you come across really innocent and you won't have been with many men, so you will be nice and tight for him." Steven told her quickly, glancing at Lee when he heard him sigh.

"But I don't belong to him." Chloe said quietly.

"You don't belong to anyone, you're not an object" Lee told her.

"I can't believe he said that." Chloe muttered sadly.

"Why couldn't you have just kept quiet?!" Lee snapped at Steven. Steven rolled his eyes as Lee glared across the room at him.

"I don't really come across like that do I?" Chloe asked quietly.

"There's nothing wrong with having some innocence, it's an endearing trait." Nathan told her.

"Did you think the same as Jonny when we first met?" Chloe asked Lee quietly, her heart sinking slightly.

"No of course not." Lee replied quickly.

"I don't know what I thought really, I can't describe it because I've never felt like that before. It was a mixture of instant attraction and feeling a strong connection with you, even before we spoke." Lee explained. Chloe nodded slowly, smiling slightly at how cute he was sometimes.

"Changing the subject slightly, why did you pull Chloe away from me, when I'd already told you I wanted her with me?" Lee asked, quickly rounding on Steven.

"The two of you were looking like you were really in love...." Steven started.

"There's nothing wrong with that." Lee interrupted.

"No, I know, but I could hear some of the crew whispering and they were gossiping about the two of you. I know you both want to be a secret." Steven quickly explained.

"You were trying to look out for me?" Chloe asked. Steven nodded slowly. Chloe could feel her eyes filling with tears as she suddenly realised how much the four of them cared about her. Nathan had assisted her earlier with Jonny and Steven had been watching her back during the photoshoot. In that moment she suddenly realised how lucky she was to have them as her 'adopted family'.

"I really want to prove a point to him." Chloe muttered angrily as Jonny walked into the room, wiggling his eyebrows at her when he walked past.

"Just forget about him, he's really not worth it." Lee told her quietly.

"I could get drunk and be sexy during the next part of the shoot." Chloe said, smiling slightly.

"Or at least I could try and probably fail." she quickly added.

"Please don't. I definitely won't be able to hide how attracted to you I am if you do that." Lee said quietly.

"I was only joking anyway." Chloe told him. Her eyes wandered across the room as she saw Bobby sitting silently in the corner eating a sandwich. She couldn't help but feel sorry for him when she noticed him run his hand through his hair and sigh sadly.

"I need to speak to Bobby." Chloe said quietly.

"Is that a good idea?" Lee asked. Chloe turned to face him, frowning at his words.

"Because of the outfit." he added quietly.

"He's not like Jonny, I'll be fine." she reassured him. Before he could argue with her, she quickly walked away from him. Bobby smiled at her as she sat next to him.

"How are you doing?" she asked him.

"Alright I guess." he said quietly.

"Mum still isn't any better, it's just difficult isn't it." he added sadly.

"I totally understand." Chloe sighed. As she watched him closely, a look of deep sadness and pain etched on his face, she couldn't help but remember how helpless she'd felt when her mother had been diagnosed as terminal. The months that she'd spent slowly watching her mother fade away before her eyes, suddenly flashed through her mind again. Bobby was such a kind person; he didn't deserve to be in this situation.

"I wish there was something I could do to help." she admitted, gently looping her arm through his and resting her head on his shoulder, in a desperate attempt to provide a small amount of comfort.

"Just knowing that I can talk to you helps." he said quietly.

"I just don't know what I'm going to do without her, she's all I have." he whispered, his eyes filling with tears.

"I know, I'm here for you though." she told him gently.

"I know you are." he smiled, quickly pulling her into a hug. Chloe sighed to herself as she heard him sniff, clearly trying to fight back the tears.

"You know you can call me anytime you need anything." she whispered. Bobby nodded slowly, reluctantly letting go of her. He kept his gaze fixed on the floor, quickly wiping the tears from his eyes, hoping that Chloe hadn't noticed.

"I can't believe you had to step in for one of the models." he smiled, trying to change the subject.

"Me neither." she smiled.

"You looked a bit uncomfortable." he said.

"It's not really my scene is it." she admitted.

"You need to be comfortable in your own skin." he told her.

"You look really pretty, just own it." he told her.

"Thank you." she said quietly.

"Also, I think Lee might like you." he stated.

"Really?!" Chloe squeaked, feeling slightly nervous that her secret had been discovered.

"I don't think he does." she added quickly.

Bobby raised his eyebrow sceptically.

"It's quite obvious from the way he looks at you." he told her. Chloe instinctively looked over at Lee, who quickly looked away from her.

"See." Bobby chuckled. Chloe fell silent, not entirely sure what to say.

"Just be careful, he's a tool." he warned.

"The way he used to strut around the place. He bullied everyone too, although you always got the worst of it." he reminded her.

"He's mellowed a bit since then." she pointed out.

"Hmmm." he said sceptically.

"I think it's a front anyway." she said quietly, feeling slightly sad when she thought back on those times.

"Yeah maybe." he said, not entirely convinced. The two of them stopped talking as Sam walked into the room.

"Right, break is over everyone. We need to get back." he announced to the room. Chloe sighed and reluctantly stood up, her heart sinking slightly at the thought of being half naked again, especially in front of Jonny, after what he'd said about her.

"Remember girl, you're a babe.... just own it." Bobby told her.

Chloe smiled slightly to herself as she stood in the changing room, gazing shyly at her reflection in the mirror. Even though she felt exposed wearing the revealing outfit, she couldn't help but enjoy the effect that it was having on Lee. He'd barely been able to tear his eyes away from her the whole day. Every time that she'd locked eyes with him, she was able to see the deep longing that he was feeling for her. This was the first time in her life that she truly believed that someone was attracted to her. She quickly pulled her clothes on over the top of the outfit, unable to resist the urge to surprise him when they got home.

As soon as she was dressed, she quickly walked back into the hall, smiling mischievously to herself.

"That was quick." Lee told her when she reached him and Nathan.

"I was keen to get changed." Chloe said quickly.

"Are you jogging home?" Nathan asked, referring to her normal routine.

"Not tonight she's not." Lee said quickly, suddenly feeling slightly desperate to get her home as soon as possible so that he could finally show her the effect she was having on him.

"I'll pick you up round the corner." Lee added.

"I can give her a lift if you want, if you don't want to be seen leaving together?" Nathan offered in hushed tones.

"No, it's fine. I'll meet you outside the coffee shop." Lee said firmly, before quickly walking away.

"He's a bit snippy today." Nathan said as soon as Lee had left. Chloe nodded.

"You'd better not keep him waiting, he seems pretty keen to get you home." he chuckled.

"I know." Chloe giggled.

"Thank you for earlier." she said, quickly pulling Nathan into a hug.

"It's fine, you're my little sister, I'll always have your back." he told her. Chloe smiled and sighed happily.

"Now come on, before you really do drive him mad." he chuckled, gently pushing her out of his arms. Chloe nodded and quickly walked across the hall, Nathan following closely behind.

"Chloe!" she heard Jonny's voice call from behind her. As soon as she heard his voice, she could feel herself becoming angry, when she remembered the disgusting things that he'd said about her.

"What?!" Chloe snapped, quickly turning to face him. Her stomach churned in disgust as he quickly jogged over to her and held out a piece of paper.

"My phone number, in case you change your mind." he said, winking at her. Chloe glanced down at his hand, smirking slightly as she saw his expression when she refused to take it.

"I'm going home to my boyfriend now. He doesn't treat me like a piece of meat." Chloe said quickly. Nathan gently placed his hand on her back, trying to calm her down. The last thing he wanted was for Chloe to become so angry that she accidentally blurted out the truth about her and Lee. Chloe started to walk towards the door, quickly stopping and turning back to face Jonny when a thought suddenly popped into her head.

"Oh, I'm keeping the outfit by the way." she told him, a small smirk playing on the corner of her lips as she slowly lifted the corner of her blouse, deliberately showing him that she was still wearing it. Jonny's eyes were fixed on the glimpse of the bottom of her corset. Chloe slowly looped her thumb through the lace panties and pulled them higher, making sure that he could see the lace above her leggings.

"Jesus." Jonny whispered hoarsely, quickly stepping towards her.

"Chloe." Nathan said quickly as he watched Chloe slowly step towards him, stopping when her face was mere inches from his. Chloe glanced down at his lips and bit her lip seductively. Jonny slowly inched his face closer to hers. Chloe waited until their lips were almost touching before she quickly placed her finger on his lips.

"I know what you said about me, and you are *never* going to have me." she whispered smugly. Jonny sighed angrily, slowly shaking his head.

"Well, it's your loss." he said, quickly recovering himself.

"I don't think it is." Chloe stated, before quickly walking away.

Chapter Fifty-Four

"I can't believe you did that to Jonny." Lee laughed when Chloe told him what had happened after he left. He glanced at Chloe as she sat in the passenger seat of the car.

"I maybe got a bit carried away." Chloe giggled.

"Sounds like you kicked his arse, I wish I'd been there to see it." he chuckled.

"I don't know what came over me, I've never done anything like that before." she admitted.

"The things he said about you were disgusting, I'm not surprised you were angry. I had to resist the urge to hit him when he said them." he told her.

"I really hate guys that think women are put on this earth to supply them with sex. And as if I would ever cheat on anyone, especially when I know how it feels to be cheated on." she ranted angrily.

"Although apparently he can make me feel things that you can't." she smirked sarcastically. Lee scoffed sceptically.

"He said that." he laughed.

"Yep, not about you specifically obviously but he whispered in my ear that he can make me feel things that my boyfriend can't." she told him.

"Does he want to bet." he replied quickly, sounding slightly angry.

"He's right though to be fair." she said quietly.

"What?" Lee frowned, quickly glancing at her.

"You don't make me feel like I want to vomit." she pointed out. Lee smiled slightly.

"Eww, the thought of sleeping with him is so gross." she grimaced, screwing up her face in disgust.

"I bet he still thinks that I want him." she added thoughtfully.

"It doesn't matter what he thinks, I know that you would never cheat on me." he told her. Chloe sighed angrily and fell silent, trying to get Jonny out of her head.

"Although I do worry that one day you'll wake up and realise that you can do so much better than me." he added.

"That'll never happen, you're everything I ever wanted." she smiled at him.

"If you do leave me for someone just make sure it's someone like Bobby rather than Jonny. At least Bobby seems to really care about you." he stated.

"I'm not going to leave you." she said firmly.

"You can't start getting insecure, that's my role in this relationship." Chloe laughed. Lee glanced at her for a moment, before bursting out laughing.

"I'm not normally, it's just been really difficult watching everyone check you out all day." he admitted.

"Just Jonny, and he would sleep with any woman." she pointed out.

"It wasn't just him; it was pretty much everyone. Even Steven and Adrian checked you out." he told her.

"No, they didn't!" she protested.

"They definitely did, more than once too." he insisted. Chloe fell silent, thinking for a moment.

"Even if they did it doesn't matter, you're the one who gets to take me home." she told him. Before Lee could respond Chloe gently placed her hand on his leg, her fingers slowly tracing along the inside of his thigh. She smiled to herself as he gasped and began to squirm slightly.

"What's gotten into you today?" he asked her, his voice slightly hoarse. Lee kept his eyes fixed on the road, trying not to get distracted by what Chloe was doing.

"I don't really know." she admitted.

"I have a surprise for you though." she added as they approached a set of traffic lights.

"Uh oh." he chuckled. As soon as the traffic light turned red, Chloe quickly unfastened the buttons on her blouse, moving the fabric to one side so that the corset was visible. She glanced at Lee, clearing her throat so that he would look at her. His eyes widened when he gazed at her and saw that she was still wearing the outfit from earlier.

"You can't do this to me, I need to focus on the road." he mumbled. Lee reluctantly tore his eyes away from her, desperately trying to focus on the road.

"Shit." he mumbled as he tried to pull away and stalled the car. Lee quickly restarted the car and eventually pulled away.

"That was your fault you know." he said quietly, glancing at Chloe and quickly averting his eyes. He took slow breaths, trying not to think about how beautiful she looked. He'd never been so aroused in his life, it had been difficult enough for him, trying to resist her all day, but now that he had her to himself, he was struggling even more.

Lee quickly took hold of Chloe's hand and held it tightly, to stop her from stroking his leg. Chloe smiled mischievously as she firmly pulled his hand towards herself and held it in place on her lap. She slowly moved his hand to her abdomen, allowing him to feel the soft material of her corset.

"You're killing me Chloe." he breathed, unable to resist stroking small circles on her abdomen.

"You'll be okay, we're almost home." she giggled. Lee glanced at her for a moment before impulsively swerving into a layby. He quickly switched off the engine, removed his seatbelt and leaned towards her.

"Wait!" Chloe said quickly.

"What do you mean wait, you've been teasing me all day?" Lee frowned.

"I know, but we can't have sex here, someone will see us!" she exclaimed. Lee laughed, gently resting his forehead against hers, their lips mere centimetres away.

"I just wanted to do this." he told her, quickly kissing her deeply. As Lee kissed her, he gently placed his hands on her hips, wishing that he could press her body against his.

"It's nice to know where your head is at though. I quite like this wild side." he admitted when he eventually stopped kissing her.

"I don't know what's happening to me." she laughed.

"I'm a bad influence, that's what's happening." Lee laughed, putting his seatbelt back on.

"Just hold that thought until we get home." he grinned, quickly pulling away. Chloe gasped as the force of Lee pulling away at high speed threw her back in the seat. Chloe was certain that he was breaking the speed limit, in his haste to get them home.

As soon as Lee pulled into the driveway, he switched off the engine and quickly climbed out of the car. Chloe slowly began to do up the buttons on her blouse, fearful that she would be seen by the neighbours. She glanced up as Lee opened her door and took her hand, quickly pulling her out of the car.

"I need to do up these buttons first." Chloe protested.

"You won't be out here long enough for it to be an issue." he told her. Chloe squealed as he quickly picked her up, placing her over his shoulder.

"What is it with everyone picking me up today?" she giggled as he carried her towards the house. Lee unlocked the door and quickly entered the security code before stepping inside the house and gently setting her down. Lee quickly removed his jacket and shoes, frowning as he saw Chloe walking in the opposite direction to him.

"Where are you going?" he called after her as she pulled off her shoes and leggings and began to climb the stairs.

"I figured you'd want to head straight upstairs." she frowned.

"No." he told her firmly, smiling slightly at her confused expression.

"I can't wait that long." he added, quickly taking her hand and leading her into the living room, quickly pushing the door closed behind them. Chloe giggled as Lee sat on the sofa, quickly pulling her onto his lap, his hands gently resting in place on her hips. Lee gazed at her longingly as she unfastened the remaining buttons on her blouse and let it slowly fall to the ground. She rested her forehead against his, their lips virtually touching enjoying the fact that she was teasing him slightly.

"You're so beautiful." he whispered. Chloe smiled and placed her hands under his shirt, her warm hands stroking his bare skin. She quickly took the material of his shirt between her hands and lifted it over his head. As soon as Chloe removed his shirt, Lee kissed her passionately, feeling slightly relieved that he was finally able to give into the feelings that he'd been fighting all day.

Chloe shivered in pleasure as Lee's hands trailed up her back, eventually coming to a stop when he reached the bare skin on her shoulders. His hands quickly trailed back down, as soon as he reached her hips, he roughly pulled her body closer to him. Chloe wrapped her arms around his neck, gently stroking his hair. Chloe hesitated for a moment, suddenly feeling slightly embarrassed.

"Are you okay?" Lee asked quickly, instantly noticing the change in her body language.

"Yes, I was going to try something, but I'm really not good at being sexy." she said quietly.

"Just do it anyway." he told her. Chloe pressed her body tightly against him, holding onto him, and slowly rotated her hips. Lee quickly rested his head on her shoulder, a small groan of pleasure escaping him.

"That noise was so hot." she whispered in his ear. She could feel Lee trembling against her, his hands gripping tightly onto her corset as she continued rotating her hips.

"I can't do this anymore Chlo." he mumbled a few moments later. Chloe instantly stopped, sitting back slightly.

"Am I doing something wrong?" she asked nervously.

"No, I just can't wait any longer." he said hoarsely. Before Chloe could respond he placed his hands on her hips and quickly turned her around. She could feel his warm breath on her neck as he fumbled with the laces on her corset. Chloe slowly reached down and removed her panties. She frowned to herself as she could still feel Lee trying to undo the laces.

"Sod this, it can stay on." he said quietly, sounding slightly frustrated. He gently pushed her onto the sofa, before quickly pulling off his trousers and boxers. Chloe slowly laid back and watched Lee as he carefully positioned himself on top of her, taking care not to crush her. A small whimper escaped Chloe's lips as he quickly pushed into her without warning. Without hesitation he quickly pumped in and out of her, gently placing a soft kiss on the top of her breasts. Lee couldn't help but smile to himself as he watched the woman that he loved slowly come undone underneath him. As he gazed into her deep blue eyes, he couldn't help but notice the mischievous glint in them.

"What?" he asked.

"Nothing." she said quickly. Before he could say anything else, he felt Chloe tighten her walls around him.

"Fuck." he gasped quietly. A small giggle escaped her lips. She couldn't help but smile at his expression. It was evident the deep longing that he was feeling for her.

"Stop doing that." he begged when she did it again.

"I have a strong pelvic floor remember." she laughed.

"That's because of your bloody tricks." he whispered. Chloe nodded slowly and quickly did it again.

"If you keep doing that, I won't be able to last very long." he whispered hoarsely. Chloe raised her eyebrow sceptically. He quickly increased the pace, determined to make sure that he didn't release before Chloe. She arched her back into him, letting out a small whimper.

"You're so hot when you do that." he told her, smiling slightly to himself. He still couldn't believe that he was the one who got to make love to her. He knew what a privilege it was to have someone like her, especially for someone like him. Chloe slowly wrapped her legs around his hips, her hands holding tightly onto the sofa cushion.

"You don't have to hold it in." he told her.

"I'm waiting for you." she squeaked.

"I love you." she whispered, not able to hold back anymore. As soon as she said those words, Lee couldn't hold back anymore. He groaned quietly as they both released together. Chloe smiled as he collapsed against her, gently resting his head on her chest.

She slowly wrapped her arm around his head and gently stroked his hair, the two of them trying to get their breath back.

"I love you so much." he told her breathlessly. She sighed quietly and rested her head on top of his. Lee sighed in contentment and reluctantly sat up, fearful that he was crushing her. He watched Chloe as she sat up beside him and rested her head against the side of his shoulder. He stared at her, smiling at how striking she looked.

"What?" she smiled, glancing up at him as she felt him watching her.

"I just can't believe my luck sometimes." he admitted. She smiled shyly, gently placing a tender kiss on his lips. Chloe shivered as he placed a soft kiss on her neck. Her skin tingled as he sat sucking her neck. Eventually he pulled away, smiling in satisfaction to himself. Lee picked up his shirt and quickly pulled it on.

"What are you grinning at?" she giggled.

"I might have left a mark." he told her proudly. Chloe rolled her eyes.

"It's okay, I can cover it with makeup." she told him.

"You don't need to do that, let Jonny see it." he said, beaming at her like a child.

"Wait, is that why you did it?" she giggled.

"Maybe." he smiled proudly.

"You're welcome." he added before kissing her softly. The two of them jumped and quickly sprung apart as the living room door opened. They quickly looked across the room and gasped as they locked eyes with Emma. Lee picked up the nearest cushion and quickly placed it on his lap, glancing behind himself at Chloe who had shuffled behind him. He shifted slightly, making sure that her half naked frame was completely hidden behind him.

"Oh my god, I'm really sorry!" Emma said quickly, sounding slightly panicked as she locked eyes with Lee.

"It's fine, what can I do for you?" Lee asked.

"I came to ask if I can go home early, my son has been taken ill at school." she said quietly, clearly feeling uncomfortable.

"Yes of course." Lee told her.

"I'm really sorry again." Emma said.

"I'm sorry Chloe." Emma added, locking eyes with Chloe who was peering over the top of Lee's shoulder. Emma quickly left the room, clearly keen to escape the awkward situation. As soon as she left the room, Lee burst out laughing, quickly pulling on his trousers in case she came back. Chloe groaned and rested her head against his shoulder.

"Oh my god, do you think she knows what we just did?" Chloe asked quietly, her cheeks colouring.

"I'd imagine so, since we're both half naked and sweaty." Lee said sarcastically.

"I can't believe I forgot she was here today." he added.

Lee quickly turned to face Chloe, smiling at how adorable she looked.

"You're so cute." he chuckled.

"It's not funny, I'm so embarrassed." she said quietly, staring at her lap. Lee sighed to himself. He couldn't help but feel sad that her insecurities had come back, he'd seen a different confident side to her today, she'd seemed happier and now she was back to feeling ashamed and embarrassed. He wanted nothing more than for her to be confident in her own skin, to be able to live her life without worrying about what other people thought of her.

"Oh god, what if she saw my body." she whispered.

"She didn't." he said quickly.

"You don't know that." she said sadly.

"Yeah, I do, I checked behind me when she came in, you were hidden behind me." he explained.

"Okay good, thank you." she said, breathing a sigh of relief. Lee watched her closely as she picked up her panties and quickly pulled them on.

"I thought you were starting to get more body confidence anyway." he said quietly.

"I am with you; it doesn't bother me when you see me anymore. But not other people." she explained.

"I feel very privileged." he said, smiling slightly.

"You make me feel special." she said quietly.

"That's because you are special, I want to cherish you." he smiled at her.

"To think a few weeks ago I thought that you didn't want me and today you were desperate for me." she said, smiling slightly.

"I did tell you what you do to me." he laughed. Chloe sighed happily and wrapped her arms around him, closing her eyes as she sat in his arms.

"It's meant to be nice weather at the weekend, we could go to the beach." he suggested.

"I can't, I have Kirstie's slumber party weekend thing remember." she told him.

"Oh yeah, I forgot about that." he admitted.

"I'll hang out with Nathan then; we can finish writing the songs for the album." he added thoughtfully.

"Or I could say that I don't feel well, and we could go to the beach." she suggested, removing herself from his arms so that she could gaze into his eyes.

"That's a bit mean, Kirstie has been good to us." he pointed out.

"I know, I just don't want to be away from you." she sighed.

"You'll be fine, it'll be fun." he told her.

"Wait, Michelle isn't going to be there is she?!" he asked quickly.

"Not that I know of, I don't think Kirstie would invite her after last time." she replied.

"Good, I don't want you near her." he stated.

"It's been a few weeks to be fair, she's probably forgotten about it." she pointed out, suddenly feeling slightly nervous about the fact that Michelle might be there.

Chloe hadn't seen or spoken to her since the weekend that Lee was away in Germany. She still couldn't understand why she'd tried to pull her away from the man that she loved by making up lies and using Chloe's insecurities against her. Chloe glanced at Lee as she felt him getting angry, clearly just speaking about Michelle was enough to make his blood boil. She knew how protective he was of her and he couldn't stand the idea that Michelle might do something to hurt her or come between them again.

"Even if she is there, it doesn't matter, she can say what she wants, it doesn't matter. I know that you love me and how lucky I am to have you." Chloe told him, gently taking his hand in hers and playing with his fingers.

"I don't trust her." he said quietly.

"Nor do I, but I trust you and that's what matters." she said.

"Anyway, I have to shower." she added quickly standing up, her hand still holding onto his. Lee glanced at their hands, frowning slightly.

"Are you coming then?" she asked, raising her eyebrow.

"You want me to shower with you?" he frowned in confusion. He couldn't help but wonder what had happened to Chloe, she'd been gradually getting more confidence over the past few weeks, but he'd never seen this slightly wild side to her before. Chloe nodded.

"Besides you need to help me get this corset off." she smiled.

"If I can get it to come off this time." he laughed. He couldn't help but smile at her proudly as he quickly stood up and followed her upstairs.

Chapter Fifty-Five

Chloe sighed sadly to herself as Lee took her hand and slowly led her up Kirstie's driveway. Even though she'd been looking forward to Kathleen's surprise baby shower for the past couple of weeks, she had been feeling differently the past few days. She wanted to be at home with Lee, in her own little sanctuary where she didn't feel vulnerable. It didn't make any sense to her, why she was feeling this way, nothing had happened or changed to suddenly make her feel like she did. As soon as they reached the doorway, Lee quickly rang the doorbell, glancing at Chloe as she wrapped her other arm through his arm, clinging to him slightly.

"Chlo, you need to tell me what's going on?" he sighed, getting slightly frustrated. She'd been acting clingy for the past few days and even though he'd asked her several times what was going on, she'd always insisted that she was fine. But he knew that something wasn't right with her, she held onto him tightly every chance that she got, almost like something had happened to make her feel vulnerable. He couldn't ignore the feeling in his gut that she wasn't telling him something.

"Nothing is going on." she said, snapping him out of his thoughts.

"Yeah, so you keep saying, but there's obviously something." he sighed.

"I just love you that's all." she whispered, feeling slightly teary. Lee rolled his eyes angrily; he couldn't stand feeling like she was keeping something from him. Chloe smiled at Kirstie as she opened the door and gestured for them both to come in.

"How are my favourite couple?" Kirstie beamed.

"We're fine. How are you?" Chloe asked.

"All good, I'm so excited for tonight." Kirstie said happily.

"You love a surprise don't you." Chloe chuckled. Kirstie nodded quickly, clapping her hands together in excitement.

"A surprise, I thought you were having a slumber party?" Lee frowned.

"It's more of a surprise baby shower for Kathleen." Kirstie told him.

"Hi guys." Louise smiled as she walked out of the kitchen and into the living room.

"Oh Chloe, it's been so long." Louise sighed as she quickly pulled Chloe into a tight hug.

"I know, you've been busy doing gigs though haven't you." Chloe said, smiling at Louise when she let go of her.

"It's been crazy busy; I literally feel like I haven't stopped the past few weeks." Louise agreed. Louise quickly turned and smiled at Lee.

"You alright babes?" he smiled, hugging her gently.

"I'm good, are you being good to my girl?" Louise asked, winking at him.

"Of course." he smiled.

"Since you guys are here, maybe you could help me set up?" Kirstie piped up, feeling slightly stressed when she looked around and noticed how much she still needed to do.

"Sure, what can we do?" Louise said.

"There's a box of decorations over there that need putting up, maybe you and Chloe could do that?" Kirstie suggested. Louise nodded and quickly rummaged through the boxes.

"I'll go and put the food on, Lee do you fancy wrapping the presents?" Kirstie asked.

"Yeah, that's fine, where are they?" he frowned, looking around the room. Kirstie quickly opened a cupboard and pulled out several bags of presents, handing them to Lee.

"Bloody hell." he laughed when he saw the huge pile of presents that he now had to wrap. Kirstie smiled slightly and quickly walked into the kitchen.

"Are you going to have time to wrap all of that stuff, won't Nathan be expecting you?" Chloe asked.

"I'm sure he won't mind if I'm a bit late." Lee replied.

"Maybe I could help you with them?" Chloe suggested, desperate to spend as much time with him as possible.

"You need to help Louise with the decorating." he reminded her. Chloe nodded slowly and reluctantly walked over to Louise. Lee quickly carried the bags into the kitchen and placed them onto the dining table. Kirstie smiled as she handed him the wrapping paper and sticky tape.

He sat silently for a few moments, concentrating on the task at hand. Lee glanced at the door, smiling as he locked eyes with Chloe through the glass panel. Her face lit up when she saw him mouth 'I love you' to her.

"You two are adorable." Kirstie giggled, clearly noticing. Lee turned to face her, smiling slightly at her words.

"She's just.... I don't know.... I don't even have the words." he muttered, not quite able to express how madly in love with Chloe he was.

"I know, I can tell." Kirstie smiled, clearly realising how Lee felt about Chloe.

"She's not been herself the past few days though." he said thoughtfully.

"Maybe she's under the weather." she said.

"No not like that...she seems really clingy, it's almost like she feels vulnerable." he told her.

"That's probably because she loves you." she smiled.

"I don't think it's that, she's not eating much either, I mean she never really eats that much but she is eating less and when I ask her about it she says she feels sick." he explained. Kirstie frowned, suddenly feeling a little concerned for her friend.

"Have you asked her?" Kirstie asked.

"Yeah, loads of times, she says she's fine." he sighed.

"I keep worrying that something has happened that she's not telling me about." he added.

"Like what?" she frowned.

"I don't know, I've been racking my brain the past few days." he muttered.

"Maybe you could ask her for me, she might tell you." he added thoughtfully.

"I can try, but to be honest she's more likely to open up to you than me." she pointed out.

"I'm just a bit worried about her." he sighed, his gaze wandering to where Chloe was standing on a chair, hanging bunting on the wall. Lee's eyes snapped down to his phone as it buzzed loudly. He smiled to himself as he opened an email from Matt and gazed longingly at the pictures from the photoshoot. Lee couldn't help but smile to himself proudly as he was reminded once again how beautiful Chloe was. Flashbacks swirled around his head as he remembered how difficult it had been to resist her that day and the moment that he'd finally been able to show her how much he'd been struggling. Making love with her was the best sex he'd ever had. Being able to hold her in his arms, and feel her body pressed against his was what he longed for. Even though he'd never been in love before, he knew in his heart that what they had was special. They would literally move heaven and earth for each other.

"Are you alright?" Kirstie asked, snapping Lee out of his thoughts. He blinked quickly and reluctantly tore his eyes away from staring at the photographs, desperately trying to focus on something else, before he accidentally revealed how attracted he was to Chloe.

"Yeah, sorry I got distracted." he muttered.

"Chlo, come here a minute!" Lee called. Chloe glanced up when she heard his voice and quickly walked into the kitchen, smiling at Lee when she saw him. She hesitated for a moment before walking across the room, sighing in contentment as she sat on his lap. Lee placed his arm on her shoulder, gently holding her close. She smiled happily as she rested her cheek against his.

"Do you need me for something?" she asked quietly.

"I need to show you these." he told her, holding his phone in front of them. Chloe peered at it, gasping slightly as she saw the pictures from the photoshoot.

"Oh no, I look so awkward." she said quietly, hiding her face in his arm.

"You look stunning." he breathed, gently placing a kiss on her cheek.

"That one's hot." he muttered. Chloe slowly lifted her head and sighed as she gazed at the picture of the two of them. She couldn't help but remember that it was one of the first pictures from the shoot, when she'd been stood in front of Lee, his arms wrapped around her tightly.

"I prefer the ones where I'm a bit more hidden." she said quietly, quickly looking away from the picture. Chloe shivered as he placed his hand under her hair and gently stroked the side of her neck. She sighed in contentment and turned to face him, resting her forehead against his, their lips virtually touching. Lee glanced down at her lips longingly, his gaze wandering back to his phone as Chloe placed her finger on it and swiped to a different picture.

"That one is better." she smiled when she eventually found a picture where she was standing at his side, most of her frame hidden behind him. Lee sighed quietly and placed his hand on her hip, Goosebumps rose on her skin as Lee carefully lifted the corner of her top and placed his hand against her bare skin, slowly stroking a trail along her spine. Chloe trembled slightly as his hand gradually made its way higher.

"Stop it." she whispered, trying to fight the urge to kiss him. She was still very conscious of the fact that Kirstie was in the room. He smirked at her, his hand slowly making its way back down. Lee glanced over at Kirstie as he saw her leave the room. Lee sighed as he softly rested his head against her chest, smiling slightly when he realised how fast her heart was beating.

"Are you sure you want me to stop?" he mumbled, chuckling slightly.

"Yes." she said quietly.

Why?" he smiled, enjoying the fact that he was teasing her.

"Because we're in public." she said quickly. She knew that he loved nothing more than trying to do things that made it difficult for her to resist him.

Lee shrugged and raised his eyebrow at her, without hesitating he planted a series of soft kisses on her neck.

"Lee seriously." she said, trying to protest, but not quite able to bring herself to move away from him.

"I'll start doing it back to you if you keep on." she warned him playfully. She smiled to herself as he burst out laughing.

"It's too late, I'm ready to go anyway." he chuckled, glancing down at his groin. Chloe followed his eyeline, smiling slightly as she rolled her eyes.

"It really doesn't take much does it." she said quietly.

"Not with you it doesn't." he whispered in her ear. Chloe quickly glanced round as she heard Kirstie's footsteps returning. Lee placed his hands on Chloe's hips and quickly pulled her into the middle of his lap.

"Are you using me as a human shield?" she giggled.

"Yep, although the problem is it's turning me on more." he muttered.

"You should look at the pictures some more, that'll help." Chloe laughed, pretending to be serious for a moment before she burst out laughing. Lee tried to pretend to be mad at her, but he couldn't resist joining in with her infectious laughter. Chloe giggled as he quickly wrapped his arms around her waist and held her against him tightly, placing his chin on her shoulder.

"You mean the photographs of my impossibly hot girlfriend." he told her, swaying her from side to side playfully.

"Ooh, are you talking about the photos from that shoot you told me about?" Kirstie asked as soon as she walked back into the room.

"Yeah, Matt emailed them." Lee said, glancing at Chloe when he felt her body language stiffen.

"Cool, can I see them?" Kirstie said excitedly. Chloe sighed to herself as she felt Lee watching her closely, clearly waiting for her permission.

"I'll see them on the album anyway surely." Kirstie frowned when Chloe didn't respond. Chloe nodded slowly, her heart sinking a little when she realised that Kirstie was right. Until now she hadn't really processed the fact that the pictures would soon be made public. Lee glanced at Chloe, before slowly handing Kirstie his phone.

"The pin number is Chloe's birthday." he said, his eyes fixed on Chloe as she sat silently, picking her fingernails once again.

"I hadn't really registered that the pictures are going to be seen by a lot of people." Chloe told Lee quietly.

"All the men will want to sleep with you and all the women will want to be you." he said quickly. Chloe sighed and remained silent, clearly not believing him. Lee took her hands in his own, squeezing them gently.

"Oh my god Chloe, you look so beautiful." Kirstie gasped as she scrolled through the photographs. Chloe smiled slightly, her cheeks colouring.

"Your body is literally to die for." Kirstie added, feeling slightly envious as she gazed at Chloe's perfect figure.

"I keep telling her that, but she doesn't believe me." Lee said proudly, gently placing a kiss on Chloe's cheek.

"I wish I could pull off an outfit like that." Kirstie said quietly. Chloe remained silent, not entirely sure what to say.

"What are you guys doing?" Louise asked as she walked into the room.

"Looking at the photos of the photo shoot." Kirstie said.

"What photo shoot?" Louise frowned.

"Chloe had to step in for one of the models for our album cover shoot." Lee explained.

"Wow!" Louise gasped when she peered over Kirstie's shoulder and stared at the photographs.

"I can't believe you hide your body all the time, I'd flaunt it if I had your figure." Louise quickly added.

"She doesn't realise how breath-taking she is." Lee said quietly, gently stroking her hair.

"You're a lucky man." Louise smiled, winking at him.

"Can we talk about something else please?" Chloe asked quietly. Kirstie nodded and silently handed Lee his phone back. Lee gasped quietly as he glanced down at the phone and saw Chloe staring into his eyes, her leg draped over his, Lee's hand gently resting in place on her bare thigh.

"I think I need a cold shower." Lee muttered, quickly switching his phone off.

"Are you struggling?" Kirstie laughed. Lee nodded slowly, trying not to look at Chloe. Chloe sighed quietly and gently wrapped her arms around his neck, resting her head against his shoulder, longing to be close to him.

"You can use the spare room if you need too." Kirstie teased, smiling slightly at how much she could see Lee was visibly struggling to control himself.

"Don't encourage him." Chloe giggled.

"The ironic thing is that it's Michelle's old room and the bed is still there." Kirstie laughed. Lee joined in the laughter as he considered it for a moment. Even though he was longing for some time alone with Chloe, he knew that she would be embarrassed by the thought of her friends knowing what was going on.

"He's actually considering it, look at his face!" Louise exclaimed. Kirstie and Louise looked at each other, the two of them still not able to control their laughter.

"I really should go." Lee muttered; his voice slightly hoarse. Chloe giggled quietly and kissed him gently. He reluctantly pushed her off his lap and onto the chair, quickly leaning down and placing a tender kiss on her lips.

"I love you." Chloe whispered.

"I love you too, I'll pick you up tomorrow." he told her.

"If you can wait that long." Kirstie laughed.

"I'll be fine, I have the photographs." Lee winked. He smiled slightly as Chloe's cheeks coloured.

"Give my best to Kathleen." Lee called as he reluctantly walked away.

Chapter Fifty-Six

Chloe fell silent as she watched Lee walk away. She couldn't help but feel like she wanted to follow him. Even though she knew she was being unreasonable, it was only one night after all, she couldn't help the way she felt.

"I'm surprised he managed to walk away from you." Kirstie said, snapping Chloe out of her thoughts.

"He was definitely struggling to resist you." Louise agreed, smiling warmly at Chloe. She couldn't help but feel happy for Chloe. She'd seen such a change in her since she'd been with Lee and she knew in her heart that he was the reason behind the twinkle in her eye.

"He's a very sexual person that's all." Chloe said quietly, her cheeks still flushed.

"He's definitely worse with you though." Louise giggled. Chloe quickly looked at the floor, her cheeks colouring even more. Her head snapped up as she heard a knock at the front door.

"Ooh, that'll be Kathleen!" Kirstie squealed excitedly as she quickly rushed to answer the door. Chloe and Louise couldn't help but smile at Kirstie's infectious excitement as they followed her to the door. Chloe's stomach plummeted as the door opened and she saw Michelle standing silently beside Kathleen. Chloe felt sick to her stomach as she stood in front of the woman who had done nothing but hurt her every opportunity she got. She knew that she would never be able to forgive what she'd said about her or the fact that she constantly tried to take the man that she loved away from her.

"Oh, hi, we didn't know you were coming Michelle." Kirstie said, sounding slightly awkward as she gestured for them to come in.

"Well, we spoke about things a few weeks ago and we have agreed that it was Mark's fault, so we are going to move past it." Michelle said quickly, choosing not to mention that despite everything she was still secretly seeing Mark.

"Yes exactly, so let's drop the subject please." Kathleen said quickly as she walked into the living room and gazed around in wonder at all the decorations and presents.

"Oh my god, is this for me?!" Kathleen exclaimed when she suddenly noticed the large sign in the living room that read *baby shower.*

"Well, nobody else is having a baby." Louise laughed.

"Aww thanks so much guys." Kathleen said, her eyes filling with tears as she quickly hugged everyone.

"I need to put the food in the oven and then we can open your presents." Kirstie announced.

"Chloe, do you want to help me?" she added, jerking her head towards the kitchen, trying to subtly tell Chloe that she wanted to talk to her. Chloe nodded and followed Kirstie, relieved to get away from Michelle.

"I can't believe *she* is here." Kirstie hissed as soon as they were alone.

"No, me neither." Chloe sighed.

"I swear I didn't know she was coming along." Kirstie said quickly, feeling slightly sorry for Chloe as she watched her hovering awkwardly.

"I know, I really don't want to be here." Chloe admitted, glancing into the living room when she heard laughter.

"But I don't want to make things awkward for Kathleen's day." she added thoughtfully, sighing quietly to herself when she realised that despite the fact, she wanted nothing more than to go home, she needed to stay and do the right thing.

"No that's right, I don't want her here either, but we need to tolerate her for Kathleen's sake." Kirstie agreed.

"Just don't tell Lee that she came." Chloe said quietly when she suddenly realised how angry Lee would be at the idea of Chloe being exposed to Michelle once again. Kirstie nodded slowly.

"Shall we take the presents in?" Chloe asked, when Kirstie finally finished putting the food in the oven.

"I think I got a bit carried away." Kirstie laughed as Chloe picked up as many as she could carry, and Kirstie picked up the rest of them.

"Oh my god, Lee's done such a bad job of wrapping some of these." Chloe smiled when she suddenly noticed how poorly some of the presents had been wrapped. Kirstie laughed and quickly followed Chloe into the living room. Kathleen gasped at the mound of presents as they carefully placed them on the table in front of her.

"Don't blame me for the wrapping, Lee did them." Kirstie giggled.

"Some of them are quite neat." Louise laughed, frowning slightly as she realised that the standard of wrapping had got progressively worse.

"Did he get bored?" Kathleen laughed.

"No, he got a bit distracted." Kirstie smiled. Chloe squirmed slightly as Louise and Kirstie turned to stare at her, both giggling quietly to themselves.

"Ooh, what happened?" Kathleen asked, her curiosity getting the better of her.

"He got an email from Matt." Chloe said quickly, before anyone could say anything else.

"Yeah, with the pictures from your photoshoot." Kirstie laughed. Even though she knew how much Chloe squirmed when people spoke about her and Lee, she couldn't resist the opportunity to prove a point to Michelle. She still hadn't forgiven her for trying to drive a wedge between Chloe and Lee.

"You did a photoshoot?" Kathleen asked, turning to Chloe.

"Yes." Chloe said quietly.

"She looked stunning, which is why Lee got so distracted." Kirstie told them.

"Aww bless him." Kathleen smiled warmly.

"How is Lee anyway?" Michelle asked nervously, trying to make the effort to build bridges with the group.

"Fine thanks." Chloe said shortly, not really in the mood for speaking to her, particularly about Lee.

"Maybe you could show us the photos?" Michelle tried again.

"I don't have them, Lee has them." Chloe said bluntly.

"They'll be on the album though when it comes out won't they?" Louise asked, smiling reassuringly at Chloe.

"Yes, it'll be a little while before the album is out though." Chloe said, smiling back at Louise.

"Chloe, I actually wanted to say that I owe you an apology." Michelle said quietly, sounding slightly nervous.

"Please don't, I don't want to hear it." Chloe said quickly.

"But..." Michelle tried again.

"You need to open your presents." Chloe prompted Kathleen, trying to shift the focus off herself. Kathleen smiled at them and slowly began to open her presents. Chloe could feel Michelle's eyes burning a hole into her head as she watched Kathleen opening her presents.

"Ooh the food is done!" Kirstie exclaimed as she heard the timer ringing from the kitchen. As Kirstie left to prepare the food, Louise quickly followed her. Chloe sighed to herself as she sat silently with Kathleen and Michelle. Kirstie returned a few moments later and quickly handed out the food.

Chloe sighed as she watched Louise and Michelle dancing in front of the television as they played a game on the console. Chloe quickly snuggled into the sleeping bag as everyone laughed and messed around.

"Are you okay Chloe, you're very quiet?" Kathleen asked her quietly.

"I'm fine, I just don't feel very well." Chloe said quietly. She swallowed quickly, trying to fight the nausea that she was feeling. She wasn't entirely sure if it was a result of being in Michelle's presence, all she knew was that she was going to be sick. She quickly climbed out of the sleeping bag and ran along the hall to the bathroom, only just making it in time to vomit into the toilet.

"Where did Chloe go?" Kirstie frowned, after Chloe ran past them.

"I don't know, she said she wasn't feeling well." Kathleen said quickly.

"Maybe she went to the bathroom then." Louise said. Kirstie quickly stood up and walked down the hallway, frowning to herself as she could hear Chloe vomiting from the bathroom. As soon as Kirstie walked into the bathroom, Chloe raised her head slowly, a pained expression on her face.

"Do you have a hair band?" Chloe asked quietly, as she tried to tuck her hair behind her ears. Kirstie nodded and pulled one off her wrist, quickly tying up Chloe's hair for her. Chloe smiled her thanks, before vomiting again. Kirstie watched sadly as Chloe rested her elbow on toilet seat and rested her head against it.

"I feel rotten." she admitted quietly.

"You look very pale; I hope it wasn't the food." Kirstie said worriedly. She sighed as Chloe began to vomit yet again. Chloe rested her head on the toilet seat, too weak from vomiting so many times to raise her head any longer.

"Maybe I should call Lee?" Kirstie suggested, an edge of concern present in her voice.

"No don't do that, I'm okay." Chloe said quickly.

"Just give me a few minutes and I'll be out." she added, smiling falsely.

"I can't leave you." Kirstie said quickly. Her heart broke a little for Chloe as she continued to vomit.

"I'm calling Lee." Kirstie said quickly, before leaving the room to get her phone. Chloe couldn't argue with her because she couldn't stop vomiting. A few moments later, Chloe was finally able to lift her head slightly, taking deep breaths to try and get her breath back. She couldn't help but feel slightly nervous at the thought of Lee coming to Kirstie's house and being face to face with Michelle once again.

Michelle squirmed in her seat as the front door opened and Lee quickly walked in.

"Where is she?" he demanded, glancing at Kirstie as soon as he entered the room.

"In the bathroom." Kirstie said quickly. Lee strode past her, not even looking at or acknowledging anyone else in the room, as he was too focused on finding Chloe. He gasped as he walked into the bathroom and saw her resting her head on the toilet seat, her chest rising and falling quickly as she tried to get her breath back. He quickly crossed the room and knelt beside her, gently placing his hand on the small of her back, to provide some comfort. Chloe raised her head slowly and placed it on his shoulder.

"What happened Chlo?" he asked her softly.

"I don't know, I just really don't feel well." she sighed, closing her eyes. She swallowed slowly, beginning to feel nauseous again.

"You don't need to be in here." she said quietly, before vomiting again. Lee gently massaged her back, wishing that he could do something to help her.

"And you don't need to see this." she coughed.

"I'm not going anywhere." he told her gently. Chloe rested her head against his shoulder once again and closed her eyes, too weak to stay awake.

"I think we need to get you home." he told her. Chloe fell silent as Lee stood up and placed his hand under Chloe's elbow, carefully helping her to stand. Chloe linked her arm through Lee's, leaning on him slightly for support as they walked through the house.

"Is she okay, I can check on her?" Michelle offered, stepping in front of them as soon as they walked into the living room. Lee could feel himself becoming angry as he finally realised for the first time that Michelle was there.

"You can move out of the way." Lee snapped. Michelle opened her mouth to argue but quickly closed it again and moved aside so that they could pass.

"And you can stop pretending to care." Lee added, turning his attention back to Chloe as he helped her leave the house.

Chapter Fifty-Seven

As soon as Chloe arrived home, she quickly ran into the house and ran upstairs to the bathroom as she felt the urge to vomit once again. Lee sighed sadly to himself as he made his way inside. He quickly poured Chloe a glass of water and made his way upstairs, leaning against the bathroom door frame, watching Chloe closely as she intermittently vomited. Chloe let out a small sob as the exhaustion finally set in.

"Don't cry Chlo." he said softly, his heart breaking a little as he watched her.

"I'm so exhausted." she muttered. She quickly pulled a bag out of the bathroom cupboard and placed it into the bathroom bin. Chloe slowly stood up and picked up the bin, staggering slightly as she walked into the bedroom, perching on the end of the bed.

"You need to get some rest." Lee told her as he squatted in front of her and gently brushed away her tears with his thumb.

"I feel too nauseous." she admitted. Lee sighed and quickly sat on the bed beside her. Chloe watched him as he sat against the bed frame and crossed his legs, before gently pulling her onto his lap. Chloe sighed and relaxed her back against his chest, feeling comforted by his presence.

"Try and get some sleep." he whispered in her ear, placing a soft kiss on her neck. Chloe nodded and closed her eyes for a moment. As soon as she closed her eyes, she could feel the room starting to spin, so she quickly opened them again.

"I'm sorry that you got dragged away from your writing session, I did tell Kirstie not to call you." she said quietly.

"She did the right thing; I want to be here for you." he told her.

"But there's nothing you can do; I just have to wait until it wears off." she pointed out. She glanced down at the bin on her lap as she suddenly felt another wave of nausea hit her and she vomited again.

"Why don't you go back to Nathan's, you don't need to see me like this?" she said breathlessly, her cheeks colouring in embarrassment.

"I'm not going anywhere." he said quickly, glancing down at his phone as it vibrated beside him.

"Kirstie wants to know how you are." he told her.

"She's worried that she might have given me food poisoning." she said, smiling slightly.

"Maybe she did." he said thoughtfully.

"I really need to brush my teeth." Chloe said quietly, when she swallowed and realised that she could taste vomit. Lee rummaged in his jean pocket and silently handed her a piece of chewing gum.

"Although you should probably have some water first." he said, quickly reaching over to the nightstand and picking up the glass of water. Chloe smiled at him as he held the glass in front of her and gently tipped it up so that she could take a few sips.

"Thank you." she muttered as he placed the chewing gum in her hand. She quickly placed it in her mouth, sighing in relief as the disgusting taste in her mouth finally started to dissipate. Chloe closed her eyes for a moment, finally able to relax. Lee carefully wrapped his arms around her waist, desperate to hold her tightly, but trying not to squeeze her too hard in case he made her feel nauseous again.

"Oh, I forgot to tell you, Michelle was asking to see the pictures of the shoot." Chloe told him.

"How does she even know about that?" he frowned.

"Kirstie told her, she was trying to prove a point to her I think." she said.

"Good, I can't believe she was even there." he said shortly, an edge present in his voice.

"She wasn't meant to be, Kathleen invited her, nobody was particularly happy about it." she explained.

"Oh no." Chloe whispered as she felt yet another wave of nausea coming. She quickly spat the chewing gum into the bin, fearful that she might choke on it. Chloe coughed as she brought up the water that she'd just drunk. Lee gently tapped her back as she continued to cough on it.

"Oh my god." she whispered when it finally subsided again.

"I felt like I was drowning." she added.

"Maybe I should take you somewhere." Lee said thoughtfully, suddenly feeling slightly afraid.

"I'm fine, it might even just be a bug." Chloe said, trying to reassure him.

"In which case, you should probably keep away from me." she quickly added. Before Lee could respond, Chloe closed her eyes and instantly fell asleep, the exhaustion finally taking its toll.

Chloe bolted awake, frowning to herself when she noticed sunlight streaming in the bedroom window. She glanced behind her and smiled when she noticed that Lee was sleeping peacefully. She frowned as she looked down at her lap and saw that the bin had been safely placed on the nightstand. Chloe glanced at her watch and saw that it was five am, she'd been asleep for hours. She slowly climbed off Lee's lap, taking care not to wake him and wandered into the bathroom.

Lee frowned to himself as he awoke with a start and realised that Chloe was no longer on his lap. His heart plummeted as he heard her vomiting in the bathroom.

He sighed and quickly walked into the bathroom, leaning against the door frame as he watched her closely.

"When did you start vomiting again?" he asked her when she eventually stopped.

"A few moments ago, I got up to use the bathroom and then it started again." she said breathlessly.

"Right, this is getting ridiculous now, I'm taking you to hospital." he said as she continued to vomit.

"Chloe Evans please!" the doctor finally called, after what had felt to Chloe like hours spent sitting in A and E. She'd never been more embarrassed in her life than she had been, sitting in a busy reception area, intermittently vomiting into a bin. Chloe quickly followed the doctor, trying to escape the embarrassing situation.

"Okay, so my name is George, I'm one of the doctors here, tell me what's been happening." he said as Chloe perched on the bed, glancing at Lee as he sat on the chair beside the bed.

"I was at a friend's house and suddenly started to feel sick, then I've been intermittently vomiting ever since, even though I haven't eaten anything since yesterday evening. I can't even keep water down." Chloe explained. George nodded slowly and quickly checked her vitals.

"I'm going to be sick again." Chloe warned him. George quickly picked up a dish and placed it under her mouth.

"Have you taken anything or eaten anything unusual?" he asked her when the vomiting subsided. Chloe shook her head slowly.

"Okay, first I'm going to give you an anti-emetic injection to stop the vomiting, and I'll put you on fluids for a little while because you are quite dehydrated. Then we'll do a blood test to see if we can find out what is causing it." George quickly explained.

"I'll go and get a nurse to organise that." he added before quickly walking away. Chloe glanced at Lee when she realised that he'd barely spoken since they had got to the hospital.

"Are you okay, you're really quiet?" she asked him when she saw him sitting silently staring at his hands.

"Yeah, I'm just worried about you." he said quietly.

"I'll be alright, it's nothing to worry about." she told him, gently holding out her hand to him. He smiled at her and took her hand in his own, and gently placed a soft kiss on it. The two of them fell silent as a nurse arrived and quickly got to work setting Chloe up on fluids and giving her the injection.

"Okay, I'm just going to take some blood from you now." she explained. Chloe nodded, watching closely as the nurse methodically filled several tubes with blood and quickly walked away to run them. As soon as she left the cubicle, Lee quickly stood up and perched on the bed beside her, smiling down at her as she rested her head on his shoulder and closed her eyes. Lee glanced at his phone as he received another message from Kirstie asking how Chloe was doing. His gaze returned to Chloe who was sleeping peacefully on his shoulder. He quickly kissed her forehead, smiling slightly as she fidgeted slightly. Lee took her hands between his and placed them on his lap, gently playing with her fingers. His eyes snapped up as George returned to the cubicle, carrying a clipboard.

"Chlo." Lee whispered, trying to gently rouse her. She blinked slowly and yawned as she glanced up at George.

"Sorry, I didn't mean to wake you, but I have your results." George smiled, glancing between Lee and Chloe.

"And?" Lee asked nervously.

"And... you're pregnant." George announced.

"What, no I'm not." Chloe muttered.

"Yes, you are." George insisted.

"But..." Chloe started but trailed off, not entirely sure how to process what he'd just told her. She glanced down at her hands as Lee quickly let go of them and turned to face her, his jaw set.

"I thought you said you're on the pill?" Lee said accusingly.

"I am." she whispered, beginning to panic slightly.

"Like all contraception the pill isn't one hundred percent accurate. There definitely wasn't a time that you forgot to take it?" George asked her. Chloe racked her brain, struggling to think because she was still in shock. She'd been taking the pill constantly since just after her and Lee had started dating. She gasped as she suddenly remembered that on the night Michelle had upset her and she'd gone to bed early, she'd forgotten to take the pill.

"Oh my god." she whispered when she suddenly remembered that he'd come home early as a surprise shortly afterwards.

"You came home from Germany early." she added.

"Wait, so you're saying this is my fault!" Lee said angrily.

"No, but I've just remembered I forgot to take it one night when you were away.... because I was upset.... and then you came home early.... and....oh my god...what have I done." Chloe rambled.

"It's okay, it's a lot to process." George piped up, trying to reassure them.

"Even if you take the pill without missing any, there is a risk that you can fall pregnant, but obviously if you miss one, the risk increases." he added.

"What are our options?" Lee asked him quickly. Before George could respond Lee quickly pulled out his phone and counted back the weeks to when he was away in Germany.

"She's about seven and a half weeks." Lee told him.

"If you decide you want to terminate the pregnancy then you can book an appointment for that to be discussed with your GP. You'll have up until you are twenty-four weeks to have one." George explained.

"Take some time for it to sink in before you make any decisions." he added, before walking away to attend to other patients. As soon as George left, Lee quickly moved away from Chloe and put his head in his hands, sighing deeply.

"I'm really sorry, I'm such an idiot." Chloe whispered, as she reached out and placed her hand on his arm. She jumped slightly as Lee quickly stood up and walked away from her. Chloe felt her heart pounding against her chest as he walked away from her. She curled up in a ball and pulled the blanket under her chin, hugging it slightly, to try and gain some form of comfort. Warm tears quickly rolled down her cheeks as she lay on her own, trying to come to terms with what she'd just been told.

Chapter Fifty-Eight

Chloe sniffed and pulled the blanket over her head, desperately trying to shut out the world and pretend that none of this was happening. She was suddenly struck with fear as she knew in her heart that she wasn't ready to be a mother. The thought of being responsible for something that would be completely vulnerable filled her with a deep sense of dread. She had no idea how to take care of a baby, she'd never even held one before. Chloe slowly lifted the bottom of her shirt and stared, transfixed, at her abdomen. She sighed as she slowly traced small circles on it, still not quite able to comprehend that she was carrying a baby inside her. Tears rolled down her face again as the enormity of the situation suddenly hit her. This was the biggest commitment of her life that she would be making and even though she was terrified and wasn't ready for it, she knew that she couldn't face the idea of terminating the pregnancy. The situation that they were in was *her* fault and she knew that. She needed to grow up and face her responsibilities for her own mistake.

Her thoughts wandered to Lee as she thought about his reaction and how he'd asked the doctor about their options. She couldn't help but think that he wanted her to terminate the pregnancy, to eliminate what he perceived as a problem that Chloe had caused. Her thoughts swirled as to what to do, she knew there was a chance that she was going to have do this alone....as a single mother. The thought made her feel sick to her stomach with fear. She curled into a ball, desperately wishing that she could turn back time and fix things. So that they could go back to the way things were. Chloe began to sob uncontrollably, her heart longing once again for her parents.

Lee couldn't stop pacing outside the hospital as he tried to process what he'd just been told. He'd never in a million years thought there was a chance that Chloe was pregnant with his child, but now that she was, he wasn't entirely sure how to process it. He couldn't help but feel slightly frustrated that they were in this situation as a result of Chloe's actions. If she had been more thorough with taking the pill, then none of this would have happened. Lee had never pictured himself being a father, it was something that he'd never imagined happening to him and he'd never wanted it too. It felt like he was having an out of body experience as he thought about having a child, that would be completely reliant on the two of them. The more that he thought about it, the more afraid he became. His father had abandoned them when he was a child, and he had no role model and no idea how to be a good father. Lee's hands shook when he finally stopped pacing and glanced into the hospital as his mind wandered to Chloe and what she must be feeling. Despite the temptation he felt to run away from everything that was happening, he knew that he had to do the right thing and check on Chloe.

"Chloe." she heard Lee's voice whisper from beside the bed. She slowly peered over the top of the blanket, glancing at him for a moment, before quickly looking away, her guilt intensifying as soon as she saw him.

"Have you been sick again?" he asked her quietly. She shook her head, before slowly sitting up and wiping her tear-stained cheeks, not quite able to bring herself to look at him. Chloe's eyes snapped up as George walked into the cubicle and silently checked her vitals, clearly picking up on the tense atmosphere.

"You've been on the fluids for a couple of hours, and you're no longer dehydrated so I'll remove your IV line and you can go home." he quickly explained. Chloe nodded, not entirely sure where the past two hours had gone, time was passing in a blur as she still didn't feel like she could process anything.

"These are some anti-emetic tablets to take, if the vomiting gets bad again." George said, quickly handing Chloe a box of tablets, as soon as he removed her IV line.

"So, I can go home now?" she checked. George smiled and nodded slowly. As soon as Chloe got confirmation that she could go home, she quickly stood up and walked down the corridors, desperately trying to get out of the hospital. Lee frowned in confusion, before standing up and quickly following her. The two of them remained silent as they walked across the carpark and climbed into Lee's car.

"I am so sorry." Chloe whispered as soon as they were on the road.

"Yeah, I'm sure you are." Lee said shortly. Chloe sighed and fell silent again. It felt like someone had punched her in the chest when he snapped at her. Even though she knew what she'd done, she couldn't help but feel slightly upset that he was angry with her. As soon as they pulled up at the house, Chloe quickly hurried into the house, desperately trying to get away from the tense atmosphere. She started to climb the stairs but paused halfway up when she couldn't take it any longer. Lee glanced up at her as she turned to face him.

"Do you want me to leave?" she whispered nervously, slightly afraid of the answer.

"No of course not." he whispered, suddenly feeling slightly guilty for the way he'd made her feel. He knew in his heart that she hadn't fallen pregnant on purpose and she seemed just as upset about the whole thing as he was.

"I don't want to lose you, I'm just shocked and I don't know how to process it." he added. Chloe breathed a sigh of relief, her legs suddenly felt weak, so she quickly sat on the stairs, her eyes fixed on her hands.

"I can't terminate the baby; I know you asked the doctor about it.... but I just can't." she mumbled, her eyes filling with tears.

"I was asking for both of us, it's always good to know the options." he said quietly, leaning against the wall and watching her closely. Chloe nodded slowly, the tears that she'd been trying to hold back slowly spilling down her face.

"Another option could be that we put the baby up for adoption once it's born." she said thoughtfully.

"What?" Lee whispered, suddenly feeling slightly uncomfortable at her words.

"Since I can't bring myself to terminate the baby, maybe it's an option. Then the baby will get all the love and care that it needs." she continued, rambling slightly.

"Why is that an option?" he asked, swallowing the lump that was rising in his throat.

"Because I can't lose you." she sobbed, finally giving into the emotions she had been holding back.

Lee sighed quietly and slowly sat on the stair in front of her. He placed his chin on her knees, suddenly feeling racked with guilt that his reaction had managed to upset her.

"Getting our baby adopted is not an option." he told her gently, feeling slightly sick at the thought of someone else raising their child.

"Well, what are we going to do then?" she sobbed.

"I don't know." he said softly.

"This is all my fault." she whispered when she finally stopped sobbing.

"You didn't do it on purpose." he sighed, resting the side of his head on her lap. He sighed quietly as she gently stroked his hair, her hands trembling slightly. Lee quickly bit his lip, trying to fight the tears that were filling his eyes, his head a complete scramble of fear and guilt.

"I'm really sorry." Chloe whispered.

"I know, it's okay." he whispered back.

Chapter Fifty Nine

Lee smiled at his Mum as she sat beside him on the sofa and silently handed him a cup of tea. He sighed to himself as he sat in silence, staring into space.

"Right, what's going on?" Sheila quickly asked.

"What?" Lee laughed, smiling slightly at her.

"Oh, c'mon Lee, I've known you a long time, spill." she said, sounding slightly impatient.

"You haven't broken Chloe's heart, or something have you?" she asked quickly when Lee still hadn't responded.

"No Mum, I haven't." he said, rolling his eyes.

"Well, what is it then?" she tried again, starting to lose her patience. Lee quickly took a sip of his tea and took a deep breath, not entirely sure how his Mum was going to take the news.

"She's pregnant Mum." he said quietly.

"Oh my god!" she exclaimed excitedly.

"I'm going to be a Grandma." she added, quickly pulling Lee into a hug, squeezing him tightly.

"Why don't you seem happy about it?" she continued when she saw his expression.

"I'm just so scared." he whispered.

"Why are you scared? It's a good thing." she frowned.

"Because I don't know how to be a Dad, I don't even know what it's like to have a Dad." he admitted sadly.

"Just because your Dad was useless, doesn't mean that you will be." she said quickly. Lee shrugged, quickly taking another sip of his tea.

"But what if I mess everything up and I let the baby down and I let Chloe down." he muttered. Sheila sighed to herself as she watched him closely and saw his eyes filling with tears. She quickly leaned over and pulled him into a hug.

"I just don't know what to do Mum." he whispered in her ear as the tears that he'd been fighting slowly rolled down his cheeks.

"The two of you will figure it out together, and you know that I'll help you." she reassured him.

"The main thing is making sure that you don't repeat your father's mistakes which you won't. You've always had a big heart and been very caring, ever since you were a child." she continued. Lee sniffed and quickly wiped his eyes when he sat back, sighing quietly to himself.

"Don't you remember that baby rabbit you found that was injured, but you were determined to nurse it back to health." she prompted him.

"Yeah, it died." he said shortly.

"That's not the point, the point is that you cared enough to spend three days taking care of it when a lot of people wouldn't have given a damn." she said quickly.

"And I know that you and Chloe have only been together a few months, but you know that you love her, and you've known her for years." she continued, trying her best to reassure him. Her heart was breaking a little as she watched her only son in such turmoil.

"It would have been nice to have had some more time for me to cherish her though." he sighed.

"You can still do that; it'll probably bring you closer." she pointed out.

"Yeah maybe." he said quietly.

"Just do your best and that will be good enough, the fact that you are scared is a good thing, it shows that you care already." she said. Lee nodded slowly.

"I hadn't thought of it like that." he said thoughtfully. Sheila smiled warmly at him, sensing a slight change in him that maybe he slowly relaxing.

"How is Chloe doing with the news?" she asked.

"Fine I think, she hasn't said much the past few days. She's been busy with work." he told her. Sheila raised her eyebrow sceptically, quickly realising that Chloe was clearly throwing herself into her work to distract from how she was feeling. She couldn't help but feel surprised that Lee hadn't come to the same conclusion. Clearly, he was too distracted to be able to figure anything out.

"Oh Lee, you need to make sure you're there for her. She doesn't have a family she can speak to like you do, you're all she has." she told him.

"Yeah, I know." he agreed.

"I'll take her out for a walk or something at the weekend." she said thoughtfully.

"Wait here a minute." she added, before quickly standing up and walking away. Lee sat silently, lost in thought. His Mum's words were swirling around his head, maybe she was right, maybe he could be a good father if he put his mind to it. He smiled at Sheila as she quickly returned, a photo album in her hand. Lee glanced down at his lap as she slowly handed him a grey blanket covered in stars.

"What's this?" he frowned.

"That was your favourite blanket when you were little." she told him.

"You also used to chew it when you started teething." she laughed. Lee smiled slightly, gazing down at the blanket thoughtfully. His eyes snapped to the photo album as Sheila slowly opened it and smiled fondly at Lee's baby pictures.

"That moment when you hold your child for the first time is so magical." she muttered thoughtfully. Lee wrapped his arm around her shoulder and smiled at the pictures.

"It really is, just you wait. You'll see." she told him.

"I love you Mum." he sighed, gently resting his head against hers.

Lee sighed to himself as he quickly walked into the studio, his Mum's words still swirling around his head. He knew that she was right, he had neglected Chloe and hadn't given much thought about how she must be feeling. He couldn't help but feel a pang of guilt. It had never been his intention to disregard her feelings, but he'd been so distracted and consumed by fear that he'd been unable to think about anything else.

Even though the boys had a few days off, he remembered Chloe telling him that she would be going into the studio again because she had a lot of paperwork to catch up on.

"Hey, what are you doing here?!" Matt called, when Lee walked past his office.

"Don't you like having time off?" Matt laughed as Lee walked into his office.
"I'm here to see Chloe." Lee told him.

"Well, she's not here as far as I know." Matt said, frowning in confusion.

"She must be here somewhere; she's been working extra lately because she said she'd fallen behind and had things to catch up on." Lee frowned.

"Chloe never falls behind on things, she's too organised." Matt pointed out.

"Besides I haven't seen her for a few days, she came in one day to help me organise the tour schedule for the band and she really wasn't herself, so I told her to go home and take some time off and come back when you guys are back to work." Matt explained.

"What do you mean she wasn't herself?" Lee frowned.

"She was distracted and teary." Matt said.

"Is something going on with the two of you?" he quickly added.

"No, everything is fine." Lee said quietly, his mouth suddenly feeling very dry. He couldn't help but feel hurt that Chloe had been lying to him about where she was going. As soon as Lee reached his car, he rested his elbow on the car door and chewed his thumbnail, racking his brain as to where Chloe could be and why she hadn't told him the truth. His heart pounded against his chest as he took out his phone to call her and sighed in frustration as it rang out. He quickly rang Kirstie, desperately hoping that she was with her.

"Hello?" Kirstie answered.

"Is Chloe with you?" Lee asked as soon as she answered the phone.

"Well hello to you too." Kirstie laughed.

"Is she with you?" he asked again.

"No, I'm at work." Kirstie told him.

"Is everything okay?" she added.

"Yeah fine." he said, before quickly hanging up. He quickly flung his phone onto the passenger seat and angrily hit his hand against the steering wheel in frustration. He had no idea what to do or where to look for her next. Lee quickly picked up his phone and called Sheila.

"Hi honey." she said when she answered the phone after a couple of rings.

"I can't find Chloe and I don't know where else to look." he blurted as soon as she answered.

"What do you mean you can't find her?" she asked.

"I went home to talk to her like you said and she wasn't there, then I remembered that she said she was going to work, but Matt said he hasn't seen her for a few days." he rambled, starting to panic slightly.

"And I called her best friend and she's not there either." he added.

"She wouldn't have gone to Nathan's would she, since the two of them are close?" she suggested.

"No, he's away in Bournemouth for a few days visiting family." he said quickly.

"Oh my god Mum, what if she's left me." he whispered, his eyes filling with tears at the thought of losing her.

"She won't have done that sweetheart." she said quickly.

"You just need to think about where she would go for some time out." she added thoughtfully.

"I don't know." he said quietly, not able to think clearly because he was so worried about her. His heart pounded against his chest as he contemplated life without her.

"Well, who did you go and see first?" she prompted.

"You...I've only told you. We're keeping it a secret for now." he said quietly.

"Okay well since she's going to be feeling scared, maybe she's gone to see her parents." she suggested.

"Do you know where they are?" she added when Lee fell silent.

"Nope." he said quietly.

"Maybe you could ask one of her friends then, I'd bet she's gone to see her parents." she told him. Lee nodded slowly, suddenly feeling a new sense of hope that at least he had somewhere else to check.

"Thanks Mum." he said, quickly hanging up and texting Kirstie to ask her where Chloe's parents were. She messaged back almost instantly, giving him the name of the cemetery. Lee drove quickly, feeling more and more sick as he sped towards the cemetery. He had no idea what he would do if she wasn't there. As soon as he pulled up at the cemetery, he quickly climbed out of the car and walked along the walkway, his eyes scanning the horizon, desperately hoping that he would catch a glimpse of her. He breathed a sigh of relief when he finally noticed her, sitting with her back against the side of one of the headstones, her earphones in as she concentrated on the notebook that was on her lap. As Lee walked towards her, he could feel his temper slowly simmering as he thought about the fact that she'd been secretly spending the past few days here. It was bad enough that she'd lied to him about it, but he couldn't understand why she would think it was sensible to spend time somewhere and not tell anyone where you are.

"What are you doing here?" Chloe frowned, quickly pulling out her earphones as soon as she saw Lee.

"Looking for you, you could have told me you were here, rather than lying to me." he said shortly.

"What difference does it make, you went to your Mum's anyway?" she snapped defensively. She couldn't understand why, when the two of them had barely spoken for the past few days, why he suddenly wanted to know her every movement.

"I know, but you knew where I was, what if something happened and I ended up looking for you in the wrong place." he pointed out. Chloe nodded slowly, sighing quietly to herself when she realised that he was right.

"I just knew that you would want to come with me to make sure that I was safe." she said quietly. Lee nodded slowly and sat in front of her on the ground.

"And this is my little sanctuary where I go when I want to be alone." she added. She sighed in frustration as he sat watching her closely. She knew now that he was here, he wasn't going to go home and leave her to her own devices.

"What are you writing?" he asked her as he glanced at the notebook on her lap.

"I'm trying to figure out a baby shopping list." she told him shortly, not really in the mood for speaking to him, particularly about the baby. She sighed deeply before quickly standing up when she realised that he was going to sit and watch her until she eventually went home anyway. Lee frowned for a moment before quickly following her.

"When we get home, I'll make dinner and we can talk, there's things we need to figure out." he told her, quickly taking her hand. Chloe pulled her hand away from his grasp, stopping in her tracks as she turned to face him.

"So, you've decided it's time to talk then have you." she said sarcastically, her temper fraying slightly that after the past few days of him being short and disinterested with her, that when he suddenly decided it was time to talk, he expected her to be willing. He stared at her silently, shocked by her outburst and not entirely sure how to respond. She rolled her eyes at him and quickly climbed into the car.

Chapter Sixty

Chloe bolted awake as she heard a sharp knocking on the bathroom door.

"What is it?" she asked, knowing that it would be Lee checking on her yet again.

"You've been in there ages, are you okay?" he asked, sounding slightly concerned.

"I'm fine." she said shortly. She glanced at the door as she noticed Lee trying to turn the doorknob, sighing in frustration when he realised that the door was locked.

"You're not feeling sick, again are you?" he asked.

"No, I'm having a bath." she said impatiently, feeling slightly frustrated that he wouldn't leave her alone. Ever since they had returned from the cemetery, he'd been fussing over her, constantly watching her during dinner, almost as if he was feeling guilty for being so distant and harsh with her for the past few days.

"Okay, I'll make you a cup of tea for when you are done." he told her. Chloe sighed quietly as she heard his footsteps walking away. Even though since she'd been home, some of the frustration that she was feeling had started to fade, she still wasn't sure how to be around him. But she knew in her heart that he was right, they needed to have a conversation and make a plan at some point and maybe now was as good a time as any. She quickly climbed out of the bath and pulled on her pyjamas. Before she could talk herself out of it she slowly made her way downstairs. Lee glanced at her as she sat on the sofa beside him, picking her fingernails nervously.

"I've been thinking about what you said in the cemetery about wanting some time alone and I think we need to make a deal not to lie to each other.

If there's a problem and you don't want to talk to me about it, that's fine, but we at least need to know where the other person is, in case something happens." Lee explained to her, still feeling a little bit hurt that she'd lied to him.

"Okay, I'm sorry." she said quietly.

"I just really needed to be with my Mum." she whispered sadly, her eyes filling with tears.

"I know, I understand. But I just want you to be safe." he told her gently, his heart breaking a little for her as he suddenly realised exactly what she must be going through. It was bad enough for him, not having his father around, but he couldn't imagine not having his mother around either or any family at all. Chloe nodded slowly, the tears that she'd been fighting slowly rolling down her cheeks.

"I'm sorry, I'm sorry about everything!" she sobbed, burying her head in her hands as she sobbed to herself.

"It's okay, you don't have to apologise, this is as much my fault as it is yours." he told her gently.

"No, it's not, I was the one who forgot to take the pill." she argued.

"You didn't do it on purpose though." he said quietly.

"You seem calmer about it now." she said tentatively, slowly wiping away her tears, even though they were continuing to fall.

"I've had a few days to get my head around it and speaking to Mum really helped. She made me realise that it's normal to feel scared and confused." he told her.

"And I'm really sorry for how I reacted, I was just panicking about everything, not knowing how to be a father and I was worried that I was going to let you or the baby down." he continued.

"So, I ended up being short with you when I shouldn't have." he added.

"It's fine." she said quietly.

"But I think I've got my head around it now." he told her. Chloe glanced up at him, finally looking him in the eye for the first time since they'd started the conversation.

"So, what do you want to do?" she asked nervously, slightly afraid of the answer.

"I think I want to be a Dad." he said quietly. Chloe stared at him silently, suddenly feeling a huge wave of relief as he said those words. Even though she was terrified of becoming a mother she couldn't help but feel better at the thought that they would be facing parenthood together.

"I thought that you would decide to leave me." she whispered, almost as if she was speaking to herself.

"I thought you'd left me today, when I couldn't find you." he said, smiling slightly. Chloe shook her head slowly. She glanced up at him as he shuffled along the sofa, until he was sitting against her and gently wrapped his arm around her shoulders.

"I think we can do this Chlo." he whispered, trying to convince himself almost as much as her. Even though he felt better since speaking to his Mum, he still had a few doubts swirling around his head.

As Chloe sat and stared at him, she found herself wishing that she was able to tell him how terrified she still felt. She was longing for some reassurance from him, but she knew in her heart that she couldn't bring herself to tell him. He'd only just got his head around the idea himself and the last thing she wanted to do was to unsettle him again, particularly when a part of her was still afraid that he was going to run for the hills and leave her behind.

"Do you feel better about it now that we've had a few days to think?" he asked her, quickly placing a soft kiss on her forehead. Chloe sighed to herself, not entirely sure how to answer him.

He just didn't seem to get it, he'd been to his Mum's and been given a pep talk from someone that loved and cared about him, Chloe felt like she had nobody to talk too. She'd always felt like Lee was the only person that she could talk to about things that had happened in her past and how she felt about things and now she couldn't even bring herself to open up to him. She wanted to protect him from feeling her fear as his own. She loved and cared about him far more than she did herself.

"It's just a bit overwhelming isn't it." she whispered, resting her head on his shoulder and snuggling against his collarbone, desperately trying to comfort herself somehow as tears rolled down her cheeks again.

"Mum said that even though she knows she'll never come close to your Mum, that if you need to talk about anything, she's there for you." he told her, sensing that she still wasn't feeling entirely happy with the situation. Chloe couldn't help but think about her Mum and how she would do anything to be able to speak to her again. Even though she knew Sheila was trying to be kind, she couldn't help but feel slightly uncomfortable about the idea of speaking to her about things, in case she repeated it to Lee. Chloe sighed and quickly laid down on the sofa, placing her head in Lee's lap and closing her eyes. She couldn't stop herself from wishing that she could fall asleep so that she could escape the intense range of emotions that she was feeling. Chloe's eyes snapped open as she felt Lee place his hand under her shirt and slowly trace small circles on her abdomen.

"I still can't believe there's a little baby in there." he said thoughtfully.

"Me neither." she said quietly.

"I think the baby is going to adore you." she said, smiling falsely at him as she tried to bury her feelings and pretend that she was excited about becoming a mother. Lee carefully removed Chloe from his lap so that he could lay down beside her. Chloe sighed sadly as he moved down the sofa so that he could rest his head against her abdomen. She'd been hoping when he laid down beside her that he was going to hold her tightly to provide her with some comfort, but clearly, he had no idea how much she was still struggling to come to terms with everything.

"God, I hope I don't mess this up." he muttered thoughtfully.

"Why would you think that you're going to mess it up?" she frowned.

"Because like I said to Mum, I've not really had a Dad. And what if I turn out to be like him." he said quietly.

"You won't, you're going to be an amazing Dad." she said quietly, trying to reassure him. Lee sighed quietly as she softly stroked his hair.

"Do you really think so?" he asked, raising his head to look at her. Chloe nodded slowly, smiling slightly at his adorable expression.

"I can picture you running around, having fun with a child." she said quietly, smiling at the thought of it.

"Imagine if we have a mini you, she'll be so cute." he said smiling as he thought about the idea of their daughter. Chloe smiled slightly as she watched him gazing fondly at her abdomen. She could clearly see that he was slowly falling in love with their child.

"Although if we do have a girl, you're going to be *so* overprotective." she smiled.

"Especially when she starts to date." she laughed.

"That won't be happening." he said quickly, smiling at Chloe when she raised her eyebrow. Lee watched Chloe as she slowly sat up and pressed her forehead against his.

"You don't have anything to be scared of, I've known for a while that you are the one, I want to be the father of my children." she told him. Lee smiled at her, feeling slightly emotional. Those few words that Chloe had just said, meaning the world to him. He placed his hand on her cheek and kissed her lips gently.

"It's just a lot sooner than we would have liked." she added when they eventually broke apart.

"We can make the best of it though." he said quietly.

"Is there any point in us going away next weekend?" she asked quickly, trying to keep herself talking before she got upset again.

"Yeah, why wouldn't we go?" he frowned, raising his head to look at her.

"Because I can't do anything, I can't go in the hot tub, I can't drink, and the girls were speaking about going zip-lining, but I can't do that either." she sighed.

"There are things you can do though." he pointed out.

"And besides, you were so excited about going to the zoo." he added. Chloe nodded slowly.

"We'll still have a good time." he told her.

"We just have to make sure that we're careful what you do and what you don't." he added.

"And that we don't let on to the others that you are pregnant." he continued when she didn't respond.

"I'll be careful." she said quietly.

"I'll always protect the two of you anyway.... I promise." he told her gently. Lee quickly glanced at her, sighing sadly to himself as she burst into tears again.

"What can I do?" he asked sadly, his heart breaking a little as he watched her cry.

"Just hold me.... please." she whispered. Without hesitating Lee moved so that he was lying beside her. As soon as he was beside her, Chloe wrapped her arms around him and snuggled herself against his chest. Lee wrapped his arms around her and held her close.

"I really wish my parents were still here, they'd have been such good grandparents." Chloe whispered thoughtfully.

"Why don't you go back and speak to them again tomorrow, I could come with you if you want?" he suggested.

"Or I can stay behind." he added a few moments later when Chloe remained silent.

"It's fine, you can come along." she said quietly.

Chapter Sixty-One

"Oh my god, this place is amazing!" Kirstie exclaimed as she climbed out of the car and gazed around at the beautiful lodge that was nestled in the forest.

"The internet definitely didn't do it justice." Ben agreed, finally realising what all the hype was about.

"At least since Louise and Peter are running late, the four of us get to pick the best bedrooms." Ben added, smiling slightly as he wrapped his arm around Kirstie's shoulders. Chloe slowly climbed out of Ben's car, smiling at Lee as he gently took her hand and squeezed it.

"I'll take that." Lee said quickly as Chloe reached into the back of the car to pick up her suitcase.

"I'm quite capable." she argued, as he quickly took the suitcase from her grasp. Lee raised his eyebrow at her as they walked into the chalet, his hand still holding onto hers protectively.

"Ooh, these bedrooms are awesome!" Ben called from down the hallway as he explored the chalet.

"There's going to be so much sex happening in these bedrooms on our romantic couples' getaway." Ben beamed, peering around the corner and winking at them cheekily.

"Stop it, we've only just arrived." Kirstie giggled.

"I'm just calling it like it is." Ben chuckled, before disappearing down the hallway again. Kirstie rolled her eyes at him as he walked away. Chloe quickly glanced around, before walking into one of the bedrooms. Lee followed her into the bedroom and placed their luggage on the bed.

"It's so hot today." Lee said quietly, as he removed his shirt and fanned himself with a leaflet. Chloe nodded slowly and unzipped her suitcase. She quickly pulled out her denim shorts and a tank top and stared at them as she laid them on the bed. She couldn't quite decide if she had the confidence to wear them in public. Before she could talk herself out of it, she quickly changed into them, starting at herself in the mirror. Chloe turned sideways, gently running her hand over her abdomen.

"I'm not showing, am I?" Chloe quickly checked with Lee as she felt him watching her closely.

"No, not yet." he told her.

"I can't wear this anyway, they are too short." she said, trying to pull down the shorts slightly.

"I think the outfit looks good on you, I'd just leave it on." he reassured her, smiling slightly at how beautiful she looked even when she was dressed in something casual. Chloe nodded slowly and quickly pulled on her trainers, jumping slightly as Ben opened the bedroom door.

"Are you guys ready?" he asked.

"Ready for what?" Chloe frowned, glancing at Lee as he pulled his shirt back on.
"We have to go and explore the complex." Ben said excitedly.

"Oh, and also there are push bikes outside for us to use." he added, before disappearing again.

"I think he's been on the energy drinks." Lee chuckled. Chloe smiled slightly as she quickly pulled her hair into a messy bun. She jumped slightly as Lee stood behind her and carefully wrapped his arms around her waist, placing his chin on her shoulder and making eye contact with her in the mirror.

"I love you so much." he whispered in her ear.

"I love you too." she whispered back, placing her arms over his.

"You'll need to be careful when you're cycling though." he told her, carefully stroking soft circles on her abdomen.

"I'm not going to fall off." she said, sighing slightly.

"C'mon you guys!" Ben called again.

"We have to go." Chloe told Lee as she reluctantly removed herself from his arms. Lee sighed and followed Chloe as she walked along the hall. As soon as the four of them climbed onto the bikes, Ben beamed at them and cycled off into the distance.

"I really don't know what's gotten into him today." Kirstie laughed.

"He's just a big kid isn't he." Chloe giggled as Ben turned around to face them, beaming at them. The three of them laughed as he wobbled slightly and had to turn his attention back to where he was going.

"Yep." Kirstie agreed, frowning to herself as Ben suddenly came to a stop and waited for them to catch up.

"We need to have a race." Ben announced, sounding slightly excited.

"What, me and you?" Lee asked.

"Well, the girls need to get involved too." Ben pointed out.

"I'll sit this one out." Chloe said quickly, as she glanced at Lee.

"You can be the judge." Lee told her.

"Why don't the two of you just do it and we'll catch up?" Kirstie suggested.

"Right, ready.... set....go!" Ben called out, laughing slightly as he cycled away before Lee had a chance to react.

"You're a bloody cheat!" Lee called after him as he cycled away, trying to catch up.

"They are such kids." Kirstie laughed as she watched them. Chloe nodded slowly, rolling her eyes as the boys jostled for position.

"Are you okay Chloe, you're quiet today?" Kirstie asked her.

"I'm fine." Chloe said quickly.

"If you need to talk about anything you know where I am." Kirstie told her, not entirely sure if she believed her.

"Hey, you know what we should do, we could hide behind a tree so that when they eventually stop dicking about, they can't find us." Kirstie added, trying to lighten the mood when Chloe didn't respond.

"Lee will freak out if I do that." Chloe said, glancing up at Lee as him and Ben finally came to a stop and Lee turned to face her. Kirstie frowned at Chloe's words, not entirely sure what she was suggesting.

"Who won then?" Chloe asked when her and Kirstie eventually caught up.

"He did, but he cheated." Lee said, rolling his eyes at Ben.

"What have you done to your face?!" Kirstie exclaimed when she saw a cut on Ben's cheekbone.

"I think it was a stone that got flung up when I was going for it." Ben chuckled, smiling at Kirstie as she carefully examined it.

"You're such an idiot." Kirstie laughed, before quickly placing a kiss on his lips. Chloe glanced down at her phone as it buzzed.

"Louise and Peter have arrived." she announced as she read the message.

"We'd better head back then." Kirstie said, before quickly climbing back on her bike.

"You've met Peter before at the ball, haven't you?" Chloe asked Kirstie as the four of them cycled back to the lodge.

"Not really, I just saw him dancing with Louise." Kirstie replied.

"From what she's said though, he seems like a nice guy." Kirstie said.

"Maybe we should set up a table and we can interview him.... like a panel." Ben laughed.

"Aww no, that's a shame. The poor guy is probably really nervous about meeting us, particularly you two." Chloe pointed out, glancing at Ben and Lee.

"Why, particularly us?!" Ben exclaimed, pretending to be offended.

"Because of the fact that you are both famous." Chloe said, smiling slightly at Ben's falsely wounded expression. As soon as the four of them reached the lodge, they safely stashed the bikes and made their way inside. Chloe hung back in the porch, smiling at Ben as he wrapped his arm around Kirstie's shoulder and led her inside.

"You alright Chlo?" Lee asked her quickly. She nodded slowly, before quickly wrapping her arms around his neck and hugging him tightly.

"What was that for?" he asked, when she eventually let go of him.

"I just love you." Chloe said, smiling up at him. He smiled back at her, glancing behind her as he heard Ben calling to them. Lee quickly took her hand and led her inside to join the others. Louise squealed and pulled Chloe into a hug as soon as she saw her.

"This is Peter." Louise said gesturing towards Peter, who was hovering uncomfortably on the edge of the group, looking slightly nervous.

"Hello, I'm Chloe." Chloe said politely, quickly walking over to shake hands with him.

"Lee." Lee said shortly. Chloe glanced at Lee, trying to give him the silent cue to be nice to him.

"It's so good to meet everyone, I've heard a lot about you all." Peter smiled, still looking slightly nervous.

"It turns out that we've actually met before." Ben told the group.

"Really?" Lee frowned.

"Yeah, he was a backing dancer for us a few years ago." Ben explained.

"It's such a small world, how are the boys?" Peter asked.

"They are good, we're taking some time out from the band at the moment, Mark is doing musical theatre I think." Ben said, feeling slightly uncomfortable speaking about Mark in front of the group when he knew how they all felt about his behaviour towards Kathleen. The atmosphere suddenly felt tense as everyone fell silent.

"I'm kind of hungry, do we have any food in?" Louise piped up.

"Nope not yet." Kirstie said.

"We should probably do a grocery run at some point." Ben suggested.

"Ooh, why don't you boys go food shopping, and we'll stay here and have girl time?" Louise said excitedly.

"That would be cool, we could get glammed up and go to a bar when you're back or something." Kirstie said quickly.

"And we have a makeup artist." Louise smiled at Chloe. Chloe couldn't help but smile at them. Despite everything that was going on, she was determined to try and enjoy this weekend, and their excitement was infectious. Peter and Ben nodded slowly, glancing at Lee who remained silent.

"Maybe I should stay behind." Lee said, his eyes fixed on Chloe as he felt slightly nervous about leaving her side.

"I'll be fine, go out with the boys, you could always get a pint or something while you are out." Chloe smiled at him reassuringly.

"Yeah, that sounds like a plan." Ben beamed.

"I really think I should stay." Lee insisted. Chloe sighed quietly to herself.

"Can I talk to you a minute?" Chloe asked Lee, holding out her hand for him to take. Lee quickly took her hand and followed her into their bedroom, watching her closely as she closed the door behind them.

"I think you should go out with the guys; you'll have a nice time and it'll give you a chance to check out Peter, which is what you wanted." she told him as soon as the bedroom door was closed.

"I know, I just don't want to leave your side." he admitted.

"Why?" she frowned.

"Because I need to keep you safe, you're carrying precious cargo." he told her, as he perched on the end of the bed, placing his hands on her hips and carefully pulling her towards him.

He sighed in contentment as he wrapped his arms around her and rested his head against her abdomen.

"I'll be here though; nothing is going to happen." she told him as she softly stroked his hair.

"You don't know that." he whispered.

"And I made a promise to keep you both safe." he added. Chloe smiled slightly to herself, her heart fluttering as he said those words.

"I know, but that doesn't mean that you have to be with me all the time, you have your own life too." she sighed.

"You are my life Chlo." he said. Chloe sighed to herself as she quickly squatted down in front of him. Even though she'd always loved his protective side, she couldn't help but feel that he was taking it a little too far. Even though she wanted nothing more than to be in his comforting presence, she knew that he needed some time to unwind.

"Right, stop stressing. This is supposed to be a fun weekend and we are meant to be pretending to everyone that everything is normal." she said quickly.

"I know you are worried about everything, but there will be plenty of time for that when we get home. We need to make the most of being here." she continued. Lee smiled at her, his heart swelling with pride.

"Nathan is right, you are more mature than me." he said thoughtfully.

"Promise me you'll call if anything happens?" he added, taking her hands in his.

"You know I will." she told him, slowly standing up and pulling him with her.

"Now go and have fun with the boys." she added. Lee smiled slightly at her words. He couldn't help but feel a surge of pride at how much more confident she was compared to when they first got together. He knew in his heart that she was right, and he knew that the girls were with her, so if something did happen, she wouldn't be alone. Lee knew that he was smothering her slightly, but he couldn't help it, since he'd found out about her being pregnant, she somehow seemed even more vulnerable to him than normal. He kissed her softly on the lips, before sighing deeply and resting his forehead against hers.

"You should go." Chloe whispered reluctantly as she heard Ben's voice calling down the hallway. Lee nodded slowly placing another soft kiss on her lips before walking away.

Chapter Sixty-Two

"Have you seriously made a hot water bottle?" Louise laughed when Chloe walked into the living room carrying a hot water bottle.

"You'll be boiling, it's roasting today!" Kirstie agreed.

"I know, but I have cramps." Chloe told them, as she sat on the sofa beside them and carefully placed the hot water bottle on her abdomen.

"Uh oh, have you told Lee yet?" Louise giggled.

"Told him what?" Chloe said quickly, suddenly feeling nervous that they had discovered her secret.

"That you're on your period, so he won't be getting any weekend away sex." Louise giggled.

"I don't think he'll be too bothered." Chloe said quietly, feeling a wave of relief wash over her, mixed with a pang of guilt that she couldn't tell them the truth.

"Anyway, I thought you were making tea?" Kirstie frowned.

"I was, but then I realised that we don't have tea bags." Chloe sniggered.

"I'll text Ben and ask him to get some." Kirstie said as she quickly pulled out her phone.

"Right ladies, when are we doing this makeover then!" Louise said excitedly.

"We can do hair, makeup, nails the whole works." she added, not quite able to contain her excitement. Before Chloe or Kirstie could respond, Louise quickly dashed out of the room and returned a few moments later with a heap of products. Chloe slowly picked up the makeup and rummaged in the products.

"I think I need to shave my legs too." Louise said thoughtfully as she gazed down at her legs.

"Wow, you really are going all out." Kirstie laughed.

"I want to look hot for Peter." Louise admitted, her cheeks colouring slightly.

"Aww, you're really into him, aren't you?" Kirstie smiled. Louise nodded, unable to wipe the wide smile from her face.

"Why don't you wax instead?" Chloe suggested.

"Nah, that's too painful." Louise said, grimacing slightly.

"It's not actually too bad and it makes your legs nice and soft." Chloe told her.

"You wax?" Louise asked. Chloe nodded quickly, bursting out laughing as Louise reached over and gently stroked her calf.

"Oh my god, your legs are really soft!" Louise exclaimed.

"I also use a special oil in the bath to make my skin really soft." Chloe smiled.
"It's one of the only good things about my job, you know what products to use for things." she added.

"I was actually going to ask what you use to on your hair, it's always looks really shiny and soft?" Kirstie piped up.

"I have some of the conditioner in my room, I can get it for you later." Chloe told them.

"Do you both want to go for a smoky eye look?" Chloe offered as she quickly picked up a makeup brush. Louise nodded excitedly.

"Yes please, I'll go and get the hair products, then I can do hair while you do makeup." Kirstie told Chloe. Chloe nodded slowly and began to work on Louise's makeup.

"I love how you are like the group product guru." Louise smiled.

"It's more of a recent thing to be honest, it's a lot of pressure to look half decent when you are dating someone famous." Chloe sighed.

"I guess it must be, I hadn't really thought of it like that." Louise said, smiling sympathetically at her.

"Especially when you know they can have anyone they want." Kirstie agreed as she walked back into the room.

"It's worse because they are both so good looking." Chloe pointed out.

"Yeah, I know." Kirstie said quietly, as she sat behind Louise and began to work on her hair.

"I sometimes wish that Lee was just a regular guy, so that there aren't so many women wanting his attention all the time. And we could be a regular couple without having to be a secret from everyone at work." Chloe admitted.

"Do you ever feel like that about Ben?" Chloe asked, glancing at Kirstie.

"I guess in some ways it would make things easier, but it's who he is and what he loves. He's worked so hard to get where he is, and I could never take that from him just for an easy life. I love that he is so passionate about music and has a job he adores." Kirstie explained.

"I love him, and he wouldn't be the same person if he didn't have the band and his music." she added.

"Oh my god that's so cute!" Louise exclaimed.

"I feel kind of bad now, I hadn't thought of it like that." Chloe admitted quietly.

"Not that I'd ever ask Lee to leave the band or anything, it would just be nice to be normal." she added.

"Is everything okay with the two of you, he seemed really stressed when he phoned me the other day?" Kirstie asked.

"We're fine, I stupidly lied to him and said I was going into work, but I was actually at the cemetery. So, he was a bit annoyed that he couldn't find me." Chloe explained.

"It was my fault for lying." Chloe added quickly when Louise and Kirstie glanced at each other.

"It's amazing though, how happy you both are in your couples." Louise said quickly, smiling at them.

"You can talk, you seem quite into Peter." Kirstie said, wiggling her eyebrows at Louise.

"I really am, it's early days, but it's going well." Louise smiled.

"It's just a shame that because we've both got such busy schedules, we don't get to see each other that much, although I met him a few months ago at the ball, this is only our third date, if you can call a weekend away a date." Louise told them.

"Wait....it's your third date?" Kirstie said, smiling in satisfaction when she finally finished straightening Louise's hair.

"Yeah, why?" Louise frowned.

"Well, that explains why you are going all out to look good." Kirstie laughed.

"Tonight's the night." Kirstie teased her.

"The first time you sleep with someone is always a worry isn't it, like what if they are really bad at it." Louise giggled.

"I know what you mean." Kirstie agreed.

"And then you end up having to fake it." Louise said, rolling her eyes.

"We've all been there." Kirstie laughed. Louise nodded in agreement, joining in with Kirstie's laughter.

"You've gone very quiet Chloe." Louise said thoughtfully.

"I'm just concentrating." she lied, not quite able to bring herself to tell them that she couldn't really contribute to this conversation because she wasn't as sexually experienced as them. Once again feeling like she was on the outside of the group.

"Okay you're done." Chloe told Louise.

"I can do your hair while Chloe does your makeup if you want?" Louise offered Kirstie. Kirstie nodded and quickly moved to sit in front of Chloe.

"You'll need to give us details tomorrow." Kirstie said to Louise a few moments later.

"And we'll keep our fingers crossed for you that you don't have to fake it." Kirstie giggled.

"At least if I do have too, I'm quite good at it now." Louise laughed.

"Really?" Kirstie frowned.

"Yeah, check this out." Louise said proudly. Chloe could feel herself squirming as Louise gave them a demonstration. She glanced at Kirstie as she burst out laughing.

"That's pretty good actually." Kirstie said.

"Wait, there's more." Louise laughed, before doing it again. Chloe's eyes snapped up as Lee and Ben walked into the room, both carrying bags of shopping, Peter following closely behind.

"What's with all the noise, we could hear you from outside?!" Ben exclaimed.

"Louise was showing us how she fakes an orgasm." Kirstie laughed. Lee and Ben glanced at each other for a moment, both looking slightly confused.

"I hate to break it to you boys, but all women do it at some point." Louise said, laughing when she saw their expressions.

"I can take the food." Peter said quietly, reaching out to take the bags from them. Chloe watched him quickly leave the room, clearly keen to escape the conversation. She couldn't help but feel sorry for him, he barely knew the group and was probably feeling very uncomfortable with what they were discussing. She glanced at Lee as he threw himself down on the sofa beside her.

Ben walked over to Kirstie and stood behind her, placing his hands on her shoulders.

"Are you honestly trying to say you have to fake it because I think we both know I do more than enough to make sure that you don't need too." Ben chuckled.

"No, I don't have to with you, but I've had to with people in the past." Kirstie told him. Ben raised his eyebrow and smirked at Lee, almost as if he was daring Lee to compete.

"I'm not being funny, but there's no way Chloe is faking." Lee said quickly. Chloe suddenly felt a tight knot in her stomach as Lee said those words and everyone turned to stare at her, waiting to see what her response would be. She could feel her cheeks colouring as she thought for a moment.

"How do you know, maybe I am." Chloe said quickly, trying to deflect from her own embarrassment. She couldn't help but feel slightly relieved as everyone stopped staring at her and stared at Lee instead. Lee stared at her for a moment, slightly shocked by her comment.

"Because I would be able to tell." he insisted.

"And besides I taught you everything you know." he quickly added. Chloe winced, her heart in her mouth as he said those words and she glanced up at Ben, Kirstie and Louise, who were frowning in confusion at them.

"About how to have good sex, since Andy was so bad." Lee said, thinking quickly, when he realised what he'd said. Chloe sighed as she carefully put down the makeup brush.

"Oh no, was Andy really that bad?" Louise laughed. Chloe leaned back on the sofa, quickly racking her brain for what to say. She really hated when Lee came out with comments that put her in this position.

"I don't really feel comfortable talking about it." Chloe said quietly, quickly deciding that she wasn't going to lie to her friends, but nor was she prepared to tell them the truth.

"Speaking of which, Chloe told us the news." Kirstie said, smiling at Lee.

"She did?" Lee said, frowning at Chloe as his heart pounded against his chest. He couldn't help but feel surprised that she had told them about the baby, when the two of them had agreed to keep the secret for now.

"Yeah, that there'll be no hot weekend away sex for you since she's on her period." Louise giggled. Lee glanced between Chloe and Louise, even more confused than before.

"I've got cramps, so they figured out that I'm on my period." Chloe said quickly, before Lee could say anything that gave something away. Lee's eyes flickered to Chloe's abdomen, where she was still gently holding the hot water bottle against it, his eyes widening nervously.

"It's okay, it's normal." Chloe said, trying to speak in code to him so that he didn't start to worry that something was wrong with her or the baby.

"Oh well, I guess I'll be the only one trying to prove a point tonight then babe." Ben said, smiling to himself as he quickly kissed Kirstie on the lips. Chloe quickly stood up and walked into the kitchen smiling warmly at Peter as he glanced at her.

"Do you need any help putting the food away?" Chloe asked.

"I'm okay thank you, I have it under control." he smiled at her.

"They can be a bit intense when you first meet them, particularly the boys, but don't worry, you'll soon fit in." she smiled at him, trying to reassure him. She sighed quietly to herself as she realised yet again that even though she'd been friends with them for a long time, she still felt slightly on the outside of their little group. Chloe was a very different person to them, she was very shy and private person that didn't like to discuss her personal business, whereas they were very bubbly and open people that had no qualms speaking about their sex lives in front of each other.

"Yeah, they seem like nice people." he smiled back at her.

"They are. Did you guys go for a pint in the end?" she asked him.

"No, we just went to the supermarket. Lee wanted to get back." he told her. Chloe sighed deeply.

"Chloe, where have you got too?!" Kirstie voice called from the living room.

"I'd better get back, you're probably safe to come back in now, hopefully the subject has changed." she chuckled.

"We need to do your hair and makeup Chloe, so that we can head out." Louise said as soon as Chloe and Peter walked back into the living room.

"Well, I was thinking that I could just stay behind and get an early night." Chloe said quietly, not looking forward to being in a bar and getting grilled as to why she wasn't drinking alcohol.

"No, you have to come along, I have a surprise for you!" Kirstie protested. Chloe sighed and nodded slowly.

"I can do your hair if you want?" Louise offered.

"No, it's okay. I'll get ready in my room." Chloe said, suddenly feeling like she needed some time out.

Chapter Sixty-Three

Chloe rummaged through her makeup collection as she sat at the dressing table. As soon as she located the product, she needed she quickly applied her makeup, trying to hold back the tears that were filling her eyes. She was finding it exhausting trying to pretend that everything was fine and that she was coping okay with the idea of having a baby. Constantly having to wear a mask of happiness was starting to take its toll, particularly when she even felt like she had to pretend in front of Lee. He was so stressed lately that the last thing she wanted to do was add to his already full plate by confiding in him about her intense fear that she was still struggling with. Chloe glanced up as Lee walked into the room and rummaged in his suitcase for a change of clothes.

"We're going to have to be so careful that they don't get suspicious of you not drinking." Lee said thoughtfully.

"I know, that's why I don't see the point in going." Chloe sighed.

"But it's not like I'm going to be left alone to stay here is it." she said, feeling slightly angry that she always ended up being pressured into doing things that she didn't want to do.

"No probably not." he agreed, quickly changing his shirt.

"It should be okay as long as we are subtle, we can do things like Mocktails and pretend it's a real one or say you've got vodka and lemonade or something." he added. Chloe nodded slowly, sighing quietly at the thought of having to lie to her friends yet again.

"I think Kirstie was a bit worried that you were upset after being questioned on Andy." Lee told her.

"I'm not upset, it just makes me uncomfortable." she said quietly.

"And you need to be more careful what you say in front of people, that's the third time you've almost told my friends my secret." she told him.

"I know, I just have no filter sometimes." he said quietly.

"Yes well, it's bad enough that you told Nathan, but if you tell anyone else, I will never forgive you." she warned him.

"I would have thought that it's something to be proud of. Personally, I'm proud to be the one that you chose." he told her. Chloe sighed to herself as she realised that yet again, he didn't seem to understand her. She didn't want people to sit in judgement on her, just like people had when she was at school when she dated but refused to sleep with any of the guys until she fell in love with them. Chloe had lost count of the number of times over the years that disgruntled people had called her a nun or teased her for being frigid, so she preferred to keep it to herself.

"It's none of their business though." she said, putting down her makeup brush and quickly making a start on her hair. Lee watched her for a moment, not entirely sure why she wasn't proud of herself for having the strength of character to hold firm in her morals. He'd met many women over the years but never one like her.

"Are your cramps any better?" he asked her, changing the subject when he sensed that she didn't want to talk about it anymore.

"Kind of." she said quietly.

"Are you sure it's normal?" he said.

"Yes, I read about it in a pregnancy book, sore breasts, feeling nauseous all the time and fatigue all of which I have are normal too." she said impatiently, gradually becoming frustrated by his constant fussing. She couldn't help but feel like every time she tried to forget what was happening, he would do something to remind her of the situation. Chloe could feel Lee watching her closely as he sat on the end of the bed. She deliberately avoided eye contact with him as she pinned her hair in place to one side, smiling in satisfaction as the gentle curls rippled down her neck.

"Do you need a fresh hot water bottle?" he asked her.

"No, I'm fine. Will you please stop fussing me all the time!" she snapped. Chloe jumped and glanced up at the bedroom door as it opened and Kirstie walked in, glancing between the two of them as she sensed the awkward atmosphere.

"I need to steal you, so I can give you your surprise." Kirstie said glancing down at the gift bag in her hand and smiling at Chloe excitedly.

"I'll go and wait in the lounge." Lee told them, glancing at Chloe for a moment before leaving the room. Chloe couldn't help but feel guilty that she'd snapped at him, she knew how much he loved and cared about her and that he only wanted to take care of her, even more so now that she was pregnant, but that didn't stop the frustration that Chloe was feeling. Chloe glanced at Kirstie as she felt her watching her closely, a thoughtful expression on her face, almost like she was trying to figure something out.

"What's the surprise then?" Chloe asked, noticing for the first time that Kirstie had changed into her dress.

"Well, I brought you a little something because I feel really guilty about giving you food poisoning a couple of weeks ago." Kirstie said.

"You didn't give me food poisoning; it was probably just a stomach bug." Chloe said quickly, sighing to herself as she lied once again.

"Maybe but I still feel bad, so I want you to have this." Kirstie insisted, handing Chloe the bag. Chloe smiled and quickly peered into the bag, gasping as she pulled out a fitted white lace dress, almost identical to the one that she was wearing on the night that her and Lee had met.

"I remember seeing it in the picture and how Lee remembered the dress you were wearing, so I thought you could surprise him." Kirstie explained. Chloe stared at the dress, feeling slightly emotional at how thoughtful a gift it was.

"Thank you so much." Chloe whispered, quickly pulling Kirstie into a hug.

"You're welcome, you'll look so beautiful in it, he won't be able to take his eyes off you." Kirstie smiled. Chloe smiled slightly, trying to pretend to be excited to go out, when all she wanted to do was curl up in bed and go to sleep.

"Put it on then and I'll zip you up." Kirstie prompted. Chloe nodded and quickly walked into the bathroom. Even though her confidence was growing, she still didn't feel entirely comfortable undressing in front of Kirstie, particularly when she had such a visible scar on her abdomen.

"Wow, it really suits you!" Kirstie breathed as soon as Chloe walked out of the bathroom. Kirstie quickly walked up behind her and zipped up the dress. Chloe looked at herself in the mirror and smiled slightly as she stared at herself in the dress. She couldn't help but feel a small surge of confidence as she looked at her reflection. Chloe carefully bent down and pulled her black pumps out of her suitcase and slipped them on.

"We should probably take jackets too shouldn't we, just in case?" Chloe asked.

"Yeah, I would, since we have to walk to the main complex." Kirstie said. Chloe nodded and picked up her leather jacket, quickly checking the pockets to check that she had money.

"Shall we go then?" Chloe said quickly, hoping that the sooner they went out the sooner they would get home and she could go to bed. Kirstie nodded and followed Chloe into the living room. Kirstie couldn't help but fix her eyes on Lee as Chloe walked into the room, so that she could see his reaction to the dress. She smiled to herself as Lee did a double take at her, raising his eyebrow as he couldn't resist staring at her.

"I just had a Deja vu moment." Lee whispered to Chloe when she walked over to him.

"I had one too when I put it on." Chloe smiled at him. Lee smiled, still not quite able to stop himself from gazing in wonder at how perfect she looked. Lee placed his arm around her waist and held her close against him.

"You're so stunning." he whispered in her ear, so that nobody else could hear. Chloe turned to face him sighing quietly as she placed her head against his chest. Lee gazed down at her longingly, still not quite able to believe that he was the one she loved.

"C'mon lovebirds, we're going." Kirstie giggled as she walked past them.

Chapter Sixty-Four

"Ooh let's sit here!" Louise said excitedly as she spotted a table in a quiet area of the bar, surrounded by sofas. The six of them quickly sat down, cosying up in their couples.

"This place is so nice; the lodge is amazing too." Kirstie said.

"Yeah, nice shout suggesting it Chloe." Ben agreed.

"I had no idea what the park was like, I just knew that I wanted to go to the zoo." Chloe giggled.

"I'm actually really grateful that you guys invited me along." Peter said, smiling around at the group.

"You're welcome, you're part of our little gang now that you are with Louise." Kirstie smiled at him.

"I have to admit, I was very nervous to meet you all." Peter admitted.

"Really, are we that scary?" Ben teased.

"No, I just knew how close you all are and that your opinions mean a lot to Louise, so I wanted you all to like me." Peter explained, smiling at Louise.

"As long as you treat her right, we'll like you." Lee said quickly.

"And if you don't then watch out." he added. Lee gasped quietly as Chloe elbowed him in the ribs, trying to remind him to behave himself. Chloe could see that Peter was a very sensitive person and the last thing she wanted was for Lee to frighten Peter away from Louise, particularly when Louise clearly liked him a lot.

"Louise did mention that she's like a little sister to you." Peter said.

"So, who were you most nervous to meet?" Chloe asked, quickly changing the subject before Lee could dig a deeper hole.

"It was actually you." Peter said, looking at Lee.

"Why me?" Lee frowned in confusion.

"I have quite a lot of dancer friends, some of which danced with Eclipse and to be honest mate, I heard a lot of bad things about you." Peter explained. Chloe glanced at Lee nervously, not entirely sure how he was going to react.

"But Lou assured me that you are just misunderstood and so far, I agree with her." Peter continued.

"I think it's more that this one has melted me." Lee said, smiling at Chloe as he wrapped his arm around her shoulder and linked his fingers through hers.

"You always say that but it's not true." Chloe said quickly.

"I'm going to get the first-round in." Peter said, quickly standing up.

"It's okay, I can get them." Lee said sharply, glancing at Chloe.

"I'd really like too as a thank you for everyone." Peter insisted.

"What does everyone want?" Peter asked. Chloe could feel her heart pounding against her chest as everyone told Peter what drinks they wanted, all of which were alcoholic. She had no idea how she was going to get away with not having alcohol, without the others becoming suspicious.

"Chloe, how about you?" Peter asked, snapping her out of her thoughts. Chloe could feel Lee watching her closely.

"Can I just have water please?" Chloe said nervously, her stomach knotting as she waited for the inevitable questions.

"Are you not drinking Chloe?" Ben frowned.

"I want to make sure that I am not hungover for the zoo tomorrow, since I've wanted to go for a few years." Chloe explained.

"You can have one though surely?" Louise asked.

"Speaking of the zoo, I downloaded a map." Chloe told them excitedly, as she pulled a piece of paper out of her pocket, glancing up at Peter for a moment as he walked away to get the drinks. Chloe couldn't help but sigh in relief when she realised that she'd managed to successfully distract the group enough to avoid being questioned. She carefully laid out the map on the table.

"Is that a map of the zoo?" Louise asked.

"Yes, it looks awesome, it has different sections because it's so big. There's an Asia section which has bears and stuff and the African section looks amazing!" Chloe told them excitedly.

"You're such a nerd Chloe." Ben laughed. Chloe smiled slightly.

"We'll probably need to get up early though as it's a forty-minute drive from here." Chloe told them.

"The speed Ben drives it'll be over an hour." Kirstie teased. She burst out laughing as Ben glared at her playfully.

"Maybe I'll go with Peter and Louise then." Chloe laughed.

"It's better to get somewhere safely than not at all, you should see Mr sports car over here, he would probably do it in twenty minutes." Ben teased Lee.

"There's no point having a sports car if you don't floor it." Lee laughed.

"You're such a show-off, with your big flashy house and fancy car." Ben said, rolling his eyes playfully.

"Just because I have expensive taste doesn't make me a show-off." Lee argued, a small smile playing on the corner of his lips.

Peter smiled at them as he returned to the table, carefully carrying a tray of drinks.

"Okay so I got everyone what they asked for, but I also got some wine for the table for us to share." Peter said, quickly handing each of their drinks and a wine glass. Chloe reluctantly took the glass that he was handing to her and placed it on the table.

"Are you guys going to be able to drive tomorrow if you're having a beer and a glass of wine?" Lee asked, glancing at Ben and Peter.

"Yeah, it should be fine." Ben said quickly.

"I was just thinking that Chloe and I could stay sober and drive your cars?" Lee offered, starting to panic slightly as Peter filled up Chloe's wine glass.

"That's probably not a good idea, I haven't driven since I was about eighteen." Chloe said quietly, realising what Lee was trying to do, but not quite able to stop herself from telling them that she probably wouldn't remember how to drive.

"Oh yeah, I forgot about that." Lee said quietly, suddenly remembering that she'd been unable to afford a car.

"I'll have to take you out in the sports car at some point." he added, trying to distract the group so that they wouldn't ask Chloe about why she hadn't driven for so long. The last thing Lee wanted was for Chloe to get upset when she was reminded about her past living situation.

"Erm, no thanks, I'd be scared I'd crash it." Chloe said, smiling slightly.

"He'd probably break up with you if you did that." Ben laughed.

"I know he would." Chloe giggled.

"No, I wouldn't, it's just a car." Lee said, laughing along with them.

"That car is your baby." Ben teased, as he continued laughing. Chloe instantly stopped laughing as he said those words, the smile slowly fading from her face.

"No, it's not." Lee said, subtly squeezing Chloe's hand reassuringly. As the others started to talk amongst themselves Lee's eyes scanned the table. He quickly realised that the wine bottle in the centre of the table was empty. As he glanced at his glass and Chloe's, he suddenly realised that Peter had given Chloe more wine than Lee, clearly trying to be a gentleman and prioritize the ladies. He knew that it was only a matter of time before the others started to wonder why Chloe wasn't drinking it. He considered knocking over the glass and pretending that it was an accident, but he knew that would be delaying the inevitable and they would only buy her another drink or give her their wine instead. Lee quickly picked up Chloe's glass of wine and downed it in one, smiling at the group as they stared at him.

"Chloe doesn't like wine, she's more of a cocktail girl." Lee said, quickly standing up and walking over to the bar.

"Since when don't you like wine?" Kirstie frowned as Lee walked away from them.

"I've gone off of it lately." Chloe said quietly, as she picked up the zoo map from the table and carefully folded it, so that she didn't have to look any of them in the eye.

"I actually need to use the bathroom." Chloe said, quickly standing up and hurrying to the bathroom.

"Where's Chloe?" Lee asked when he returned to the table.

"Toilet." Ben told him. Lee nodded and placed Chloe's drink on the table. Lee's head snapped up as he saw Chloe walk out of the bathroom. His heart pounded against his chest as he saw a group of men at the table wolf whistling her. He watched closely as one of them reached out to take her hand as she walked past. Chloe paused and turned to face them, speaking to them for a few moments before smiling and walking back to the group and sitting beside Lee.

"What did they want?' Lee asked her quietly as soon as she sat down.

"To buy me a drink, but obviously I said no." Chloe said quietly, glancing at the others to check if they'd overheard. Chloe breathed a sigh of relief when she realised, they were still speaking loudly to each other. Lee gently stroked Chloe's cheek with his fingertips, glancing behind her as he saw the group of men intermittently glancing over at Chloe and then talking amongst themselves, clearly speaking about her. Lee could feel his blood slowly simmering.

"Do me a favour and kiss me or something?" Lee said quickly.

"Why?" Chloe frowned, glancing behind her and following his eye line. As soon as Chloe turned to face them, they winked at her and gestured for her to come and join them.

"Right, I've had enough." Lee said, quickly standing up.

"Just leave it!" Chloe said quickly.

"Where are you going?" Ben asked.

"Bathroom." Lee said shortly.

"Oh, for god sake." Chloe muttered under her breath as Lee walked away. Chloe turned her back on them, not quite able to bring herself to watch.

"Where's he going?" Kirstie frowned when she noticed Chloe's body language.

"To tell those guys to back off probably." Chloe sighed.

"Why, what did they do?" Louise asked.

"Asked to buy me a drink and then they kept gesturing for me to come and sit with them." Chloe said.

"But I can handle it, he doesn't need to overreact all the time." she added, sounding slightly exhausted.

"It definitely seems like an overreaction." Louise said.

"I mean, I know he's an overprotective person when he cares about someone, but that's a bit much." she added.

"I think he's a bit over sensitive to it because it's been happening a lot lately, what with Shayne and Jonny a few weeks ago." Chloe said thoughtfully.

"Who's Jonny?" Kirstie frowned. Chloe quickly filled the group in on what happened with Jonny during the photoshoot.

"And he was vile, he wouldn't back off, even though I told him I had a boyfriend several times." she told them.

"He sounds gross." Kirstie agreed.

"He is, it always seems to happen to me, I'm sick of it." Chloe said

"It's because you're really pretty, you drive most guys crazy. I remember when all the bands joined up with Matt's record label and we all met Eclipse, and you.... how long ago was that now?" Ben frowned.

"I'm not sure, but I think it was just before I split up with Andy." Chloe said thoughtfully.

"Yeah, that's right, because they stopped when they found out you had a boyfriend." Ben agreed.

"What stopped, what are you talking about?" Chloe frowned.

"A group of the guys, all of which wanted you had a bet on to see who could get you first." Ben told her.

"No, they didn't." Chloe laughed, not believing him.

"They did, because there were a few of them that wanted you and they couldn't decide who should get to ask you out first, they decided to all have a shot and see what happened." Ben insisted.

"Which ones was it?" Chloe asked quickly as she felt herself becoming more and more angry.

"If I tell you then you none of us can let on that we know, it needs to stay between the six of us." Ben said, glancing around at everyone as they nodded quickly.

"Right well obviously Shayne was one of them, so was Mark, Dougie and I'm pretty sure one of Nightmare were involved I think." Ben said thoughtfully.

"Please tell me it wasn't James?" Chloe asked nervously, feeling slightly uncomfortable about the fact that James might have been involved, since the two of them had been good friends when they worked together for a couple of months.

"No, it definitely wasn't James, I think it might have been Charlie, in fact I'm pretty sure it was his idea." Ben told her.

"I remember some of the guys moaning to Matt about how come you were only working with Eclipse; I think a lot of them wanted to spend more time with you." Ben added.

"This is making me feel a bit ill." Chloe admitted.

"It's disgusting, you're not a prize to be won." Kirstie piped up.

"I'm so sick of it, I don't understand why guys think they want me all the time." Chloe said, beginning to get angry.

"Erm hello, look at you." Louise smiled, still not quite able to understand how someone as beautiful as Chloe, clearly had no idea how stunning she was.

"Also, I'm fed up with guys trying to get into my pants all the time, I have a heart and a mind, not just a vagina!" Chloe said angrily, her temper finally snapping. Peter's cheeks coloured as he looked around awkwardly. Ben, Louise and Kirstie burst out laughing, none of them able to believe that Chloe had said that.

"What did you put in that cocktail?!" Louise asked Lee as soon as he returned to the table. Lee frowned in confusion when he saw Chloe with her arms folded across her chest, an angry expression on her face.

"I didn't put anything in it." Lee said, glancing at Kirstie and Louise who were having a fit of the giggles.

"I'm so confused." Lee admitted.

"Chloe just had a rant and said vagina and it was hilarious." Ben laughed.

"We've officially corrupted her." Louise laughed.

"I can't believe I said that." Chloe said, smiling slightly.

"I'm just so mad." she added.

"I didn't start anything, I just told them to stop hitting on my girlfriend." Lee said quickly, assuming that Chloe was angry with him for confronting the group of guys in the bar.

"We've moved on from that." Ben said.

"Although it was a bit uncalled for when I can handle them. I keep telling you I can fight my own battles." Chloe snapped.

"Calm down Chloe, we'll get you another drink." Ben offered, feeling slightly guilty that he'd caused her to be angry.

"No thank you, I think I need to walk it off." Chloe said, before quickly standing up and pulling on her jacket.

Chapter Sixty-Five

"You don't need to come with me." Chloe sighed as she glanced behind her and saw that Lee was following her.

"I'm quite capable of finding my way back to the lodge." she added, sounding slightly frustrated.

"I don't think any of the guys would let their girlfriends walk through a forest on their own in the dark." Lee said defensively. Chloe rolled her eyes at him.

"What were the others laughing at while I was away from the table?" he asked her.

"Ben was telling me that apparently some of the guys from the bands we worked with before wanted to ask me out and because they couldn't agree who got the first shot, they all decided to go for it, and the others put bets on who would be successful." Chloe ranted as she angrily strode along the pathway.

"Really, which ones?" he frowned.

"Dougie, Mark, Shayne and Charlie." she said.

"And I assume you were involved?" she said accusingly.

"No of course not, I don't even remember hearing anything about that." he said quietly, feeling slightly hurt when she scoffed sceptically.

"You don't seem surprised." she insisted.

"That's because I'm not, I keep telling you that a lot of guys fancy you." he said.

"I wasn't involved in it Chlo, I promise." he told her.

"They probably didn't tell me and the other Eclipse boys because we'd been working with you for a few months by that time, and the five of us were good friends, so they probably realised that if we knew about it then we would tell you." he explained. Chloe nodded slowly, calming down a little when she realised that he was right.

"I'm just really pissed off, it's like Kirstie said I'm not a prize to be won!" she said angrily.

"And I do actually have feelings and a personality, it feels like everyone just wants to get in my knickers and it's winding me up!" she said, continuing to rant. Lee frowned at her as he listened to her rant, in all the years that he'd known her, he'd never seen her so angry and he'd never heard her swear before.

"Admittedly Mark and Shayne are like that, but I don't think Dougie and Charlie are. They probably wanted to date you." he told her. Chloe sighed and fell silent.

"Make sure you don't leave me then, now you know that all these guys like you." he chuckled.

"There's more chance of you doing that than me." she said quietly.

"That's never happening. I realised the other day when I thought you'd left, that I have no idea what I'd do without you." he said quietly.

"Whereas I think you'd be fine without me, and you'll probably find someone else pretty quickly, especially since everyone wants you." he added.

"Well, they won't soon when I start showing." she said shortly, suddenly feeling her temper growing again. Lee glanced at her, slightly confused by her random outburst.

"What's wrong Chlo?" he asked her gently.

"I don't know, I'm just so angry." she admitted quietly.

"These pregnancy hormones are really messing with my head, one minute I'm fuming and the next I want to burst into tears." she added. Lee smiled at her sympathetically and gently wrapped his arm around waist, pulling her close as they walked, to provide her with some comfort. He frowned to himself as she suddenly stopped dead in her tracks. His brow furrowed in concern as she took deep breaths.

"I think I'm going to be sick." she said. Before Lee could say anything, she quickly walked off the track and stood behind a tree. Lee sighed to himself as he heard her vomiting. He couldn't help but feel sad for her, it broke his heart a little to see the woman that he loved struggling, especially when she'd already been through so much in her life. Chloe glanced up at Lee as he appeared beside her, carefully placing his hand on her back as she doubled over and vomited again.

"I'll be okay." she reassured him, when she finally stopped vomiting.

"You don't really keep anything, down do you?" he said worriedly.

"It's probably just the drink, I'll take one of the tablets when we get back." she told him.

Chloe slowly straightened up and rested her back against the tree as she tried to get her breath back. She smiled at Lee as he watched her closely, quite clearly trying to resist the urge to smother her. She quickly removed her jacket, frowning to herself as she suddenly felt very warm.

"I'm sorry I keep being snappy with you." she said quietly.

"It's okay, I understand. I just wish there was something that I could do to help." he said sadly. Chloe nodded and slowly walked back towards the track. Lee quickly fell into step beside her, quickly reaching out to grab her forearm to steady her when she tripped. Chloe winced slightly at his tight grip on her arm. As soon as she recovered herself, Lee quickly let go of her arm.

Chloe sighed in relief as they finally reached the lodge. As soon as they were inside, Chloe quickly walked into their bedroom, sat at the dressing table and began to remove her makeup.

She glanced at Lee in the mirror as he stood behind her, placing his hands on her shoulders. Her skin tingled under his touch as he began to softly stroke her neck with his fingertips. Lee smiled to himself as she shivered when his hand reached her hair. Chloe watched as he expertly removed her hair pins and watched as her loose curls tumbled onto her neck.

"You look even more beautiful than normal tonight." he told her, watching her closely as he softly stroked her hair. Chloe locked eyes with him in the mirror and sighed as she stood up.

"Are you trying to get in my pants too?" she said shortly, before quickly walking into the bathroom to brush her teeth.

"You know it's not like that with us Chlo, I love you." Lee told her as soon as she emerged from the bathroom.

"I know, I'm sorry." she sighed as she stood in front of him.

"You don't have to keep apologising; you can't help it." he told her. Chloe smiled and slowly turned her back on him, gathering her hair in her hand and holding it to one side.

Her skin tingled as she felt Lee's warm breath on her neck. He hesitated for a moment before slowly unzipping her dress, his fingers brushing down her spine as he did so. Lee placed his hands inside the dress, resting them on her hips as he carefully pulled her body against his.

"I'm having another Deja vu moment." he whispered in her ear. Chloe nodded slowly, struggling to concentrate on what he was saying as he placed a series of soft kisses between her shoulders, slowly making his way to her neck. Chloe gasped and looped her arm behind her, placing her hand on the back of Lee's head as he kissed the sweet spot on her neck. Eventually Lee carefully turned her to face him, smiling down at her as she kicked her shoes off.

"Do you remember the last time I helped you out of a hot dress?" Lee asked her, smiling slightly as he thought about their first date.

"Yes, I do." Chloe smiled.

"You're so much more confident now though." he breathed as she slowly removed her dress and stood in front of him in her underwear.

Even though she'd undressed in front of him numerous times, she still took his breath away, almost like he still hadn't built up a resilience to her beauty. He couldn't help but smile to himself when he realised that she was wearing the white lace set that was his favourite.

"I kind of wish we could go back to when we first started dating." she admitted, wrapping her arms around his neck.

"Why?" he frowned.

"Because it would be nice to go back to before things got complicated." she said, sighing deeply.

"I know." he said quietly.

"We'll get through it though." he added, as he removed his shirt. Lee placed his hands on her waist and kissed her softly, quickly deepening the kiss.

"I really need to pee." he laughed when he eventually pulled away. Chloe giggled as he quickly ran into the bathroom.

"Just hold that thought until I get back." he called. Chloe smiled and slowly walked over to the bed. She sighed as she laid down and turned onto her side, resting her eyes for a moment as she waited for Lee to return.

As soon as Lee emerged from the bathroom, he removed his trousers, glancing at Chloe who was curled up on the bed, her back to him.

"Chlo." Lee said softly, frowning to himself as he made his way to his side of the bed, frowning to himself as he laid down beside her and saw that she had her eyes closed. He couldn't help but smile at how adorable she looked as she slept. He sighed in disappointment and carefully pulled the bed sheet over her, taking care not to wake her. Lee couldn't tear his eyes away from her as he watched her sleeping peacefully. He slowly reached out and brushed her hair out of her face. Until Chloe and him had started dating, he'd had no idea it was possible to love someone as much as he loved her, he would literally do anything for her.

"I love you Chlo." he whispered, placing a soft kiss on her lips.

Chapter Sixty-Six

"Oh my god, you've made a bloody mess!" Lee exclaimed as he walked into the kitchen and saw Ben making an omelette. Lee shook his head as he gazed around at the kitchen counters that were strewn with mess.

"You're only making an omelette; how did you manage to get onion peel everywhere." Lee sighed.

"I've put onion in it obviously." Ben laughed. Lee sighed as he began to clear up Ben's mess.

"You're like a bear with a sore head today." Ben chuckled as Lee angrily scooped the mess into his hand and flung it into the bin.

"That's because it's ridiculously early." Lee said as he quickly made himself a coffee.

"How come you're so chirpy?" Lee asked.

"Because as of when we get home, my girlfriend is moving in with me." Ben beamed. "That's awesome mate." Lee said, quickly high fiving Ben.

"We went for a walk in the woods last night and I asked her. And then she showed me how much she appreciated my commitment to her." Ben beamed, wiggling his eyebrows at Lee.

"Is that why you want her to move in with you, so that you can have sex more often?" Lee laughed.

"Speak for yourself." Ben said, pretending to be offended but with the hint of a smile playing on the corner of his mouth.

"That is not why I asked Chloe to move in with me." Lee said quickly.

"Don't tell the girls about it yet though, as I think Kirstie is pretty excited to tell them." Ben said. Lee nodded as he took a sip of his coffee and leant against the kitchen counter.

"I remember that time that you thought I was into Kirstie because I was spending a lot of time at her house." Lee chuckled.

"What's that got to do with anything?" Ben said, sounding slightly defensive.

"I just wondered if asking her to move in with you is your way of telling the world that she's with you." Lee teased.

"No not at all, I just love her and I'm ready to take the next step." Ben told him.

"I know, all banter aside, I'm really happy for the two of you." Lee smiled, feeling slightly nostalgic when he remembered how happy he'd been when Chloe had agreed to move in with him.

"How was your night?" Ben asked Lee.

"Pretty uneventful." Lee replied.

"Oh yeah, that's right, you're having to take a few days off aren't you." Ben laughed, trying to sound like he'd forgotten.

"What a shame that you miss out on hot weekend away sex." Ben added, continuing to tease Lee. Lee rolled his eyes, trying to resist the urge to rise to the bait.

"Although it'll be a relief for Chloe to have a few days off having to fake it." Ben said, bursting out laughing when he saw Lee's expression.

"Well Kirstie must have given up trying because I didn't hear a peep last night and given your news, I would have thought you'd be doing something right." Lee said, smiling slightly. The two of them glanced up as Peter walked into the kitchen, smiling at them.

"You lot really love talking about your sex lives, don't you?" Peter chuckled.

"Well, you can feel free to contribute." Ben laughed.

"I think I'll pass." Peter smiled.

"I feel rough." Louise announced as she walked into the room. Peter smiled at her and wrapped his arm around her shoulders as she leant against him.

"You did get a bit carried away with your drinking didn't you." Peter laughed, smiling at how adorable she looked.

"I was only borderline drunk." Louise smiled, gazing up at Peter before quickly placing a kiss on his lips.

"Morning everyone!" Kirstie called happily as she walked into the kitchen.

"Someone is happy this morning." Louise smiled.

"I had the best evening ever last night." Kirstie said, smiling at Ben. Ben beamed and raised his eyebrow at Lee smugly. Kirstie smiled at Ben as he fed her a piece of omelette on his fork.

"Speaking of which, I need to speak to you girls." Kirstie said to Louise, glancing around the room when she suddenly realised that Chloe wasn't there.
"Where's Chloe?" Kirstie frowned.

"She's in the bedroom." Lee told her.

"Did she calm down in the end?" Peter asked.

"Yeah eventually." Lee said.

"I feel really bad, I was trying to give her a bit of a confidence boost and I ended up making her really mad." Ben said quickly.

"It's fine, I think it just reminded her of when our choreographer made her feel like a piece of meat at the photoshoot. I think underneath it she knows that not all of them just wanted her for sex." Lee explained.

"No definitely not, a couple of them were keen to date her. Especially Dougie, he felt a strong connection with her." Ben said. Lee nodded slowly, swallowing the lump that was rising in his throat as he tried to process Ben's words.

"Did he?" Lee frowned.

"Yeah, didn't you notice the way he used to look at her?" Ben chuckled. Lee shook his head slowly, feeling slightly sick at the thought of someone else having strong feelings for Chloe.

"C'mon, let's go and find her." Kirstie said, quickly taking Louise's hand and walking towards the hallway.

"No, leave her!" Lee called sharply. Kirstie turned to face him and frowned at his sharp tone.

"She might still be sleeping." Lee quickly added.

"Well, she needs to get up anyway, we have to get to the zoo." Louise pointed out.

"Yeah, but not right now though." Lee said.

"We need to leave fairly soon, and she'll need time to get dressed and stuff." Louise insisted.

"Fine, I'll go and see if she's awake." Lee sighed before quickly walking away.

Lee smiled at Chloe as he saw her snuggled up under the covers. She slowly opened her eyes and smiled at him.

"Sorry did I wake you?" he asked as he squatted in front of her.

"No, it's okay, I was just dozing." she told him.

"I'm just so tired." she yawned. Lee smiled at her as he leaned towards her.

"Don't, I'll have morning breath." she giggled, quickly turning her head away before he could kiss her.

"I don't care." he laughed, quickly kissing her before she could protest.

"You might want to get dressed, the girls want to talk to you, and I wouldn't be surprised if they don't burst in." he smiled at her when they eventually pulled apart. Chloe sighed and slowly climbed out of bed.

"I probably won't have time to shower will I, we need to head off soon?" she said thoughtfully.

"I'll just have a quick wash then." she added, before Lee had a chance to respond. He watched her as she picked up a fresh set of underwear and walked into the bathroom. Lee perched on the end of the bed as he patiently waited for her to return.

As soon as she emerged from the bathroom she walked over to stand in front of Lee, sighing in contentment as he wrapped his arms around her hips and pulled her close, gently placing his head against her abdomen. Lee shivered as she reached down and softly stroked his hair.

"I kind of accidentally ended up teasing you a bit last night, didn't I?" Chloe said, smiling slightly.

"Yeah, a bit, but it's fine." he smiled.

"It just means I'll be more ready to go tonight." he laughed. Chloe giggled and rested her head against his, smiling to herself as she felt him place a soft kiss on her abdomen.

"We have to go for your scan a few days when we get home don't, we?" he said thoughtfully. Chloe nodded slowly, suddenly feeling a tight knotting sensation in her stomach as she was reminded once again of their situation. She still hadn't come to terms with what was happening and was plagued with intense fears. She found herself wishing once again that she could tell Lee how she felt, but she knew that she couldn't bring herself too.

The last thing she wanted was to cause Lee's fears to amplify, as she was terrified that he was going to wise up and leave her.

"I'll have to make an excuse to Matt as to why we need the afternoon off." Lee said, snapping her out of her thoughts. Chloe bit her lip, trying to hold back the tears that were filling her eyes.

"Maybe I'll just tell him I have a hospital appointment and you want to come with me." he continued thoughtfully.

"That could work." she whispered, sniffing quietly.

Lee slowly raised his head to gaze at Chloe, sighing quietly to himself when he saw that her eyes were full of tears.

"Don't cry Chlo." he whispered sadly, his heart breaking a little as he watched her cry. Chloe blinked slowly, unable to hold back her tears any longer.

"Today is not a day for tears, we're going to the zoo." he told her, trying to cheer her up as he slowly wiped away her tears with his thumb.

"I know, I'm fine." she said, smiling falsely at him. Lee stood up and gently pulled Chloe into his arms, holding her tightly as she cried. The two of them jumped as they heard a knock at the bedroom door.

"Chloe, can we come in?" Louise's voice called.

"I need to get dressed." Chloe told Lee, quickly removing herself from his arms and picking up her shorts and a shirt.

"Hold on a second!" Lee called, sounding slightly frustrated as he heard another knock at the door. Chloe rolled her eyes and quickly pulled on her clothes.

"You look really beautiful." Lee told her, smiling at her as she ran a brush through her hair and tied it up. Chloe smiled up at Lee as he gazed at her longingly.

"I really like the new 'short' shorts." he smiled as he ran his hand up her bare thigh.

"I thought you would." she smiled back.

"No more tears okay." he whispered, gently kissing away the last of her tears. Lee sighed as he heard Kirstie and Louise talking amongst themselves outside of the door.

"You can come in now!" he called. As soon as they heard Lee's voice, they quickly opened the door and hurried into the room.

"You can leave, we need girl chat." Louise told Lee, trying to sound stern. Lee nodded slowly, smiling slightly.

"Do you want me to get you some breakfast Chlo?" he offered.

"Yes please." Chloe said quietly. Even though she felt nauseous she knew that she had to eat something.

"What do you fancy?" he asked her.

"Maybe just some cereal." Chloe said. Lee nodded and rummaged on the counter, before handing her one of the anti-emetic tablets. Lee gently pulled her into a hug.

"If you take it now, it'll have time to work before you eat." he whispered in her ear. Chloe nodded and sighed in disappointment when he let go of her and left the room.

"Are you alright Chloe?" Kirstie asked worriedly as soon as Lee left the room.

"Yes, why?" Chloe replied.

"You look a bit teary." Kirstie tried. She couldn't seem to ignore the gut feeling she had that something was going on between Chloe and Lee. The way that he seemed to be acting more protective of her than normal, almost like he was showing possessive tendencies.

"Everything is fine." Chloe insisted as she quickly swallowed the tablet. Kirstie fell silent for a moment, watching Chloe closely, not entirely sure that she believed her.

"Anyway ladies, I have news." Kirstie announced excitedly, when she realised that Chloe wasn't going to open up.

"Ooh, sounds exciting." Louise said as she sat cross legged on the bed. Kirstie couldn't keep the smile off her face as she sat on the bed beside Louise.

"Come and sit with us Chloe." Louise said, patting the bed beside them.

"I can't I have to get ready." Chloe told them as she pulled on her socks and trainers.

"Do you ladies need sun cream?" Chloe offered as she began to put on the sun cream.

"Yeah, maybe actually, I hadn't thought of that." Kirstie said.

"Anyway sorry, I went off topic, what's your news?" Chloe asked.

"Ben asked me to move in with him!" Kirstie squealed excitedly. Louise let out a little squeal of happiness and quickly pulled Kirstie into a hug.

"Wow, that's amazing, Kirstie. I'm so happy for you." Chloe smiled.

"I'm so happy, I just can't believe it." Kirstie told them, smiling widely.

"It's so exciting though." Louise agreed.

"He makes me so happy; I just can't believe my luck." Kirstie continued.

"It's all thanks to you." Kirstie smiled at Chloe.

"I didn't do anything." Chloe frowned.

"I met him backstage at your work." Kirstie insisted.

"Matt set up you all coming to the gig, not me." Chloe argued.

"I'm still very grateful to both of you." Kirstie smiled.

"So, when do you move in?" Louise asked.

"When we get back, I think." Kirstie smiled. Louise let out another squeal of excitement and hugged Kirstie again.

"We need to celebrate tonight." Louise said.

"I'm thinking takeaway, drinks and hot tub night?" Kirstie suggested. Chloe opened her mouth to explain to them that she wouldn't be able to participate, but quickly closed it again when she remembered that she had to keep the secret.

"That sounds like fun." Louise grinned.

"We can draw straws over who gets to have sex in the hot tub." Louise said, wiggling her eyebrows at Kirstie.

"Well, it won't be me." Chloe said quietly, glancing up as Lee walked back into the room and handed her a bowl of cereal. Chloe smiled as she glanced down at the bowl and saw the mound of chopped fruit on top of it.

"Thank you." Chloe smiled at Lee.

"Ben is getting stressed about the time so I think we need to go." Lee told the girls.

"Okay let's go." Louise said as she quickly stood up and walked out of the room.

"I can eat this in the car." Chloe told them.

"Are you coming with Ben and me?" Kirstie asked them.

"Yeah, we could do actually." Lee said.

"C'mon you lot, we're going!" Louise's voice called from the hallway.

Chapter Sixty-Seven

"She's really in her element isn't she." Louise smiled at Lee as they watched Chloe up ahead gazing in wonder at the exhibit.

"She's always loved animals." Lee told her, smiling at Chloe as she turned to face him, and he noticed that the twinkle in her eyes had returned. Louise jumped and glanced up at a tree as she saw a lemur staring at her.

"I can't believe I agreed to do this walkthrough." Louise sighed as she walked along the pathway, gazing around nervously.

"Who ever thought of the idea of getting the guests to walk through an exhibit with a bunch of lemurs and kangaroos needs to be fired." Louise added.

"I think it's a nice idea that the guests get to walk with them and feed them some fruit." Peter laughed as he quickly took Louise's hand and squeezed it gently.

"Also, they are wallabies." Lee corrected her, smiling slightly. Kirstie let out a little squeal of excitement as a lemur jumped onto her shoulder. She giggled and glanced at Ben.

"I think it wants your fruit." Ben laughed.

"Where's Chloe?" Lee asked.

"Up ahead I think." Ben told him as he handed the lemur a piece of fruit. Ben locked eyes with Kirstie as the lemur eventually jumped off her shoulder. Kirstie slowly leaned in and placed a kiss on Ben's lips.

As soon as the five of them rounded the corner, they came to a stop, smiling as they noticed Chloe squatting on the floor, surrounded by lemurs. She laughed as one jumped onto her shoulder and another onto her lap. Lee watched her closely, feeling a surge of pride when he realised how much the animals clearly adored her.

"Oh my god, look at her." Kirstie said, summing up what Lee was thinking.

"She's amazing isn't she." Lee breathed.

"I'm sorry, I don't have enough hands to feed all of you at once." Chloe said as she handed out the fruit. She smiled happily as one of the lemurs approached her and gently took the slice of melon from her hand, gently wrapping it's hand around her finger as it gazed up at her.

"Excuse me, those are mine." Chloe laughed as the lemur on her shoulder started to play with her sunglasses.

Lee glanced at Kirstie as she slowly took out her phone and took a picture, trying not to disturb Chloe in the process.

"Animals really adore her don't they." Peter smiled.

"Can you send me the picture?" Lee asked Kirstie, as he struggled to tear his eyes away from Chloe. Kirstie nodded, smiling slightly when she noticed Lee staring at Chloe.

"I've run out of fruit now sorry guys." Chloe told the lemurs sadly as she slowly stood up. Chloe slowly turned to face the group, her cheeks colouring when she noticed for the first time that the five of them were watching her. She stared at the ground as she slowly walked back towards them.

"Why is everyone staring at me?" Chloe frowned.

"Because you're adorable." Lee told her.

"You're like a little animal magnet." Ben teased her.

"Animals can sense when someone loves them, they are a lot more intelligent than humans give them credit for." Chloe said quietly.

"Hey, look there's the wallabies." Peter said as they rounded another corner and spotted a group of wallabies in the clearing. Louise let out a little squeal as the wallabies came over to them, clearly checking if they had any fruit. Lee watched closely as the wallabies gradually got closer. He reached out and grasped Chloe's forearm, quickly pulling her towards him, out of harm's way.

"What are you doing?" Chloe asked quickly, when Lee's hand remained in place on her arm.

"They kick." he whispered in her ear.

"They aren't going to hurt me." Chloe sighed.

"You don't know that." Lee argued. Chloe sighed in frustration as she watched the rest of the group feeding the wallabies, glancing down at Lee's hand that was still holding onto her arm tightly. As soon as the wallabies wandered away, Lee slowly let go of Chloe's arm.

"So, I have permission to go now do I?!" Chloe snapped. Lee remained silent, glancing at the rest of the group when he noticed them staring at him. Chloe shook her head angrily and walked away from him. He couldn't help but feel slightly guilty that he'd spoilt her fun, it was the last thing that he'd wanted to do, particularly when she'd been so sad lately, but at the same time he felt an overwhelming need to protect her and their baby. Even though he knew in his heart that he was being unreasonable, he couldn't help but feel afraid that something could happen that might cause Chloe to lose their child. He knew that it was his responsibility to make sure that they were both safe. Everyone remained silent as they left the walk-in exhibit, clearly picking up on the tense atmosphere as they watched Chloe walking a few metres ahead of them.

"There seems to be a lot of families in the zoo today." Kirstie said, desperately trying to think of something to say to fill the awkward silence. She smiled at a group of children as they ran past, shrieking in excitement to see the animals.

"I've always wanted children." Kirstie said thoughtfully. Kirstie quickly turned to Ben when she realised what she'd said, suddenly feeling slightly nervous that she might scare him. Ben smiled at her when he noticed her watching him closely, a nervous expression on her face.

"I'd actually like to have kids at some point too." Ben smiled at her.

"Oh my god, do you have something you need to tell us?!" Louise exclaimed.

"Now we know why you're moving in together." Peter teased.

"Calm down, one step at a time." Ben said quickly.

"I didn't mean right now anyway." Kirstie laughed as she wrapped her arm around Ben's waist.

"She's on the pill anyway." Ben announced, bursting out laughing when Kirstie elbowed him in the ribs.

"I hate to break it to you, but the pill isn't a hundred percent effective." Lee told them, his eyes fixed on Chloe as he saw her sit on a bench and gaze silently into the lion enclosure.

"How about you Lou?" Ben asked.

"Definitely not for a while, if at all. I'm too focused on my career at the moment." Louise answered.

"Yeah, well that's what you said about a man, but we all know how that turned out." Kirstie laughed, smiling at Peter.

"I'm very career focused too. We both have such busy schedules as well don't we." Peter said. Louise nodded, smiling at him. Even though it was still early days for her and Peter, she couldn't help but feel relieved that she'd found someone with the same life goals as herself. As soon as the group caught up to Chloe on the bench Lee stood behind her and placed his fingers on her shoulders. Chloe flinched for a moment before relaxing when she realised that it was him.

"I'm sorry, I'm trying really hard not to smother you." he whispered in her ear, fearful that the others might overhear.

"I know you are." Chloe sighed. Lee rested his chin on her shoulder and stared into the exhibit with her.

"Do you guys mind if we abandon the group for a bit?" Louise asked.

"No of course not." Kirstie smiled.

"Go and have some couple time." Ben teased them, wiggling his eyebrows at them. Louise held up her middle finger at him as her and Peter walked away. Kirstie and Ben glanced at each other and burst out laughing. Lee watched Chloe closely as she slowly stood up and gazed down at the zoo map.

"What are we going to see next?" Kirstie asked her.

"Well, the giraffes and zebra are that way, and the elephants are that way, so it depends what you want to see first?" Chloe asked, pointing as she spoke.

"Let's go and see the elephants." Ben said. Chloe nodded, glancing down at her hand as Lee took it gently.

"Oh my god it's huge!" Ben exclaimed as they reached the elephant enclosure.

"That's what she said." Lee grinned.

"Indeed, she did." Ben laughed, smiling at Kirstie for a moment before winking at Lee. "Have you never seen an elephant before?" Chloe laughed.

"Nope." Ben said. Ben glanced over his shoulder as he heard a girl scream a few metres away from them. The girl was speaking excitedly to her friends as the group stared at them.

"I think we've been spotted by some fans." Ben quickly told Lee, glancing nervously at Kirstie and Chloe. Lee followed Ben's eyeline, his heart pounding against his chest as they began to run towards them. Lee glanced nervously at Chloe, quickly racking his brain for what to do. Lee quickly placed his hand on Chloe's waist and pulled her towards himself.

"Quick, take a selfie of us." Lee told her.

"Why?" Chloe frowned.

"Just do it." he told her sternly. Chloe sighed and quickly pulled out her phone, posing with Lee as they took a selfie together. Chloe jumped and dropped her phone as a group of excitable, shrieking girls suddenly appeared in front of them.

"Oh my god, I can't believe you guys are here!" one of them exclaimed. Chloe could feel herself beginning to panic slightly as the girls surrounded them, the more fuss that was made, the more people spotted Ben and Lee in the park and rushed over. Kirstie tried to squeeze out of the circle, gasping and falling to the floor as a fan ran into her in her haste to get to Ben. Ben quickly squatted down in front of Kirstie and offered her his hand, carefully helping her to stand.

"Are you okay?" he mouthed. Kirstie nodded as she slowly stood up, glancing down at the grazes on her hands.

"You need to be more careful, that was uncalled for." Ben warned the fan. The fan shrugged and quickly threw herself into Ben's arms. Ben locked eyes with Kirstie who smiled at him reassuringly, trying to subtly tell him that she was okay and not to cause a fuss over it.

"Everyone needs to calm down, you'll all get a turn with us." Lee said sternly, feeling his temper rising slightly as soon as he'd noticed Kirstie on the floor and realised that it could have been Chloe.

"Oh my god, Lee!" the fan shouted when she suddenly noticed him for the first time. She quickly let go of Ben and dashed over to Lee, barging past Chloe on her way past. Chloe staggered slightly, quickly reaching out to grab the railing to steady herself. Lee watched Chloe, breathing a sigh of relief when she steadied herself. He took deep breaths, trying to control his temper as he turned back to the fan, who was gazing up at him happily.

"You really have form don't you, first you knocked someone over and then you nearly knocked someone else over." Lee snapped, trying in his angry state not to reveal that Chloe was his girlfriend.

"She's had her turn though." the fan shrugged. Chloe glanced at Lee as he slowly shook his head. She could see how close he was to losing his temper and the last thing she wanted was for him to accidentally reveal the truth about the two of them. Chloe quickly pulled Lee into a hug, desperately trying to do something to calm him down.

"I'm alright, just leave it.......please." she whispered in his ear. She smiled to herself as she felt him relax.

"It was nice to meet you." she smiled at him when she quickly removed herself from his arms. Lee smiled at her, glancing at Kirstie as he saw her quickly take Chloe's hand and pull her away from the group of fans.

"We need to go this way; the boys can catch us up." Kirstie said quietly as she led Chloe down a different track.

"Oh, wait, my phone is still on the floor, I dropped it when the fans came over!" Chloe said, quickly stopping dead in her tracks.

"It's fine, I'll text Ben and ask him to get it." Kirstie said, continuing to lead Chloe away in case she decided to go back for her phone.

Chapter Sixty Eight

"Are you alright, I saw that you got pushed over?" Chloe asked Kirstie as they sat on a bench on a hill above the elephant enclosure.

"I'm fine." Kirstie said quietly, choosing not to mention that she was a little shaken.

Chloe sighed to herself as she gazed into the distance and saw Ben and Lee still surrounded by fans.

"This is what I meant the other day when I said I hate that Lee is famous." Chloe sighed.

"It's definitely one of the downsides, but they seem to be in their element, now that they don't have to worry about us getting hurt." Kirstie smiled as she watched Ben and noticed how happy he looked chatting to the fans.

"I guess so." Chloe said quietly.

"I can't help feeling like it's going to get worse when Eclipse go on tour." Chloe said thoughtfully.

"Which part is worrying you?" Kirstie asked.

"People finding out about us mostly, when their fan base gets bigger again and it potentially goes back to like it was when Eclipse were first together, we won't be able to do anything or go anywhere without someone recognising him." Chloe explained.

"And as there are more and more fans, they'll get younger and prettier. Everyone will want him." Chloe continued.

"None of them will be able to compete with how he feels about you though." Kirstie said quietly, trying to reassure her. Chloe sighed and fell silent.

"Speaking of which, is everything okay with the two of you?" Kirstie asked.

"Yes, why?" Chloe frowned, reluctantly tearing her eyes away from watching Lee and turning to face Kirstie.

"He just seems like he's being really intense with you recently." Kirstie prompted.

"He's always been overprotective." Chloe said quietly.

"It's more than overprotective though when he's pulling you away from the wallabies and having a go at some guys just because they offered to buy you a drink." Kirstie said, trying to get Chloe to open up.

"It's tripping over into being a bit possessive." Kirstie continued.

"No, he's not like that." Chloe said her eyes filling with tears as she began to panic slightly. She had no idea what to say to reassure Kirstie without telling her the truth about the situation.

"He wouldn't even let us come and find you in the bedroom the other day without going to get you, and when we did come in, you'd clearly been crying." Kirstie continued, trying to prompt Chloe to open up.

"I'm worried about you Chloe." Kirstie added when Chloe didn't respond.

"It's not his fault, he's just being overprotective because he's stressed." Chloe said, sounding slightly teary. Chloe sighed as she gazed over at Lee again. She couldn't stand the idea of her best friend thinking badly of the man that she loved, particularly when he hadn't done anything wrong. Even though she found it frustrating at times when he was overprotective of her, she knew that it was coming from a place of love. He loved and cared about her so much that he couldn't stand the idea of anything happening to her. She knew that side of him had been amplified as a result of her pregnancy and the promise he'd made to protect her and the baby.

"He shouldn't be taking his stress out on you though." Kirstie said, misunderstanding what Chloe was trying to say. Chloe sighed quietly as she realised that she would have to tell Kirstie about the baby. Even though her and Lee had made a deal not to tell anyone apart from Sheila, she couldn't stand the thought of Kirstie thinking bad of Lee, particularly when he was her rock at the moment.

"I know that he loves you, I'm just worried about you Chloe, you seem miserable underneath the facade you're putting on." Kirstie told her.

"That's not Lee's fault though, it's mine." Chloe said quietly. Kirstie frowned at her words and waited for her to continue, able to sense that Chloe was about to open up to her.

"If I tell you something, you can't tell anyone, not even Ben." Chloe said sternly.

"No of course not." Kirstie frowned, suddenly feeling slightly nervous about what Chloe was going to say and the idea of not being able to tell Ben.

"I shouldn't even be telling you, so you need to promise." Chloe insisted.

"I promise." Kirstie said.

"I'm pregnant." Chloe blurted, before she could talk herself out of it.

"Oh my god!" Kirstie exclaimed, quickly clapping her hand over her mouth.

"How far gone are you?" Kirstie asked, her eyes darting to Chloe's abdomen as she quickly recovered herself.

"We haven't been for the dating scan yet, but I stupidly forgot to take the pill that night when Lee was in Germany and Michelle had upset me. Then Lee came home the following night, so in theory nine and half weeks." Chloe said, rambling slightly.

"So, this isn't Lee's fault, it's all mine. He's just trying to deal with it the best he can." Chloe added.

"And hopefully he doesn't decide that he can't be a father and kicks me out." Chloe said sadly.

"He won't do that Chloe." Kirstie said, gently placing a hand on Chloe's shoulder.

"It's all too soon though and he's always said that he doesn't want children." Chloe told her, sighing sadly to herself.

"The ironic thing is that I think he'll be a really good Dad." she added.

"If he didn't want the baby, he wouldn't be acting so protective over you." Kirstie pointed out.

"He's probably just scared, having a baby is such a big commitment, and it's a lot to get your head around when it's not planned, but you'll both be amazing parents." Kirstie told her.

"I won't be, I have no idea what to do, I've never even held a baby before." Chloe said.

"I'm just so scared that I'm going to mess all of it up and lose Lee in the process, and it'll all be my fault.... he's all I have.... I can't lose him Kirstie." Chloe continued.

"Have you told Lee how you feel?" Kirstie asked.

"No, I can't." Chloe whispered.
"But he'll be able to reassure you." Kirstie pointed out.

"Maybe but I still can't tell him how afraid I am....he's only just getting his head around it himself, the last thing I want to do is dump my fears on him too." Chloe explained.

"But that's what people in relationships do, they open up and talk to each other about things." Kirstie argued.

"Otherwise, if you bottle them up they get worse." Kirstie added when Chloe fell silent.

"And he's told you how he feels, and you've been reassuring him presumably?" Kirstie asked. Chloe nodded slowly.

"I've told him loads of times that I think he's going to be a good Dad and he hasn't once said to me that I'll be a good Mum, I think he realises that I won't be." Chloe sighed, slowly wiping away the tears that were flowing down her cheeks.

"And I know I should be grateful; a lot of women would love to have a baby and so many fans would love to be in my position.

"Fans are always commenting on things that they want to have his babies...." Chloe started but trailed off.

"Yeah, but that's just fans being stupid, they've never even met him." Kirstie pointed out.

"And here's little old me carrying Lee Knight's baby and wishing that I wasn't." Chloe continued thoughtfully, almost as if she hadn't heard what Kirstie had said.

"Oh god that sounds so bad, I didn't mean that." Chloe whispered.

"I don't think it's that you don't want the baby, you just don't know how to deal with the idea of being a mother and the fear is taking over." Kirstie said quietly.

"I'm afraid of losing Lee too.... I love him so much that I don't want to live without him." Chloe admitted.

"I don't think you're going to lose him, but I think you need to tell him how you feel." Kirstie said quietly. Chloe shook her head slowly, biting her lip to try and fight the tears that were filling her eyes. Kirstie sighed and gently pulled Chloe into a hug.

"Don't stress about it, the two of you will be amazing parents." Kirstie whispered in her ear.

"Having a baby is amazing, you just need to try to relax and enjoy the process. It'll bring the two of you closer." Kirstie said quietly when she eventually let go of Chloe. Chloe's eyes flickered upwards as she noticed Ben and Lee walking up the hill towards them. Chloe quickly wiped her cheeks, hoping that Lee wouldn't notice that she'd been crying.

"Hey, nice of you guys to join us." Kirstie smiled as soon as they reached them. Ben smiled slightly and handed Chloe her phone.

"Thank you." Chloe said quietly.

"Are you alright Chlo?" Lee asked worriedly when he saw her eyes were filled with tears. Chloe bit her lip and nodded slowly, desperately trying to hold back her tears.

"I think she just needs a hug." Kirstie said. Lee took a step towards her, smiling slightly as Chloe quickly stood up and flung herself into his arms. As soon as she was in Lee's arms, she could no longer hold back the tears she'd been fighting.

"I think we need to give them a minute." Kirstie whispered to Ben as she quickly took his hand and led him over to a different exhibit.

"What's going on?" Lee asked her as soon as they were alone.

"I'm fine, just please don't leave me." she said in a small voice.

"I'm never going to leave you." he whispered in her ear as he softly stroked her hair. Chloe gazed up at him as he placed his hands on either side of her face and lifted her head to look at him.

"I thought we weren't having tears today." he told her softly, gently wiping away her tears with his thumb. Chloe smiled slightly as she stared into his eyes.

"I love you." she whispered.

"I love you too Chlo." he whispered back.

"I need to tell you something." she said nervously.

"What is it.... are you and the baby okay?" he asked quickly.

"Yes, we're fine." she reassured him, placing a soft kiss on his lips.

"I told Kirstie about the baby." she announced.

"I know we said we weren't going to tell anyone, but she'd noticed that you were acting differently, and she was really worried about me.... because of her job I guess, she was worried that you were being possessive.... rather than protective....and I didn't want her thinking bad of you, so I told her the truth." Chloe rambled nervously, feeling slightly guilty that she'd gone back on their deal.

"I've never been possessive of you." he said quietly, feeling slightly hurt that Kirstie thought that of him.

"I know that." she told him.

"I'm sorry that I told her." she said quietly.

"It's fine, I'm glad you have someone to talk too about everything." he sighed as he carefully pulled her into his arms.

Chapter Sixty Nine

Lee smiled to himself as he walked into the living room, holding the cup of tea that he'd made for Chloe, when he realised that she was curled up, fast asleep on the sofa. He sat beside her carefully, taking care not to wake her. Lee placed his hand on her leg, smiling down at her fondly. He couldn't help but smile as he thought about how happy she'd been at the zoo when she was feeding the lemurs, he hadn't seen her smile like that for a couple of weeks. Lee knew that she was stressed about the pregnancy, even though she was trying to hide it from him. He took out his phone and gazed down at the picture of Chloe feeding the lemurs, wishing that she realised how beautiful and amazing she was.

"Right, what are we ordering from the takeaway?!" Louise said loudly as she burst into the living room followed by Peter, Ben and Kirstie.

"Ssh." Lee said quickly, glancing at Chloe who was still sleeping soundly.

"Oops sorry." Louise said quietly.

"We've found a Chinese that's not too far away, so write down what you want, and I'll go and get it." Ben said, handing Peter a notebook.

"Can I come along, I can nip to the supermarket and stock up on alcohol?" Louise asked. Ben nodded slowly.

"I'll come too." Peter smiled at Louise as he wrapped his arm around her waist.

"We need to wake Chloe and ask what she wants." Ben said.

"She's fine, I can write hers down, I know what she normally orders." Lee said as he took the notebook that Peter handed to him and quickly wrote down the order.

"Are you coming with us Kirstie?" Ben asked.

"No, I think I'll stay here." she told him. Ben nodded and quickly pecked Kirstie on the lips before walking away, closely followed by Louise and Peter. Chloe's eyes bolted open as she heard the front door of the lodge close behind them. She slowly lifted her head, glancing up at Lee.

"Are you okay?" she asked when she noticed him watching her closely.

"Everything's fine, go back to sleep." he told her softly, sensing that she wasn't yet fully awake. Chloe smiled as she placed her head on Lee's lap and snuggled against him. Lee remained silent and methodically stroked her hair, trying to help her fall back asleep. He knew that she'd been struggling with fatigue as part of her pregnancy and being at the zoo all day had zapped her of her energy. Lee smiled to himself when he realised that she'd fallen asleep once again. He glanced up at Kirstie as he felt her staring at him.

She smiled warmly, a warm feeling spreading in her heart when she saw how much love Lee had for Chloe.

"Chloe told me that she spoke to you about the baby." Lee said quietly, speaking in hushed tones so that he didn't wake Chloe.

"Yeah, she did, I couldn't believe it when she told me." Kirstie admitted.

"Nor could we when we found out." he said, smiling slightly.

"It must have been a big shock." she agreed. Lee nodded slowly, glancing down at Chloe as she fidgeted in her sleep.

"You do realise that I would never do anything to hurt her." he whispered, biting the inside of his lip as he suddenly felt a wave of emotion wash over him.

"I know that, I just worry about her. My job makes me more sensitive to things." she admitted.

"I could never hurt her, she's too precious to me." he said firmly.

"I've just been so worried that something bad is going to happen. And I promised her that I would protect her and our baby." he added.

"I understand, but maybe you need to rein it in a bit." she suggested.

"Yeah, I probably do." he sighed.

"I'm grateful that she has you looking out for her." he smiled at Kirstie. She smiled back, the two of them falling silent as Chloe opened her eyes and slowly sat up, squinting slightly as she adjusted to the bright light.

"What were the two of you talking about?" Chloe asked as she slowly rubbed her eyes.

"About the baby....and I was just about to tell Lee that I think the two of you will be great parents." Kirstie said. Lee smiled, quickly turning to face Chloe as she sighed and fell silent. Lee watched her closely as she sat beside him, gently stroking his hair.
"I actually had a dream about our child last night." Lee announced.

"Really?" Chloe frowned.

"Yeah, she was so beautiful she looked just like you and she was always out in the garden looking at the wildlife." he said, his eyes glazing over slightly as he spoke about it and the dream suddenly came flooding back.

"She'll be hanging off your neck more like it." Kirstie laughed.

"A daddy's girl, like me." Chloe smiled.

"It was weird though because I went out to find her in the garden and when I saw her, I felt an overwhelming surge of love that was still there when I woke up." he told them.

"Oh my god." Chloe whispered, her heart swelling with pride as she watched the expression on his face as he spoke about their child. The way his face softened with so much love.

"What?" Lee frowned.

"You're going to be such a good Dad." Chloe said, sobbing slightly. Lee smiled at her and placed a soft kiss on her forehead.

"So, you're having a girl then?" Kirstie asked.

"We don't know, it's too early." Chloe answered.

"I just have a feeling." Lee admitted.

"I think that's because you want a girl." Chloe smiled.

"Yeah, I do, I want a mini you." he told her.

"I think you guys are going to do just fine." Kirstie announced, smiling at the two of them. She could clearly see that Lee's face lit up whenever he spoke about the baby and despite Chloe's intense doubts that she was feeling, even her expression seemed to soften slightly.

"Also, you'll have a lot of help from all of the baby's aunties and uncles." Kirstie added, beaming at them.

"Nathan is going to be so excited when we tell him." Lee smiled.

"We have to wait until I'm twelve weeks though, just in case." Chloe reminded him. Lee nodded, smiling down at Chloe as she rested the side of her head against his shoulder. Chloe's head suddenly bolted off his shoulder as a thought suddenly occurred to her.

"Speaking of Nathan, what's going to happen about the tour?" Chloe gasped.

"What about it?" Lee frowned.

"Well, it starts in January, I'll be six months pregnant by then." Chloe said quietly.

"So?" Lee asked.

"So, I can't be on the road all the time, especially since the tour is two months, that's going to be pushing it." Chloe pointed out. Lee fell silent, suddenly realising that Chloe was right.

"I'll need to stay behind." Chloe said thoughtfully.

"There's no way in hell that's happening." Lee said sharply.

"I'm not going to be away from you for two months, particularly when you're pregnant." he quickly added.

"Well, you can't pull out of the tour, I'll never forgive myself and the boys will never forgive me." Chloe said quietly.

"We can figure it out nearer the time." Lee said quietly. Their eyes snapped up as the rest of the group returned with the food. Chloe frowned to herself as Peter and Louise were laughing loudly at something, Louise staggering slightly as they walked into the kitchen.

"They were drinking in the back of the car." Ben told them as he walked past. Ben quickly returned from the kitchen and handed each of them a beer, before returning to the kitchen.

"Here we go again." Chloe sighed, glancing down at the beer in her hand. Chloe frowned as Lee quickly stood up and ran into the bathroom, before quickly returning a few moments later.

"Swap me." he told her, holding out his hand for her bottle and quickly giving her his bottle.

"What did you do?" Chloe frowned.

"Emptied it down the sink and filled it back up with water." he said, smiling slightly.

"That's actually really clever." Chloe laughed.

"And don't worry, I made sure I gave it a good rinse out." he told her, beaming proudly with himself.

"Well cheers then." Chloe smiled as she clinked her bottle against his and took a long swig.

"Slow down, I don't want you getting drunk." he laughed, winking at her. Chloe raised her eyebrow at him as she took another swig.

"The food is done!" Ben called from the kitchen.

Chloe sighed to herself as she sat on the decking and watched the rest of the group having fun in the hot tub. She felt like she'd been sitting there for hours, watching them slowly getting more and more drunk. The only exception being Lee who'd decided not to get drunk in case Chloe needed him for something.

"Chloe, come and get in and have a drink with us!" Louise called for what felt to Chloe like the hundredth time.

"I don't want to get in, I told you I have a sore head, which is also why I don't want to get drunk." Chloe said shortly, her temper starting to fray a little. The last couple of days were finally starting to take their toll. Even though she knew that most of the group didn't know her situation, she was becoming exhausted by the constant peer pressure.

"I hate to be the mum of the group here, but aren't we supposed to be travelling home tomorrow?" Chloe asked as Ben opened yet another beer.

"We have the lodge until the evening though, so we can sleep it off and we should be good to drive by then." Ben told her, rolling his eyes slightly. Chloe sighed and shook her head, feeling slightly frustrated as she stared into the night. She tuned out their conversations, trying to ignore how excluded she felt thanks to the fact that she couldn't participate.

"You and Chloe need to settle it though." Ben laughed. Chloe's ears pricked up and she turned to face them when she heard her name.

"What do I have to do now?" Chloe sighed.

"Remember how we were speaking this morning about drawing straws over who gets the hot tub?" Louise asked.

"Vaguely, but you're all in the hot tub anyway." Chloe replied.

"No, I mean, which couple gets to get frisky in it after everyone else gets out." Louise laughed.

"Yeah, exactly and since you two aren't in the running, you get to decide." Ben said, his words slurring slightly.

"I really couldn't care less, why don't you sort it out amongst yourselves." Lee said quickly.

"You guys are impartial though." Peter pointed out.

"I also don't care." Chloe snapped.

"Don't get snippy just because you guys are having to take a few days off." Ben laughed.

"Ben and Kirstie then, they are the ones that are celebrating." Chloe said as she quickly stood up and walked away, trying to get inside before she said something she was going to regret. As soon as she reached the bedroom, she breathed a sigh of relief that she could finally relax, without having to lie or pretend anymore. She was finding it mentally draining having to be on her guard all the time. She couldn't wait to get home and relax for a few days. Chloe quickly ran herself a bath, trying to find a way to calm herself down.

Lee watched Chloe as she walked away from the group, her jaw set in frustration. He knew that she was finding it hard work being around the group when she couldn't participate and had to lie to them all the time.

"I can't believe we won the vote!" Ben cheered, winking at Kirstie.

"Me neither." Kirstie grinned.

"Yeah alright, don't rub it in." Louise pouted.

"No, don't worry I'll be saving the rubbing for later." Ben beamed.

The four of them glanced at Lee as he quickly stood up and climbed out of the hot tub. He remained silent, quickly walking away from them before they could question him. The last thing he wanted was to be accused of being possessive of Chloe again, but at the same time he wanted to be by her side. Lee frowned as he walked into their bedroom and noticed that she wasn't there. He walked into the bathroom, smiling to himself when he saw that she was in the bath, her arms resting against the side of the tub as she read a book. As soon as he walked into the room, she glanced up at him and smiled.

"Budge up a bit." Lee told her as he removed his swimming trunks. Chloe quickly did as he asked, glancing at him as he climbed into the bath and sat beside her.

"What are you reading?" he asked as he peered over her shoulder.

"A pregnancy book, I'm trying to be prepared." she told him. Chloe sighed deeply as Lee placed a soft kiss on her shoulder, her skin tingling as she felt his warm breath on her back.

"Do you think my breasts are bigger?" she asked him, putting down the book and glancing down at herself.

"Hmm...maybe." he frowned. Chloe glanced down at herself as he placed his hands on her breasts and gently felt them. Lee frowned to himself as Chloe burst out laughing.

"What?" he chuckled as he watched her place her head in her hands, unable to control her laughter.

"Why are you laughing?" he laughed.

"I meant for you to look at them, not use it as an excuse to grope me." she giggled.

"I couldn't help myself." he laughed. Chloe rolled her eyes playfully at him, sighing in contentment as he placed his hands on her lower back and began to gently massage her.

"You have a lot of tension in your muscles." he said quietly.

"There's a lot to be tense about isn't there." she sighed.

"I know, we will be okay though." he told her. Chloe nodded slowly, glancing at Lee as he laid down in the bath. Chloe sat between his legs and carefully laid on top of him, smiling happily as she rested her back against his chest. Lee smiled down at her as she placed her head on his shoulder. He wrapped his arms around her waist, holding her tightly against himself before placing a tender kiss on her lips.

"I can't wait to get back home and relax for a few days, without having to be careful what we do and say all the time." she admitted, sighing quietly as Lee stroked soft circles on her abdomen.

"Me too, I'm looking forward to going for the scan too, so that we can finally see our baby." he said softly, gazing down at her longingly. Lee's eyes flickered to her lips as she gazed up him, her eyes filling with tears.

"It's kind of amazing to think that our love for each other has made a little person." he said thoughtfully, his gaze wandering to her abdomen as he continued to stroke it softly.

"True, I hadn't thought of that." she smiled gazing up at him lovingly. Lee stared into her eyes as he gently pressed his forehead against hers, their lips virtually touching. Chloe gasped as Lee placed his hand on her leg and slowly ran his hand up the inside of her thigh, smiling slightly as he reached her sensitive area, and a small whimper escaped her lips. Chloe squirmed slightly as he stroked her, his eyes fixed on hers as he watched her closely. Lee smiled to himself as he felt Chloe trembling against him, she gasped as he used his other hand to slowly trace a trail up her abdomen and along her sternum.

"I love you." he whispered in her ear, smiling in satisfaction when she continued to tremble and whimper as she laid on top of him. Chloe reached for his hand that was on her chest, quickly linking their fingers and squeezing his hand tightly as he continued to stroke her. She closed her eyes, a small moan of pleasure escaping her lips when Lee increased the pace, his lips placing a series of soft kisses on her neck.

Lee couldn't stop himself from staring at her longingly as she slowly came undone on top of him, his lips mere centimetres from hers. She frowned slightly as she made a move to kiss him and he turned his face away from her slightly.

"Kiss me." she pleaded, as she let out another small whimper.

"No, I want to watch you." he said hoarsely. Chloe placed her hand over his hand that was between her legs, gripping onto it tightly as Lee expertly massaged her.

"Are you making sure that I'm not faking?" she gasped, smiling slightly.

"No, I know you don't." he smiled. Chloe nodded slowly, biting her lip as she felt the pressure building. Lee seemed to sense that she was close as he softly blew on her neck, trying to keep his own breathing steady as he fought the deep longing that he was feeling for her. Chloe finally released, calling out his name as she did so.

"Ssh." he chuckled, fearful that the rest of the group would hear her.
"We're meant to be taking a break remember." he reminded her.

"They are too drunk to notice anyway." she said breathlessly. Before Lee could react Chloe quickly turned over, placing her legs on either side of him and pushed herself onto him. Lee groaned with pleasure as she leant down and placed a series of soft kisses on his chest. As she began to slowly kiss her way along his neck, Lee quickly placed his hands on her hips, moaning in pleasure as she began to move her hips back and forth. Chloe smiled when he shivered under her touch as she ran her hands down his chest.

"You're so beautiful Chlo." he told her as she brushed her hair out of her face and gazed at him for a moment.

"I love you." she whispered as she leant down to kiss him.

Chapter Seventy

Lee opened his eyes slowly, trying to adjust to the bright sunlight that was streaming in the window. He frowned in confusion when he glanced at the window and saw that the blinds were open. He turned over in bed, his heart pounding slightly when he saw that Chloe was no longer beside him. Lee breathed a sigh of relief as she walked out of the bathroom, smiling at him as she walked past.

"Good, you're awake." she said as she perched on the bed and quickly pulled a hairbrush through her hair.

"Oh Chloe, come back to bed." he groaned tiredly.

"Chlo." he tried again when she didn't respond. Chloe glanced down at him as he fidgeted in bed and placed his chin on her lap, gazing up at her with a puppy dog expression.

"I can't, we have to get ready otherwise we're going to be late." she told him, trying to be stern, but unable to stop herself from smiling at his adorable expression. Chloe laughed as he groaned and rolled onto his back, rubbing his tired eyes. Lee placed his arm behind his head as he watched Chloe pull on her jeans and a top. He smiled slightly to himself when he noticed how fitted her clothes were. He couldn't help but remember a few months ago when she constantly hid her body under hoodies and baggy jumpers, but now she had the confidence to wear fitted clothes. His heart swelled with pride at how confident she was slowly becoming.

"What?" Chloe asked, locking eyes with him in the mirror, when she noticed him staring at her.

"I was just thinking about how amazing you are." he said quietly. She smiled slightly, her cheeks colouring as she turned to face him. Lee frowned to himself as his eyes wandered to her abdomen.

"Is it me or are you showing?" he asked her, frowning when he noticed a small bump.

"Am I?" she frowned, following his eyeline and glancing down at herself.

"Oh my god, so I am." she whispered, her hand shaking as she ran her hand over her tiny bump.

"This is actually happening." she whispered, glancing at Lee as he nodded.

"No pressure." she said quietly, suddenly feeling another wave of fear wash over her. Lee quickly stood up and walked over to her, stopping when he was stood in front of her. He placed his hand over hers, frowning slightly when he noticed that she was trembling

"It'll be okay, you'll be a great Mum." he reassured her.

"Really?" she whispered, glancing up at him, her eyes filling with tears as he said the words she'd been longing to hear for the past few weeks.

"Of course, you will, you have the biggest heart out of anyone I've ever met, and you've managed to love me even though I was a dick to you for six months." he said quietly. Chloe smiled slightly, placing her other hand over the top of his and gently playing with his fingers.

"I really wish Mum was here to show me what to do." she said thoughtfully.

"I know, you've had a good role model though, from what you've told me, it sounds like your Mum was amazing." he smiled at her. Chloe nodded slowly.

"Your little bump is so cute." Lee said thoughtfully as he felt yet another surge of love for their unborn child.

"I'll need to change into something baggy." Chloe piped up.

"Why, it looks cute?" he frowned.

"Because we are going to Kathleen's afterwards to meet her baby and they might notice." she reminded him.

"Oh yeah, I forgot about that." he said.

"You need to get dressed, otherwise we're going to be late." Chloe protested as Lee pulled her into his arms and held her tightly. Lee sighed as he reluctantly let go of her, watching as she glanced at her watch.

"Oh my god, we have to leave in ten minutes!" she exclaimed.

"Shit." Lee muttered, before quickly running into the bathroom.

"Right, my name is Kim, I'll be showing you your baby." the sonographer told Chloe and Lee as soon as they walked into the room.

"So, Chloe, if you can pop yourself onto the couch and lift your shirt for me?" Kim asked, smiling kindly when she noticed how nervous Chloe looked.

"I'm assuming you're the father?" Kim asked, raising her eyebrow at Lee.

"Yes, Lee." he told her, holding out his hand for her to shake.

Chloe's heart pounded against her chest nervously as she laid down on the couch and slowly lifted her top, her cheeks colouring in embarrassment when she saw the sonographer stare at her scar for a moment before quickly recovering herself. As soon as Lee sat on the chair beside the couch, Chloe quickly reached over to take his hand, smiling slightly when he squeezed it gently, trying to reassure her.

"Okay, this is going to be a bit cold." Kim warned Chloe, before squeezing some gel onto Chloe's abdomen.

"This is your first baby isn't it?" Kim asked. Chloe nodded slowly.

"Okay so what I'm going to do is I'll find your baby and check that everything is as it should be, and then I'll take some measurements that will allow me to date your pregnancy and then I can give you a due date." Kim explained.

"We think she is about ten weeks." Lee told her.

"I should be able to check for you." Kim told them. Chloe glanced down at her abdomen as Kim placed the probe on it and gently moved it around, her eyes fixed on the screen as she searched for the baby. Chloe gasped as she heard a fast heartbeat echoing around the room.

"There you go." Kim said, slowly turning the screen to face Chloe and Lee. Chloe glanced up at the screen, gasping as she saw a small baby on the screen.

"Oh my god, that's our baby." she sobbed, turning to face Lee. Lee nodded slowly, his mouth suddenly feeling very dry as he stared at the screen.

Lee quickly pulled the chair closer to the couch so that he could rest his chin on her shoulder as they stared at the screen together, both feeling slightly overcome with emotion.

"Is the heartbeat meant to be that fast?" Lee asked quietly, trying to distract himself from the powerful emotions that he was feeling.

"Yes, that's normal and everything else looks normal too which is great news." Kim said, smiling happily at them.

"I think you're right about being ten weeks pregnant, so your due date will be the eighteenth of March." Kim told them. Lee glanced at Chloe as he saw a stray tear roll down her face, her eyes fixed on the screen. He bit his lip, to prevent himself from becoming emotional.

"I love you both so much." Lee whispered in Chloe's ear. Chloe smiled at his words, her heart pounding against her chest. As she stared at the screen, everything suddenly felt real. She was carrying Lee's baby inside her and seeing his expression made it clear just how much he adored their baby already. Chloe smiled as the baby moved on the screen, closing her eyes for a moment as she listened to the soft heartbeat, the idea of being a mother suddenly feeling not quite so terrifying.

She couldn't help but feel a swirl of excitement for the day that she was finally able to hold their child in her arms.

"Okay, so that's everything, your midwife will let you know about your injections and the next scan." Kim announced a few moments later. Chloe nodded and watched as Kim slowly wiped the gel from Chloe's abdomen. Chloe quickly pulled her top down, feeling more relaxed now that her scar was covered.

"Here's some pictures of your baby." Kim stated, handing them to Lee. He smiled his thanks at her, watching Chloe closely as she carefully climbed off the couch. As soon as she stood up, Chloe quickly took Lee's hand as they left the room and walked down the hallway together.

"We have a while before Ben and Kirstie pick us up don't, we?" Lee asked Chloe as he quickly checked his watch.

"We have a couple of hours." Chloe told him.

"Do you want to go out for lunch?" he asked as they climbed into the car.

"That would be good." she smiled at Lee as he pulled out of the carpark.

"As long as it's somewhere quiet." she added.

"Yeah, we don't want a repeat of what happened at the zoo." he agreed. Chloe shook her head slowly.

As soon as they reached the cafe, Lee took Chloe's hand and led her over to a table in the corner.

"I've just thought of something, I'm going to need to get another car." he said thoughtfully as the two of them sat down opposite each other.

"Since my car only has two seats." he added.

"We can wait a few months though can't we, then I can save up some money and pay half." she asked.

"You don't need to pay half; I'd rather you save for something you really want." he told her.

"Like for example, a zoology course so that you can fulfil your dream of being a zookeeper." he suggested.

"I don't want to do that anymore." she told him.

"Why not, you're brilliant with animals?" he frowned.

"I know, but I want to be able to go on tours with you. Otherwise, we'll regularly be apart for months at a time." she pointed out.

"I don't want to stand in the way of your dream though." he told her.

"You're not, it was my dream, but that was years ago. My new dream is to be with you and the boys and our little family." she told him, smiling down at her abdomen as she affectionately placed her hand on her small bump. Lee smiled at her words, his heart pounding against his chest. He still couldn't believe how remarkable she was and how someone like him had managed to win the heart of someone as special as her.

"Anyway, going back to the car, can we wait for a bit please?" she asked, feeling slightly guilty at the thought of him buying something that she wasn't able to contribute too. Even though her debts had been cleared she still didn't have very much money, and needed some time to be able to save up for things.

"If that's what you want." Lee agreed, snapping Chloe out of her thoughts. Lee sighed sadly when he realised that she wasn't going to feel comfortable with him buying things for her and the baby. He knew that she liked her independence and felt guilty that she was taking money from him, but Lee knew that he had more money than he would ever need, so he wanted to use it to spoil her and their baby.

"I just don't want people to think that I'm with you for your money." she sighed.

"Nobody thinks that Chlo." he told her.

"Yes, they do, especially since I was homeless before we started dating." she pointed out.

"I don't want to sound big headed, but I have more money than I need, and what's the point in having it, if I can't treat the people I love." he said. Chloe sighed quietly, sensing that it meant a lot to him to be able to buy them a bigger car.

"And plus, I could buy one with all the safety features and stuff." he added.

"Okay fine." she agreed against her better judgement. The two of them fell silent as a waiter appeared to take their order. Lee frowned at Chloe as she ordered a glass of water and a salad.

"You don't usually eat salad." he frowned as soon as the waiter left.

"I know but I really fancy celery." she said, smiling slightly.

"I think the cravings have started." she giggled when he screwed his nose up. Lee smiled at her as he rummaged in his pocket and took out the scan photos, before carefully placing them on the table.

"What are you doing?" Chloe frowned as he took out his phone and took a picture of the photographs.

"I thought I'd send a picture to Mum." he told her. Chloe smiled at him.

"It felt so strange seeing the baby on the screen." she told him.

"I know, it was incredible." he agreed.

"I can't wait until we can tell everyone, I want to shout it from the rooftops." he added, smiling slightly.

"Please don't do that." she laughed.

"No, but seriously, I'm looking forward to being able to tell our friends." he laughed.

Chloe nodded slowly.

"Aren't you?" he frowned.

"Not really, they'll probably think that I've trapped you on purpose or something, particularly when Michelle finds out. It'll be another thing that she can stir up about." she sighed.

"Oh well, who cares." he said quickly, glancing at the waiter as he returned and handed out their food.

"I can't wait to be a Dad." Lee beamed as soon as the waiter left.

"Maybe we should go shopping and get all of the things we need this weekend?" he added.

"I think we should wait until I am twelve weeks, otherwise it's bad luck." Chloe told him, smiling at how excited he was.

"Okay fine, can we discuss names then?" he tried excitedly.

"No, stop it!" Chloe said quickly.

"Why, I don't like keep saying *it.*" he protested.

"Say *the baby* then." she suggested.

"And besides we don't know what we are having yet, so we can't decide on a name anyway." she added.

"We can speak about the surname, though can't we?" he asked.

"I guess so." she said quietly. Lee laughed as she placed a piece of celery in her mouth and closed her eyes, sighing in pleasure.

"I think we should use my surname." he told her.

"Oh really?" she said sarcastically.

"And what if I want my surname?" she smiled, teasing him. Lee glanced at her quickly, a smile forming on his face when he noticed the cheeky twinkle in her eyes.

"Since I'm going to make you my wife one day, it makes sense to use my surname." he said matter of factly. Chloe spluttered on her water.

"What?!" she said when she eventually recovered herself.

"I'm going to make you my wife on day." he smiled.

"We've only been together six months." she said quickly.

"I know that's why I said one day." he smiled.

"And besides every day that goes by I fall in love with you more than the day before. Six months ago, when I told you that I was in love with you, I didn't think it was possible to love you anymore than I did.... but I was *so* wrong." he admitted, smiling at her. Chloe smiled at his words as she carefully leant across the table and placed a soft kiss on his lips.

"I love you." she whispered against his lips.

Chapter Seventy-One

"Hi guys, how's it going?" Kirstie asked as Lee and Chloe climbed into the back of Ben's car.

"We're good, how are you?" Chloe asked.

"Fine thanks." Kirstie smiled, wishing that she could ask Chloe about her baby but knowing that she couldn't in front of Ben.

"How are you getting on living together?" Lee asked, wiggling his eyebrows at them as Ben pulled away.

"Ah, it's just bliss." Kirstie said, smiling widely at Ben.

"Yep, she cooks for me and does all my laundry." Ben chuckled, glancing at Kirstie as he teased her.

"No, I don't you liar!" Kirstie exclaimed, slapping his arm playfully. Chloe couldn't help but smile at how adorable the two of them were together.

"I'm so excited to hold Kathleen's baby." Kirstie squealed in excitement.

"Me too." Ben said, smiling at Kirstie briefly, before turning his attention back to the road.

"I feel a bit guilty that she gave birth when we were away." Chloe said quietly.

"I'm pretty sure she will understand." Kirstie said, turning in her seat to face Chloe and smiling warmly at her.

"Has she found out who the father of the baby is yet?" Lee blurted, frowning at Chloe as she quickly glared at him.

"It's okay, Ben knows about the situation." Kirstie said, smiling at Chloe when she saw her panicked expression.

"Yeah, Mark spoke to me about it." Ben told them.

"And the baby is David's thankfully." he added.

"Aww, that must be a relief for Kathleen." Chloe smiled, thinking of the three of them as a little happy family.

"I expect so, I think she was hoping the baby would be David's." Kirstie agreed.

"Ooh, I'm so excited!" Kirstie said as they pulled up outside Kathleen's house and climbed out of the car. Ben chuckled and quickly took her hand. Chloe glanced at Lee, her heart plummeting when she noticed Michelle's car parked outside the house.

"Maybe we should come back another day." Chloe whispered to Lee as they stood behind Kirstie and Ben and waited for Kathleen to answer the door. Lee frowned for a moment and followed her eyeline, sighing quietly when he noticed that she saw staring at Michelle's car.

"She wouldn't dare start on you again." Lee said quietly, gently placing his arm around her waist.

"Hi everyone!" Kathleen exclaimed when she opened the door and gestured for them to come in. Lee kept his arm in place protectively as Kathleen led them into the living room. Lee glared at Michelle across the room when he noticed her sitting on the sofa, silently warning her not to say or do anything to upset Chloe.

"So, this is Daisy." Kathleen said as she walked over to the moses basket and carefully picked up her daughter, smiling at Kirstie as she quickly stepped forward and held out her arms.

"She's so cute." Kirstie said as she gazed down at Daisy. Ben smiled at the expression on Kirstie's face as she stood beside him.

"I think I want one." Kirstie smiled as Daisy stared up at her and gurgled happily.

"I think you'll be a great Mum." Ben smiled at her as he watched her. Kirstie glanced up at him and smiled.

"Let's do it." he whispered in her ear.

"Really?" Kirstie whispered.

"Yeah, why not." Ben said, smiling at her excited expression.

Chloe sat awkwardly beside Michelle on the sofa, glancing at Lee as he perched on the arm of the sofa beside her, clearly not wanting to sit close to Michelle.

"When was she born?" Chloe asked Kathleen, smiling slightly at Ben and Kirstie as she watched them fussing over the baby.

"She's almost a week old now." Kathleen replied.

"Yeah, she was born when you guys were away on your trip." Michelle piped up.

"Which I didn't get invited too." she added bitterly under her breath.

"Why would we invite you, we wanted to have a nice time." Lee snapped. Michelle turned to glare at him, her temper rising as Lee smirked slightly. Lee's eyes flickered up as Kirstie walked over to him, still carrying Daisy in her arms.

"Do you want to hold her?" Kirstie offered Lee. He nodded slowly and held out his arms to take the baby. Chloe smiled to herself as she watched Lee gently cradling Daisy. He rocked her slightly as she began to stir, smiling as she wrapped her hand around one of his fingers. Kirstie glanced at Chloe as she noticed her watching Lee closely, a look of admiration on her face. Chloe's eyes darted to Daisy as she gurgled.

"Why don't you hold her Chloe?" Kirstie suggested when she noticed how nervous Chloe looked. Kirstie couldn't help but hope that by holding Kathleen's baby, Chloe might feel a little less terrified by the idea of having her own baby. Chloe shook her head quickly.

"It's okay, she won't bite you." Kathleen giggled, teasing her.

"I've never held a baby before; I'll probably make her cry." Chloe said quietly.

"Or worse drop her." Chloe added. She glanced up at Lee as she felt him watching her closely, her cheeks colouring as everyone stared at her.

"You'll be fine, you won't drop her." Kathleen said, smiling reassuringly at Chloe.

"If you're worried, hold her sitting down." Kirstie told Chloe, trying to reassure her.

"Stand up a second." Lee told her gently. Chloe quickly did as he asked, watching him closely as he sat in her place on the sofa. Chloe smiled slightly as he jerked his head towards his lap, gesturing for her to sit on it. She tentatively sat on his lap, sitting forward so that she didn't crush Daisy. Lee carefully placed his arms over her head, slowly lowering Daisy into Chloe's outstretched arms. Chloe gasped as she held Daisy, smiling down at her as she fidgeted. Lee's arms remained in place around Chloe's as he attempted to help her feel safe holding Daisy.

"Don't let me drop her." Chloe whispered, starting to panic slightly when she noticed her hands shaking.

"You won't drop her." Lee whispered softly in her ear. He watched Chloe as she gazed down at the Daisy, smiling widely when Daisy smiled up at her.

"See she likes you." Lee told her. Chloe smiled slightly, not quite able to believe how small and vulnerable Daisy seemed.

"Holding a baby suits you both, you look like a little family." Ben told them. Chloe's eyes flickered upwards, suddenly feeling nervous that Kirstie had revealed their secret to Ben. She locked eyes with Kirstie, trying to read her expression, Kirstie slowly shook her head, giving Chloe the subtle signal that she hadn't said anything to him. Chloe's cheeks coloured as she suddenly noticed everyone staring at them.

"They do actually don't they." Kathleen said fondly.

"I know who to call if I need babysitters." she added. Chloe glanced at Lee for a moment as he rested his chin on her shoulder. She sighed to herself and relaxed against his chest.

"Are you ready to try on your own?" Lee asked her gently. Chloe nodded slowly, her heart pounding nervously as Lee slowly moved his arms away. Chloe gasped slightly as she suddenly had the responsibility of Kathleen's baby resting solely on her.

"See, we said you could do it." Kathleen smiled. Chloe nodded slowly, her eyes filling with tears as she was reminded yet again of her own situation. As she gazed down at Kathleen's baby, she couldn't help but feel like with Lee by her side, maybe everything would be okay after all.

Chapter Seventy-Two

Chloe glanced at Lee and smiled at him when he quickly let go of her hand as soon as they were within sight of the studio, fearful that they might be seen.

"I think Nathan knows something is going on, he keeps asking why I'm so cheerful." Lee told her as they walked.

"You didn't tell him, did you?" Chloe asked quickly.

"No, I said that I'm excited about the album coming out." he chuckled. Chloe smiled slightly.

"I'll be twelve weeks in a few days, we can tell him then." she reminded him. Lee nodded slowly, smiling slightly at how feisty she was slowly becoming. Lee fell into step behind her as they walked into the studio. Chloe smiled as Adrian and Steven waved at her from across the studio.

"I should warn you; Jonny is in a foul mood today." Nathan told them as he stood beside them. Chloe rolled her eyes and quickly beckoned for Adrian and Steven to join them. They smiled as they walked over to join them.

"I have the final track list for the album for you to check." she said as she handed each of them a sheet of paper. Lee's heart pounded against his chest as he noticed the song that he'd written about Chloe on the album. He wasn't entirely sure how he felt about the idea of the whole world knowing how he felt the day he realised that Chloe was leaving them. Chloe glanced up as Matt walked over to join them.

"Is that the track list?" Matt asked her. Chloe nodded.

"I have the final draft of the album cover." Matt said, winking at Chloe as he handed one to her. Chloe smiled down at the cover as she saw the pictures of her with the boys and the models.

"Scroll to Lee's acknowledgement section." Matt told her. Lee peered over her shoulder as Chloe quickly flicked through, gasping as she laid eyes of a picture of her posing with Lee. The two of them gazing into each other's eyes as Chloe draped her leg over Lee's hips, his hand resting in place on her bare thigh.

"That's the one I said I really liked." Lee said quietly.

"I mean look how stunning you are." Lee whispered.

"He's going to be in a rush to get you home again tonight now." Nathan laughed. Chloe glanced around nervously, fearful that they might have been overheard, breathing a sigh of relief when she realised that everyone was too busy going about their business to notice.

"If you guys are done gossiping, I need you boys!" Jonny called from across the room.
"What for now?" Steven asked.

"Choreograph the routines." Jonny said shortly, rolling his eyes.

"But we've done all the fast-paced songs, there's just the ballads." Adrian frowned.

"So, we still have to choreograph them." Jonny insisted.

"You do realise that we are in our thirties, and these routines that you are doing, are very fast paced." Nathan sighed.

"Tough." Jonny snapped.

"Before you guys go are you happy with the album track list, so that I can get it submitted?" Chloe asked. Adrian, Steven and Nathan nodded.

"Can we put Broken as the last track Chlo.......e?" Lee asked, quickly adding the extra letter when he realised what he'd said, quickly pointing at the song on the list.

"Yes, that's no problem." Chloe smiled at him.

"Thank you." he smiled at her, quickly walking away from Chloe before he felt the overwhelming urge to kiss her. Chloe walked over to the bench and spread out her paperwork, glancing up at the Eclipse boys as she heard Jonny shouting at them. Her heart sunk as she watched Jonny force them to run the routines repeatedly, the four of them gradually looking more and more exhausted.

"Maybe you should work on a slower song for a bit?" Chloe suggested when she couldn't stand seeing them struggling any longer.

"Like one of the ballards that you said you needed them to work on?" she added when Jonny didn't respond. Jonny sighed and slowly turned to face her.

"What's it got to do with you?!" Jonny rounded on her.

"I am their day manager, and I don't want you running them into the ground." Chloe said firmly.

"Oh whatever." Jonny said shortly. Chloe smiled in satisfaction as he began to teach the boys the moves.

"Okay so, point to the crowd, try and pick a fan and look them in the eye as you do it." Jonny told them.

"Then make a heart with your hands on your chest." he continued. Chloe giggled as Nathan locked eyes with her and rolled them impatiently. She jumped slightly as Jonny switched on the stereo and the chorus began to play. Chloe locked eyes with Lee as he began to sing the chorus.

Her heart pounded against her chest as he sang pointing at her as he executed the dance moves. Chloe smiled slightly, quickly looking away from him, pretending to be engrossed in her paperwork. She glanced at Bobby as he sat beside her silently.

"I didn't realise you were back today, isn't it too soon?" Chloe asked him worriedly.

"Mum wouldn't want me to sit at home feeling sorry for myself." Bobby replied.

"I know, but you need to take some time for yourself though." she told him gently.

"That's the problem though, my life is so empty without her." he sighed.

"It will pass eventually; you just have to try and remember the good times that you had with her and not the times when she was sick." she said thoughtfully. Bobby nodded slowly, his eyes filling with tears. Chloe rested her head on his shoulder and gently wrapped her arms around his neck, trying to provide him with at least a little bit of comfort. Chloe glanced up at him as he rested his head against hers, sighing quietly to himself.

"Are you okay?" he asked her as she rubbed her abdomen, wincing slightly.

"I'm fine, it's just cramps." she told him. Chloe could feel her heart pounding against her chest, something in her gut telling her that something wasn't right. She gasped, glancing at Lee as the pain in her abdomen intensified.

Chloe sighed to herself as she saw that Lee was still rehearsing, completely oblivious to how she was feeling.

"I think I need a minute." she said, slowly standing up. Chloe could feel Bobby watching her closely as she stood up. She took a few steps, crying out in pain and doubling over as the pain intensified.

"Are you alright?" Bobby asked, quickly standing up and placing his hand on her elbow to support her weight.

"I need to get to the bathroom." she told him, gritting her teeth in pain. Bobby nodded, helping her as the two of them quickly made their way to the bathroom.

As soon as Chloe was inside the disabled toilet, she locked the door and dropped to her knees, crying out in pain as she felt a popping sensation in her abdomen. She curled into a ball, clutching her abdomen, watching helplessly as her white jeans slowly stained with her blood.

Lee's head snapped up as he saw Chloe stand up and double over, a cry of pain escaping her lips. He saw her speak to Bobby before the two of them walked away. His heart pounded against his chest when he realised that something was wrong. Lee quickly turned to face Jonny when he impatiently clapped his hands in front of Lee's face.

"And you're back in the room." Jonny said sarcastically.

"Fuck you, that's the woman I love!" Lee stated, before quickly running out of the studio, desperately trying to find Chloe. Lee skidded to a stop when he saw Bobby walking towards him, making his way back into the rehearsal room.

"Bobby, where's Chloe?!" Lee exclaimed, as soon as he saw him.

"She needed to use the bathroom, she has a stomach upset I think, I'm sure she won't be long." Bobby told him, completely oblivious to the situation.

"I think I might have upset her speaking about my Mum...." Bobby started.

"Which bathroom Bobby?!" Lee interrupted quickly.

"Disabled toilet I think." Bobby told him, frowning slightly at Lee's behaviour. Lee ran along the hallway, skidding around the corner slightly in his haste to find Chloe. As soon as he reached the toilet, he turned the handle, cursing under his breath when he realised that the door was locked.

"Chloe, it's me." he said quickly, tapping his hand against the door.

Chloe's head snapped up as she heard Lee knocking at the door. She could tell from his panicked tone that he knew something bad had happened.

"Chloe." he called again when she didn't respond. Even though she knew she needed to let him in, she couldn't bring herself to tell him what had happened. She knew how attached he was to their baby and how devastated he was going to be when he discovered that she'd lost the baby.

Warm tears rolled down Chloe's cheeks as she stared at their baby as she held it in her hand. Even though she'd had her doubts at the beginning she'd never wanted this to happen, she loved their baby.

"Chloe, I swear to god if you don't open this door, I'm going to kick it down!" Lee called angrily, snapping her out of her thoughts. Chloe sighed, knowing that he meant it and if she didn't let him in, he would find a way to get into the bathroom anyway. She hesitated for a moment before reaching out and slowly unlocking the door.

As soon as Lee heard the click of the lock, he quickly burst into the room, his heart plummeting as he saw Chloe sitting on the floor with her back to him, her white jeans stained with blood.

"We need to get you to hospital." he told her, quickly placing his hand on her elbow and pulling her up.

"No, stop it." she said, squirming away from his grip, wincing slightly as she landed roughly on the floor.

"It's too late anyway." she whispered, as tears flowed freely down her cheeks. Lee dropped to his knees when he finally realised what had happened. He glanced at Chloe as she turned to face him.

His eyes wandered to her hand that was in place on her lap when he saw that she was holding something. Chloe followed his eyeline, her heart breaking a little for him.

"We don't have a baby anymore." she whispered. She snuggled her body against his chest, the enormity of the situation finally hitting her. Lee placed his hand under hers, unable to bring himself to tear his eyes away from their baby.

"Our poor baby!" she sobbed. Lee glanced down at her as she rested her head against his chest and began to sob uncontrollably. Chloe gripped Lee's shirt with her other hand, trying to hold onto something to gain some comfort. Lee rested his head against hers, unable to fight the tears that were filling his eyes as he realised that they'd lost their baby. His heart felt like it was going to shatter at the thought of it. His heart broke further as he gazed at Chloe and realised how devastated she was. Lee glanced around as he heard footsteps approaching, he pushed the door closed and quickly slid the bolt along to prevent anyone from walking in on them. He quickly wrapped his arms around Chloe, holding her tightly against his chest as she continued to sob. He reached up to his face and quickly wiped away the tears that were rolling down his cheeks, before Chloe could notice.

"We need to get you home." he whispered in her ear. Lee glanced at her trousers, trying to think quickly when he realised that Chloe couldn't walk through the studio when her jeans were quite clearly stained with blood.

"Don't leave me." she pleaded, clinging onto him tightly as he stood up.

"I'll be back." he told her, trying not to look at her as he quickly left the bathroom.

Chapter Seventy-Three

As soon as Lee left the bathroom and closed the door behind himself, he sighed and placed his back against the door, slowly sliding down it as his legs buckled from underneath him. He pressed the back of his head against the door and closed his eyes, trying to erase the image of Chloe, on the other side of the door. He knew that he would never forget the sight of her, stained with her own blood, gently holding their baby in her hand. It almost seemed intangible that they no longer had a child on the way. The two of them had spent the past few weeks, trying to get their head around the idea of being parents and it almost seemed like as soon as they came to terms with the idea, their baby was stolen from them. Lee placed his head in his hands, digging his fingernails into his scalp angrily, trying to fight the way he was feeling in order to be strong for Chloe. He glanced behind him and sighed quietly as he heard Chloe sobbing on the other side of the door.

Lee quickly stood up and walked in a trance to his locker, rummaging through until he found his spare trousers. He quickly picked them up, pulling on his jacket at the same time. Lee glanced up as Matt walked into the room.

"Oh, there you are!" Matt exclaimed when he saw him, frowning slightly when he noticed how pale Lee looked.

"Jonny is kicking off about you disappearing." Matt told him. Lee shrugged silently, not really in the mood to speak to anyone.

"I really don't give a shit right now." Lee admitted quietly.

"Where's Chloe?" Matt asked, sighing slightly at Lee's attitude.

"Bathroom." Lee replied shortly.

"You might want to give her a heads up that everyone is now gossiping about you and her." Matt told him.

"I really don't want to talk about this right now, I'm taking Chloe home for the day, she's not feeling well." Lee said firmly. Matt opened his mouth to argue that Lee needed to stay and work on the rest of the choreography, but he quickly changed his mind when he noticed how emotional Lee was slowly becoming. Even though Matt had no idea what was going on, he could tell from Lee's face that it was something serious. Matt quickly closed his mouth and nodded slowly, smiling sympathetically at Lee as he quickly walked past him.

Lee frowned to himself as he walked around the corner and saw Nathan knocking on the door of the disabled bathroom toilet.

"Is Chloe okay, she won't let me in?" Nathan asked quickly.

"She's fine, just leave her." Lee snapped.

"In fact, do me a favour and see if you can find a small box." he added. Nathan frowned at Lee's waspish tone but decided not to press him. Nathan nodded and quickly walked away.

"Chloe, it's me." Lee called as he tapped lightly on the door. As soon as he heard the click of the door lock, he quickly walked into the room. Chloe glanced up at him for a moment before returning to staring at the ground.

"You need to put these on over your jeans Chlo." he told her gently as he handed her his sweatpants. Chloe nodded slowly, staggering slightly as she stood up and carefully pulled on his trousers.

"Where did you put our baby?" he asked her quickly when he suddenly noticed that she was no longer holding their baby.

"Wrapped in a towel on the counter." she muttered. Lee glanced up as Nathan barged into the bathroom. Chloe stared at Lee, a look of panic in her eyes as Lee cursed himself under his breath.

In his haste to check on Chloe he'd forgotten to close the door behind himself. Lee could feel Chloe and Nathan watching him closely as he took the box from Nathan's grasp and carefully placed the towel inside.

"What's going on?" Nathan asked nervously, glancing between Chloe and Lee.

"Nothing, we're going home." Lee said shortly, holding out his hand for Chloe to take. Chloe quickly took his hand, gasping slightly as Lee pulled her out of the bathroom with him, hurrying to get to the car before anyone else saw them. As soon as they reached Lee's car, he quickly handed Chloe the box, before climbing into the driver's seat. Chloe winced as she climbed into the passenger seat and carefully placed the box on her lap. She slowly traced small circles on the lid of the box, still not quite able to process what had happened. Chloe glanced at Lee as he drove them home in silence.

She knew that he was upset by the loss of their child but for whatever reason he was trying to hide it. He'd been so excited about the idea of becoming a father and had quickly grown attached to their baby, so Chloe knew that he was hurting. Lee jumped slightly as she took his hand that was resting on the gear stick and held it tightly. Lee glanced at her for a moment, before turning his attention back to the road. Chloe squeezed his hand gently, wishing that she knew what to say or do to comfort him.

"I love you. " she whispered, lifting his hand to her face and placing a soft kiss on it. Lee glanced at her for a moment, sighing quietly to himself when he noticed that she was crying. Lee bit the inside of his lip, desperately trying to fight his emotions. The last thing he wanted to do was give in to his feelings, particularly when he had to be strong for Chloe.

As soon as they reached the house, Chloe slowly climbed out of the car and walked inside, Lee following closely behind her.

He watched her closely as she carefully placed the box on the counter before slowly turning to face him.

"Are you okay?" she asked him, knowing that he wasn't but trying to get him to talk to her.

"I have no idea; I don't know how I feel." he admitted quietly. Chloe nodded slowly, watching him closely.

"I need to get myself cleaned up." Chloe told him, before reluctantly walking away.

Lee nodded slowly, sighing to himself as he watched her walk upstairs. He knew that she was hurting and that she wanted him to open up to her about how he was feeling, but he couldn't even process what had happened, let alone talk about it. Before Lee realised what, he was doing he climbed the stairs and followed her to the bathroom.

Chloe jumped and whirled round in the shower as she heard the toilet seat slam shut. She locked eyes with Lee as he sat on the toilet and watched her closely, a look of sadness on his handsome features as he watched her clean herself up. As soon as she was finished, Chloe climbed out of the shower and wrapped a towel around her naked frame, gazing down at Lee as he stared up at her.

"I think we need to bury our baby." he told her. Chloe's heart broke for him as she saw his bottom lip wobble. She took his hands in hers, sighing quietly when she noticed that his hands were shaking. Chloe quickly knelt on the floor, resting her chin on his knees and gazing up into his deep blue eyes.

"You need to talk to me." she told him softly.

"There's nothing to say." he said quickly. Chloe sighed, staring at his hands as she gently played with his fingers. She sighed and rested the side of her head on his knees, closing her eyes tightly, wishing that she could wake up and discover that it was a nightmare.

"I'm really sorry." she whispered, suddenly feeling a wave of guilt that she'd lost their baby. Lee sighed and stroked her hair softly.

"I wish you'd let me into the bathroom, maybe I could have done something." he said thoughtfully.

"You couldn't have, it was too late." she said quietly. Chloe stiffened for a moment as Lee leant forward and rested his head on hers. She sighed quietly as she gently wrapped her arms around his head, holding him tightly against her, wishing that she could do something to take their pain away.

Chapter Seventy-Four

Chloe sighed and ran her hands through her hair as she carefully placed her phone on the table. She placed her arms on the table and rested her head against them, closing her eyes tightly, wishing that she could sleep. She'd spent most of the night tossing and turning until eventually she'd cried herself to sleep. Chloe lifted her head as she heard movement, glancing at Lee as he walked into the dining room and sat beside her.

"Did you manage to speak to the midwife?" he asked her.

"Yes, I have to go for a check-up tomorrow." she told him quietly, not quite able to look him in the eye. In the past few hours, Chloe had begun to feel incredibly guilty for what had happened, she knew it had been her responsibility to carry their baby and she couldn't help but feel like she had failed in her duty.

"Why?" he asked quietly.

"Because they need to check that everything has progressed as it should, otherwise I might end up with an infection." she told him.

"When is the appointment?" he asked her, swallowing the lump that was rising in his throat.

"Tomorrow at two." she said quietly. Chloe sat in silence for a moment, sighing quietly to herself as she felt Lee's eyes burning a hole into her head. She still didn't quite know how to process the loss of their baby, all she knew was that if she had been taking the pill like she was meant too, none of this would have happened, their baby wouldn't have died and the man she loved wouldn't be hurting as a result. Chloe's eyes wandered to the garden as she stared out of the window, remembering the moment only the day before when they'd buried their baby in the flower bed. In all the years that Chloe had known Lee, she'd never seen him so quiet, almost like he was lost and didn't know what to do.

Chloe had lost people that she loved in the past, but this was the first time Lee had experienced the death of a loved one and she knew that it was hitting him hard.

"When are we going to tell your Mum?" she asked him nervously.

"I'll tell her myself." he said dismissively, following her eyeline as she stared into the garden.

"Are you sure, I don't mind coming along to support you?" she asked, trying to mentally reach out to him and wishing that he didn't keep pushing her away.

"I said I'll do it!" he snapped. Chloe glanced at him, slightly confused as to why he was being so dismissive and snappy with her when she was only trying to help him. She knew from her experience with grief that they needed to rely on each other and not push each other away. Chloe quickly stood up, suddenly feeling the overwhelming urge to keep her mind occupied. Lee didn't even tear his eyes away from staring at the garden as she stood up and walked away.

Lee stood up and began to pace as he felt himself slowly growing more and more angry. Chloe had spent the whole day in the study organising Eclipse's tour schedule for them and now she was working out in the gym as if she didn't have a care in the world. He couldn't help but feel like she didn't even care that they'd lost their baby. He had so many emotions going around in his head that he didn't know how to process them. The loss of their baby had devastated him, he'd been so excited to have a baby with Chloe and now everything had been ripped away from them. He felt a deep surge of anger at the thought that their baby had been cruelly stolen from them, even though he'd done everything he could to keep his promise to Chloe that he would protect them both.

Lee sighed to himself, running his hand through his hair angrily. He stopped pacing as Chloe walked into the kitchen, quickly picking up a glass and filling it with water. Chloe glanced at Lee as she felt him watching her closely, his jaw set in frustration.

"Are you okay?" she asked him quietly.

"I think I am going to go out." he said shortly.

"Why?" she frowned, starting to feel slightly upset about the idea of being left alone.

"Because I need a few drinks." he snapped, trying not to lose his temper with her as he felt his temper slowly rising.

"Please don't.... please stay with me." she said sadly, her eyes filling with tears. Lee shook his head angrily.

"You don't even care about any of this, so why should I care what you want!" he exclaimed, his temper finally snapping. Chloe stared at him for a moment, in a state of numb shock as she tried to process his words.

She watched in horror, not entirely sure what to do as Lee quickly stormed out of the room and slammed the front door behind himself. Chloe sighed to herself as she walked into the living room and sat on the sofa, her mind racing with Lee's words. He hadn't spoken to her like that for months, she knew that he was hurting and lashing out at her, but that didn't stop the hurt that she was feeling. Chloe curled up on the sofa and picked up a cushion, hugging it tightly against herself, wishing with all her heart that she could curl up in Lee's arms.

Chloe bolted awake, sighing to herself when she realised that she was still on the sofa, waiting for Lee to come home. She glanced at her mobile when she suddenly realised that it was ringing. She frowned to herself when she looked at the display and saw that Nathan was calling her.

"Hello." she sighed when she answered the phone.

"Chloe, I need your help!" Nathan said quickly as soon as she answered the phone.
"Why, what's happened?" she asked nervously, feeling slightly worried by Nathan's tone.

"I'm with Lee in a club, he's so drunk that he's causing fights, so I need you to come and calm him down." he told her. Chloe sighed quietly to herself.

"He's an adult, he can do what he wants." she said quietly, still feeling hurt by what Lee said to her.

"Yeah, but Shayne is in the club and I'm worried what he will do if he sees him." he explained. Chloe's stomach dropped when she heard Nathan's words. Even though she didn't want to leave the house, she knew that she needed to do something. She couldn't help but feel afraid that given everything that was going on Lee would lose his temper with Shayne if he saw him.

"He'll probably kill him." Chloe whispered, almost as if she was speaking to herself.

"Yeah exactly." Nathan agreed.

"Text me the club, I'll get a taxi." she told him, quickly standing up and grabbing her jacket as she ran out of the front door.

As soon as Chloe reached the club she hurried inside, frantically searching for Lee. Chloe's heart plummeted when she noticed Shayne walking through the crowd of people in the club. She followed his eyeline gasping to herself when she realised that he was heading straight towards Lee and Nathan. Chloe hurried across the club, squeezing between the people, desperately trying to reach Lee before Shayne.

Lee sighed to himself as he downed yet another shot. He could feel Nathan's eyes burning a hole in his head.

"Have a drink and lighten up a bit." Lee told Nathan, rolling his eyes at him. Nathan sighed as he watched Lee continuing to drown his sorrows. He knew that Lee was hurting because of what happened, but he couldn't help but wish that he could convince him to go home and be with Chloe, so that the two of them could process their pain together. Nathan's stomach plummeted as he glanced over Lee's shoulder and saw Shayne striding towards them purposefully.

Lee frowned and turned to see what Nathan was looking at. He suddenly felt a deep surge of anger as he saw Shayne walking towards them.

"What the hell is he doing here?!" Lee exclaimed.

"Don't start anything." Nathan warned. Shayne smirked at Lee as he stood beside them and leant against the bar casually.

"What are you doing here?!" Lee asked angrily.

"It's a public club." Shayne replied condescendingly.

"Yeah, but that doesn't mean you have to stand right by us." Nathan pointed out.

"Well, feel free to move." Shayne said shortly.

"Where's your beautiful stylist tonight?" Shayne asked, smirking at Lee.

"At home." Lee snapped, trying to control his temper that was slowly rising.

"Really, I thought I saw her a few moments ago." Shayne said, smiling slightly when Lee frowned and glanced around the club.

"Maybe I should go and find her." Shayne smirked, quickly straightening up.

Lee quickly reached out and took hold of Shayne's shirt, quickly pulling Shayne towards himself.

"Chloe isn't here and if she was you wouldn't dare get near her!" Lee said, his tone full of menace. Shayne smirked in Lee's face, almost daring him to make a move.

"Lee, let go of him." Chloe said from behind him. Lee quickly let go of Shayne and pushed him out of his personal space. Chloe moved to stand in front of Lee, so that she was between Shayne and Lee.

"What happened to your face?" Chloe asked, as she reached out and softly stroked the cut on his cheek.

"Just a fight, what are you doing here?!" Lee asked, sounding slightly angry.

"We need to get you home." Chloe told him, feeling slightly sorry for him when she realised how drunk he was, clearly trying to escape the pain that he was feeling inside.

"I don't want to go home." Lee snapped.

"Oh well, maybe you would like to dance with me then Chloe, just for old time sake." Shayne said from behind her. Chloe rolled her eyes and kept her back to him, choosing not to rise to the bait. She knew that he was trying to wind her and Lee up and she refused to give him the satisfaction.

"Chloe?" Shayne asked.

"No thank you." she said quickly, her eyes fixed on Lee as she noticed him slowly becoming angry again.

"Back off." Lee warned Shayne, glaring at him over the top of Chloe.

"She's way out of your league anyway." Shayne smirked.

"I mean look how beautiful she is." Shayne said in Chloe's ear. Her skin crawled as she felt Shayne softly stroking her hair.

"Don't fucking touch her!" Lee shouted when he realised what Shayne was doing. Shayne locked eyes with Lee, smirking at him as he continued stroking Chloe's hair.

Lee quickly made a move to grab Shayne, stopping when Chloe moved to block him.

"Lee, you need to calm down." Chloe told him sternly.

"He's not worth it." she quickly added. Lee reluctantly tore his eyes away from Shayne and finally locked eyes with Chloe, feeling himself calm down slightly as he looked at her.

"Let's just go." Nathan said, placing his hand on Lee's shoulder, and quickly steering him out of the club. As soon as the three of them were outside the club, Lee stopped in his tracks.

"Aren't we going home?" Chloe asked him.

"I told you, I don't want to go home." Lee said shortly, leaning against the wall as he staggered slightly. Chloe's eyes filled with tears as she watched Lee glaring at her angrily.

"Why?" she asked, not entirely understanding why he was so against the idea of coming home with her.

"Because I want to stay out." he snapped.

"Please come home." she pleaded, desperately hoping that he would agree. Not only did she want him to come home so that he was beside her, she also wanted to know that he wasn't going to stay out and get himself into any trouble.

"Lee." she tried when he closed his eyes and reminded silent.

"You do realise this is all your fault, if you'd been taking the pill like you were supposed to, then none of this would have happened." he said matter of factly, finally opening his eyes to look at her.

"Lee, stop it!" Nathan said firmly, glancing at Chloe as he heard her let out a small sob.

"You need to take Chloe home and look after her." Nathan added. Lee smirked and shook his head.

"It's always about *her* isn't it.... why do I always have to take care of her, and she couldn't even take care of our baby!" Lee shouted. Chloe stared at him for a moment, in a state of numb shock.

"I can't believe you just said that." she eventually whispered, unable to hold back her tears any longer. Lee shrugged and walked away from her, heading down the street. Chloe let out a small sob as she watched Lee walking away. Nathan sighed in frustration and quickly pulled Chloe into his arms, squeezing her tightly when she began to sob.

"It'll be okay Chlo Bo." he whispered softly in her ear.

"I just want to go home." she admitted, slowly removing herself from his arms.

"Do you want me to take you home?" Nathan offered, suddenly realising that Chloe would have to make her own way home in the dark.

"No, it's fine. Stay with him and make sure he's okay." she said, pointing at Lee who was still staggering down the street. Nathan nodded and reluctantly walked away from Chloe, hurrying to catch up with Lee. Chloe quickly wiped away her tears, before beginning the long walk home.

Chapter Seventy-Five

Chloe sighed as she closed the front door behind herself and slowly slid down it, her legs suddenly feeling weak. She rested her head against the door, finally releasing the tears that had been threatening to overwhelm her all day. Being at the hospital had finally made everything feel real for her. She couldn't help but remember the last time she was there, when her and Lee had seen their baby moving and heard it's soft heartbeat. She'd have given anything to have had Lee by her side at her check-up, but he still hadn't returned home, even though she'd been trying to call him all day. The only contact she'd had was a text from Nathan telling her that Lee was at his house and he was safe.

Chloe knew that Lee blamed her for the loss of their baby and quite frankly she could understand why, she blamed herself.

She couldn't help but wonder if she'd done something to cause the miscarriage. Chloe sniffed and angrily wiped away her tears, the doctor's words still spinning around her head. Even though the doctor had told her numerous times that the miscarriage wasn't her fault and unfortunately these things happened quite often, she still couldn't stop the guilt she was feeling. Chloe slowly stood up and walked into the garden, collapsing to the ground in front of the flowerbed where they'd buried their baby.

"I'm so sorry little baby." she whispered, picking up a small amount of the fresh dirt and squeezing it tightly in her fist.

"I should have protected you better." she sobbed. Chloe curled into a ball and sobbed quietly, clutching her abdomen, wishing that she could have her baby back. She laid on the grass for what felt like hours, finally falling silent when she didn't have the energy to cry any longer.

Chloe jumped as her phone sounded, alerting her to someone ringing the doorbell.

She quickly stood up, staggering slightly with exhaustion and walked through the house. She frowned to herself as she opened the front door and stood face to face with Ben and Kirstie.

"Oh no, what's wrong?" Kirstie asked as soon as she saw Chloe's face.

"I'm all good." Chloe said, smiling falsely.

"Did you forget that we are meant to be going out for a double date?" Ben chuckled, when he noticed how confused Chloe looked.

"Yes, I did." Chloe said quietly, gesturing for them to come in, feeling slightly pleased that she finally had some company.

"We might need to take a rain check though." Chloe said quietly, feeling slightly guilty that she'd let them down but not quite able to bring herself to leave the house.

"Lee isn't even here anyway." Chloe added, sighing when she remembered how Lee had been treating her.

"Is he at work?" Ben asked.

"No, he's at Nathan's." Chloe said quietly, desperately trying to fight her tears and pretend that everything was okay.

"I'll get you guys a drink." Chloe added as she led them into the kitchen. Kirstie and Ben glanced at each other as they followed Chloe into the kitchen. They couldn't help but feel like something was going on with Chloe.

"Is white wine okay?" she asked them as she took three wine glasses out of the cupboard.

"Sounds good." Ben beamed. Kirstie nodded slowly, frowning to herself when she noticed Chloe pouring three glasses of wine. As soon as Chloe poured her glass of wine, she quickly drank half of the glass.

"Can I use the bathroom?" Ben asked. Chloe nodded slowly as she downed the rest of her glass of wine.

"Chloe, what's going on, why are you drinking?" Kirstie asked quietly as soon as Ben left the room.

"It's fine, we don't have a baby anymore." Chloe said quietly, her eyes filling with tears. She quickly poured herself another glass of wine, trying to keep her hands busy in order to stop them shaking.

"I lost our baby a couple of days ago." Chloe added.

"Oh my god Chloe, I'm so sorry." Kirstie said, her mouth suddenly feeling dry.

"It's not your fault, it's mine." Chloe said shortly as she picked up her glass of wine and walked into the living room. Kirstie watched her closely as she picked up Lee's hoodie from the sofa and quickly pulled it on, before sitting on the sofa.

"It's not your fault Chloe, you shouldn't blame yourself." Kirstie said gently as she sat down beside her. Chloe remained silent, gently pulling down the sleeves of Lee's hoodie so that it was covering her hands, trying to find a way to comfort herself.

"I think I've lost everything.... the baby has died, and Lee hates me." Chloe said quietly.

"And I just don't know what to do." Chloe continued, sobbing slightly. Kirstie watched in horror as Chloe covered her face with her hands and began to sob uncontrollably. Kirstie wrapped her arm around Chloe's shoulders and pulled her close, rubbing her arm to try and provide some comfort. Kirstie could feel her own eyes filling with tears as she watched her friend breaking down in front of her, Chloe's sobs full of such anguish that Kirstie's heart was breaking for her.

"He really hates me Kirstie!" Chloe sobbed.

"I'm sure he doesn't." Kirstie told her. Chloe quickly wiped her eyes, breathing deeply to try and get her breath back.

"He does, he told me it's all my fault and basically said that I didn't do a very good job taking care of the baby." Chloe said quietly.

"It's only been a couple of days, he's probably just angry with what's happened and is lashing out." Kirstie pointed out. Chloe nodded slowly, sighing to herself.

"He's probably struggling as much as you are but isn't expressing it very well." she added.

"I can't imagine what the two of you must be going through, it must be horrendous." Kirstie continued when Chloe fell silent.

"I wish he'd let me be there for him though, we need to pull together." Chloe said thoughtfully.

"I'm also really hurt that he didn't come with me to the hospital." Chloe admitted.

"Didn't he?" Kirstie frowned.

"No, I had to go for a check-up today and I couldn't get hold of him." Chloe explained.

"You should have said, I would have gone with you." Kirstie said, smiling sympathetically, feeling slightly sorry for Chloe that she'd been alone.

"It's fine." Chloe said quietly.

"What are you guys talking about?" Ben asked as he came bounding into the room and threw himself down on the sofa, his smile quickly fading when he noticed the tears that were slowly rolling down Chloe's face.

"Oh no, what's happened?" Ben asked.

"Nothing, it's fine." Kirstie said quickly.

"It's okay, it's not like it matters anymore." Chloe said quietly.

"I had a miscarriage." she added.

"Oh shit." Ben said quietly, not entirely sure what to say.

"I didn't realise you were pregnant." he added.

"We were keeping it quiet until I was twelve weeks." Chloe muttered, her eyes filling with tears again as she suddenly had another flash back of the scan.

"Please keep it quiet though, only you guys know and Lee's Mum." Chloe told him. Ben nodded slowly.

"And I suppose Lee will have told Nathan." she added thoughtfully. Ben sighed quietly as he watched Chloe crying softly to herself. He couldn't help but feel like Lee should be with her.

"It'll get easier Chloe, I promise." Ben told her as he quickly pulled her into a tight hug. Chloe quickly let go of Ben when she heard the front door slam. She glanced up, her heart pounding as she saw Lee staggering along the hallway. Chloe quickly stood up, watching as he perched on the staircase, resting the side of his head against the wall and sighing deeply. Chloe quickly walked over and knelt in front of him. Even though she was still hurt by what he said to her last night and the fact that he hadn't come with her to the hospital, she still needed to know that he was okay.

"Your face is really swollen." she sighed when she saw how swollen his cheek bone was.

"I'll get some ice." Ben said, quickly standing up and walking into the kitchen.

"I'm sorry for everything." Chloe whispered, glancing down at his hands when she noticed that they were shaking. She couldn't help but feel a pang of guilt that her actions had caused all of this. Lee remained silent, staring at the ground that was slowly spinning. Chloe smiled her thanks at Ben as he returned with the ice and handed it to her. Lee flinched slightly as Chloe gently applied it to his cheek. She reached out to take his hand, sighing quietly when he quickly moved away from her.

"You hate me, again don't you?" Chloe whispered. Lee shrugged, still not able to bring himself to look at her.

"Fine, put ice on your own face!" Chloe snapped, angrily placing the ice in his hand, before quickly walking away.

Chapter Seventy-Six

Chloe sighed deeply as she watched Lee pull on his jacket and leave the house, without even so much as a word to her. The two of them had barely spoken for the past few weeks. Every time that Chloe tried to get Lee to open up or even to speak to her, he was snappy and dismissive with her, almost as if he didn't have time for her anymore. It felt like someone was punching her in the chest every time that he snapped at her, Chloe couldn't help but be reminded of all those months ago when she'd worked for him and he'd continually pushed her away. Despite the fact it was nowhere near to the same extent, Chloe couldn't help but feel that he would never forgive her for losing their baby.

She had no idea what to say to him or how to fix the situation, all she knew was that she had never felt so alone. She was grieving the loss of their baby too and needed him now more than ever.

Chloe quickly opened the front door when she heard the doorbell chiming, smiling at Kirstie and gesturing for her to come in.

"I passed Lee on the way out, he looks a bit better." Kirstie told her.

"I wouldn't know, he doesn't speak to me." Chloe sighed.

"Or go anywhere near me, he's been sleeping in the spare room for the past few weeks." she added sadly.

"Why?" Kirstie frowned.

"I don't know, I think he just hates me so much that he doesn't want to be around me, but he would probably feel guilty if he kicked me out." Chloe explained.

"I keep thinking that maybe I should get my own place." Chloe added.

Kirstie frowned at her words, not entirely sure where this was coming from. Chloe loved Lee with all her heart and Kirstie couldn't understand why she was considering giving up on their relationship.

"I'm just exhausted with hitting my head against a brick wall." Chloe sighed, almost as if she knew what Kirstie was thinking.

"You need to talk to him Chloe, you can't give up on what the two of you have." Kirstie insisted.

"I've tried, he doesn't want to talk to me, and I barely see him anyway, he goes out drinking every night and then sleeps most of the day." she explained.

"I even tried giving him the information of the bereavement counselling that they gave me at the hospital, and he wasn't interested." she continued.

"It's like everything that I do annoys him, he got mad at me the other day because I said the *baby,* rather than using the name he gave the baby." she ranted.

"He named the baby?" Kirstie asked.

"Yep, Riley." Chloe said.

"That's cute." Kirstie said, smiling slightly.

"It's starting to get like it was before, I'm walking on eggshells all the time, the only time he speaks to me is when he's being snappy." Chloe said quietly, her heart breaking as she told Kirstie what had been going on. She couldn't believe that it had come to this, she'd never considered life without Lee but she couldn't help but feel like she was slowly losing him.

"Do you want me to ask Ben to have a word with him?" Kirstie offered.

"No, there's no point. Nathan has been trying I think." Chloe said.

"Part of me would love to be able to take care of him, since he took care of me after the stabbing, but he won't let me, he just keeps pushing me away." she continued.

"I honestly don't know what to suggest." Kirstie sighed, feeling slightly sad at what was happening with Chloe and Lee. She knew that the two of them were perfect for each other and couldn't help but feel sad that this had driven such a big wedge between the two of them.

"Also, I keep thinking that maybe he's cheating on me." Chloe said quietly.

"What, why would you say that?" Kirstie said quickly.

"Because he's not been getting anything from me for the past few weeks and I know how high his sex drive is." Chloe said thoughtfully.

"I don't think he would cheat on you, because he knows that if he did, he would lose you forever." Kirstie pointed out.

"Anyway, I'd better get back to work, I just popped in to check on you." Kirstie said, glancing at her watch.

"I have to be at Bobby's anyway." Chloe said.

"I'll come and see you on my way home." Kirstie said, quickly pulling Chloe into a hug.

Lee sighed deeply and reluctantly climbed out of bed to face yet another day of pain and anguish. With every waking moment, he couldn't stop thinking about their baby, the constant images swirling around his head. Even though he'd never known grief before he couldn't help but feel in complete turmoil. The sadness, anger and guilt all rolling into one.

He frowned to himself as he walked through the house and noticed that Chloe was nowhere to be seen. Since he'd got home in the early hours of the morning, he'd just assumed that Chloe was in bed, but he couldn't help but feel slightly nervous when he suddenly remembered that he hadn't seen her keys hanging on the hook last night when he'd returned. He suddenly felt a pang of fear that he'd lost her, maybe in his attempts to push her away, he'd finally pushed her too far. He knew in his heart that he didn't blame her, he was just so broken and so racked with guilt that he'd been unable to keep his promise to her and the baby, that he'd pushed her away. He wasn't strong enough to take care of himself let alone her.

Lee quickly walked into the hallway as he heard the front door close. He frowned when he noticed Chloe's dishevelled appearance.

"Have you been out all night?" he asked her. Chloe nodded slowly, slightly confused as to why he was suddenly speaking to her.

"Where have you been?" he demanded.

"I went to the cemetery last night and I fell asleep." she told him, rubbing the sleep out of her eyes.

"And before you even think about moaning that I didn't tell you where I was, you have been going out for the past few weeks and not telling me where you are going." she added, her temper starting to rise.

"I was just wondering if you spent the night at Bobby's, since you've been going there a lot lately." he snapped back.

"Yes, I have, because supporting someone through their grief, is helping to distract me from my own." she said shortly.

"Even though according to you, I don't care." she added angrily.

Lee swallowed the lump that was rising in his throat. He felt another wave of guilt wash over him when he realised that he'd said that to her. He couldn't help but wish that he could turn the clock back and not take his anger at the world out on the person who was the most precious to him.

He couldn't help but think about the conversations he'd had with his Mum and Nathan over the past few weeks, both telling him repeatedly that if he continued to push Chloe away then he was going to lose her forever. He couldn't bear the thought of life without her. Lee watched her as she quickly climbed the stairs, hurrying to get away from the tense atmosphere.

"Chlo!" he called after her, suddenly making a snap decision.

"What?" she said shortly, stopping in her tracks and slowly turning to face him.

"Pack a bag." he told her.

"Why, are you finally kicking me out?" she asked nervously.

"If so, can you wait a few days, I've seen a few flats that are in my price range, but I haven't been to look at any of them yet." she added, rambling slightly as she began to panic slightly at the thought of having to return to her park bench. Lee stared at her for a moment, feeling slightly sick when he realised that she'd been preparing to potentially move out and leave him.

"My Mum suggested the other day, that we should go away for a few days and I think it's a good idea." he said when he'd eventually recovered himself.

"Okay whatever." she sighed, before continuing to climb the stairs.

"Make sure you pack warm!" he called after her.

Chapter Seventy-Seven

Chloe gazed around at the mesmerising landscape as she stood outside the lodge where her and Lee would be staying for the next few days. Even though she was excited to be in Norway, since she'd always wanted to go, she couldn't help but feel slightly nervous about the trip. She had no idea how Lee was going to be with her, and she couldn't help but feel uncomfortable around him, almost like she didn't trust him as much as she used too. She quickly pulled her suitcase out of the back of the jeep that Lee had rented and perched on the it, staring in wonder at the fjord in the distance, surrounded by mountains. She couldn't help but feel a sense of calm when she realised how peaceful it was, like she was in her own little sanctuary away from civilisation. Chloe glanced up at the sky as she heard an eagle screech, smiling to herself as she watched a golden eagle soaring above the fjord.

"What are you looking at?" Lee said from behind her, snapping her out of her thoughts.

"Just admiring the view." she said quietly.

"Do you want me to take your suitcase?" he offered when she eventually stood up.

"No, I can do it, I'm quite capable." she said shortly. Lee nodded slowly and followed her into the lodge. Chloe walked around the lodge, gasping as she walked into the bedroom and saw the large window that looked right across the fjord. She glanced at Lee as he walked into the room and placed his suitcase on the bed.

"Wow, that view is amazing!" Lee breathed as he walked over and stood beside her.

"I know, I would love to live somewhere like this." she told him.

"In the middle of nowhere." he said, smiling slightly at her.

"Yep bliss." she sighed.

"Maybe we can move to the countryside at some point?" he suggested, glancing at her nervously. Chloe shrugged. Lee's heart sunk slightly when she shrugged. He couldn't help but feel afraid that as a result of his actions she was contemplating a future that he wasn't in. Ever since she'd let on to him that she'd been looking for her own place, he hadn't been able to stop thinking about how he could lose her. It was bad enough losing their baby, but he knew that he wasn't strong enough to lose Chloe. He sighed sadly to himself as he watched her slowly leave the room.

Chloe frowned to herself as she walked around the lodge and suddenly noticed that it only had one bedroom. She sighed when she realised that the company must have got Lee's booking wrong.

She rummaged in the cupboards until she eventually found a spare blanket and walked into the living room, smiling slightly when she saw the large open fireplace with three sofas set up around it in a U-shape. She slowly began to rearrange the cushions, laying out the blanket and carefully tucking it in.

"What are you doing?" she heard Lee say from behind her. Chloe jumped and quickly turned to face him.

"Don't do that, you made me jump!" she snapped.

"Sorry, I didn't mean too." he said quietly. Chloe nodded and continued tucking in the blanket.

"Wait, are you making a bed?" he frowned.

"Yes, I think they must have made a mistake when you booked it, there's only one bedroom." she told him. Lee frowned at her words, not entirely sure what she meant.

"I only booked one bedroom." he told her.

"Well, why did you do that?" she sighed.

"You've been sleeping in the spare room for the past few weeks to get away from me." she added sadly.

"Yeah well, if you want to share a bed we can." he said quietly, feeling slightly guilty.

"Or if you prefer, you can have the bed and I'll take the sofa." he offered when she didn't respond.

"No, I want the sofa." she told him shortly, not quite able to lower her barriers that she'd built up as a defence for his behaviour towards her. Lee nodded slowly, resisting the urge to argue with her that she should have the bed. He knew that he had a lot of things to make up to Chloe, but he had no idea how to do so. All he knew was that he couldn't lose her, so he had to find a way to repair the relationship that he'd fractured, before it was too late.

"Would you like a cup of tea?" he asked her, trying to break the uncomfortable silence. Chloe nodded and followed him into the kitchen.

"It's cute how they've stocked all the cupboards and stuff." Chloe said as she sat at the kitchen island.

"And the fridge." Lee agreed, opening the fridge and placing a bottle of wine on the counter.

"I'd rather have wine than a cup of tea." she said, smiling slightly. Lee nodded in agreement and quickly poured two glasses of wine, before placing one in front of Chloe.

"I've never heard of Krumkake before." he frowned as he picked up a packet of what looked like waffles shaped like a cone.

"It's probably a delicacy." she said quietly as she sat picking her fingernails awkwardly. Lee nodded slowly, sighing quietly to himself as he watched her. He couldn't help but wish that things were back the way they used to be between the two of them.

"Apparently there's a hot tub outside." he told her.

"Is there?" she frowned.

"Yeah, I remember seeing one when I booked it." he said.

"I didn't realise, I didn't bring a bathing suit." she replied quietly.
"You could go in it in your underwear." he suggested.

"There's only me here, so nobody else will see you, especially since we are a few miles from civilisation." he tried when she didn't respond. Chloe nodded slowly before picking up her glass of wine and walking outside. She smiled slightly when she noticed the hot tub on the decking overlooking the fjord. Chloe couldn't help but wish that she never had to return to the city. She felt a deep sense of relaxation when she was in the countryside, surrounded by beautiful scenery and silence, rather than the hustle and bustle of a busy city. Chloe jumped as Lee walked up behind her in his swimming trunks and climbed into the hot tub.

"I can't believe how early it gets dark here." he said quietly as he gazed thoughtfully at the sun slowly setting in the sky.

"That's because it's winter, you only get a limited window of daylight." she replied, perching on the edge of the hot tub.
"Although on the plus side November is the start of the killer whale season." she added, smiling slightly at the thought of seeing killer whales.

"Hopefully we'll see them tomorrow on the boat trip." he said, smiling when he noticed her eyes light up, like they always did when she spoke about animals.

"Are you coming in then?" he asked her, raising his eyebrow when she glanced at him. Chloe sighed quietly and slowly nodded. She could feel Lee watching her closely as she slowly removed her clothes.

"Jesus." he muttered under his breath as he stared longingly at Chloe's figure. He couldn't help but notice that she was even more toned than normal, thanks to the amount of time she'd been spending in the gym recently.

"What did you say?" Chloe asked as she climbed into the hot tub.

"Nothing." he said quickly, his voice slightly hoarse as he continued to stare at her, desperately trying to resist the urge to pull her into his arms.

He quickly crossed his legs and switched on the jets, trying to hide the effect that seeing her perfect body was having on him. Chloe quickly took a large sip of her wine and placed the glass on the edge of the hot tub, glancing at Lee as she felt him watching her closely.

"What?" she asked shortly, when she couldn't stand it any longer.

"Nothing." he said, quickly looking away from her. Chloe glanced up at the darkened sky, smiling to herself when she noticed the northern lights, rippling through the sky above the fjord. She folded her arms against the side of the hot tub and rested her chin on them, staring up at the sky.

"I've just realised you would have been exactly twenty weeks pregnant today." Lee said randomly, when he suddenly realised what the date was.

"Yes, I know." Chloe said, keeping her back to him.

"We'd have been able to go for a gender scan to find out what we were having." he continued thoughtfully.

Chloe sighed quietly to herself, wishing that he would stop talking about their baby.

"I was so looking forward to being a Dad." he sighed.

"I know you were." she replied quietly, her eyes filling with tears.

"I never thought of being a Dad before but being with you has made me realise how much I want a family." he told her, staring at her back, wishing that she would turn to face him.

"Maybe we can try again in the future." he said nervously. Chloe remained silent for a few moments, clearly thinking deeply.

"I don't think that's such a good idea is it." she said shortly. Lee watched her as she quickly stood up and climbed out of the hot tub.

"Chlo." he called softly, his heart plummeting as she walked away from him. Lee sighed and ran his hand through his hair in frustration, his fear that Chloe was going to leave him intensifying.

First, she'd been dismissive when he'd mentioned moving to the countryside and now, she didn't want to speak about them starting a family together. He couldn't escape the feeling that she didn't want to be with him anymore and was contemplating a life without him. Lee wiped the tears from his eyes and climbed out of the hot tub, sighing to himself when he walked into the living room and saw Chloe curled up on the sofa, huddling under the blanket. She glanced at Lee as he crossed the room and squatted in front of her.

"Please come and sleep in the bedroom, it's much warmer because it has the heater." he pleaded, his heart sinking slightly when he noticed that she was shivering.

"Fine." she said shortly, quickly standing up and striding into the bedroom, carrying the blanket under her arm. Chloe could feel Lee watching her closely as she climbed into bed, quickly shuffling right to the edge of the bed when she felt him climb into bed beside her.

She stared into the darkness, tears beginning to roll down her cheeks like they did every night when she laid down alone with her thoughts. She couldn't remember a time in her life when she had ever felt as lonely as she had the past few weeks. Even when she was living on a park bench, she hadn't been as miserable as she was now.

Lee glanced at Chloe and sighed sadly as he heard her crying softly to herself. His heart broke for her when he realised that the way he had been treating her for the past few weeks had probably made an already difficult time for her even worse. Lee quickly wiped away the tears that were filling his eyes and turned his back on Chloe, trying to forget about what he'd done to her.

Chapter Seventy Eight

Chloe slowly opened her eyes, blinking slowly as she adjusted to the bright light that was coming in the window. She frowned to herself when she realised that she was curled up against Lee, her head resting gently against his chest. She lifted her head, cringing slightly as she locked eyes with Lee.

"Sorry, I didn't mean to do that." she said, quickly shuffling away from him, back over to her side of the bed.

"You don't have to apologise." he told her gently, feeling slightly disappointed when she moved out of his arms. Chloe quickly climbed out of bed, feeling slightly awkward being beside him. Lee watched her closely as she rummaged in her suitcase, searching for some clothes.

"Did you sleep well?" he asked awkwardly.

"I slept fine." she said shortly, quickly walking into the bathroom and closing the door. Lee sighed quietly to himself when she closed the door, the more time that passed the more upset he was becoming with the way things were between himself and Chloe. He desperately wished that he could turn back time, so that he could stop himself from hurting her. The last thing he'd ever wanted was to do anything to hurt her, she was too precious to him. Lee's eyes snapped up as she walked out of the bathroom, fully dressed in her warm clothes. Chloe glanced at him as he walked over to her and stood in front of her, gazing down at her silently, trying to fight the deep longing that he was feeling for her. Lee placed his hands on her waist, slowly stepping closer towards her, staring down at her lips. Chloe sighed and quickly moved away from him. Lee watched her sadly as she silently walked out of the room.

Chloe sighed as she sat at the kitchen island, eating the bowl of fruit that she'd prepared. She couldn't help but feel slightly guilty that she'd rejected Lee, especially since she knew how it felt when he'd been doing that to her for the past few weeks. She just couldn't bring herself to be close to him, she'd built her walls too high as an attempt to protect herself from the hurt that she was feeling. As much as she longed to be in Lee's arms, she didn't feel comfortable around him anymore. Warm tears rolled down Chloe's cheeks when she suddenly realised that maybe her relationship with Lee was irreparable.

"We should probably leave." Lee said shortly as he walked into the room, finally unable to hide the frustration that he was feeling any longer. Chloe nodded and quickly followed him out of the lodge, remaining silent as she sat in the passenger seat of the car. Lee glanced at her intermittently, trying to resist the urge to ask her what he could do to fix things.

The last thing he wanted to do was to upset her, particularly when he knew how excited she was about seeing the killer whales.

As soon as they reached the harbour, Chloe quickly climbed out of the car and walked over to the boat, smiling happily as she walked across the gang way and onto the boat.

"Hello, I'm Erik." the boat driver told them, holding out his hand for them to shake.

"I'm Chloe." Chloe smiled.

"Lee." he told him.

"So, have you seen Killer Whales before?" Erik asked, as he started the boat and pulled out of the harbour.

"No never, but I've always wanted too." Chloe said excitedly.

"It's a magical experience." Erik smiled at her.

"I can imagine, they are supposed to be really intelligent as well aren't they." Chloe smiled, as she sat on the edge of the boat, peering over the edge excitedly, desperately hoping that she would get to see the whales.

"Indeed, they are." Erik smiled at her infectious excitement.

"I heard that they have an extra part of the brain that has developed to process emotions, so they are actually more emotional than we are." Chloe continued.

"Really?" Lee frowned, trying to join in with the conversation. Chloe nodded slowly, finally falling silent.

"Depending on which pod we see, there's one particular pod that one of the whales is really friendly and quite often comes up to the boat." Erik told them.

"Wow." Chloe breathed, feeling even more excited than before.

"That would be amazing." she added. Chloe glanced at Lee as she felt him watching her closely.

"What?" she asked.

"You're just really cute." he smiled. Chloe's cheeks coloured as she quickly looked away from him and returned to staring out at the ocean.

"Is that them over there?!" Chloe squealed excitedly, as she pointed towards the horizon, her heart soaring as she saw a collection of fins rising out of the water. Erik followed the direction she was pointing, nodding quickly. Chloe fell silent as she gazed in wonder at the whales, not quite able to believe how close she was to them.

"Oh, here comes Lillian." Erik told them, smiling down at one of the whales that swam over to the boat and stared up at them. Chloe smiled down at her as she sat mere inches from a Killer Whale, not quite able to believe how close she was to it.

"Lillian is such a sweet name for her." Lee smiled.

"She'll probably let you stroke her." Erik told them.

Chloe smiled as she gazed into Lillian's eyes, gasping slightly as she made a series of clicking noises at her, trying to communicate. She carefully placed her hand on Lillian's head, a small sob escaping her lips as she stared at her. She couldn't help but feel like Lillian was gazing into her soul and was able to see just how broken Chloe was. Erik and Lee watched Chloe closely as she began to sob quietly, tears streaming down her face as she softly rested the side of her head against Lillian's.

"Be careful Chlo." Lee said quickly, feeling slightly nervous that Lillian might do something to hurt Chloe.

"I don't care if she eats me." Chloe said, breathlessly, unable to stop the sobs that were escaping her lips, her whole body shaking with the effort. Erik glanced at Lee, slightly confused as to what was going on.

Lee stared at Chloe, unable to take his eyes off her as he watched her pouring out her soul. He couldn't help but feel guilty that Chloe clearly felt more comfortable letting down her barriers to a whale than to him. He knew that it was his fault, he was the one who had pushed her away so much that she now didn't want to come back to him. Lee quickly walked down the end of the boat, no longer able to watch the woman that he loved sobbing her heart out, when there was nothing that he could do to fix it. As soon as he was at the opposite end of the boat, Lee sat down and placed his head in his hands, his stomach churning with how helpless he felt.

Chloe slowly sat up, her cheeks colouring slightly when she noticed Erik watching her closely, a look of concern on his features.

"I'm really sorry about that." she muttered, not quite able to look him in the eye. He smiled at her reassuringly, not quite sure what to say to her.

"We've had a bereavement recently." she told him, sighing slightly as Lillian swam off to join the rest of the pod. Chloe glanced around the boat when she suddenly realised that Lee was no longer beside her. She sighed to herself when she noticed him sitting at the end of the boat, silently watching the whales.

Even though she was finding it difficult to be around him recently, because he'd pushed her away so much, she couldn't help but feel disappointed in him that she'd broken down in front of him and he didn't even seem to care. He hadn't done a single thing to comfort her or even to check that she was okay. Before everything had happened, he would have done anything to comfort her, but now it was like he didn't even care about her. Clearly, he blamed her so much for the loss of their baby that he had fallen out of love with her but didn't have the courage to end things himself.

"Can we head back please?" Chloe asked Erik. He nodded slowly and quickly turned the boat around. Chloe sat in silence, slowly tracing circles on the decking with her finger, her thoughts in complete turmoil over what to do. All she knew was that she couldn't live like this anymore. As soon as the boat docked in the harbour, Chloe hurried onto the shore, quickly walking towards the jeep. She jumped slightly as she heard the central locking unlock. She glanced behind herself for a moment, sighing quietly when she saw Lee walking behind her.

The two of them remained silent as Lee drove them back to the cabin, neither of them sure what to say to the other. As soon as they reached the cabin, Chloe hurried out of the car and walked towards the cabin, stopping for a moment to allow Lee to walk past her.

"What are you doing?" he asked, turning to face her and frowning as she sat down in the snow.

"You'll freeze to death." he tried when she didn't respond.

"I'll be fine, I need to make a call." she said dismissively, staring at him until he left her alone and went inside.

"Can't you do it inside?" he frowned.

"Nope." she said quietly. Lee remained silent for a moment, slightly confused as to why she was acting so strangely.

"Shall I get you a blanket and make a hot chocolate then?" he offered.

"Yep, do that." she snapped, breathing a sigh of relief when Lee nodded and reluctantly walked away from her.

As soon as he closed the door behind him, Chloe quickly pulled out her phone and called Kirstie.

"Hey, how's Norway?!" Kirstie said excitedly as soon as she picked up.

"I don't have much time, my phone is low on battery, but I need you to do me a favour." Chloe told her.

"Yeah sure." Kirstie said worriedly. She could tell from Chloe's voice that something was wrong.

"Can you book me an earlier flight please?" Chloe asked.

"We don't get internet here, otherwise I would do it." she added.

"Oh no Chloe, is it that bad?" Kirstie sighed.

"I just want to come home." Chloe said, her eyes filling with tears.

"Why, what's happened?" Kirstie asked.

"Things are just too far gone." Chloe said quietly.

"I got more comfort from a whale than I do from him." Chloe said.

"There's no point in being here, he clearly doesn't love me anymore." she continued, letting out a small sob.

"Of course, he does Chloe." Kirstie sighed, wishing that she was beside Chloe so that she could provide her with some comfort.

"Can you just book the flight please; I'll pay you back when I get home?" Chloe said quickly.

"I need to get home and start packing." she continued.

"Where are you going to go?" Kirstie asked worriedly.

"I'll stay at a hotel or something for a few days until I get my own place." Chloe said, quickly wiping away the tears that were steadily flowing down her cheeks.

"You're welcome to stay with us." Kirstie offered.

"No, it's okay, I don't want to intrude, I could probably stay with Nathan anyway if I can't get a hotel since it's a bit last minute and I don't have a car." Chloe explained.

Kirstie sighed quietly to herself as she listened to Chloe. It was clear that she was trying to be efficient and organize everything in an ill-conceived attempt to hide how upset she really was.

"Okay well, I'll ask Ben to pick you up from the airport." Kirstie told her. Chloe frowned, quickly taking her phone away from her ear and glancing down at it when she heard it beeping.

"My battery is about to die." Chloe told Kirstie when she returned the phone to her ear.

"Okay, I'll text you the flight details once I've booked it." Kirstie told her.

"Thank you." Chloe said before quickly hanging up. Chloe gasped and turned around as she heard glass smashing from behind her. Her heart plummeted when she locked eyes with Lee....

Chapter Seventy-Nine

Lee sighed sadly as he slowly poured water onto Chloe's hot chocolate and picked up a blanket. He couldn't help but wonder what was so important that she had to make a phone call outside in the cold. He frowned to himself as he walked towards the front door of the cabin, trying not to listen to Chloe's words, but not quite able to help himself.

"Things are just too far gone." Chloe said quietly.

"I got more comfort from a whale than I do from him." Chloe said.

"There's no point in being here, he clearly doesn't love me anymore." she continued, letting out a small sob.

Lee gasped as he heard her words. He slowly opened the door, staring at her silently, not quite sure how to process what he'd just heard. How could Chloe possibly think that he didn't love her anymore?

She was the most important person in his life and meant the world to him. He felt a pang of guilt when he realised that he had pushed her further away than he'd thought, so much so that she was doubting his feelings for her. Lee was snapped out of his thoughts when Chloe continued speaking:

"Can you just book the flight please; I'll pay you back when I get home?" Chloe said quickly.

"I need to get home and start packing." she continued.

"I'll stay at a hotel or something for a few days until I get my own place." Chloe said, quickly wiping away the tears that were steadily flowing down her cheeks.

As soon as Lee heard her words, it felt like someone was stabbing him in the chest repeatedly, like there was a knife between his ribs that was slowly being twisted.

He'd never thought about a life without her by his side, without being able to hold her in his arms. Lee's hands shook as he suddenly realised the enormity of the situation, reality finally setting in that he was about to lose Chloe forever. He gasped, watching helplessly as the mug of hot chocolate fell to the floor. Lee glanced up, locking eyes with Chloe as she turned to face him, her cheeks colouring when she saw him standing on the doorstep.

Chloe felt a pang of guilt as she locked eyes with Lee and saw the expression on his face. In all the years that she'd known him, she'd never seen him looking so sad and scared at the same time.

"I was going to tell you." she said quietly, feeling slightly guilty that he'd overheard her conversation.

"Tell me what?" he muttered, still not quite able to process what was going on.

"That I'm going home." she told him, slowly standing up and brushing the snow off her trousers. Lee watched her as she carefully walked past him into the cabin.

"And then when I get home, I'm moving out of your house." she added.

"You're leaving me?" he asked nervously as he followed her into the bedroom.

"I don't want too, but I don't know what else to do, neither of us are happy." she told him, her eyes filling with tears as she thought about life without him. Lee remained silent, watching her closely. Chloe gasped as Lee suddenly dropped to his knees in front of her, his legs finally buckling from under him. Before Chloe could react, Lee wrapped his arms around her legs, holding her tightly, almost as if he didn't want to ever let her go.

"I'm already broken Chloe; I can't lose you as well." he whispered. Chloe watched in horror as he sobbed his heart out, still clinging tightly to her legs. Warm tears rolled down Chloe's cheeks as she watched Lee completely breaking down in front of her. His sobs filled with such anguish that she felt her heart breaking for him. She'd never even seen him cry before, let alone break down. Chloe placed her hands on his arms, trying to extract herself from his tight grasp.

"Let go a minute." she said softly.

"I can't." he said breathlessly, fighting to get his breath back as he continued to sob.

"Please don't go." he whispered sadly when he finally stopped sobbing. As soon as Lee loosened his grip slightly, Chloe slowly knelt beside him, watching him closely as he slowly lifted his head to look at her. She couldn't help but feel a pang of guilt that she was clearly breaking his heart. Even though she thought he didn't love her anymore, she could clearly see that wasn't the case. She'd never seen him so devastated. She carefully wrapped her arms around his neck and pulled him close, sighing to herself as she held his head against her chest, softly stroking his hair to calm him down.

"I'm sorry." she whispered, suddenly feeling another wave of guilt wash over her that she was hurting him.

"You have nothing to be sorry for, this is all my fault." he muttered against her chest. Lee sighed sadly as Chloe held him tightly, slowly stroking his hair.

"What can I do to fix things?" he said quietly, finally asking the question he'd been dying to know the answer too for the past few days.

"I don't know." she said quietly.

"Maybe if we talk about everything and see what happens?" she suggested quietly. Lee nodded. Chloe glanced down at him as he slowly raised his head from her chest, and gently rested his head against her forehead, sighing quietly as he gazed down at her lips. Chloe flinched slightly as he placed a soft kiss on her lips.

"What is it?" he asked her when she gasped quietly.

"I forgot how good it feels when you kiss me." she admitted quietly. Lee smiled slightly, closing his eyes and sighing in contentment as he inhaled her familiar scent.

"I am so sorry for everything, I never wanted to hurt you." he said quietly. Chloe sighed and sat back, watching him closely as he wiped away his tears.

"I know." she whispered.

"I was just so angry about what happened." he admitted.

"And you blame me." she said sadly.

"No I...." he started.

"I know that it was my fault, you didn't need to remind me." she interrupted.

"It's not your fault." he said quickly.

"Of course, it is, I'll carry the guilt for the rest of my life." she told him, her eyes slowly filling with tears.

"It's not your fault." he repeated sternly, his heart breaking a little at the thought of her feeling guilty for something that was beyond her control.

"I will never forgive myself for saying that it was your fault." he added. Chloe nodded slowly, wiping away the tears that were rolling down her cheeks.

"I don't even remember that night to be honest." he told her.

"What night?" she frowned.

"The night you came to find me in the club. Nathan told me what happened afterwards and what I said to you and I was so mortified that I ended up getting drunk again." he explained.

"And then you missed the hospital appointment." she said quietly.

"I know." he muttered.

"I am so sorry about that." he added. Chloe nodded slowly.

"I've never felt as alone as I have these past few weeks." she told him, feeling slightly guilty that she was adding to the guilt that he was already feeling, but she knew that for their relationship to have any chance of being saved, she needed to be completely honest with him.

"And when something like this happens you need to pull together, we could have taken care of each other, but you wouldn't let me." she continued.

"I know, I've just been struggling with all of the emotions, and I pushed you away, not because I blamed you but because you were a constant reminder of the guilt that I was feeling for what I'd said." he explained.

"But then it became a viscous circle because I pushed you away more to avoid feeling even more guilt, but then I felt worse because I knew that you needed me." he continued.

"And I wasn't even strong enough to take care of myself, let alone you." he said quietly.

"You don't need to take care of me all the time, we should take care of each other." she sighed, Lee's words from the night in the club swirling around her head as she remembered how he'd told her that she couldn't even take care of their baby.

"Don't cry." he said sadly. Chloe sighed and slowly wiped away her tears.

"I know how attached you were to the baby and I just wanted to take care of you, like you always do me." she admitted sadly. Lee swallowed the lump that was rising in his throat as he thought about their baby and how he would do anything to bring their baby back.

"And I am so sorry that I lost your baby." Chloe said, letting out a small sob as she fell forwards, resting her forehead against his shoulder. Lee carefully wrapped his arms around her small frame, holding her tightly.

"You didn't do anything wrong; I am so sorry I said that it was your fault, I'll never be able to take that back." he whispered in her ear, gently stroking her hair.

"I was feeling guilty before you said what you did. I feel like you have done so much for me over the past few months and when I needed to step up, I couldn't even protect your baby." she explained, snuggling her head against his collarbone, cherishing the feel of being in his arms and suddenly realising just how much she had missed him.

Chloe glanced up at Lee as he carefully picked her up and carried her over to the bed. As soon as he carefully set her down, she curled up beside him, snuggling into his chest. Lee curled up against her, gently resting his head on top of hers, sighing in contentment as he inhaled her familiar scent.

"The baby was ours not just mine, I should have protected you both better." he sighed quietly, his eyes filling with tears. Lee sighed as he heard Chloe sniff. He snuggled his head against hers.

"I made you a promise and I didn't keep it." he whispered.

"It's not your fault, you did everything you could." she muttered, glancing up at Lee as she felt his warm tears falling against her face.

"Maybe we both need to stop blaming ourselves." Chloe said quietly.

"I just want our baby back Chlo." Lee whispered, closing his eyes as the exhaustion finally set in.

"Me too." she agreed, sighing deeply.

Chapter Eighty

Lee frowned to himself as he slowly opened his eyes and realised that Chloe was no longer curled up in his arms. He quickly sat up and switched on the lamp, starting to panic slightly that maybe she had left him during the night. His heart pounded against his chest as he quickly climbed out of bed. Lee breathed a sigh of relief when he saw Chloe sitting outside on the bedroom balcony, silently watching the sun rise over the fjord. He quickly pulled the blanket off the bed and walked over to her. Chloe turned and smiled at Lee as he gently placed the blanket around her shoulders and sat beside her.

"What are you doing out here?" he asked her softly.

"I don't sleep much anymore." she said quietly.

"It's so beautiful here." Chloe breathed, trying to change the subject, her eyes fixed on the sun that was slowly rising above the mountains.

"You'll be sad to leave here won't you." he said, smiling slightly when he noticed how relaxed Chloe seemed, despite everything that had happened. Chloe nodded slowly.

"Speaking of which, what time is your flight home?" he asked her nervously, feeling sick to his stomach once again when he thought about losing her.

"I texted Kirstie when I woke up and told her that I'm staying." Chloe told him, smiling slightly when she saw Lee take a deep sigh of relief.

"So, you're not leaving me?" he asked, his heart pounding against his chest.

"No, I never wanted to leave you, I just thought that you didn't want me around anymore but didn't want to say." she explained.

"Of course, I want you around." he told her.

"And I'm sorry I made you feel like I didn't." he quickly added.

"You don't have to keep apologising." she said quietly.

"Just promise me something." she said quietly. Lee nodded slowly and waited for her to continue.

"You can't keep pushing me away all the time, you did it when you found out that I was pregnant and when you realised that you had strong feelings for me. It can't be a case of whenever anything happens in our lives you pull back from me every time. If you open up to me about things, then hopefully we won't find ourselves in a similar situation again." she explained.

"Okay I promise, and I promise that I'll never hurt you again." he told her. Chloe nodded slowly, not entirely sure if she believed him or not. She couldn't help but remember the last time he'd said those words to her, back when they first got together and yet he'd pushed her away yet again.

Even though she knew it was as a result of grief, that didn't stop the hurt that she was feeling. Chloe nodded slowly, sighing quietly to herself.

"We can come back from this can't we Chlo?" he asked, sensing her trepidation.

"I think so." she said quietly. Chloe glanced at Lee for a moment when she suddenly noticed that he was shivering. She quickly moved the blanket so that it was wrapped around the two of them, sighing quietly to herself as she rested the side of her head on his shoulder. Lee gazed down at her longingly, desperately wishing once again that he could turn the clock back and change the way that he'd treated her. Chloe slowly lifted her head when she felt him watching her, her cheeks colouring as she made eye contact with him.

"I love you so much Chlo." he whispered, suddenly feeling slightly emotional. Chloe's eyes flickered to his lips as he slowly moved towards her, almost like he was nervous.

Her heart pounded against her chest as Lee placed his hands on her neck and kissed her lips softly. Chloe sighed quietly when they eventually pulled apart, suddenly realising how much she had missed being close to him. Even though there was a small part of her that didn't trust him as much as before, he still meant the world to her.

"What do you want to do today?" he asked her softly, staring down at her lovingly as she rested the side of her head against his shoulder.

"Maybe we could go exploring, there's a forest over there." Chloe suggested, pointing to the forest in front of the fjord. Lee nodded slowly, gently resting his head against hers.

Chloe smiled at Lee as he took her hand and squeezed it gently. She couldn't help but gaze in wonder as they walked through the forest, the small beads of sunlight illuminating the fir trees.

"Mum and I used to come to the woods quite a lot, we collected pinecones to make decorations." she told him, smiling when she thought about her Mum and how much fun the two of them had together over the years. Lee glanced at Chloe when she let go of his hand, leaning down and picking up a handful of pinecones.

"She was very particular about the shape they had to be though." she chuckled. Chloe quickly put down the pinecones, smiling up at Lee when she noticed him watching her closely.

"Sorry, I'm being a boring nerd again." she said quietly.

"No, you're being adorable." he smiled at her. He smiled slightly when he noticed her cheeks colouring.

"Here looks like a good spot." he added, throwing himself onto the ground, smiling at Chloe as she sat beside him, crossing her legs. Lee watched her closely as she sat in silence, picking at the pinecone in her hand. He couldn't help but feel another pang of guilt when he was reminded once again that it was his actions that had made things awkward between them.

"Chlo, you know that night you came to find me in the club?" he asked tentatively. Chloe nodded slowly.   '

"Nathan said that Shayne was there." he tried, a lump rising in his throat as he thought about Shayne being anywhere near Chloe.

"Yes, you almost got into a fight with him." she told him. Lee frowned in confusion.

"Don't you remember anything from that night?" she frowned. Lee shook his head slowly. He kept his eyes fixed on Chloe, as she remained silent.

"He didn't touch you, did he?" he asked nervously, his heart pounding against his chest as he waited for her to reply.

"No." she said quietly, glancing at Lee as he heard him breath a deep sigh of relief.

"Oh, actually he stroked my hair, but that was just to annoy you I think." she added when she suddenly remembered.

"And you didn't see him after I left you?" he checked.

"No, I walked home." she replied.

"You walked home?!" he exclaimed in horror, his stomach churning at the thought of Chloe walking home, alone, in the dark.

"Only because I didn't want to wait around outside the club for a taxi when Shayne was around." she explained. Lee sighed and shook his head slowly. He placed his hands on either side of her face, his eyes filling with tears as he thought about the situation that he'd inadvertently put her in and what could have potentially happened as a result. Lee's eyes filled with tears as he gently rested his forehead against hers.

"If something had happened to you it would have been my fault." he said softly, feeling sick with guilt.

"Nothing happened, I'm fine." she reassured him.

"What if he'd hurt you Chlo." he whispered.

"He didn't, I'm fine." she told him firmly, feeling slightly sorry for him that he was clearly racked with guilt.

"Besides he probably doesn't want me anymore, he just likes to wind you up." she added, gently wrapping her arms around his neck.

"I don't believe that for a second." he said quickly.

"Don't underestimate him Chlo." he added.

"Didn't Matt tell you that he tried to take advantage of a lot of other women as well?" he asked her, gently resting the side of his head on her shoulder.

"He mentioned it briefly." she said quietly. Chloe glanced at him, as she heard him sniff quietly.

"It's okay, he didn't hurt me." she said gently, placing a soft kiss on his forehead.

"I just feel like I've let you down." he muttered.

"I have, haven't I?" he asked when she didn't respond. Chloe thought for a moment, trying to decide how to answer his question. Even though she knew that she was going to cause him to feel even more guilty than he already did, she knew that she had to tell him the truth.

"Kind of, but I understand why." she said, trying to be diplomatic and avoid telling him how much she was still hurting because of his actions.

"I still can't believe I missed your hospital appointment." he added thoughtfully, disregarding what Chloe had just said.

"Was it okay?" he asked.

"Well obviously it wasn't fun." she told him.

"Tell me." he prompted.

"They just gave me a check-up to see if everything had progressed as it should and gave me some iron tablets because I was a bit anaemic again and you bleed for three weeks." she explained, her eyes filling with tears when she remembered being alone in the hospital. Flashbacks swirled around her head to when she was sitting with the doctor and the full realisation finally hit her, she remembered how she'd turned behind her, seeking some comfort from Lee, only to be reminded that he wasn't with her.

"I will never forgive myself for not being there with you." he said quietly.

"There's no point dwelling on it though, it's done now." she sighed, trying to fight the tears that were filling her eyes. The last thing she wanted to do was to keep talking about the hurt that she was feeling because he'd let her down. She preferred to sweep everything that happened under the carpet and not think about it. She knew that if it hadn't been for the loss of their baby, Lee wouldn't have treated her the way that he did. It was purely as a result of the intense grief that he had been feeling. In her heart she knew that she still loved him deeply, but it would take time for her to forgive him and trust him fully again.

"I am really sorry." he told her.

"Can we get back to having a nice day please?" she asked quickly. Lee nodded and sighed quietly. He knew in his heart that Chloe hadn't forgiven him for what he'd done, and she was trying to carry on as normal in the hope that the cracks he'd caused would eventually fill themselves. Lee knew that there was still a risk that he would lose Chloe as a result of his actions and he was determined not to let that happen.

"We could have a race." he suggested, quickly standing up and reaching out his hand to Chloe.

"Are you serious, I don't stand a chance!" she giggled, taking his hand and laughing as he gently pulled her to her feet.

"I could give you a head start." he laughed, winking at her.

"I don't need a head start." she giggled, glaring at him defiantly.

"Right, are you ready then?" he asked, laughing as she braced herself. Chloe nodded determinedly. She smiled to herself as Lee bolted away. As soon as he was in front of her, she quickly turned around and ran as fast as she could in the opposite direction. Lee glanced behind himself as he ran, frowning in confusion when he realised that he couldn't see Chloe. He stopped dead in his tracks and turned around, worried that Chloe might have fallen over. He burst out laughing as he saw Chloe running in the opposite direction. He quickly turned around and ran after her. Chloe giggled as she heard Lee running up behind her. As soon as he reached her, he wrapped his arms around her and picked her up. Chloe squealed and burst out laughing as he spun her around playfully.

"You cheated." he laughed, carefully setting her down.

"You didn't specify which direction we were racing in." she giggled.

"Very clever." he smiled. Chloe glanced down at his hands as he placed them on her hips and gently pulled her close. He kissed her deeply, finally able to give into the deep longing that he was feeling for her. Chloe threw her head back, gasping quietly as he placed a series of soft kisses along her jaw, slowly making his way down to her neck. She smiled mischievously to herself as she slowly turned her back on him and pressed her body against his. Lee rested his chin on her shoulder, placing his hands under the material of her shirt and gently caressing her soft skin. Chloe slowly rotated her hips, smiling to herself when she heard Lee groan in her ear. She smiled in satisfaction and continued to rotate her hips, her heart pounding as she listened to Lee groaning in pleasure. Lee placed his hands on her hips, pressing her body against him tightly, closing his eyes.

He placed his hand on her back, grasping the material of her shirt in his fist, needing to hold onto something as he felt the pressure building.

"I want to be inside you Chlo." he whispered in her ear.

"We can't, not here." she told him firmly. Lee groaned and collapsed against her as he finally released.

"God, I taught you well didn't I." he whispered. Chloe shivered involuntarily as she felt his warm breath on her neck.

"I need you so bad Chlo." he said quietly, placing his hands under her shirt and softly stroking her abdomen. Chloe slowly turned around to face him, smiling slightly when she saw the longing in his eyes. Her skin tingled as his hands slowly made their way upwards, gently resting in place on the sides of her bra.

"We're not having sex in the woods." she told him sternly, a slight smile playing on the corner of her lips.

"It worked out well for Ben and Kirstie." he grinned.

"I don't care." she giggled. Lee smiled slightly.

"It turns me on more when you get feisty." he laughed. Chloe giggled, her cheeks colouring.

"We need to go back to the cabin." he told her quickly.

"Not yet I want to carry on hiking." she told him.

"There's a bit of woodland along there, that I haven't seen yet." she said, pointing along the trail, a small smile playing on the corner of her lips when she noticed Lee's incredulous expression.

"Chloe." he whined.

"What?" she asked innocently. Lee stared at her as she slowly walked away from him, making her way along the trail. He smiled at her when she turned to face him.

"I was actually joking." she laughed, raising her eyebrow at him. Before Chloe could react, Lee rushed over to her and picked her up in a fireman lift.

"I am quite capable of walking." she laughed.

"Yeah, but this is quicker." he laughed.

Chapter Eighty-One

Lee reluctantly placed Chloe back on the ground, when after what felt like an age, they finally reached the cabin. Chloe quickly walked into the kitchen and rummaged in the fridge, smiling in satisfaction when she found the bottle of wine. Lee watched her as she poured them both a glass and handed him one. He frowned to himself as she took a sip and he noticed that her hands were shaking.

"Are you alright Chlo?" he asked her softly. Chloe sighed quietly to herself, not entirely sure how to tell him how she was feeling. When he'd carried her back to the lodge, she hadn't been able to stop thinking about the fact that he hadn't been near her for the past few weeks. Doubts were swirling around her head; she knew how highly sexed he was, and she couldn't help but worry that he might not have stayed faithful to her.

"Chloe?" Lee tried again when she didn't respond.

"I need to ask you something." she said quietly, feeling slightly awkward.

"Okay." he said nervously.

"Well obviously, we haven't done anything for a few weeks, and I know that you have a high sex drive....so...have you been going elsewhere?" she asked.

Lee stared at her, not quite able to believe that she was asking him if he had cheated on her.

"Also, you've been going out clubbing a lot...so you've probably had a lot of temptation." Chloe rambled, becoming more and more nervous with every moment that passed. She couldn't help but feel afraid of Lee's answer, as she watched him staring at her silently. Chloe knew that if he ever cheated on her, there would be no going back, she wouldn't be able to forgive him and they would be over for good.

"I haven't cheated on you Chloe." he eventually said, feeling slightly hurt that she even had to ask.

"Are you sure, what if you did but you don't remember it?" she checked.

"Do you not understand my love for you at all?" he sighed.

"I don't want anyone else." he added quietly.

"You don't have to say things like that just to reassure me." she said quietly.

"Chloe, I've fallen so hard for you, my heart literally belongs to you." he told her quickly. Chloe smiled slightly, finally releasing the breath that she didn't realise she was holding.

"From the moment I realised that I was in love with you, which was when I saw you laying in that hospital bed, I haven't wanted anyone except you." he added.

"Is that why you wouldn't go out and find someone that night I overheard you and Ben talking?" she asked.

"Yeah, I was actually talking to him about you." he told her.

"Really?" she frowned.

"About how much I wanted you." he said, smiling fondly as he remembered all the time that he'd spent taking care of Chloe when she was recovering and how he'd cherished every moment that he'd spent by her side.

"In fact, there was one time that a woman I took home slapped me." he laughed, trying to lighten the atmosphere.

"Why, what did you do?" she chuckled.

"It was after I kissed you at that gig, I started fantasizing about you again, so much so that I accidentally called her *Chloe* during sex." he said, smiling slightly. Chloe burst out laughing.

"I'm not surprised she slapped you." she laughed.

"Yeah, I kind of deserved it." he laughed. Chloe smiled and walked over to Lee, perching on his lap and sighing deeply when he wrapped his arms around her waist and held her tightly. She brushed her hair to one side, smiling slightly when Lee began to kiss her neck softly.

"I love you." he whispered softly in her ear. Chloe reached over and picked up her glass of wine, quickly downing it. Lee gently stroked the stray hairs off her neck, smiling slightly when she shivered.

"Are you trying to get drunk?" he chuckled, when she quickly poured herself another glass.

"No." she laughed.

"I've never actually seen you drunk before have I?" he frowned. Chloe shook her head, turning to face him and smiling at him cheekily as she took another deep gulp.

"It's probably for the best, I get quite wild." she giggled.

"Really, I'm intrigued now?" he said, raising his eyebrow at her.

"I tend to make sure that I only get drunk when I have someone with me that is sober enough to stop me doing stupid things." she laughed.

"If you want to get drunk, I can keep an eye on you." he offered.

"No, it's fine." she said quickly. Lee frowned at her as she quickly put down the wine glass and pushed it away from her so that she wouldn't be tempted.

"Surely you trust me to keep an eye on you?" he frowned at her.

"It's fine, I don't want to get drunk." she said dismissively. Lee stared at her, not entirely sure how to process what was happening. He couldn't help but feel like Chloe no longer trusted him to take care of her.

"You do trust me to take care of you, don't you?" he asked nervously.

"Kind of." she sighed, realising that he wasn't going to drop the subject.

"I'm just afraid that you are going to push me away again that's all." she explained when she noticed how hurt he looked.

"I know, I need to rebuild your trust." he agreed.

"I'm probably just being insecure again." she said quietly.

"No, you're not. It's my fault, I'm sorry I made you feel so unloved." he said softly.

"It's okay, I understand that you were hurting." she said, gently placing a kiss on his forehead. Lee smiled at Chloe as she carefully climbed off his lap and held out her hand to him.

"Where are we going?" he frowned, taking her hand and slowly standing up.

"We need to finish what we started in the woods." she said, smiling at him.

"You did remember to take the pill, didn't you?" he asked her as she led him into the bedroom. Chloe nodded slowly.

"Remind me not to go that long without making love to you again." Lee said breathlessly, carefully resting his head against Chloe's chest. Chloe wrapped her arm around his head and softly stroked his hair.

"I don't think you will forget." Chloe said quietly.

"No probably not." he smiled. Chloe sighed quietly to herself as she closed her eyes tightly. Her heart was still pounding against her chest as she thought about how grateful she was that Lee had finally come back to her. The last few hours that the two of them had spent making love to each other, had reminded Chloe once again, of how much she loved Lee. Even though there was a small part of her that didn't trust him a hundred percent, she knew that it was just a result of fear that he was going to push her away once again, and she knew that her heart couldn't take it again. Chloe glanced at Lee as he slowly sat up.

"I need to shower." he told her.

"Do you want me to pass you my hoodie?" he offered, smiling slightly to himself when he remembered how much Chloe liked to curl up in his hoodie.

"What hoodie?" she frowned.

"My one from Eclipse's last tour, that you always wear." he said.

"I didn't bring it." she told him.

"Really?" he frowned in confusion. He knew how much Chloe liked wearing his hoodie, so he couldn't understand why she would decide to leave it at home. Chloe shrugged as she quickly stood up and pulled on her pyjamas. Lee thought for a moment, before deciding not to press her. He knew that he had a lot to make up to her and could only hope that she wouldn't decide to leave him before he'd had the chance to show her how sorry he was.

Chloe quickly climbed back into bed and snuggled down under the covers, glancing up at Lee as he walked into the bathroom. As soon as Chloe was alone, she pulled down the sleeves on her pyjamas so that they covered her hands, carefully picking at them with her fingernails. She slowly wiped away the tears that were steadily flowing down her cheeks. Whenever she was alone, her thoughts always wandered to their baby and how it had felt to lose a part of them. She quickly reached over and flicked off the lamp, so that Lee wouldn't notice her tears when he emerged from the bathroom.

Lee frowned to himself when he emerged from the bathroom and he noticed Chloe quickly wiping away her tears. He quickly climbed into bed beside her and placed his chin on her shoulder.

"Come here Chlo." he said softly. Chloe slowly turned over and snuggled into his arms. She heard Lee sigh quietly as he held her tightly. Lee placed a soft kiss on the top of her head, before resting his head against hers, his heart breaking slightly at seeing her hurting.

"I remember Mum told me once that when you lose a baby you are never whole again." she said quietly. Lee glanced down at her as she slowly lifted her head to look at him. "And I think she was right." she continued.

"Yeah probably." he agreed.

"Try and get some sleep Chlo." he added sadly. Chloe sighed quietly, wiping away the last of her tears and snuggling into Lee, smiling slightly when she felt him wrap his arms around her and hold her tightly.

Chloe jumped and quickly opened her eyes as she felt Lee pull her into his arms and squeeze her tightly. She frowned to herself when she felt his heart pounding against her back and his warm tears against her cheek. She switched on the lamp and glanced behind her at Lee, frowning slightly when she saw how scared he looked.

"What's wrong?" she asked quickly, feeling slightly nervous about his answer. He remained silent, watching her closely as she turned over to face him. Lee slowly reached out and tucked her hair behind her ear, his hands trembling slightly as he thought about his nightmare.

"Lee, what's going on?" Chloe asked worriedly when she noticed that his hands were shaking.

"I had a bad dream." he told her, taking deep breaths to try and steady his nerves. Before Chloe could respond, he wrapped his hands around her waist and held her tightly against himself.

"Whatever it was, it was just a dream." she told him softly, wrapping her arms around his neck and gently stroking his hair.

"It was horrible, it felt so real." he whispered in her ear.

"Do you want to talk about it?" she asked him gently.

"It was about Shayne, I think it was because we were speaking about him earlier." he sighed, closing his eyes for a moment, wishing that the images that were swirling around his head would desist.

"He raped you in front of me, and there wasn't a damn thing I could do about it." he continued, his voice breaking slightly. Chloe gasped slightly as Lee squeezed her even tighter.

"It's okay, it was just a dream." she whispered when she heard him sniff. Chloe sighed when she realised that Lee was crying quietly. Even though she knew he was upset because of his nightmare, she couldn't help but think that his reaction to it was as a result of the guilt he was feeling for the way he'd treated her and the fact that he was still devastated by the loss of their baby.

"He wouldn't do that anyway, he just got carried away that night." Chloe said quietly, trying to reassure him.

"You're right, he wouldn't do it, because he knows I'd fucking kill him." Lee said menacingly. Chloe's heart fluttered slightly as he said those words. She'd always loved how protective Lee was of her and the fact that she knew he would do anything for her. Chloe carefully removed herself from Lee's arms and gazed at him.

"It was just a bad dream, I'm okay." she told him, carefully stroking his face with her fingertips, trying to provide him with some comfort. Lee closed his eyes and sighed in contentment.

"I know, I'm sorry I woke you. It just really scared me." he said quietly.

"It's fine." she told him.

"Although I'm kind of wide awake now." she said, smiling slightly.

"Me too." he admitted.

"I'm sure we can find something to do." she smiled cheekily, raising her eyebrow at him. Lee smiled at her as she sat up and slowly removed her pyjama top, maintaining eye contact with him the entire time.

"You're getting worse than me." he laughed.

Chapter Eighty-Two

"Hey lovebirds!" Ben exclaimed as Chloe and Lee sat opposite him and Kirstie at the beach cafe.

"Hi, how's it going?" Lee asked.

"Things are amazing." Kirstie beamed, smiling at Ben as he gently wrapped his arm around her shoulders.

"How about you guys, how was Norway?" Kirstie asked.

"It was good, we aired a lot of things and said a lot of things that needed to be said didn't we." Lee said, glancing at Chloe who nodded slowly.

"It's such a beautiful place, words can't even describe it." Chloe breathed, smiling slightly when she remembered how relaxed she had felt being in those surroundings.

"You didn't want to come home, did you?" Lee smiled at her.

"Nope, we've only been home a few days and I want to go back." Chloe admitted.

"And seeing the Killer Whales was an amazing experience." Chloe added.

"Did you see the Polar Bears, like you've always wanted too?" Kirstie asked. Chloe shook her head slowly.

"It was a last-minute break so there were no spaces left on the Polar Bear trips." Lee explained.

"You can go back and do that next time though can't you." Ben smiled.

"Well, I was actually going to suggest that maybe after the tour is over, I take a few months out from the band and we go and live there for a bit?" Lee suggested, watching Chloe closely.

"Really?" Chloe frowned.

"Yeah, you were so at home there, I liked seeing you happy." Lee told her.

"You would really do that?!" Chloe said excitedly.

"It seems only fair, we do the tour and then we have a bit of time just me and you, doing something that makes you happy." Lee said.

"As long as the boys don't mind." Chloe said quietly.

"They won't, we were speaking the other day about taking some time off after the tour anyway." Lee told her, smiling slightly when he saw her eyes light up at the thought of going back to Norway. Chloe leaned towards Lee and placed a soft kiss on his lips. Chloe's cheeks coloured as a waitress appeared at the table to take their order.

"I need to use the loo." Lee said as soon as the four of them had placed their orders.

"Are the two of you back on track now?" Kirstie asked as soon as Lee walked away.

"Kind of." Chloe said quietly.

"It's so painful when you lose a baby, we're both just trying to get through each day." Chloe added.

"And he feels so guilty for pushing me away, but I do get it, even though it hurt." she continued. Kirstie nodded slowly. She couldn't help but feel like Chloe still hadn't fully forgiven Lee for his behaviour towards her.

"I think the two of you will be okay." Ben smiled at her.

"It just takes time." Kirstie agreed. Chloe nodded in agreement.

"Even though, it's been a difficult few months, I know how lucky I am to have him." Chloe said, glancing up as she saw Lee walking back towards the table.

"He's lucky to have you too, I would say." Kirstie smiled at her.

"I can't believe it's Christmas in a few weeks." Ben said, quickly changing the subject as Lee approached the table and quickly sat down.

"I know, I just love Christmas." Kirstie smiled.

"What are your plans?" Lee asked, glancing up at the waitress when she returned and handed out their food.

"We were thinking of having a quiet dinner just the two of us since it's our first Christmas together." Ben said, smiling at Kirstie fondly.

"We'll probably need to go and see both of our Mum's at some point too." Kirstie said, smiling back at him, her stomach swirling with excitement as she thought about their first Christmas together.

"What are you guys doing?" Ben asked, reluctantly tearing his eyes away from Kirstie and turning to face Chloe and Lee.

"We haven't spoken about it, yet have we?" Lee said, turning to Chloe.

"No, there's been too much going on." Chloe agreed.

"I normally go to my Mum's, so we can do that if you want?" Lee suggested. Chloe nodded slowly.

"I would like to go and see Danny at some point too. It's horrible being alone in the park at Christmas, watching all the happy people on their Christmas Day walk." Chloe told him. Lee smiled at her, his heart swelling with pride when he realised once again how kind Chloe was.

"Is he still sleeping rough?" Kirstie asked sadly.

"Yes unfortunately. Eclipse haven't released the single he wrote yet, but Matt and I have been trying to sort something so that he gets paid in advance, rather than having to wait for royalties." Chloe explained.

"I did offer him one of the spare rooms, but he didn't want it." Lee told them.

"He's very independent." Chloe said, smiling at Lee. Chloe slowly put down her knife and fork and turned to gaze out of the window. She couldn't help but stare at the beach longingly, as she watched the seawater crashing against the rocks.
"I really want to go on the beach." Chloe admitted.

"It's the middle of winter, it'll be freezing!" Kirstie exclaimed. Chloe shrugged and quickly stood up.

"C'mon, stop being a bunch of wimps." Chloe giggled. Kirstie glanced at Ben who was beaming at her excitedly as he stood, offering Kirstie his hand. She laughed slightly as she took his hand. Lee quickly placed the money for the meal onto the table and stood up, wrapping his arm around Chloe's waist and following her outside.

"Oh my god it's bloody freezing." Kirstie muttered as she sat on the sand and quickly zipped up her jacket.

"Winter is the best time to come to the beach." Chloe said, laughing when she saw Kirstie's incredulous expression.

"Because you pretty much get the beach to yourself." Chloe continued. The three of them watched her as she took a run up along the sand and expertly performed tricks.

Kirstie couldn't help but smile at how much happier Chloe had been since her and Lee had returned from Norway. Even though she knew that the two of them were still hurting from everything they had been through, she could now see a glimmer of happiness in their eyes.

"What do you have against people?" Ben asked Chloe, snapping Kirstie out of her thoughts.

"Nothing, I just don't like crowds." Chloe said.

"But you live in London." Ben laughed.

"It wasn't my choice to move here." Chloe said quietly, sighing to herself when she was reminded of the time that she'd moved to London with her family, as a desperate and futile attempt by her father to save her mother's life. They watched Chloe closely as she quickly pulled off her shoes and socks.

"Are you going in the water?!" Ben exclaimed when he noticed Chloe rolling up her trousers. Chloe nodded quickly.

"You do realise it'll be freezing." Kirstie laughed.

"I'm not going all the way in, it'll be fine." Chloe said. Before any of them could react, Chloe turned on her heel and ran towards the water.

"She's finally gone crazy." Ben laughed as he sat beside Kirstie and wrapped his arm around her shoulders, holding her close when he noticed that she was shivering.

"She gets a bit excitable when she's at the beach." Lee smiled, watching her fondly, his mind wandering to the last time he was at the beach with her, when she'd opened up to him and the other Eclipse boys about her family situation. He couldn't believe how much had changed since then. Lee watched Chloe longingly as she slowly walked into the sea, stopping when the water reached her knees.

Chloe sighed in contentment as she stood, staring out at the ocean, enjoying the feel of the cold water on her legs. She jumped slightly, glancing behind her for a moment when she felt Lee wrap his arms around her waist and hold her tightly. Chloe quickly squirmed out of his arms and turned to face him, smiling cheekily at him.

"What?" he smiled at her, knowing that twinkle in her eyes all too well. She beamed at him and bolted down the beach, Lee laughed, quickly running after her. Chloe squealed as Lee picked her up and spun her around playfully.

"I'm so happy that the two of them are doing okay." Kirstie smiled as she watched Lee and Chloe messing around in the water.

"Me too." Ben agreed.

"They are too cute." Kirstie smiled. She laughed when she saw Chloe jump on Lee's back and wrap her legs around his hips, giggling as Lee supported her legs and ran deeper into the water.

"We have to stop at the chemist on the way home." Kirstie told Ben, eventually tearing her eyes away from Chloe and Lee.

"Why?" Ben frowned.

"Because I'm late." Kirstie told him, glancing at Chloe and Lee nervously, in case they overheard.

"What....*late.... late*?" Ben checked. Kirstie nodded, smiling slightly when she noticed his eyes light up hopefully.

"Oh my god, maybe it's third time lucky." he said excitedly.

"Maybe, don't get too excited though, just in case I'm not." Kirstie said quickly. Ben nodded slowly. Ben glanced down at his phone when he felt it buzzing.

"What is it?" Kirstie asked when she saw Ben gazing down at his phone, his brow furrowing in concern. He silently handed Kirstie his phone. She gasped and clapped her hand over her mouth when she saw what he'd been looking at.

"How are we going to tell them?" Kirstie whispered, her eyes filling with tears as her gaze wandered to Chloe and Lee who were still messing around in the sea.

"I don't know, but I think we need too." Ben said, sighing deeply.

"They've only just started to be happy again." Kirstie said quietly.

"They are going to find out anyway, and it's probably better if it comes from us." Ben pointed out. Kirstie nodded slowly. Ben took a deep breath, getting ready to call Chloe and Lee over.

"Wait!" Kirstie said quickly.

"Just give them a few more minutes." she added.

Chapter Eighty-Three

"Chloe!" Ben reluctantly called out to her a few moments later.

Chloe turned and gazed up the beach when she heard Ben calling her. She reluctantly climbed off Lee's back, smiling up at him as he turned to face her.

"I love you so much." Lee whispered, leaning down and kissing her deeply.

"I love you too." she whispered back.

Lee took her hand as they walked back up the beach towards Ben and Kirstie. Chloe frowned to herself when they reached them, and she noticed that Kirstie's eyes were full of tears.

"What's going on?" Chloe asked nervously, glancing at Ben who was staring silently at the ground, slowly playing with the grains of sand. Ben sighed deeply and picked up his phone.

"The press have photos of the two of you at the airport." Ben told them, holding out his phone so that Chloe could see the pictures.

Chloe's heart plummeted as she gazed at the images of her curled up asleep in Lee's arms as they waited in the departure lounge. She scrolled through the images on Ben's phone, trying to stop her hands from shaking.

"Oh my god." Chloe whispered when she noticed an image of the two of them kissing.

"There's an article too." Ben said reluctantly, his heart breaking a little when he glanced up and saw that Chloe's eyes had filled with tears.

"With only a few weeks to go before Eclipse kick off their tour, band member Lee Knight took a much-needed break from his hectic rehearsal schedule to enjoy a romantic getaway to Norway with a mystery woman.

Known for being a notorious lady's man with an eye for beautiful young models, it came as something of a surprise to discover that his new fling doesn't fit that bracket at all. Dressed casually in jeans and a top she can only be described as a plain jane. Although it was clear that the two of them were enjoying each other's company, it begs the question, how long will it be until Lee moves onto the next in a long line of women that he's been linked too." Ben read.

Chloe quickly let go of Lee's hand and began to slowly step backwards, shaking her head as she tried to process what she'd heard. As soon as she blinked, the tears that she'd been fighting, slowly rolled down her cheeks.

"How the hell did they know where we were?!" Lee exclaimed angrily, his temper starting to rise when he noticed how upset Chloe was.

"I don't know, but obviously someone leaked it." Ben said.

"Your phone has been going mad with notifications, so I'm guessing it's social media." Ben added, gesturing to Lee's jacket that was still on the sand where he'd left it before going to join Chloe in the sea. Lee took a deep breath and quickly pulled on his jacket, slowly pulling his phone out of his pocket, his stomach churning when he saw the hundreds of tweets he'd received from fans, all giving their opinions on Chloe. Chloe watched Lee closely as he stared at his phone, his complexion slowly turning pale. She quickly walked over to him and peered over his shoulder, gasping as she read the selection of posts stating that Lee must be desperate to get with someone who looks like her.

How did someone like her manage to get our gorgeous Lee to take her to Norway.

That moment when you realise that Lee couldn't find a model to go to Norway with him, so he picked some random.

"I think it's safe to say his standards are dropping." Chloe said thoughtfully, not realising that she was speaking aloud.

"Don't read them Chlo." Lee said, snapping out of his trance and quickly pocketing his phone. His heart broke a little when he noticed the steady stream of tears that were rolling down her cheeks. Lee reached out to take her hand, frowning slightly when she quickly moved away from him. Chloe quickly rummaged in Lee's jacket pocket and pulled out his car keys. As soon as she found them, she picked up her shoes and ran towards the car, staggering slightly as she tried to run at full speed on the sand. She winced in pain when she twisted her ankle, but she continued to run, desperately trying to get to Lee's car, so that she could hide from the world.

"I knew this would happen." Lee muttered angrily as he watched Chloe running towards the car.

"This is partly why I distanced myself from her all those months ago." he added, feeling himself starting to panic.

He'd been trying to avoid this ever happening as he knew how sensitive Chloe was and how much she would struggle to cope with her life being made public and being judged for everything that she did. Lee's eyes snapped up as he heard his car door close.

"Hopefully it won't be a big deal and the fans won't pay much attention to it." Kirstie said, sighing sadly. Ben and Lee glanced at her and raised their eyebrows sceptically.

"You just have to ride the storm until everyone gets bored." Ben pointed out.

"That's easy for us to say though, we chose to be in this business, Chloe is so sensitive, she won't cope with it." Lee said sadly.

"I need to go and see if she is okay." Lee sighed, his eyes wandering to his car once again.

"We'll head off and pop over to see you both later." Ben said, quickly standing up and offering his hand to Kirstie.

Lee nodded and quickly walked along the beach towards his car, sighing quietly to himself when he noticed Chloe sitting in the passenger seat, slowly wiping the tears from her cheeks.

Chloe glanced up at Lee as she saw him walking towards the car. Her hands shook as she stared down at her phone, her eyes scanning Lee's Twitter feed as she read tweet after tweet about her and Lee, her heart hurting at the barrage of negative opinions. She'd been afraid of this moment for a while as she knew the fans wouldn't like and approve of her. Chloe glanced up at Lee as he climbed into the car beside her. Lee watched her closely, not entirely sure what to say to make her feel better.

"I don't think your fans like me very much." she said thoughtfully, resting her leg on the seat and massaging her sore ankle.

"It doesn't matter what they think." he told her, gently wiping away her tears with his thumb.

"Well basically they think I'm fat and ugly and you're dropping your standards!" she said angrily, quickly flinging her phone onto the dashboard and sighing deeply.

"That's complete bullshit though!" he said angrily.

"You're so beautiful Chlo." he added softly. Chloe nodded slowly, quickly folding her arms across her chest, trying to protect herself from the world and how exposed she suddenly felt.

"Don't believe a word of what they are saying, it's completely untrue." he tried, desperately trying to say something to comfort her.

"We're never going to hear the end of it now are we." she said, running her hands through her hair as she felt herself beginning to panic once again.

"It'll pass eventually, it always does." he told her.

"Can we just go home please?" she asked quietly. Lee nodded slowly, and quickly pulled out of the carpark. He couldn't help but feel slightly guilty that he was the one who had brought this into Chloe's life, at the worst possible time, when the two of them were still grieving the loss of their baby.

Even though Chloe was one of the strongest people that he knew, he couldn't help but feel afraid that something like this would be more than she was able to cope with. She was a self-conscious person that liked to live under the radar, and Lee knew from experience how much the media liked to drag up dirt about their victims and how Chloe's private life was potentially going to be broadcasted across the tabloids for everyone to read. He really wished that there was something that he could do to protect her from the fan backlash that he also knew was inevitable, but he was completely powerless.

As soon as they arrived home, Chloe pulled up the hood of her jacket and hurried into the house, desperately trying to get inside before somebody saw her. She couldn't help but feel self-conscious and suspicious of everyone, almost like she knew that her picture could be taken at any moment. Lee frowned to himself as he watched Chloe slowly climbing the stairs.

"Don't you want some dinner?" he asked her.

"No, I just want to go to bed." she said shortly as she continued to climb the stairs, not even turning to acknowledge him.

"Chlo!" he called after her. Chloe ignored him and quickly walked into the bedroom, longing to curl up under the covers and hide from the world. She'd worked in the entertainment industry for several years and she knew that this was only the beginning. She dreaded to think what was going to be dragged up about her next. She quickly changed into her pyjamas and climbed into bed, pulling the covers over her head, in an ill-conceived attempt to shut out the world. She closed her eyes tightly, trying to ignore the insecurities that were slowly swirling around her head again. She'd always known that Lee was way out of her league, but it still hurt when it was pointed out to her by complete strangers.

Chloe jumped, snapping out of her thoughts as Lee climbed into bed beside her and burrowed under the covers with her.

"Come here Chlo." he said softly, gently pulling her into his arms. Chloe sighed and turned to face him, snuggling into his arms.

"I'm sorry Chlo, I never wanted this to happen." he said quietly.

"I know, it was always going too though wasn't it, we were naïve." she sighed, snuggling her head into his collarbone.

"I love you." she whispered against his chest.

"I love you too." he said quietly, softly stroking her hair.

"I had another dream about us the other night." Lee told her, trying to change the subject and distract her from her thoughts.

"Really?" Chloe asked.

"Yeah, I made you my wife and we had a little family." he said, smiling slightly as he was reminded of how perfect the dream was.

"How many children did we have?" she asked, smiling up at him.

"Four." he smiled.

"That's way too many." she giggled.

"I know, I don't want to put your body through that. Two would be enough I think." he told her. Chloe's smile slowly faded from her face as she thought about the idea of falling pregnant again and how terrified she was of history repeating itself. She knew that she couldn't cope with losing a baby again.

"Don't get too excited, I might be like my Mum and have problems carrying to term." she said quietly, her eyes filling with tears at the thought that she might not be able to provide Lee with the family that he desperately wanted.

"The fans are right, maybe you should go and find someone better, someone that is beautiful and can give you everything you need." she added sadly, her eyes filling with tears. Before Lee could respond Chloe turned onto her side, facing away from him so that he wouldn't see the tears that were slowly rolling down her cheeks.

"That is so untrue Chloe." he said, shuffling over to her and resting his chin on her shoulder.

"I'm the one who doesn't deserve you." he added, placing a soft kiss on her cheek. Lee sighed sadly to himself when he rested his face against hers and felt the tears rolling down her cheeks.

"Don't listen to them Chlo, they don't know what they are talking about." he whispered. Chloe sighed quietly as she felt Lee wrap his arms around her and pull her close. She closed her eyes, trying to stop thinking about the article and all the things the fans were saying about her.

Chapter Eighty-Four

Chloe sighed as she sat at the kitchen island and carefully wrapped her hands around her coffee mug. Her eyes felt like they were full of sand every time that she blinked. She'd barely slept all night, unable to stop the fans comments from swirling around her head. Even though she knew the fans opinions didn't matter to Lee....they mattered a great deal to her. They had opened all of Chloe's insecurities from before and she couldn't help but wonder, in the back of her mind, if the fans were right and Lee did deserve someone much better than her. Chloe frowned to herself as she gazed down at her phone and saw a barrage of fresh posts on Lee's social media. She quickly placed her phone on the counter and turned it upside down, staring at it intently as she tried to ignore the temptation to read the tweets. Chloe jumped as the front door opened and Nathan walked into the kitchen.

"Oh good, you're awake." Nathan said as soon as he laid eyes on Chloe.

"What are you doing here?" Chloe frowned, watching him closely as he quickly made himself a cup of coffee.

"Where's Lee?" he asked, completely disregarding Chloe's question.

"Still in bed, it's early." she said, taking a sip of her coffee.

"Let's go and sit in the living room, it's more comfortable." he said, picking up his coffee mug and walking into the living room. Chloe rolled her eyes and followed him, still not entirely sure what he was doing at Lee's house so early or why he was acting so strangely.

"Are you going to tell me what's going on yet?" Chloe asked Nathan as she sat beside him on the sofa.

Nathan sighed deeply and rummaged in his pocket, slowly pulling out a rolled-up magazine. Chloe's eyes flickered to the magazine, then back to Nathan's face, her heart plummeting when she figured out that there was yet another article about her.

"Lee's mystery woman revealed." he said sadly.

"Oh god." Chloe whispered.

"You probably shouldn't read it, but basically they know about you being homeless before you and Lee got together, and they know about the stabbing. They've basically made it sound like you are sleeping with Lee so that you get to live in luxury and that he feels sorry for you because of the stabbing and the fact that you are an orphan." Nathan explained.

"Great." she whispered, her eyes filling with tears as she felt her heart slowly breaking. "That explains all the new tweets this morning." she said quietly.

"Yeah, the fans are kind of going a bit crazy. I've been getting them too." he told her. Chloe quickly climbed off the sofa and strode into the kitchen, snatching her phone off the kitchen counter and quickly walking back into the living room. Nathan watched her closely as she sat down and stared at her phone.

Chloe's eyes filled with tears as she read the barrage of vile tweets from Lee's fans calling her ugly and a whore who was only with Lee for his money.

Nathan watched Chloe closely, his heart plummeting when he saw her eyes fill with tears. He glanced down at her wrist as he saw her gripping it tightly with her other hand, digging her fingernails into her soft flesh and slowly scratching a trail down her arm. Nathan gasped as he saw a small amount of blood on the fresh scratches she'd made. He watched in horror as she began to frantically scratch at them, clearly trying to hurt herself because she felt that's what she deserved.

"Chloe don't." he said sadly, quickly reaching out to take her hands between his and holding them tightly.

"Why, it helps?!" Chloe exclaimed, suddenly feeling sick to her stomach at the thought of all of her friends and a large amount of the population of Britain knowing almost everything about her and her pitiful excuse for a life.

"Am I really that bad, that I deserve all of this?!" she sobbed.

"No of course not, they are jealous of you Chlo Bo, because they want to be you." he reassured her. Chloe glanced up at Nathan as he gently pulled her into his arms and held her tightly as she sobbed quietly against his chest.

"I don't know if I can cope with this on top of everything else." Chloe whispered. Nathan sighed and rested his chin on the top of her head, glancing up at the doorway as Lee walked into the room and sat on the sofa.

"What's happened now?" Lee asked as soon as he saw Chloe curled up in Nathan's arms. Chloe glanced up at him as she heard his voice and quickly shuffled along the sofa. Lee watched her closely as she slowly wrapped her arms around his neck and snuggled against him. Lee wrapped his arms around her waist and pulled her onto his lap, sighing sadly when he realised how upset she was. Chloe sniffed and angrily wiped away her tears, trying not to show Lee how upset she was. She knew that he already blamed himself for putting her in this situation and the last thing she wanted to do was cause him to feel even more guilt. Chloe jumped and glanced down at her phone as it buzzed loudly.

"See these are the ones that really hurt." she said sadly, tears rolling down her cheeks again.

"Show me." Lee said softly. Chloe sighed and slowly handed him her phone.

"If only the ugly bitch had died when she was stabbed, then poor Lee wouldn't be saddled with a hanger on." Lee muttered.

"That's vile." he added, an edge of anger present in his voice.

"I'm not a hanger on, am I?" she asked nervously.

"No of course not....and you're not ugly either." he told her. Chloe sighed quietly, resting her cheek against his.

"That comment has fourteen likes already." Chloe said quietly, her voice breaking slightly as she thought about all the people out there who wished her dead, just so that she was away from Lee.

"I think I'm going to be sick." she said, quickly climbing off Lee's lap and running upstairs. Lee sighed sadly as he watched her go.

"This is all my fault." Lee said, running his hand through his hair angrily.

"I should have resisted her better." he added.

"I feel partly responsible too, I encouraged you to tell her how you felt." Nathan admitted.

"I just don't know how she's going to cope with all of this, I'm really worried about her." Lee said, gazing thoughtfully upstairs.

"I know, and this is only the beginning." Nathan sighed.

"Do you remember when Steven got a girlfriend?" he added. Lee nodded slowly, his stomach churning when he remembered how badly Steven's girlfriend was trolled for months on end.

"It's going to get worse when the tour starts too." Lee said, swallowing the lump that was rising in his throat. Nathan nodded slowly, smiling sympathetically at Lee when he noticed how sad and frustrated, he looked. He knew that Lee would do anything to protect Chloe, but in this situation, there was nothing that he could do. Lee quickly reached over and picked up the magazine. He sighed to himself, his stomach churning when he read the article, tearing down the woman that he loved.

"I just don't understand where they are getting all their information from?!" Lee said, angrily flinging the magazine onto the coffee table.

"Yeah, I was thinking that when I read it, it seems very thorough." Nathan agreed.

"We have a spy in the camp." Lee said thoughtfully, racking his brain as to who it could be.

"I just don't understand why anyone would want to do anything to hurt her." he added, sighing quietly to himself.

"I think in this case, it's probably for the money." Nathan pointed out.

"Oh probably, tear down a good person just for a pay out." Lee muttered angrily.

Nathan and Lee instantly stopped talking when Chloe walked back into the room. Lee watched her closely as she walked back into the room, quickly pulling down the sleeves on her hoodie, like she always did when she felt uncomfortable.

"We should probably go to work, shouldn't we?" she asked quietly, glancing between the two of them awkwardly.

"I can drive us if you want, to save taking two cars when we are all going to the same place anyway?" Nathan offered. Lee nodded and quickly stood up his eyes still fixed on Chloe. He couldn't help but feel sad about what was happening to her, she hadn't been herself since they lost their baby, but now she was a shadow of her former self. Over the last few days, Lee had watched the confidence that she'd built up over the past few months, slowly ebb away. She was back to hovering nervously, unable to look people in the eye, and hiding her amazing figure under baggy clothes. He hadn't seen her smile since the day at the beach and he knew that he was partly responsible, his lifestyle had brought all this negativity into Chloe's life, that she was now struggling to cope with. He'd never felt so powerless, he'd always been able to protect her, but in this situation, there was literally nothing that he could do. Chloe glanced down at her hand as she felt Lee take it and squeeze it gently.

Chloe sighed and ran her hand through her hair in frustration as she sat on the windowsill at the studio, surrounded by paperwork. She'd spent the whole morning trying to figure out the tour schedule for the boys, but she couldn't seem to think straight.

"What are you doing Chlo Bo?" Nathan asked as he sat on the floor in front of the windowsill. Chloe glanced up as Adrian and Steven sat beside him, the three of them rummaging in the lunch bag.

"Trying to figure out the damn schedule and it's not happening." Chloe said angrily.

"I thought we already know what dates we are doing at certain venues?" Adrian frowned. Chloe sighed in frustration, glancing up at Lee as he walked over and sat on the windowsill behind her. Chloe smiled her thanks as he handed her a sandwich.

"We do, but I need to sort out transport and stuff." Chloe said, answering Adrian's question. She quickly put down the sandwich and stared at the paperwork, desperately trying to focus her mind.

"Do we get to stay in fancy hotels?" Steven asked.

"No, Matt said no hotels, except if you are doing more than one night at that venue." Chloe explained.

"Great." Nathan sighed. Chloe quickly pushed the paperwork away, finally deciding that she needed a break from staring at it.

"Budge up a bit." Lee said quietly. Chloe quickly did as he asked, watching closely as he turned sideways on the windowsill and crossed his legs. He raised his eyebrow at Chloe, smiling slightly when she sat on his lap and sighed to herself.

"Hang on, so are we literally going to be living on a bus for two months?!" Steven exclaimed, suddenly realising what Chloe was telling them.

"Yes, pretty much, I don't think there's money in the budget for hotels." Chloe told them.

"Hey Matt!" Steven called, gesturing for Matt to come over and join them.

"What's the problem?" Matt asked as soon as he reached them.

"Are we living off a bus for two months?" Steven asked.

"Yep, I'm afraid so. There won't be time for a hotel anyway, because you'll be sleeping on the bus while you travel to the next location." Matt explained.

"That's ridiculous, what if we want to go out or something?!" Steven said angrily. Chloe sighed and rested the back of her head against Lee's shoulder, not quite able to summon the mental strength to have an argument.

"You'll have the daytime, up until you have to be at sound check." Matt pointed out.

"We can't exactly go clubbing or anything though can we." Steven sighed. Lee rolled his eyes at them and stared down at Chloe, he wrapped his arm around her shoulders and gently stroked her neck with his fingertips.

"It's alright for him, he has a girlfriend that's coming on tour with us." Steven snapped, gesturing to Lee. Lee's head snapped up, as he frowned slightly at Steven's words.

"So, what you mean is, you want to go out and find ladies." Nathan said quickly.

"Well yeah." Steven said.

"Oh, for god sake." Lee muttered, becoming slightly frustrated by the tension Steven was causing.

"Erm excuse me, you used to do it." Steven reminded him.

"And like I said, your girlfriend is coming with you, so you won't be bothered will you." he added.

"Yeah, well we're not exactly going to be having sex with the three of you only a few feet away are we." Lee said shortly.

"You've done it before to be fair." Adrian laughed.

"Things are different now." Lee said quietly, turning his attention back to Chloe who was staring up at him silently. Steven shook his head as he stood up and quickly walked away.

"What's gotten into him today?" Nathan frowned.

"I'll go and talk to him." Adrian sighed, before quickly walking away, Matt following closely behind.

"They won't bring women back to the bus, will they?" Chloe asked quietly.

"Oh probably, especially Steven." Nathan told her.

"That's going to be so awkward." Chloe said quietly, her cheeks colouring at the thought of it.

"The bigger problem is how I'm going to be able to keep my hands off you for two months." Lee admitted.

"You'll be fine, there are public places that you can be discreet." Nathan told them. Chloe opened her mouth to argue but quickly closed it again, not entirely comfortable having this conversation with Nathan. She could feel Lee watching her closely, clearly picking up on how uncomfortable she was feeling.

"We'll be fine." Lee said quickly. He knew that Chloe wouldn't feel comfortable with the idea of them doing anything in public and despite the temptation he knew he would be feeling, he wasn't prepared to do anything that would make Chloe feel uncomfortable. She meant far more to him than himself. Chloe turned to face him, raising her eyebrow sceptically.

"As long as you're with me, I'm happy." he smiled reassuringly. Chloe slowly wrapped her arms around his neck and gently kissed his lips. As soon as they pulled apart Chloe sighed in contentment and rested her forehead against his, gazing down at his lips longingly.

Chloe jumped as she saw a flashing out of the corner of her eye. She frowned and quickly turned to gaze out of the window, gasping as she locked eyes with a photographer. Chloe squirmed and tried to hide herself against Lee's larger frame.

"For god sake." Lee muttered angrily, gently pushing Chloe off his lap. He quickly stood up and took Chloe's hand, pulling her away from the window. Lee stood against the small amount of wall between the windows that ran the length of the studio, quickly pulling Chloe close so that she remained safely out of sight.

"Matt!" Lee called across the room. Matt turned to face him and quickly crossed the room, raising his eyebrow questioningly.

"There's media outside, you need to get rid of them." Lee said shortly. Matt sighed, glancing at Chloe sadly when he saw her eyes filling with tears.

"I can distract them while the two of you sneak out the back." Matt offered.

"I'll do it." Nathan said, quickly handing Lee his car keys as he walked past.

"This is getting ridiculous now!" Lee said angrily when he glanced at Chloe and saw her eyes were full of tears. He slowly pulled up her hood and gently tucked her hair inside.

"Can I work from home for a few days please?" Chloe asked Matt, suddenly feeling like she needed to hide from the world for a while.

"Yes, that's fine, I'll need Lee here though, we have to start practicing using the set and stuff." Matt said, glancing at Lee. Chloe nodded slowly. Matt quickly peered out of the window, silently giving them a thumbs up when he noticed the journalists speaking to Nathan. Before Chloe could react, Lee took her hand and strode across the studio, quickly pulling her after him.

Chapter Eighty-Five

Chloe sighed deeply as she sat silently on the sofa, staring at her phone. She quickly pulled her legs towards herself and wrapped her arms around them, trying in vain to protect herself. She couldn't quite process that the pictures of her and Lee at the studio were already online, when it had only happened a few hours ago. Even though she knew it wasn't healthy for her to keep scrolling through the fan's tweets, she couldn't seem to stop herself. Her heart sunk further and further into her chest as she read the barrage of hate about her. She'd lost count of the number of times she'd been told how ugly and fat she was, and how she would never be good enough for someone like Lee. A small sob escaped her lips as she read a series of tweets between two fans speaking about her:

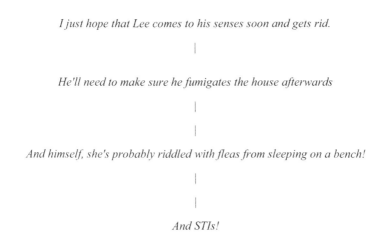

I just hope that Lee comes to his senses soon and gets rid.

He'll need to make sure he fumigates the house afterwards

And himself, she's probably riddled with fleas from sleeping on a bench!

And STIs!

Chloe pressed her phone against her heart, desperately trying to ignore the deep hurt that she was feeling. Even though she'd never met any of these people, their extremely negative opinions of her were still slowly tearing her apart. She gripped onto her phone tightly, trying to release the pain that she was feeling inside. She slowly fell sideways, no longer having the strength to hold herself up, quickly curling up on the sofa and sobbing quietly to herself.

Even though she knew in her heart that the things being said about her weren't true, that didn't stop them from destroying her confidence. Chloe knew that she couldn't deal with the constant character assassination much longer, it was slowly tearing her apart.

Lee's stomach dropped as he walked into the living room and noticed Chloe curled up on the sofa, quietly crying to herself.

"What's wrong Chlo?" he asked her, squatting down on the floor in front of her.

"Nothing I'm fine." she said shortly, quickly wiping the tears from her cheeks.

Lee sighed sadly, frowning to himself when he reached out to softly stroke her hair and she squirmed away from him. He pulled his hand back, watching her closely as she glanced at him.

"I wouldn't want you to catch anything." she said sarcastically.

"What are you talking about?" he frowned. Chloe sighed and remained silent. Lee slowly took Chloe's phone out of her hand and stared at it, a deep feeling of anger building inside him as he read the tweets. He remained silent, not entirely sure what to say or how to process what he'd just read. Even though he'd always known that the fans would dislike Chloe, purely out of jealousy, he hadn't expected them to be so vile and below the belt to her. Chloe flinched slightly as Lee leant forward and carefully rested his head on top of hers, desperately wishing that he could do something to take her pain away.

"I'm so sorry for all of this." he whispered when he heard her sniff sadly.

"I'm just sick of it." she admitted quietly.

"Don't take any notice of them, they don't know what they are talking about." he sighed.

"And as for this.......it's bollocks!" he said, quickly lifting his head and angrily switching off Chloe's phone.

"You're the purest person I've ever met." he told her, softly kissing her tears away. Chloe closed her eyes and sighed quietly, trying to forget about everything that was swirling around her head. She knew that Lee loved her with all of his heart, but the more time that passed the more she was beginning to believe that she didn't deserve him and that he could do so much better than her.

"You need to stop reading what they write about you, you're torturing yourself with it." he told her, sighing quietly to himself when he remembered how every night since the media outed them, Chloe had been up most of the night, obsessively searching social media to read what was being said about her.

Chloe nodded slowly, realizing that he was right, but knowing in her heart that she couldn't stop herself. In her mind it seemed better to know what was being said about her, rather than living in ignorance. Chloe jumped as she heard the timer ringing from the kitchen. Lee reluctantly stood up and walked into the kitchen.

Chloe glanced up at Lee and slowly sat up when he returned to the living room and handed her a plate of food.

"Thanks." she said quietly. Lee watched her sadly as she slowly pushed her food around her plate.

"Chlo, you need to eat." he prompted her.

"I'm not hungry." she said quietly, carefully placing her plate on the coffee table.

"You've not been eating much for the past few days." he said sadly. Chloe shrugged, as she sat, silently picking her fingernails. Lee angrily put his plate onto the coffee table and shuffled over to sit beside her. She didn't even react when Lee wrapped his arm around her shoulders and held her close.

"I love you so much." he whispered in her ear, gently snuggling his head against hers. Chloe nodded slowly, her eyes filling with tears once again.

She glanced down at her hands as she felt Lee take them in his own, gently playing with her fingers to prevent her from picking her fingernails.

"Don't let them do this to you Chlo." he whispered, softly placing a series of kisses on her neck. Chloe slowly turned her body to face him and snuggled against him, desperately trying to seek some comfort. Lee laid down on the sofa, carefully pulling Chloe into his arms. Chloe sighed in contentment, closing her eyes softly.

"I can't believe they said that about me." she said quietly against his chest.

"If only they knew the truth." he sighed.

"Do you remember the night you gave me your virginity?" he asked her, trying to steer the conversation away from the fans and their vile tweets.

"I'll always remember it." she said, glancing down at her necklace fondly.

"You hated it didn't you." she giggled when she remembered how stressed he'd been about the whole process.

"Only the fact that I was going to hurt you, I still appreciated how lucky I was that you chose me." he told her, gently stroking her hair. Chloe wrapped her arms around his neck and kissed his lips softly. As soon as they pulled apart, Lee reached down and stroked Chloe's necklace, smiling slightly to himself when he remembered that night. Chloe sighed as the two of them fell silent, her thoughts wandering back to the fans again.

"One good thing that's come out of all of this, is that I got a letter from my cousin the other day." she said quickly, trying to keep her brain occupied.

"What cousin?" he frowned, softly stroking her hair.

"Amy, she's a younger cousin on my Dad's side, we used to be really close, but we kind of lost touch when we moved to London, because I was distracted with everything that was going on." she explained.

"And she saw the articles and wrote to me at the studio." she continued.

"That's amazing Chlo, I'm really pleased." he smiled, his heart filling with pride that she finally had a member of her family in her life.

"Is she still in Nottingham?" he asked. Chloe nodded slowly.

"Maybe we could go away for a few days, then you'll get to see her and get a break from everything?" he suggested.

"We can't go away; you go on tour in a few weeks and there's still a lot of preparation to do." she sighed. Even though she was tempted to take him up on his offer, she wanted nothing more than to disappear for a few days, she knew that he'd made a big commitment to the band, and she wasn't going to be the one to pull him away from it.

"Yeah, I guess." he sighed, feeling slightly guilty that he couldn't even take her away for a few days to give her a break from everything.

"Don't feel guilty, I'll be okay." she told him, clearly sensing how he was feeling. Chloe slowly sat up slightly and kissed his lips softly, her heart pounding as he quickly deepened the kiss, placing his hands on her hips and pulling her onto his lap.

Lee sat up, quickly placing his hands on her waist as he planted a trail of kisses along her jawline, slowly making his way down to her neck. Chloe sighed in pleasure and wrapped her arms around his neck, gently stroking the hair on the back of his neck. Lee quickly grasped the bottom of her hoodie, and slowly lifted it over her head. He frowned to himself and quickly took hold of Chloe's wrist, staring down at the scratches on her arms.

"Chlo, what are these?" he asked worriedly.

"It's nothing." she said quietly, her cheeks colouring in embarrassment as he stared at the self-inflicted wounds on her arm. Lee gently pulled her arm towards himself and placed a soft kiss on her scratches, his heart breaking a little when he realised that they were clearly caused by fingernails. He couldn't bear the thought that Chloe had been hurting herself because she was struggling so much.

Lee slowly lifted the bottom of Chloe's shirt and placed his hands on her bare skin, smiling slightly when he felt her goosebumps. Before Chloe could react, he kissed her intensely, his hands slowly lifting her top. He broke the kiss for a moment to remove her top, before he quickly returning to kissing her lips. Chloe quickly turned her face away from him, her cheeks colouring as she stared down at her exposed torso. Lee methodically kissed a trail along her collarbone, his hands fumbling slightly as he reached around her, searching for her bra so that he could unclasp it.

"Wait!" Chloe said quickly, when she realised what he was doing. Lee instantly stopped and sat back, watching her closely as she stared at her lap. He frowned to himself as she picked up her hoodie and held it over her torso, her cheeks colouring in embarrassment.

"What's wrong?" he frowned.

"I don't know." she said quietly.

"I've seen you before." he said quietly, his heart breaking a little when he noticed her hands were shaking. He couldn't help but remember all those months ago when she was embarrassed to undress in front of him.

Her confidence had come on leaps and bounds since then, and he couldn't help but feel a deep sense of sadness that she felt the same way about her body as she had at the beginning of their relationship.

"You haven't been like this for months." he told her sadly.

"I've had a lot of people tell me that I'm fat and ugly lately though." she whispered. Lee nodded slowly, sighing sadly to himself.

"Which is ridiculous, you're none of those things." he said sadly.

"You're the most beautiful person I've ever met." he added. Chloe raised her eyebrow sceptically, sighing quietly to herself.

"And your body is flawless." he added. Chloe glanced down at his hands as he placed them on her hips and gently pulled her onto his lap.

"I'm sorry that I'm being stupid." she whispered in his ear, sighing quietly as he wrapped his arms around her and held her tightly.

"It's not your fault, I'm angry at what they are doing to you." he sighed. Chloe nodded slowly. Lee watched her as she quickly climbed off his lap and walked over to the doorway, smiling to herself when she switched off the light. She quickly returned to the sofa and discarded her hoodie. Chloe glanced at Lee, smiling slightly when she saw his face dimly lit by the light coming from the fireplace. She returned to her original position on his lap, feeling more relaxed now that there was barely any light in the room.

"I wish you would realise how beautiful you are." he whispered in her ear.

Chloe smiled at Matt as she opened the front door and gestured for him to come in.

"How are you doing?" he asked, as soon as he saw her.

"Alright." she said quietly, quickly leading him into the dining room.

"It hasn't been the same at the studio without you." he told her, as he rummaged in his bag and pulled out a folder full of paperwork.

"It's been nice not having to leave the house for a few days." she admitted.

"Have you not been out at all?" he asked quickly. Chloe shook her head slowly.

"That's not healthy." he said worriedly.

"It's better than being photographed though and giving the fans more ammunition to shoot me with." she pointed out. Matt nodded in agreement, sighing quietly to himself when he noticed how miserable Chloe looked.

"Anyway, I have the paperwork you asked for." he told her, handing her the folder.

"Thank you." she smiled.

"Oh, and this got delivered to the studio for you." he smiled, handing her a letter.

"It's probably from my cousin." she said, smiling slightly. Chloe frowned as she took the letter from Matt and gazed down at it, not entirely sure who's handwriting it was.

She could feel Matt watching her closely as she quickly opened the letter, her stomach dropping when she noticed that it was from Andy.

"What's wrong?" Matt asked when Chloe gasped.

"It's from Andy." she said quietly.

"What does that twat want?" he asked, frowning when he noticed Chloe slowly turning pale.

"He wants money." she muttered.

"Huh?" he frowned.

"He wants me to pay him ten thousand pounds otherwise he will be speaking to the press about me." she explained.

"He must have been approached to sell an article or something." she added thoughtfully.

"I don't have that amount of money." she said.

"There's nothing he can say anyway though, he broke up with you and he was the one who treated you badly." he pointed out.

"I don't think he'll go through with it anyway; he probably just has more debts that need paying off." she sighed.

"I don't think he hates me enough to do that." she added, trying to convince herself as much as Matt. Matt opened his mouth to respond, quickly closing it when he heard the front door close. Chloe jumped and quickly stuffed the envelope into the folder.

"You can't tell Lee about this?" Chloe said under her breath.

"Why not?" Matt frowned.

"Because he'll probably feel like he has to pay him, to protect me and I don't want to take his money." she said. Matt nodded slowly, not quite able to bring himself to tell her that he had a bad feeling that she hadn't heard the last from Andy.

Chapter Eighty-Six

Chloe ran her hands through her hair in frustration, digging her fingernails into her scalp, in an ill-conceived attempt to remove the thoughts that were swirling around her head. Her eyes flickered to the magazine on the counter, a deep sense of rage swirling in her stomach as she stared at Andy's smiling face. Even though she knew Andy wasn't the nicest person in the world, she'd never for a moment thought he would be capable of something like this. Warm tears slowly rolled down Chloe's cheeks, that she was powerless to stop. Chloe jumped as she heard the doorbell ring. She quickly walked along the hall to answer the door, smiling slightly at Kirstie as she gestured for her to come in. Chloe silently walked into the kitchen, Kirstie following closely behind.

"You've seen the article then?" Kirstie sighed as soon as she saw the magazine on the kitchen counter. Chloe nodded slowly.

"I can't believe he did that to you." she added.

"I know, it's the biggest pile of bullshit I've ever read." Chloe said angrily.

"He's the one who built up all the debts in my name and he's trying to make out it was me and that he tried to help me with my gambling problem!" Chloe ranted.

"I didn't even know you were in debt." Kirstie frowned.

"Yes, but only because of him, I ended up on the street because of him and he has the audacity to make out it was all me." Chloe said quickly.

"Also did you read the part about the fact that I supposedly cheated on him all the time and went with anyone that would buy me drinks?" Chloe asked.

"Yeah, I did, I noticed the fans are lapping that up." Kirstie sighed.

"Because it reaffirms their belief that I'm with Lee for his money, so that he'll pay off my debts." Chloe said, shaking her head sadly.

"And they've been calling me a whore for the past few days, so now they think they have 'proof'." Chloe added, gesturing inverted commas.

"What does Lee say about it?" Kirstie asked sadly, feeling sorry for her best friend. In all the years that she'd known Chloe, she'd never seen her looking so run down.

"I don't know if he's seen it yet, he's at the studio." Chloe said quietly.

"He's going to be furious though." she added. Chloe fell silent and scanned the article again, unable to help herself. Her eyes slowly filled with tears as she read all the lies that her ex-boyfriend had said about her. She knew in her heart that anyone who read the article and didn't know her, would likely believe every word.

"The part that really hurts is when he mentions my Dad." Chloe muttered, pointing at the article. Kirstie peered at it her heart sinking as she read Andy's comment stating that if her father could see her now, he would be so disappointed with her behaviour.

"He's just trying to hurt you; your father would be proud of everything you've achieved and how strong you are." Kirstie said.

"Besides if he would be disappointed in anyone it would be Andy, since your father thought that he was going to take care of you and all he did was break your heart." she continued. Chloe nodded slowly, quickly wiping away the tears that were steadily flowing down her cheeks.

"I wish I'd taken out a loan now and paid him, it would have been so much easier than having the world hate me." Chloe admitted sadly.

"What do you mean?" Kirstie frowned.

"He wrote to me a few days ago, threatening to go to the press if I didn't give him ten thousand pounds." Chloe admitted.

"But I naively didn't think he'd actually go through with it." she added.

"He really is despicable isn't he." Kirstie said, shaking her head slowly.

"I don't think I can do this anymore Kirstie." Chloe admitted, feeling a wave of relief that she'd finally admitted it to someone.

"What do you mean?" Kirstie asked.

"I can't cope with being hated by the world when I haven't done anything wrong. I haven't even been outside for the past week, all I do is sit inside, reading all the hate about me." Chloe said quietly.

"I don't know what to suggest, it's a really difficult situation." Kirstie said, sighing sadly.

"I don't know what to do either, but I know I can't live like this anymore." Chloe sighed.

"Just don't do anything impulsive." Kirstie told her. Chloe nodded slowly. Kirstie sighed and quickly pulled Chloe into a tight hug, squeezing her gently to try and provide some comfort.

"I'm really sorry, I have to get back to work." Kirstie said, feeling slightly guilty that she was having to leave Chloe when she was upset.

"It's fine, I'll be okay." Chloe said, smiling falsely.

"I'll come over and see you on my way home." Kirstie told her. Chloe nodded and sighed sadly as she watched Kirstie slowly leaving the house. As soon as she was alone, her thoughts wandered to the fans once again. Before she could help herself, she picked up her phone and scrolled through the mound of posts about her. She gasped as she read them:

If she really cared about Lee, she would leave him! #moneygrabber

People like her give women a bad name, she should do the world a favour and kill herself.

Chloe stifled a sob that was rising in her throat, as she tried to process their words. Her stomach churned as she watched fan after fan agreeing that she should kill herself so that Lee would be *rid of her.*

"Fine." she whispered impulsively. Before Chloe knew what, she was doing she stood up and rummaged in the medicine cabinet, breathing a sigh of relief when she finally clasped her bottle of sleeping tablets in her hand. She stared at the label, sighing quietly to herself when she remembered all those months ago when she'd been given them at the hospital. She smiled fondly when she remembered how Lee had barely left her side when she was recovering. She numbly filled a glass with some water and slowly tipped the sleeping tablets onto the counter, slowly moving them around with her fingers. She couldn't cope with her life any longer and she knew that this was the only way to make the pain that she was feeling stop.

Chloe jumped as her phone rang, cursing to herself as she dropped the glass of water and watched it smash on the floor.

She sighed to herself when she read the display and saw that Lee was calling her.

"Hello." she answered, trying to put on a steady voice and pretend that everything was okay.

"You okay Chlo?" he asked quickly.

"Yes, why?" she lied.

"Matt has just shown me Andy's article." he told her, a note of anger present in his voice.

"You don't believe any of it do you?" she asked quietly.

"No of course not." he told her.

"It's the most disgusting thing I've ever read." he added angrily. Chloe nodded and sniffed quietly, trying to fight her tears, but no longer having the strength.

"Don't cry Chlo." he said sadly, his heart breaking for her.

"Do you want me to come home?" he offered.

"No, you have to work, I'll be okay." she whispered, her voice breaking slightly as she glanced at the tablets that were still strewn across the counter. Chloe couldn't believe how far she'd fallen, that she'd strongly considered taking her own life, in the same way that her father had done. She knew in her heart that if her parents could see her now, they would be turning in their graves. They'd never wanted Chloe to be unhappy, to slowly be destroyed in the same way as her father, to the point where the only option seemed to be to end things. She knew that she had to get away from everything, before her life was destroyed. A small sob escaped Chloe's lips when she suddenly realised what her only option was.

"Do you know where Andy lives?" Lee asked, snapping her out of her thoughts.

"Yes." Chloe sighed, her mind wandering to the letter she'd received from him, with the address to bring the money too.

"Why?" she added.

"So that I can go and kick his arse!" he told her, his temper slowly growing when he realised how upset Chloe was by what Andy had done to her. Lee hadn't liked Andy from the moment Chloe had told him what he'd done to her when they were together, but he knew that the article was causing her heart to break all over again. He desperately wanted to punish him for hurting the person that he loved.

"Just leave it." she said quietly.

"Anyway, I have to go, Kirstie is coming over." she added, feeling a pang of guilt that she was lying to him, but realising that she had to get him off the phone before she completely broke down.

"Okay, I'll be home in a bit." he told her sadly.

"Okay." she muttered.

"You know how much I love you right?" she asked, suddenly realising that this was the last conversation she was going to have with him.

"Yeah." he sighed.

"And I'm really sorry." she whispered.

"Sorry for what?" he said, frowning at her words.

"I don't know." she lied, placing her hand over her mouth to stifle the sob that almost escaped her lips. Even though she knew in her heart, how miserable she would be without Lee in her life, she'd come to realise that it was her only option, since she couldn't live like this anymore. It was slowly destroying her.

"I love you Chlo." he told her.

"I love you too." she whispered sadly, quickly hanging up the phone before she could talk herself out of it. As soon as she hung up, she placed her head in her hands and began to sob, finally able to let out the emotions that she'd been keeping in check. When she eventually recovered herself, she slowly lifted her head and stared into space, her brain working overtime. Chloe knew that if she was going to leave, she had to do it before Lee got home. Even though she felt a pang of guilt that she was leaving him without even saying goodbye, she knew that she couldn't bring herself to say goodbye to him.

She also knew in her heart that he would try and convince her to stay and she couldn't allow that to happen, things were too far gone, she needed to escape before she lost her sanity completely.

Before she could talk herself out of it, Chloe ran upstairs and began to frantically stuff her clothes into her suitcase, tears streaming down her face the entire time. She couldn't believe that the media and fans had pushed her to breaking point and had finally managed to drive her away from the man that she loved. She'd wanted to spend the rest of her life with Lee, to eventually become his wife and raise a family with him, but now that dream had been shattered and there was no going back.

Chloe quickly zipped up her suitcase, sighing in relief at the thought of finally getting away from everything. Even though her heart was breaking at having to leave Lee, she couldn't help but feel a small glimmer of hope that she would soon be able to escape this oppressive media storm that was slowly sucking the life out of her.

She quickly hurried downstairs, dragging her suitcase behind her and rushed into the kitchen to collect her phone. She perched at the kitchen island and quickly scribbled Lee a note, feeling yet another wave of guilt that she was doing this to him, but knowing in her heart that it was her only option. She sighed quietly as her tears slowly dripped onto the letter, smudging the words slightly. She quickly folded the note, trying to hurry, in case Lee came home before she left. Chloe glanced down at the necklace that was around her neck and reluctantly removed it, her heart breaking slightly when she remembered the night that Lee had given it to her, when she'd made, what was to her, a big commitment to him. When she'd finally realised that she'd found someone that she loved and could trust enough to give her virginity too. She carefully placed it beside the note, her heart breaking as she stared at it, silently stroking her bare neck. Chloe took a deep breath and quickly walked out of the house before she could talk herself out of it.

Chapter Eighty-Seven

Lee quickly walked up the driveway, desperate to get home and check on Chloe. Ever since he'd spoken to her on the phone, he'd been unable to shake the feeling that she was struggling more than she was letting on to him.

"Chlo!" he called as he walked into the house. He frowned when she didn't reply, his heart pounding against his chest when he suddenly realised how silent the house was. Lee's heart pounded against his chest as he walked into the kitchen and saw a pile of tablets strewn across the kitchen counter, he quickly picked up the bottle, gasping to himself and quickly throwing the bottle into the sink when he realised that they were Chloe's sleeping tablets. He felt sick to his stomach at the thought that she had taken some of the tablets. He knew that she'd been struggling with everything, but he'd had no idea that she'd been struggling that much. His heart sunk even further when he noticed a neatly folded note on the counter.

Lee's eyes filled with tears when he picked it up and noticed Chloe's necklace beside it. His hands shook as he slowly opened the note and read it:

Lee,

Firstly, I'm really sorry that I've had to do this, the last thing I ever wanted to do was to hurt you. I know that I at least owe you a goodbye, but I couldn't bear to see the hurt on your face, and I knew in my heart that you would convince me to stay. I never wanted to leave you but being in this environment is slowly destroying me and I can't take the hate anymore. I need to get away, before my life is destroyed completely.

I'll never be able to thank you enough for everything that you have done for me, I hope you know that you saved me from the darkest of times and being with you helped me to finally feel like myself again.

I hope that you understand and know that I will always love you.

Chloe x

Lee sniffed sadly, trying to fight the tears that were slowly rolling down his cheeks. He slowly picked up her necklace and gripped it tightly, staring at the engraving of their names on the back.

"Oh Chlo." he whispered, curling his hand into a fist as he gripped onto her necklace tightly, unable to stand the thought that he'd lost her forever. He quickly pulled out his phone to call her, sighing quietly as it rang out. Lee slowly slid down the counter, his legs finally giving way when he continued to call Chloe, and it continued to ring out. He angrily wiped away the tears that were rolling down his cheeks.

He racked his brain for what to do, all he knew was that he couldn't let Chloe go. He didn't want to imagine his life without her. Lee quickly called Kirstie, silently praying that she would pick up.

"Hey." Kirstie said.

"Thank god." Lee whispered.

"Have you seen Chloe?" he added quickly.

"I saw her at lunch time, but not since then." she told him, frowning slightly when she realised how upset he sounded.

"Is something wrong?" she quickly added.

"Chloe has gone." he said, his voice breaking slightly.

"What do you mean gone?" she frowned.

"She's left, I don't know where she's gone." he whispered, a small sob escaping his lips.

"Oh my god." Kirstie whispered.

"Did she say anything about it to you earlier?" he asked, feeling a slight glimmer of hope that Kirstie might have some idea where Chloe was.

"No." she said sadly. Before Kirstie could say anything else, Lee quickly hung up the phone, pressing the top of it against his head in frustration, the realisation finally hitting him that he was never going to see Chloe again. He couldn't quite comprehend his life without her by his side, without being able to know that she was safe every day. To never be able to hold her close and tell her how much he loved her.

Chloe sighed sadly, her eyes filling with tears as Lee tried to call her for a fourth time. Her heart was breaking every time that his name was displayed on the screen and she didn't answer him. She knew that she was breaking his heart, but she couldn't bring herself to answer his calls. She knew that if she heard his voice, she would no longer be able to remain firm in her decision to leave. She stared out as the landscape rushed by, listening to the steady rhythm of the train as she slowly made her way to Nottingham. She quickly wiped away her stream of tears, glancing at her phone once again, her heart sinking even further when she heard Lee's amazing voice singing Broken as he tried to call her yet again. She sighed sadly when she noticed that Lee had left her a voicemail. Chloe quickly put the phone to her ear, gasping to herself when she heard his voice:

"Please come home Chlo, I miss you so much already. I know you are struggling but I'll leave the band if I have too, I will do anything to have you back." he said sadly.

"Please Chlo, I love you." he added, his voice breaking at the end. Tears rolled down Chloe's cheeks as she heard him let out a small sob, before quickly hanging up.

She returned to staring out of the window, watching the raindrops slowly trailing down the window, wishing with all her heart that things didn't have to be this way. Even though she'd only left a few hours ago, she missed Lee terribly, it felt like she had left her heart behind with him. She knew that as long as she lived, she would never meet someone like Lee, someone who cherished her and would do anything he could to protect her.

Eventually the train reached Chloe's stop, she quickly stood up and picked up her suitcase. She silently stepped onto the platform, smiling slightly when she noticed Amy waving to her amongst the crowd. Chloe quickly hurried over to her, quickly pulling Amy into her arms as soon as she reached her.

"Are you okay?" Amy asked Chloe when she realised that she was crying.

"No, not really." Chloe admitted, shaking her head slowly, biting her lip hard to try and stop herself from bursting into tears.

"C'mon, let's get you back to mine and then we'll talk." Amy said, gently taking Chloe's hand and leading her towards the car.

Lee began to pace the kitchen angrily, still holding Andy's letter tightly in his hand, trying to control the intense anger that he was feeling. As soon as he'd read the article that Andy had written, he'd felt a deep surge of anger towards him, but that didn't compare to the anger he now felt at the fact that he'd lost his reason for existing because of him. His anger had grown even more when he'd rummaged through Chloe's remaining belongings, hoping to discover a clue as to her whereabouts and he came across Andy's letter. He couldn't understand how anyone in their right mind would want to do anything to hurt Chloe's sweet soul. Lee was snapped out of his thoughts when he heard the front door close loudly, and Nathan walked into the kitchen.

"What's going on?" Nathan asked as soon as he walked into the room.

"I need you to come with me to Andy's house!" Lee said, his tone full of venom.

"Why?" Nathan frowned.

"Because Chloe has gone, and he needs to pay." Lee snapped.

"But...." Nathan protested.

"And it's this little fucker's fault!" Lee hissed, angrily flinging the letter across the counter. Nathan frowned, feeling slightly sick to his stomach as he read the letter.

"He blackmailed her!" Nathan exclaimed. Lee nodded angrily.

"I don't think it's a good idea for you to go over there." Nathan tried, feeling slightly nervous about what Lee was going to do. In all the years that he'd known Lee, he'd never seen him so angry.

"I'm going with or without you." Lee said shortly, before quickly walking away.

Printed in Great Britain
by Amazon

17976342R00373